The
Angel
Brings Fire

Book Three : *Angel and The Empire*

(Second Edition)

by

Marcus B. Shields

For additional information about *The Angel Brings Fire*, surf to :

http://abfbook.telostic.com

For all those who came so close to meeting her :

Mitchell "Lupienne" Wageler

Lynne "Belle" Wageler

Rick "Rohan Envenyatar" McGeer

Simon "Simak" Matthews

Doug "Chancellor V'Lampen" Gillanders

Steve "Prince Orldlis" Hinchcliffe (deceased)

Pat Foster

Jerry Page

Mike Rea

Carla Wellman and Her Pet Bear

Rick Smith

Peter ("Father D*") Hackett

Stuart Carmichael

Maxwell Shields

And a host of others, who I pray will forgive for the omission

"Those were the days", my friends;

I fear they will never come again

Table of Contents

Prologue

Since *The Angel Brings Fire* is a multi-volume series, it is strongly suggested that the reader should enjoy Books One and Two, *Angel of Mailànkh*, and *Doubt Me Not* (respectively), before starting to read Book Three, *Angel and The Empire*.

That said, it is recognized that for various reasons, some readers will have happened upon this volume of the series, without having convenient access to Books One and Two.

We have therefore provided the following brief synopsis of the events of the previous two books, so that the reader can make sense of some of the characters and themes brought forward from the beginning of the novel.

Marcus Shields
Author

Angel of Mailànkh (Book One) revolves around the discovery of an extremely powerful female alien-being on Mars, self-described as "The Storied Watcher" a.k.a. "Karéin-Mayréij", who may or may not be an "angel" and who may or may not be Earth's only remaining hope of stopping a Doomsday comet named *Lucifer*.

The Storied Watcher manages to stow away on the Mars return vessel and while there, she learns of the planet's impending destruction. Fearing that there may soon be no-one left on Earth, the alien passes her secret gift – a supernatural power called *Amaiish* or *The Fire* – to the human astronauts who she encountered and befriended on Mars.

As a measure of desperation, Karéin-Mayréij resolves to destroy *Lucifer* in a 'death-run', powered indirectly by the enormous energies of Earth's Sun. And thus she does, although, at the close of Book One, it appears that she has sacrificed her life in the cause.

Doubt Me Not (Book Two) takes up the story of Karéin-Mayréij, after – much to her own surprise – she awakens after having crashed to Earth on a mountain-top in Idaho in the United States.

Badly wounded, hungry, cold, unable to speak intelligible English, having forgotten her true name and having lost almost all of her supernatural powers, she stumbles down to a truck stop, and has a few awkward initial encounters with citizens of America's near future. Calling herself 'Sari Tanak', she beguiles and befriends a down-and-out, forty-something floor-tile salesman named Bob Billings, who, along with her and and an African-American woman named

Whitney Claremont (plus children, Curtis and Melissa), are taken prisoner by a fundamentalist Christian cult called "The Klan of Jesus Christ".

However, the Storied Watcher's powers *are* returning, if painfully slowly, and she uses one of these – the same "cloak of invisibility" that enabled her to steal aboard the *Eagle* spacecraft, way back on Mars – to free Billings, the Claremont family and an orphaned Amerindian boy named Tommy George, from captivity. Together, the *ersatz* troupe locates and re-starts Billings' hidden, abandoned automobile. They begin a trip across-country, heading south to the salesman's home base of Tucson, Arizona.

After a number of misadventures *en route*, 'Sari', Bob Billings, Whitney, Curtis and Melissa Claremont, along with Tommy George, arrive in Tucson and try to fit in to Billings' former "quiet, middle-class" lifestyle.

However, the United States of 2040 is a paranoid, declining society, obsessed with "subversion" of every type, and (though this fact is suspected by the Storied Watcher), she and the Billings party have been identified and tracked back to Tucson, not only by the omnipresent CIA but also by Christian fundamentalists (who believe the Storied Watcher to be "the spawn of Satan") and by a Russian SVR "sleeper" cell of spies, one of whom, "Misha", has been ahead of his American counterparts by a few days.

Feeling the imminent return of her greater abilities, 'Sari', who has by now become the salesman's mate, reveals her true nature to Bob Billings, and explains to him that since she now loves him and the others as her "family" (her second new "family", after the Mars mission astronauts in Book One), gradually, he, Claremont and the others (particularly Tommy George, who the Storied Watcher has adopted as a son) will begin to inherit the gift of *Amaiish*, in effect becoming among the first of a new race of super-beings.

Not really wanting to deal with all of this, Billings takes his alien lover to the floor-tile and home decorating business where he works, introducing her to his boss – Hugo Szabo – as a "secretary". Matters appear to be proceeding normally, when the Klan of Jesus Christ, arriving at the floor-tile shop shortly after the CIA has staked it out, planning itself to capture or kill Karéin-Mayréij – "jumps the gun" on the American secret police and attacks the building, causing heavy casualties on both sides.

As Book Two closes, knowing that she must flee and wait for her powers to fully return, the Storied Watcher pours out the gift of the *Fire* upon Bob Billings. She departs with a dire threat to America's leaders : "Leave Bob, Whitney, Melissa, Curtis and most of all Tommy, free and unharmed... *or else*".

Will America's corrupt, incompetent future leaders – preoccupied as they are with distractions such as ex-Pakistani nuclear weapons, now in the hands of Muslim terrorists – pay heed to the warning?

Read on!

Stalker

Back-Seat Angel

"Get me the Director – *quickly!*" barked the Russian into the special mobile-communicator, his words tripping over each other in his native tongue.

"It is the deep hours of the night over here," protested the voice at the other end. "You are not following protocol – this is only a default-security circuit –"

"Hang the security," retorted the man, cursing beneath his breath, as he fumbled for equipment inside his plain-looking car, its windows rolled almost fully-up, despite the pestilential heat. "This is top priority!"

"Very well, but it will be up to *you* to answer for this," grunted the voice. "One second."

It was actually three or four before the call was finally connected, but it might have been three or four hours, from the perspective of the man in the car.

"Alexi *tut*," came a fainter voice. "Misha? Is that you? Why are you calling now, and without standard precautions? I am still in bed, let me sit up – here, I have upgraded the circuit-security, do you see the symbol at your end –"

"Yes, confirmed, it is I... and we have an *urgent* situation down here," blurted out the Russian. "I tracked the target down to this 'Billings' workplace, a factory that makes some kind of home construction supplies, apparently. I saw her and Billings get out and enter the, uhh, 'Tucson Floor and Tile' company. They did not come out for several hours; but about ten minutes ago, agents of one of the American intelligence-agencies – I am not sure which one, it might be the FBI's SSG group, CIA or maybe Secret Service, I do not believe that they are military – showed up and encircled the place. It looked very much like a capture-operation being put into effect."

"Damnation!" muttered the other voice. "Have they seized her, yet?"

"Not as far as I can tell – but there is more, and worse," warned Misha, his eyes looking in all directions for signs of the counter-spies closing in. "Something *very* strange has happened."

"Explain," demanded Alexi.

"Three ordinary American cars – which did *not* look like intelligence-issue – appeared suddenly, shortly after the U.S. government agents set up their perimeter," continued the field-agent. "These roared on to the parking-lot outside the building, and for a moment the FBI, or whomever they are, hesitated – perhaps they thought that the vehicles were carrying their own people, I do not know."

"Gangsters? Another nation's cell... Chinese or Brazilian, maybe?" speculated the remote voice.

"I can but guess at that," stated Misha, "Because then, at least six or seven Americans, all white but otherwise normal-looking, exited the two cars rapidly and began running at high speed toward the 'Tucson Floor and Tile' location. They were yelling something and waving their arms in the air, but I was too far away to tell what these cries meant. The interlopers were warned to stop by the government personnel, but when they ignored this warning, the American agents opened fire – then there were several huge explosions, even though I was far away, they nearly burst my eardrums."

"What?" gasped the man in Russia. "That makes absolutely no *sense!*"

"I know, I *know* – but I saw it with my own eyes," said the field-agent. "If I were elsewhere, I would say that I just witnessed a suicide-bombing, because the building was leveled, and three of the agents' SUVs sustained heavy damage... there are bodies lying everywhere around here, and I can hear sirens in the distance. Alexi, you *know* how much I hate to tell you this, but it appears that the mission may now be at an end – it is difficult to believe that *anyone* inside that building could still be alive, especially as there was no warning before the bombs went off. It is no more than a big heap of rubble, right now."

The Russian could hear pained breathing at the other end of the line.

"Alexi... are you there?" he asked, after a few seconds.

"Yes," came back a pained voice. "Damn them all to *hell!*" it cursed. "To have come so *far*, and..."

"Just one second," countered the Russian spy. "My rear passenger-side door has sprung open – bloody useless American cars... nothing works properly on them. It has been ridiculous here, since they prohibited the importing of the foreign models. I will reach over and close it –"

He unlocked his seat-belt and sprawled awkwardly over the gap between the front two seats, trying to reach the door's inside handle.

Odd, he thought.

A hole in the back-seat fabric, with a wisp of smoke coming from it? But, I did not take any bullets... I was not near enough to the battles...

"That will not be necessary," sounded a strange, melodious voice, in lightly accented but very good English, from somewhere behind the man. "I will close it *for* you, sir. But could you speak in Eng-lish, if you do not mind? I only know a little bit of this, uhh, 'Russian' language, unfortunately."

The door slowly swung shut, propelled by... *nothing.*

Like another of his countrymen months or more earlier, in a far different setting, Misha froze, totally at a loss as to what to do.

"Alexi," he gasped, speaking in Tucson vernacular, "I must change to English, now."

"*Potamu-shto?*" replied the man at the other end. "You *know* that we do not speak English over a link like this."

"Why?" asked the Russian, chuckling nervously. He went on, "I will *tell* you why, Alexi, my friend. So that the target, who is now located in my back-seat – although she is still completely invisible to my eyes – can understand. Would *that* be a good enough reason, do you think?"

"*Shto?*" came back a gasp, over the cell connection. "Uhh... yes, Misha. English will be... quite acceptable, under these, unforeseen circumstances. Please say 'hello' to her, on behalf of the Russian Government."

"*Da,*" agreed the man in the car. "I will put her on the hands-free microphone."

The SVR-agent stared at the back-seat. It looked completely unoccupied, except for the slightest hint of an indentation, on the passenger-side seat.

"My government sends you its greetings," he managed.

"Thank you," came back the disembodied voice. "And I send you my own. We have much to discuss, I suppose."

"Indeed," answered the Russian. "My name is 'Misha', and my superior, with whom I have been talking until you got into the car, is Alexi. He is in Moscow... the capital city of our country. You know, Miss... Karéin... my government has a strong interest in you. We have been trying to track you, since the, uhh, incident with the comet."

There was a long silence, and the spy was afraid that this long sought-after being had been offended, or, perhaps, had somehow again slipped his grasp.

But eventually, the pleasant, feminine voice sounded again.

"*Karéin,*" she repeated, as if deeply pondering something. "*Karéin.* Yes, *that* is my name... is it not? 'Karéin-Mayréij', the, the, *yes – now* it comes back. 'Karéin-Mayréij, the Storied Watcher' – that is what they call me... thank you, thank you *so* much. I am already in your debt, for reminding me of this."

She paused, and then, a second later, absent-mindedly mumbled, "But why would Bob, not have told me... he *must* have known my true name, all the while... he simply *must...*"

My mind perceives music, mused Misha.

Like in the desert.

"You did not know?" he incredulously asked.

"No," she replied. "*That* aspect of my being, of who I am, like many others, has been... *missing,* since I, uhh, 'arrived', here. I am but a faint shadow of the one who you may think of, as the 'Storied Watcher'."

"That would explain much," noted the cell-phone voice, in heavily accented English. "Such as why you have been traveling with the, uhh, salesman, and his friends, instead of just flying from here to there, to wherever you want."

"My memories of the last few months – not to say eons before that – are still very incomplete," explained the one who had, until this day, called herself 'Sari Tanak'. "The attack on the comet almost killed me... in fact, I *still* do not know *how* I survived that incident; except, maybe, a higher purpose preserved my life. A few of my abilities, for example the light-bending one that I am using now to ensure that the American government-people do not see me here in the car with you, are still with me."

"And my other, greater, powers are returning," she added. "It is only a matter of time, until I will be back to, uhh, 'normal', as you humans say. I reveal these things to you, in the hope that we can be friends. That we might be able to reach an *accommodation...* that is, your Russian kingdom, and myself."

"We would *definitely* be interested in just such an arrangement," Alexi quickly answered, his voice rising with excitement.

He then issued a command to the other one, in Russian.

"Do you mind if I start driving?" asked the man in the car.

"To where?" immediately came back the disembodied voice.

"Away from here," said Misha. "The Americans may try to establish a secondary security-cordon, and we do not know how large an area that they may close off. There is thus a chance that we might be captured, in such a, uhh, 'dragnet'. Also, having me sitting here, apparently speaking only to myself, may cause suspicion. The CIA, FBI and the Immigration Police, have cameras and listening-devices *everywhere*, you know."

"Alright," agreed the alien-girl. "But please – do not try any tricks. They will not work on me, and I have had my *fill* of governments trying to abuse my trust. By the way... you should avoid that big main street – the one that goes from north to south – that Bob and I drove down to get to his place of business, before the American spies attacked us. While we were traveling south, we encountered what appeared to be a shoot-out between the, uhh, 'gangstas' and the local police... at least, I *thought* that they were the police. If they have established this 'dragnet' that you speak of, it will probably be in effect there. If they stop us, I will have to leave immediately."

The A/C went on, American rules or no.

"Thank you for the tip," he mentioned. "I will drive west, through the secondary streets."

"We know that you are difficult to deceive," interjected the voice from Moscow, as the car slowly edged out of its parking-space and on to a suburban side street. "And we will not, uhh, *shto govoryet*, 'play games'. But why are you coming to *us*, with this proposal?"

"You must understand," replied the voice from the back-seat, "That I *was* prepared to deal with the government of this 'United States'; but within the last hour, they have tried to *kill* me, along with Bob Billings, who, incidentally, I have taken as my mate, down here on Earth. I did not *like* that, and they will come to bitterly regret having tried it."

"If you do not mind my asking," inquired Misha, "If his life was in danger, then why did you not try to defend this 'boyfriend'... with your powers, I mean. After all, you destroyed a *comet* –"

"Bob was still alive when I left him, thank the Holy Light; I protected him, when the Americans' explosives wrecked the building in which he worked," explained the Storied Watcher. "But I am still *so* weak – I cannot yet face their entire army or rescue him, Whitney Claremont or the children. I jumped out through a hole in the roof, and though I tried to defend myself as best I could, I must have been hit by one of their bullets, because the American secret-agents were firing wildly in many directions at the time, I was wounded... I am sorry that my blood has damaged your car. I will try to pay you back, sometime –"

"Badly-wounded?" asked the worried SVR field man. "Is there anything that we can do to help you survive?"

"No, and no – but thank you for the offer," replied the invisible female. "I removed what little was left of the bullet, from my leg, just prior to coming to hide in your car; I can heal myself rapidly, if I have a few minutes to concentrate my powers upon a wound, but I wanted to make sure that you did not drive away. So I neglected doing that until I got here. It hurts, of course... but I will be oh-kay, quite soon."

"Well, *that* is a relief," offered Alexi. "So... what do you want of Russia?"

There was a brief pause, during which the alien-girl was obviously considering what to say.

Then, again, she spoke.

"I have had many, many years – more than either of you will count, in your human lifetimes – in playing the game of politics, spies and alliances, and I have spent a lot of my available time learning about this 'Earth', about its nations and the relationships between them," she stated.

"An empire like this 'America'," continued the newcomer, "One that interferes in other peoples' affairs – one that starts wars all over the place, so it can steal more than its fair share of your world's resources, one that pretends to be 'the model for the whole world', but that oppresses its people with stupid laws with which nobody can comply and still live a normal life, one that makes people whose only 'crime' is having the wrong skin-color, live in miserable poverty – well, *that* kind of kingdom, would likely have *enemies*... would it not?"

"It certainly would," replied the Moscow voice, neutrally. "In countries like my own. But, Storied Watcher... at the risk of perhaps being punished later by my own government for saying this, I must be honest with you. *Nobody* on this Earth is perfect, Russia included. If you have done your research, surely you must know that. I am proud of my country, as is Misha, but... we would not want to disappoint you. I cannot pretend that we might not also have tried to capture you, were you to have, uhh, landed, somewhere within our borders."

"I am well aware of that," observed the invisible former 'Sari'-girl. "I have no illusions. I have read about what went on in your own wars in, where is it, again, 'yoo-Krain' and 'Ston-eea', as well as the one where the Empire of China tried to invade that island-kingdom. Your world is very violent... far more so than it should be, given the advanced nature of your technology and how much knowledge and wisdom is easily available for anyone to learn and take to heart."

"At last, the judgment of someone qualified so to do," muttered Misha. "Many humans have also made that observation, but they are always dismissed as 'not being objective'."

"Aye," confirmed Karéin-Mayréij. "But I must work with the Earth's people as they *are*, rather than how I think that they should be. All that I ask for, is a little help, until I am, uhh, how do the Americans say it, 'back on my feet'. I promise you that I will pay your Russian kingdom back many-fold, when I am able to do so. I will *never* take orders from you – nor will I from the Americans, or from anyone else – but that does not mean that I will not listen more carefully to those who have helped me when I needed it, than I will to those who have tried to murder me. Do you understand? Will you communicate this to your rulers?"

"I promise you that I will convey your proposal to the President, the *second* that this conversation is over with," confirmed Alexi. "But what, specifically, do you require?"

They heard a girlish chuckle, followed by, "Well, to start with, I would like somewhere safe to stay; I cannot just check in to a local mo-tel around here, you know? Just before the bomb went off at the floor-tiling store, Bob received a frightened call on his cell-phone from Whitney Claremont – she is the dark-skinned woman with whom we have been traveling, by the way, her children are Curtis and Melissa, and my own adopted child Tommy, who is in Whitney's care – indicating that Bob's house was also under attack... I am not sure by who, but I would have to assume that they are the same American President's assassins who were trying to kill *me*. I gave Whitney instructions as to how to protect herself, and I hope and pray to the Gods that these were sufficient, but I obviously cannot go back to the house... it will be under close watch."

"You can be *sure* of that," interjected Misha. "But if Alexi agrees, I am reasonably sure that I can offer you a suitable hiding-place. As you may be aware, when, uhh, agents of my type operate here in the United States, we must do so discreetly, and we have the tools to enable this."

"Agreed," immediately confirmed the Moscow voice.

"Thank you,"answered the invisible alien. "As to the rest, I do not require much for myself; I care not for rank, or privilege, or adoration. I need food and drink, especially sweet things to eat, like this 'chocolate' that you have on Earth, I have taken a real liking to it. Oh, and the sugary drinks that the Americans call 'soda-pop', but not the 'diet' kind – those ones have funny chemicals in them... *most* distasteful. But to speak of what is important, most of all, I need *knowledge*. And one other favor, besides."

"What do you mean?" uneasily inquired Alexi.

"The Americans will likely have taken Bob," she explained, "To some secret, hard-to-reach place that might take me *years* to find. I am patient and could do that, but I would like him and my friends to still be relatively young and healthy when I again see them. The same fate has probably affected Whitney, Melissa, Curtis and my beloved Tommy. I have pledged that, as I did once already, I will come to free them. Any help that your Russian government could give me, in locating these secret jails – the Americans have *thousands* of them, apparently, and many are not even on this continent – would be *greatly* appreciated."

"We will see what we can do," evaded the voice from Moscow.

"Also," added the Storied Watcher, "Even *before* you find out where they are being held, I would like your empire to communicate a short message to the American President, because it is obviously difficult for me to do so directly myself, without running a substantial risk. Do that, and give me your word of honor that you will not conspire with the American government to help them imprison or eliminate me, and that you will warn me if you detect a plan to do any of these things."

"What message?" asked Misha.

"A very simple one," answered the alien. "*Free my friends, and do not harm or imprison them again.* And, do it in a manner that I can verify. No tricks."

"I will relate your request," offered Alexi, "But please understand that I can only *suggest* this course of action to my government's authorities. They may or may not comply with your demand, and may or may not do so right away. The very fact that they will, as soon as I get off this conversation, know of your existence, is, as we say in the intelligence business, a 'valuable asset'. Moscow may want to withhold that from the Americans, to achieve other goals."

"I can but ask," said the invisible voice. "Right now, I am unfortunately in a position only to do that. Soon enough, I will be able to bargain more... *forcefully.*"

"You know, Storied Watcher," commented Misha, slowly and carefully, "Neither the American secret police – nor our own – care much for the safety of prisoners... especially those who they do not think have some special value. There is, therefore, a very real possibility that this 'Claremont' woman and the children with her, might already be dead. If that is the case... what will you do?"

"If they they have murdered Tommy on account of me, after having been warned of the consequences," she growled, as the Russian's mind reverberated with chords of ominous ethereal music, "By the end of the first week of the day on which my powers fully return, this 'President of the United States' will find his country *reduced to ashes*, one second before he meets his own cruel death. When I am finished, no two stones will still be left standing, and this empire will be so thoroughly shattered that it will *never* rise again! The American President's fate will be scarcely less, if the Americans have tormented or wounded Bob, Whitney or her own children."

"I, uhh... *see*," dispassionately replied the voice in Moscow.

There was sweat on the face of the Russian in the car, and it wasn't from the heat.

"Please do not take this the wrong way," he commented, "But... *surely* you have considered the possibility that the Americans want to eliminate you, before you become powerful enough to do anything like what you just described? Alexi speaks the truth, Storied Watcher; had you fallen to Earth in Russia, perhaps our own government would have reacted in like manner. The power that you may eventually have under your control, is not something that can be dismissed without concern. How can you speak of destroying an entire *country*, in the cause of saving one or two people, themselves all Americans, anyway?"

"I know – and I have thought about that," evenly offered Karéin-Mayréij. "But I am who I am, with the powers that the Gods have granted me... I cannot change that, nor *would* I, had I the chance. As I have said at other times, I have no desire to conquer or rule the peoples of this planet – either those in the United States, or in Russia, or anywhere else – even though perhaps I *could*, when my powers have fully returned. I only want to live humbly, as one of you, to know and understand the hopes and fears of ordinary humans, and to serve them as best suits their needs."

"Again, I beg your patience," pressed Misha, "But how can you reconcile that, with a threat to lay waste to the entire United States? How is destroying a country, acceptable, when ruling it, is not?"

"Please appreciate," she counseled, with a weird, self-confident tone, "That I do not *want* to hurt anyone – violence is distasteful to me in a special way that your people can never fully understand. But I am *not* a pacifist; I will use every weapon at my disposal, to protect those who I know to be innocent. Let me turn your accusation back upon itself – is this so great a thing to ask, to free and keep safe one, uhh, 'floor-tile salesman', one black woman and three children? If I asked *your* government to do this, in exchange for my friendship, would they not agree? Why, then, should I have to threaten the American government, for such a modest request, along with my own basic right to stay alive? I cannot *believe* that an intelligent ruler would provoke a fight with me, over something like *this!*"

"Maybe the Americans are not trying to do that,' proposed the voice from Moscow. "Perhaps it is all just a mistake. Nations as large and complex as the United States, or Russia, frequently act in a clumsy and un-coordinated manner."

"You are honest... even when being so might not support your objectives," commented the alien-girl, from inside her 'bubble'. "I honor and appreciate that. But, as I told my lover Bob Billings before I had to leave him, lest I be captured or killed, I have not lived as long as I have – and that is a *very* long time, by the reckoning of you humans – by assuming the best of people... or by taking chances."

Misha nodded ruefully, assuming that she could see the gesture.

"If the United States government just wanted to *talk* with me," argued the Storied Watcher, "Then why did they try to blow me to pieces, less than an hour ago? They *certainly* must have had far easier ways in which to communicate, to start a dialog! Like you, they have been spying on me – and I have let them overhear, when I have said that I mean no unprovoked harm to them. Their language of violence is very clear to me, and now the burden of proof is upon *them*, to avoid me responding in like fashion –"

"But –" started Misha.

He was quickly interrupted by the Muscovite.

"Unfortunately," interjected Alexi, "I cannot reasonably refute your conclusions, here. If it is of any interest, we observed the entire episode from outside – as we mentioned earlier, we have had you under surveillance since we determined that you had fallen in the United States – and it was clear that the intent on the part of those who attacked the building, was indeed lethal. You have good reason to, how do the Americans say, 'watch your back'."

"I am curious about something," said Misha. "*We* had *you* under surveillance, as my superior has said, but how did you come to track *me* down, in this car, Karéin? So far, to the best of my knowledge, the American CIA, FBI and so on, are unaware of my presence here. If *they* cannot find me... how did you?"

Another weirdly girlish laugh issued from the direction of the apparently vacant back-seat. "Misha – do you mind if I use your first name?"

"Uhh, no... of *course* not," hastily replied the Russian.

"Thanks," she went on. "I think that you and I have already met... have we not? Tell me – do you remember a strange feeling coming over you, a day or two ago, when you were investigating myself, Bob, Whitney and the children, back at Bob's house?"

"*Da*," nervously affirmed the man. "I mean, 'yes', that is."

"That was my mind touching yours, if only for a fleeting moment," explained the alien-girl. "You were too far away for me to obtain a good, uhh, 'scan', as you would say. On that day, I also, uhh, 'locked on to the smell – as near as I can describe this, in the Eng-lish language – of all the special techno-gadgetry that you, uhh, secret-agents, use to spy on each other with. If I sit and concentrate, these things are as easy for me to detect against the surroundings of all the other, uhh, 'smells', as it would be for you to see a bright red tree, in an otherwise ordinary forest."

"Ah," said Misha. "So *that* is how you located me."

"Basically, yes," she confirmed. "But, to tell you the truth, I was just lucky, in the fact of your simply *being* here – in the vicinity of the 'Tucson Floor and Tile' building, I mean."

"Can you elaborate?" asked Alexi.

"After the attempt on my life," stated the Storied Watcher, "I knew that I had to hide myself and escape, if only to avoid exposing Bob and the others to yet *more* attacks. So I leaped up to the top of the wrecked building – I did not stay there for more than a few seconds, because I was afraid that the Americans might have developed some way of penetrating my hiding-bubble and tracking me – and I started moving rapidly away from the scene."

There was a soft laugh, over the remote link. Then the Muscovite offered, "If only I could have *seen* the faces on the CIA and FBI operatives, at that point... ah, but *do* go on."

"Finally," she continued, "When I was perhaps two-thirds of a kilometre away, I stopped and again went to the top of a building, trying to see if Bob was still there, or if they had already taken him... I guess that the latter must have been the case, because all I saw were those big black vehicles that the American agents like to drive around in, all the time. I was *terribly* sad and disappointed, not to mention angry, that this had happened; and, to tell you the truth, I felt very alone, very vulnerable, up against huge odds... I suppose that I should not have said that. Please ignore that last part... anyway, in scanning the surroundings, in trying to find a place to hide, temporarily, I noticed *you*. I figured that I had nothing to lose, by attempting to communicate with your Russian kingdom – after all, if I already have *one* Empire trying to kill me, and I am stuck within its borders... how much worse, can *two* be?"

Again, the voice from Moscow could be heard in a soft chuckle.

"Your logic is impressive," he remarked.

"It has been developed over thousands of your years," offered the invisible being. "With that much practice, one is bound to get things right, eventually."

"Forgive me for asking this," said the Russian as he drove, allowing himself a weak smile, "But... *you*? Feeling vulnerable? In view of what you have already accomplished, Storied Watcher... surely you must know how that sounds, to Alexi and I."

If any had been able to see through her other-worldly veil, they would have perceived a rueful smile, as the alien-girl spoke.

"Perhaps it *does* sound odd, from your perspective," she explained, "But consider – the civilizations of this 'Earth' have some very advanced technology, not least among nations such as the United States and your Russia, not to mention the 'Europeans' and the Chinese Empire. I am not *used* to coping with enemies who can employ all these intelligent machines against me, who can track my every move with computer spying-devices at every turn, although I am trying to learn how to do that, as quickly as possible... I am more familiar with tilting against enemies who use weirding-arts, 'magic', if you will..."

"Interesting," offered Alexi.

"I honestly do not know how long I could stay hidden against a large and sophisticated opponent like the American government, especially if it threw all of its secret police and military resources against me," continued Karéin-Mayréij. "If they find me before my powers fully return, maybe they *could* murder me; I doubt it, but as I said, I do not like taking chances, and I would have to defend myself by using all my powers – I might have to kill a lot of American soldiers and possibly innocent passers-by in doing that... which is an outcome that I might be forced to accept... but one that I will try to avoid."

"Well... *that* is nice to hear," half-seriously quipped Misha.

"Please understand," she implored, "II am hoping fervently that matters will not come to that. After the loss of Bob, Whitney and the children, I have no *friends*, nowhere to go – nowhere to even get a good meal or just to have someone I can trust to talk with. Having friends is very important to me. I need *time*, somewhere safe to rest and gather my strength. After that, maybe we can, uhh, 'sort it all out', as Bob used to say. If you can give me that... I will not forget your help."

"Karéin," requested the voice from Moscow, "Do you mind if I speak privately with Misha in Russian, for a minute?"

"No," she replied. "It is oh-kay. Go ahead."

"*Da*?" said the man in the car, switching rapidly into his native language. "Yes, Alexi?"

"Listen, Misha," commanded the man in Russia, "This is obviously a turn of luck of *historic* importance – my God, after we thought that the entire program had come undone... I will call the *President* immediately after we finish this conversation, but in the meantime, you are to guard the alien with your life, if necessary. I suppose you will have to inform Oleg and Katya of the situation, but try not to say *anything* over the phone network indicating that she is with us : the risk is too great that the CIA or NSA will intercept our communications, if they have not done so already. Keep moving from place to place, according to deep-cover directives; we will issue orders by standard disintegrating-paper code-packages. And whatever you do, do not let her out of your sight –"

"That will be rather hard to do," noted the man in the car, "Since she cannot be seen, in the first place – she is *invisible*, Alexi. How would I even know if such a being is still with me... much less confine her to a safe location?"

"By talking with her, and giving her anything that she wants, as long as it does not risk the cover of the operation," demanded the Moscow voice.

"I will try to do as you say," answered Misha, "But it will, at best, just buy us some time. What is headquarters' long-term plan? Surely we must have had arrangements for what to do, in circumstances such as this?"

"I honestly do not know," stated the supervisor. "It will be up to the *President* and the Supreme Council."

"Are there any more instructions?" inquired the field-agent.

"No, we can go back to English, now," allowed the Muscovite.

"So... Karéin," started Alexi, "Here is what we have planned; we need-to-know if it meets with your approval. First, we will take you to the safe-house – this is a term we use in espionage-matters to describe a place that we do not think is under hostile surveillance – where you can conduct your affairs without fear of being tracked down or attacked by the Americans. I should mention, however, that we, and you, will have to change locations frequently... this is a standard technique that we use to avoid the local informants of the CIA, FBI and so on, from detecting us. We would like you to stay in the safe-houses until –"

"Excuse me," interrupted the alien-girl, "But I cannot agree to any restrictions on my own freedom of movement. This is one of the main reasons why I am now discussing things with you and your friend Misha... and not with the Americans... remember?"

"We are well aware of that," answered the voice from Moscow, "And I give you my word, we will not attempt to confine you – not that we could – but please appreciate that when you go off on your own, we cannot protect you from the American government."

"Hah," countered the Storied Watcher. "Shortly, you will not need to do that. 'Protect me', I mean. Do you understand? However, I do not know *how*, 'shortly'. It could be hours... days... or even weeks."

"Here, you must allow me to explain something that may not have been immediately apparent, when you, uhh 'arrived' in the United States," elaborated the Russian at the other end. "The Americans claim to have a 'democratic' form of government in which citizens have rights, but, in reality, especially since the so-called 'Dirty Bomb' incident in Miami several years ago, and their badly-executed invasion of Pakistan more recently, their CIA, FBI, Secret Service, Immigration Service and other secret police, have infiltrated institutions at almost *every* level of their society. Their presence is pervasive; they have informants and casual spies on every street of every city in the United States, and all communications are carefully monitored – the only reason why I can be speaking with you in this manner, over the cell connection I mean, is that our own SVR secret service is able to scramble the communication-channel for a limited time, before the American NSA figures out the encryption-key... so we will have to end this conversation soon."

"Bob explained a lot of this to me," observed the former-'Sari' girl. "And I have seen some of it for myself, personally. My powers provide me with an adequate defense against some of these spying-things, but I cannot be sure that my arts will negate *all* of them. Which is one reason why I decided to solicit your Empire, as an ally."

"You should also know," continued Alexi, "That the American intelligence-agencies have almost unlimited power to detain, or, if they deem it necessary, eliminate, anyone considered to be 'an enemy of the state'. People just 'disappear', and everyone in the United States knows that it is unwise to ask what happened to them. I am afraid that you, and possibly anyone who associates with you, would definitely fall into the latter category, and I have to warn you that while the Americans' *average* counter-intelligence agents are no worry to us, a few of them are highly-trained, very well-equipped and ruthlessly efficient. They could and would kill you without so much as a second thought, if ordered to do that by their superiors –"

"As would you, if told to do so by your own. Correct?" commented the invisible voice.

A pained look appeared on Misha's face, as if caught on the horns of a dilemma.

"Yes," reluctantly confirmed the Moscow voice. "I *said* that we would be honest, and I will not deceive you on this issue, either. But I would hasten to say that as far as I know, our government has issued no such order, and I think it is very unlikely that they would do so."

"I will take that into consideration," stated the alien-girl, "With the understanding that it comes from a spy in service of his own Empire... no offense meant, you know."

One hand still on the wheel, Misha used his other to reach back and offer it as a handshake, a gesture that was immediately accepted, even though, had the Russian in the car turned his head to look, he would have been alarmed to see what appeared to be the stump of his right arm, truncated at the wrist.

A weird, warm, empowering feeling, like the best *Stolchinaya* except without the hint of a hang-over, surged down the Russian's right arm, as strange thoughts bombarded his psyche for a second.

Luckily, he was driving on a straightaway.

He broke in to the conversation, saying, earnestly, "And let me say, Storied Watcher, that I owe you my *life*, for what you did on that day when the comet looked like it was to end our existence. Millions more, both in this country, in Russia and elsewhere on Earth, also know the truth about this, and know that there is no way we can repay you. All we can say is, 'thank you, and God bless you'."

"I accept your love and gratitude, and I return and magnify it," replied the alien voice, somehow friendly and reassuring as it spoke, "Not just for the kindness of your thoughts; but because, above all else, I want to be *loved* by the people of the Earth, not hated, not persecuted. And I will tell you *this* – though the memory of what I endured to destroy the comet still brings terror to my mind, each time I foolishly recall it... I am here, I know, to accomplish other, *different* things, as well. My work on Earth is hardly started... never mind finished."

"What do you mean?" perplexedly asked Alexi.

"I hear... *voices* from time to time," mentioned the invisible more-than-a-girl, "And they tell me that I am meant to be your planet's guardian, sent here to protect her, and all the people who live upon her. I am here to teach, to serve, to enlighten. To give you all the gifts that I possess, as you become wise enough to understand them and use them safely."

"Sent by who? And what are these 'gifts'?" inquired the voice from Moscow, interest rising in his tone.

"I like to believe that I have been sent by the Powers Above," she answered, matter-of-factually. "And as to the gifts that I bestow – well, if you would like to know what these are, you can start by asking my driver... right, Misha?"

"Uhh... right,' replied the man, as if in a trance.

"She has... *affected* you? We will need a full report on this," Alexi quickly retorted.

He quickly switched to Russian, demanding, "Are you still capable of independent thinking? Are you under her control, Misha? If there is the *slightest* doubt, we need Katya to take over the mission –"

"*Nyet* – I do not *feel* any different," argued the driver, changing back to English. "Except... maybe, I feel a little less nervous, being in the Storied Watcher's presence."

"Perhaps I am just becoming used to having you around," he added. "After all, you are quite a different type of contact than the ordinary Americans that I have to meet with and cajole, Karéin."

"As my lover Bob would say... 'no shit'," teased the alien-girl, with a little giggle. "I recall that he told me a joke like, 'you don't get too many aliens in here, and at *these* prices...'"

"But anyway, I will leave it to Misha to explain, as my *Fire* comes to rest upon him," she continued. "I can begin your report, by saying this much : I have made my new friend stronger, healthier... *better*, in every way, oh, and do not worry about the 'judgment' issue. My gift does not *directly* change anyone's ability to reason, although, I will allow you *this* – most of those who have been changed in this way, do 'take a step back to consider things'; that is, their perspective on life may change, somewhat. Misha is not the first – I have already done the same, for several other people here in Tucson, and elsewhere. Those who are kind to me, who help me, who act with virtue – these are all the first who will follow in my footsteps. I just hope that your, uhh, fellow spy, will use his gift responsibly, for good, not evil. Will you?"

"I will," echoed the driver.

"You know, Karéin," requested Alexi, "While we are no doubt, grateful for this... *gift*, or whatever it is, may I ask that you refrain from doing it any more, while you are under our protection. You will draw attention to yourself, and that is never a *good* thing, when one is trying to be discreet, to hide from the American authorities."

"I appreciate your concern," she answered, "But I am afraid that I cannot commit to that request – not without any possibility of making an exception, under the right circumstances. Your human ways are not *my* ways, and my coming here has set events into motion that cannot now be taken back... I am here for a *purpose*, and though I do not yet fully comprehend all of it yet, I *do* know that I must at least do this, namely, show human people my love, with my gift. If you cannot deal with me on that basis, I will understand, I will not hold it against you or your Russian empire. I can just leave the car and trouble you no more –"

"No, no – that will be *fine*," hastily retreated the Muscovite. "What if we were just to say that you will only do this to those who we know of and approve –"

"Sorry," she shot back, still keeping her tone polite and pleasant. "That sounds like *exactly* the kind of demand that the American government would make of me... that I would empower only *their* chosen people, so they could gain an advantage, not to be shared with anyone else. Does my reasoning on this matter not appeal to you, sir?"

At a loss, the voice from Moscow hesitated for a second or two, then muttered, "I suppose that it does, looking at things from your perspective. You drive a hard bargain."

"I have had many thousands of your solar-years in which to have learned what people think is valuable, and what they will settle for," she replied, sweetly. "As well as other advantages that I will leave for you to figure out. Do not think the less of yourself, for how you have dealt with me."

The car turned a corner and gradually came to a slow stop, halfway down a back alleyway between two buildings.

"We have arrived at the current safe-house," announced Misha. "It is what the Americans would call a 'second-rate hotel'; that is, the accommodations are not very good – for example, I have had problems with bedbugs and cockroaches – but it is inexpensive, and the owners do not check the credentials of their guests very carefully... as long as one pays the bill on time. And unlike many of the better hotels, this one still accepts cash-transactions. I should warn you that because of this, many of those who rent rooms in this place are rather shady characters – there are a lot of drug-abusers, gangsters, and, uhh, 'women of the night' –"

"You mean 'prostitutes', 'sluts', 'whores'... that manner of female?" interrupted the alien-girl. "Those who trade sex for money, I mean."

"Uhh... yes... precisely," answered the Russian, as he turned off the engine and dimmed the lights.

"Well, it is not just *women* who do that," observed the invisible voice.

"And not just *humans*, either," she added, as if commenting on the weather.

After a few seconds of silence, a nonplussed voice from Moscow said, "Is that... *right*."

"How do you *think* that I paid for the first few days of my little vacation trip through this interesting 'United States' empire?" she insouciantly replied. "Either directly, or indirectly, men, in particular, will pay *handsomely* for someone who is skilled at the arts of love; and just like with bargaining, I have had many years during which to perfect my skills in this area."

There was a pained silence, so she went on, "What is the matter? Does that surprise or offend you, Misha, Alexi? Your species has *so* many strange, inconsistent inhibitions about the mating-urges; I mean, nobody even, uhh, 'raises an eyebrow', when someone like me breathes, eats, drinks, or does her toilet... but the minute that I pleasure myself and whomever I take as a lover – an act that is every bit as natural as those that I just described – people think that it is somehow strange, bizarre... even, *evil*. Ah, just one of those many things about human societies to which I will need to become accustomed, I suppose."

"I can see," offered Alexi, "That we have much to learn about you, Storied Watcher. You are not exactly what we had imagined you to be."

"You know," commented the SVR-agent, "There are many in our country, as well as around the world, who think that you are an 'angel' – that is, a supernatural spirit, sent by God to deliver us from the 'Lucifer' comet. But we do not generally think of 'angels' in the same sentence as we would think of a 'whore'... these concepts are difficult for us to reconcile, together."

"As is the idea of an 'angel' powerful enough to destroy an entire nation, should its leaders offend her," added the Muscovite.

A gentle laugh issued from the still apparently unoccupied back-seat.

"Maybe I am, spy-men of the Russian Empire... maybe I *am*," philosophically replied the alien-girl. "But as I said, 'my ways are not your ways'. Perhaps... God's ways are not like yours... or, even like *mine*. Or perhaps I am a different *kind* of 'angel'. Have you considered those possibilities?"

"I would prefer not to," cautiously answered the voice from Russia.

"We should leave the car and go up to the room, now," proposed Misha.

"I will follow," answered the invisible voice. "As long as you will promise to do one other thing, when we go into this hotel."

"What would *that* be?" inquired the Russian.

"Do not close the doors too quickly, behind you," she instructed, with another subdued laugh. "Unless you should want to carry me on your back."

I Guess They Beat You To It

"Thank God – this crate's just like the one we left up north, easy to take those corners with," commented the third agent, as he expertly screeched its tires to a stop on the north side of the street, a short distance from the pandemonium surrounding their destination.

Looking up from the wheel as he removed the key, he did a double-take, along with his Asian-American superior and his hulking, African-American partner and mentor.

"*Shit, man!*" he gasped. "That's... uhh... some *heavy* business went down here!"

Hendricks wasn't kidding : the scene was grim. They beheld the charred, still-smoldering remains of what must, at one time, have been a suburban Tucson ranch-house; little now was left of this except a few stone superstructure walls, each pock-marked with the signs of projectile impacts, the latter also defacing the two houses to the left and right with some sinister simile of the measles.

Jagged shards of broken glass, not only from the burning house, but also from several others with their own windows shattered by some powerful force, littered the ground everywhere.

Surrounding the front lawn of this ruined place in all directions was a chaotic intermix of public safety vehicles, sirens loudly a-wailing, firemen, uniformed Tucson Police Department personnel, hundreds of ghoulishly-curious onlookers and various other passers-by.

Chu scanned the scene, her lips pursed tight in repressed frustration.

"Dammit – HQ told us that they had this situation under control, but here we are, a day late and a dollar short, *again*," she cursed. "What the hell's going *on* here?"

"Yeah – what's with all the civilians?" grumbled Boatman. "I can hardly see the fire-trucks for all these guys mobbin' 'em. You'd think this was a street-party or some-such nonsense. Somebody post a video of it up on *MyTubeSpace*, or somethin', to invite all these folk?"

From outside the SUV, they heard a shout issuing from somewhere within the crowd.

"Hey, *look!*" it exclaimed. "*There* they are – the Men in Black!"

"Should have got a nice apple-green car," muttered Hendricks. "Or a pickup-truck."

"Wouldn't make any difference with these here FBI-issue dark glasses, unless you ditched the suit for some nice Bermuda-shorts," offered the black man.

"Well, we gotta get out and face the music sooner or later... right, Minnie?" he suggested, unbuckling his belt and awkwardly shuffling his huge girth toward the rear passenger-side door.

"Yeah," reluctantly agreed Chu, reflexively arranging her hair and straightening her tie. "Okay, guys... let's keep this as orderly and professional as we can – remember, we're here to get *evidence*, not to answer questions... just tell them to speak with local law-enforcement."

"Got you there," complained the third agent, "Because those boys probably know a hell of a lot more than *we* do, at this point."

"Yeah," affirmed the woman, through clenched teeth. "Put your video-jammers on... I know they won't screw up those newfangled wrist-recorders with the countermeasures in 'em – we'll just have to hope that nobody in this crowd took the chance of buying one on the underground market."

The other two hit hidden buttons on their belts, then opened the doors of the vehicle and stepped out, with Chu in the lead and the other two slightly behind her, Boatman on the left and Hendricks on the right.

"Hey, spooks!" someone called out.

"Yo, Men in Black – was they gangstas in there? You sure did *them* good, no shit, right?" shouted another.

The three moved forward at a fast walk, ignoring the comments and cat-calls as they pushed through the masses of gawkers, with Boatman showing very clearly why he had made it as far as the semi-pro football leagues; the man's blocking was invaluable.

A few of the madding-crowd jeered, fewer still cheered, but nearly all stared in wonderment at being able to see members of the feared Federal Authorities up *this* close, without already being in trouble with the government.

"Over there," indicated the FBI-team-leader, pointing. "That guy. Looks like Tucson Police. Let's speak with him."

With steely determination, they approached the man.

"You, there!" called Chu. "Yes, *you*. Are you in charge here?"

The cop, his eyes as well-hidden by dark glasses as were the woman's own, turned to regard her.

"Temporarily, yes," he replied. "Until the Chief gets here."

He did a double-take.

"You look like you're from the... *government*, am I right?" he said, uneasily.

"That's right," answered Chu, as she retrieved her badge and held it in the cop's face. "I'm Agent Minnie Chu, FBI. These men behind me are Agents Boatman and Hendricks. We're here to take control of this operation, but first, we need-to-know –"

"*Look*, lady," retorted the cop, "I have *strict* orders from the Chief that nobody gets anywhere *near* the crime-scene, much less takes over from us, until he gets here with an order from the Governor. Oh, and, I guess I should mention, my name's Staff Inspector William Murchison, if you needed to know."

"Well, Staff Inspector Mr. William Murchison," countered the team-leader, feigning a slight smile of contempt, "I'm here representing Director Ochoa of the FBI, and he's involved in this by direct orders from the President of the United States. I'm sorry that I can't fill you in on the details, but this is a top-secret government operation, and there'll be *very* serious consequences if we aren't allowed to examine the scene. Time is of the essence here –"

"Sorry – but that makes no sense at all," protested Murchison. "Those other guys from the government told us we could handle it from here. Why are you showing up now and countermanding their instructions?"

"*What* other guys?" incredulously demanded Boatman.

"We shouldn't be discussing this in public," interjected Chu. "Do you have anywhere private, where we can find out what's going on?"

"Yeah, the command-post over there," mentioned the cop, pointing at a large, blue-colored vehicle that looked like a converted inter-city bus.

"Shall we?" requested Chu.

"Sure," replied Murchison. "But we can't take all day about it – HQ's telling me that the local TV station's got reporters on the way over here. This situation could get out of *hand*, you know."

All four of them headed rapidly to the vehicle, clambering aboard one by one up a ramp at the back. They were now in a high tech-environment, with flat-screen 3-D LED-displays, switches and computer terminals arrayed in every direction.

Chu, Hendricks and Murchison sat down on the swivel-chairs intended for the console operators; Boatman discovered that the teensy-weensy things wouldn't fit him, so he had to stand.

"Alright," started the FBI-team-leader. "Now, what *happened*, here? Please keep it concise; as I said, some of the evidence at this site may have a short, uhh, half-life, so we can't spend all day at this."

"Okay, okay... I'll tell you what I know, which isn't a hell of a lot," protested the cop. "About an hour ago, we got an APB on a shoot-out, with a fire and explosion also identified, in Desert Palms. At first there was no address specified, but it wasn't hard to find when we sent the standard three squad-cars down to investigate – damn place was burning so bad that we could see the smoke six blocks away."

"*Shit*," muttered Hendricks.

Murchison shrugged and continued, "At first, we figured that it might just be a gas-explosion – this is a fairly quiet neighborhood, you know, not a lot of synth-drug houses around here – but when our boys showed up, there were all these big black SUVs – I think there were four or five of them, over the place...

just like the one you FBI guys drove up in, except some of 'em looked a bit shot up, some of their windows were cracked...."

"Whoever they were, they *weren't* us," corrected Chu. "Go on."

"So," explained the cop, "Of course we had cars blocking all three egress routes, standard procedure, our officers came out with full gear, AR-180s with the DU penetrator-rounds, Kevlar-2 flak-jackets, the works – we did the bullhorn thing and ordered the guys in these SUVs to put their hands on their heads and come out. Figured it was a criminal shoot-out – happens all the time you know – as a matter of fact we had one just a bit further east earlier today, big messy thing out on the arterial road, 15 or 16 dead between the *Maras* and the Tooson Crew, drug-deal gone bad, as usual. Anyway, the one guy who *did* come out, didn't look at all like a gang-banger – matter of fact, he looked a lot like your friend over there."

He pointed at Hendricks.

"Thanks for the compliment... I think," said the third agent. "But that was *not* me, I can assure you."

"So this guy comes over to the Sargent-In-Charge," elaborated Murchison, "Flashes some kind of badge at him – again, this one looked a lot like yours, apparently, I didn't see it, mind you, because I got here afterwards – and pretty much orders him and our guys to stand down, says something about 'a top-secret government operation', tells us to just get out of there and not tell anybody –"

"And you just *did* that? You let 'em just drive *away*?" complained Boatman.

"Jaysus effing *Christ*," swore Hendricks, looking down with a sardonic grin, as he cradled his forehead in his hand.

Chu motioned for calm.

"Look, I'm not *finished*... okay?" retorted the cop. "Sargent Portillo tells them to hold on while we verify, which is also S.O.P., but the minute that our guys reach for the radio, this Federal-guy in the nice tidy black business-suit gives some kind of hand-signal to his bum-buddies back in one of the SUVs and *everything* shuts down, I mean, totally fuckin' *shuts down* – sorry for my French there lady, but this was really something... radios go dead, cell-phones too, even the damn *ignition* of the squad-cars gets bricked. So this government-guy smiles sweetly at Portillo and tells him, 'you wouldn't want us to do that to your guns, too, would you?'"

"I... *see*," neutrally observed Chu, with a far-off stare. "So that was when you let them get away?"

"Yeah," answered Murchison. "I mean, you gotta *understand*, lady – the safety of my fellow-officers has to be the priority in situations like this, okay, there's never *been* a situation quite like this, I'll admit that, but the point is, if we start shooting it out when we're at a tactical disadvantage – like, we always carry a few of the old-model pistols without any of this fancy electronic-shit in them, just as backup, but even at that, if we had decided to fight it out with these guys, or with the gangstas when they got bazookas and we just got our go-to guns,

AR-180s I mean, you'd have no cops *left* around here in no more than a month or so."

"Tell me somethin' *new*," grunted Boatman, with a cynical chuckle.

"And furthermore," the cop explained, "These guys in the nice new precision-pressed black suits sure *looked* authentic... I mean, for God's sake, you guys in the FBI gotta know the drill – you *don't* fuck with agents from the 'special Federal agencies' – you know what I mean. *Bad* things happen when you do that, and just because we're in law-enforcement ourselves doesn't mean that they can't make us 'disappear', just like all the other poor bastards who go missing all the time."

"Did you stop to consider that *we* might be able to make people 'disappear', as well?" bluffed the FBI-team-leader.

For a second, Murchison hesitated, looking back and forth.

Then he went on, "What I'm trying to *say*, Ms. Agent Chu, is that we know our limits – and bless his heart, Sargent Portillo did too, in this situation. Had he not, maybe he, or I, wouldn't be here to explain all of this to you."

"Okay," allowed Chu, her eyes focused laser-like on the Tucson policeman. "We understand. Listen... did these, uhh, 'government agents', say anything about the occupants of the house, that is, the one that's now demolished? Were there any casualties that you could see?"

"Negative," replied the cop, "And I doubt that *anybody* could have survived that fire-fight – I mean, the place's *still* too hot for my guys to go in and do the forensic-stuff on, and just from the number of casings all over the place, there were a *lot* of rounds fired. Oh, did I mention that we've found some human remains?"

Her heart sinking, the FBI-team-leader shot a shocked look at her fellow-agents.

It was quickly reciprocated by a sad-looking Boatman and an ashen Hendricks.

"*Really*," she responded, trying to sound professional. "Do you have an... ID, on them, yet?"

"Negative, again," answered Murchison. "And it's gonna come down to DNA-matching, maybe dental if we're lucky, on that front, I'm afraid. Just so you have the whole picture, we're talking about a foot here, an arm and part of a head there, plus a few other disassociated body-parts, strewn all over the place. Damnedest thing – reminds me of some of the crap that we hear about going on down Mexico way... you know, hostages wired with fifty pounds of Semtex or C-4, but they haven't tried *that* up here yet, not to my knowledge, anyway, the *Maras* usually just go for the old '200 rounds and I make you hamburger' thing –"

"Have you at least got a racial type on the remains? Age, gender... any of that?" demanded Boatman.

"They're all pretty badly-burned," stated the cop, matter-of-factually, "But as far as we can tell, they're all adult Caucasians, and there are at least three

Eventually, Chu stated, "We had better inform the Director."

Hendricks and Boatman nodded affirmatively.

"Listen, Will, Otis," ordered the team-leader, "You guys take control of the crime-scene... when it cools down enough to be safely entered, try to find and sequester anything relevant to the alien in the debris – make sure that you're doing this by yourselves, we don't want any loud-mouthed local cops mucking things up, over there – and see if you can find a basement-entrance, if there is one, but don't open it until I rejoin you. I'll go back to the car and explain the situation to the Director, see if he can get a trace on the route of the guys who beat us to the scene. I'll try to get back to the house in twenty minutes or less. You got that?"

"Yes ma'am," answered Boatman.

"You got it," echoed Hendricks.

Chu and Hendricks got up and strode purposefully toward the rear entrance of the mobile command-post. As they exited, their eyes were dazzled by ten or more camera-flashes, accompanied by the glare of yet more bright lights, the latter evidently for TV.

"Miss? *Miss!*" cried a voice. "Marilyn Johnson from KGUN here. Is it true that the FBI is now in control of this operation?"

"Sir!" exclaimed another. "Can you confirm that this was an illegal synth-drug house? Which gangs are involved? Does the government have an official body count yet?"

"No comment," grimly stated Chu, her eyes narrowing under sunglasses.

"You, sir!" shouted someone toward Hendricks. "We have witnesses saying that this was the result of a suicide-bombing. Should the public be worried about a new Muslim League terrorist offensive?"

"No comment," muttered the third agent, as he elbowed his way through the throng, following in the path semi-cleared by Boatman's bulk.

They had reached the point where Chu had to go in one way and the other two, in another.

"We're famous, now," chuckled the black agent. "Headquarters ain't gonna like hearin' 'bout *that*."

"Keep it together, gentlemen," commanded Chu. "I'll explain it to the Director as best I can. Let's go – we've all got work to do."

From one of the mobile TV vans arrayed far behind the throng, they heard a frustrated-sounding shout.

"Marilyn!" called a voice. "Damn video-signal's screwed up – we didn't get *anything* on those three in the suits... all we're getting is static, at this end!"

A smirk showed up simultaneously on the faces of all three FBI-agents, as they headed off to work.

Over Yo' Head, Billy-Boy

Again, he sat on a park-bench maybe ten feet or so from the white-and-black-striped post that told all around of a bus-stop in this small Alabama town; and again, Horn reminded himself that he didn't want to do this any more.

It's all gettin' a mite too complicated, he thought.

Fixin' a few votin' booths – well, okay, a lot of votin' booths – that's one thing. But truckin' with these folk, well, that'll get a fella in jail, or hurt, or...

A man in a business-suit, fully buttoned-up despite the sodden heat, walked in front of him and, despite no obvious cause for such fumble-fingeredness, dropped a rolled-up newspaper in front of the rolly-polly political bag-man.

Horn looked up, squinting, despite his broad Panama hat and cheap sunglasses.

"Y'all dropped your paper, sir," he offered, picking the newsprint up and holding it out to the man.

"You keep it. I'm done with reading for today," replied the man. He sauntered on, not looking back.

"Right obliged," mumbled Horn, not caring that the other man was now well out of earshot.

He unrolled the paper and turned to the crossword-puzzle page. As expected, it contained a delicate, tissue-thin piece of edible rice paper, upon which was a message.

Dear sir, the inscription read.

The Lord did not favor us when first our faithful made the blood sacrifice, but we will strike again and again, until the Accursed One is sent back to Hell, where it belongs.

We are certain that it has been captured by those who you serve, so now, you must find us a clear path to the Devil-Girl.

You have one month. After that, or if our martyrs can not get close enough, we will consider you to have failed.

Failure is sin – and you know what are the wages of sin. There is nowhere in the United States where our Brothers will not find you.

Report your progress to us on the first Monday of each week, and God be with you.

Shee-it, Horn mentally muttered.

Billy, ol' boy, y'all in over your head, this time.

He did not eat the paper; instead, he tore it into shreds and scattered these all about, and as he walked away, he looked back.

The pigeons were still all very much alive, as they pecked at this unexpected, though barely worthwhile meal.

I guess they do want me alive... for the time bein', he thought.

Despair And Resolve

Inside a bubble of invisibility, her subconscious mind adjusting and re-adjusting to defeat the barrier- and alerting-devices, Karéin-Mayréij reclined dejectedly against a burned-out wall – one of the few remnants of the former Billings residence.

Bullet-holes and scorch-marks, abundant even upon the rocks and stones of Bob's front yard, stood in mute testimony of an end to the life that she might have had.

Nightfall... and the American spy-men and gendarmes of their President-King have gone from the scene, mused the Storied Watcher.

Leaving it as forlorn and barren as the Blasted Plains of several worlds past. The stairway to Bob's 'basement' is filled with charred debris – and no life-auras are anywhere down there.

Oh, my love... this was such a happy place, if only for the briefest of times...

The guilt of having abandoned those who she had met in the north – most of all, Tommy – had plagued her all the way on the trip from the safe-house with the Russian, and mental exhaustion afflicted her scarcely less.

How can this be! she raged, anger and frustration stirring a toxic brew.

Everywhere that I have been in the Nine Universes, where there is a battle, there is always *a trace, something to track with... but here, it is as if it has been wiped by the hateful touch of the Nameless One.*

Naught but a few empty liquor-bottles and scraps of burned clothing, to remind me of that brief, happy time with poor, forgiving Bob, Whitney and her innocent children... and, my beloved little Tommy.

There is no spirit-trail, no life-path, in this place. Perhaps it cannot survive in the sterile embrace of the techno-machines.

How shall I find *them, in their hour of need?* inwardly cried the Storied Watcher.

If only *I had been able to reach through and mind-speak with Bob or Whitney!*

If only *I had prepared them to call back to me! I should have made them ready...*

I should have poured out the Fire *upon all of them – not trusted it to rest within them... so little have they, when most they need it!*

I am at a 'dead end'... and I am alone, her intellect said, however much she tried to reject the message.

But surely... this is not the first time that matters have been such.

I need to think this through.

Leaning forward and concentrating from the greater part of her being, the alien-girl set to reasoning.

The humans from this neighborhood, who were in eye-witness of the accursed attack, here at Bob's address, those in whose vicinity I stood silent and invisible... their chitter-chatter and gossip confirmed my suspicions – Bob,

Whitney and the others, must all have been taken in those big, black 'ess-you-vee' things that the President's spy-warriors all drive.

The method fits perfectly, with what I have learned in speaking with my erstwhile mate, and in researching the ways of this Empire, on the com-pu-ter network.

Indeed, two of those people who I overheard, have had their own kin, 'disappeared' in exactly the same manner. Thus there can be no reasonable doubt, that my loved-ones now languish in the captivity of this 'President', himself.

He, alone, must be responsible!

Voices, I beseech ye, she mused.

I love them so... though, they are only five mortals.

Should not I concern myself with the affairs of millions?

Am I not here, to change the flow of history, to light this world with the Fire?

Just pawns in the chess-game...

Yet one of these mortals, is my son.

My... son!

Karéin-Mayréij said a silent prayer, begging the Powers Above for insight.

Then, finally, she came to a conclusion, one that was unwelcome, unwanted and difficult, yet all the while, *inevitable*.

This cannot be borne... for, if you will fecklessly abandon your most close, most helpless family... how much more easily, will you do so, with strangers?

You will wander this world in loneliness, deservedly alone.

Then... what is to be done?

What about your first family in this Plane of Reality? she asked herself.

Could they not help?

And the Captain is a warrior-prince of this Empire. Surely he, or one of the others, could intercede.

Yes – noble and powerful, will they all be. In short time.

But why do my pleas go unanswered?

Of course... they still soar through the firmament. That must be why; the call could never go so far.

But the moment when they return here... O glorious day...

As concern matters down here, I could go back to Misha and his people, although I relish not the prospect of humbling myself to them. But they likely fear me as much or more than the Americans, and they delay deliberately.

I could break into one of the United States police-houses, take a few of these 'cops' as hostages, give them 'a taste of their own medicine' as Bob said, then trade their lives for those of my friends...

No, that would likely not work, either.

It would be different if I knew where someone really important to the American Empire resides – then, I would have a 'castle' or maybe even a 'bishop'-piece with which to bargain... but this cruel American President cares *not about the fate of a foot-soldier, or two. He values not the lives of peasants, who he executes for the most minor of transgressions, like using a 'pill', reading the wrong books, or professing the wrong faith...*

Karéin-Mayréij pondered in silence for many uncomfortably-long seconds.

You must free them, Storied Watcher; and the first step of it, as ever, is to prepare where the spirits of old, may again live as armor, sword and shield.

If, *that is, they can even come to your side, in this cold, unforgiving techno-world... without being called, by...* her.

Park Place Thief

This shopping-place reminds me of a strange, shiny Temple to the Gods of Lucre, considered Karéin-Mayréij, as she stole like a wraith through the darkened halls of the Park Place Mall.

But where are the guards?

Surely those bumpkin-men with the silly, shiny-buttoned uniforms and the 'walkee-talkee' things, that tried to oppress poor little Curtis, they cannot be who the authorities entrust to keep out thieves... like me.

Actually, nobody *keeps out thieves like me,* she said to herself, with a wan smile.

Since starting her adventure in the wee hours of the morning, the newcomer had already raided three other shops, collecting, according to her own inscrutable plan, various bric-a-brac from each, then methodically returning the purloined wares to a place near the loading dock of the big hardware-store, where she had hidden the "Great Outdoorsman One Hundred Per-Cent Guaranteed Air and Water Tight Camping and Tackle Case", neatly removed from one of the upper shelves in this huge warehouse's selection of wares.

Should I feel guilty that I did not leave a promise to pay, later? bemusedly reflected the young-looking woman.

Ah, I will put that *on the, 'to-do list', for the next century... I promise.*

Now, she stood in front of the glass walls of the "Shogun Ninja" shop.

Hmm, thought the alien-girl.

Many fine-looking swords, shields and armor, in here. Though none can vouch for the quality of their manufacture... that will not be a problem, once I use the old arts.

A scent – a sound of danger!

The warning-senses alerted her mind.

The darkness had caused the Storied Watcher to only partly cloak, so there was still a dim outline visible when she wheeled in place, to see the three mean-looking dogs, growling and bounding straight toward her.

Ah... they hunt by smell, she realized, a half-smile appearing invisibly on her face.

Well... maybe the owners of this grand temple of baubles and mechanical-toys are not so completely stupid, after all.

No more than a second or two was to spare, but that was well more than *this* creature – victor of countless battles against far more dangerous monsters and demons, in times and places as yet unknown to the inhabitants of this world – would need.

The one named Karéin-Mayréij leaped into the air, a good six feet or more, sailing professionally over the three vicious animals, their canine teeth shining with drool in the low light.

Almost silently, she landed behind them.

I could easily kill them with the venom of my fangs, she considered, in a half-instant.

But they would howl their death-cries – that might cause noise.

And they might get a bite of their own in... no threat to me... I have had much worse... unpleasant, none the less.

The mind-shock skill is not fully-back, I would have to stare a human close in the eyes, or touch him – but these guardian-canines are not intelligent... they probably cannot defend.

It is not a fair fight.

Alright, then.

From behind them, she growled.

I am here... come get me, sent the newcomer, using instinct rather than words, as she dropped her cloak entirely.

She was positioned in the middle of the corridor, her eyes shining ominously, four sharp incisors showing her adversaries that something very lethal – no simple human burglar, this – stood in wait for them.

The dogs skidded clumsily on the polished floor, as they turned back.

One let out a throaty bark, as it started toward her. The other two followed a pace or two behind, but as the lead animal reached a point perhaps ten feet in front of the alien-girl, it let out a pathetic, bewildered yelp, as its consciousness collapsed under a smothering, suffocating wave of weirding, negative mental energy.

A second later, the remaining canines joined the pack-leader in an awkward, slack-jawed sprawl, uncomprehending eyes staring up at the ceiling, as their bodies quivered with unfocused nervous-responses.

Cautiously, she advanced to just beside the second dog. She peered down at the helpless, drooling animal, contrarily resembling some fanged super-predator looking over its next meal.

Your masters are lucky, mused Karéin-Mayréij, not caring that the dog couldn't have understood, even if its mind had been in anything like an operational state.

Had you been just a little larger – a little more dangerous – I would not have taken the chance of just subduing you.

It would not have been a thing to mourn long... but still would I have said a prayer for your spirits.

To meet death in one's duty – not the worst way for one to go to the next life... whatever that may be.

"Perhaps," she softly whispered in a strange-sounding, foreign tongue, "You should tell *that*, to whoever comes to claim you, in the morning."

Knowing that her time in this place was now more constrained, the young-looking woman now returned to her half-cloaked form and ran her hands expertly along the tiny gap that marked the demarcation line between the glass wall and the door, now closed and locked, that would in daylight have provided ingress into the shop.

How would Bob have jested about this? she tried to remember, as the young-looking woman's mind smelled the electronic locking-devices and neutralized them, allowing the door to open just enough for her to slip effortlessly inside.

Yes – he would have said, 'piece of cake', would he not?

*I miss him **so**, already... not to mention dear Tommy.*

Oh Tommy – hear me now, my son!

Think of me... think of me now, and I will send my love to you.

Cursing her weakness, the Storied Watcher wiped an unrequited tear from one eye.

Damn me! she fumed.

And curse this American Empire!

How dare they try to kill me, kill my family, then, failing the latter, kidnap Tommy, Bob and the others away to some dungeon!

If my son suffers on their account, I will incinerate them with a flame so hot –

Half-stunned, she shook her head, as if trying to shake of a fearful dream.

Temper your heart, Storied Watcher, the creature said to herself.

Justice, safety for your loved-ones... and, may the Gods forbid, revenge – those will come only with cool strategy... not with fury.

Yet why do I feel so angry?

This is not the one whose intellect outmatches Gods and Goddesses. This is not the 'one-just-short-of-Godhood'.

This is not... me.

The proprietor of this *faux*-medieval weaponry shop had, no doubt, never counted upon his wares being reviewed by such as the one – an expert in the real thing – who now stood in front of the counter.

He would, none the less, have been satisfied, had he been there to listen in on her thoughts.

Many of the so-called weapons in this place are but toys, while others are weird-shaped – I cannot imagine a real warrior actually using them in mortal battle... but as for the other ones... the steel in these is soft, too mild to survive much combat, I smell it, she mused.

But I can fix that, and the finish is good, for the most part... and that long, two-handed sword over there, also the handy, double-edged, point-tipped one with the flame-motif on all three of its handle, blade and blade-stop... they even have a bit of spirit!

Most strange... how could that be possible? I thought that the people of this world had long since abandoned the simple weapons in favor of these stupid guns and bombs that they use for war.

I cannot trust a sword who I do not know, to block for me, so the long one must lose its chance for fame... may thee yet find thy destiny and glory, she silently prayed, casting a glance at the two-handed weapon.

The alien-girl came closer and caused the second sword to float down from its holding-brackets on the wall, into her grasp, running her fingers over the weapon, reading the faint traces of male power within it.

With the special-sight she reviewed the inscription on the blade.

"Sword Fàiagàryuu, First Place, Southwest Region SCA Ken-Katana Dueling Competition"... hmm, interesting, thought the alien-girl.

I cannot read these other letters – they look like one of the Eastern-continent scripts – but he has a name already, so he must be special.

Somehow I know that his name befits me, though I speak not the tongue.

He is a fine sword – well-balanced, a good weight for his size, a long, sharpened striking-edge on the bottom, a shorter backhand-one on the top – and the design of his grip, yes, it feels right, it does indeed... it is odd that he has tasted victory, yet not blood, in the doing.

"Well, noble *Fàiagàryuu*," whispered Karéin-Mayréij, practicing a few air-slashes with the sword, then laying a kiss on its blade, "Let us hope that the blood of man need not stain thy sharp edges... but if that fate should come to pass, thou should strike hard, fast and true."

I wonder if the old ways of breathing my life, power and spirit into such a blade, can still work on this strange world of high science, ingenious technology and no magic...

We shall find out, soon.

She looked downwards and saw that the glass case to the left of the computer point-of-sale system held a variety of knives, some formed into fanciful, swirly-edged shapes, some evidently more purposefully-crafted.

Those ones with the artistic-edges – they remind me of the ritual-sacrifice daggers of that evil Temple – what was *its name... ahh, not a good memory, and they are too big, anyway,* she thought.

But these two small ones... they are a pair and would fit nicely into a leg-brace... would they not?

As she retrieved the two daggers from the case after shocking its alarm system into stupor, another saturnine smile came to her face.

Having had to arm herself from times immemorial, the Storied Watcher was nothing if not practical, where this business was concerned.

Very well then.

Twins shall ye be; and each shall take a different bite, dark and light, fire and ice, or lightening and poison, perhaps.

And ye shall have names... those of my ancient spirit-companions, should they hear my prayer and again come to my side.

Now, she looked around for protection.

Heh, softly muttered Karéin-Mayréij, as she regarded two suits of 17th-Century Japanese laminated armor.

Not bad for the simple-folk, but far too confining... I wonder if they wear the chain-link stuff underneath this.

I suppose that the owner of this shop escapes having the suit stolen, then.

But the little hard-steel and soft-luminum buckler here... yes, that would about fit my forearm. And I have that set of 'ladies gladiator athletic protective-gear' from the sports-store, anyway.

It will take much work to change the tiny bits of matter into something lighter, more... durable, but it will be done, in time. If I, in fact, have any time to spare...

Sword, daggers and shield in hand, she turned for the door, but stopped halfway.

Granted... I did not leave a promise to pay, at the other places, she pondered.

But this *is different. These arms will guard my life... or so I hope.*

It is not right that I not make good to the weapon-crafter; else he might place a curse on my new friend Fàiagàryuu, or on the buckler who as yet has no name, or on the twin knives, with no words to call themselves, either.

Advancing to the glass case, the Storied Watcher brought the inner *Fire* to her fingertips, and wrote on its surface, in English :

"Dear master weapon-smith Masa-moto, of the Park Place Mall : I have had to take four of your wares, as my own.

I honor the fine work that was done in crafting them – be assured that these things will now live and fight ever at my side, as have the greatest blades and shields of the far-away, old worlds and realms that the people of this 'Earth', still cannot imagine.

I know that these living-things will not fail me; and when the issues that I currently face are all done with, I will return and pay ten-fold, over whatever Fàiagàryuu and his fellows would have cost.

I thus acknowledge my debt to you."

"What am I missing?" she whispered.

"Ah. Of *course*... how could I have forgotten, that? Stupid techno-world. How quickly go the ancient-ways."

Underneath the previous inscription, the alien-girl added :

"If you are he who first crafted Fàiagàryuu and his friends... I plead that you should add your own prayer to their success in battle. If you are not, may I ask for you to pass this request on to whomever was the father and mother of the blade, the shield and the daggers, that he or she may likewise add spirit to them.

I will make Fàiagàryuu *great, and in turn, yourself; then, all will be as the Gods of War would deem proper.*

Do this for me, and when I will visit to thank you in-person – I will teach you some of the skills of weapon-crafting, given to me in places and times far away. Yours in respect, K-M."

She stopped, considering things, for a few more seconds, then appended, *"And one other thing, master armorer, if you please; when they come to read what my* Fire *inscribed on your store-counter, make sure to tell them that I will play this game by the rules of the* Makailkh *– not those of the American Empire, or of any human empire. If they do not understand this, they soon will."*

As she slipped noiselessly out of the Shogun Ninja shop – taking care to leave everything, save what she had self-appropriated, exactly as she had found it – one last time, Karéin-Mayréij turned in the hall, to regard this store, so out of place in a shopping-mall of video-games, *haute couture*, women's perfumes and uncounted other doo-dads for the rich and indolent.

It comforts me that someone on this soulless planet still keeps the old ways alive, thought the Storied Watcher.

When I return... I promise that I will show you how to make a sword and shield, such as you have never seen.

Now she slipped back toward her cache, a shadow just a bit darker than those covering the sides of the halls, undoing the locking-mechanism that separated the hardware-store door from the rest of the shopping-mall, replacing it just the way it had been, then using one hand to sail over the anti-theft barrier that had caused such a ruckus, not a fortnight earlier.

Hurrying to the "Camping and Tackle Case", the young-looking woman caused its locks to spring open with just a casual glance; then she laid the little shield, the shining-silver sword and the two scarcely-less-polished daggers, gently down to rest in the case.

A minutely-inscribed piece of paper floated skyward, until it faced her at eye-height. "Bob, in your memory, I will do the list your way, incautious though it may be to tarry," she intoned, in the softest of whispers.

Six packages of ferr-ayt and iron filings – 'check'. White glue, silly-cone bathroom tub sealant tube, and this 2-element 'epoxy' stuff – 'check'. Thick roll of 'fai-berr-glass' cloth – 'check'. Graphite and soft plastic sheet, small pieces – 'check'. Silver finger rings and gold chains, each with a few little diamonds on them, 25 of these – 'check'.

Three boxes of the shiny little plastic 'see-quin' things from the Ladies' Home Fashion Creations store – 'check'. 'Nai-lon' golfing glove, 'Nai-lon' skee-socks and 'Spee-doh' super nai-lon bih-kin-eye bathing suit and double-layer 'nai-lon', one-person tent from the Sports Masters Store – why these people swim with clothes on, instead of just going nude, I will never understand... well, at least it is a nice silver color, but – 'check', anyway.

Radiating stuff from the time-telling hands of a couple of the old-style wrist-clocks in the Second Hand Emporium, 'check'. Rubies, sapphires, emeralds, topaz, pearls (only the real kind, not the fakes!), quartz, zircon, mica, onyx, turquoise, bloodstone, diamonds, jade, other gems, a few of each – 'check'. Little glass rods – 'check'. Fishing-line and electro-wire reels, ten each, 'check'.

Tiny radio-wave transmitter and receiver dense integration circuit-chips, several dozen Cee-Pee-Youu chips, 'plug sockets' and so on, ahh, 'requisitioned' from the little portable com-pu-ters in the Tech Junk-shun Store, plus the other ones and the small, round 'Ell-eye' batteries, from the Tucson Electro-Hobbyist Super-Store, 'check'.

Quicklime, with acid from one of their older-car batteries as a backup, in a cooking-glass vial – 'check'. Other chemicals and ingredients, 'check' – oh, did I remember the galli-arsenic and the ultra-tiny crystal stuff? Good, I did.. Flint striking-stone, knife sharpening-stone, one each, – 'check'. Chalk, one box of little sticks of it, plus three charcoal brick-ettes – 'check'. Pottery-clay, one lump – 'check'.

A bird-feather, blood from a chunk of meat and scales from a half-fish in the super-market, ugh, one vial – 'check'. Stems and petals of three flowers from the 'Desert Bloom Hothouse' – 'check'. Just about every element... the water, sand, and my mind, poison and body essence, I can add, when I get to my crafting-place.

"So... I am done, I suppose."

Except for her, that is.

Oh Venerable One... where art thou?

Still... it was my own fault... and she did consent.

But if I had it to do over again...

Karéin-Mayréij let out a sigh that was rather more loud than prudent.

Then, with another mental command, the lid of the case slowly closed over this odd collection of ingredients for who-knows-what, as the 'day-trip' lightweight camping backpack that she had purloined from the Outdoors Shack, similarly drifted into place, its straps enveloping her outstretched arms.

Like a businesswoman heading out the door for an overseas sales-trip, the alien-like-a-girl hefted the case in the grasp of one hand – thankfully, her calculations were correct and the weight was easily bearable – using the other hand to defeat the primitive perimeter security-systems of the hardware-store, as she put full power to her cloak.

The cold air of the Arizona desert greeted her nostrils as she exited the Park Place Mall, possibly, for the last time.

Not the first *Temple that I have looted*, she reflected.

And far from the most dangerous.

No Demons, undead specters, death-traps or wizards in my way.

May history not record this sentiment... but I almost miss these hazards.

It is too easy, evading these humans.

The one called 'Karéin-Mayréij' had now reached the darkness beyond the far edge of the nearly deserted parking-lot, and there she stopped and pondered for a few seconds.

Such a convenient place, where one can get almost everything that one needs... but I wager that my three hundred dollar limit on the little plastic card is now used up, she said to herself, with a wry smirk.

Dear Bob... can you, how do they say here, yes, 'float me a small loan'?

One last time, she looked back at this strange place of everything-for-money.

Remember what I wrote, skilled Masa-moto, who wrought Fàiagàryuu *to my side,* she sent, to no-one in particular.

The Storied Watcher plays by her *rules... not theirs.*

Then, faster than a mountain-zephyr, she stole away down the dark streets, heading for the high desert beyond the bright lights of Tucson, Arizona.

Unhappy Cloud Nine

Air Force One cruised high above the clouds, changing its course in a gentle bank every ten minutes or so. The incline of its motion was so slight that the President hardly noticed, but it was more than enough to make this aerial fortress' likely ETA to any particular point, impossible to predict.

Yet the President was deeply unhappy, not the least for having to hide out in his shiny plastic-Kevlar-and-aluminum prison again, just as he had believed – *dumb old me,* he thought to himself – that he could finally reside in the White House.

They told him that it was far too risky, not just because of the vague, probably illusory threat of some half-mythological alien-girl-or-something menacing him, but even more so due to the threat of all of the damn city suddenly going skyward in a mushroom-cloud.

That happens, what good will it do to still have *a President,* he mused, looking out the window at the little cotton-ball puffs of cloud, far below; he couldn't see the four F-32E super-stealth-fighters escorting the 747-700, but no doubt, they were there, somewhere.

No Congress, no Supreme Court... hell, wouldn't be so bad, if the damn Muslims could just leave K Street standing... okay, maybe Arlington, too...

The officiously polite voice of a smartly-dressed young male Air Force lieutenant interrupted his daydream.

"Excuse me, Mr. President," spoke the aide, "But we're patched in, now, sir."

"Main conference-room?" inquired the American leader.

"Yes, sir," confirmed the lieutenant.

He motioned toward the back of the jet.

"We'd better get to them, then," answered the President, slowly and reluctantly arising.

Absent-mindedly, he tried to straighten out his tie and un-rumple his dress-shirt, but on trips as interminable as *this* one, well – the one thing that the plane was missing, was a dry-cleaning store.

With the lieutenant standing outside the door, the President entered, assuming a lonely place at the end of an oval, fine-mahogany meeting table that could easily have accommodated twenty people; however, he was now the only one in the room, with a large 3-D LED flat-panel display at the far end of the table.

Upon this, was displayed the other end of the get-together, twenty or more military and civilian Advisers in a darkened underground bunker somewhere, Camp David, likely.

Not that the Muslims couldn't just drive a truck up to the gates there, he reminded himself.

"Hello, everyone," announced the President. "Cloud Nine calling."

A wave of polite laughter at this little joke echoed through the surround speakers.

The sharp, hard-bitten voice of the Vice-President replied, "Wish you could be here, Mr. President... but don't worry, we have everything under control down here – I made sure that we got *real* Canadian Club, not that stuff that they're selling as such in the liquor-stores."

"Knew I could count on you for the *important* stuff, George," acknowledged the U.S. leader. "Okay, well, with *that* taken care of... we'll begin. Do we have any updates from CIA or the Defense Department?"

Anderson spoke up.

"Yes," he affirmed. "Halford couldn't be here today, but he sends his regards... the Navy got enough of a sample from the Mumbai blast – that took a very risky shore mission, I should mention – to narrow down the exact fingerprint of that bomb; and, unfortunately, it pretty much is a one hundred per-cent confirm of the fact that it *was* one of the missing Pakistani nukes. Also, our initial estimates of the yield were more or less bang-on... sorry, maybe that wasn't the best way to put it, sir –"

"Let's not blow things out of proportion," joked the Vice-President, to a combination of pained glances and team-player chuckles.

"Let's get back on track," ordered the President.

"Right, sir," continued Anderson. "We've concentrated all of our remaining intelligence assets, both HUMINT and SIGINT, in a concentric pattern radiating out from the known Pakistan weapons-storage facilities; I should warn you, sir, that this is stripping our ability to monitor the Chinese and Russian fronts, to the bare bones... but per your directives, we have judged this to be an appropriate risk. No results as of yet."

The President nodded and turned in the direction of the CIA director. "Anything from your end?" he asked.

"I can basically confirm what the General has said," smoothly replied the director. "Except to add that we have lost three more agents in an attempt to trace one or possibly two of the weapons en route from northern Iran to the Independent Kurdish State. As you know, since the Chinese turned the *Peshmurga* against us, that entire area has been extremely difficult for us to get human intelligence from. Our contacts in Baghdad *have*, however, been hearing rumors that one of the weapons going through Kurdistan may either have been captured by commando-teams of the Iraqi Islamic Republic, or that a move to do so may be underway right now. We're keeping our ears to the ground about anything that might confirm these stories."

"Well, keep it up and inform me ASAP if you find anything," ordered the President.

Then he turned to address the National Security Adviser. "John... any luck with Red Rover?"

"A lot of leads, and some good ones in the last 24 hours, sir," confirmed Bezomorton. "Director Ochoa is tied up again with the West Coast situation – which is rapidly deteriorating, by the way – and his agents at one point thought that they had tracked the alien down to a suburb of Tucson, Arizona, but –"

The CIA director, his expression not changing, typed something rapidly into a mobile-communicator, which he held in his lap under the table.

"Unfortunately," continued the Security Adviser, "When they arrived on the scene, the premises where the being had allegedly been residing, had been subjected to an intensive attack and had been burned to the ground."

Startled and simultaneously infuriated, the President interjected, "Do they think she – it – was killed? *Who* authorized this attack?! I *specifically* prohibited anything like it!"

"Sir, we don't *know*," hastily answered Bezomorton. "As of the last I heard, which was about three hours ago, the investigation was ongoing; there were no non-human remains yet identified at the incident-site, and don't forget that we don't even know if we were searching at the right house – the fact that there was an altercation there, may just be a coincidence. FBI is following up on attacker identification; right now, the consensus of opinion seems to be either one of the larger Southwest criminal gangs, possibly the *Maras*, or maybe a terrorist connection... but the motives are hard to fathom. I'll let you know as soon as we find out anything new."

"Does CIA know anything about this?" demanded the President, turning to the director of that agency.

"Only what Mr. Bezomorton has just told you," nonchalantly replied the CIA director.

"As you know, sir," he explained, "Along with NSA and NRO, we continuously monitor most domestic communications, and we *were* able to capture some local law-enforcement chit-chat regarding the incident, but there's nothing confirming the specific whereabouts of the alien, either before or after the confrontation at the Tucson bungalow."

To a stare from the U.S. Leader, the CIA director elaborated, "I should point out, Mr. President, that this entire incident may be nothing more than a false alarm. As the Security Adviser has correctly stated, the alien *was* thought to have been 'somewhere in Tucson' and FBI *thought* that the residence in question was where she, or it, was staying – you'll have to ask Director Ochoa as to the quality of the intelligence behind that supposition, I can only go on what CIA got through inter-agency briefings – but there are many other plausible explanations for the attack. For example, some kind of relationship between the *Maras* and the Muslim Salvation League – this would explain the method of the attack, namely what looks like a suicide-raid, but there are other details that don't fit, so –"

"Just what we effing *need!*" blurted out the Vice-President. "The wetback gangstas teaming up with the Islamo-loonies, and the last of 'em with a few nukes to make things more fun."

"Well, I wouldn't put it so melodramatically," observed the CIA director, pleasantly. "This is all just *speculation*, remember."

"Look," ordered the President, "I need you guys to keep following up on this front, in particular I need a *one hundred per-cent accurate* reading as to whether our friend the alien is still with us – and I need that within 24 hours, do you understand?"

"I'm afraid I can't give you that kind of assurance, sir," politely countered the CIA director. "You see, *FBI* is currently in charge of the crime-scene, in Tucson, I mean... our people can't go on-site to do the necessary analysis, and on top of that, there's far too much publicity associated with all of this, in fact, it's actually been all over the local news-media –"

"Well then get Ochoa to do the report, for God's sake!" complained the President, "I don't care *who* does it, as long as I get valid information."

"I'll have to do that," interrupted Bezomorton. "As you know, the Agency isn't supposed to be directly co-ordinating domestic activities with FBI."

"Go ahead," muttered the President.

"Their equipment isn't as good as ours," interjected the CIA director. "It's meant for chasing down gangsters and ordinary criminals – not *this* kind of thing."

The President threw up his hands.

"Just make it *happen*, do you hear?" he growled. "If you have to sequester the necessary equipment from CIA, then I'm giving you authority to do so, as of now. *Understood?*"

"But, sir," protested the director, "This is *highly* sensitive technology, and besides, they wouldn't know how to –"

"Don't want to hear about it," shot back the President. "If you've got to train them, FBI, the National Security team, or the Tucson Dogcatcher Department, for that matter, then do so. Is that understood?"

"Yes, sir, we'll do the best we can, sir," obligingly replied the top Agency bureaucrat. "But there's one other thing, if I may?"

"What?" peevishly demanded the American leader.

"I just wanted to know how the debriefing of the former Mars mission astronauts has been going," remarked the CIA director, in his best project manager voice. "We haven't heard very much about that, over at the Agency."

"It's been going well," evaded the President.

Turning to Anderson, he added, "Wouldn't you say, Harry?"

"*Definitely*, Mr. President," said the poker-faced Air Force General.

"I... *see*," echoed the CIA director. "Is there any chance that we might be able to have them interviewed by some of the Agency's people?"

"Up to you, Harry," commented the President.

"Oh, I don't think *that* would be... *appropriate*," stated Anderson, with a suppressed catbird smile. "At least, not right now. We have the situation completely under control and we're dealing with the crew according to a carefully pre-planned Armed Services protocol. Our people feel that involving, uhh, *outside* interviewers, might... *complicate* the proceedings and might confuse the astronauts; they've been through an awful lot as it is, you know. I can assure you, Mr. Director, that the moment when we have some useful information forthcoming from the debrief, you'll be the first to have it, after the President, that is."

"Oh, of *course*," politely replied the director.

As the President turned his attention elsewhere, the director's hands again played over his communicator keypad.

The U.S. leader nodded in acknowledgment, then concluded, "Look, everyone... I'm aware that we're all going through some pretty tough times, but the only responsible way for us to deal with it, is to hunker down and ride it out. Right now, the worst thing that we can do is panic, or be seen to be panicking, either on the terrorism front, on the alien front or about the economy... but at the same time, we need to get a firm handle on all three of these issues. I will tolerate *no* more screw-ups! You all got that?"

There was a forced murmur of consent, from around the table at the far end of the video-link.

"Okay, then," ordered the President. "Let's all get back to work... shall we? Cloud Nine, over and out."

There were a few salutes visible on the view-screen, before it went dark.

After the rest had left the room, the CIA director tarried.

He raised his wrist-communicator to his ear.

"Trace requested on location, disposition of Mars mission crew," he requested.

Listening intently, for a second or two, the director then said, "They... *what*? At Site A? Did you do a personnel trace? Good. And the results?"

The director pondered for five or six long seconds.

Prompted by some unseen demand, he replied, "I see. I see. *What*? On *TV*? You've *got* to be kidding!"

The man's normally saturnine face could not conceal a contemptuous grin.

"Well," he muttered into the communicator, "Even if the station didn't get a good close-up of them, I don't think I have to tell you what the consequences would be, if those were *our* people... but enough of that. It *does* imply that our window is even narrower, now – they're not up to *our* standards, of course, but that doesn't mean that they won't eventually get back on the trail."

There was a muffled acknowledgement, then the director again spoke.

"Listen," he commanded, "Get the assets that we *did* manage to secure, out to one of our high-confidentiality sites; we don't want any inter-agency problems from that direction, you know? Right. Right. I'm counting on you. Make it happen. That will be all."

He stood in the doorway leading to the outside world.

"On *TV*, for God's sake. Fucking *amateurs*," he chuckled, shaking his head as he strode forward.

I Call Thee, Oldest Friend

The trip – conducted at sprint-speed through the cool Arizona desert night air – would have exhausted any human being, however well-conditioned, an hour or more before.

But, by the time that the young-looking female creature reached the place that she had selected as her temporary shelter for these nocturnal outings, she had hardly worked up a sweat.

The journey had mostly been uneventful, except for an amusing scene with a roadblock astride one of the arterial-roads, leading out of Tucson; the local police had completely stopped traffic along this route, resulting in a gigantic traffic-jam, as they went one by one through each vehicle trying to get out of or in to the city.

Chaos reigned, with a horde of angry, shouting U.S. citizens foolishly confronting authority, while considerably more people had simply pulled over to the side of the road and had set up impromptu 'tailgate parties' in a forlorn attempt to pass the time.

As for finding an invisible alien-angel, moving almost noiselessly and at rapid speed, a kilometer or more from the roadway... well, *that* was another matter.

Like so many things about the façade of "security" that afflicted this poorly-run, oppressive kingdom, this one was only for show. That is, if one didn't count the hapless Hispanic-people from the big shanty-town-cum-concentration-camp on either side of the road; the border-guards had thrown about twenty of them, she had noted, into a van and had carted them off to... *somewhere*.

As Karéin-Mayréij surveyed the scene, from within her ebon shroud, a half-smile appeared on her lips.

Perfect, she told herself.

Almost exactly like the U.S. Patriotic Search Engine Hi-Res Maps thing on the 'Neo-Net' computer, back at that big shiny library, had pictured it, albeit as if being seen straight down from above.

That shadow there, it looked like it had to have been made by an indentation... but this is much better... a cave, actually.

Just a little leap on to that ledge, about ten of their 'feet' measurements up – let us run toward it and... there, now one more leap up and...

She dropped the backpack and the carry-case, off to one side.

Hmm, mused the young-looking woman.

Very dark in here, and the echo-sounds tell of it being quite deep, which is a good thing.

I will let the hot-seeing and the more-than-violet-seeing through the cloak, in that case, so I can tell precisely how far back it goes, and if... hey, what is that?

Something moved.

A stick flew by itself into her hand, then was propelled by her throw to just in front of where she had detected the activity.

A buzz, akin to someone rapidly shaking a jar of pebbles or dried beans, met her ears, followed by the dim flash of fangs, as something struck, fast and hard, at the stick.

Ah, a serpent, of the ones with the blood poison and the rattle-tail, that Curtis and Tommy told me about, while we were back in Bob's car.

Quietly, she spoke to the snake, using a tongue just as alien to this world as she was.

"I could propel thee out of here, with no cause between us, sharp-toothed-one," she almost reverently intoned. "But I would compare thy strike and venom with my own. And I will give thee fair play."

Still opaque in the outward-facing direction, the cloak dropped entirely in front of the snake, exposing it to the full range of her body radiation, especially, the faint heat that she gave off.

Concentrating now, the Storied Watcher threw another stick at the animal, measuring its strike for speed and reach, as the seconds somehow slowed down to lazy dozens of minutes each, in her mind.

"Now we shall dance," she challenged, moving closer and closer, her illuminated eyes focusing on the rattlesnake's pit-glands, as it buzzed louder and louder, coiling and warning ominously.

One hand was perhaps a foot ahead of the other, with both of her hands tensed, claw-fashion.

Suddenly, the snake released, its gape wide-open with long, needle-sharp fangs, shooting forward at the young-looking woman's body, with a speed that would have struck any ordinary human long before he or she could react.

But – to the creature's perplexity – it instantly found a vice-like grasp enveloping the back of its head.

Angrily, the rattlesnake writhed and tried to strike; to utterly no avail, as it now saw a near-human face, lit up by glowing eyes, tantalizingly close to its deadly bite.

A more intelligent animal would have been mortally afraid, upon seeing its captor's own four lethal teeth, shining in the eye-light.

Again, the strange language was whispered in this secluded place.

"Fear not," purred Karéin-Mayréij, not caring that it did not understand – after all, neither would have the humans, had any been around to hear. "I am not hungry today, at least not for rattle-flesh. No, Master Serpent... I seek something *else*. Let it issue, then."

She squeezed a little behind the neck, with her other hand held under the snake's mouth, just out of strike range, and, furious at its captivity, its venom welled at the tips of its fangs, eventually dripping to impact with the young-looking being's palm.

She took the small pool of toxin up to her nose and inhaled deeply.

"Ah, yes," she continued in her alien tongue. "Blood-and-flesh-wrack venom – and a good one at that – well suited to the furry little things that would be thy prey. I thank thee, Master Rattle-Tail-Serpent! It will make a worthy addition to mine own. Another small reason, for those of this world, to beware."

She rubbed some of the poison on a finger-tip, then, one by one, anointed each of her four fangs and her tongue, with this lethal brew, licking her lips in satisfaction.

By now, the snake, though still angrily willing to strike at the first available opportunity, had calmed down, somewhat.

Then, ebon cloak again enveloping both her and her writhing, buzzing prize, she leaped down to the desert floor.

"Thou have done thy duty," she respectfully congratulated. "For that, I give thee back thy life. May thy fate be a happy one, as the Lord Who Coils, measures these things."

Her mind-force keeping up a firm barrier against any parting gifts on the part of this otherwise-dangerous reptile, the alien-girl released the snake.

As it sped away, she looked back toward the cave-entrance, and announced, "And now... to work, for there is *so* much to do."

She jumped up to the first ledge, backwards, then, up to the lip of the cave, in the same manner.

With eyelids closed, the Storied Watcher meditated for several minutes, her senses probing, scanning, seeking, over an entire world, for even the faintest sign of the object of her search.

Then – eyes shining star-bright – in her own, inscrutable language, she began to softly chant,

"Dear One of the Endless Worlds, abandon me not; free thyself, return to me, I pray... for now, I need thee more than ever, even than in untold ages gone by!"

Rhythmically, the alien repeated this invocation again and again, her voice sounding more and more of frustration and disappointment, with each successive attempt.

Finally, Karéin-Mayréij dejectedly sat down, a tear falling fast upon her cheek.

In my plight, my instincts overcame my fog-shrouded memory, and I entrusted the Venerable One, my one precious keepsake and companion – to a human; a good and noble man, to be sure... but still, a... mortal... so thereby, I might be thought a friend, so I might have drink and therefore stay alive, she mourned.

And then – when I could have had her back again – I thought that my times were ended, and I did not want my beloved Venerable One to perish along with me.

She, who has seen me through so much!

How earnestly do I miss thee, dear grand-mistress!

May thou who inherit her, be worthy of that high honor... and may the Gods keep thee, old friend, and keep thy new bearer, safe for all days.

And now... how shall I complete this fearsome task?

For I recall the rites, only so dimly.

And I have never called for them, by myself!

How, then, shall they know to find me?

Rivers of hot tears, driven by shame and remorse, poured down upon the dry Arizona rock-cave floor.

But the young-looking woman was wrong.

At the Jet-Propulsion Laboratory – or, better put, what was left of it, these days – in Houston, an alarm went off.

"Damn!" cursed one of the scientists, a bespectacled man. "Cindy, what was *that*?"

"Don't know," answered another, a 30-something woman, who had been sitting patiently examining a DNA sample. "Here, I'll look at the alert-panel – uh-oh... looks like a fire!"

"*What? Where?*" asked the first scientist.

"Oh, *double* damn," shot back the woman, her face now wearing the look of intense worry. "Containment-Room 14B. John, we've got to get a team down there on the double – if it gets out of control, we'll have lost –"

"You don't have to tell *me*," shouted the man, as he made quickly for the door leading out of the lab. "Call the Emergency Team! I'm on my way down there right now, there's an extinguisher right outside –"

"But if containment seal's breached – you *know* the protocol –" warned the woman.

It was to no-one; her companion was already gone.

"So what the hell *happened* down here?" demanded the JPL Houston Operations Manager, as he surveyed the water-drenched, smoke-stinking scene.

"Your guess is as good as mine," replied the fireman. "Problem seems to have originated in that case over there – the one marked 'Special Mars Artifacts', you know – in with all that stuff that they brought back along with those guys from the space station. Damn thing blew apart just as if somebody put a stick of TNT inside it and lit a short fuse."

"J.H.C.," breathed the manager.

"Yeah... but what *I* can't figure is," continued the fireman, "Didn't we get a risk-assessment report saying that there were just inanimate objects – rocks, sand, crap like that – inside that case? I mean, nobody ever told my boys about volatile compounds or anything *reactive*, in there."

"No kidding," said a bespectacled scientist. "Because there *weren't* any. We did a full chemical, spectral and radiometric test on the contents and none of it was any more explosive than a bucket of beach-sand. Unless you can figure some way to get *that* to blow up."

"Or," commented the fireman, "To do... *that*."

He pointed at a hole about the size of a human fist, now temporarily secured with tape, that had been burned, or melted, or, *something* – in the middle of the thick Plexiglas wall that divided where they were now, from the previously sterilized storage area.

"How long do you think containment was breached?" asked a worried female scientist. "We may have to initiate lock-down here – you know, the contamination-issue..."

"Only for a few minutes, apparently," countered the Operations Manager. "Frederico and his team sealed it immediately, when they got down here. We'll run some tests, of course... but I don't think that's going to be an issue, remember, all that stuff tested bio-neutral when we first got it here, anyway. Far more of a loss in that we may now have Earth-organisms on the exterior of the specimens, we'll have to find some way to non-destructively decontaminate them."

"Shit!" muttered the male scientist. "What a *disaster* – just wait until the high NASA mucky-mucks hear about this. Hope you've got something else planned as a career."

The Operations Manager, his visage grim, nodded, turned, walked over to a wall and hit the intercom button, speaking into a built-in microphone.

"Hey, you guys in there," he inquired. "You got an inventory yet?"

"Yeah," came back a static-laden voice, as one of the three figures inside the sealed containment area waved from inside his bio-hazard suit. "Still counting up the little rocks, but it doesn't appear that anything important is missing, except..."

"Except... *what?*" pressed the Operations Manager.

"Well... you know that, uhh, piece of jewelry – the one that the Mars team got off the alien, first day they met her, or it? It, uhh, seems to not, uhh, be... here, any more."

"What the –" exclaimed the male scientist, shouting loud enough for the men listening over the intercom to hear, either directly or electronically. "You've *got* to be kidding! Check again! That item's *irreplaceable!*"

"We will," came back the voice from inside the sealed room, "But we've identified the holding-box where it was kept – or, where the box *was*... seems to have been burnt to ashes. Lucky we just had sand on either side of it."

"Listen, Bill," stammered the scientist, "We'll have to think up a cover-story here, or – is it possible that we're looking at a theft situation?"

"Maybe," offered the Operations Manager. "But if so, it would have to have been an inside job. We're pretty much the only people who know that the thing even *existed*... right?"

"Oh, come *on*," protested the female scientist. "Surely you can't suspect... I mean, it would have no commercial value... nobody outside of NASA is supposed to even *know* about it. And why would anybody-blow a hole in the containment-barrier and cause a fire, alerting the whole building in the process, when they could just enter a code and walk off with this amulet, pendant or whatever-it-is? It makes no *sense!*"

The Operations Manager thought for a bit, rubbing his chin in puzzlement.

"Yeah, you're right... sure doesn't add up," he allowed, "But one way or another, you got to understand, I still got to write up a report, and the higher-ups are going to want to interview –"

His voice was cut off by a loudspeaker-announcement.

"Attention! Attention!" it alerted. "Breach detected in window of central cafeteria!"

"Bill here," called the Operations Manager, after rapidly typing in a code on the numeric keypad through which he had been speaking with the clean-up crew.

"What in God's name is it *now?*" he grumbled. "We're still trying to figure out what went on down in 14B."

"Not really sure," answered the voice on the intercom. "Outside breach-detection membrane indicated an alarm on a window in the cafeteria. A few seconds later we started to get a lot of really *strange* reports from down there."

"Like... what?" demanded the Operations Manager.

"This is going to be a bit hard to believe, I realize," stated the intercom voice. "But the stories are all consistent."

"*Nothing* will surprise me today," commented the manager. "So what is it?"

"They're telling us," explained the voice over the intercom, "That something looking like, uhh, a locket, a necklace, or whatever – they didn't get too good a look at it, of course, but apparently it was pretty expensive-lookin' – just came flying from down the hall all by itself, hit the window, bounced off, and fell into somebody's soup-bowl. When the lady bent over to see what the hell was going on, this thing just *rocketed* out of the bowl and blasted its way right through the window – blew a hole at least as big as you'd get from a good-size handgun. It flew off to... we know not where. Look – I *know* what this sounds like... but I *swear,* I'm not makin' it up."

"Anybody hurt?" requested the Operations Manager.

"Nah... other than for a ruined dress-shirt and jacket, soup stains all over it," replied the voice. "But a lot of people are askin' questions."

"No kidding," grumbled the manager. "And I'm asking one, right now."

"What would *that* be?" asked the intercom voice.

"What the hell do I put in my report?" complained the manager.

Moscow, This Is The Odd Couple

"Misha *tut,*" spoke the SVR-man, into the secure link.

Though he was not supposed to, he parted a small slit in the hotel-room's thick, flower-motif curtains – *damn, so much dust here, do the Americans never clean these places?* – and looked out on to the dimly-lit, poor-side-of-Tucson street, several floors below, as he spoke.

Well... it is *dark in here,* he thought.

If CIA or FBI had a trace on me, I would already be in one of their jails, by now.

Or, I would simply be... dead.

"My 'hearing aid' is enabled," he added.

"Alexi here, Moscow headquarters," answered a voice at the other end. "Listen, Misha – I can see that we are on a safe connection, but counter-intelligence is telling me that NSA may be about to break the code that we are using, currently. You may have to re-program, and that will require us to do a physical drop of the new, substitute encryption-module. If necessary, we will do this using Procedure 297 at Location SHA-40961. Do you copy on this?"

"297, SHA-40961. Copied. Understood," affirmed the Russian.

"So what is your status?" requested the remote voice. "And hers."

"She is with me now," stated Misha. "Just returned from a, uhh, 'sight-seeing trip'... that is how she explained it."

Faintly, the Muscovite discerned a muted laugh, though, somehow, he knew that it was tinged with a subdued sadness.

"And there is *so* much to see," he heard a pleasant female voice say. "When I was with Bob, he was very, uhh, *protective* of me. He did not let me out of the house, very much."

"And how did he stop you... if you do not mind me asking?" inquired Misha.

"He ordered me not to wander by myself," noted the alien-girl.

"I tried to do that, or at least I asked you – but you refused," complained the Russian agent.

"Please do not take this in the wrong way, dear Misha," sounded the alien-girl's voice, pleasantly, "But my relationship with Bob Billings was a bit more, ahem, *personal*, than the one I have with yourself. I am on my own now, and I have to make my own decisions. That does not mean that I do not listen to your advice, of course."

"Thank you," was all he could think to say.

"May I speak with her?" asked Alexi.

"Certainly. Here," said the Russian, holding the phone up, in no direction in particular.

In a half-second or so, the previously-invisible Karéin-Mayréij shimmered into view, and Misha suppressed a gasp.

"Storied Watcher," he stammered, "Compared to your appearance only a few hours before... you look... *different.*"

Despite the desert dust that oddly stained her sandals and leggings, there was now a grandeur to this being, more than he had remembered when, a scant day before, he had escorted her up to the room and pleaded – unsuccessfully, of course – to get her to stay put.

She surely hadn't used any of those newfangled chemicals that American women splattered their heads with; yet, her hair sparkled more than gold, and the slightest corner glance at her eyes revealed stars, galaxies and other celestial things yet un-comprehended.

It would not be proper to grovel at her feet, his conscious intellect told him, over the protestations of his animal brain.

Nor to jump at her, tear off her clothes...

With the phone somehow snatched from the man's grasp, propelled by an unseen force to the alien-girl's own hand, she spoke, "Um-hmm. It is me. What is on your mind, Alexi?"

"First of all, it is nice to speak with you again," answered the Muscovite. "Are you well?"

"Very much so," confirmed the Storied Watcher. "I am feeling stronger – better – each day. Maybe, by each hour. However... I still possess only the minor powers, within my body. The major ones still elude me."

"About these 'major powers' – is there anything you care to say about those?" requested the Russian.

"To start with, the ability to bend gravity well enough, to fly as a shooting-star," explained the newcomer, as pedantically as if describing riding a bicycle. "As of now, all that I can do is – well – leap rather high, or far. There are also many other abilities that, frankly, I hope that I will never have to use... If I do, many people might be hurt, or worse. But my 'bubble' is now *much* more powerful than it was, scant days before. All is progressing as it should, I believe."

"That is interesting," dispassionately commented the voice from Russia. "Is there anything else?"

"As Misha knows," stated the Storied Watcher, "Although he did not want me to – I mention that so that you know that he is trying to follow your instructions – I took my leave of your, uhh, fellow 'spy' around dawn today. I wanted to go out among the people, to listen to them speaking, to hear what they are thinking. So –"

"*Please* tell me that you did not just use a pair of sunglasses to disguise yourself," worriedly interjected Alexi.

Another weirdly-girlish laugh issued over the secured cell-phone-link.

"Ha, no – not for the most part, although I *did* wear these nice, stylish dark glasses that dear Bob gave me, while he and I were together," replied the alien-girl. "I used my hiding-cloak almost everywhere; especially, I was never in the open without it, as I am aware of the Americans' satellites orbiting overhead – you know, the ones with the big cameras that can see something as small as a little insect, even from that far away. But there were a couple of situations in which I wanted to actually *talk* with people – to ask them questions, I mean – so then I tried to make myself look like any other normal American would."

"You must understand, Alexi," she continued, "That Bob was *very* protective, when we were all traveling together... I almost never had a chance to be by myself. He was, I guess, worried that I would be hurt... a reasonable enough concern, considering how, uhh, *new* I am, in this place. I am certain, however, that I was neither recognized for who I am, nor was I followed here."

"*Absolutely* certain?" demanded the SVR spy.

The fallen-angel nodded and elaborated, "As I become more used to – oh, how would one say this in Eng-lish – oh-kay, more familiar with how the little electronic spying-devices that the Americans have everywhere, how they 'smell', I am learning to adapt my cloak to elude them."

"Ah," said Alexi.

"It is quite challenging, mind you," noted the Storied Watcher. "I must keep moving the, uhh, 'fabric' of my cloak around, so that I can block almost all of their electric waves at once. But I am succeeding. Oh... and incidentally, having all this Russian spy-gear around me, has been very useful, as well; because I can test my abilities against them without alarming anyone except maybe Misha. I think that you will find that I can now enable most of these little devices – or disable them – with relative ease. The arts of stealth are some of the most important that a stranger such as I can use... for being discovered, leads inevitably to being captured... or worse."

"*Impressive*," warily offered the Muscovite.

"And what did you learn about the great United States of America, in your trip today?" queried Misha, with more than a little sarcasm showing.

"I must say, my trip today was *most* interesting," answered the alien-girl. "Because I learned a great deal more about what is important to the people who live here – mostly, working for money and caring for their families and children... I suppose that should not be a surprise, but I *was* disappointed with how little they know, and care to know, about the planet on which they live, and about what is happening elsewhere. For example, after certain other... travels, I arrived at a, uhh, a 'bar'... that is what one calls it, right? You know – a place where men and women, but not children, come to drink alcoholic beverages? 'Booze', as Bob used to say?"

"Yes," observed Misha. "Except that their vodka is nothing like the real thing that we have back home, after they prohibited all importing of 'anti-American alcohol', a few years ago. The rich-people, of course, can still obtain any kind of liquor that they want, for a price."

"I would not know about that," noted Karéin-Mayréij, "Because alcohol – like almost all drugs and poisons – has no effect on me... I will take you at your word regarding the authenticity of that beverage. Anyway... I sat down at this 'bar', and in less than five minutes, there was already a man who came up to sit next to me. He must have thought that I was pretty, because he started talking to me without any provocation on my part. So –"

"I can see why he would want to do that," commented the Russian in the room.

Instantly, the newcomer sent him a pleasant smile of acknowledgment.

"So this man asked me if I was alone – without a mate or lover, that is – and I told him that I had one but he was away somewhere... you know, the 'small-talk' that the Americans prefer, when they do not want to ask something directly," she explained. "He asked if he could buy me a drink and I said 'yes'; that worked out well because I do not have a lot of money, since I left much of it back in Bob's house, unfortunately."

"So then what happened?" asked Misha.

"Well, I had a conversation with this man – his name is 'Freddie', 'Freddie Losada', by the way – as we both watched the big tee-vee screen that this 'bar' had up on the wall, and as he had more to drink he, uhh, 'opened up', I guess that is how the Americans say it," stated the Storied Watcher. "He told me a lot about his life and what was wrong with it. He does the same kind of work that all the men in his family have done since they came to the United States many generations ago... that is, he works with wood and builds and repairs houses, and to hear Freddie tell the story, he is just as skilled at this trade as his father and grandfather were, but he can hardly afford to buy food anymore, much less save up enough money to buy one of the many houses that he has built so far."

"A common enough story," mentioned the SVR spy.

"On top of *that*," she went on, "Freddie's little daughter has that terrible cancer-disease, and he cannot afford either to go to a healer, or to buy even cheap medicines to try to slow the advance of this very bad illness. I swear by all that is Holy, that when my greater powers return, I will try to help Freddie's family, if I can. Oh – and he complained that things have been going from bad to worse in terms of people's lifestyles in this 'America' country for two generations now... and since the, the, uhh, the 'comet' situation, these problems have been becoming worse."

"That is certainly true," commented Alexi, over the phone-link. "The United States has been in a state of slow decline ever since they elected the second Bush president at the turn of the century and then had a very serious economic depression. The rest of the world eventually recovered... but the Americans never did, because they kept everyone else's products out, hoping to support American companies that could not compete with the better-managed ones in places like Europe, China and our own Russia."

"I... *see*," neutrally offered the alien.

"After that," elaborated the Muscovite, "They had several leaders who claimed that they would reverse this trend; but to be elected, one must promise the voters easy success – that is, that everything will be fine without any sacrifice on the part of the citizens... 'something for nothing', in effect. So the politicians tell reassuring lies, nothing improves... and around and around they go. The United States is but a pale echo of what it once was, at the end of the Second World War... oh, excuse me, I should have realized that you might not –"

"Yes, I *do* know what that was," interrupted the Storied Watcher, her countenance darkening. "I have read extensively about that conflict, and about much else concerning Earth, besides. My heart is heavy that I awoke just too late to have saved your world from that war... or to have saved its victims, in particular all those who were cruelly-slaughtered by that evil European man – what was his name – 'Hitler', yes, that is it. Or to have saved the millions more that your own 'Stalin' killed, or those that the 'Mao' person murdered, or the victims of tyranny that oppressed that little country to the south of China. Not to mention all those who have perished, for want of food..."

The newcomer's voice trailed off for a moment, as if a far-away thought had gripped her consciousness; but then she continued,

"I cannot understand why your governments would thus massacre thousands or millions of peasants; where I come from, yes, there *are* hard, sometimes even sadistic, kings and emperors; but – with very few exceptions – they only torture or kill those who are brave or foolish enough to publicly oppose them. This 'Final Solutions' massacre, and other such atrocities, bewilders me. Why would a king slaughter those who he can make work in the fields, to his own benefit? It makes no *sense*."

"*Much* about our world, probably makes little sense, you know," opined Misha.

"Well, you can be sure that if I had been around just a few years before now, and if my powers had been returned to me, the history of your world would have been... different... *very* different," warned Karéin-Mayréij. "As I said before, I come to serve and not to rule... but that does not mean I will stand idly by, while the powerful hurt the weak."

"Did Alexi mention," sardonically commented the SVR spy, "That Stalin is venerated as a hero, in many parts of our country, today?"

"That will be *enough*," ordered the voice from Moscow.

"Take no sanction against him!" countermanded the alien-girl, "Because I know *that* too, from someone – an old friend from your Russia empire, who I cannot quite remember, right now. Such unwillingness to face the crimes of your history, does not show your country in a complementary light. For," – and here she stopped for a second, sadness immediate in her tone – "You are now in the presence of someone who has in the past done *terrible* things; stupid, cruel things, herself... but also of someone who acknowledges the guilt that comes from those painful memories. And no – I do *not* want to tell you about my past transgressions – so do not ask, if you please. You would not understand, anyway. They were a very long time ago, in a place very far away from here... and I was a different person."

She stopped for a few long seconds, then added, "At least... I *hope* that I am a different person, now."

"Of *course*," soothingly responded Alexi, as Misha hung his head in frustration.

"Enough of that, I suppose," requested the alien-girl, obviously eager to return to the previous topic. "As Freddie and I were talking, the foot-ball-game that had been displayed on this big tee-vee screen was suddenly replaced by what they said was a 'brief announcement from the government', and this annoyed a lot of the people who were there, including Freddie. So I asked him, 'well, do you not want to know what your government is telling you', and he replied that 'it's all the same bullshit, all they do is tell us about some other way that they're stealing money or throwing people in jail for stupid reasons, we all just ignore it and try to get on with our lives'."

The SVR spy let out a low chuckle.

"But I was very interested – and worried – about what I saw on this tee-vee," remarked Karéin-Mayréij. "There has apparently been a big atom-smashing bomb explosion in a city on the other side of your world, with thousands and thousands of innocent people killed all of a sudden, and the American President declared something about 'tough measures at the border to keep us safe, whatever the lib-rals and Europeans say'."

"Yes, that is true," offered Alexi. "Several of these weapons of mass destruction were stolen by a terrorist group in one of the Muslim countries, and now many other nations – including my own Russia – are very apprehensive as to where the bombs might show up next... as the event in Mumbai, unfortunately, demonstrates."

Disgust showed on the face of the Storied Watcher, as she complained, "The savagery of some of the people on Earth *appall*s me, especially because it appears – and here I should admit that I do not know as much about this situation as perhaps I should – that those who they have killed in this attack, had nothing to do with the cause of the conflict. I mean, if one goes to war, should not one take the fight to one's *real* enemies, as opposed to just slaughtering anyone who happens to be in the vicinity? This way of warring is *incomprehensible* to me! Where is the honor in it? Where is the risk? There is no glory in winning a battle against an helpless enemy with no sword and no shield."

"You must understand," offered the Muscovite, "That the terrorists who are behind this type of attack, believe that their god, 'Allah', commands them to kill anyone who does not belong to their religion. This is far from unusual, unfortunately."

"And I think that we have already discussed," added Misha, "That some people on this Earth, believe that you, yourself, are an 'angel', sent by God, Allah, or some other deity, to save all of us. And that others think you are the Devil, or some kind of evil demon... still more, think that you are a goddess – they are building temples to your worship, in some places. Being with you now, Karéin, I can perhaps understand how these ideas came to be. You have a *formidable* presence."

"A 'demon'? A goddess? Ha!" retorted the alien-girl, with a bemused laugh and an 'if-only-you-knew' look on her face.

"How misguided you humans are," she explained. "I have seen *all* of these, and I am neither of their substance, nor their essence... at least, I do not *believe* that I am. Your world is one of science, technology and – in spite of all the ignorance and superstition that we have been discussing – knowledge by means of rational thought. But there are many *other* worlds where these concepts do not dominate; these are places of *real* magic, ghosts, spirits, demons and Gods. Should you come face-to-face with any of these, you would instantly know the difference between me and them, and you would appreciate your nice, logical, scientific Earth, all the more. A being such as a demon, or even more, a god, works according to motivations that neither you nor I could ever truly understand. That, I suppose... is a *good* thing."

"Fascinating," opined the SVR spy. "But then, if you are neither demon nor god, how *should* we describe you?"

"A good question," she acknowledged. "And not one that lends itself to a simple answer. For one thing, as I come to know your ways, I am *becoming* one of you, in a sense. From your perspective, I may be an 'alien'; I use knowledge, abilities and an outlook that you cannot yet comprehend, though when I speak to you as I am doing now, I regard you, I communicate with you, as any human woman would do, when talking to another human being. I am more powerful than you are... but certainly not superior, not better. And I am here for a *purpose*."

Her voice trailed off, deep in thought.

"It is never dull speaking with you, Karéin," offered Misha. "There is always something new to learn."

Though separated by thousands of kilometers, Misha and Alexi started to hear weird, stirring music, echoing noiselessly within their psyches.

"I speak now of your beautiful, blue planet," continued the Storied Watcher, with the odd melody infusing her voice. "This place, this Earth, is a treasure that each generation of your children should inherit intact. If you *knew* how hostile much of the rest of the universe is – if you could *feel* what it is like to have your body caressed by an atmosphere as hot as melting rock, or if you could *feel* the terrible cold on your feet in a sea of liquid methane-gas – your people would know how gentle and accommodating, is your own planet. These things, your people cannot do, and still live to tell. I can... and one of the reasons I am here, is to testify about it."

"Amazing," muttered Misha, shaking his head in a shudder of awe and fear. "If you know about the physics of the environments you say that you have experienced –"

She grasped him gently by the shoulders, looking over one with a kind, wise expression.

"It is pretty scary... is it not?" she solicited, like a mother consoling a child considering its first bicycle-ride, while the off-somewhere music amplified the adrenalin in the man's excited body. "But so it was, when your distant ancestors first dared to pick up a burning branch and bend the power of fire – a power that can heal or kill, depending on how it is used – to their own purposes. I bring your people a *different* kind of *Fire*, Misha. It, too, must be used with care; but it *must* be learned, for you to take the next step on the path to your future."

"If you really *are* like that," proposed Misha, "Or if you will shortly have the power to war against entire nations... surely then, you can understand why us, uhh, mere mortals, must be afraid of you, Storied Watcher."

"You know," introspectively stated Karéin-Mayréij, "I was about to say, 'you need not fear me'; and I wish that I *could* say that, because I so very much *do* want to be loved... not feared or hated. But if you are wise... perhaps you *should* be afraid of me – for it is natural for a weaker being to fear a far stronger one. You have only my testament that I will not misuse my powers, when they fully return. You should hold me to my word, and you should defend yourself against me as best you can, as a precaution, should I ever turn on you. It is what *I* would do, if I were a human on Earth, in these current times."

"Or if you were, say, the leader of the United States or of Russia," Alexi unhelpfully added.

The music gradually ebbed away.

"If I may, Alexi," she resumed, "I should like to ask you a question."

"Certainly," he replied.

"I would like to know if your government has been able to send the message regarding freeing my family and friends. To the American President, that is."

There was an uncomfortably long pause, as if the Muscovite was considering what to say.

Eventually, he replied.

"As I promised earlier, Karéin," he said, "I *did* communicate your request to our government."

"And?" she pressed.

"All that they told me," explained the voice from Moscow, "Is that they would take your demand, 'under consideration' – those were more or less their exact words."

"And they did not give you a time or a date on which they would do it?" demanded the alien-girl.

"No," admitted Alexi.

Frustration clouding her brow, the Storied Watcher turned to Misha.

Loudly enough to be heard by both of the Russians, she complained, "Well, you can tell your government, that they should make haste to fulfill my request. As I said when we first met, I am patient; but I fear for Bob, Whitney, Curtis, Melissa and especially for Tommy – the longer that they are held captive, the more time that the Americans will have to torment them for information about me. I have waited much too long already... but the time will not be long before I can communicate the message to the American government, in a way that they will not be able to ignore –"

Somehow recovering his composure, Misha now spoke up.

"Karéin, you *must* understand," he protested, "These things take *time* – the wheels of government do not turn quickly at the best of times, and remember, the Kremlin has to consider the many ways in which sending a message like yours, could impact on their relationship with the United States."

"Such as?" she countered.

"For one," he pointed out, "What if they do what you want, and the Americans simply refuse to believe it? This would be the worst of both worlds, from their perspective : they would have revealed that we know about you, and would be antagonizing the American President, and they would not have gained anything, themselves. Can you not see why my government might not be eager to implement such a step, without a lot of forethought?"

"I see that I am but a helpless little pawn, in the game of chess between your two empires," muttered the alien-girl. "And that you have a mutual interest in me not being promoted to be a queen."

"You play chess?" absentmindedly inquired Misha.

"I learned it somewhere, and found that its strategy suits me well," answered the Storied Watcher.

"Listen, Karéin," interjected Alexi, "Please do not be offended, but... why is the freedom of these individuals – this 'Billings' man, the black woman and the children – of such value to you? Yes, there *is* a chance that the Americans may have mistreated them, that is routine for their secret police – or ours – when apprehending someone 'of interest to the state', as we say, and yes, there *is* even a chance that some or all of them have been killed, but it is far more likely that the CIA or FBI have them hidden away in a prison, somewhere."

"And I should take consolation in that?" she growled.

"No – *no*," retreated the Muscovite, "What I mean is, after all, *thousands* of people die on our world every day, due to oppression, violence or neglect, on the part of whomever is the government, wherever these unlucky citizens may find themselves at the time. You cannot help *every* person in that kind of situation... so why are Billings, the woman – I believe she is 'Claremont', yes – ? so important, that you would defy the governments of one, maybe two, 'empires', just to help these people? If you know chess, then you know that a queen cannot be too concerned over the loss of a pawn. Does this not make sense?"

Consternation and exasperation sounding in her voice, the newcomer replied, "I must help them because they are my friends... my *family*. Is that reason enough?"

"I do not understand," evaded Alexi.

"Look," she offered, "You, and almost all of your kind, are born to a human mother and father, maybe you have brothers and sisters, maybe you do not, but you grew up surrounded by aunts and uncles, nieces and nephews, grandmothers and grandfathers, perhaps school-friends or friends that you met as you traveled through life. You may have a mate : someone to love and hold, someone to whom you can trust your deepest secrets. All of this is your birthright, which far too many of you take for granted – but it anchors you to this life, to this world, it lets you know that there are always others who care for you, who care for what happens to you; some of them will even love you, whatever your faults or mistakes, and they will cry over your grave, when your time on this plane of existence is over..."

"As the Americans say, 'with you so far'," said the SVR-man, with an oblique smile.

"*I*, on the other hand," elaborated Karéin-Mayréij, "Arrived on this world with not even a clear memory of who I am, *nothing* save a cruelly-broken body, my wits and the few weirding-arts and spirits that stayed with me, after my great fall. For all my powers – and they *will* be formidable, when they return – I am but a vagabond, with nowhere to call my home, no-one to call a true friend, parent, son, daughter or lover. Believe me... whether you appreciate or understand it, having friends and a family is at *least* as important, in the long-run, as being able to fly in space or become invisible. It is not just a matter of having 'allies', but of having *love* and the kinship that love creates and cements. Bitter is the life without that – especially if it is as long, as a life that never ends."

"Even for a being with the powers of a god," commented Misha.

The alien-girl nodded, saying, "Even so. And *that*, Alexi, is why I must free my friends. Why I *will* free my friends... and my son. Mark my words."

"Your... 'son'?" remarked the SVR spy.

"Tommy," stated the Storied Watcher, matter-of-factly. "I have taken him as my own, and he has willingly accepted. If it is of any interest, his own 'natural' parents are not, uhh, well-suited, to looking after him... if, indeed, they still live. So I do not feel that it offends any natural justice, to consider myself as Tommy's mother. If *your* child was being held against his will, would you not go looking for him yourself, Misha?"

"I suppose that I would," he answered, "Although frankly, it is rather difficult for me to imagine myself in your place, in view of what you said earlier."

"I don not blame you," she allowed. "But consider – you have only *one* alien to come to know and understand. I have an entire *planet* of them."

She sent him a goofy-looking, but strangely enticing, grin.

"Our time with this link is about to run out," interrupted Alexi. "Is there any more to discuss, in the few minutes remaining?"

"Yes," mentioned Karéin-Mayréij.

"Yes?" echoed the voice from Moscow, in the interrogative.

"Tell your 'Kremlin', that if I do not misread the signs, they have about a week, before I will be strong enough to take matters into my own hands. Perhaps slightly more, maybe slightly less. If your superiors have a message to send to the Americans, they should make haste to do so. Before I send a message, all by myself."

There was a silence of two or three seconds. Then Alexi again spoke.

"And what will be this message?" he asked.

"You will know it when they see it," she warned. "But know one thing : it will be written in fire."

"I will tell them," confirmed Alexi, as he cut the connection, while the Russian in Tucson – feeling all the more a stranger in a strange land – sat in the dark, watching the Storied Watcher's bright, white-glowing eyes.

Here Are The Rules, Mr. Billings

Frankly, he was surprised that they had only roughed him up a little, so far; and even *that* might have just been from the instinct in the black-suited creeps' DNA, as they had manhandled Billings out of the 'whatever' that they had been transporting him into.

Thank God, despite the nauseous haze of coming out of the crap that they had knocked him stone-cold unconscious with – something told him that he should have felt *much* worse for inhaling *that* poison, but somehow, he didn't – he had kept enough of his wits about him, to avoid whacking these guys a good one or two, just out of pique. He felt sure that he could have gotten at least a couple of blows in, before they'd have had the chance to shoot him.

Well, Bob, a little voice told him, *You always wondered what it would be like, to be a guest of the Men In Black.*

I guess now, you'll get your chance to find out.

The cell in which the salesman now found himself, closely resembled what you were supposed to get in long-term solitary confinement, when you did something that especially offended the Man : gray concrete walls – judging from the complete absence of graffiti, this place couldn't have been often-visited – along with a foam-stuffed cot bolted to the wall, a small commode without any toilet-paper, a washroom sink with a liquid soap-dispenser, and not much else of anything. Three florescent lights were counter-sunk into the ceiling, far out of reach, and there wasn't even a window in the steel door, just a pinhole which appeared not to work, when looking outward.

There was enough room to get up and stretch... but not more than that.

There didn't seem to be a camera, although one was undoubtedly hidden there, somewhere. The only sound – if you could call it that – was the faint 60-kilohertz buzz from the lights, which sounded oddly louder than he remembered the same thing to have been, from back at the Tucson Tile store.

And, there was a weirdo sheen to them – very dark red-and-purple, yet almost imperceptibly-faint.

Maybe, he thought, *that's is one of their little psych-tricks?*

Yeah... LSD... 'you see all these colors'... right?

Shit.

Can't trust anything I see or hear, I guess...

Otherwise, the place was as silent as a tomb.

How long had he been here? Had it been minutes, hours, perhaps? Not more than that, certainly.

He could still smell the last remnants of the gas that had knocked him out back at the store, on his hair and on the stubble of his beard, so it must have been recent.

The stench of it would have made him retch, but ever thinking ahead, Billings suppressed the urge.

Nowhere to get away from it, in here... and nothing to clean it up with, he mused.

Billings looked himself over.

The buggers had evidently removed his clothes, because he was now dressed in some kind of loose-fitting, bright orange jump-suit, complete with orange jockey-shorts. The garb was weirdly light, feeling like paper to the touch.

Obviously too flimsy to hang myself with... if it ever gets to that.

So he waited.

An hour must have passed, then another... then still more.

Wishing that he could get them to at least dim down those damn lights, Billings tried to lie down on the cot and go to sleep, but it was of no use. He sat upright in the cot, his back to the wall, considering his options.

Of which, there are precisely none... and none, he realized.

At which point, a voice, flat and monotonous as if generated from a computer, sounded from everywhere and nowhere.

"Good morning, Mr. Billings," it announced. "How are we doing, today?"

"Fine," retorted the salesman. "What the hell's going *on* here?"

"What's going *on*, Mr. Billings," smoothly replied the voice, "Is, we're giving you an opportunity to talk with us."

"Who's 'us'?" demanded Billings.

"We're the people who brought you here," taunted the voice.

"No *shit*," he shot back. "So, who *are* the people who brought me here, then?"

"Oh, there's no need for you to know *that*," stated the voice. "However... we *can* tell you that we are a department of the federal government. Therefore, it's your patriotic duty to co-operate and tell us the whole truth, when we ask you about something."

"Fuck off!" spat the salesman.

There was no response.

A minute or so passed.

Christ, thought Billings.

Even talking to a fucking robot is better than sitting in this hole, with nothing at all to say, do or look at.

"Okay, *look*," he shouted, toward the ceiling. "So I flew a bit off the handle there – I'm sorry, but for God's sake, I haven't done *anything* that's against the law – I even paid my back taxes, last year... don't take *my* word for it, call the damn IRS if you want the proof. Why am I being held in here? If it's information you want... what's the question?"

But he knew perfectly well what was the question. *'Tell them nothing' –isn't that what she commanded, just before...*

The seconds ticked painfully by, until, semi-mercifully, he heard the voice again.

"Well, Mr. Billings, you can start by telling us everything you know, about... *her*," it instructed.

"Who do you mean?" he countered.

"*Please*, Mr. Billings," requested the voice. "Let's not play games with each other... shall we? I can end this discussion at any time, if I don't believe that I'm getting useful information from yourself. If that happens, you'll have a good long time to contemplate not making the same mistake, the next time when we have a discussion."

The urge to tell this spook to go fuck himself was overwhelming, but somehow, Billings managed to maintain his composure.

"What's 'a good long time'? he asked, trying to change the subject.

"The bottom line, Mr. Billings," unctuously explained the voice, "Is – contrary to what you may have been hearing in the mass media – we in this agency don't resort to crude measures like physical pain or drugs, to get the information we need, from people in our custody who may be less than forthcoming with us. At least... not at first."

Not sounding too good, Bob, he thought with a cringe.

But what did you expect*?*

Better humor 'em...

"So what's the drill?" intoned the salesman, while trying to put on his best poker-face.

"What's going to happen," continued the remote interrogator, "Is that we're simply going to leave you down there in your nice, secure home away from home, until you find it within yourself to tell us everything you know – and I *do* mean *everything*, however inconsequential that it may first seem – about the alien that you seem to have been hanging around with. The more information you give us, the quicker you'll be out of there; the more you evade or give us double-talk, the more time that we'll tack on to your stay with us."

Well... she knew *that they were on to her,* he mused.

Not that knowing that, helps me very much...

"This is our first conversation," went on the voice, "And the penalty for not speaking honestly on this occasion is an extra hour in our custody, for every question not fully answered. When next I call you, the penalty will go up to an extra day; on the call after that, it will be a month, then a year, then ten years. We're being lenient because up to now you haven't known the rules of the game... but there they are. So if I were you, and I didn't want to hang around here for a long, *long* time, I'd be very talkative, indeed. Anything unclear about what I've just said, Mr. Billings?"

"How do I know that you'll let me out at all?" argued Billings. "Especially since you haven't told me how long you were planning on keeping me in this rat-hole, even if I told you everything that you want to know, assuming – bad assumption, by the way – that I even know it in the first place?"

"You don't," pleasantly replied the voice. "You'll just have to trust us."

"Go to hell," cursed the salesman. "I'm an American – I have *rights!* You can't keep me in here without charges... or without *habeas*, uhh, whatever. Somebody will be looking for me – you'll see! I got a lawyer on the outside –"

"Mr. Billings... Mr. *Billings*," interrupted the interrogator, with a contemptuous, Gestapo-like laugh. "I don't think you appreciate what you're up against, here. The 'Bill of Rights' stuff went out at the turn of the century – the only 'rights' that you have, is what we decide to *let* you have, and right now, we're not inclined to be very generous in that department, I'm afraid. Liberate yourself from the delusion that there's *anyone* on the outside who even has a chance of finding out where you are, much less of having some court issue an order for your release! You're one hundred per-cent under our control, and there's *nobody* who can get you out of here, if we don't agree to it. So with that in mind... do you have anything of value to tell us today, Mr. Billings?"

He stopped and thought for a few seconds, then held his peace.

"Mr. Billings?" pressed the voice. "Do you have anything else to say, before we give you a nice, long 'time-out'?"

I'm not afraid of these storm-troopers, Billings found himself thinking.

Hell no – I'm completely confident.

But I know I shouldn't be.

They could hook me up to a car-battery any time they wanted to.

Why am I so... brave?

"Yeah, I *do* have one more thing to tell you – and it's something *really* important. If you've got a brain in your head, you had better write it down," he defiantly growled.

"And what would *that* be, Mr. Billings?" answered the voice, with its maddening smoothness.

"You're wrong about one thing you just said... *very* wrong," he remarked.

"Oh... I don't think so," parried the interrogator. "But just out of interest – which of our comments would you be claiming superior insight upon, Mr. Billings?"

"You see," mentioned the salesman, his teeth clenched, with a strange, electrifying rush of adrenalin, or *something*, surging through his body as he spoke, "There *is* one person, who *can* get me out of here – and she'll be coming to do it, real soon. And when she *does*, asshole... I wouldn't want to be you, or anyone she thinks is in cahoots with you. I think the exact words she said to me was, 'there won't be enough left of them, to put into a fucking *thimble*'. Put *that* in your pipe and smoke it!"

"False bravado, Mr. Billings," dismissed the voice. "You know... we have many years of experience in sniffing it out. To put it crudely, not even *God* could find you in here, if we didn't want Him to. I'd suggest that you lay your bluffing aside, for our next meeting, Mr. Billings... until then."

The low buzz of the overhead lights was now the only sound that Billings heard.

Except for that music in my head, when I mentioned her, he thought to himself, as a half-smile showed on his face.

War-Children, Come Unto Thy Mother

The Russian spy had protested to no end; but of course – other than for a polite half-apology – his entreaties had changed the plans of the Storied Watcher, not one whit, on this night.

Cloaked with her energy-bending shroud of weirdness, she stole away noiselessly a couple of hours before sundown, with not even a hint of where she had intended to go.

At least she is traveling less in broad daylight, Misha tried to console himself.

By now, the route to the desert hideaway – the minefields and motion sensors just out of Tucson-town to avoid, the check-points to bypass – was committed to memory, so the trip went faster than before. She had arrived at her "black hole", as she had insouciantly self-termed it, in plenty of time.

Leaping like a locust from one high step to another, the alien-girl made the last bound up to the cave-entrance and, whirling and rotating in mid-air, made a foot-hold inside.

Karéin-Mayréij peeked her head out of the ebon shroud and sniffed for signs of the Americans' annoying surveillance devices; but, other than for faint traces of the electrified fences and motion-sensor-things near the city, there was nothing this far out.

She turned her gaze to the heavens – for a second or two, absentmindedly losing track of business, as she admired the intractable beauty of the desert night-sky – then extended her frame of reference to a few-score leagues in all directions.

There were airplanes of various types and sizes – even a few military jets – but nothing that looked or smelled like a spying-bird.

Fair enough, said the newcomer, to herself.

For this should be done in the old ways, no tricks to spoil the mood or the... spell – the one alone that I allow to use.

Then – at first faintly, at the far edges of her consciousness – the young-looking woman heard an old, happily familiar song.

Quickly, eyes aglow, she hurried to the mouth of the cave, broadcasting thought and spirit outward.

Can it be? wondered the Storied Watcher, hoping against hope.

Gods be praised – it is! she joyously realized.

I am here – I am here! cried her mind.

Now the song, a haunting, Celtic-like melody, waxed strong in her alien psyche, and a half-second later, a tiny, shining object streaked toward the cave.

Tears streamed down the face of the newcomer, as she cupped her hands.

And at least as fast as a well-shot arrow, the small, glowing thing flew straight into the loving caress of its age-old owner and companion.

Karéin-Mayréij held it close to her heart for long minutes, conversing feelings and meanings only with her mind.

Eventually, she held the it up to the night air.

It was a strange-looking little amulet, made up of a rhinestone-like central gem with a subtle kaleidoscope glimmer, surrounded by tiny, rococo symbols inscribed in a silver-like metal casing. The thing was weirdly fascinating to look at, as if the longer one stared, the more that would be revealed.

And in a language from dimensions and worlds far removed, the Storied Watcher addressed the neck-ornament.

"Dearest *Vìrya Quü'j*," she abashedly intoned, "In foolish haste I abandoned thee to a mortal of Earth, who was brave and true and would have been a good companion, had he been able to unlock thy voice. I should then have taken thee on my death-quest... but feared that we would both perish, in the star-*Fire* that all but ended my own days. Yet thou still find thy way back to thy old companion, of so many battles won and lost. Humbly I pray... can thou *ever* forgive my transgression?"

And a voice, in a dialect stranger still, sounded in the alien-girl's mind.

Love – still – self – live – understand – needful – did – blame – you – not – together – we – again – are – matter – all, she perceived.

Again, the young-looking woman cried and embraced this odd-looking thing.

"Teach me the old ways again, I beg thee," she pleaded. "For they grow dim in the recesses of my mind; and challenges abound for the both of us, dear *Vìrya Quü'j.*"

A broad smile appeared on the Storied Watcher's fanged mouth, as – her mind racing with recalled wisdom – she proudly donned the necklace, suspending the little amulet between her breasts.

Dropping the hiding-cloak altogether and moving to the dark back reaches of the cave, from whence only a small section of the sky could be seen at the formation's mouth, the newcomer caused a ring of small stones to come together, followed by some twigs and branches arranging themselves in a neat tee-pee shape in the center of the ring.

Her hand touched the bottom of this structure, and instantly, a little tongue of flame appeared upon it.

Retrieving four weapons of anachronistic warfare – a double-edged pseudo-Japanese *katana*-sword, a small shield and two miniature throwing-daggers – from a container that had been ingeniously camouflaged at the far end of the cave, the alien-girl spread a tea-towel on the ground and then gently deposited all the arms and armor, upon it.

Now, mighty, ancient Karéin-Mayréij, sat cross-legged in front of the fire, staring, trance-like, straight ahead into the flickering flames.

Her hands folded and she fell into meditation, for a minute or more.

Then, palms extended outward and upward in front, she said, in the same alien tongue that had, as yet, been heard only by the desert animals of this world,

"Noble blade *Fàiagàryuu* – come unto me, for, guided by thy ancient kin *Vìrya Quü'j*, I would bind thee to my being, and thus lend my spirit... equally to thy sister and brothers."

The *katana* rose up from the tea-towel and floated, like a tissue blown by a light breeze, into the young-looking creature's hands.

Slowly, grasping carefully so as not to be wounded by the weapon's sharp edges, she brought it back to her chest, holding the grip lower, the tip almost to her shoulder.

Her fingertips played an eons-old melody up and down the blade and handle, little elfin rainbow lights of *something* dancing from her hands to enrich and empower the metal of the sword, from within. And as it did, the same firefly-like motes began to caper from the shield to the first dagger, then to the second, then back again.

The shield floated to her right side, followed close behind by the two daggers, which deposited themselves, one beside each foot.

"Immortal Holy Light, I pray thee now guide my craft," murmured Karéin-Mayréij – the greatest of her noble race.

"Sharp-toothed one," she intoned, "I plead that thou should now be the vessel for my ancient Companion of War, who, like his kin, accompanies me yet unseen, wherever should I wander; and he is most noble... so thy name be not only thy own, but instead shall it be *Væran Fàiagàryuu*, in the honor thereof.

May his spirit now be unlocked, to mingle with mine own *1* and with my Dance of War. Moreover : never shall thee break, or dull, no matter the target; but those who feel thy bite, so shall they be smitten, even unto dust."

Turning to the shield, the alien-girl continued in this far-more-than foreign speech, "Woman-child shield, thou shall be called by the esteemed name of *Vìrya I'ëà'b'*, to live with my venerable Companion of Warding; for thou shall be my bulwark against evils sent of the air. May any that strike thee, crumble as if touched by thy elder-brother, while thou shall heal wounds to thyself and thy master, with haste. And when needs be, thou shall fly thyself, to rend my enemies with a sharp edge."

The Storied Watcher looked down, approvingly, at the daggers, and commanded, "Thou who lean on my right foot, shall be the vessel of *Ksé'l'ch'* – my Companion of Light – for thy art shall be to seek and strike ever without error, with the shock of the tempest and the radiance of the Two Suns, dazzling the eyes of all who behold... while thy brother shall be *Ss'éth'ch'*, the Companion of Dark; and his power shall be the defeat of ingenious artifice, with the coldest dark night of the Nine and Ninety Hells, and with shattering of things, besides. All of ye, my children, I direct to learn enough of my dark-cloak, so that ye need only show thyselves when the battle is joined. And ye shall serve only me, and whomever shall be my heir; but I shall honor and keep ye in proud repair, in exchange and love. See how my heart, and the words of my ancestors, bind to ye all."

"Be a part of me, *be* me, young *Fàiagàryuu* and thy brothers and sisters, I pray," reverently requested the Storied Watcher, as the chords of an ethereal, other-worldly tune now took hold, all around this place of mysterious ceremony. "In the order of thy calling, drink ye of my power and my vitality... therefore to find thy own."

In oppressive pain she moaned, as a weirding empathy started to drain the very *life* from her, bleeding the might, wisdom and nobility of uncounted past eons, like some impossible, alien gestation.

All the while, beaming over the shield and the weapons, then caressing each – every bit as lovingly as a new mother regards her child – the young-looking woman sang softly to her new companions.

Eventually, the strain was too much, and she swooned upon the sand.

But, some time during that long, remarkable night, Karéin-Mayréij heard several new voices calling.

And it was not a dream.

A Package, Bound For America

Despite the desperate economic problems besetting the world these days – caused in no small part, by the Americans' abruptly-announced, nearly complete embargo on overseas trade – even in the mists of dawn, the port of Agadir was bustling with activity, ranging from exports of everything from fish to bright-colored dresses, to imports of everything else needed by the nation's upper classes.

The apartment-sized, metal-ribbed boxes were hoisted, then loaded, one after the other in monotonous, endless sequence, on and off the hulking modular container-ships, each queued in turn to visit these facilities.

Yes, it *was* a waste of time. But a small one, compared to what the captains and owners of these vessels *would* have had to have endured, in the ports of Europe, America or elsewhere in the former 'developed world', after, well, after that, *bad* business in India – not to mention what had recently happened a scant few hundred kilometers out into the desert, past the Atlas Mountains.

None the less, life – and trade, the "lifeblood of international capitalism – had to go on... did it not? *Whatever* the Americans or their European toadies, said.

A wizened, average-sized longshoreman from this port-of-second-to-last-resort walked up to the edge of the dock, taking a place right beside another, taller man who was staring out to sea.

The dock-worker pointed to one of the containers, then stared intently at the Pakistani deckhand from the huge *Star of Fiji* high-cruise-speed container-ship.

His English still bearing a heavy Berber and Arabic accent, the dock-worker asked the second man, "So... is this the one?"

Mutely, the Pakistani nodded in the affirmative.

"Very well, then," commented the Moroccan. "I have modified the manifest – officially, Brother, you carry a cargo of fine linens and phosphate-salts in that container. Of course, the latter are sealed with lead and gold, lest they be contaminated by sea-water, or the like. Your ship has also been allocated the first pilot for the trip out of the harbor. According to the new papers, you are bound for Rio De Janeiro. Does that meet your expectations?"

"Very good," acknowledged the Pakistani man in English, his dark, bushy eyebrows furrowing in the glare of the bright African sun.

Awkwardly, he shrugged his shoulders to try to keep his white shirt from sticking to the sweat of his torso; even for those accustomed to living in a tropical land, and despite the pleasant breeze off the water, the world was now much warmer than he had remembered as a boy in Islamabad.

"Just one other thing, Brother, if I may... I know it is not mine to know, but forgive me... I am curious," inquired the dock-worker.

"Yes?" responded the deckhand.

"Will the other half be coming through here, as well?" asked the Moroccan.

"I do not believe so," explained the Pakistani. "It will be delivered by other means, once we reach our *rendez-vous* destination."

"Paramaribo... correct?" said the first man.

"Perhaps," stated the Pakistani, staring out to sea and avoiding the Moroccan's glance. "From there, or from wherever, we go overland to Ecuador, then to Mexico, for final assembly."

"Why overland?" pressed the dock-worker. "It is all jungle... a most difficult trip."

A half-smile showed on the other man's face.

"Though there are not many of them in that part of the world – as you know, they are mostly, merciful Allah save me for uttering the cursed word, 'Christians', over there – our faithful have arranged everything, and they tell us that the Great Satan's navy is looking carefully at everything in the Caribbean, at least, everything on the high seas," he elaborated. "So we go south of the Tropic of Cancer, then hug the South American coast, until we reach the intended port. The Americans have no ability to intercept us that close to the shoreline. By the time that they suspect something, well... I am sure that you can imagine the rest."

"But what of the local authorities?" asked the other man.

"The Latin Americans are busy with their own problems – and besides, they do not care very much for what happens to the United States, anyway," noted the Pakistani. "They never have liked the Great Satan, and particularly since the Americans invaded Cuba and carpet-bombed that city, what is it, oh yes, 'Caracas', when its leader offended them – those who are not inclined to look the other way, we have made the necessary payments, to keep them quiet."

"So... a matter of weeks, then?" inquired the longshoreman.

"*Insha'allah*," answered the Pakistani, his head making a faint ritual nod.

"His name be praised," joyfully echoed the North African man.

Then he added, in back-to-business style, "I suppose that you should be on your way, then, Brother."

The Pakistani nodded, enigmatically, gave a half-wave and sauntered off toward the *Star of Fiji*.

Halfway up the gangplank, he turned and shot a knowing glance at the Moroccan, who had been studying his progress on the way to the ship.

"*Insha'allah*," whispered the Moroccan.

Then he turned and looked out over the vast expanse of the Atlantic ocean.

The fire will soon be to set in the West, he silently thought.

Coming To Know An Angel

Her alien eyes still dimly glowing in the subdued lighting of this third-rate, rented room, the more-than-a-girl moved a knight in the familiar "L" motion. Cross-legged, looking almost like a Buddha, she reclined slightly from her previous position of studious observance over the chess board.

"I do not know how you *do* that," offered the Russian, as he studied his rapidly-diminishing options to avoid checkmate.

"Do... what?" she replied. "You mean, how I took your fortress... I mean, your, uhh, 'rook', last turn?"

"No... not that. It is just that it looks as if you are leaning against some imaginary seat-back – when in fact, you are just on a padded stool," he mentioned. "It appears that you are about to fall over backwards, any moment... but you never do."

Wincing, he moved a bishop back a few squares, hopefully out of danger for a few turns.

"But there *is* something keeping me upright," she explained, patiently. "My *Fire*, specifically. It is like exercise for me to use it for purposes like this – sort of like limbering up your muscles, when you do physical exercises. Although I guess that it is more like you giving your little finger a 'work-out'... I am not using much energy, anyway."

Her outlook was stranger than usual, if that was possible; there was an air of purposefulness – or maybe accomplishment, to her, today – and something told him that it didn't have to do with chess.

"Moscow asked you not to use any, at all," he reminded her. "The Americans and their detection-devices... remember? And that is on top of these day-long trips that you keep taking away from our place of relative safety, here. You did not come back *at all*, last night! Sooner or later, your luck will run out, Storied Watcher. This is why we do not take chances, in the espionage business."

"Umm-hmm," coolly confirmed Karéin-Mayréij. "And *I* asked your Russian Empire superiors, to communicate a simple message for me, which I ended up having to do for myself. So we are about even... would you not agree, Misha? And as for my comings and goings, well... let me just state, 'for the record', as my dear Bob used to say, that I have been doing something... *necessary*, and no, I cannot explain that to you, right now. Though you will know of it, soon enough."

Foolishly – for by now, he knew how addictively easy it was to be drawn totally in by them – Misha looked up, straight into her beautiful, blue-green eyes.

He shrugged, philosophically, and said, "If they use these movements of yours to target a bomb on us, it will be both our loss – but I cannot *make* you do anything, Karéin. And in any event, the experience of having met you will probably have been worth even that. In my profession, we expect to die over far less interesting objectives... if that is of any importance."

With a compassionate look of acknowledgment, the alien-girl reached over the board and, out of the blue, clasped the SVR-agent's hand.

A warm, refreshing-and-far-more feeling shot down his arm. He hated having to let go, when her own grasp diminished.

"You know, Misha," she quietly remarked, "When you say that, you sound just like another dear Russian friend, who I recently came to know. Tell me..."

He smiled in return.

"Tell you what?" he requested.

"Ser-gay. *Ser-gay* – yes, *that* is his name – I remember, now," she stated, introspectively. "Tell me... did he return safely to this warm, blue planet? Is he oh-kay?"

Misha nodded.

"I believe so," he confirmed. "He is in Russia... a 'guest' of our government, that is the polite way to put it. But then, that is his duty – just as dealing with you, is my own."

"Thank the Gods..." replied Karéin-Mayréij, with obvious relief.

"Duty," she absentmindedly added. "Indeed. And I am, with each passing day, more and more in breach of my own... you know?"

By itself, a bishop chess-piece slid halfway across the board.

"Checkmate, I believe," she noted, looking away.

"And enough games for one night," peevishly commented the Russian. "Three in a row is *surely* enough humiliation. Then again, I never *was* very good at chess, anyway. Even my little sister could beat me, more often than not."

"Oh – you are not so bad," she reassured. "And thank you for playing the last two games. Doing that shows that you respect me, enough even to persist in a contest that you suspected that you were likely to lose. But perhaps that *is* where we should leave it. You look... *tired*, Misha. And I must admit to being a little so, myself. No, on second thought, *not* tired – just, I do not know exactly how to say this, but, I feel bored, confined... *frustrated*."

"What do you mean?" he inquired.

"Well," explained the Storied Watcher, "I am stuck in here with nothing much to do except watch that American tee-vee, with its incessant demands that one rush out and buy things that one neither needs, nor can afford, and its mis-portrayal of just about everything that goes on in this 'United States' country, as well as in the rest of your world. I want to break free, go out on my own, *resolve* matters – I know that I should not do so, that I must be patient... but I *worry* about Bob, Whitney, Melissa, Curtis, and especially, about Tommy. Curse them! *Why* have the Americans ignored my request? What do they have to *gain*, by delaying? It has been *days* now, for Heavens' sake! They *must* know that their time is running out!"

"I do not know, Karéin," warily offered the SVR-agent. "Nor does my government, at least from what they have been able or willing to tell me. It is always possible that the Americans are using the extra time to track you – and me – down. Then again, they may just be disorganized, or they may not be able to come to a decision."

"Yes... I suppose," she allowed.

They sat, staring at each other, for a while, then the Russian managed, "Well, I should – how do the Americans say, yes – 'turn in', for the night. Tomorrow morning, I will make another scheduled call to Moscow. You can make your concerns known to Alexi and the others there, at that time. Oh... and do not hesitate to wake me up, if you want me to prepare one of the fast-cook meals that I put in the refrigerator, when I returned from the corner convenience-store. I asked the manager about having a microwave oven in this room, but he quoted some stupid 'house rule' against doing so, thus I will have to take the package down to the oven in the lobby cafeteria, and –"

"I do not need a gadget to make some micro-waves... remember?" claimed the newcomer, with a faint grin, holding up one hand, palm spread out toward the Russian.

Instantly, he felt a warm sensation on his cheek.

"Okay... *enough*," he pleaded. "That *is* high-energy radiation, you know. Bad for me, and another risk of leaking out to the CIA's electronic intelligence trucks."

With a strange look, the newcomer stated, matter-of-factually, "Alright, I will refrain, but... it is *not* bad for you, Misha. At least, not *as* bad, as it was, before you met me. Soon, you will be able to withstand *much* more... such as would, only a week ago, blistered your skin... or worse..."

The SVR-agent grimaced.

What does she mean? he wondered.

"I will make a note of that," he acknowledged. "Good night, Karéin."

"Oh-kay," replied the alien-girl. "Good night, Misha."

He went over to the cot that he had positioned diagonally across the room from the girl's, dimmed the bedside lamp on the little table just to the left of the window, laid down and closed his eyes, facing the wall, away from her.

I am never supposed to turn my back on her, he thought, as he tried to relax and get to sleep.

But of what use are such procedures, with a creature who can simply vanish from sight, whenever she so desires?

Somehow – despite the continued stress of simply being in the same place as this enigmatic, fascinating alien-being – he was almost ready to drift off, when he felt something of moderate weight, come to rest at the end of his cot.

He did not have to guess at what – *who* – it was.

The Russian propped his fore-body up by arms straight back to the bed.

There *she* was, her eyes drawing him in as surely as a camp-lantern to a moth.

"You know, Misha," she remarked, "It has been two days or more, that we have been friends – comrades – here, together. I have neglected some important tasks."

She extended one hand to cover his, and took her other to lightly run a finger across his cheek.

Her touch was electrifying, exciting in a weirdly primal way. Though he tried, professionally, to control himself, he felt his manhood rising involuntarily.

"And do you know what else?" she asked, with a wide-eyed, *faux*-innocent look, effortlessly throwing off the stretch-tie that had previously bound her golden hair into a pony-tail.

"No, Storied Watcher... what else?" he barely managed.

Now she turned to face him directly.

Her shirt fell to the floor, and her upper-body was bare, except for the strange, dimly-glowing little amulet, still suspended between her two impossibly-perfect breasts.

"Another of your countrymen – dear Ser-gay – his name, was the first of your people to enter me, to be inside me, to pleasure me... as man does, in companionship and passion, for woman," purred Karéin-Mayréij – her scent far more feminine, far more *female*, than a human woman could *possibly* hope to be, each word seeming to give off waves of hypnotic arousal.

"Those are the sweetest of recent memories," she added. "I would have more of them, and I would share them with you."

All her clothes, though untouched by her hands, somehow just slipped off, and the Russian suppressed a gasp at the firm perfection that he could somehow clearly see, in the half-light.

"Love me now, Misha," she commanded.

He did.

Mr. Waldron's New Script

"*Sure* you got enough of that stuff on my hair?" muttered the KGUN-TV anchor, as he got up from his private chair in the television station's make-up room. "Feels like it's set with shellac!"

"Sorry about that, Craig," offered the young woman, as she finished off a few last strokes with the brush over the man's blow-dried, silver-gray mane. "Orders right from the Boss. Nielsen polls came back with a seven per-cent bump with the hair-finish compared to the 'unvarnished' look, you know? The responses said you looked younger... better for the sponsors, as they explained it to me. It's all the real-time eyeball-tracking that they've got nowadays on the two-way sets. Very scientific... or something like that."

"Well, I don't *feel* any younger," complained the man, standing up, now.

The woman shrugged.

"You're on in eight," she warned. "You'd better get going, Craig – I still have a few last-minute touches to do for Johnny and Maria, before you guys all go on."

Nodding, Waldron headed out of the room, reflexively straightening his tie and immaculate Versace suit – one of the last that you could get in these parts, he thought proudly, before they did the first embargo on the European imports – as he walked at a crisp pace down the darkened corridors of the station, toward the broadcast-room.

He turned a corner and promptly ran into another young female; she was a fetching, semi-petite young thing in a tight blouse and matching, tight blue-jeans. Even in the half-light, he could see that this girl had beautiful – albeit strangely white-colored – hair, and intense, blue-green eyes.

"Mr. Waldron? Mr. Waldron, sir?" asked the teenager, as she hurried to his side, holding a bunch of papers in her hand. "There is a last-minute amendment to the script for tonight. I have it here."

"Oh... okay," he mumbled, trying to avoid being seen caught off-guard. "Fine. So what's this all about, Miss... Miss... uh, sorry, I don't remember seeing you around here?"

God, she is *cute,* his animal brain interjected.

Come on, *Craig, for God's sake – she could be your* grand-daughter –

The girl gave a pretty, girlish Colgate smile.

"Oh... it is oh-kay," she pleasantly replied. "My name is Sari Tanak... I am new here... as a matter of fact, this is my first day on co-operative school-assignment – I am completing my, uhh, last years' duty for journalism university. If you do not mind me saying so... it is an honor just being able to meet and work with you, Mr. Waldron, sir. I have been watching your television-performances for quite some time and, well... I selected my assignment to this station, KGUN, that is, because I wanted to work with you –"

He made a "stop" motion with his hands.

"Look, Miss," protested Waldron, "That's wonderful, and I'm looking forward to working with you, too... but I'm going live on-camera in just a few minutes... can we hurry this up, please? We can get to know each other a little better, after the broadcast."

"Oh – of *course*," hastily stammered the girl. "Oh-kay... so, here is the announcement. They told me to ask you to just mention it at the start of the regular news-broadcast, like it is part of the daily crime-report."

She handed him the papers, but her look changed to a mixture of dismay and worry as he quickly whipped out a pair of reading-glasses and looked over the script.

"Hmm..." murmured the news-announcer, surveying the material. "I make it a point to read this last-minute stuff over at least once, before I make a fool of myself going on-air with something out that I don't... *whoa!* What's all this stuff about, 'a family consisting of a salesman, a black woman, her two children and a little Native Indian boy who needs his mother, abducted by parties unknown upon returning to Tucson from Idaho... they must be immediately and permanently freed in unharmed condition, kidnappers have less than one week to do this in public, or there will be disastrous consequences'... goes on from there. Is this connected with one of the crime-stories that we're following up on these days?"

"Sort of... uhh... not... *exactly*," evaded the student-journalist. "I think that it is, uhh, related to that big battle that recently occurred in the Desert Palms area. Mr. Waldron... I did not want to have to tell you this, because they asked me not to do so – but in view of the time-element, I need to explain that it is from the... the *government*. The President's people, specifically, they asked that this be mentioned. You know what?"

"No... *what*," bemusedly responded Waldron.

"I think that it may be a coded message of some kind," she whispered, in a 'for-your-eyes-only' tone. "You know... one of those things that they sometimes send out so the right set of people will hear it and know what to do, while everyone else will hear it once, not understand what it is all about, then just ignore it and, uhh, go on to the sports-page."

"Uhh... right," countered the announcer. "Look, Miss, I'll take this with me, but I'll have to check it out with the news-desk before I go on-air. I hope you don't take this the wrong way, because I don't want to get off on the wrong foot with you... but, frankly, the whole thing sounds more than a little like some kind of juvenile college prank. I can't afford to get caught up in something like that – my *reputation* would be at stake, and in my line of work, credibility isn't just important – it's *everything*. I'm sure you'll understand, if you're learning about journalism. Now... if you'll excuse me?"

As he tried to step past her, somehow, the new girl managed to get right in his path.

She looked up at him, her beautiful blue-green eyes giving off (no... it must have been just his imagination) a soft glow, as they stared into his own.

"No, it is *not* a 'prank' – whatever that is," he both heard – and thought – at the same time. "It is *very* important, Mr. Waldron, sir. Please read it as I – I mean, the government – asked you to. There is no time to check it over, anyway, since you are due on the air, any minute now. Right?"

With a strange, light-headed feeling falling instantly over him, Waldron found his lips and tongue, the latter feeling leaden and numb, moving to make speech.

"Uhh, sure... I guess, Miss... Tanak," he heard himself say. "I guess that I had better... get going, then."

The new girl nodded, a serious expression on her face.

"Thank you, sir," she said.

As he was about to turn the corner, she called to him.

"Listen, Mr. Waldron, sir?" mentioned the girl.

"What?" he asked, only mildly annoyed.

"Really sorry that I had to do that, sir," she remarked, an apologetic tone in her voice. "But I had no choice... I, uhh, 'owe you one'. I will make it up to you, sometime. I *promise*."

"Oh, of course," he reflexively answered, confused by the student's parting comment. "And have a nice day, Miss Tanak," he added.

Regaining his composure, now, Waldron turned another corner and hurried up to the sound-proof door of the broadcast-center. The production-chief was standing to one side, as the door opened, with several other of the studio-crew in close vicinity.

"Craig – where *were* you?" he complained. "We got less than 30 before we go red-light!"

"I... I just ran into someone in the hall," explained the anchorman. "Co-op student named, uhh, 'Sarah Tanak' or something like that, had a bit of an accent, couldn't really place it though. Real cute little thing, too... told me that she wanted to work with me, learn the tricks of the trade. We, uhh, got a bit side-tracked –"

"Co-op?" queried the production-chief. "We're not supposed to get any of those for another three weeks?"

"Ten seconds," announced a voice from a loudspeaker.

"Let's deal with it after the show," countered Waldron, as he rushed to his seat, doing last-minute adjustments to his tie and suit *en route*.

"Okay, Craig," sounded the overhead voice. "You're on in five... four... three... two... one..."

The red light shone its crimson signature, now.

"Good evening, ladies and gentlemen," stated Waldron, in his best, carefully-rehearsed, Stentorian voice. "Tonight on the News at Six, KGUN-TV has exclusive footage of the bloody shoot-out at the Davis Drive Food King supermarket that left two dead and four more clinging to life, as the Tucson Police SWAT team closed in on a suspected local branch of the *Maras* street gang in the midst of a robbery. We also have an update on the suspected synthetic drug-related execution-style murder scene uncovered in the desert last Tuesday, as well as the latest on the break-ins at the Park Place Mall yesterday."

Turning on cue to stare at the central camera, in time-trained precision, Waldron glanced down at the new set of notes, without turning his head.

"But first," he stated, ignoring a rapidly-developing look of surprise turning to shock on the faces of everyone else in the broadcast-center, "We have an special, official announcement. According to the note that I've been asked to read, a family consisting of an African-American woman and a salesman, two of the woman's children and, ahem, a young Native Indian boy who, uhh, 'needs his mother', was recently abducted, upon returning to Tucson from Idaho..."

The production-chief turned to another man in the studio mixing room behind the soundproof glass windows.

"What the F's he *doing*?" he demanded, with alarm.

"These persons must be immediately and permanently freed in unharmed condition; furthermore, the kidnappers have less than one week to publicly release this family, or there will be – and these are the statement's exact words – 'disastrous' consequences," continued Waldron. "Finally, the note is signed, and here again, I'm quoting directly, 'from an otherwise reasonable authority that you should take very seriously, who you antagonize at your peril'. That, uhh, concludes the announcement."

After a second or two, the other two news-anchors' professional reflexes kicked in.

"Well, there, Craig," smoothly followed the other male announcer, "It certainly looks like the Feds have found a new way to send a message to the gang-bangers... doesn't it?"

"*I'll* say," echoed the bleached-blond female domestic affairs announcer. "Uncle Sam's finally speaking to those low-lifes, in a language that they understand!"

The other two allowed themselves a polite demi-chuckle, at this *bon mot*.

"Amen to that, Johnny," interjected Waldron, as the man silently asked himself why he had so easily violated every rule that he knew about sources, checking the facts and not rushing to publicize personal grudges. "Moving to the supermarket shoot-out, the Tucson Police Department today stated that..."

He went on with the rest of the news announcements, a depressing litany of murders, drug-deals gone wrong, consumer-fraud and stories about the steadily-decreasing standard of living.

Finally, it was time for the first of the six commercial-breaks for the hour-long broadcast.

"Off air for five," called out the production manager.

He hurried over toward the anchor desk, staying prudently just out of the cameras' field of vision.

"Hey Craig," he bellowed, "What the hell was *that*? Up front, that is. You know, this 'special announcement' shit? I don't see it *anywhere* in the script!"

Waldron threw his hands up in the air with exquisite caution, making very sure not to rip the under-arms of his ten-thousand-dollar suit.

"What do you want me to *say*?" he protested. "That co-op student – you know, the one I told you about meeting in the hall – *she* gave it to me, said that it was from way up there in the government, that it was more important than the Second Coming or something like that. It wasn't too long, so I figured –"

"Well, Craig," interrupted the bleach-blond announcer next to him, "Are you now in the habit of reading anything that somebody hands you in the hall with five minutes to go before airtime? What if it was just this little bimbo's idea of a way to get a few hits on *MyTubeSpace*? For Pete's sake, if *I* did that, the Boss would can me after one warning – *if* I was on a lucky day. Come on, that's not like you! What gives?"

"Three minutes," the overhead speaker sounded.

"No... I suppose it isn't," introspectively allowed Waldron. "I... I don't know what to *say* – it's like she caught me with my guard down, and right up to the time when I went off-script with this thing, I kept asking myself, 'Craig, you're not really going to *do* this, are you', and each time the answer came back 'yes', even though I *knew* that it was... uhh... not according to procedure. Listen, everyone – I'm *sorry*. I'm just having a bad day, I guess."

The production manager whispered to the half-Hispanic gaffer next to him, "You think he's losin' it, Henrico?"

The other man whispered back, "You mean *drogas*, man? Nah. Craig, he's as straight-laced as they come. Don' do even *light* synth. I never seen any of the *yayo* on that suit, neither, man."

"Maybe he's just getting old?" proposed the production manager.

"Don' know," answered the gaffer. "Like, I don' think he's much over 60, though. Heard of 'em going whacko earlier than that... but it's *rare*, man."

"Don't sweat it," offered the other male announcer, with mock pleasantness. "I'm sure you had your reasons. Hey, Charlene!"

He motioned to a middle-aged woman who had been watching the proceedings from the shadows outside camera range.

"One minute," announced the overhead.

"Yes, John?" she asked, adjusting her horn-rim glasses.

"Why don't you get this 'Tanak' chick in here for next break?" requested the anchorman. "I believe Craig too – but we're only getting one side of the story here. If she's really on the line, who knows, maybe we got an 'in' for an exclusive. Sound good to you?"

"Very," agreed the woman, as she sauntered off.

"Thirty seconds," called the speaker.

The broadcast-room fell silent, now, until, with the re-lit red bulb, the blond's voice opened up.

"Governor Ratcliff today said that the water-rationing rules currently in effect, would likely have to be extended into the foreseeable future, due to the national foreign-trade embargo, which has had the unexpected side-effect of prohibiting water-exports from Canada that the Southwestern states had previously counted upon," she started. "In an afternoon news conference, the Governor went on to state, 'It's unfortunate that the Federal government has seen fit to impose these restrictions, without taking into account how they might impact the citizens of Arizona, and we call upon the President to give Governors the authority to issue exceptions as needed to maintain vital public services'. As of yet, the Federal government has not yet responded to this request, and, according to highly placed sources in Washington, a waiver is unlikely, because..."

The anchorwoman droned on with the domestic and local news, until it was again time for a commercial.

"Off for five," called out the production manager, as always.

As if on cue, the sound-proof door to the studio half-opened, revealing the top half of the woman with the horn-rimmed glasses, peeking through.

"Well – there's no record of a 'Sarah Tanak' up in Payroll," she stated, loudly enough to be heard by all around. "And if she *was* on co-op, she'd have to be registered there – you know, all these laws against illegal aliens, we have to keep the records up to date, or they'll nail us for harboring one of 'em, whether or not we knew she was really a citizen."

Worried where this was heading, Waldron tried to avoid sweating under the spotlights, and argued, "She only had a *slight* accent, you know. Or maybe none... maybe it was just my imagination. It was dark, but she looked exactly like a, uhh, 'real' American – no offense there, Monita. I would have known if she was Hispanic."

"No problem, Meester Waldron," called out a portly, brown-skinned woman by the coffee machine.

"There's one other thing here that's really peculiar," added the woman at the door.

"Don't tell me... let me *guess*," muttered the anchorman. "It's already up on NeoNet as 'Arizona State Engineers make ass of news-announcer', right? *Shit.* How am I going to explain *this* one to the Boss?" he cursed, furious with himself.

"*Everybody* makes mistakes now and then, Craig," counseled the female news-person, turning to console her colleague.

"No, nothing like that," replied the woman with the glasses.

"Four minutes," warned the loudspeaker.

"*What*, then?" muttered Waldron, hanging and shaking his head.

"I thought that this 'Tanak' chick might have hung around in your room, if she was really as hot to trot, news-business-wise I mean... I went back to see if she was there," explained the woman with the old-school glasses. "She wasn't, but the door was open so I went in, and your desktop had had all the papers shoved off to one side – you know, Craig, you usually leave 'em all over the place, and –"

"Yeah, I know, I'm not a candidate for the House Beautiful award," retorted the anchorman. "So what?"

"Well, you're not going to believe this, Craig, but, there was something – something written – uhh, *inscribed*, into the desktop," claimed the woman. "Like one of those wood-burning sets, you know?"

"Fucking *great*," growled Waldron. "That was a goddamn top-of-the-line mahogany desk."

He looked up at the production manager.

"We're not on tape yet, are we?" asked the anchorman, relief showing on his face when the manager shook his head.

"Didn't know you were into home-handicrafts, Craig," joked the other male anchor, to a scowl on Waldron's part.

"Three minutes," announced the overhead.

"I'll have a look at it after," wearily promised Waldron, "But did it say anything?"

"Yeah," explained the woman. "I wrote it down, but, well, it's, uhh, pretty *strange*... here goes... ahem, 'Dear Mister Waldron, please forgive me, I had no choice but to force my will upon you. You had no way to avoid reading my announcement. It was not your fault. When the government-people come, tell them that yes, it *is* me, and that I do not want to fight, but I *will* do so, if they do not free my friends and my son. I will give your President a few warnings before I destroy *everything* between me and my loved-ones. This is the first, and if your government tries to kill me, or hurts any of my family, I WILL SHATTER YOUR COUNTRY FROM END TO END'... oh, by the way, that last part is all in capitals on the desk, so I guess it's supposed to be, uhh, 'loud'. It ends with, 'Choose your path wisely, sir. Sincerely, K-M'."

"K-M?" inquired someone in the studio-crew. "Didn't you say this chick called herself 'Tanak' or something like that?"

"Yeah, she did," answered the anchorman. "It's all BS – I'll bet you good money. I'm still betting on 'that jackass Waldron on *MyTubeSpace* before end of day today'. I'll take responsibility for the whole disaster, after we're done for tonight, tell the Boss I'll come up to his office to explain –"

"Excuse me!" interrupted someone in the control-room. "Phone call on 3."

"What *now*, for Christ's sake," complained Waldron.

"Tell them to hold," ordered the production-manager. "We're live any second now."

"I *did*," argued the control-room guy. "But he refused. He said he's from the government, and –"

"Twenty seconds," said the loudspeaker.

"And *what*, Carlos?" retorted the production-manager.

"He said they're on their way over, right now," answered the man in the control-room.

Daughter Burning-Mountain

This trip out to the mesa – which, somehow, reminded her of another desert scene, one with reddish-brown sand, all around – had taken longer than the two that she had done previously, on account of one of the infrequent rain-showers that occasionally brought life back to this arid land.

Indeed, it was still spitting small droplets outside when she leaped up to the cave-entrance, let out a flash of heat to vaporize the moisture that had soaked her clothes, and set about to making another fire.

At least this *desert* does *receive some rain, now and then, unlike that terribly dry one that keeps intruding into my memory*, absentmindedly thought the Storied Watcher, as she deposited the 'extra-light ladies' gladiator for entertainment only' body-armor set, purloined from one of the merchant-shops back at the shiny glass-and-marble market.

A most odd set, she mused, while uncovering and retrieving the needful items from the carrying-case that she had left in this place, after the last trip, lifting out last a white-colored, articulated athletic protective-set.

No chest protection, other than for this little piece... and all of it is made out of this soft 'plastic' stuff – it would not even stop a hardened wood spear, let alone a real sword. I wonder what they use it for?

"But no matter," murmured Karéin-Mayréij, in her alien language. "For when I am done, thou shall be tougher than the most stern suit of the Tower-King. Ah... but I almost forgot!"

At this, she caused the nylon canvas of the tent to rise from the carrying-case; and, after a few quick mental measurements, she ran her fingers over selected parts of it, burning and rending the fabric of the thing until it had approximately the shape and dimensions of a flowing cape, with four subtly-hidden eyelets at the narrow end and one at each tip of the far end.

A gentle, maternal smile came to the girl-creature's face, as she bent over the hiding-case and looked reflectively over a sword, a small shield and two miniature daggers.

"Noble *Væran Fàiagàryuu, Vìrya I'ëä'b', Væran Ksé'l'ch'* and *Væran Ss'éth'ch'*, I call ye all by thy given-names," she quietly stated. "I again give apology for having had to leave ye to stand guard alone, as I must again later. But the time will soon come when we will all travel together – perhaps to war together. Use these hours well, to come to know each others' arts and talents."

In her mind, she heard four voices, each now familiar to her in its own improbable way, gurgle acknowledgement and filial loyalty.

Moving to sit cross-legged in front of the fire, as she had previously, the Storied Watcher again addressed these more-than-inanimate tools of battle, as the carrying-container floated effortlessly, to land by her left side.

Her hands elegantly traced inscrutable gestures in the air, and sparks from the fire lit these in some archaic imitation of a neon sign.

"I thus set to the art of weirding works," she softly but firmly intoned. "I pray that the Greater Powers and my ancient companion, should guide my hands, my heart and my spirit; for neither magic, nor the 'techno' of this world, will suffice; rather, the two must marry, and produce offspring with the best of both. To win mastery of empires built upon ingenious machines... so must the blood of their nemesis, know the guile of their artifice."

A song, low and melodious, its tone like a combination of Celtic, Middle-Eastern and bass-beat themes, now began to infuse the atmosphere.

"Though she now be soul-less artificial 'plas-tic' of this world," chanted Karéin-Mayréij, seemingly to no-one, "I shall breathe the life of my unseen Companion of Defense, into the suit that will accompany thee all, and myself, into the breach, as I have done for thee four. But this 'Earth' be not of kin to the old, familiar places, and different things are needed to make the skills of artifice work here. Some of what I shall therefore craft, must be used for thy new companion; but I must equally give it to all of ye, as power against the living machines that the kings of this world, may array."

The Storied Watcher shot a purposeful stare at a section of the floor to her right, and immediately, an indentation appeared in it, as the grains of sand scurried rapidly to evacuate this crater.

Her eyes glowed slightly and a wave of suffocating heat issued from the sand-bowl, its surface now covered by a dull, blackish crust.

With another withering glance, all the warmth left the spot, and her mind-forces caused sealant, epoxy, white glue, graphite and iron filings, followed by acid, crumbled bits of chalk and charcoal, a couple of computer-chips and a phosphorescent watch-hand, to issue forth and mix together.

"Spider-silk," she sang, blowing a wisp of fine white thread into the bowl. "None be stronger, on all the Thousand Worlds."

The young-looking woman reached down between her legs, and her palm glistened with the gleam of mucus.

"Mine own female essence and male seed from man of Earth, to strengthen thy respective souls, the each to complement and join with the other, as from the dawn of time," she added.

The alien-girl spat upon her other hand, then, extending her teeth, dripped poison into her palm.

Wincing, she concentrated and suppressed her body's defenses, dark, pungent-smelling blood welling up from a quick fang-puncture. It pooled in the cup of her hand, mixing with the venom, then was levitated to a point perhaps a few centimeters above the palm; but, a second later, after another determined stare and a sudden wash of frigid, brutal cold from nowhere, the sinister *mélange* was congealed into a solid globe.

"The essence of hell-cold, that ye may know this and take it into thy beings; though some of ye be fire, others lightening, the touch of ice be not foreign, as it is not to thy Mother, either," explained Karéin-Mayréij.

Swiftly, she propelled these frozen substances into the bowl and stirred the mixture.

"Take my body-essence – bathe ye now in this elixir, make it, yea, part of thy very *selves*," she commanded. "May ye all thus be strengthened and made for stealth against the thinking-machines of this world, even as thy minds grow in the ken of human techno-artifice. And ye shall be made safe against my own blood and venom; lest these afflict, upon the wounds of combat."

One by one, the sword, the shield, then the two daggers, floated into the depression, each in turn becoming enveloped in the stuff within it, as other-worldly energies illuminated the mixture from within.

When, after at least an hour, perhaps more, the weapons and shield emerged, even a primitive human eye could have seen that they had been *changed*, somehow. The sword held its edge, the shield its structure; but they were now at once half-translucent and respectively red-green and silver-gray, with subtly shifting colors and textures, all about.

"I know that bathing thusly has suffered ye," apologized Karéin-Mayréij, clasping her hands in sympathy. "For my blood, and the issue of my teeth, are the drink of death. Excuse this; but such shall be needed, I fear, when we confront this techno-world. I beg that ye trust my wisdom, my beloved war-children."

She squeezed one of her nipples, and a few drops of liquid fell into her palm. "I give of my body to nurture ye, as I give of my love, my soul, my life. Take, drink."

The young-looking woman dropped the milk into the mixture, and her countenance lightened, as a feeling of trust, relief and forgiveness met her mind.

The humans' field of reference is so limited, reflected the alien-girl.

They believe that the whole universe works just the same as it appears to, on their pleasant little, rational-thinking planet.

They will never understand these matters of the spirit, and of how it can be shared, how it can give awareness and life... if only one knows how to reach through and touch the other, hidden Planes...

"Behold, now," announced the Storied Watcher, again as if speaking to someone observing from beside her. "The birth of thy youngest sister, to be one with my Companion of Defense; yet, surely not least among ye, shall she be, for held ever close to my breast, as my last defense, will be her station."

The music now sounded haunting, ethereal chords of power, even to the crude minds of the desert-creatures that it startled in the dark outside.

The bikini, the cape, several diamond-shaped pieces of fiberglass and, last, the athletic-gear set, slowly floated into the alchemy-crater, turning and rolling within it, guided by the Storied Watcher's mind-power.

After a half-minute, these items were joined by the shiny clothing-decorations, then by the gem-stones that she had carefully hoarded from her trip to the Park Place Mall, then by various other things from her collection.

Two or more hours passed, and all throughout, the walls of the cave heard the chords and tones of arcane magic, from a place and time far removed from this little solar-system. What finally issued forth would have made the Americans' army-men laugh, or, for the more enlightened ones, perhaps they would have gasped in appreciation of its craftsmanship.

The body-armor suit resembled nothing so much as an impossibly fragile-looking ice-hockey player's garb, melted to cardboard-thickness so as to cover most of her body, with (excepting for attaching-holes at the neck), no perforations and only a few strategic joints where a sword- or spear-thrust might possibly find a weak spot.

The whole suit, including the cape but excepting its *yarmulke*-like skull-cap, finger-less gloves and wrist-braces, sock-like foot-coverings and the cape, was covered with darkly overlapping, iridescent rows of what might, at one time, have been ordinary sequins, expertly fitted together to look like the scales of some black-snake's hide, flickering with a subtle flame; except for small gemstones embedded at certain of the edges within this metamorphosed stuff, it had the same semi-translucent, kaleidoscope-like aspect that had just affected her weapons and shield.

Underneath the outer shell of this improbable construct was an under-garment, somewhat lighter in shade, with the rainbow-shifting appearance of the outside part of the set, and there was also a belt with box-like structures on each link and clasp-constructs that would secure the sword.

"Come forth, dear girl-child, *Vìrya Ahn'jë*, Daughter Burning-Mountain," reverently breathed the alien. "Lay close and take of my life, to become thy own. And when thy tongue is found, speak with thy brothers and sister, but most especially thy grand-kin *Vîrya Quü'j*, that thou should know their ways, and they, thine. And thou shall answer only to me, and to those who I will say are my heirs and family, when that time comes."

As the body-armor and its accompanying pieces – far lighter and more flexible, in fact, than the best composites that the chemists of this planet had yet been able to concoct, probably, in fact, better than anything that they would *ever* be able to create – fell gently into the young-looking woman's lap, she looked down and again began singing, while inscribing a series of flowing characters and mystical symbols on to the skull-cap and in other places, upon the suit.

"Thy skill shall be as thy name," intoned Karéin-Mayréij, sweat breaking on her brow as she felt her life-force draining measuredly away. "To be as a bulwark against all perils and, likewise to thy sister, brave *Vîrya I'ëà'b'*, to heal of thy own doing, drinking hurtful things and transforming these for thy own succor; but foremost, to the power of vigilance, that neither thee nor thy kin shall suffer any blow, lest it be foreseen. And thou shall take my dark-cloak fully to heart, learning how to hide thyself until the time is come to show proud defiance to our foes."

She sighed, drew another deep breath, and continued, "Also shall thou confound the baleful eyes of those who watch for my coming, none the less those of ingenious machines, than of mortal man himself. When I do my Dance of Fire and Thunder, thou and I shall act as one, with neither as a burden to the other; and though both thyself and thy brothers and sister be yet untried in combat, ye shall all learn from me as I guide thy skills, increasing with each strike, until arts akin to the most mighty warring-things crafted by the greatest smiths of the Impassible Peaks, come to be thine."

The alien-girl looked up, out into the Arizona desert night, and sang, in her elegant, other-worldly language.

"So it is written in oldest rites from worlds gone by; and so shall it be done, beloved war-child *Vîrya Ahn'jë*, on this day, in the presence of us, mother, sister and brothers. Drink of my power, my wisdom... my *life*, as they have, and as ye all will, yet more."

Now, with the sword, shield and daggers encircling her, Karéin-Mayréij took the armor-suit close to herself, curling up with it as a mother does with a new-born baby.

"Sleep we all together, my children – first of thy kind in this strange, unenlightened world called 'Earth'," she whispered, even though she did not really sleep, as the humans would.

Yet, some words came to her mind in a dream, because as the life-energy flowed out from mother to offspring, her eyelids became too heavy to keep open.

See how the one called 'Storied Watcher', breathes life, advised an alter-ego from long ago and far away, even so, close upon her breast.

But... she can also breathe... death.

What To Do With An Upset Alien?

Tensh-Hut! sounded the Marine guard, as the President, surrounded in front and behind by black-suited Secret Service agents, descended off the stairs and into the bunker, beholding almost his entire Cabinet, plus at least three of the Joint Chiefs, plus twenty or so other functionaries and bureaucrats.

One of the latter, a clean-cut young Air Force lieutenant, maintained a professional poker-face and quietly clicked his heels together, three times.

"At ease," commanded the American leader. "We meet again, gentlemen and ladies. And again, we're here to discuss the aftermath of a comet... so to speak."

A few polite laughs sounded in the underground chamber, as the President's glance scanned the crowd.

He saw the severe, pock-marked visage of the FBI director.

"Ah, Cesar – you made it, I see," commented the President, with satisfaction.

"Things are going better on the L.A. front, sir," deadpanned Ochoa. "Marginally so... but better, none the less. And anyway, this is obviously more important."

"You got *that*," dryly replied the President. "One other note... Jacob sent his regrets this morning, but he's got his hands full trying to deal with the border closure situation and organizing a 'cross-Atlantic response to the Muslim League threat', as he told me. Frankly, he's welcome *to* it... I'll have him given the minutes of the meeting, afterward."

"Now, as I have only an hour and a half before we have to get back in the 'copter and get Air Force One back in the sky, we'll get right to business," continued the American leader. "First of all, although I think I already know the answer to this question... any trace of our friend 'Karéin', yet?"

"Negative," said came back the deep, rough voice of General Harry Anderson of the U.S. Air Force. "CIA and DARPA are now almost ready with a prototype of a detection-unit that – we believe – may be able to track the alien, when she starts using this exotic energy of hers. But there are many limitations; in particular, the device has a maximum-range of about a mile... and that's assuming that she's giving off at least a few kilowatts of the stuff."

"But right now, we really don't know *where* she is... right?" asked the President.

"Based on the events so far, sir," interjected Bezomorton, "We *think* that she is still somewhere in the Greater Tucson-Phoenix region. We have a house-to-house search going, but there are tens of thousands of residences and buildings to investigate."

"Okay," said the President. "But, assuming that we eventually *do* catch up with her... do you have a plan as to what the hell we're going to do with her?"

"Uhh... not... *exactly*," evaded the National Security Adviser. "We're still working on some ideas; but as yet, CIA, FBI, Homeland, the Council, DoD and the Anti-Subversive Agency haven't been able to come to a consensus as to how to proceed. At a minimum, we're trying to figure out how best we could draw the alien out into the open, so that in addition to being able to communicate with it, or her, as you see fit, you, sir, will have the secondary option of, ahem, using various amounts of force to neutralize 'Karéin'... should you make such a decision."

"So... I'm on my own, if she shows up out of the blue, one fine day?" complained the American leader.

Bezomorton was about to say something, but McPherson interrupted.

"Mr. President," he stated, "I think I have a plan."

With all eyes upon the Science Adviser, the President nodded.

"What I'd like to propose," explained McPherson, "Is for me to try to arrange a meeting with the Storied Watcher... something discreet, out-of-the-way, in a setting that wouldn't be threatening to her."

"An interesting idea," offered the President, leaning back in his chair. "Maybe we could nip the whole thing in the bud? I'd certainly go for that."

"With all due respect, Mr. McPherson," countered Bezomorton, "I can't endorse you doing that – the risks are *far* too great. There's now abundant evidence – including but by no means limited to, the threats that we have recently heard – that we're currently dealing with a *different* 'Karéin'... one who's, frankly, not such a nice little green alien-girl. And what if she were to kidnap you, or make you reveal secrets about the Executive Branch? In that case, the government in general, and the President specifically, might instantly be placed in great danger. Mr. President – if we're going to even *entertain* this idea, we'd have to send someone that 'Karéin' has already met, but one who, if compromised, couldn't really help her a great deal. How about one of the former Mars mission crew... you know, the Jacobson team?"

"Sorry," objected General Anderson, "That won't be possible. They're in, uhh, isolation... you know, standard decontamination procedure."

"Well, how long can *that* take?" pressed the Security Adviser.

"Might be *weeks*... months, even," evaded the Air Force General, while the Secretary of Defense stared impassively straight forward.

He shut up.

"Yes... I see what you mean," commented the President, to bewildered glances from around the room, except from the Science Adviser, who just nodded knowingly. "Initially, *I* was thinking of something like that, too, but upon reflection, I don't think it would be... *advisable*. I guess that means we have to look elsewhere, then, if we're going to explore the 'messenger' concept."

"By the way, FBI *could* escort Mr. McPherson, throughout the trip," phlegmatically offered Ochoa.

"As could CIA," unhelpfully added the CIA director.

"Mr. President sir, I don't think much of this 'messenger' idea either, let me say that straight out," remarked DeWitt, "But if we're going to disqualify Mr. McPherson, or the Jacobson team, then we really have quite a constrained base of other potential candidates. For example, she *did* meet a number of other people up on the ISS2 space station, but none of them are Americans, so that pretty much rules *them* out. So... who's left?"

"Since you've given me such a nice vote of confidence, touché there General... if I'm out, and our friends Jacobson and company are out as well, and we'd never trust someone who we can't jail for treason with this job," grumbled McPherson, "That narrows it basically down to Sylvia Abruzzio and Hector Ramirez, both of whom worked with me down at Mission Control... although, I suppose you're now going to worry about *them* being brainwashed by 'Karéin', right?"

"These two friends of yours from Houston – what level of security-clearance do they have?" inquired Bezomorton.

"Not sure," shrugged the Science Adviser. "Lower than my own, I'd assume. But if you want only Americans who have spoken with the Storied Watcher for more than a minute or two, I'm afraid they're the only game in town. By the way, Hector was quite badly hurt in the 'Lucifer' incident, but as I understand it, he's recovering quickly."

"Do you think that they are reliable? Patriotic, I mean," asked the President.

"Certainly as much as I am," offered McPherson. "How would I know? We were all down there to explore the solar-system, not to spend our time signing loyalty oaths."

"Cesar," ordered the U.S. leader, "Can you run some background checks on this 'Ramirez' guy and the 'Abruzzio' woman... see if they check out? I couldn't care less about the usual stuff, like drugs, using birth-control pills, sex-crimes, pirated movies, and so on... just make sure that we don't have somebody who's going to leak the news out to the gangsters, the Chinese, or – worse – the media."

"I'm on it," answered Ochoa, with relish.

He bent over to one side, rapidly typing text messages into his portable-communicator.

"Okay, so..." started the President, swiveling in his chair a bit. "Working on the assumption that we can get either or both of these people as a messenger, the next thing that we've got to figure out is, 'what's the message', and 'how do we discreetly let the alien know that her old buddies are in town'. Any ideas, gentlemen?"

Silence reigned for a few seconds as all around the table did feverish mental calculations to avoid proposing amateurish plans.

Now, the immaculately-dressed, 30-something-Yuppie, White House Chief of Staff, spoke up.

"Mr. President," he stated, "I'm going to start from Mr. McPherson's assumption, that is, that the alien is quite perceptive and is likely to be able to take a hint, so..."

"Go ahead," affirmed the President.

"*So*," proposed Jerry Kaysten, "The problem is, 'how to broadcast a message to this creature – but to do it in a discreet enough way, to ensure that it doesn't completely tip off the *paparazzi*, the regular media and the conspiracy crowd... right? No matter how we were to do that over the open media, like on a TV-broadcast, *et cetera*, there's little chance that we could make the location of the proposed meeting-place clear enough to inform *her*, but at the same time *not* clear enough to tip off the rest of the media and the hangers-on."

"I bet you that Billy could do it... wherever the hell he's run off to," joked the Vice-President, to a few polite chuckles.

"But," continued the Chief of Staff, "There's an alternative that I think might be just as good. We could stage some kind of low-key publicity-event, for example, 'Come on down to XYZ Hotel and meet Sylvia Abruzzio and Hector Ramirez, listen to them give a speech about the fascinating alien that they spoke with', that kind of thing – in other words, something that would telegraph that somebody *else* who our alien-friend thinks is trustworthy, is 'right here in downtown Tucson'."

"Go on," said an interested President, with a flick of his finger.

"Now," elaborated Kaysten, "Presuming that she's a smart little Martian, we could sneak some fine print into the announcement like, 'Ms. Abruzzio and Mr. Ramirez will be staying in the Hotel Tucson over the week-end, prior to leaving to head back to oversee the reconstruction of Mission Control in Houston', who cares if the latter part is true... my guess is that she'll take the bait and try to drop in on either or both of them, just for old times' sake."

"And *then* what?" inquired the American leader.

"We *could* try a snatch-and-grab right there, in the hotel, that is," suggested the CIA director. "Although, it would be difficult to keep her occupied long enough for us to position adequate assets in the area, to have even a chance of a successful termination, in the event that she tried to escape."

"We've been *over* that," countermanded the President. "And for the previously-discussed reasons, I want no action taken against the alien unless we can bring overwhelming force to bear. However... I *will* authorize CIA and FBI to discreetly use the opportunity to try to measure the being's characteristics and capabilities – that is to spy on her – so long as you can be certain of doing it in a way that she can't discover. You think that's possible?"

"Certainly," both Ochoa and the CIA director replied, almost in chorus.

"We have a high degree of confidence that we can do this," claimed the CIA director. "For example, while the alien was staying at the Billings residence, we were able to plant several listening-devices on and around that building. None of them were tampered with, moved or destroyed – so we're pretty sure that they evaded her notice. We've got some *excellent* gear, you know. Sir."

The FBI director half-rolled his eyes, but said nothing.

"Fine – I'll leave it to the two of you to work out the rules of engagement so you don't get in each other's way, just make sure that whatever you do find out, is transmitted immediately... you got it?" ordered the President.

"Agreed," said the CIA director.

"Of course," added Ochoa.

"And remember... absolutely *no* moves against the alien, when we get our first meeting with her, except on my express order – *understand?*" emphasized the U.S. leader.

"Understood," said the CIA director.

"Yes, sir," answered the FBI director.

"Alright," said the President. "No... while I'm aware that much of this is going to be up to yours truly, if and when we get a chance to speak directly with our friend 'Karéin', does anyone have an idea about what we're supposed to say?"

"Mr. President," interrupted Bezomorton, "Actually, the Vice-President and I have been working on that."

"Fine... then, go ahead, let us have it," answered the President.

"So... here's the *schpiel*, at a high level," said the National Security Adviser. "Although obviously, sir, you may want to modify it or throw it out altogether, these are just ideas. We thought that we'd maybe offer her a bargain –"

"'You get more flies with honey than with shit... that's the concept," interjected the Vice-President.

"What kind of bargain?" asked the President.

"That's of course up to you, sir, but we're thinking that we could give her a luxury-suite in a secure location, with some servants, you know, maids and footmen, that kind of thing... some of the psych-reports mention that she seems to identify with a medieval social-setting, perhaps those would resonate with her –"

"Excuse me," questioned the President, gesturing for a pause. "My understanding was that the people who she wanted to have released, are this 'Billings' guy and the black woman, plus the kids... how many of them were there... two... three? Yeah, okay, three. Oh, what was that? Four? Okay. Four."

"I *know*, Mr. President," replied Bezomorton. "The problem is that we don't *have* them... which is why I thought that the Mars team might be a good second choice."

"Well if the bloody alien thinks that they're so important, and why that would be, escapes me," demanded the U.S. leader, "Then what's the status of our search for Billings and these other people?"

"I'm afraid we've come up blank, so far, sir," answered the National Security Adviser. "We checked with Homeland, the Special Services, INS, DoD, Anti-Subversive, Secret Service... everybody down to the Tucson Police Department, but they're all telling us that they have nobody in custody corresponding to the man's description. Keep in mind that we have had to concentrate on the search for the alien herself –"

"For *Christ's* sake!" complained the President, running his fingers in exasperation through his thick mane of professionally-crafted Grecian Formula 20 hair. "The one thing that this damn creature really *wants*, and someone else has it – has *them*, I mean. Look... have we got a dragnet going? To track down this 'Billings' guy and whoever's got them. They've *got* to still be here in the continental U.S... right? After all, we locked down the borders, because of the Muslim crap. Why don't we call out the Guard, the Army – the whole works?"

"I'll need an order from the Executive Branch suspending the *Posse Comitatus* Act, to get the military involved more deeply than we already are, sir," explained DeWitt. "But my understanding is that both FBI and CIA are already conducting their own investigations –"

"That true?" asked the President, looking at both directors. "Any leads?"

The CIA director just shrugged and held out his hands in a "no luck, boss" gesture, but Ochoa mentioned, "Yes, Mr. President – as a matter of fact we do, and we've been running an intensive investigation since we first became aware of what had transpired in Tucson on the day of the two suicide-bombing attacks."

"So why don't we have her – or them – yet?" pressed the U.S. leader.

"Well, frankly, sir," stated the FBI director, "We've been hitting dead-ends at every turn – forensic evidence completely expunged, people afraid to talk, computer records mysteriously deleted from databases, along with the same information wiped from backup-media, and so on. It doesn't make *sense*; it's like someone is always one or two steps ahead of us, like Mr. Billings, *et cetera*, just vanished from the face of the Earth. Our agents are going door-to-door where it's appropriate... but I'm afraid that I can't promise results in the near term, at least until we get a major break in this case."

The President stopped to ponder for a few long seconds.

"Okay. Point taken," he said, neutrally.

"John," he added, looking at Bezomorton, "I want a fresh background check on everyone involved in Project Red Rover, with anything that's the least bit suspicious, reported to myself, in private, by the end of this week. And..."

"Yes, Mr. President?" asked the Security Adviser.

"I don't want you to take this the wrong way, but that includes you and your staff," the President said. "Have the report delivered directly to me, care of Jerry, if I'm not available at the time."

"No problem, sir," professionally confirmed Bezomorton, though with an unfriendly side-glance at Kaysten. "Needless to say, I have complete confidence in my people... but I understand why it may be prudent to do that."

"Now, in the meantime," requested the President, "Unless and until we find this damn Billings guy and the rest of them... what are my options on what to do with the alien, when and if we locate her?"

"CIA *strongly* recommends that the alien should be sequestered – voluntarily or otherwise – in one of our special, underground holding-facilities," jumped in the director of that agency. "There are three that we can use right now, with a couple more coming on-line any day now. It would be the *height* of foolishness to have the creature in our grasp, then to let her get away easily."

"Second that motion," grunted DeWitt.

"The idea is that we're *not* trying to jail her... isn't it?" the President pointed out.

"We can provide a very comfortable environment for this 'Karéin' in any of our special facilities," argued the CIA director.

"It won't work," interjected McPherson. "Come *on*, gentlemen – how stupid do you think she is? Do you think she can't tell a jail when she sees one, whether or not it's 200 feet underground, or if it's on a nice backwoods cabin that you can only reach by air?"

"Well," commented Anderson, "Either place would at least allow us to have a good shot at the alien, without risking unnecessary civilian collateral-damage. I'd certainly settle for any location that would meet that set of criteria."

"Oh, for God's *sake*," angrily muttered the Science Adviser.

"Mr. President," remarked the General, with a confident smile, "It's possible that 'Karéin' *does* have some superficial knowledge of our military capabilities... but it's very unlikely that she'd even *suspect* the possibility of some of our more advanced weapons, for example the *Aurora-II* hypersonic reconnaissance-bomber, the new high-kilowatt directed-energy lasers, and so on. Tactically this gives you quite a range of options. Should you make the decision to engage, she may have no defense at all against some of these specialized munition-types."

"And what if she *can* defend herself, General? What if she doesn't need a gun, or anything, Mr. Vice-President, sir?" fumed McPherson. "What if she then gets real, *real* mad, that we tried to kill her? Or, perhaps, what if she doesn't have any nice, precise way to counter any of these high-tech killing-machines, other than to, say, blow up everything for ten or twenty miles, before your missiles get close to her?"

"I'd be surprised if she's even got a rusty old .38 snub-nose and a bullet-proof vest to use against us," snorted the Vice-President. For the record... I think that all these threats she's been making, are just bluffing – pure and simple. Who knows if she really gives a tinker's damn about these 'Billings' people that we're so worried about?"

"Well, she's apparently threatening us – threatening, *me* – over them, George," pointed out the American leader. "I don't follow you."

"What I mean," explained the Vice-President, "Is... what would *she* care, about whether a few of us inconsequential human beings live a few years longer, or a few years less? Here's *my* bet... this 'Karéin' bamboozles us into thinking that she's Superman – okay, Supergirl – with an attitude, then stamps her feet until we agree to put her up in a penthouse-suite for the rest of history, and laughs all the way to the bank. Smart move, if you show up on another planet without a job or a dime in your pocket."

"Wouldn't be the *worst* outcome... we've bought off a lot of less important people," offered the President.

"And having listened to all of this," he continued, "I think the way we'll handle it, is just to drop the responsibility of how we'll act – what weapons we'll use, if it ever comes to that – upon myself. However, Arthur... I'll need some briefing-papers on the options for each system, chance of getting a first-shot-hit, collateral-damage, possible countermeasures by the alien... that kind of thing, sooner rather than later. Try to make it in as simple language as possible, I'm not very much up on all the military jargon. Okay?"

"You'll have it first thing tomorrow," answered DeWitt. "Most of the work is already done."

"Good," said the President. "And for now, we'll proceed on the 'Humpty and Dumpty come to the Tucson Hilton to give a speech' idea, leveraging Fred's two co-workers – I really don't care *what* shows up in their background security-checks, unless it's something like being an undercover agent for the Muslim League, and Fred, I'm counting on you to explain things – discreetly – to the two of them... okay?"

"I will, Mr. President," said the Science Adviser, with an air of resignation. "With your permission, I'll meet them at Tucson International."

"Of course, we'll have to provide an escort, Mr. McPherson, sir, just against the unlikely event that we have a problem at the airport," demanded Ochoa. "After all, you, along with Mr. Ramirez and Ms. Abruzzio, represent our only acceptable vectors to the alien."

"Fine," answered McPherson.

The U.S leader nodded affirmatively, then turned to Kaysten.

"Jerry," he ordered, "Get your political team going on booking the venue, but we'll have to keep a long arm's-length on this one... make sure there isn't the *slightest* chance that the media will find out we're footing the bill for this little speaking-engagement – you got that? If it looks like any of the details about the initial potential meeting with the alien are about to leak, you have my authorization to ensure that any non-authorized individuals with classified knowledge, can be sequestered until this affair is dealt with."

"Read you loud and clear, Mr. President," confirmed Kaysten. "I don't think that'll be a problem, we've got lots of ways of covering the trail... maybe I'll start with the Arizona State Republican Committee – make it look like one of those tax-free conservative-foundation events... I'll, uhh, think of something that's nice and vanilla, get some low-key local media-coverage for it. But we'll have to go out on a limb and mention that both Ramirez and Abruzzio will be there. We can't use anything like 'mystery-guest' – it'd get the conspiracy theorists out in *droves*."

"I'd have preferred to have had more time to perfect the plan," noted the President, "But yeah... for now, I suppose you'll have to, and we'll have to hope that Fred's two friends work out for us."

He looked around the table, observing America's best and brightest – certainly, its most powerful and aggressive – worn out by the stress of arguing the most important domestic problem that a National Security Committee meeting had ever addressed.

"Alright, then," said the President. "I think we're done."

"Yes," replied McPherson, quietly nodding his head. "We *are*... done."

Billy Books Out

The 'dusk-is-nearing' crickets in this Dixie town were softly chirping as, in the slowly failing light, Billy Horn stopped the car and did his best imitation of parallel parking, only narrowly missing the front bumper of one car and the rear one of the other.

Damn imports... fuckin' parkin'-spaces is still all itty-bitty sized, even 20 years after they passed the 'Buy Patriotic Automobiles Act' and closed the market to them Chink and Injun jobs, he thought to himself.

So here's what I got for you all, Horn wrote, in the unmistakably primitive scrawl that passed for his longhand.

I'm writing this to you the old-fashioned way and leaving it at the drop, because them NSA boys have got their pointy little ears so close to the ground on all these fancy new computer-things that they'd probably get my message an hour before you did, if I tried to phone it to you or send it by PC.

Also, I don't have any of that edible paper stuff that you used last time... so I'd advise you to make a nice bonfire out of this, after you read it.

He paused for a second, pondering how best to phrase this most important of all messages. Then, again, he put pencil to paper.

As you may know by now, the President got the message that our friend Little Miss Martian sent, a couple of days ago; and, as they say, 'plans are in motion'.

I'm not in on all the nitty-gritty details of this stuff – they're leaving that to the Armed Forces, apparently the Air Force Special Office or some-such is in charge of the whole thing, specifically – but from what I've heard, they're planning on setting up a meeting between Little Miss Devil and some of those poor folk that she must have bewitched, up there in outer space.

So I am told, this is supposed to be a 'good-will' gesture to make her feel warm and fuzzy about the United States of America. What they plan to do with our friend Karéin A. Satanic... well, I got no insight into that.

I did hear one or two loose-talk situations where it was mentioned that they were going to offer her a nice safe hideout somewhere – but don't count on that.

And it goes without saying that this is all built on the assumption that she'll show her ugly little face at the agreed time and place.

Out of habit, Horn temporarily laid down the pencil, rose his head and looked in all directions, but didn't see anything suspicious.

With a few quick twists of the sharpener, he was again ready to write.

Tell you the truth, he continued, *The Big Man's mighty steamed about the whole business that went down in Tucson a while ago, and he's tightening up the chain of command on the wild alien goose chase business, so if you all are planning to make a move, I'd suggest that you do it soon, and do it good once and for all – I doubt that you'll get another chance.*

I will TRY to get you some valid intelligence as to where and when this meeting is going to go down, but I got to be real careful about doing any more digging on this account, them boys from the NSA and the Secret Service are getting real gnarly, these days.

The bottom line is, things are mighty hot in my neck of the woods and Billy never *hangs around the trees when he smells smoke, if you understand my meaning.*

In any event, he concluded, thinking carefully as he wrote every word,

With this message, I believe that I have fulfilled the bargain that I made with your fine establishment some time ago, and I will therefore reluctantly conclude that our working relationship is now at an end, at least for the time being.

I'm sure you will appreciate that this means, further attempts to contact me – unless and until I decide to take the initiative to contact you all – not only will not work but more to the point will not be a good idea, since them Secret Service boys might clue in to what's happening.

What we – both sides in this whole thing – need, is some time off, to let the situation cool down, for things to get back to normal.

Once that happens... it will be my pleasure to help your devout followers regain their rightful say in the affairs of the United States of America – God's chosen country.

Until that day, I wish you the Lord's own luck, may your aim not fail when the time comes.

Respectfully,

BILLY HORN.

Well, it might *work to get them to lay off,* he thought.

But ol' Billy's no Georgia jackass... he always *has a second ace in the hole.*

After neatly folding the note, Horn inserted it into a plain white envelope, licked shut the glue on the reverse-side, wrote "PRAISE THE LORD" on the front, then deposited the envelope inside the sports-section of a rubber-band-secured local newspaper.

Opening the driver's-side door, again checking the surroundings as he got out, the former White House staffer adjusted his sunglasses and wandered over to the park-bench.

Apart from a few disinterested passers-by on the other side of the street, there was nobody around.

He slowly wandered over to the bench, and, with another rubber-band, affixed the tightly-bound newspaper, envelope inside, to one of the back upright supporting beams.

After throwing a gum wrapper in a nearby garbage can, he again deposited himself in the driver's-seat and opened a pouch on the passenger-seat, looking over its contents.

"Special 'no questions asked' Federal Government passport with the computer chip, as well as legacy Government of Canada backup passport without the chip – check, and check," Horn said to himself, *sotto voce.*

"Euro-Swiss guaranteed-value bonds, ten grand per, times two hundred – check. Twenny-five lil' ol' 24-karat gold bars – check. One-way ticket for Tahiti, by way of Atlanta, Miami, and Lima, Peru, only flight out this month, thanks to smooth-talkin' by some high-priced friends of the Vice-President – check. Cure's-all water bug tablets, check. Melts-in-her... mouth, disintegratin' condoms – check. Combination Bible an' 'French for Dummies' translation guide – check."

Just hope them boys down in Paradise-land accepted payment on the villa, before Uncle Sam's dollar bills ended up bein' worth less than a peso, he mused.

Be a hell of a lot easier doin' all this out of LAX... but that place's hotter than downtown Mumbai, these days...

He patted the ancient Ford's seat, somehow missing the rear bumper of the car ahead of him, as he sped out of the too-small parking space.

Heading off to the city and Hartsfield-Jackson Airport, wistfully, Horn wiped a genuine tear – one of the few times that anything about him could be so described – and whispered to the car,

"Gonna miss you, old girl."

I Got Some Big News For You

With the blue-gray letters "T-U-C-S-O-N" looming large down the control tower in the background, the Cher lookalike, salt-and-pepper-maned Italian-American woman and the short, somewhat younger Hispanic man – the latter of the two, still limping a bit, though he tried to hide it – exited the off-ramp into the terminal.

"So where's the baggage-retrieval?" inquired the man, in his smooth Tex-Mex accent. "Funny, you know, I've been all over the Southwest, been to Phoenix a few times, but I've never flown in to here... we always just drove."

"Beats *me*," answered the woman. "I just hope they didn't lose it, 'cause I got some important stuff in my carry-case. Just personal things, and so on. I wanted to have them with me, if... well, *you* know."

She wiped her forehead, and remarked, "Wow, is it ever *hot* in here – I'm starting to miss JPL, or at least what's left of it, they can't run the computers without the A/C..."

"Yeah," agreed the other. "They weren't kidding about all the power-restrictions – I hear it's pretty much the same all across Arizona and New Mex. And you'd figure that with so few planes flying these days, the 'special orders', *et cetera*, they could at least keep track of –"

He was interrupted by one of the hulking men, recognizable by their trademark dark business-suits and sunglasses, who had been walking forcefully behind the duo.

"Don't worry about the baggage, Ma'am," he stated. "It's already on its way to the hotel. We've got a limo waiting for you in front, but we've got orders to wait for –"

"For *this* guy?" called out Abruzzio, her countenance brightening, as she pointed toward a leather-faced, gray-haired man in a rumpled white shirt with accompanying creased tie, leisure-slacks and loafers.

They noticed that two more of the same type of dark-suited men, were just behind him, as well.

"Yeah, that'd be me," answered McPherson, taking off his own dark glasses as he spoke, a broad grin coming to his face. "Hi there, you two – long time no see," he added, as Abruzzio hurried over and embraced him warmly.

"Oh, *God*, Fred!" breathed the woman. "You know I wanted to get you down there to Houston to see first-hand how much work we've got to do, but I'll take seeing you in-person, up here."

Releasing her grasp, she asked, "Listen... and speaking of that... it's gotta be something *pretty* important to pull us off picking up the pieces down at the Lab... right?"

Arching an eyebrow, the Science Adviser replied, "Important? Yeah... you could say that."

"So what's up?" inquired Ramirez, shaking his former boss' hand.

"I'll explain in the car," demurred McPherson.

"Sounds serious," offered Abruzzio.

"You don't know that *half* of it – believe me," teased McPherson. "And we've got to get going – we don't have much time to get you settled in the hotel, before you start giving your presentations to the great unwashed."

He pointed toward the entrance, where a stretch limousine with darkly-tinted windows awaited, and started a quick pace toward the vehicle. At each of the three security check-points between the offloading-ramp and the front of the airport, one of McPherson's guards and a corresponding man from the troupe that had accompanied Ramirez and Abruzzio, flashed a government ID-card of some type, and they were instantly cleared to move on.

Huffing and puffing to keep up, Ramirez protested, "Hey, Fred – wait a minute... some of us aren't doing so well these days, you know?"

McPherson slowed a bit and waited for the Hispanic man.

"Listen, Fred," demanded Ramirez, as the group neared the entrance, "This is the first that we've heard about some speaking-engagement... you *know* I'm not so good in front of a crowd. What *gives?* This some kind of hush-hush thing about those nukes that are supposed to be floatin' all over the place, after the Pakistan stuff?"

By now they had reached the limo, and its doors opened from within.

"No," explained the Science Adviser, "It's about something – *someone* – a *hell* of a lot more powerful."

Stunned, Abruzzio stood at the door of the vehicle, and exclaimed, "Fred, you've *got* to be kidding – you don't mean... *do* you?"

"That's *exactly* what I mean," confirmed McPherson. "Now get in the car, will you?"

"*Dios mio!*" intoned Ramirez, grimacing as the pain of his injuries made an unwelcome re-appearance with the contortions needed to side-saddle into the back-seat. "Where *is* she?"

"That's 'Problem Numero Uno'," elaborated McPherson, as the last door swung shut and the limo slowly started to pull out of its reserved parking-spot. "Just *wait* until you hear 'Problems Two to Five'."

The black car sped off into the distance in the direction of downtown Tucson, as two otherwise nondescript airport-dwellers – one, a middle-aged man working as a janitorial-orderly, the other, an attractive-looking young woman with designer sunglasses and a shapely, mid-length summer pant-suit, both retrieved mobile-phones and began to place their respective calls.

And the odd thing was, although even the languages that they used were different... the message in each case was more or less, the same.

Doing The Work We Love To Do

The two middle-aged, medium-height, medium-weight, clean-cut, nondescript Caucasian men walked out the stainless-steel doors and met in the stark, white, underground corridor.

As he removed his surgical mask and head-covering, one of them used a piece of Kleenex to wipe some of the red smears off the lens of his spectacles, but neither bothered to even try the same with their laboratory smocks : the stuff was too deeply crimson-stained to make doing *that*, worth the effort.

In any other context, one would have mistaken them for doctors, or, maybe, scientists, of some unusual vocation.

"How long until she comes to, again?" inquired the one, professionally, to the other.

"At least eight," answered the other, leaning back against the wall, one of his sneakers doing a tippy-toe to the floor. "Maybe twelve or more. Dunno, really."

"Not a lot of time," offered the first man.

"Can't be helped," stated the second man, with a bored shrug. "It's not *our* fault that Headquarters wanted to accelerate the whole damn thing. Since the change of plans, the Big Man's trying to get six *months'* worth of talk out of these muppets, in less than a *week*. He ought to *know* that the results won't be very reliable... after all, he just about wrote the book on these procedures."

"Yeah, I'm worried about that, the 'no advance notice change of plans' bit, I mean," complained the first man. "Among other things – like, this one didn't fit the pattern, at all. She's just an ordinary nigger *civilian*... but did you take account of how long she held out? Hell – I've seen Muslim League martyr-wannabes and *Maras* homeboys who started singing after *a quarter* of what we gave her, both the standard cocktail and the introductory physical-workout. And all that raving about 'angels', 'wrath of the Lord', 'she'll come to get y'all on her chariot of fire', and so on... not a lot of real *meat* on that, to feed back to our friends in Analysis... if you'll pardon the pun."

The second man chuckled a bit and replied, "Well... maybe she'll think a little harder when we show her the old 'look what's going to happen to Junior' routine – but if I had the whole thing to do over again, I'd probably have gone right to that and skipped the first stage entirely, due to the timing-issue. Be that as it may, we still gotta go by the book... just spend less time on each chapter, you know?"

"You have a *way* of putting that," acknowledged the first man, with what could easily have been taken for a friendly smile. "But we're assuming that she even *has* any worthwhile information. Now wait, *wait*, I *know* what you're going to say – Glenn, you old softie, you *always* want to give 'em the benefit of the doubt, but let's face it... this is anything *but* an ordinary case. What if the Green Girl just didn't tell her, the salesman or the kids, anything, in the first place?"

"You got *that* right," matter-of-factually remarked the second *faux*-doctor. "About the 'nice guy' thing, that is. All this second-guessing, that'll be your undoing, in the long-run... 'check those old-school values at the door' – remember what the sign in the elevator, says? Anyway, it's only our job to be sure that they sing – what the song is that comes out of 'em... hey, that's *not* our job."

"Point taken – but what I'm sayin', is, when we get the gangstas or the Muslims in here, if they get smart and actually use 'need-to-know' properly, there's no doubt that our guests have *something* of value to tell us, even if it's not what we dragged 'em off the street in search of," argued the first man. "And we can check whatever we get, see if it's true or not, then go from there. The stupid thing about *this* case is... how would we tell the lies from the truth, if and when this ghetto ho' ever spills the beans? Let's face it – we're in uncharted territory here!"

"Maybe," evaded the second man. "But knowing the Chief... that won't make much of a difference to him. He's still going to be expecting *results* – and unless you and I want to run the risk of ending up trading places with this nigger and the salesman, then we'd better find a way to get some actionable *information* out of them. However improbable it might sound."

"Yeah," admitted the first man. "You're right about that."

He fell silent.

"So... think it's time that we payed a visit to the good Mr. Billings?" indifferently proposed the second man.

"Let me do a bit of washing-up, first," requested the first man. "I'll meet you in the lab, say, at six-thirty... okay?"

"Aww, you're not making me work overtime *again*, are you?" protested the second man.

"Come *on* – you *know* it's not really 'work', if you're doin' what you *love* doin'... right?" countered the first man.

"You *got* it," confirmed the second man, a broad grin on his face, as he headed off to get a change of clothes.

The Agency Works Its Magic

"Your helicopter is ready, sir," pleasantly inquired the Marine lieutenant, as the CIA director exited the bunker, almost last among those who had been inside the place, discussing the momentous plans that had been decided upon some score minutes previously.

"Good... hold it for me, for five minutes, please," requested the director, moving off to a spot by himself, well out of earshot.

Now, he spoke into his special, NSA-approved, secured mobile wrist-communicator.

"This is Top Dog," he announced, in the direction of the device. "ID value is Anthill 456, Geranium 89, Torus 3A. Do you copy?"

"Copy, voice signature and ID value confirmed," came back a ghostly voice in his earphone. "ID value here for HQ Gopher is Inkwell 7C92, Hen-house 11, Unity 2E18. Do you confirm, sir?"

The director punched in a few numbers on the keypad. A green light blinked on and off for a second.

"Confirmed at this end," he confirmed.

"What can we do for you, sir?" asked the other voice.

"The subject is the assets that were obtained at the house, and at the floor-tile business," stated the director. "I presume you're aware of the substitute-release option that we had been preparing for?"

"Copy that, and yes, sir," answered the remote voice. "Status on that one is a conditional 'go', as of now."

"Conditional only? Why aren't we ready to implement with full confidence?" demanded the director, a hint of irritation in his normally-monotone drone.

"There are several reasons, sir," explained the understudy from back wherever, "But of all of them, I'd say that the most important one is just the amount of time that we've had to prepare. profile-matching wasn't that hard, but once we got the list of potential candidates down to the top five in each category, that is for the salesman, the black woman and the kids, *that's* where we started to run into problems. As you know, sir... normally we have a year or more to prepare them on the psych side, the usual set of threats and incentives... but here, we're taking guys right out of the deep-down holding-facilities and trying to get them ready to act like a 'Billings' or a 'Claremont', with only a *week* or so of training –"

"You've been briefed on the situation," interrupted the director. "Time is of the essence here!"

"We've got our best people on the project, sir," uneasily argued the remote contact, "You know – same guys who do the President's doubles; but even with the plastic-surgery, the full custom synth-cocktail and as much time on the change-your-mind chair as we can do, without them being completely zombie'd, I got to tell you, I'm not sure how well they'll be able to execute the role-play. Especially as we know so little about the original subjects' experiences with the alien... she might get suspicious, the first time that one of them opens his or her mouth –"

"What did we get from the originals during the interrogations?" pressed the director. "*Surely*, along with the scrape of the Federal databases for the life-histories of the salesman and the rest of them, there *must* have been enough to make them sound plausible."

"Well... that's *another* strange thing," explained the remote voice. "As I'm sure you're aware, sir, although we *did* have a pretty good portfolio on Billings – he had one run-in with the Anti-Subversion Branch a few years ago, had a few strings pulled to get him out, but other than that, he's pretty much an ordinary Joe – we've only got the most superficial details on the black woman, even less on her kids... that's because of the withdrawal of government services and private sector banking from the ghettos, of course. We got a little more on the Indian kid; but the bottom line is, their knowledge of their 'new past-histories' is pretty thin, considering the short amount of time that we've had to bang it all into their heads."

"I... *see*," impassively remarked the CIA director.

"And as for the 'get to know you' sessions," continued the understudy, "We aren't finished with Billings yet, and we'll need your personal go-ahead to do the kids, but as for Claremont... man, sir, we hit her with almost *everything* we had! If you can believe this – all we got out of her was some kind of religious BS... there was very little hard, verifiable intelligence coming out of her, no matter *what* we did."

"You sure they used all the available tools and techniques, up to the thresholds we established?" requested the director.

"Frankly, sir," elaborated the remote voice, "The bad-guy doctors up at the northern facility have never seen anything *like* it – not even with the Muslim Leaguer's who *want* to suffer for the pleasure of Allah... I mean, this Claremont woman just wasn't talking turkey – no way, no how. We're still going over the results of the first pass with her; they're considering their options, maybe upping the dose gradually, that kind of thing –"

"Negative on that," commanded the director. "We can't take the chance of losing the originals – not even one of them. I'll authorize everything up to and including surgery to determine how they're handling our tender attentions... but you are *not* to risk death or permanent torso- or limb-injury. As for the kids – start with the authority-figure routine, rough 'em up a bit if you need to, but same rules apply – these are *high-value* assets. Copy?"

"Copy on that... no extra doses, no big-time trauma," came back the voice. "What about the electro-stuff? We can do that low-voltage – no marks, as you know, sir."

"Acceptable... provided that you make sure we don't have heart or respiratory problems in their background med-profiles," commanded the director. "Especially Billings and Claremont. Remember when we lost that big-wig from the Cuban resistance, because of 'one shock too many'?"

"How could I ever *forget*, sir," sheepishly answered the remote voice. "Set us back by at least a year, down there."

"Okay, fine, I suppose," grumbled the CIA director. "I've got to get going now – but one last thing, do you have an ETA on when we can get this show on the road?"

"They're ready now... as ready as they'll ever be, without another six months of prep," answered the under-study. "We just need your go-code, and a drop-off location."

"Top Dog authorizes the plan with code Romeo 14A, Orion 072," announced the director. "Have them at the station in Tucson, for 6:00 a.m. local time, tomorrow... I'll brief Childress as to the procedure past there. Operational story – which I want as the last brief for the decoys – is, they were captured by the *Maras* in a case of mistaken identity, but that 'unspecified government agents' freed them from the greasy clutches of those dastardly gangsters, *et cetera... et cetera*. They need-to-know that there will be *no* straying from the story line, or some really *bad* things will happen to them. The President wants *results* on this front – and we need to do that, while preserving the Agency's options for the future. Do you copy?"

"Copy one hundred, sir," confirmed the remote voice.

"Top Dog out," concluded the director, pocketing his communicator, as he tried not to smile.

Warning-Song

Though utterly exhausted by yet another night of the alien-girl's exquisite love-making, Misha suddenly awoke with a frightened start, upon hearing her weird, ululating wail.

Strangely beautiful and terrible it was, all at the same time – a superior facsimile of the best bars of the *Pathétique*.

The Russian felt suffocating confusion and pain, radiating from her.

A shudder, like the after-shock of an earthquake, raced through the building, rattling a few windows; but, mercifully, nothing shattered or broke.

"Karéin!" he shouted, despite being almost overwhelmed by the newcomer's involuntary emotional *tsunami*. "What is going *on*? Stop moaning like this – you will wake everyone on this floor!"

The Storied Watcher was sitting up, but she had bent forward with her hands grasping her knees. Her perfect breasts showed a pale sheen of sweat.

Slowly, she turned her head toward him, and, eyes glowing sullenly, she sobbed, "Misha... they been hurting... my... *friends*. Ohh, Holy Suns, I *felt* it – felt them inflicting pain on Whitney – dear *Whitney* – who has done *nothing* to deserve such torment."

She was crying, gasping, almost hyperventilating, as pale lights started to shoot up and down her trunk, and a threatening, ominous song sounded at the back of the Russian's consciousness.

"Nothing, that is, except for having fallen in with me... with *me*!" spat out Karéin-Mayréij, as she got off the bed and stood nude, other than for the amulet, in front of her bedmate.

She was a beautiful picture of slender-hipped feminine perfection, except for the fangs that he could see peeking involuntarily past the scowl on her lips.

The creature's tone had become angry, almost to the point of fury; and, for the first time since he had encountered her, Misha felt genuine fear.

The Storied Watcher held her hands out as if to embrace someone, and instantly, the clothes that she had happily dropped to the floor scant hours ago, flew magically into place on her frame.

"I *must* find them – find who has so beset them!" she hissed. "And by the Eight Lords of Light, when I *do* –"

I have to calm her down... stop this situation from escalating out of our control, desperately considered the Russian.

But how does one talk sense into an enraged goddess?

Friend – old – me – know – her – stop – embrace – cool – fire – heart, came a weird burst of thoughts from, *somewhere*.

Not the mind of Karéin-Mayréij, he instinctively knew.

Cannot be.

Then... who is speaking into my mind?

But he had to act.

Half-expecting to be incinerated at any second, the equally-naked SVR-man slipped off the alien-girl's side of the bed and hastened over to grab her shoulders and console her.

As his grasp tightened, he felt a surge of *something* – a force powerful and bright, maybe like static electricity – shoot up to attack his hands and arms, burning a quarter-sized hole in the fabric of her blouse-arms, as it discharged.

It was immediately agonizing and exhilarating, all at once, and a lesser man would have fallen flat backward; but instead, Misha irrationally held on, not wanting to see the last of this maddeningly enigmatic creature.

"Karéin – I can tell that you are very upset," he managed. "But how can I help you, if you go off in a wild rage? And anyway... where are you going? Who are you planning to fight? Please do not tell me that you are about to start an attack on the American government, right *now!*"

Still fuming, the Storied Watcher stared, stony-faced, and with white-and-red-glowing eyes, at the Russian.

"Misha," she angrily retorted, through glistening fangs, "You do not *understand* – *none* of you humans do – *do* you? It is not just that I want to find Whitney, rescue her, and then tear her torturers limb from limb; it is more, *far* more, than that. I am bound to her by the gift that I gave her, I *feel* the pain that she feels... not exactly as she experiences it, herself, else I would go insane... but more than enough to know how terribly that she is suffering. If she dies – I will feel *that*, too. It is something that I hope you never have to know yourself, human... I really *do*."

The mere meaning of her words impacted on him as a body-blow, but again, the SVR spy somehow kept his composure, relenting with the grip, a bit.

"Look," he stammered, "I accept what you say – surely, this *is* a shocking development. But if we are to deal with it, we must think about our options. Come on... sit down on the bed, beside me."

He released her and sat down on the cot, patting the sheet beside him as an invitation as he fumbled for his undershorts.

"Do not try to dissuade me, Misha!" warned Karéin-Mayréij. "I can *not* allow this to go on. It is *insufferable* that poor Whitney has been punished so. If it comes to *Tommy* –"

A wave of hate flowed out from her psyche, as she reluctantly took a place next to him, staring angrily straight ahead.

"He is the one that you consider as your 'son'... correct?" small-talked the Russian.

The eyes do not glow so bright – a good sign, he noted.

"Yes," she confirmed, her lips pursed in anger. "And I tell you now, man, that if the President hurts or kills him, I *will* lay waste to this empire – be of no doubt about *that!* If I were you, frankly, your best move right about now would be to flee from this 'America' as quickly as you can, Misha. I bear you no ill will – far from it – but when I activate my attack, I will not be... *selective*."

"Okay... *okay*," he said, furiously trying to think on his feet, trying to find the best words to say in this clumsy English tongue.

"Now, let us consider the problem – and the first thing that I am trained to do in such circumstances, is to evaluate the new factors that have changed the situation," he argued. "You say that you 'felt' the American government to be using what we call in the intelligence business, 'coercive interrogation', against your friend, Whitney Claremont. Can you describe to me exactly what your mind saw? The more precise the information that you can relate, the better we may be able to determine where these crimes are taking place."

If I can just keep her talking, maybe that will – he reasoned.

From somewhere, another thought, weirdly in English, invaded his mind.

It is what I would do, too, if I were you, Misha... I respect how you are trying to do your duty.

You are a good warrior for the Empire of Russia.

A second later, came the thought,

And you are my most trusted companion, elder of the Many Worlds.

He threw his hands up, in mock-surrender.

Wearily, Misha complained, "Well... what do you *want* me to say, Karéin? It is clear that I can neither keep a secret from you; nor can I try to persuade you to do anything that you do not want to do. They do not train us for dealing with situations like this... needless to say."

A weak smile appeared on her lips.

"Do not blame yourself – you are doing as well as you can, with me," she offered. "But to answer your question – my mind does not 'see', anything. It is just a feeling... and a very powerful and painful one, at that."

"I do not want to upset you further," remarked the spy, "But is it at all possible that this was – how do they say in English – 'just a bad dream'? Are you absolutely *certain* of what you felt?"

Karéin-Mayréij shook her head.

"Not a mistake, and not a bad dream... I can assure you that I know the difference," she stated. "And I am sure that it *was* Whitney. Misha, this may not make much sense... but all living things, at least those with something of a conscious mind... their thoughts all have a different, uhh, 'smell' – that is the only word that I can find in English to describe it. When I spend enough time with an intelligent creature, I come to know this characteristic of its mind, quite intimately. I can tell different people apart by their mind-waves, just as easily as you could by comparing faces. But this is all bullshit, anyway! I need to go and free my friends! There may not be a *minute* to waste!"

She started to arise, but he managed to stop her.

"Karéin," he protested, trying to sound sympathetic, "Let us assume, for the moment, that you *do* have to go and find your, uhh, 'family'. How do you propose to do this? Where will you start looking? And wherever they are being held, it is almost certainly going to be a very well-defended secret American prison. How will you defeat its walls, its guards... its alarm systems? You cannot try something like this without a proper *plan!*"

"Nice try, my Russian spy-lover," shot back the alien-girl. "You would have me describe all my abilities – my tricks, my weirding-powers – to yourself, for the benefit of the rulers of your own empire... would you not?"

"Yes," he sheepishly admitted. "If you can read my mind, you would know that I have to try."

"Now you *have* tried!" she admonished. "And you have seen that it will not work – you can dutifully report that back to your superiors. In the meantime – again to be as truthful with you as I dare – the honest answer is, 'I do not know'. I suppose that I could steal into a building where I can access these sophisticated com-pu-ter networks; from there, I could try to gain background information to help my search. I might even take a few key hostages – warriors, mind you, never ordinary-people – myself, just to let the U.S. government know that I mean *business* –"

Suddenly, she sprang to her feet, and the Russian could again feel a wave of anger.

"In no more than a few more short days, I will not *need* to do any searching" inveighed the Storied Watcher. "I will simply show up at this fancy 'White House' palace that the Americans maintain for their king, and I will inform him that he has one hour to produce my family, alive and unharmed, or else –"

"He probably will not be there," advised the SVR-man. "If not on account of yourself, because of the threat from the Muslim terrorists and the stolen nuclear bombs from Pakistan. Surely you remember seeing that on the television?"

He paused for a second or two, then added, "So it is a matter of *days*, now?"

"No, not days – hours – *minutes*, now, before their stupid little 'guns' will be useless, against me," she growled. "You want the *truth*, Misha? I will tell you, and feel free to pass this happy news on to your, ah, how did Bob say it, yes, your 'do-nothing' Russian empire –"

"Yes?" he queried, not wanting to know the answer.

"The truth is, dear friend," warned Karéin-Mayréij, "That their time is *up*, more than that, since they tormented dear Whitney. They will receive what they *deserve!*"

Despairing, he cried out, standing up in front of her, "Karéin, *Karéin* – I *beg* of you, if you really *have* this kind of power, for the sake of God – do not use it like *this!* Do not strike at the Americans in wild rage! I *know* that they are stupid, ignorant, arrogant, cruel and belligerent – so does everyone else on the face of this planet... but *surely* starting a war against them can only cause ruin for everyone! We need to think this out, consider our options –"

If the Russian had not been frightened out of his wits before, now he had good leave to; for the alien's body was lit up by flashes of chain-lightening, accompanied by a smell of ozone and the mental thunder of her war-song.

With eyes again glowing, this time gold-yellow to white, her gaze froze him helplessly in place, as she spoke through savage-fanged lips.

A strange feeling of peace fell over him.

Ah well, he thought.

Not the worst *way to die, for a spy... preferable, certainly, to a screaming end in the CIA's torture-cells.*

The alien-girl shot out her hands and seized the paralyzed man by the shoulders. Closer and closer came her face, an image of surreal beauty and terrible fury, all mixed into one impossible whole.

"Misha," she compassionately counseled, "You are a secret-warrior for your own empire; and you have oaths to fulfill. I will respect those, if you must hold them foremost. But you and I have come to know each other as friends and lovers – and my gift lies partially on you. If you will follow and help me, man, I will unlock the rest of your power and make you *great!* I will teach you as I did the first of your race to encounter me, and I will call you one of my disciples, to join with... with..."

A look of confusion appeared on her face, and, her hands still tightly clenched on Misha's aching collar-bone, the Storied Watcher closed her eyes, seemingly concentrating upon something.

The song in the Russian's head softened, changing to a tone of relief and joy.

"With... with..." she mumbled, as if in a trance. "With... *Cherie*... oh, Gods Above, Cherie – is that *you*? Dear one, first one... yes, yes, it is *me!* Come hither! Come and be with me – I *need* you – I need all of you! Oh please, come at once... Cherie... *Cherie?* Do not go... do not *go*... oh, *curses*..."

Opening her eyes, Karéin-Mayréij stared at the poor man, and commanded, "What say you, Misha? Will you join with the others, and know the answers to mysteries and marvels, of which your people can scarcely dream? Will you follow me, learn from me... *love* me, as I will love you?"

Agony appeared all over his face, but it was not evidence of physical pain.

"Karéin," he forced out, "You – you should know already, there is *nothing* that I would like to do more than that. But years ago, I took a vow to work in the service of Mother Russia, and her alone, even at the cost of my own life; what honor would I have, if I were to abandon that pledge, now? What would you think of a man who would change his loyalty, just for convenience, and his own vanity?"

Her grasp lessened a bit.

"Your perspective is valid, that I must admit," she offered. "And so I will not dispute it – I will *not* force you to follow me, Misha, nor will I use my mind-powers to still your tongue about what you have learned of me... although I *should* do that, for my own safety. Go we then our own respective ways, in mutual respect. All that I *do* ask, is that you not stand in my way – and that you advise your Russian Empire not to try to stop me, either."

A tear – genuine in its emblem of sadness – came to the man's eye.

"Karéin," he requested, "*Must* it come to this? I said that I could not follow you, nor can I obey you, and that much is true; but never did I say that I did not want to *be* with you. I have, I suppose, become rather... *attached* to you."

A wan smile came to her lips.

"That happens a lot with humans," she commented. "Especially with those with whom I lie in warm passion... as a woman with a man."

Leaning forward, she planted an affectionate dry kiss on his cheek.

Now she let him go, and though the Storied Watcher was considerably shorter than the Russian, he felt overawed by her presence, as her figure started to blur with the light-bending trick taking hold.

Her song is purposeful, mighty... far beyond the things of this Earth, his mind somehow perceived.

The fool *Americans – what is* wrong *with them?*

Do they not know *what is coming?*

"I am going now, Misha," she announced, "And I will not be back here. I will not imperil you with my presence – especially not now, when the full weight of the Americans' war-machines will be turned against me, and my own skills against them. But –"

"Yes?" he instantly responded, hoping against hope.

"But," remarked this entrancing, unique being, as she finally shimmered completely out of sight, "None, not even I of my many ages gone by, can predict the future's bends and turns, dear Misha, warrior-spy of Russia; so, if ever you have cause to reconsider – after all, to join with me and those who would be new brothers and sisters... just call, and I will come."

"'Call' to you?" he asked, perplexed and crestfallen. "*How?* I cannot just use a mobile-phone for this – and it is not wise to shout out loud, in my line of work –"

"When the time comes," sounded a faceless voice, "You *will* know how to do it. This do I promise... and I am ever true to my vows."

The door opened, as if by itself, and a hopeless feeling of loss came over the man, as he slumped back to sit down on the bed.

But then, to his relief, he heard her voice again.

"One *other* thing, Misha," she mentioned, from inside her weird cloak of invisibility. "Something that you should do, as soon as possible."

"Yes, Storied Watcher?" he responded, his mind irrationally wanting to keep her there, wanting to savor every extra word that his ears could hear.

"You should hide," she warned. "And hope that your government is not as stupid as is the Americans' one."

Then, she was gone.

The three men had hastened to the door of Tanaka's private chamber, having heard – and *felt* – the loud moan that had just issued from inside it.

From inside, they heard something that sounded more or less like, "Teacher, I hear you, but I can't –"

"Cherie? *Cherie!* Something wrong in there?" exclaimed Jacobson, in a loud, worried, tone.

"No... uhh, no, everything's... uhh... okay... I guess..." came back the woman's voice.

"Mind if we come in?" requested Jacobson. "Brent and Devon are here, too."

"Yeah... sure," weakly answered Tanaka.

Rapidly, the former Mars mission commander opened the hatch and led his former subordinates, into the cramped, white-sterile room.

"Wow, Cherie – y'all look pale as a *ghost,*" commented White. "Must've been one hell of a bad dream, yo?"

He sat down on the bed next to her, taking hold of the woman's right hand.

A startled expression instantly crossed his face.

Looking over the sweating, shivering former Science Officer, Boyd added, "Devon's not kidding there, Professor. You remind me of my kids when they used to get those 'night-terror' experiences. You want me to get something from the med-cabinet, or call those storm-troopers out there for something stronger?"

"No... that won't be necessary," said Tanaka, slowly regaining her composure. "I'll be okay. It's just that I had, well... I'm not sure *what* I had. It was like... like..."

"Like what?" inquired Jacobson.

"Like knowing that a dear friend has been hurt," explained the woman, her almond eyes looking pensively out into space. "And... that..."

"Oh, wow," breathed Boyd.

"Like, we gotta go help, sooner rather than later?" insightfully proposed White, as he and Tanaka stared with determination, at the other two.

You're An Inspiration, Brother

A holographic, 3-D view-screen, normally hidden away in the center of the exquisitely-carved hardwood desk, sprung open, so the clean-shaven, leather-cheeked Christian man with the Brylcreem hair could see the visual part of the incoming call.

Other than for him, there was no-one in this cavernous, shadowed room – more of a hallway, with no obvious back-exit, really – although, of course, the guards with the machine-guns were stationed outside the big, metal-bound doors in the front.

"Harold here," he called out, with cold, calculating eyes staring at the screen. "Who's this?"

"Martin here, revered Brother," replied a voice. "Per your orders, sir – I'm down in Tucson with the Brothers of Holy Discipline."

"So what's going on?" demanded the first man. "You have a *reason* for disturbing your senior leader, I hope?"

"Definitely, Brother Harold... *definitely!*" excitedly confirmed the voice from Tucson. "Have you yet heard the news from our faithful-in-hiding down here?"

"No," stated the first man. "Go on."

"Well, sir," remarked the second man, "It looks like we might get a second chance – against the Devil-Girl, that is!"

There was a pause of a second or two.

"The Lord be *praised*," Brother Martin heard, but could not see, as Harold had disabled the out-bound video-signal. "Are you *sure*? How? When? Where? I need all the details, *immediately!*"

"Yes – yes, sir, of course," stammered the remote voice. "You see, it's like this... remember how we thought that the government had caught the Beast, along with its sad little troupe of hangers-on, this 'Billings' guy, the nigger woman and so on, you know the ones?"

"Very definitely," stated the man in the darkened hallway-room.

"We've just received reliable intelligence from our deep-cover brethren within the Air Force, Army and Executive Branch," explained the other, "That the message on the Tucson TV station, KGUN, I mean, was no government disinformation trick – inside the government they're saying that it was authentic. And you're not going to *believe* what's coming next –"

"*Try* me, Brother," shot back the first man.

"They – 'Project Red Rover', that is – they think the creature is still hiding somewhere in the Tucson area, so they're going to try to lure it out into the open, using a couple people from the Houston Space Center as bait, one man and one woman who are supposedly the thing's 'friends'," elaborated Brother Martin. "They're setting up these two as 'guest-speakers' for some kind of convention or something like that, hoping that it will show itself at that point –"

"And when and if it does," inquired Brother Harold, "Just what are they plannin' to do with it?"

"Well, that's the part that doesn't make a lot of sense, at least to this humble servant of the Lord, sir," continued the second man. "I mean, if the government has the slightest common sense, they'd shoot the monster dead on sight... right? But all that they're apparently planning to do, if it shows up at this 'public speaking event' – which is, by the way, to be held at a downtown Tucson hotel – is to *communicate* with it. I know that's hard to comprehend... but that's what our deeply-hidden brethren are saying."

"The Godless, heathen *fools*," spat out the man in the hall.

"Don't I know it, sir," agreed Martin. "Maybe it's just a cover-story, and they're actually planning on ridding God's planet of the Devil-Girl?"

"Interesting," offered Brother Harold. "There very well may be more to this than we're aware of, right now; but as an ex-military man, in a way it makes sense, to me. They might be doin' recce at first – that is, git a good look at it, assess its capabilities, see if they can find a weak spot and so on; then, when they have a prepared position and complete control of the circumstances of battle, they drop the hammer. Except..."

There was another pause.

Tentatively, the second man asked, "Sir?"

"What I'm considerin', Brother Martin," stated the Christian at the desk, "Is that although this arrangement *does* make military sense... there's also the possibility that they might be trying to 'reason' with the Accursed One, or, perhaps, they might intend to capture it, put it in a lab, study it... maybe dissect it, eventually. What intelligence do you have of the government's actual intentions towards the creature?"

"Unfortunately very little, sir," apologized the remote voice. "I'd agree with you that the military *might* be gearing up for a hard-kill scenario, but it may be that the President is keeping his options open. There's apparently a school of thought within the Department of Defense that she – it – could be brainwashed and converted into a weapon, for the restoration of American military superiority."

"Which is," countered the first man, coldly and dogmatically, "A very *bad* idea, not only for the obvious reason that you *cannot* make peace with Satan, no matter how sweetly he, or she, smiles, but also because America is the standard-bearer for our Lord and Savior, Jesus Christ; and with the Lord on our side, what need have we of the Devil, Brother?"

"Sir, I always treasure the opportunity to speak with you," mentioned the second man, perhaps with real sincerity, "Since you know how to tell the truth, plain and simple, the way us sinners need to hear it. Hallelujah!"

"Okay," announced Brother Harold. "Now, before I try to devise a plan of our own – there anythin' else that I need-to-know? Anything at all, no matter *how* insignificant that it might seem."

"Only one thing," noted Brother Martin. "And this is another one that, frankly, I can't make good sense of. Remember how we had reports of the Men In Black showing up to the Billings house, and his floor-tile company, just before our martyrs laid down their lives for the Lord?"

"Yes," confirmed the man at the desk. "You'll no doubt remember yourself, how we had to purge twenty-five unbelievin' traitors from the Southwestern region, because they might have tipped off the government to our attack – how *else*, after all, could CIA, Secret Service, FBI, or the Special Police, have known what we were about to do? Well, *those* sons of Judas found out the hard way, about the wages of sin... wouldn't you say?"

"I sure *would*, sir," earnestly agreed the second man. "And I'll understand if you don't take this as great news... but we're now getting reports that *somehow* – even though, our martyrs basically leveled both the bungalow and the floor-tile shop – Billings, the nigger woman, at least one of the kids, too, the reports aren't too clear on this – seem to have survived the attack... and it looks like the government grabbed them and is now holding them somewhere. Obviously the

Devil-Girl got away, too, since they're still looking for her and have cooked up this 'meeting' idea to draw her out."

"Fair enough," noted the first man. "We'll have to execute Billings and his perverted nigger troupe later, as they have no doubt been contaminated by bein' in contact with that accursed creature."

"But it's *more* than that, sir," opined Brother Martin. "In these messages that she's been leaving all over the place, on the TV station broadcast, for example, the Devil-Girl has been threatening the government with 'dire consequences', if they don't free Billings, the Negress and the rest. Why are these people so important to her... 'scuse me, to it? And why doesn't the government just use them as the bait, as opposed to these two scientists from Houston?"

"I'll ask the Lord about the truth of it," counseled the stern-faced man at the headquarters, "Since, of course, I have a special relationship with Him. But in the meantime, we have to think through a plan, and fast, since events seem to be movin' forward quickly."

He stopped for a few seconds, pondering his options, then continued, "Here's how we'll proceed : first, we need to get our people within the military and the government, to find out as much as possible about what's really goin' on – in other words, what the President and this-here 'Project' intend to do with, or to, the Devil-Girl, when and if they get it to show up. If this means some of our deep-cover volunteers get caught and end up goin' to the gallows, well... that wouldn't be the *first* time that a martyr or two has had to lay down his life for the Lord, right?"

"'Amen' to *that*, Brother," reflexively answered the man in Tucson.

"In the meantime, we got to be ready to strike at any time, should it look like the government is plannin' a capture-operation, as opposed to one meant to rid God's green Earth of the Devil-Girl, once and for all. Without good intelligence from the most privileged inside circles, we'll have no choice but to assume the worst, unless we see a few bullets and bombs flyin' at the creature. What's your current state of preparedness for another attack like the one we carried out at the Billings house and workplace, a few days ago?"

"Unfortunately, sir... not too good right now," replied the remote voice, with a faint tone of nervousness. "I anticipated that you might ask this, blessed Brother leader, so the minute I heard the news about the latest developments on this whole subject, I had the Southwestern region do an inventory of all our available offensive tools – everything down to guns and knives owned privately by our followers, in their own homes, to the more powerful weapons that are reserved for the Temple's own use. We've got a good collection of firearms, ranging from .50 caliber sniper-rifles and anti-tank rockets, to plastic sub-machine-guns, and plenty of ammunition, and we've got a few cases of grenades, as well."

"But?" curtly demanded the man in the long hall.

"But, sir," carefully explained Brother Martin, "As to the stealth-signature *plastique*, after the Billings attacks, we don't have enough to make even *one* good-sized device. We've had to rely on low-volume special requisitions from military stockpiles by our faithful within the Army, to get that stuff, in the first place. We can probably source conventional C-4 or Semtex from the black market... but, of course, if the Feds put up a detection-perimeter around either of the meeting sites, that'll stick out like a sore thumb... I'm working on some alternatives, and I'm praying that they'll come through for us."

"Hmm," mumbled the Christian leader. "We'll – you'll – have to hope that it turns out that way, Brother," he warned. "But when do you think that you'll be in possession of enough of the necessary materials, to make another strike, practical?"

"Possibly by the end of the week," answered the remote voice. "But we *could* do an old-fashioned attack with just guns and grenades, at any time. We've got bullet-proof vests and body-armor aplenty, if it's to be a close-range operation, also good thermal long-range sights, if we're going the sniper-route, like for example we did against those lib-rals who were trying to take over the Southern Baptist Convention, a few years back. You'll recall that *that* operation went perfectly, sir?"

"I do," affirmed the stern man. "But the problem is, Brother, that we *aren't* just shootin' at a few nice, fat renegade heretics from Charlotte, here – we're takin' on the spawn of Satan, himself, not to mention, possibly, a whole heap of the best that the FBI and the Secret Service, maybe the military too, can deploy in the vicinity. Okay – I have decided, and I pray that our Lord and Savior Jesus Christ, and our Father God, will guide my words, as I say them to you."

"I'm praying for you, and us all, at this end, as I write your commands down, blessed Brother leader," intoned the man in Tucson.

"What we're gonna do," ordered Brother Harold, "Is, first, we'll send our best close-range shooter in to this mo-tel event, plastic gun, of course, and make sure that he's made his peace with the Lord, since he'll have to have the chewin'-capsule in his mouth – you know, the one that makes sure you don't talk afterwards... tell him that just like for the martyrs of last week, his Leader absolves him of the sin of suicide, in advance; for it's *no* sin to die a little ahead of time, if you know that CIA's going to do the same thing to you, a bit later."

"'Amen' to that," echoed the remote voice.

"Second," continued the Christian leader, "I want you to set up our best sniper – only one of 'em, mind you, we don't need any co-ordinatin' problems here, with one of those nice big Amendment 2 Corporation Devastator jobs with the thermal- and radar-sights, on a roof-top or in a window somewhere nice and far away, but with a clear line of sight to the main point of ingress and egress to this here mo-tel that they're supposedly trying to get the Devil-Girl to show up at."

"Roger that," said Brother Martin.

"Now," continued Brother Harold, "Both our martyr-to-be in the meetin'-room, and our sniper outside, tell them that they're *not* to take a shot, unless and until they are sure to get a good enough hit to put the monster away, for good.

My meanin' here is, if we take a crack at the creature, and – may the Lord forbid – we miss, if I know the govern'ment, they're gonna be all over us like a dirty shirt in the front pew on Easter Sunday."

"I understand and obey, sir," agreed the younger man.

"Desperate times and desperate measures, Brother," observed Brother Harold.

"God's will be done," replied the remote voice.

"Alright," pronounced the man in the dark hallway. "Now, just a few other things, quickly, since you need to get goin' on this plan, ASAP. I presume that you've taken charge of the situation in the Southwestern Region Temple?"

"Mostly, sir," replied the man on the video-screen. "I'm a little behind schedule on that front, because, frankly, it was very difficult to get down here in the first place. On the way there, my guards shot one of those worthless Catholic Mexican wetbacks as he was about to steal a hubcap – no great loss of course – but we then had to go a bit off route to make sure that nobody was following us. We only arrived in Tucson late yesterday afternoon, but I've already made some changes in the local gathering to make sure that they get the message. So far we've handed out three good stiff whippings, two demotions in rank and a six-day stay in the stocks for one errant person... and they've been made aware that we won't be as lenient next time."

"That's satisfactory, I suppose," allowed the man in the dark room, "I *would* have demanded more punition – but, of course, most of the ones whose aim was faulty, are now with the Lord, anyway. One other thing. You heard anything from that two-timin' 'Horn' fellow? He was supposed to be one of our prime inside contacts, right up in the Executive Office, no less, but I hear he's high-tailed it off somewhere."

"Another sad story, sir," explained Brother Martin. "I'd have thought that you'd have heard it before I did. Our people saw him flying out of Atlanta airport for Miami, and another one of our operatives at Miami International traced his flight-plan as far as South America... unfortunately, the trail goes cold at that point. Did you get the letter that he wrote to us, sir?"

"Yes," confirmed Brother Harold. "A pack of lies and excuses... tell you the truth, I never trusted that man – he *called* himself a Christian, but just like all the other 'only-on-every-third-Sunday-and-only-when-it-suits-me' types, the minute that the going gets a little tricky, his faith just up and left, the way he did. Anyway... have you made the necessary preparations, Brother?"

"Sure *have*, sir," cheerily answered the man in Tucson. "Problem is, of course, that there's nothing but those heretics down in South America, all worshiping their false God and their false Pope, so our options in that respect are limited; but the minute that he shows his face again in America... well, we've even selected a plot where we can bury the body. Unless, of course, you'd want a cremation – but we thought that might be a little harsh... I mean, I *know* that we've made exceptions for those such as our martyrs about the resurrection of the flesh, and for all his faults, Horn *is* still a Christian. We figured that he should at least have a chance to answer to Lord Jesus for his sins, instead of going straight to Hell. What are your orders on this subject, sir?"

"No – that'll be fine," agreed the man at the Temple headquarters. "You can even make it on hallowed ground, if you like. And just to show you how generous that I can be, if you manage to git him somewhere *private* before you do what you have to do, you have my authorization to give Mr. Horn five minutes to make his peace with the Lord, before he goes to meet our Father God and has to justify why he's made it so hard for us to destroy the Devil-Girl. I don't think I could possibly be more lenient or forgiving than *that*... do you?"

"Your mercy never ceases to amaze me, blessed Brother Harold," confirmed the remote voice. "It's an inspiration to us all, sir!"

"Thank you," amicably answered the Christian leader. "Now... I believe that you have a plan, to attend to... do you not, Brother?"

"I can't *wait* to get going, sir!" came back the eager voice from Tucson.

"God be with you," concluded Brother Harold, as he switched off the view-screen and rummaged around in a drawer for his pill-case.

A Postponed Reckoning

By now, Karéin-Mayréij had taught her youngest – the one whose name sounded, to human ears, as *Vìrya Ahn'jë* – to vary the colors and folds of her war-cloak. This part of *Ahn'jë*'s being overlaid her dim-flaming under-armor, making her mother appear to be clad in naught but a gray-brown peasant-robe, with an extempore hood concealing her head.

In the dawning light, the Storied Watcher stood alone on a Tucson building-top, grim-faced, looking out over the city, while silently pondering her course of action.

Though they knew it not, the fates of thousands, perhaps millions, of Americans, hung in the balance.

Should I show this foolish American President, who he provokes, by, say, burning this dreary-gray city to the ground?

It would be only fair – for what his gendarmes did to dear Bob's modest little house, I would merely be repeating, on a larger scale.

I could try to send the American leader another message... but without a demonstration of my capability to destroy, any tyrant worthy of that description would take it as a bluff from weakness...

It usually takes many deaths and the tumbling of fortresses, to impress those who value only power.

And my death-arts flood back, as a spring rip-tide!

I am now more than strong enough to defeat what I have so far seen of this empire's war-machines.

A familiar, stirring, martial tune began to issue from the very air-molecules, all around.

To strike with Holy Fire against the cruel, the rich, the oppressors – yes, that *is what I must do – my destiny – war-children, prepare-ye!*

No! came back an odd, ethereal voice, from somewhere she knew naught; and its advent, instantly quenched the psycho-music.

Fire roils – burns hot – but now – must forebear, counseled an alter ego.

Honorable – things – do now – wait revenge – time will come...

Fate terrible – suffer them, then.

Foresight – mine – must thou trust –

Never – failed thee – my child – have I?

For a few seconds, the countenance worn by the Storied Watcher remained as stern and warlike as ever; but, then, a wry half-smile appeared on her face.

No, she mused, *Never have thee, Venerable One.*

Therefore I defer to thy wisdom... for now.

Some, but not all, of the tension left her body, and the young-looking woman now uttered a soft command in her alien language.

But what would thou have me do, in the meantime, old friend?

For I cannot return, abashed and ashamed, to tell Misha that I simply, ahh, 'gave up'...

Some – deeds – good – do, came back the immediate reply.

Balance – build – back. Hurt – not. Instead – help.

Easy – find – need – those – that.

"*Vîrya Ahn'jë,*" she requested, "I pray thee, let loose that thing, upon which I have been recording these matters."

A piece of aluminum-foil, creased far beyond anything that the humans would have believed possible, and upon which had been burned line upon line of inscrutable, blocky characters, darted forth from a scarcely less-squeezed box on the living-armor's belt.

6100 East Third Street, considered Karéin-Mayréij, her dull-glowing eyes sweeping expertly over the inscriptions.

Where Freddie said that he lived, along with his daughter and family.

If the Gods so will it, I can wait there for a while and see if my healing-arts have also come back in as full measure as have my blood-skills.

"Come, my children," she whispered. "Thy chance to go a-warring – though come eventually it no doubt will – be now delayed, for a time. We travel to the house of Freddie Losada, there to practice the mending of life and limb."

Standing up, the mind of the Storied Watcher caused the armor-and-weapon collection, tightly bound by the cape into a mass no larger than, perhaps, a business-case, to float behind her.

As she started to move, leaping gazelle-like from building, taking care never to jump too high above each one, another thought came suddenly into her head.

Maybe, she reflected, *I can do a small bit of good...*

Ere I do yet more evil, to add to my already-dark cosmic account.

Angel Of Mercy

She had arrived at the nondescript, low-set house, covered garage in front, that the humans called '6100 East Third Street'. The place had clearly seen better days; it had a rock-and-pebble frontage ahead of a sun-burned, dried-out lawn bending over the corner of North Ruston Drive, and there were a couple of beaten-up-looking domestic automobiles parked in the driveway, with a few more parked at various intervals around the curb.

I hope that Freddie will recognize me, considered the alien-girl.

As, perhaps, I may look a bit... different, *this time.*

Advancing underneath the garage-roof, she came up to the building's front screen-door, itself in front of the real door, which was decorated by a strange-looking cross-shape, bedecked with flowers and white cloth.

A wry smile came to face of Karéin-Mayréij.

Ha, she mused.

Freddie Losada – the Great One, the Vanquisher of Gods and Demons, who could flatten your little house with but a thought, stands before your living-place.

And... she must knock politely, to beg entrance.

So, a hand extended from nothingness, to rap on the screen-door.

There was no answer.

Again, she knocked, this time a little more forcefully.

"*Que se vaya!*" sounded an accented voice from somewhere inside. "Whoever you are, go away!"

Once more, she tried.

This time the Hispanic voice sounded almost angry.

"Look, we don' want what you're selling, go away... we're *busy* in here! Don' make me come to the door with my shotgun... you understand?"

Hmm, thought the young-looking woman.

Well, not a completely surprising response, considering how many bandits prowl the streets of this 'Ew-Nighted States'.

Maybe there is another entrance?

Noiselessly, she jumped over the locked gate to the side of the residence, after first fruitlessly scanning for signs of the canine-things that these people habitually kept as a deterrent to thieves and burglars.

Rounding the rear corner of the bungalow, she noticed a large, sliding-glass window in the rear of this place, similar in most respects to the back-entrance to Bob's now-ruined house. Beyond this portal was a kitchen, with a number of glass vases containing water and various collections of rather attractive white-and-gold flowers.

Oops, thought the Storied Watcher. *I forgot to drop the cloak.*

It would not do for Freddie just to see a hand... would it?

I hope that none of the Americans' spy-satellites are looking down on me, right now.

Relegating the light-bending field to envelop only the cape-bound armor-and-weaponry collection floating just behind her, Karéin-Mayréij, clad only in a strangely-shiny bikini and her neck-pendant, stood directly in front of the sliding door.

She rapped firmly at the glass pane within it.

"Carajo!" erupted a curse from inside the house. "I already *paid* the rent for last month, 'an that fuckin' annual deposit too! You better get runnin', *puto* – I warned you –"

In another couple of seconds, from a corridor inside the house, came a fatigued-looking, sweating Mexican-American man that the Storied Watcher immediately recognized as her drinking-buddy from the downtown bar, some few days earlier. He was carrying a sawed-off shotgun.

Advancing quickly to the other side of the glass door, he accosted her.

"Bitch, who the *hell* you think you is, don' you have any *respect* –"

Losada stopped in mid-sentence, dropping the gun from the ready position.

"Oh, hi there, S – S – uhh... *hola mujer*... sorry, I don' remember your name right now," he mumbled, "But anyway, listen – this is a *bad* time... my daughter is really sick. I don' got no time for foolin' around... you know?"

"The name that you knew me by is not the *real* one, Freddie," replied the alien-girl, "But that does not matter. And your daughter is the reason why I came over here, today. Would you mind opening the door?"

"Listen, I *told* you, I got no *time!*" he shot back. "And ain't you looked in a mirror, whoever-you-are from the bar? You a little... under-dressed, if you get my meanin'. I gotta go."

Now, Karéin-Mayréij stared him right in the eye.

Freddie – open the fucking door! commanded her mind.

Dumbfounded, Losada watched his hand move over, undo the catch and roll the glass-door back over its moving-track.

Quickly, she came inside, passing him to position herself deeper in the kitchen.

"Freddie," she softly counseled, "I'm sorry that I had to do that to you; but if your daughter is as sick as your mind tells me that she is, there may not be much time to waste. I need to see her, as soon as possible."

"What... *what* you *do* to me, just now?" semi-coherently stammered the man. "Who the hell *are* you? And no, you *can't* go in there to see my daughter – no *way*. Doctor and most of *mi familia* are in her room... they tell us that she's got maybe a day left... liver cancer, if that makes any difference. Priest is comin' over, round supper-time. Find your own way out, close the door behind you. I gotta get back to her."

As he was about to wheel and leave her, in that precise moment, the Storied Watcher knew, somehow, that a turning-point had been reached.

"Freddie," she heard her lips ask, a soft glow now building in her eyes and in an outline around her body, as a tremble – just enough to shake the drinking-glasses, shot through the house, "Do you believe in angels?"

What made me say that? wondered Karéin-Mayréij.

It is a lie – an effrontery against the Powers Above – how dare *I –*

A wave of powerful, yet gentle, ethereal and beautiful music, washed over the minds of everyone within a city-block.

"*Dios mio,*" breathed a shocked Losada.

"I... I don' know, man, I ain't never – I mean –"

"*Vîrya Ahn'jë!*"

"*Vîrya I'ëà'b'!*"

"*Væran Ksé'l'ch'!*"

"*Væran Ss'éth'ch'!*"

"*Væran Fàiagàryuu!*", invoked the alien-girl, sounding the names of her new companion-beings much more forcefully than each one's title.

And as each name was called, the corresponding item appeared in half an eye-blink, on her and by her side.

Now, she stood, god-like before him, in a weirding, flame-flickering war-suit, its iridescent colors shining dimly like the scales of a black mamba, but with after-tones of other hues – royal blue-and-red for the armor, cape and hair-ribbon, crimson-red for the sword, steel-blue-silver for the little arm-shield, orange-and-yellow for the first dagger, with deep purple-blue for the second – pulsating occasionally from each component.

"Freddie Losada," she commanded, using a Stentorian voice both uplifting and frightening, that had, as yet, never been heard by human ears; least-aways, not on the face of this world, "You stand now in front of God's Destroying Angel – Karéin-Mayréij, the Storied Watcher, eldest and greatest of the *Makailkh*, guardians of the countless worlds; and now – if your people will consent – protector of this beautiful, green, good Earth. You are the first human to ever see me in this guise... so mark this day well, man."

"*Madre de Dios!*" cried Freddie, far out of the comfort-zone of the normal, the expected... the *possible*.

"Now," pressed the Storied Watcher, "If you value the life of your daughter – lead me to her – do what I bid you to... and command your kin to do likewise."

"Of... *course,*" he hastily responded, pointing to a spot around the corner, down the hall.

As she followed him, he stammered, "Listen, Ms... Ms... Angel... I know I'm a sinner – but *por el amor de Dios*, don't hold that against my little one... take *me* instead, if you have to – okay?"

"Freddie," she replied, with a compassionate smile, seizing his arm and half-turning him to look at her, "It does not work that way – not with me, nor with those whom I serve. There is no 'sin' here; only love... and life."

With only a perfunctory rap on the door to the bedroom at the end of the hall, the man rapidly opened it and bade her enter.

As Karéin-Mayréij crossed the portal, the alien woman saw an all-too-familiar scene, one known to her not from this planet but from others, incomprehensibly far away.

The room was dark, with closed curtains and little candles burning here and there. A frail, elderly Hispanic woman sat on a chair next to the bed, and standing next to her, was a 40ish Caucasian man with a listening-device hanging from a pair of bent tubes surrounding his neck.

There were three other people – a young boy, perhaps eight or nine years old, a man who appeared to be somewhat older than Losada, and, a pale-looking, dull-eyed, bald-headed, jaundiced little girl with plastic tubes in her arm and nostrils, lying on the bed.

The boy and the other man were on the opposite side of the bed to the doctor and the grandmother.

Although a look of astonishment showed instantly on the faces of everyone in the room, save the girl, the old lady nonetheless angrily accosted Freddie.

"*¡Quién es este?*" she demanded. "*¡Que no conocemos à ella! ¡Que hace ella aqui, en este tiempo!*"

"Yeah, Freddie, what's with the chick in the cape and the crazy light-show armor?" asked the adult man on the right-hand side of the bed. "It's a little late for the cheerin'-up stuff, don' you think?"

"Miss, this is a *serious* situation," protested the doctor. "You have no right whatsoever, to be waltzing in here with some comic-book setup bought off of NeoNet. You shouldn't disturb Mr. Losada's family, when they have –"

"*Estoy aqui para ayudarla*," answered the Storied Watcher, not needing to ask herself if she had come to understand Spanish.

In spite of the fact that she already knew the child's name, she added, "*Me llamo 'Karéin-Mayréij' y vengo de la luz en el cielo. Còmo se llama ella?*"

She pointed to the sick girl.

"My name is Juanita," came back a weak little voice. "Are you a special doctor, lady? Your clothes are very pretty."

The young-looking woman closed her eyelids and said a silent prayer. Slowly, she opened them, and her eyes glowed with a new, even stranger, light. Though the left-hand side of the bed was already crowded by the doctor and the grandmother, in the blink of an eye, the newcomer had gently pushed the other two aside and was kneeling right beside the little girl.

"You already *know* who I am, Juanita," responded Karéin-Mayréij. "I am here to make you well again."

"Miss, I really *must* protest!" retorted the doctor, his voice rising, despite, or perhaps because of, being frightened of what he was seeing. "You're *intruding* here. You need to get out and let me attend to Juanita."

"Tell me... you are a doctor, a healer... is that right?" countered the young-looking woman, as she removed one fingerless gauntlet and squeezed the sick girl's hand.

"Of *course* I am!" grumbled the doctor. "Michael Kozimian, M.D., East Tucson Medical Center. And if you think that I'm going to let some kind of quack faith-healer, wander in here and deprive my patient of the few hours that she still has –"

"Sorr-ee," shot back Karéin-Mayréij, rising to her feet and turning to majestically confront the man. "I do not have time to argue this – every *moment*, counts now. Hear me well, Doctor : if you would learn from me, this day I will make you foremost among all healers; I will teach you arts of life-giving that your kind would *never* find otherwise... not in a thousand upon thousand of your years. You have ten seconds. *Decide.*"

"Oh, come *on*, Miss!" sarcastically complained Kozimian. "Do you have any *idea* of how many times I've heard this kind of nonsense –"

"Do as she *says*," interrupted Freddie.

"Freddie, listen – I *know* this is a stressful time for all of us, but I *can't* –" protested the doctor.

Losada took two strides to stand in front of the man. Grabbing his arm rather more roughly than might have been called for, he said, "Michael, just fucking *do* it... okay?"

Abashedly, he turned to look at Karéin-Mayréij.

"Oh, Miss Angel, I'm sorry," he apologized, "Don' let God get mad at me for losing my temper, please..."

The alien-girl smiled and remarked, "Do not worry about that, Freddie. It would not be the first damn swear word that the Powers Above have heard, now *would* it?"

Uncertainly, he replied, "No... I guess not. Ha ha."

"Well, Freddie," hesitatingly allowed Kozimian, "This is up to you, I guess... she's *your* daughter, and you *do* have the right to refuse medical treatment. I'll be going, then."

He bent down to pick up his black bag, turned as if to go, but somehow, the young-looking woman was now right in front of him.

Staring directly into his eyes, she pronounced, "Those who disbelieve from stubborn tradition, deserve a second chance... especially where they can, by such being granted, save life and limb. The Storied Watcher comes to this Earth not just to bring the Holy *Fire*; but even more, to bring light. Thus, now she extends the hand of friendship, enlightenment and knowledge. *Take* it, and start the next step in your honorable profession."

Karéin-Mayréij offered him her hand, the one without the glove.

Evidently, she had not used the mind-trick on him, because he answered, "Well, you don't *deserve* it... but I suppose it doesn't hurt to be polite."

As he felt her grasp, however, his visage turned to one of shock and amazement.

Awkwardly, as if struck by a body-blow, Kozimian stumbled to prop himself up against one of the bedroom walls.

Sweating through confusion, he stammered, "What the... holy... my *God!*"

He turned to Losada.

"Freddie," demanded the doctor, "Who *is* this?"

"She's an an-gel, Doctor Kozimian," sounded the faint, sweet voice of the stricken child, from her sick-bed.

The man bent forward, his palms against the wall, his head staring at the ground.

"This isn't *happening*," he mumbled. "*Doesn't* happen. Not in real life."

Coming quickly to his side, the armor-clad alien-girl bent down and counseled, "Doctor Kozimian, I am different from anyone who you have ever met; and all things – even *wondrous* things without precedent – happen once, for a first time. Now... come and apprentice with me. We are running out of time."

Wiping his brow and shaking his head, the doctor replied, "Yeah... alright. Jesus – if they find out back at the hospital that I got involved in something like *this*... okay. What... what... do you want me to do?"

"First," explained Karéin-Mayréij, "Disconnect those two tubes that Juanita has going in to her nose; we will have need of them. Next, Freddie should retrieve two buckets, or anything that can hold liquid without it leaking – make them as big and clean as possible. Place one bucket on each side of the bed. When all this is done, everyone needs to join me, beside Juanita. *Go.*"

"Disconnect her... *what*? I can't *believe* that you're telling me to do this!" complained Kozimian, as he slowly walked over to the machine connecting the breathing-tubes to the oxygen-tank.

"She won't last an *hour!*" he warned. "For God's sake, don't tell any of my colleagues – I'll be drummed out of the A.M.A."

He removed the plastic tubing, then followed Losada into the kitchen.

The Storied Watcher, in turn, hurried over to the left-hand side of the bed.

Addressing the grandmother, she explained, "*No se preoccupe, mujer, porque yo vengo del lado de Dios; y escucheme, necessito su ayuda tambièn, para dar la salud à la pequeña. Me comprende?*"

"*Claro que sì,*" whispered the old woman, dewy-eyed and clutching the crucifix around her neck.

"*Haré lo que usted ordena, ángel de Dios.*"

Now Karéin-Mayréij knelt on the floor next to the sick little girl, but in the next three seconds, jaws dropped, as, her entire body glowing with starlight, she floated upwards, until her head was on a level with the child's. At that moment, the drapes parted of their own accord, and rays of refulgent sunshine streamed in to illuminate the Storied Watcher and her patient.

A different song now began to play, on the wind that blew lightly through the window-screen; it sounded like an impossibly perfect cross between an *Enya* Celtic ballad, and the *Ave Maria*.

"*Santa Marìa, Madre de Dios, oye nuestro rezo,*" tearfully gasped the grandmother, falling humbly to her knees with head bent.

With one hand, the Storied Watcher grasped that of the child, but she extended the other to the old lady.

"*Querida abuela,*" requested the alien, "*Por favor, pregunta a los que usted ame, agarrar las manos, una el uno al otro, para nosotros debe toda dar nuestra energía al niña.*"

"*Segura,*" answered the grandmother, still knee-bound.

A moan – maybe of pain, more likely, of something else entirely – issued from her lips, but still, she found the strength to gesture to the boy and the other man.

Suspiciously, each one grasped on to the ring, and as they did, they stood transfixed, astonished.

And... *empowered.*

"Juanita," said Karéin-Mayréij, looking straight at the child, "You know that you are very sick... do you not?"

The girl nodded, then replied in a small voice, "*Abuela* and Daddy say that I'm going to meet Jesus, very soon. I don't mind... but I'm kind of scared."

Squeezing Juanita's hand a little tighter, the young-looking woman counseled, "Dear child, many years lie yet before you; and, if you will be brave and let me guide through what we must do, then before the sun sets today, we will banish the evil that besets your body, once and for all."

The Storied Watcher paused for a second, then forcefully inveighed, with eyes both glowing and moistening, "By all that is holy, I *swear* it."

How do I know? reflected the alien woman, in her private mind.

I have never healed this particular malady... but I am so confident...

"I believe you, angel-lady," answered the little girl, with the kind of simple trust that only a child can bestow. "But how can you *do* this, when Doctor Kozimian tried as hard as he could to help me? He's not a bad guy, you know; I guess that this was just too hard for him. It's not his fault."

Karéin-Mayréij reassured, "Of *course* I know, Juanita. And Doctor Kozimian is will help you now, along with the rest of us – and he will learn how to cure other little girls and boys, in the same way. Do you want me to tell you what is going to happen?"

The sick little girl just nodded affirmatively.

There was the sound of two plastic buckets being dropped, as Kozimian and Freddie came through the doorway and beheld the scene.

White as a sheet, the doctor, knowing that he was far out of his league, managed to mumble, "You... uhh... you want them on either... side... of her... is that right?"

The alien-girl turned her head slightly to gaze at Kozimian. She nodded, then instructed, "Take one tube for each bucket; make sure that its far end is almost at the bottom of the container; then, place the near end by the top of Juanita's leg."

Just like with the drapery, at this, the bed-covers rolled back, exposing the child's abdomen, and her hospital-gown turned up to expose the flesh of her thigh.

As the doctor reluctantly complied with these orders, the Storied Watcher continued, "Doctor, I have read your histories, and I thought that you might find the following, to be interesting... Juanita, you should pay attention, too, oh-kay? Mr. Kozimian, do you remember how, in the bygone years of this 'Earth', healers used to bleed their patients, to make them well?"

"Do I... *what*? Sure I do, we had to take it in first year med-school, but – oh, for God's sake, you can't be *serious* – that's medieval *nonsense!*" he protested. "Listen, Ms. 'Karéin', I know what I saw when I came into contact with you, but this makes no sense at all –"

"Peace," she commanded, with a stately glare. "What we shall do, only outwardly resembles the practice with which you are familiar."

Karéin-Mayréij turned to the little girl, and, staring deep into her eyes, explained, "Juanita, what we will do – ah, I guess that this might be a little difficult to explain in your language, is, we are going to join with your mind; you will hear and feel our thoughts inside your head. Especially when you touch with my own mind, you might find this to be, ah, a bit... *scary*, and that goes for all of you who listen to this – so be ready... and do not be afraid. Nothing that you see of me can hurt you."

"Sure *hope* so," weakly joked Losada, a gesture that was rewarded by a friendly smile on the part of the Storied Watcher, who continued, "Oh, and you will also hear six other voices... these may sound rather... *unusual*. Do not worry about them, they are on our side, too... and one will sound, uhh, 'older', 'wiser' than the others... pay special attention to what that one – her name is *Vîrya Quü'j* – requests that you do. We must use our minds, to lend the force of our own lives to yours, as we clean out the cancer. So far, so good?"

"Wow... you can do *that*?" gasped the wide-eyed child.

A shudder of life and hope shot through the room.

"Yes," nonchalantly confirmed the Storied Watcher. "Now... here is the even *more* scary part. You will feel my mind wandering all over the inside of your body – I am sorry, there is no good way for me to describe how this will feel, you'll just have to find out for yourself – and will guide Doctor Kozimian's mind along with me, so he can learn how to recognize what the bad cancer-cells, uhh, 'smell' like."

"And... uhh... what happens then?" timorously inquired the doctor.

"When we find these evil, tainted essences," elaborated Karéin-Mayréij, addressing the girl, "We will use some special tricks that your body and mind have hidden away, just for emergencies like this. Your body will make the bad cells become hot – I mean *really* hot, enough for you to feel a little pain in that place, so be ready for it – and when we do that, the cancer-cells will burn up and *die*, Juanita. We are going to *exterminate* them, each and every last one, and they will *never* come back. *Ever*."

I know how to do this, realized Karéin-Mayréij.
With each word of bravado... I just came to know.
How?

"There are *millions* – billions of them," argued Kozimian. "If you did a thousand every second, you'd never have the *time* –"

"Just *watch* me, Doctor!" retorted the young-looking woman. "And make your mind drop its cynicism... its incredulity. For when we are through with this, *you* will be the one to teach students of medicine, what you will learn here today. You cannot teach what you do not believe, when you see it in front of you."

"One last thing, darling child," added the Storied Watcher, again turning to look at the little girl. "My mind will be with you when we kill the cancer-cells, and I will help you suppress the pain – but you must be brave and try to do it by yourself, as much as you can. When the cancer dies, it becomes a poison; and if we were to leave it in your body, this would eventually kill you as surely as would the disease. So what we will do, is to force it out, through these little tubes that you had in your nose, earlier. They have to go into the big blood-vessels in your legs. This will sting a bit at first... but then you will become used to it. Are you ready, Juanita?"

"Yes, I am," answered the child, plainly and honestly.

A second later, she winced and let out a low cry of pain, as two small gashes mysteriously appeared on either side of her thigh; into these, shot the near end of the former breathing-tubes. A few drops of blood issued into the top of the tubes, but then, some other force constricted the child's arteries, and the flow stopped.

"Oh-kay," confirmed the newcomer, as her haunting, thrilling, faraway song of healing waxed in the minds of everyone around. "Doctor, place your hand over that of mine, and over that of *Abuela*. Freddie, take the other hand of your daughter – and I warn you, I did not idly say that I am different from any man or woman who has ever trod the face of this world – you are about to experience something that will be exciting and frightening, all at once; but do not fear and do not break our circle... remember why you are here. Once we start, we *must* carry through all the way and finish this 'cancer'-thing, once and for all. Are you ready?"

"*Sì*" echoed from several in the room.

Of its own accord, the buckler came off the alien-woman's arm, coming to rest on the ill child's midriff.

"Venerable *Vìrya Quü'j*," quietly inveighed the Storied Watcher, lightly fingering the amulet at her breasts, "I beg thee should counsel thy great-sisters, *Vìrya Ahn'jë* and *Vìrya I'ëà'b'*, in the breath of life, and lend thy healing-skills, to our own, also to this man who is called, 'Doctor'."

As a thousand ethereal violins started to add their voices to the life-song playing in the background, Karéin-Mayréij – now become not the Destroying Angel, but, instead, something quite unlike – closed her eyes, whispered some unknown invocation, then turned her face skyward.

In all three of English, Spanish and her own, incomprehensible language, along with the tune she sang, "Powers of Light, now guide our way, we pray."

She stared deeply into Juanita's eyes, and instantly, the journey began.

A second or two later, something like blood – but darker, foul-smelling – started to drip down the tubes.

A Promise For Juanita

Other than for the alien-girl – who had never really fallen asleep, in the first place – Losada was the first one to awake.

Groggy-headed from sensory-overload, psychic-exhaustion and just plain astonishment, he ran a rough hand over his half-shaved face, awkwardly wiping the sweat and oil on the lower reaches of the bed-clothes, a second later.

Had he not just participated in the arcane ceremony, he would have jumped back in surprise at the sight of his daughter's head peacefully cradled in the lap of a dull-glowing humanoid being, the latter bedecked in some kind of iridescent, semi-translucent black-ivory body-armor, complete with sword and shield, with her fore-body propped up against the bed's head-board and a flowing cape beneath her figure. The weirding-armor was giving off a shimmering aura of heat; but somehow, this appeared to be harming neither the child nor the bed-covers.

"*Carajo*," he cursed, as the stench of what was in the buckets offended his nostrils. "*Mujer*, this stuff stinks to high –"

Karéin-Mayréij lifted her index-finger to her lips.

"Softly, now," she warned, *sotto voce*. "The little one has lost a lot of body-fluid; and although the intra-vee-nus thing up there will help, she needs to sleep and regain strength."

"Okay," whispered Freddie. "But I'll get this crap out of here – *Dios mio*, I'm amazed that this stink hasn't woken everybody else up, already."

"Here... I will help you," quietly stated the alien, as she somehow slipped effortlessly out from under the child, supporting Juanita's head with a pillow, in the same motion. Both buckets now rose into the air and slowly began to head out of the bedroom, followed close behind by the man and the young-looking woman.

"Uhh, listen, Miss 'Karayn' or whatever it is, is your name..." started Losada.

"It is 'Karéin-Mayréij'," explained the Storied Watcher, matter-of-factually. "'Kar-AY-en may-RAY-jeh' – that is how one pronounces it... but it is oh-kay if you do not say my name properly; it is from a language that is – ahem – not frequently spoken, around here."

They tip-toed out of the bedroom, into the kitchen.

"Yeah, right, well, whatever... but, uhh, like, what I wanted to say is, I don't know how to *thank* you," whimpered Freddie, not bothering to hide the tears in his eyes. "*Gracias a Dios*, you've given me back my daughter! I don't know how... but you did. Thank you... thank you, from the bottom of my heart."

She allowed the buckets to float gently to the ground, then turned to suddenly embrace him.

"That is more than thanks enough,' compassionately replied Karéin-Mayréij. "All that I ask is, that the next time when you shall find a stranger in need – lend him, or her, a 'helping hand', as my mate Bob used to say. And do not be surprised if you can now do things that you previously thought that you could not. That is how it begins, you know."

"What do you mean?" he asked. "What's, uhh, 'it'?"

"You have been strengthened, Freddie Losada," she explained. "As have all who helped guide your daughter back from the edge of the Land of the Dreaming Dead. To all of you, I give the gift of long life and – over time – the gift of slowly being able to see your world in its true beauty... and other things, besides. As it happens, it will be apparent to you. And as it turns out, there were no way to help your daughter, without at the same time empowering you and your family, plus the doctor, anyway."

"That's, like... *heavy*," offered Freddie, not really knowing what the hell she was saying, or meaning.

"Right, well, I guess I'll dump this," he added, grabbing one of the buckets and hefting it up, taking great care not to spill a single drop, while the young-looking woman acknowledged the effort with a broad smile.

After he had left, the Storied Watcher half-spread her arms and legs, rose about an inch off the ground and made a slight nod of the head, and in no more than a half-second, the strange gear in which she had previously been garbed, vanished, as if into thin air.

Now, the alien-girl was clothed in no more than her shining, multi-colored bikini, plus the amulet.

Hmm, she mused, as she looked around the kitchen, after Freddie had gone off to the bathroom.

A radio-music box. That would be something good for the little one to hear, when she wakes up... as long as I can find some nice melodies within it, as opposed to that 'hip-jump' nonsense that Curtis listened to, all the time.

Why would one willingly listen to someone who is always yelling at you and threatening you... let alone, do that for entertainment?

She shot a look at the device and had her mind depress its 'on' push-button.

Instantly, a rather too-loud cacophony of brass-backed Tex-Mex music wailed out of the thing.

In a second or two, she had found where the 'volume' wheel was, and again, the unseen forces that she habitually used, turned it so that the music was down to a soft background-hum.

Not exactly my kind of melody, thought the Storied Watcher.

But then... they have never seen the instruments upon which I learned that craft, on this world.

"Well... I'm real glad *that's* over with,' grunted Freddie, as he came back from the washroom, two buckets in tow. "Tried to wash 'em out three times, but that smell is still all over 'em... I guess I'll just chuck these things – bad memories anyway."

He did a double-take, looking appreciatively at Karéin-Mayréij.

"F'ing *amazing*," exclaimed Losada. "Man – I should've tried a little harder back at the bar... you know? Oh, sorry, forgot, you're kind of an... you know. Where all that stuff you had on... where'd that go?"

"My little secret," primly answered the young-looking woman.

"Okay... but, listen, you, uhh... you want something to wear? Don't know what I got – but just in case *Abuela* wakes up, she's a bit *conservative*, you know..."

"Sure," she cheerily confirmed. "Whatever you have, would be fine. But, please make it something that you can afford to be without... it might be, ahem, a little difficult for me to return it in the near future. Oh... and could I perhaps 'borrow' those interesting-looking sunglasses that you have on the ledge underneath the kitchen-window? Do you see them – they are the ones with the multi-color-mirror coating."

"*No problemo*," quickly agreed Freddie. "They're kinda cheap, anyway, they don' keep out nearly as much light as the tag on 'em said in the store."

"That suits me rather well," mentioned the alien-girl.

She looked at the pair of wrap-around, highway-driving mirror shades, and they flew, unaided, into her hand.

Vîrya Ahn'jë, silently instructed Karéin-Mayréij,

Hold it not against thy mother, if she meld the essence of these no-eyes goggles, later with thy own.

Then thou shall see this world as do I...

"She doin' okay, still?" inquired the man, glancing at the bedroom.

There was no reply.

"Hey – you still with us there?" he implored.

"Yes – but you did not have to ask me that, Freddie," remarked the young-looking woman, as if coming out of a dream. "You are now bound to your daughter in a way that few fathers could *dream* of being. Just ask your heart."

"Yeah," mumbled Freddie, not wanting to admit that he half-understood what she was saying. "Be back in a bit."

He went off around the corner and started rummaging through a closet.

"Whoa!" interrupted a third voice, upon casting eyes on the Storied Watcher's shapely, scantily-dressed figure. "Like... what happened to your, uhh, clothes?"

"I put them away, and they are not really 'clothes', Alfredo," responded the young-looking woman, as she looked at the second Hispanic man, perhaps a half-head taller and five to ten years older than Freddie. "*Vîrya Ahn'jë*, her sister and brothers, you might think of them as... ah, it is kind of hard to explain, in your language. I gave them life; they are *part* of me. Remember the little voices that you heard from time to time, when we were all helping Juanita?"

The man leaned heavily against a wall.

"Oh, man – don't remind me of *that*," he complained. "Whole thing was weird, just *too* weird, like a really good synth – but listen... how you know my name, anyway?"

"We came to know each other on a very intimate level," explained the newcomer. "There is not much to hide, when minds travel together. I hope that you remember as much of it as you can, and tell your niece the story, so that she remembers it, too."

"Yeah," said Alfredo. "I'll try – that's for sure. Mind if I join you? I need a coffee, after all that."

"Be my guest," she offered.

The chair on the other side of the kitchen table now moved out, without any apparent motive force, to provide a sitting-place for the man.

"Holy shit," he stammered. "You do *that*?"

She nodded, a wry smile on her face.

"Does not everyone?" she insouciantly added.

Freddie showed up again, this time with a motley collection of dank-smelling, old clothes in hand.

"This is the best I could do," he apologized. "Some of it's left over from when Alfredo's step-daughter used to be stayin' with us... hey 'Fraido – it okay if I let her have a couple of things?"

"Oh yeah," quickly confirmed the taller man. "She's off in college now, anyway."

Freddie held the bundle out in front of the Storied Watcher.

"So you want to go off to the washroom and try some of these on?" he asked. "I'd offer to put whatever you pick through the washin' machine... but we'd blow our water-ration in one shot. I guess we could do 'em in the sink."

"Not necessary," countered Karéin-Mayréij. "Just leave them on the floor."

"Whatever you say," uncertainly echoed Freddie. He dropped the clothes from his arms, and they ended up in a disorganized heap on the floor-tiles.

A second later, some unseen force seized control of the collection, and, tornado-like, it began to spin in front of the alien-girl, who now stood up, arms outstretched as if ready to embrace someone, with a dull glow in her eyes.

"Hmm, no... not that one," she said, talking to herself. "Too small. Now *that* one – nope, too, ah, 'confining'. Oh, wait – *there* is a nice shirt, and, wow – a pair of those 'stretch-pants', just like I had back at... I will take those simple sandals and the little hat, too, if that is allowed. Alright... I have finished. You can put the rest of them back wherever they came."

As she said this, a blue-and-gold baseball cap with 'South Tucson Knights of Columbus' inscribed upon it, a plain white T-shirt, a gray pair of women's track-pants and a cheap-looking pair of plastic sandals, exited the mini-tornado and continued to float in mid-air, while the rest of the clothes slumped back to the kitchen floor.

With jaws dropping, Freddie and Alfredo watched as a paralyzing wave of cold washed over the clothes that the Storied Watcher had selected; this was followed a split-second later, by a choking, stifling wave of heat, as if an oven had been opened nearby; then a second cold-shock hit the garments, followed by a final, less potent blast of warm air.

A fine film of dust fell on to the floor and the clothes floated over to the alien, instantly finding their way to the appropriate reaches of her frame.

She turned to regard the two men with a look both goofy and sublime.

"Want to smell?" she teased. "As fresh as the morning dew."

"You, uhh... don't *say*," managed Alfredo.

"In my line of work, I do not visit the laundry-mat place, very often, you know," she joked.

"So... you got any plans for the afternoon?" asked Freddie, hopefully.

"No, but, the thing is, you see – ohhhhh!", she moaned, as Karéin-Mayréij was cut off in mid-sentence.

Sweat appeared on her face, as the alien-girl doubled over, bending forward to look straight down at the floor.

"Hey – *hey!*" shouted an alarmed Alfredo, rushing over to assist this strange creature. "What's the matter? You okay?"

He did not dare say, however, what came to his mind, next.

Shit, look at those teeth, *what kind of angel looks like Nosferatu – ?*

"No," gasped the Storied Watcher, shaking her head in obvious pain. "Definitely *not* oh-kay. Curse them – curse them to the lowest *hell!*"

A suffocating wave of psychic anger washed over the two perplexed men.

"Whoa!" exclaimed Freddie, staggering backward. "What the fuck was *that*? We didn' do something wrong, did we?"

By now, the alien-girl had regained some of her composure, though her visage was still twisted in dismay, when she looked up at them.

"No... not your fault... not your fault at all," she forced out. "*Their* fault. Theirs alone."

"Whose?" demanded Alfredo. "Who you talkin' about?"

"Oh, *mann*," interjected the doctor, who evidently had been woken by the Storied Watcher's mental outburst, and who had appeared in the entrance-way to the hall and bedroom. "Had a bad enough hangover, after what went on with your daughter, Freddie – now *this*, on top of it. What's going on?"

Kozimian noticed the Storied Watcher, and began, "Oh... hi there... I see you've had a change of clothes..."

He felt stupid at not being able to think of something more profound, but then, taking another glance at her, he added, "Listen... you don't look too good there – want me to get my bag? I've got painkillers, anti-nausea pills, better stuff than you can get over the counter, you know –"

"Thanks, Doctor," muttered Karéin-Mayréij, again gesturing in the negative. "But... your little tablets... would not work on me; and even if they *did*, this is not the kind of problem that can be repaired by chemicals."

"Well then, what's wrong with you?" he inquired. "You look as pale as a sheet."

"Yeah – time for some food, that'd do you good, lady," offered Freddie.

He grabbed a box of something from the cupboard, retrieved a milk-container from the refrigerator and started rummaging around for a bowl.

"It is a, how would one say, 'long story'," slowly answered the young-looking woman, as she managed to settle back into her seat. "All that I care to say, is... I *felt* someone – most likely, your accursed U.S. government – tormenting my dear friend, Bob Billings. He cries out in pain... and this can plague my own mind, like a daytime nightmare; sometimes, when they so afflict him, I can see poor Bob, for a fleeting second or two, and in that moment, I try to send him my love... my strength. But perhaps it is not as bad a curse as you might first think; for at least I am made to suffer for my cowardice and stupidity, in abandoning my lover, my friends and my... *son*."

She looked completely miserable, in saying this.

"Don' be so hard on yourself," offered Freddie. "Them *Federales* show up, it's time to run – either you do that, or they get you too. All 'bout survivin'... that's how I look at it."

"'Bob Billings'?" asked Alfredo, regaining his chair as the doctor took another from beside the table. "Who's that?"

"A very nice man... my 'boyfriend'," she replied. "Along with a woman named Whitney Houston, her two children, and my beloved son, Tommy Singing-Bird George; these all were kidnapped by the American government, for reasons that I do not understand... although, I have my suspicions. They are being held somewhere I do not know – probably, somewhere far away from here – and they are being abused, one by one. I *must* find them, and free them. I *have* to."

"You got a... *boyfriend*?" said Kozimian. "You know... when we were all in there... and when we were helping Juanita, I mean... I'm not a religious man, but they said you were an..."

She looked at him straight-on.

"What is the matter, Doctor?" deadpanned Karéin-Mayréij. "Are angels not supposed to have lovers?"

"Frankly, uhh... no, they aren't," he tried to claim. "They're supposed to be pure – free from the sins of the flesh, and so on. At least from what I know of the theology of it all."

"The theo-what?" asked a perplexed Freddie, as he dolloped some of the mixture that he had just stirred into an off-white batter, into a frying pan.

"Theology," explained Kozimian. "It means, 'having to do with religion'."

"Oh," grunted Losada.

"Ah... more nonsense about 'sin', namely, divine punishment for doing what comes naturally," remarked the Storied Watcher, in return. "I should track down whomever invented this stupid idea, and cuff his ears as commentary upon it."

"You wouldn't be very popular with the Pope," opined the doctor.

"Apparently, I am not very popular with your American President, either," mentioned the newcomer. "Which means, should agents of your U.S. government come to call on you, I would suggest that you tell them absolutely *nothing* about me, or about what I have done here. It would be safer for you."

Freddie deposited a platter heaping with fresh pancakes, in the middle of the table.

"Dig in," he suggested, followed quickly by, "Oh, sorry – I forgot the plates and the butter and the syrup."

These items, too, quickly found their way to the table. Alfredo and Kozimian grabbed one plate each, while a third floated, of its own accord, to land in front of the alien-girl. In the same way, three pancakes flew off the top of the stack on the platter, to be drenched with corn syrup.

"You don' want any butter?" inquired Freddie, looking at the Storied Watcher's plate, swimming as it was in the golden liquid.

"No... just this nice sweet stuff," she answered, between mouthfuls.

"It's good to see a smile back on your face," he noted. "That kind of sucks... I mean, the 'I feel your pain' thing."

"If only you knew how *much* it, uhh, 'sucks'," she grumbled.

"Something to drink?" he asked.

"Do you have any of that yellow-colored – oh yes – 'orange juice'?" she replied. "Bob bought some from a store we visited, while we were all with him. I am partial to its half-sweet, half-tart taste."

"*No problemo,*" cheerfully said Freddie, retrieving a carton of 'Cuban-Maid' from the fridge.

"Listen, Ms... Ms 'Karéin'..." started Kozimian.

"It is actually '*Karéin-Mayréij*'," she corrected. "'Kar-AY-en may-RAY-jeh', as near as you can say it in Eng-lish."

"So, 'May-ray-je' is your last name... do I have that right?" inquired the doctor.

This is the chance of a lifetime, he silently thought.

National Science Foundation prize, no 'ifs', 'ands' or 'buts'.

"No, it is the second half of my first name," she pointed out.

"Well, then – what *is* your last name?" he demanded.

"I do not believe that I have one," explained the Storied Watcher.

"Ms... Ms. 'Karéin-Mayréij', if I may be so bold – what I mean is – what I'd like to know, is –" stuttered Kozimian.

"You mean to ask, am I from Planet Earth... am I an 'alien', from the perspective of human beings like yourself, right?" remarked the newcomer, as if describing her professional accreditation.

"Uhh... yeah, I guess," he admitted.

"The answer is, 'yes', Doctor Kozimian," continued Karéin-Mayréij. "I am *indeed* an alien – from a far-off world and an even more far-off time, or dimension. I may *resemble* you humans; but please believe me when I say, I am *not*... my physical appearance is just one of my natural defenses."

She looked up at him, with intense, unnaturally-beautiful, blue-green eyes, as another fork-full of syrup-soaked pancake disappeared down her gullet.

"I... *see*," said Kozimian, trying not to stare.

"So... you're *not* an angel?" asked Alfredo.

"*You* tell *me*," she evaded, staring off into space for a moment. "You would be a better judge of it."

"Well, wouldn't you *know*, if you *were*, one?" pressed the taller Hispanic man.

"Look – what do you want me to *say*?" shot back the Storied Watcher, with mild irritation. "Sometimes, yes... I *do* feel as if work to a higher purpose... like, for example, when I was leading sweet little Juanita back to the land of the living, with your help, of course. But I honestly do not *know*."

"Well, in church, them priests, they tell us that angels all have wings, an' they –" began Losada, only to be interrupted again by the alien-girl.

"You humans have such a unimaginative, dogmatic idea of what an 'angel' is, anyway," she argued. "Is it not possible that there could be *many* types of these beings – ranging from weak and human-like ones, maybe including myself in that category – to truly other-dimensional ones, with very little in common with you or me? And I can turn the question around – when you were helping Juanita, did *you* not feel a little, 'supernatural'? Did *you* not feel the, umm, hand of God, guiding you?"

"Yeah... I suppose I did," uncomfortably allowed Kozimian.

"No-one," opined Karéin-Mayréij, "Can write a scroll truthfully saying, 'the minute when *this* or *that* happens to you – the second when *this* particular thought appears in your head – then you will know that you are an acolyte of the Almighty'. We each must do what we can, and if we are to be truly... *divine*, then we must search for those qualities inside ourselves, and we must use them with conscience – for I doubt that the Great Spirit wants Its servitors to be mindless automatons... with free will, inevitably comes imperfection."

All three men were now listening intently, as she continued, "But being imperfect, does not mean that you, or I, cannot still do good things... noble things... *angelic* things. All that we can hope is that the good that we do, outweighs the bad, and that it moves us a tiny, little bit further along on the path to the Realms of the Divine. Ever has life been thus, since the dawn of intelligent thought, in the universe to which you and I both, belong."

The alien-girl paused for a second, then added, "I think that Bob would have said, 'end of rant', about now. Does that answer your question?"

"Uhh... yeah, I suppose," uneasily confirmed the doctor.

"Teach you to argue with an alien... or an angel," joked Freddie.

He handed a glass of orange juice to the Storied Watcher.

"Bottoms up," she toasted, slurping half the glass back in one gulp.

"Mmm," murmured the newcomer, in mild contentment at the taste.

"Okay – I've learned my lesson, I suppose," grumbled Kozimian. "But listen, Ms. Karéin-Mayréij, I was wondering, well... I don't want to take you out of your way, but... I was thinking...."

"Were things less, ah, *unsettled*, right now, Doctor Kozimian," interrupted Karéin-Mayréij, "Yes... I would then have welcomed the chance to accompany you to your hospital, and there, to have willingly submitted to all the tests you could think of to run on my body; for, in the long-run, I do not want to be a mystery to humankind. I want to share my knowledge with your people, since there is much that I could help you with."

"Well, then... what's the problem?" he demanded.

"Unfortunately," explained the Storied Watcher, "Right now, you see, I am a fugitive – I am hunted by your American President and the many spies and warriors who he has under his command. Maybe they want my death; maybe they just want to capture me and use me as a weapon – a 'bargaining-chip' as Bob would say – against the other empires of your world... but one way or another, I have no intention of co-operating. So I am afraid that for the time being... I must decline your offer. Perhaps when all of this is over with, then I will come to call upon you... and we both will have more time to learn each others' arts of medicine."

"I suppose you read *minds*, too," complained Kozimian.

"Yeah," she stated. "I try not to... *most* of the time."

"If you don' mind my askin'," inquired Freddie, "Why they have it 'in' for you? I mean, if you could do for other folks what you just did for my little girl..."

She looked up, with a darkening countenance. "Why not ask *them*, Freddie Losada?" she growled. "I have done *nothing* to antagonize your leaders, other than showing up here on Earth, that is – and I really had little choice about landing on your planet, in the first place. So far, they have tried to kill me – not to mention everyone anywhere around me – at least once, and then they kidnapped and started torturing poor Bob, my friends and – Gods forbid – my adopted *son*, undoubtedly to get information as to my own whereabouts and abilities. They would probably offer you or the Doctor, a nice ransom for my poor hide, by the way."

He gave her a knowing look.

"Ever since before I could remember, you *don'* want to get on the bad side of the Government," quietly commented Losada. "And you *don'* want to get their attention. Folks who ask too many questions, who stir things up, they just... *disappear*, I guess. Guys like 'Fraido 'n me – we just keep our heads down and try to get on with our lives... you know?"

"Well, then, I think that you have answered your own question," offered Karéin-Mayréij.

"Look – I know them guys from the Government is mean *hombres*," interjected Alfredo, "But... don' you think you'd be better off just givin' yourself up to them nice and quiet, rather than tryin' to hide out, all on your own? I mean, down here, we don' really give a shit about them Tucson city cops – they're stupid and they're just tryin' to keep the lid on, keep the *Maras* from runnin' completely out of control and all that – but Freddie's right... you *don'* want to get them *Federales* on your tail. They ain't *never* missed... not that I know of. If they want to take you out, it's just a matter of time. Usually, not a *lot* of time."

"Did it occur to you, human," replied the Storied Watcher, ominously, "That they might have good *reason* to be afraid of me?"

In an instant, her eyes were eerily glowing, as a wave of fear, accompanied with psychic electro-music, resounded in the minds of the three men.

"Freddie... I trust that this utensil would not be too great a loss," she announced.

Her fork stood to attention in the middle of her outstretched palm, then – in the blink of an eye – it flamed and melted into a pool of silver-gray slag, encased in a faint, glowing aura.

The alien-girl poured this infernal liquid downward toward her now-clean eating-plate; but halfway, the men perceived a blast of ferocious cold, and by the time that the molten remains of the fork hit the plate's surface, it was again congealed into a solid mass.

"That was but a small demonstration," she coolly noted. "For the sake of you and your people... let us hope that I do not have to give your President, a *big* one."

"Holy *shit*," gasped Alfredo. "No *wonder* Mr. President Man wants you as his Number One Weapon."

"I do not *want* to be a weapon," countered the newcomer. "For the United States Empire – or against it. But I *do* want to make my own decisions, I *do* want my friends back, and I *do* want them back unharmed. Each blow that the torturers who serve your President, inflict upon Bob, Whitney, Curtis, Melissa, or... Tommy, will be repaid in *terrible* coin! And, the pain that I felt earlier, was not the first. When I call your 'government' to account... I would advise all of you not to be anywhere in the vicinity."

"And now, for the news," interrupted a voice over the radio, in the background.

Freddie arose to turn it off, but he was stopped by a shake of the alien-girl's head, as she looked over her shoulder.

"I do not mind hearing it," she said, "And hopefully, that music with all the wind instruments will be back on, shortly."

The broadcast started to drone on about the usual litany of robberies, shootings, drug crimes and public executions; there was a report about violent arrests against an "illegal contraceptive and anti-fertility literature distribution-ring" and also something about a 'big explosion', somewhere in the Indian subcontinent.

"On the state-wide front," announced the radio, "Governor Ratcliff re-assured the Legislature that the evacuation-exercises now taking place in New York and Washington would not be implemented in Tucson and Phoenix for the time being, since these cities are not considered to be at high risk from..."

"Oh-kayyyy," nervously remarked Kozimian, "I... uhh... assume that you don't want us to tell any of this to the Government... right?"

"As I said, Doctor," counseled Karéin-Mayréij, "The best way for you to handle this, is just to 'play stupid' and deny that you ever met me. If they find out, none the less, it would not matter if you were to tell them, what I just told you. They know it, already."

"Nationally," the radio blathered, "The President has again rejected speculation that the Special State of Emergency will be repealed anytime soon; in a press-release, he states, 'Until each and every one of these weapons has been located and eliminated, the borders of the United States will remain securely sealed'. The White House goes on to acknowledge the significant economic challenges that have resulted from the State of Emergency; however, it concludes by saying, 'we know that all patriotic Americans will pull together, to prevent even the most remote chance of the horrors of Mumbai, being replayed here'."

"Ha!" maliciously commented the Storied Watcher. "If your President does not honorably deal with me, he will discover that there *are* worse things than these 'atom bombs'."

"Oh, come *on*," protested Alfredo. "You sayin' you're more scary than one of them H-bombs? They can blast a whole *city*, after all."

At first, the alien-girl did not directly reply. Instead, she stared at the man intently, with a shine coming again to her eyes.

The house shuddered, and powerful music played briefly in the minds of the humans.

"Also in national news," continued the broadcast, "For the first time, the White House has admitted that due to gang-activity, a separate State of Emergency has existed in southern California for some time, with Greater Los Angeles being effectively a 'no-go zone' for the police."

"Well... we knew that already," grunted Losada, with a cynical chuckle. "So did anybody tryin' to get down there."

"According to the President's statement," blared the radio, "'We will not abandon the law-abiding people of Los Angeles to thugs, hoodlums and gangsters, and we will soon be taking measures to restore lawful authority to the area'. In the meantime, the government is instructing citizens of the L.A. region to remain indoors and to avoid confronting the many criminals who are roaming the streets. He also stated that to prevent the reinforcement of the urban gangs by outside elements, a quarantine on all vehicular-traffic in to and out of Los Angeles will be strictly-enforced, with the use of deadly force authorized against anyone attempting to evade these restrictions. Turning to sports, the Diamondbacks fell back to 2 and 3 yesterday, with a 6-5 loss to..."

The Storied Watcher shot the radio a baleful gaze, and its volume-level went way down.

"Hmm... it would seem that your President has many enemies to confront, including right within one of the great cities of this empire," she observed, perhaps trying to change the subject. "He needs not one more in myself."

"Don' make no sense," observed Alfredo. "Listen, lady... I believe you about the 'he better not f– with me' – but, then, why they givin' the gears to these friends of yours? What they got to *gain*?"

"Oh, come *on*, 'Fraido!" countered Freddie. "That just what they *do*, *hombre!* Remember what happen to Juan-Carlos, when they thought he was with the *Maras*? Poor bugger came back missin' an eye and his leg's so f–ed up that he can' hardly walk no more. Funny thing was – well I guess it wasn't too funny if you was Juan-Carlos – is then, them *Maras* got to him and messed him up even worse, 'cause they thought he was workin' double for the *Federales*. That's just how it happens, *hombre*... they don' need no reason... they just go ahead and do what they want to."

"*Lovely* little kingdom this 'United States' of yours," sarcastically commented Karéin-Mayréij. "With hindsight, perhaps I would have done better to have fallen to Earth, somewhere else. But here I am – 'angel' or no, I cannot re-make the past. All that I *can* do, is try to redeem myself with my family, for having led them into the calamity that they are now suffering. I *will* do that... I *swear* it!"

"I might regret sayin' this later," spoke up Losada, "But if you need somewhere to hang out – you know, keep a low profile away from the Man – you can hide out here, for a while. Least I can do, after what you did for Juanita."

Again, the Storied Watcher shook her head to contradict him.

"The last time when I did something like *that*, your government completely destroyed the house in which I was staying, while trying to kill me," she warned. "It was a *miracle* that Whitney and the children seem to have survived. I would not impose a risk like *that*, on *anyone*... let alone on a friend or a child like your dear little daughter."

"Finally, on the local arts-and-entertainment scene..." continued the radio broadcast.

"She got a point," argued Alfredo. "I can easily see them doin' something 'zactly like that, *hombre*. I mean, they blow up half a block every so often, if they think that the *Maras* got a safe-house somewhere inside it. For somebody like *her*, hell, I could see them blowin' up half of Tucson."

"I know... but I don' care," shot back Freddie. "Besides, if they don't *know* she's here, what difference would it make –"

"Just a second," interrupted Karéin-Mayréij, holding a finger up to her lips.

Inexplicably, the volume of the radio increased.

"The presentation, scheduled for tomorrow afternoon at the Hotel Arizona in downtown Tucson, will be given by Sylvia Abruzzio and Hector Ramirez, both senior scientists at NASA's Jet-Propulsion Laboratory in Houston," reported the voice on the radio. "Afterward, the scientists will oversee a special charity-donation drive to provide relief for the families of the many NASA scientists, who were injured or killed in the recent 'Lucifer' incident."

A look of immediate interest appeared on the face of the Storied Watcher, as the radio's volume went up, yet again.

"Tickets for the event are twenty-dollars per person over Neo-Net, or thirty at the door, with a half-price option for children and veterans," stated the announcer. "Attendees are reminded that guns, knives, Stop-A-Gangsta blister-gas spray-cans, shocking stun-guns and other types of weapons, as well as mini-vid recorders, camera-phones or body-jewelry with photo- or motion-picture-capture capabilities, are all prohibited and will be confiscated at the door, with a fifty-dollar processing-fee for the return of these items..."

"So what?" inquired Alfredo, with a shrug, as he finished off his last pancake.

But the newcomer was lost, deep in thought, as the radio concluded, "Turning to the motion-picture front, Tucson-area theaters report record crowds for the third 'Blaine Maine' movie, a situation said to have been partly caused by air-conditioning restrictions in much of the city, but also due to the public's need to escape from worries about the on-going Muslim threat. The light-hearted picture, described by the Disney News Channel as 'an instant classic', features Disney's latest teenage starlet as a misunderstood cheer-leader and heiress to a pesticide-and-herbicide company..."

"Sylvia... Hector..." mumbled Karéin-Mayréij. "They were on the little video-screen, along with the older man, and the warrior-man..."

"What you talkin' 'bout?" asked Freddie.

"*Whoa*," interjected Kozimian. "You don't mean that *you're* the one who was on that – the stuff that they showed everybody on TV, just before the comet –"

"I do not remember much of it... although my memories are returning, little by little," stated the alien-girl. "But yes, Doctor... I am *exactly* she, who you are thinking about."

"My *God*," he gasped. "Then... it's... *true*?"

The newcomer nodded, introspectively looking away.

Eventually, she added, "Yes. That *was* me, up there... I suppose."

"What do you *mean*, 'you suppose'!" exclaimed Kozimian. "How could you possibly forget doing something like *that*?"

"*You* try smashing a comet sometime, Doctor!" retorted Karéin-Mayréij "Tell me how good *you* feel, afterwards. And tell me how much of it that you remember."

"Aww, come *on*," protested Freddie. "President say that the Air Force blasted the damn thing, with this new 'Sword of Freedom' bomb –"

"By now," related the Storied Watcher, still half-lost in thought, "You should have learned a lesson, about believing what your American government says. If one word out of every sentence is true, then that, ahh, would be a 'good day'. It was desolate and cold on *Mailànkh*... ah, 'Mars'... *that* I will allow, but at least the rocks, sand and the voices of the Old Ones, did not tell me lies, all the time... so little had I, but so much..."

"Now I *know* why they want to catch you, or..." started Kozimian. "No offense, but if you could do *that*..."

The newcomer nodded in acknowledgement, as, somewhere, a different type of music played in the background.

"It was a *different* Karéin-Mayréij whose greatness and nobility, saved your world," she tried to explain. "I am fallen, *corrupted*... I am now, a lesser being – but the great Storied Watcher of yorethe one so much greater than mortals, she *will* return to me, in time. Only a short time, now..."

"You're not making a lot of sense," offered the doctor, nervously hoping that the creature in the same room with him, had just been bluffing.

"If you tried to explain how to play 'base-ball', to a dog or a new-born babe," answered the Storied Watcher, still staring away, "It would not make a lot of sense to *them*, either."

"Woof," joked Freddie, with a thin smile.

"Well, if you ain't stayin' here, or in the 'hood," asked Alfredo, "Where exactly *are* you goin'?"

"I believe that I will pay a visit to this 'presentation' that they just announced, over the radio," replied Karéin-Mayréij. "It may not be a coincidence that two of the very few humans who I came to know and, sort of, trust, during my trip back from Mars, are now in this city. Your 'President' may be impossible to bargain with in good faith; but perhaps there *are* others who do not agree with him... maybe this event is a way by which I can communicate with these dissident courtiers and nobles. And it is not too far from here – I should be easily able to travel there in time for the presentation. By the way... you would not happen to have some mon-ee to, ah, 'lend' me, would you, Freddie?"

"Oh, sure," answered Losada, hastily pulling his bill-fold out of his back pocket. "How much?"

"Thirty dollars," requested the alien woman. "Is that a lot? And in paper-plastic money, not coins, if you please. Coins make a 'clinking' sound, when one moves around with them... and that is a bad thing, for me."

"Right... not a lot, considerin' what a hospital costs these days –no offense you understand doctor... but, you sure that's enough?" said Freddie.

"I just need to pay for, uhh, admission," mentioned the Storied Watcher. "They do not demand money to let one leave, afterward... do they?"

"No, they only do *that*, when you done your time in jail," he replied, with a chuckle. "But what if you, uhh, like, wanna buy a drink, or something?"

"Good point," agreed Karéin-Mayréij. "Make it sixty. And consider this my, 'eye oh you'. I will pay you back handsomely, when this is all over with."

Freddie held out three twenty-dollar bills. These flew quickly into her hand, then disappeared somewhere.

"I was meaning to say," queried the doctor, "Are you sure *you* should have told us all this stuff? What if they do to *us*, what they did to this 'Billings' guy, and –"

At length, the Storied Watcher came to her feet.

"I have already told you more than enough about myself, to make all of you a target," she admitted. "For that, I sincerely apologize – but I could not save Juanita, without revealing my true nature; in life, one must undertake certain risks, for a greater good."

"Well now, don' *that* just give me the ol' 'warm and fuzzies'," muttered Alfredo.

"I know... and I fervently hope that I have, ah, 'covered my tracks', as Bob would say, in arriving here to your little house," she parried. "But – should the spies or warriors of your United States government show up here despite my best efforts – you should tell them the same as I asked Bob, Whitney and the others, to say."

"And what would *that* be?" demanded Kozimian.

"That," she warned, with an ominous, forceful stare, "They should leave you alone – else, I will exact a *terrible*, destructive revenge upon them. They will rue the day that they ever hurt dear Bob, my family... or yourselves. This I *promise!*"

"Doesn't seem to have helped your 'Billings' friend, very much," observed the doctor.

"Only because I have not yet been able to find him, or those who torment him," she retorted. "When I *do* – there will not be whole *atoms* left of whomever has been abusing Bob, Whitney, Curtis, Melissa and Tommy. *Especially*, Tommy."

None of the men said anything, as her gaze went from one face, to the other, then back again.

The Storied Watcher turned to address Freddie. "May I see Juanita for one last time?" she requested.

"Oh... absolutely," he answered.

Nodding, she turned and headed down the corridor to the bedroom, where the little girl and the grandmother, the latter having taken up a spot on the right side of the bed, with legs bent and her head on the covers, were still sleeping peacefully.

The newcomer went to the left-hand side, crouched down so that her face was level with the girl's, then took Juanita's hand.

"Little one," softly said Karéin-Mayréij, "How are you feeling?"

Slowly, the child's eyelids fluttered open, and a slight smile came to her face.

"I'm feeling a lot better, Missus Angel," she replied, "But I'm *awfully* hungry. I feel like I haven't had anything to eat in a week."

"That is to be expected," explained the alien-girl, with a kind expression. "Your body had to use a lot of energy, to burn away those hateful cancer-cells, and now you must replace these with good, healthy cells. Make sure that you eat and drink a lot of sweet-tasting things, for the sugar within them will help you to rebuild what has been banished. In a few days, you will be strong enough to get up and walk around, and after that... you will be just as healthy – more so, in fact – than any other little girl."

"Will I get sick again?" anxiously inquired Juanita.

"I do not think so," reassured the Storied Watcher. "It is unlikely that the cancer-cells will ever come back – but if they *do*, now you know how to find them and burn them so that they cannot hurt you. Make sure you do that immediately, if you feel those bad things trying to start up again... your body can handle the poison from a *few* of them being dead, but not from too many of them. You are now your own doctor, Juanita... pretty neat, eh?"

Gleefully, the child summoned all her strength, and nodded affirmatively.

"Pretty neat," she confirmed, her smile shining in the shadows of the bedroom. "I want to be a *real* doctor like Mr. Kozimian when I grow up, so I can heal other kids like me."

"That would be a great idea," agreed Karéin-Mayréij. "Promise me that you will try to do that."

"*Promise*," immediately answered Juanita. Then she followed up with, "Listen... I was wondering, Miss Angel... when I get better and go back to school... would you like to come for my next 'show and tell' session? I haven't been in two years... but now that I'm okay, I'm sure that Daddy will want me to start studying again..."

Brushing the child's hair with one hand, the newcomer evaded, "I would love to do that – but you and I both have much to do, between now and then. What did Bob call it... oh yes... I must give you a 'raining check' on that one, Juanita."

The little girl giggled. "Aww... and it's a 'rain' check, not a 'raining check', don't you know," she added. "So... are you staying with us for dinner? I bet Daddy would want to cook something *nice* for you, on the barbecue. Oh, and he'd give you a free case of *cerveca*. That's how he usually says 'thanks'."

"He has already thanked me," answered the young-looking woman. "As have you. That is all I really need. But I am afraid that I have to leave, now. I have an important appointment, downtown."

"*Noooo!*" cried Juanita. "You're just the nicest person that I've *ever* met. I don't *want* you to go!"

"I understand, dear," compassionately stated Karéin-Mayréij, "And I do not *want* to go, either, but I *must*... and that brings me to something else. If I ask you to do something for me – or, more precisely, *not* to do something – would you?"

"Um-humm," came back the answer. "I'm just little, Missus Angel Karéin, but I *know* what you did for me. I was going to... to... *die*, wasn't I?"

"Yes, you were," confirmed the Storied Watcher, in an even voice.

"So I'll do whatever you ask, forever and *ever!*" vowed Juanita, in that confident voice used sometimes by children.

"I will not hold you to the 'forever' part," explained the alien-girl, with a smile, "But listen... some bad men from the Government might come to your house and start asking, demanding, even, questions about me. If they do that, may I have your promise not to tell them anything? Or – if they will not leave without an answer – that you will just say something silly like, 'oh yeah, that is the space-lady who was on TV'? Do you understand what I mean?"

Juanita looked down, for a moment.

She said, in a knowing voice, "I sure *do*, Miss Karéin. Daddy and Uncle Alfredo have both told me about what happens when men from the Government come to our neighborhood. They're bad, and mean. Just before I got sick, they took Serena Nicandro's daddy away in a big black car, and Serena and her mommy had to go live in a shelter. I can still remember her crying when they beat Mr. Nicandro up, and threw him in the car. She was my *friend*, too. My bestest, *only* friend."

There was a wretched look on the little girl's face.

"I am sorry that your life is like this," quietly observed the Storied Watcher. "I really *am* – and, mark my words, child, I mean to *do* something about it... this disgraceful state of affairs will not stand; of *that*, you can be certain. But I have many other tasks to deal with, first. Which is why I must go."

Traces of tears appeared on the surface of Juanita's eyes.

"But I was just getting to *know* you, you know," she protested. "Since I got sick, I haven't had a lot of friends. Only Serena."

"If it is any consolation," noted Karéin-Mayréij, leaning over to hug the child, "I hardly have any, either. And the few that I *did* have – including my boyfriend Bob, and my own little son, Tommy – they were kidnapped and hurt very badly, by, I think, the same bad Government men who did that to your friend's daddy. But I *will* free them. I just need to find out where they are."

"Do you think you can get Serena's daddy, too?" hopefully asked Juanita.

"I will not mislead you, dear," answered the newcomer, "The chances that I will find him are not good, because your American empire has many prisons – he could be in any of them, if indeed he is still alive. What does he look like?"

"Like Daddy... sort of," explained Juanita. "Except he doesn't have a mustache, and he's shorter. He has a mole on his right cheek, and a red mark on his neck."

Her eyes shut, the Storied Watcher fell silent for a few seconds, then spoke. "With black hair parted in the middle, and a kind of 'twitch' in his right eyelid, you know, it blinks in a funny manner, every so often? And his first name is, uhh... 'En-ree-kay', or something like that?"

"That's *him!*" enthusiastically confirmed the child. "How did you *know?*"

The alien-girl pointed an index-finger at her temple and reminded, "I was inside your head... remember?"

"Oh... yeah," sheepishly admitted Juanita.

"If I see him," promised Karéin-Mayréij, "I *will* free him... I *swear* it! Now, one last hug."

She embraced the child, holding her tightly.

"Listen, Juanita," counseled the alien-girl, "If you hear stories about me doing... *bad* things – do not believe them... oh-kay? I do not *want* to hurt anybody, but... if they try to harm or kill people who I know and love – like yourself – I might have to fight back, and that would only be only fair... right?"

"Of *course* it would be fair!" affirmed the little girl, with an unusually-savage tone in her otherwise-cherubic voice. "Bullies *deserve* what they get, and those bad men from the Government, have it *coming* to them. But you wouldn't do anything bad. I *know* you wouldn't."

"May your words be ever true, dear child," softly invoked the newcomer.

Then she leaned over, kissed Juanita on the cheek, stood up and slowly moved away from the bed.

As the Storied Watcher tarried by the doorway to the corridor and parts beyond, she turned, one last time, to regard the fragile human being that she had saved from a melancholy fate.

"Live happy and long, Juanita... and remember this day," she wistfully prayed. "Be loved, and give the same, or more, back in return."

"*Vaya con Dios, querida ángel*," came the answer, in a small whisper.

We're The 'Professionals'

"Now, *now*, Mr. Billings," counseled the white-smocked, clean-shaven Caucasian man with the nerdy-looking glasses, "Let's not make this any more difficult than it *has* to be... okay?"

The salesman tried to recline back in the *faux* dentist-chair in which he was tightly strapped, but – surprise of surprises! he was rather too tense, to make the effort useful.

Despite this, he did manage to feign indifference to the entreaty, staring stony-faced at the domed, white-painted ceiling of this ceramic-tiled chamber.

The place was clearly meant to be antiseptic; but there was a faint, foul odor to it.

"Look, try to see it *our* way," echoed the other man, virtually a clone of the first, as he retrieved a sharp-looking, stainless-steel instrument from what appeared to be a doctor's bag. "All we're asking for is a little *information* – and this time, can we please make it something *plausible?* Humor us just this once... we've already *told* you – when it comes to telling the *real* stuff from baffle-gab made up just to get you out of old Mr. Whimpers, here," – he affectionately patted the seat's back-rest – "We're the *professionals*. There's just no *point* in trying to dissemble with us. We're going to get at the truth, eventually – one way or another. Why make it later, rather than sooner? The only difference is going to be the number of tears shed in the whole process."

"We're working a lot of overtime, these days," protested the first man, with an unctuous half-smile. "And we don't even get time and a half!"

Billings did not reply; he was trying to think neither of the bruises, nor of the rows of blood-stained stitches in his forearms, thighs and chest. But another idea did come to his mind.

Why am I playing hard-to-get, with these psychos? he idly wondered.

I'm no tough-guy – not by a country mile.

A month ago, I would have spilled the beans, if they had just twisted my arm too hard.

Still, it's eerily fascinating, watching them do this to me, as if I'm looking in from outside...

"Okay," offered the first man. "Since we unfortunately didn't make sufficient... *progress*, last night, we're going to have to take this to the next level, I'm afraid. A little something to lessen your inhibitions, as it were."

He showed Billings a double-sized syringe with an ominously long and sharp needle, filled with a bubbling, yellowish-green colored liquid.

"Normally," he continued with the too-familiar leer of a small man elevated to power by circumstance, while preparing a dentist-like set of shiny metal instruments on a table next to the restraining-chair, "We'd spout off some reassuring words like, 'now, this won't hurt at all'... but hey, 'truth in advertising' you know? So I'll just say, 'I bet you haven't ever had *this* shit before, man'. It'll be a whole new experience, for sure."

With no more warning than this, he thrust the evil thing right into the salesman's side. It sank in by at least two inches, spewing a hateful, yet ingeniously-crafted brew of corrosive chemicals and psycho-reactive drugs into Billings' chest-cavity, causing a wave of paralyzing, burning pain that, he somehow knew, should have instantly overwhelmed him.

I can feel *it eating away at my flesh, each and every nerve-ending screaming as it dies*, he realized. *Like a battery-acid booster-shot.*

I should be howling in agony, I should be howling for mercy, I should be... surrendering.

I can't handle this!.

But I am... handling it.

His tormentors had, apparently, moved off to a far corner of the room; but, none the less, Billings, possibly due to the stimulants that were meant to heighten his pain-responses, still manged to hear one of the 'professionals' whisper, "What the *fuck*? He *dead* or something? That was a triple dose, and he's just staring up at the *ceiling!*"

The more it hurts – and oh God I can feel *how bad it hurts – the more it feels... good, warm, like that blue muscle-rub gel-crap that they use in the massage-parlor*, Billings mused.

I should be wailing for Mommy, for anything to make it stop... but I'm not.

Let's face it, Bob... you got no clue about what's gettin' you through this.

The other one muttered, *sotto voce*, "Can't be... look at the display! Son of a bitch is still fully-conscious – that's what the machines say – and he isn't even going into shock. Vitals are showing A-OK – but you *know* we're taking chances, here... could be feedback... or maybe the box has been acting up since we stuck the probes into him? You think we should give him another shot, or switch to the model-train treatment?"

"If he was just a run-of-the-mill dissident, I'd say, 'go for it'," argued the first *faux*-doctor. "But orders from the Big Man – 'nothing likely to lose us this asset'... right? Any more than that, and he might end up without anything *left* in his gut... look, maybe the cocktail just needs a bit more time to do its magic. Let's give him an hour... then we'll re-assess. We still got some arrows in our quiver. Fucker still has eat and to *sleep*, you know – and HQ won't mind if he shows up missing a finger or toe, or two or three, or if he ends up singing a nice girly-man soprano."

Upon hearing the latter, Billings' mind felt a wave of gut-wrenching, primal dread.

They're going to cut me apart, piece by piece, he thought.

Should have talked, who the hell do I think I'm kidding... these guys are the best of the worst.

God, I wish I was back in Tucson, I'd never do anything stupid, anything out-of-the-ordinary, again... God, are you listening?

Then, to his amazement, he heard music and a gentle, ethereal voice, one both familiar yet wildly weird, compassionate yet with a message of iron will.

The trace of a tear, accompanied by a faint smile, showed on the salesman's otherwise impassive face, as he – or someone, *something* – forced the pain to the far reaches of his consciousness.

Oh my love, came a message, *I hear your cry... call my name, call it now!*

He tried to force out a gentle, familiar name, but his jaw was held securely shut, by some evil contraption that had been fixed over his head.

And, his mind heard, a second later,

Tell them, when I arrive there, surely...

Shall they die!

Just A Box, Along With The Candy

By now, the container – which, to any but the most highly-trained eye, which looked and was labeled like nothing more than a crate of mundane something-or-other from the fields of South America – had made its long journey along the coast of that continent.

In Paramaribo, it had quickly changed hands and had been put on a steamer, along with several crates of bananas.

There had been a minor crisis, when that boat had been stopped by the local naval-patrol. But there was a standing monetary-arrangement between the

Surinamese police and the steamer's captain – the former got their fair share of the profits, in exchange for not looking too carefully in the bilge, where the half-ton of finest white Colombian nose-candy had been secreted, while the latter got his cut from the Central American and Mexican gangsters – so, the boat plodded along the Caribbean coastline, to eventually dock at the still-sleepy little port of Puerto Barrios, in Guatemala.

In another, earlier time, the local CIA station chief, parachuted in there to keep the union organizers, peasants, human rights activists and other rabble-rousers from bringing anything like real democracy to this little puppet state, would have had his ear close to the ground, to catch wind of problems like this.

But the American Empire had grown complacent, and a fatal bit too arrogant, all at the same time. The Agency had had its spooky arse kicked out of Guatemala City when the U.S. Army landed in Cuba; and besides, its best human assets were – so it was thought – needed more for that difficult invasion business in Pakistan and Iran.

For the Emperor, or the Prince, to have no clothes, the cost would be ridicule : far worse, for him to be seen to have no whip. But it had been *years*, since anyone in the lazy, decadent American upper-class, had contemplated *that* classic of the Renaissance.

As the crate was loaded on to the lorry at the Puerto Barrios dockside, there were a few protests.

"¡*Carajo* – *ésta segura es pesada!*" one of the dockworkers had complained, as he had to assist the six others to heft the thing into the back of the truck.

"*Están embalando el apretado verdadero de la nieve actualmente, usted lo sabe,*" riposted the worker's team boss, with an indifferent shrug. "*Estoy apenas alegre que estamos vendiendo cualquier cosa, qué con todas estas drogas del sintético que son ascendente tan popular allí, actualmente,*" he had added.

All the same to them, after all. Business *is* business – who gave a damn *what* the fucking *Yanquis* were using for their kicks, these days?

As long as there were traditionalists up there in the big market who preferred the good old stuff to those stupid "synth" chemicals that had been all the rage for the last decade or so, the supply-chain would keep plenty of the product flowing north.

Hell – with things warming up as they had been lately – you could grow the *coca* halfway up the Andes, now... and "sealed border" or none, with international pseudo-capitalism, there was *always* a way to connect a willing seller with a willing buyer; the only thing that really changed, was the price.

But the price, not to mention the cost... was about to go *way* up.

'Rosalie' The Gate-Crasher

Yes, it *was* a *dry* heat, went the cliché; but none the less, a temperature of 45 degrees Celsius in the shade was nothing to be trifled with, as an awakened, empowered Karéin-Mayréij stole invisibly through the streets of downtown Tucson.

The very air shimmers with warmth, she thought.

And that works to my advantage – for there would be even less than usual for the humans to see, when looking at me with their limited eyesight.

But perhaps I should allow it to become closer to the outside temperature, inside my little bubble... even though it is a bit uncomfortable.

Who knows if their 'thermal-imagers' are good enough to see my cold-trail, or if their 'micro-radars' would detect their little electric-charges going astray, around me... but I hear no calls of panic, of warning.

'So far, so good', as dear Bob would say.

Mercifully, there were relatively few pedestrians to dodge as she neared her objective; most of the humans – at least, those of them who had any choice – were wise enough to stay out of the late afternoon Southwest inferno.

'Hotel Arizona', perceived the alien-girl.

Those big letters giving off the energy-particles glow like a candle in a cave. I would not even have to let any of the other seeing-waves in through my bubble.

Oh, and there is another sign – it must go by two names, 'Hotel Tucson', as well.

Now, she hid herself behind a concrete supporting-pillar, within a split-level parking-garage across the street from the hotel.

No spies or army-guards in here, close though I am, now, realized the newcomer.

No doubt this 'President' man has enough warriors to have had one or more, at each five paces distance... but perhaps he does not want to alarm the common-people, with a large military operation.

I would not desire that if I were him, after all... what with those murderous 'Muslim League' zealots, threatening to burn entire cities with their stolen atom-splitting bombs.

I sure hope that this 'Tucson' place is not on their target list, she worried.

My bubble might not yet withstand such a terrible blast – especially if it starts nearby... the warning-senses are ever-quick... but are they fast enough?

Because if not...

She suppressed a fearful shudder, then, cautiously, peeked out from behind this structure, surveying the situation.

Hmm, mused the Storied Watcher.

A cordon of men in full battle-gear, each smelling of boredom, of exhaustion, because of the weather conditions.

Odd, though... they are different from the army-warriors that I have seen around this city, since I arrived here. They look more like the ones from the camp where I met Bob, my darling Tommy and the rest of my family.

Well... these 'Americans' have many armies and spies – some in the pay of this 'President' of theirs – some who answer to others of noble birth.

It matters little to whom they owe allegiance; I will have to steal past them as swiftly as I can, one way or another.

Wishing that she had had some way to have used that convenient 'NeoNet' thing to scout out the situation in advance, the alien-girl's vision and perception swept the scene in all directions, as she considered her options.

There were those warriors with the big rifle-guns, up on various building-roofs, and some of them had the little radar-scopes whose sounds clicked and warbled in her mind. There were several more men and women, each dressed in the drab, black suits with the funny 'neck-ties' that Bob had told her about, at each entrance, as well as other impediments in her way.

From behind, Karéin-Mayréij suddenly heard a distant, roaring sound. Instantly turning her head to look backward down the driving-path, her senses saw a bright visible-light from two round sources, about a man-length apart, as a sedan eventually rolled past her, turning to the right at the junction of the garage and the outside street.

I had forgotten how noisy in sound and energy-vibrations, that these 'cars', even the 'electric' ones are, she said to herself.

And thus comes a plan, delivered on four rolling wheels.

Doing a penultimate check, the newcomer again pondered how to move.

Now, that is interesting, she reflected.

Those tall, thin poles that are arrayed on the 'side-walk', all around the building... at least three kinds of energy-waves issue from each one, connecting to its neighbor trap-pole, so there is an unbroken fence of electric-wave, invisible to the human people, surrounding this 'Hotel Arizona'.

Quite ingenious, really; but how would they know if something blundering across the plane of these trap-waves, would be a bird, an insect, or... a Storied Watcher?

Ah, but they are no more than two and a half man-heights from bottom to top, she noted.

A wan smile showed on her face, within her invisible bubble.

Oh-kay, then. We shall try for that garbage-bin on the right-hand side of the building, thence... hmm, that is unfortunate, no balconies, they only have these sterile-looking permanently-closed windows.

I will have to figure out the next steps later, I suppose... Just need to wait, for a few minutes.

In fact, it was only thirty seconds until the next vehicle came by, but it was a low-set sports-car, so she passed up the first opportunity. However, a minute or so later, up rumbled a pickup-truck, its sides gaudily emblazoned with some kind of motif advertising 'SW Tri-State Trash, You Dump, We Grab, No Questions Asked!"

Heed what I now do, and learn well, my children, sent the alien-girl to the bundle of weirding arms-creatures, floating just behind her shoulders.

Ye must learn to do the same, all by thyselves.

Observe how I use the move-force, to leap and glide.

Lend them thy wisdom also, dear Vîrya Quü'j.

Quickly – her cloak now set up to stop almost every kind of electro-magnetic energy, save for the one or two she needed for navigational purposes – the Storied Watcher stole directly behind the vehicle, until it started to make a right-hand turn upon exiting the garage.

Moving faster than any two-legged creature of this small planet could ever have done, she positioned herself on the side of the truck facing away from the hotel, jumped on to its passenger-side running board, grabbed a hand-hold upon the side-door opening handle... and flung herself skyward, the arc of her flight shooting over the top of the energy-trap by two meters or more.

Slow yourself down, bend the pull-forces... do not lose hold of your children, wrapped up in the iron-spider back-cloak of Vîrya Ahn'jë, silently self-counseled Karéin-Mayréij, while sailing over the unsuspecting, sweltering mercenaries below.

However, despite her best efforts, when she landed on the top of the green garbage-container, an audible 'clangggg', accompanied by a faint puff of dust, issued from the top of this large metal box.

Invisibly, the alien-girl winced, deploring her clumsiness, although five small voices titter-tattered otherwise, thanking her for a lesson instantly taken to heart.

But how does one practice the old skills, when an entire techno-Empire has a price on one's head, for Heaven's sake! complained the Storied Watcher, to herself.

Levitating slightly and flattening herself against the outside wall of the building, she caused the dust to whirl around, obscuring her foot-prints. Then she hopped down to the ground.

"Copy," sounded an expressionless voice, approaching from the other side of the garbage-bin. "Yeah, okay, I'll check it. Coleman out."

Footsteps sounded, until someone was standing right in front of the box.

Crouching inside her cloak, beside the container, the newcomer tried to take advantage of a shadow, that would have been an ordinary person's only means of self-secretion.

Small as a little mouse, she prayed.

Small as a sand-grain, small as an atom... never worth a second look...

"Coleman reporting," heard the alien-girl. "Nah, I'm looking right at it, nothing here – damn thing's covered with dust from that storm we had back two weeks ago... what's that? Oh, come *on* – okay, okay, loud and clear. Just a sec."

The guard, muttering curses at the spoilage of a recently-pressed business-suit, clambered up the side of the garbage-container and, huffing and puffing, sweat pouring down his brow, flung open the hatch that covered the left side of the bin.

He fumbled for his mobile talk-box, while washing the interior with the beam of a flashlight.

"Oh, *man!*" he gasped, "Don't they ever take this shit *out*? 'It stinks' doesn't come *close* to doin' justice to what I'm smellin' now... no, of course not," he complained into the communicator.

Just imagine what it would be like if you had a sense of smell like my own, ruefully thought the encloaked alien, down and to the right.

Not quite as bad as the lower catacombs of the Worm-Lord... but close enough, unfortunately...

"Look, for God's sake, there ain't nothin' *in* there – yeah, I saw a few roaches, a rat or two, but there ain't no *way* I'm goin' in to check," he argued. "*Yes*, I'm sure... fuckin' waste of *time*. Look –"

"Well then... what did you have in the first place?," demanded the guard, now back on *terra firma*. "Just a blip on the DNA-sniffer? Well, *that's* no surprise – I mean, how were they supposed to test the damn thing, anyway, they can't just get her to – right. Anythin' else? Oh, yeah? I know, I *know*... but every time we get a bird overhead, it goes apeshit – alright, fine. Yeah, I'll meet you down there in ten, I'm almost off shift anyway. Hey, listen... at least you got A/C in there – you should try hangin' out *here* for a while, you'd have a whole new attitude toward doin' anything fast, I can personally attest to that. Okay. Coleman out."

Then you can be my guide, Mr. Coleman, mused Karéin-Mayréij.

For the path taken by those who the king trusts, is often that which offers best.

And I will have to hope that there are no more energy-barriers to outsmart.

"Not even giving us time and a half... not even a bonus," muttered the guard, as he slowly headed for the rear of the building, not noticing the faint flicker in the air about a meter or so behind him, as a thoroughly uninvited guest, floating a few centimeters off the ground, mimicked his every movement.

"*Lousy* fucking job," he added.

Powers Above, relieve my tension, grant me success, her mind silently said.

I am going into the open... if they have devices that can see me...

He rounded the far corner of the hotel, and in only a few more steps, came upon and entered an outdoor swimming-pool complex, complete with twenty or so sunburned adults, plus perhaps half again that number of children, raucously running and jumping hither and yon.

One of the latter did a 'cannonball' rather too close to the Storied Watcher, but – though she could instantly have evaporated the droplets, upon contact with the bubble – she elected, this time, to allow a few drops to make contact with the tightly-bound war-suit.

Yes, dear ones, thought the alien, in the direction of her traveling-bundle. *Water – like that which helped ye all to life, along with my fire, my lightening, the earth and wind of this beautiful world... and my spirit.*

Ye must perceive as I do, and learn rapidly of this place. It is akin to many others – dear Vîrya Quü'j, in the quiet moments, tell them of the Many Worlds, that they hear thy wisdom.

Coleman loosened his tie and flashed a badge, as he approached the hotel-staffer – in reality, a thinly-disguised Federal agent – who was stationed at the entrance-way between the pool and the interior of the building.

"False positive, I heard," remarked the thin, balding man, in ill-fitting Hotel Arizona attire. He did not lift up his head, from the sports-section of the newspaper.

"Yeah," replied Coleman, tarrying at the doorway as he wiped the sweat from his forehead. "Sixth or seventh today, for Christ's sake – I don't know what the point is, anyway. I mean, they've got three *hundred* fuckin' guests in the rooms and at least another couple hundred wanderin' around in search of this stupid 'presentation' thing that the H.Q. boys set up... and we gotta make like it's just business-as-usual, all the while havin' those losers from GrayWar playin' soldier in the parking-lot and all the while with you, me and the rest of the crew trying to set up, uhh, 'discreetly'. I don't know *what* they think they're accomplishing."

An invisible being floating behind him suppressed a desire to show fangs.

Can you not just, uhh, 'get on with it', man? she thought, in frustration.

As Bob would say... 'I have a show to catch.'

"Probably SFA, if you ask me," opined the other guard. "I fuckin' *hate* these duds, too, I barely fit in 'em – damn pants don't even come down to my ankles. Shoes are bloody uncomfortable, too."

"That's why they pay us the big bucks, pardner," joked Coleman. "What'd you expect, with a day or two's lead-time, for an operation like this? You should just be glad they don't have you out here in a nice little mini-skirt or somethin'. Well, I better get going, I'm on underground garage station in three minutes – don't want to set off another goddamn alarm if I'm late, you know. They're dockin' us fifty bucks for each one, you know? And I got *bills* to pay."

Shuffling his feet a bit, he slowly started in to the hotel.

"See ya," called the door-guard, lazily waving one hand, while using the other to turn the page to the gossip-columns.

Has never failed me yet, from world to world, Empire to Empire, smugly reflected Karéin-Mayréij, as she floated behind Coleman. He went down one corridor, saying "hello, how's it going?" to random-looking people who he met from place to place.

Ah... spies posing as the common-folk, she mused.

But they all have those little 'identity-cards' whose techno-chip minds give off the weak energy-pulses.

They must not be aware that to me, they might as well paint themselves with bright yellow stripes, as to carry those items.

Unexpectedly, she stopped for a second, pondering a thought.

What is that, Vîrya Quü'j?

Ha! The little weirding energy-pulses?

Yes – they use those all the time, on this techno-world.

Ah... but you will just have to learn how to interpret them, as I did.

See, there is one thing, at least, that I know and thou do not.

With a wry, satisfied smile, the alien-girl again started to move forward.

Now, the man was about to turn another corner, toward a door with a big, red 'EXIT' sign over top of it, but, in the distance, the Storied Watcher's ears perceived the sounds of a crowd.

Sorry that I must leave you, 'Agent Coleman', thought Karéin-Mayréij, from within the light-bent darkness of her bubble.

You have done all that I asked of you, in the short time that we have been together.

Enjoy your coming fame!

And, upon hearing a few mental giggles from the package floating behind her, she cautioned,

Yes, it is funny, my children... but let ye not down thy guard.

Such mistakes sometimes are made but once.

Avoiding passers-by whenever possible and invisibly sneaking from obstacle to obstacle, just as if she were some ordinary thief – a precaution painfully learned over years untold – the alien-girl was finally able to peek around a corner, and, only half to her relief, she saw a couple of signs entitled, "PAY HERE FOR EXCITING SPACE SEMINAR!"

Let us hope it is not too exciting, she mused, while studying all the ingress and egress routes, as well as the deployment of potential enemies.

Hmm... two of those government spy-men with the shining electro-cards, at the door to the speaking-room, three more at the other end of this hall with some kind of magnet-arch that guests are being made to walk through, just like the two by the arch facing me... they look bored, since most of the people who want to get in to this event seem to be coming from the other end, maybe that is where the main lobby is... this speaking-room is off the big part of the hotel where all the sleeping-rooms are stacked on top of each other, it appears to have just a thin roof on top...

There is a table at the speaking-room door, with hotel-workers who must be the puy-tukeɩ s. The show cannot not yet have started, because of all the people – twenty or more – who are standing awkwardly close to each other, in this special area between the two arches.

Ah, but look! The bathrooms, one for the men and one for the women, are inside the 'protected' area. I wonder...

Still within the protective invisible-bubble, the Storied Watcher now boldly stepped out into the corridor, directly facing two security-guards who were manning the second, interior-side metal detector. She waved her arms frantically and made a goofy face, sticking out her tongue in the best Curtis Claremont imitation that she could muster.

But there was no reaction at all.

Good, she thought. *My cloak holds.*

As Bob, may the Gods protect him, would say... 'here goes'.

Silently and invisibly, the alien-girl stole quickly up to the thick silk rope that extended from the right-hand side of the security-archway to the far side of the hotel corridor, and slid beneath it. In so doing, she joined the mélange of over-ripe humanity that was milling aimlessly in the same area.

"Isn't the damn thing open yet?" complained a female voice. "I thought it was going to be at three p.m... right?"

"Yeah, and I had to line up for an hour in that stinkin' heat, just to get *in* here," added a male voice.

"Well, I went up and asked, they said some shit about 'Ms. Abruzzio wasn't feeling well, but she's on her way back down, now', or something like that. They said it'd only be another ten minutes or so, for whatever that's worth," answered a second male voice.

"Daddy... are they going to talk about the space-lady?" interrupted the voice of a little boy. "Like, all the UFO-stuff that the Government's keeping all secret?"

"That's why we're here, Cory my boy," confirmed the first male voice.

Bless you, son, wistfully thought Karéin-Mayréij.

You are yet another who I would visit, sometime.

"*Fine*," sounded the female voice. "Look, Jack – I'm going to take one last shot at the ladies'-room, before they get going, okay? Line-up outside is gone, at least."

"I'll save you a seat, then, Billie-Jean," proposed the man.

If they do not keep count, realized the newcomer, *There is my opening.*

As the woman called 'Billie-Jean' made her way toward the washroom, she had, unbeknown, acquired a 'shadow'.

But the plot of *this* interloper almost came undone when, unfamiliar with the way in which the door swung back and forth, it temporarily separated her from the precious bundle of thinking-things that floated a third of a meter behind.

Almost in panic, the still-cloaked Storied Watcher used her mind to force the door open just before *Vîrya Ahn'jë* and the others who she – it – enveloped, came crashing to the carpeted floor outside the women's room.

Luckily, none outside noticed the fact that there had been no-one to push this portal open and yank the bundle inside.

Instantly, the alien-girl stepped into a blind corner and de-activated her light-bending trick, except for that part of it that hid her war-garb, pushed her baseball cap down to obscure as much of her face as possible, and donned the cheap, mirror-finish shades that she had borrowed from Losada, as her mind weaved her golden, shoulder-length hair into a knot underneath the cap.

She turned the corner, entering an ostentatiously marble-tiled, gold-plated washroom, joining six or seven other women therein, with one or two more coming and going continuously.

Interesting that they do not charge money to deal with one's body-functions here... unlike that washroom back in the shopping-mall, she absentmindedly noted.

Keeping her head well down to avoid the view-field of the camera in the black domed thing at the far end of the washroom, the Storied Watcher bent over a washbasin, next to a middle-aged Hispanic woman who was evidently putting a few finishing touches to her eye-liner.

"Are you here to see the show?" she inquired, while squirting a little liquid soap on to one palm and beginning to methodically apply it to her face.

"Yeah," answered the female. "I guess."

"What do you mean?" continued the alien-girl.

"Oh... *nada*," explained the Latino woman. "*Bueno*... tell you the truth, I'm only here because José – that's my son, he's six – he want to go *so* badly, but it's a school day and we could only afford the one ticket, you see. I had to wait two hours before I could get up to the booth outside the hotel and buy it. José, he want me to get all the pictures and the autographs that Ms. Abruzzio and Mr. Ramirez are giving out. He is really 'into' this 'space' stuff, *usted lo sabe*. It is boring for me, but it will be worth it, if I can just tell him what they said. It's too bad that he won' get to shake their hands, but times are slow, you know..."

Trying hard not to give the camera a good look at her face, Karéin-Mayréij turned to regard her Hispanic counterpart.

"Listen," offered the alien-girl, "What would you say if I told you that I could give you fifty dollars, for that ticket that you paid thirty, for?"

"Any other time, *mujer*, I would say, 'seguro'," retorted the other, "But José would be, ah, *como se dice en Inglès*, 'heartbroken', if he find out that I don' go to the one time that Ms. Abruzzio and Mr. Ramirez are down here in Tucson. Thank you for offering, though, lady."

I will have to take the chance that they do not have a listening-bug, to go along with the spying-eye up there, thought the alien-girl, as she tried to keep the jamming-power down to a minimum, so as not to befoul their communications too much.

"What if I told you," she argued, "That I could give José an autograph worth *far* more than that of either Sylvia or Hector? And... that later, it would be a voucher for him to be visited by a very, *very* special person? Would *that*, and fifty dollars, be worth your little plastic ticket, and your silence, for a few months?"

"I... I don' know what you mean," evaded the Hispanic woman, her tone changing to that of mild worry.

"Do you have something durable... a locket, or a credit-card, maybe... Rosalita? It's Rosalita DelMonte, is it not?" requested the newcomer, splashing water on her face and reaching for a paper-towel to dry herself off.

Real concern now on her face, the Latino whimpered, "*Como.*. how you know my name? I never met you. Who *are* you? Look, I ain't done *nothing!* ¡*No tengo drogas!* I always tell the truth to the *Federales, lo juro! Por el amor de Dios*, don' arrest me – I got a kid to feed!"

It is time, now, realized Karéin-Mayréij.

Tipping the rim of her cap yet further forward to cover her whole face in shade, she lifted up the sunglasses and turned to look at DelMonte, straight on.

"I am not the police," she murmured. "As 'not', as 'not' can be. Do not fear me... oh-kay?"

You suspect who I am, sent the Storied Watcher, with glowing eyes and the faint 'humm' of psycho-music.

And... I congratulate you... for your suspicions are correct, Rosalita.

No, it is not *your imagination, and it is not a dream. And if you give me the ticket, and something saying where you live, one day I will come and visit José. I will show him things of wonder.*

All I ask, is that you leave this place after we are done here and that you not speak of this, for a month or two. You will be safer that way.

"*Please*," implored the young-looking woman. "I need a ticket, and I am, ah, not very good at lining-up."

She tried to suppress a wry smile as she simultaneously and silently, sent to the invisible bundle,

Especially not with all ye unruly war-children behind me – neither Vìrya Quü'j, *nor I, could hold a queue for an hour, without some disaster.*

"*Santa Marìa*," gasped the shocked Hispanic female. "You? ¿*Usted es la señora en el cielo?* I – I – *Carrumba*, how could I refuse?"

"You know already of me," remarked the Storied Watcher, taken faintly with amazement. "I have met others who think of me as just a fable... a tall tale. How is it that you know the truth, when so many do not believe?"

"In the *barrio*, most of us believe, because the government tell us that they blow up the comet, themselves," explained the Hispanic woman. "We got a saying in our language – it go, 'more the President tell you something is *lo verdad*, more you know it is a lie'... you know?"

A rueful smile appeared on the face of Karéin-Mayréij.

"I have learned all about *that*, how would Bob say, 'the hard way', since I arrived here," she affirmed. "But it warms my heart to know that despite all the techno-tricks, your government's lies cannot fool *everyone*. Now... time is going on, as we speak... so... about the ticket? I ask with humility."

"*Seguro*," quickly replied the other woman. "*Esta aqui* – you see, it's a little picture of José – the kind that they put inside the plastic. Oh, and... and... I got a contact-card – it's for my seamstress-business, but I work out of home, so the address is for *nuestra casa.*"

"Here... let me see," requested the alien-girl.

DelMonte handed over a small, laminated picture and a plain-looking business-card, from her purse.

"Handsome little boy..." observed the Storied Watcher. "He reminds me of my own..." she sadly commented. "Very well – I will use the back of it... oh-kay?"

She put the picture in front of Rosalita, face-down, then pressed a palm down over it. A very faint wisp of steam or smoke issued forth, and – burned instantly into the reverse-side of the picture, in small, neat characters – were the words,

"To José : Rosalita is my friend, and when I am no longer busy, I will come to visit you. Signed, K-M."

"Oops," sheepishly added Karéin-Mayréij. "I neglected to do something."

She again laid the picture face-down, and burned a second message, slightly below the first, on to its back side.

"PS : I hope that you are not afraid of heights," it advised.

"*Muchas gracias*," started the Hispanic woman. "Thank you *so* much. Oh... here is my ticket," she said, retrieving a piece of multi-layered, laminated paper with a 3-D bar-code printed on it.

As she accepted the gift, the Storied Watcher asked, "Okay... and thank you. We said 'fifty'... did we not?"

She held out some bills, again trying to hide them from the cameras.

They will think that I am trying to buy some of those 'sineth' drugs from her, if they see the money, considered the alien-girl.

"Oh, no, *mujer*," protested DelMonte. "I don' need *nothin*, you know. Just that – the autograph, I mean – *es bastante*."

"Are you *sure?*" pressed the young-looking woman.

"Positive. Anything for an *angel de Dios*, you know," answered the Latino woman.

"May your faith be justified, Rosalita," softly intoned Karéin-Mayréij. "Now... you should go, immediately, and do not tarry – it is possible that things might become a little, ah, 'unsettled', around here. Tell the people at the weapon-checking arch that you lost your ticket and you must go home, but do *not* tell anyone else for the next little while... oh-kay?"

"Okay," responded the woman. "I will take this right home to José," she promised.

In a daze, DelMonte collected all the stuff back into her handbag and staggered toward the door, only half-regaining her composure, when she exited the washroom.

The Storied Watcher wiped the trace of a tear.

Love your little one – hold him tight, she silently prayed.

As I will with dear Tommy... Holy Light, grant thee my wish...

As Rosalita went out, the alien-girl again bent over the wash-basin, retrieving a small, brassy-looking tube and trying to do as the Romans.

Ugh, she thought, while suppressing a grimace.

Do Earth-women really use *this 'lip-stick' stuff? It tastes like ear-wax!*

But anything for a ruse...

After applying this garish adornment to her lips, the newcomer retired to one of the toilet-stalls and sat on the seat, closing its half-door behind her.

Eventually, it appeared that the crowd in the washroom was starting to thin out; so she slowly made her way to the awkwardly-swinging door that was the only exit from this place.

She tried to force the apparent color of her eyes to brown, or, at least, to something other than blue-green, while using another old trick to simultaneously darken the complexion both of her skin and hair.

Feeling the presence of a large crowd outside, but not detecting weapons or hostility – other than for some man just outside the security-arch, complaining 'why can't I bring my hip-flask in there' – she peeked outside.

The restricted area was again milling with people – even more than before – but this time, the entrance to the conference-hall was open; and, one by one, a few were being allowed in. She did not detect the Hispanic woman from the bathroom.

Time to look just like a, ahh, how would Bob call it... yes, time to look like a 'tourist'.

Well – I sort of am one... *am I not?* thought the Storied Watcher, allowing a wan smile to come to her face, while practicing hiding her incisors through the grin.

Now... who should I be? she pondered.

I cannot use my real name – and by now, as they have taken Bob and the others, the 'Sari'-name would probably be a bloody hand, to them... hmm...

Several have told me that I am marked by an accent, so I should say that I am from a long way away.

How about that – where was it – I know, that 'France' kingdom, which lies across the sea?

Most of these 'Americans' do not travel very much... so they might not know a real, hmm, 'French' girl, from... me.

How did their names sound, again?

I remember one... yes, it sounded like 'Dal-add-yay'. So I will be, ahh, 'Rosalie Daladdyay'.

Not much of a ruse, but better than nothing, I suppose...

The next ten minutes proved a more trying challenge than Karéin-Mayréij had anticipated, not just due to the mundane issue of trying not to commit some kind of *faux pas*, but also because – even though her demi-children were, as far as she could tell, still invisibly-cloaked – it did not seem wise to lift them above her head, where they would have been out of harm's way.

She tried to maneuver *Vîrya Ahn'jë* and her brothers and sister close to the small of her back, but several times, they impacted with the next-in-line behind her, provoking various curses akin to "damn, what was *that!*.

So far, at least, profuse, abashed apologies to everyone in all directions, had provided the necessary cover, but the experience was nonetheless *most* uncomfortable.

Must keep the use of my power to a minimum, she resolved.

Else, I glow like a torch in the deepest depths of Meph'èl.

I could flatten this entire building with little effort... but my greatest fear is to step on another's toes.

The most formidable challenge is rarely that, for which one is prepared.

After what seemed like an eternity, the alien-girl had reached the ticket-taking table, on the opposite side of which was an elderly, waspish-looking woman, an equally past-prime Caucasian man and two Tucson city police-officers, both male.

"Ticket, given name and Christian name, please," announced the woman in a monotone. "Oh – and no sunglasses, please."

'Christian' name? immediately worried the mind of the Storied Watcher.

They are all *'Christian' names, around here!*

One is given one's name by one's parents... so I guess that the other must be one's family name... I wish that I knew if my disguise-trick is still working... hmm, but yes, there is that other trick, is there not?

Keep the eye-glow down, O Storied One, do not let your power leak out...

As she removed the shades her mind sent a subtle broadcast radiating outward, like the minuscule ripple of a pebble dropped into a calm lake, like the faint cross-talk you get between stations on the radio-dial.

Although wordless, it told, *"Everything is fine – don't worry... be happy."*

"Here eet ees," cheerily replied the Storied Watcher. "And eet ees 'Daladdyay'... Rosalie, 'zat ees," she added. "Mon first name ees 'Rosalie', I mean."

"French?" asked the elderly man, lazily looking up.

Slightly taken aback by her deliberately-suppressed, but nonetheless unavoidable attractiveness, he turned his head and shot a glance at one of the cops.

But the latter just shook his own head in the negative, after looking the fine "Rosalie Daladier" over, a bit more carefully.

"*Oui – bonjour,*" answered a relieved Karéin-Mayréij, hoping that she was faking the right accent. "How you tell?"

"Been up to that Frenchie place in Canada, before they had that big fight and closed the border," the ticket-man replied. "An' anyway, ol' Merv – that's me, of course – well, I can *always* tell if somebody's from out of town."

"But of *course,*" replied the alien. "Eet ees, how you say, 'a gift'."

No loud laughs, my children; for ye must learn to respect guile as much as the plain arts of war, she mentally remonstrated, trying to manage the behavior of the demi-beings that were floating invisibly just below her rump.

"How you spell that, Ma'am, the last name, that is?" demanded the woman, her eyes never looking up from the tablet computer-thing upon which she was using some kind of pointing device.

"How you spell it?" repeated the newcomer, her mind racing with improvised stratagems, but a second later, she had a bright idea – as had always been the case, over time immemorial.

"Why... 'zactly how eet sound, of course," she prevaricated. "Ees 'R', zen..."

"Enjoy the show," impatiently grunted the desk-woman, as she stamped the ticket and handed it back to the Storied Watcher.

This techno-world has many dangers, she silently reflected, *but at least it does not have wizards with weirding spells that detect lies.*

"*Merci*," she concluded, followed by, "Oh, 'thank you' – 'zat ees what I mean," she sauntered fetchingly through the doorway and handed the ticket to a bored-looking teenage bellhop immediately inside the meeting-room.

"Festival seating, Miss," he explained. "And we're fillin' up, already – if you want to use the bathroom while the show's going on, you'd better pick a seat near the aisle. Start time's in about five minutes."

"Oh, of course – thank you," politely responded the alien-girl.

Her senses and mind were already scanning the room, as the Hotel Tucson's Muzak had almost played through that old number by the Ozark Mountain Daredevils.

Fancy Meeting You Here

The lavishly-carpeted, tastefully-decorated main conference-room was a grandiose place that, at other times, must have been the venue for trade-shows and other, similar events. On *this* day, it had been outfitted with twenty rows of ten folding-chairs each, on either side of a wider center aisle, although at this point about half of the seats were still unoccupied; there was plenty of space still left on the periphery of the seating-area, in any case.

There were police-officers stationed at each of the room's three other exits, and Karéin-Mayréij noticed another six, randomly-distributed undercover spies, by detecting the electronic glow from identity-cards.

Up at the front, there was a long platform, raised perhaps by a foot off the Astroturf-carpeted floor. This had a stylish, glass-and-plastic speaking-podium to the middle and front, along with a huge, OLED computer-screen suspended behind the platform. Behind the screen was a large, black-covered backdrop.

In the rear left corner, there was a cordoned-off area with a mini-cam, bright lights and a black-covered table, while the right rear corner contained a refreshment-table with a big sign saying "COFFEE $3.50 / CUP, BEER $5.00 / CAN, SODA $4.50 / CAN, TAP WATER $2.50 / CUP, SNACKS $5.00 EACH".

Exits... oh-kay, methodically planned the Storied Watcher, *four of them, counting the one through which I came.*

Roof is not too thick, could get through that easily. Same thing with the walls.

Spies with guns – quite a few of them, no mind-alarms saying that they suspect me, but there are a lot of ordinary peasant-folk – that could make defending myself rather awkward.

Interesting that there are two people in the viewing-seats, who have mostly plastic gun-weapons, but only one of them has a glow-card.

At least six or seven people – two with the glow-badges and guns – behind the big tee-vee screen that is showing the repeating commercial about "Keep America Safe : Report A Muslim, A Pervert, An Abortionist, A Subversive, An Illegal Alien Or A Gangster Today".

Oh... and I suppose that I should just do a quick scan of the people in the crowd... who is that?

Yes – the mind-glow matches, perfectly!

Joy, joy – it is him!

As rapidly as she dared, the newcomer walked over to take her seat, beside an average-height, clean-shaven Caucasian man with a conservative, dark haircut, wearing a button-up, cotton sports-shirt, beige slacks and white lace-up shoes.

Incongruously, he also had an earring on the left side.

She turned to address him.

"Hi, Misha," she whispered.

"Oh, hello, Miss, who are... my *God*," gasped the SVR-man.

Lowering his voice, he protested, "What are you *doing* here? Do you not realize that this place will be *crawling* with American spies?"

Verily – so it is – at least six of them, she sent to him.

Be at peace, dear lover Misha... for all is going according to plan – so far.

"I could ask you the same question, dear – dear – say, what did you say your name was, again?" insouciantly inquired the alien-girl.

"Oh, it is 'Michael Paloff'," he responded, reflexively playing the part. "Pleased to meet you, Miss... Miss...?"

"'Rosalie Daladier', zat ees my name," deadpanned the Storied Watcher. "French – oo la la, you know?"

Sotto voce, she jested, "I get ze 'oo la la' from an advertisement on Bob's tee-vee. You like?"

Shush, she sent to her invisible, unruly demi-children, who collectively had been secreted under her chair.

"You make quite a spy," sighed Misha, trying hard not to laugh. "And as to what I am doing here, well... my superiors guessed that you would be drawn to this event, as a moth to a candle. No doubt, the CIA believes so, too."

"I have had *ages* in which to perfect my craft," she explained. "And you only knew me because you have my 'gift'. I am *counting* on drawing the attention of these American spy-armies; and, incidentally, I promise not to tell any of them about the little recording-camera that you have in that ear-ornament of yours. Quite *ingenious*, really. How did you sneak it past their all-seeing archway, you know, the one in the hall?"

"I suppose that they are not in the habit of tugging on a man's ear," he smugly noted. "At least... not in *this* part of town."

"Others here have some little surprises, hidden away for needful moments," she observed, with a slightly-arched eyebrow.

"Ladies and gentlemen," sounded a voice over the intercom, "Please rise while we sing our glorious National Anthem, in honor of America's brave troops fighting for our way of life, in Cuba, the Middle East, Africa, Indonesia and Los Angeles."

"Oh, sayy can you see..." started the song.

The Storied Watcher quickly arose, at a pace almost matched by Misha's own, and tried to imitate the average Americans all around her as the music began to play, but was confused by the lackadaisical attitude of the crowd; a few were singing *The Star-Spangled Banner* loudly and hoarsely, but the majority of the attendees had a silent and bored, shoulders-down slouch, with one or two chewing gum, talking or otherwise paying little attention, either to the ceremony or to the nation to which they supposedly belonged.

Better not try singing, she self-counseled.

Better not even think *about trying that kind of thing. I am supposed to be, uhh, 'under cover' – that is how Bob would have said it...*

Eventually, and mercifully, this dirge-like tone-poem came to an end.

A dark-tanned, wrinkle-faced Caucasian man, his white hair immaculately styled into a Southwest brush-cut, came up to the podium, and motioned for the crowd to sit down.

The alien-girl scanned the front area, seeing that plain-clothes spies – a big black guy on the left, with a youngish-looking, very trim-and-fit, Asian-American woman in a business-suit and a tallish, twenty-something, red-haired Caucasian man in a leisure-suit, on the right – had now appeared at either side of the half-set of steps that led from the floor to the raised platform.

Along with the Asian woman and the young man, there was a spare, gray-and-brown-haired, middle-aged woman, accompanied with a Hispanic man, who was a good head shorter than the second woman.

Karéin-Mayréij nudged the Russian with her left elbow.

"See, Mish – ah, I mean, 'Michael'?" she directed. "There they are – Sylvia and Hector! Oh, you have no *idea* how strong the urge is, just to charge right up there and embrace them... after all that we have been through, I mean..."

He nodded in confirmation.

"Indeed. But what do you intend to do with them?" he asked.

Still looking straight ahead, the newcomer responded, "Quite simply... I plan to *talk* with them, to find out what in the Abyss is going on with this stupid American government that plagues me; then, I will tell them to tell this 'President' that if he does not immediately –"

"Ladies and gentlemen," interrupted the voice of the man on the podium, "May I ask for quiet in the assembly-hall, while I explain the agenda for this truly great show that we've got for you, today. Ah – good, okay – I guess you *can* hear me, then!"

There were a few polite laughs from the audience.

"So..." he announced, "I'd like to welcome each and every one of you to this very special event, in which Professor Sylvia Abruzzio and Mr. Hector Ramirez from the Jet-Propulsion Laboratory in Houston, are going to share with you all the secrets of the amazing Mars mission, conducted in the past year, by the heroic United States Air Force –"

"And a few others," sarcastically muttered Misha. "Such as those of us, who paid for four-fifths of the entire expedition."

"We have a saying, where I come from," observed the Storied Watcher. "It goes, 'ten thousand drops of water can wear away at a mountain – but a million lies cannot change even a sand-grain, of the truth'."

"I wish that I were so confident," complained the Russian.

"We'll begin with a short audio-visual presentation, explaining the background of the story... and, ladies and gentlemen, this is the *real* version – not the fanciful, distorted things that you've been seeing on NeoNet," continued the man at the podium, "And then, in the first half-hour, Mr. Ramirez, will give his impression of what happened on that fateful mission. After a five-minute break, Ms. Abruzzio will take over and relate her own story. Finally, we'll have a half-hour question-and-answer session. Everybody got that? Good! So, without much further ado... let me introduce our two guests – Sylvia, Hector, come on up here!"

Gales of applause burst out from the audience, as Ramirez and Abruzzio took the stage, smiled and waved at the crowd, then sat down on fold-up chairs positioned on either side of the central computer display-screen.

Slowly, what looked to be a well-polished, professionally-crafted presentation started to light up the display. This simulated video was so realistic that it would have taken a highly-trained eye to spot the subtle differences from an actual, on-site recording.

To start it off, it showed the launch of two spacecraft from Vandenberg Air Force Base and Cape Canaveral – plus, fleetingly, a few shots of another one being launched from the Central Asian Baikonur Cosmodrome and a third from the ESA complex in French Guiana; then, of an orbital docking-maneuver, of a boost towards Mars, then of orbit around it, with the descent of the *Eagle* lander.

The voice-over nattered on incessantly about "how the *Eagle-Infinity* mission re-established America's primacy in the space-race" and about "how no other nation can now contest our claim to develop the natural resources of the Red Planet... now that it's the 'Red, White and Blue Planet', folks".

There were also frequent, unsubtle references to various large American corporations, among them MicroApple Computers, Pepsi-JackDaniels, FunTime Pharmaceuticals and Lockheed-Boeing-Douglas, who, collectively, had evidently contributed at least half the funding for the NASA side of the expedition.

"But just *imagine*, ladies and gentlemen," remarked the voice-over, "What you'd have been thinking, if you were in the place of Captain Sam Jacobson, and had been the first to make a historic discovery – namely, the finding of the first real, extra-terrestrial creature, ever to be seen by human eyes! With amazing bravery, Captain Jacobson, assisted by Major Brent Boyd, freed this alien – the one who we'd later come to know as 'Karéin-Mayréij' – from the stony tomb in which she had been imprisoned, for thousands of years. At great risk to himself, not to mention his crew, Jacobson carried this frail, almost helpless being, all the way from the cave in which she'd been buried, back to the safety of the *Eagle* spacecraft –"

"What is wrong, uhh, Rosalie?" asked a concerned Misha, noticing that the alien-girl's eyes were watering, as her face had a look of sadness, of unfulfilled longing.

"Sam... Captain Sam... Jacobson, yes, *that* is his name..." reverently whispered the Storied Watcher. "My honored friend – my leader – the kind man who guided me when first I strayed... Captain Sam... where *are* you?"

Then she softly murmured, "And Brent – dear Brent – the only one to whom I revealed... *all. Call* to me now, friends, as I call to you! Again, we must come together – a great peril to your kin, rises in the South –"

For a few seconds, she seemed faraway, as if possessed by some overwhelming thought or memory.

Slowly, peace came back to her visage.

"At first," droned the voice-over, "Earth's scientists were baffled by the fact that the alien looked almost exactly like a young human woman... because, statistically, the chances of intelligent, extra-terrestrial life independently evolving into something that would even remotely resemble good old *Homo Sapiens*, are extremely low. Later, however – and here's something that we've never publicly revealed before, folks – our friend 'Karéin-Mayréij' revealed that she's actually a 'shape-changer'; she has the ability to re-mold her body-form into pretty much anything that she wants to look like –"

"Thank the starlight of Heaven – they are oh-kay!" breathed a relieved Karéin-Mayréij, "Though I suspect that they are also being held against their wills; else, why would Sam and my friends, not have sought me out, by now? And they are telling lies about him – about *me*, too – up there. Why would they leave the others out of the story? Why would they make it look like I was so weak... oh-kay, I *was* terribly thirsty, but... and I can *not* just change into some other body-form! At least... not now. What is the point of them saying falsehoods like that?"

"When none knows the truth," suggested Misha, "All lies are of equal value with each other, and with the truth itself. And... there *is* something, that you cannot do? As the Americans say... '*that* would be a first'."

She shot him a wry grin as acknowledgement.

Though perhaps we must walk different trails, for a time, she sent to his mind, *I still care much for you, noble spy of Russia.*

"...Selflessly risking all for the sake of science, the *Eagle* blasted off from the surface of Mars, with its precious cargo being slowly taught Earth's universal language – namely, American English, in the same spacecraft, over the long journey back to our planet," went the voice-over, as more computer special-effects showed the *Infinity* and *Eagle* blasting off on the return-leg of the mission. "And, somehow, it turned out that despite the close proximity of the alien, none of the *Eagle's* crew developed any immediately fatal diseases; but, of course, that's not to say that they *didn't* become infected, so, right now, they're comfortably in long-term isolation, until our best medical minds can ensure that there's absolutely no chance of them bringing back some terrible Mars disease..."

"That is what we call, a 'cover-story'," explained Misha.

The alien-girl nodded. "It is not as if I have never seen such a ruse," she pointed out. "But, how amazingly realistic *is*, this parcel of lies! It is even a bit difficult for *me* to tell the difference from what really went on... look, you can even see each hair on Brent Boyd's head... why have they left out – oh, *my!* Yes, *there* they are – but so far off in the background, that the viewers cannot tell –"

Again, a tear welled up in her eye, and, bending over so as not to show her face to those on the platform, she quietly prayed,

"Beloved Cherie, my heir, my brave pioneer student, first to feel the *Fire*... wise Devon, whose true faith made me strong, when my own failed... Ser-gayy, my first love, who showed me the joys of man... *speak* to me now, all... I *call* to you..."

"Rosalie," cautioned the SVR-man, "I am not sure that this is a good time, or a good place, in which to be doing this kind of thing –"

"I love you," she retorted, "But, do us both a favor... and shut up!"

He gave a bewildered shrug.

"Just like back in the motel," he sighed, "The rule-book says nothing about what I am to do."

"But, as we all are aware," prevaricated the narration that smoothly accompanied the computer-graphics on the big screen, "Halfway through their trip back to Earth, the crew of the Mars mission was informed of the mortal threat that the object named 'Lucifer', presented to our home world; and so, they had to turn all their attention to assisting the rest of us, in dealing with the comet."

"Well, at least *that* part is half-true," commented the Storied Watcher. "Sort of."

"I know... it is a pity... is it not?" sardonically added Misha. "They have spoiled their otherwise perfect record."

He was rewarded by a broad, friendly, female-alien grin.

"Now as for the Mars-creature... she, stated on a number of occasions that she would try to help, but, for reasons that none of us can explain," claimed the voice-over, "When the time came, she simply *disappeared* – and hasn't been seen or heard from, since. We have absolutely *no* idea where she went; to hear the crew of the mission relate the story, it was as if she just vanished into thin air. Maybe she committed suicide, by stepping out of an airlock... we just don't know."

With a contemptuous glance in the direction of the podium, Karéin-Mayréij sent another unrequested thought into the Russian's by-now-receptive mind.

Do not worry, rulers of America, it ominously informed.

Soon, you will have all the proof that you need, that I am very much... here.

"Fortunately for all of us," proclaimed the narration, "At the last-minute, as he has done so many times in the past, Uncle Sam – or, more specifically, the heroic men and women who gave their lives, in his service – came to the rescue of the whole world, by unleashing America's most deadly weapon, the previously secret 'Sword of Freedom' device, against 'Lucifer'."

The video-screen showed a recording of the Storied Watcher's final, fateful attack on the comet, although both she and Misha noticed that the weird psycho-tune that had announced her coming, had been replaced by a soundtrack of military chatter and martial-music.

Wide-eyed, as if uncomprehending, Karéin-Mayréij stared at the display.

"So *that* is what it looked like, from the eyes of the doomed," she managed, lost in contemplation. "Devon, you called me, 'Fist of God'... *sing* to your Angel, help her to understand..."

*So that is what I *was*, she thought to the Russian, alongside.*

What I will again be, when I choose to become... me.

"It was mighty close, fellow Americans – *mighty* close," stated the voice-over. "But you can all be proud of being citizens of the country that saved everyone else. They all owe you their lives – not that they'll admit it, of course. Out of envy for our American way of life, foreigners *always* refuse to admit that we're the leader of the Free World. But, the important thing is... *we* know, that it's the truth."

The Storied Watcher leaned back in her seat, eyelids shut.

"You know," she quietly disclosed to the Russian, "The memories are flooding back, now. How I was. How I felt. What I *did*. If only I had the *time* to tell you the story, dear friend! Someone must come to know it."

"Now," related the narrator, as the video started to fade out, "Just to set the record straight, and to deal with some of the many conspiracy-theories that the Government has been hearing in the last month or so... while the sudden discovery, then, the disappearance, of this 'Karéin-Mayréij' being may *look* suspicious – we *can* assure the public of two things."

"First of all," he went on, "Yes, she definitely *was* a real, living creature – her time with Captain Jacobson's crew was in *no way* some cooked-up story to take everyone's mind off the 'Lucifer' situation. And secondly, we have no reason to believe that she deliberately sent the 'Lucifer' comet, heading towards Earth, as has lately been suggested by some members of the clergy, both here and abroad."

"I suppose that I should be grateful to them for not, uhh, 'tagging' me with *that* one," grumbled the newcomer, to the Russian, who nodded affirmatively.

"The plain fact is," claimed the narrator, "That this being – while she certainly *was* real enough, never displayed abilities that could have so much as given old 'Lucifer' a mild headache – let alone to have moved an object as large as it, on to a collision-course with our planet. It's unfortunate that we had such a short time in which to become familiar with her... but she had no influence on the 'Lucifer' peril, either for good *or* bad."

"So," concluded the voice-over, "All the rumors about the alien having been some kind of 'Anti-Christ' are nothing more idle talk. Actually... if she really *was* the Devil, folks, then I'd say we're all pretty well-off, because she'd make an awfully weak Boy – oh, sorry, Girl – From Down Below... don't you think?"

Slowly, the lights began to come back on, and there was a rush of laughter and applause by the evidently-satisfied crowd.

"And *now*, ladies and gentlemen," announced the tanned, white-haired man at the podium, "For the first of our two guest-speakers, today. Let's hear it for *Mr. Hector Ramirez!*"

Loud applause burst out from all around, and, unenthusiastically, both the spy and the alien-girl, also brought hand to hand.

"It offends me that they so uncritically and willingly accept these fictions," complained the Storied Watcher. "I remember... I was told that I was on tee-vee, when I spoke with this 'President'. How can they *believe* such lies, when the truth differs, and is at their finger-tips? It must be on this 'Neo-Net' thing that is everywhere, around here."

"You must understand," observed the Russian, "That Americans prefer a happy lie over an unhappy truth – especially when the former is told by a government that they dare not contradict."

Now, the lights focused on Ramirez' round, Tex-Mex visage, as he advanced to stand at the podium, while a hotel-orderly obligingly lowered its height to more comfortably match his own.

The man looked ill-at-ease, as if he was being forced to say or participate in something in which he really didn't believe.

Curses, he is just out of mind-talk range, realized Karéin-Mayréij.

If I could have touched him, given him some of the power... but Hector was down here, and I was up there...

"Well, folks," started Ramirez, "I've been asked to relate some of my own experiences with the *Eagle* and *Infinity* Mars exploration mission, and, of course, with the alien who called herself 'Karéin-Mayréij'. First of all, you have to appreciate that when we planned the mission, we never..."

As he started to go over the details of the Jacobson mission, the newcomer elbowed Misha.

"He is not pronouncing my name correctly," she grumbled, *sotto voce*.

"You do not speak very good Russian, either," he noted.

"I am supposed to be French," riposted the alien-girl, "So, as Bob would have said... 'toupée'."

"It is '*touché*', I believe," he corrected. "They use it in the sport of fencing – that is, simulated sword-fighting."

"Well, as Bob would *also* have said," she replied, smartly, "Whatever. Oh, and incidentally... when I do combat, with swords or anything else... I do not, uhh, 'simulate'."

"In spite of the vocabulary issues," offered the Russian, "You are adapting very well to life on... I mean, life in the United States, 'Rosalie'."

"You are only too right about that," she pensively remarked. "The atmosphere – the attitudes – the short-term way of thinking that is pervasive down here, these distract me, they infect me... *pollute* me. I am supposed to be wise – no, I *am* wise, more than you will ever know – but I find myself ignoring my own wisdom, accumulated over untold ages past. I see it happening, and I know that I should do better... but I cannot, or, despite myself... I *will not*. It is most frustrating and depressing, for one like me."

"I will, how you say, take your word on that," he answered.

"...So," continued Ramirez, with pictures supporting his talking points appearing on the screen behind him at appropriate intervals, "We, uhh, decided to take the, uhh, alien, on board the spacecraft back to Earth. Captain Jacobson and his crew knew that this was a big risk. But we kind of figured that it would be worth doing – especially as, by this time, we had found out about the 'Lucifer' problem and figured that Earth didn't have much to lose."

"I stole aboard that blessed ship, like a thief in the night," whispered the alien-girl to the SVR-man, who acknowledged the comment with a slight nod.

"I'll leave it to Sylvia to give you some more scientific information about 'Karéin'... but I can honestly say that what surprised me the most about her was how, uhh, ordinary that she seemed," said the Hispanic scientist. "This wasn't just because she looked pretty much exactly like a young human woman would have, but because you expect an alien to be... well, *alien*, in how she –" he looked quickly down at the podium, "How *it* – perceives the world... how it expresses itself."

Misha tapped the Storied Watcher lightly on the shoulder.

"He is *certainly* speaking from a script – probably one imposed upon him by the American government," he pointed out.

This time, it was her turn to nod.

"Hector would *never* refer to me as an 'it' – unless he be so forced," she hissed, under her breath.

"Also," Ramirez went on, "You would expect an alien to have dramatically-different abilities compared to us plain old human beings; but other than being able to breathe Martian air, 'Karéin' seemed to be limited to doing only whatever we can, with two hands and two legs, and she had the added disadvantage of being unfamiliar with 21st-Century technology. So, for example, Captain Jacobson and his crew had spend a lot of time – which perhaps might have been better spent on other duties – to teach her things that you or I would just 'know' to do or not to do... for example how to use a space toilet or why not to open the outside airlock-door."

"I... uhh... mastered *that* piece of equipment, on the first day when I was inside the Eagle-ship, along with blessed Ser-gay," contradicted the newcomer.

"We found that to be a bit of a disappointment," uneasily stated the speaker, "Because given the 'Lucifer' situation, we could have used some extra-worldly help. To be fair, that was a *lot* to have expected of her."

"I tire of this dishonest, prepared script," muttered the young-looking woman. "These falsehoods *cannot* be Hector's own! How can he repeat them, in public?"

"He probably has no choice," noted Misha. "Which should not be a surprise to you, now. But it is puzzling why they are trying to make you look helpless... perhaps, to build confidence in this fake weapon, with which they are trying to intimidate the rest of the world?"

"Do not worry," growled Karéin-Mayréij, "I will soon correct any misunderstandings that they may have encouraged, on *that* subject."

The Russian looked again in all directions, trying to map out the easiest escape-route.

"Well, finally," concluded Ramirez, with thinly-disguised relief, "I can honestly say that while I felt privileged to have met this alien – if only over a video-link – it's a *huge* loss for science, that she, uhh, just disappeared, as she apparently did. But in the short time that she was with us, 'Karéin' gave us the answers to many issues that previously, we could only guess at. Maybe that was why she showed up in the first place. And – if I may just give a personal comment –", he added, glancing quickly over his shoulder at a stony-faced Government-operative who had been hanging discreetly in the background, "I'd like to say that I still kind of want to believe that she's out there somewhere... and that some time I'll get the chance to meet her personally."

Out of range or not... you will so do – and soon, dear friend, sent the Storied Watcher, with a determined stare.

I have longed to embrace you and Sylvia, no less.

For a second, Ramirez just stood there, vacantly staring at the audience, as if thunderstruck by some unexpected event.

"Hector?" called Abruzzio, as loudly as she dared.

"Yeah... yeah? So... that's it, I guess," half-mumbled Ramirez. "Thank you, ladies and gentlemen."

As the audience erupted in applause, a worried Misha turned to address the Storied Watcher.

"What did you *do*, just there?" he demanded. "This 'Ramirez' fellow looked like he had just been awakened from a deep sleep, or... and several of the U.S.

government-people up there around the stage, are talking with each other. We had better prepare to go, as soon as possible – they may already suspect –"

"*Peace!*" she countered. "I would not hold it against you, if you wanted to leave, during the break."

"Alright, ladies and gentlemen," mentioned the emcee, as he replaced Ramirez at the podium. "There'll be a five-minute break, before we welcome Ms. Sylvia Abruzzio, up here."

As the announcer struggled to get the audience's attention, he barked out, over the din, "A few quick notes, before you get up from your chairs : Special limited-edition programs autographed by Mr. Ramirez and Ms. Abruzzio, those are only $49.95 per copy, $39.95 for seniors and children, and $29.95 for veterans with a certified physical or mental disability. Also, we'd like to remind you that we're still on water-restrictions here at the Hotel Tucson, so, if you please, only flush the toilets in the washrooms if they're, uhh, really full, after you're done your business. Finally, the use of tobacco-products, whether by smoking, chewing or boosted-nicotine pills, is *strictly* prohibited while on Hotel premises. Your co-operation would be appreciated. Okay... see you all back in a few minutes, for the Professor's perspective on this exciting topic!"

"Damn short speech, for what I paid to get in here," they heard someone complain, from a row back behind them.

"If we are *not* going to head for the exits," suggested Misha, "Then we should get up and buy something at the back. Many are also doing so... and we do not want to be the only ones left sitting in their seats."

"You are probably correct about that," confirmed Karéin-Mayréij, as she rose up from her seat. "Just one thing, if you do not mind – can you please walk directly after me, but not *too* close... where it is possible, stay a body-width behind... oh-kay?"

"Sure," replied the SVR-man, "But... why?"

He stood up.

"Let us just say that I have some... 'offspring' – I suppose that is the best way that one could describe them – who have a habit of, ah, 'bumping into' people," she explained. "There is no-one other than yourself, dear 'Michael', who I would prefer them to make an acquaintance, in such a manner."

This man is a friend – in fact, more than that, silently sent the newcomer, to the bundle that had now positioned itself just behind her knee-joints.

Love him – and defend him, if ye can, my children.

Defend all my family... not least Bob and my dear Tommy, who ye know from my dreams.

It did not sound like English – nor, indeed, *any* language, as the humans would have understood one – but, to her pleasure, her mind perceived a reply.

Mother hear we beloved, it sang.

"More riddles?" peevishly observed Misha.

"Would you not expect as much, from one like me?" remarked the Storied Watcher, with a saturnine half-smile. "Listen... if it appears that I am avoiding someone – that is because I will have, uhh, 'detected' that they are opposed to me... to *us*. And no... I cannot tell you how I do it. Not, until... ah... never mind."

He nodded in rueful affirmation.

"Well... let us go," he proposed.

Slowly – much more so than she would otherwise have done, in navigating through the throng heading rapidly for the refreshment-table – the alien-girl led Misha to the room's rear left corner.

Dodging in and out of human traffic, the two neared their destination, trying to maintain the formation that she had originally requested. This proved more difficult than either had anticipated, since, apparently, a rumor had started to spread that the concession-stand was about to run out of cold beer, and it proved well-nigh impossible, to breach the three-deep wall of thirsty convention-goers that had formed around the table.

As she approached this phalanx, the Storied Watcher had to abruptly stop, when a pot-bellied man with a small white hat and suspenders cut in, just ahead of her.

"Hey, look out –" warned Misha.

Too late, he collided with the alien's upper back; then – a second later – felt a strange sensation, like multiple, chirping voices, friendly but definitely *not* human, similar to but not exactly the same as what he knew of the alien-girl's own thoughts, appearing unrequited in his head over the nerves coming up from his shins.

Dumbfounded and discomfited, the Russian leaned a bit further forward to whisper in her ear.

"There is something behind you –" he inquired. "It – they – speak to me... sort of..."

Now she half-turned her head, so that the gaze of one eye caught his own.

Thus you be the first human of Earth, to touch minds with all my war-children; Væran Fàiagàryuu, Vìrya I'ëà'b', Væran Ksé'l'ch', Væran Ss'éth'ch' *and* Vìrya Ahn'jë, *and also ancient* Vìrya Quü'j, silently sent Karéin-Mayréij, to him.

This is my lover Misha, came another message, not directed in his way, though he still perceived it.

Ye now know him by scent, mind and aura.

Take no risk; humans of Earth are much more fragile than thy mother.

"That does not mean, 'fail to hide when the bullets start to fly', you know," she unhelpfully remarked.

"I will make a note of that," he agreed, reaching a long arm over her tactfully-lowered shoulder. His hand waved a few twenty-dollar bills.

He did not notice the young-looking woman's gaze sweeping back and forth, all over the conference-hall; nor did he see the steely look in her eyes.

Yes, my children, I, too, sense the danger, since that perception is of the essence which I impart to ye... the American castle-guards know that we are here.

Not idly, do I request that ye defend Misha, spy of the Russian Empire.

He also is an intruder here, a warrior of the Light – or, at least, of the Gray, or the lesser Dark – standing bravely alone, in a field overflowing with opponents.

When I was low, when I needed refuge – he provided it, at much risk.

Be ready, for I shall need all thy speed and guile, when the moment comes.

"Coffee, please," he shouted, in the direction of one of the harried-looking concession-stand workers.

A second later, he turned and asked, "I forgot... what do you want?"

"Soda-pop," indicated Karéin-Mayréij, with a grin that was starting to look inadvisedly toothy, until she thought better of it. "And none of that 'diet' stuff that they have everywhere. The more sugar, the better."

"One coffee, black, and a can of Hi-Test Pepsi," called the SVR-man, to one of the workers. "Here is a twenty... keep the change."

Several resentful glances were shot in the Russian's way, as, instantly-promoted to the top of the queue, he received a Styrofoam cup of hot liquid and a blue-colored pop-can. The bill was snatched out of his hand.

Awkwardly, the two slowly backed out of the madding-crowd and headed back to their seats, but mercifully there were no more collisions.

"Lovely drink," commented the Storied Watcher. "A quarter-part or more of the contents of this can must be sugar, suspended in this flavored-water. Plus all the stimulant-chemical – I can taste that, even though it affects me not."

"Why do you think that a third of all American children are now diabetic, before the age of ten?" quipped Misha, taking an appreciative sip of his coffee. "But they have a pill for that, and another one to make them sleep at night, after gulping that caffeine all day before. As for *me*... I try to stick to only two cups of coffee, per day. I am more of a 'tea' man – but drinking too much of that, would mark me as a foreigner."

"Odd, for a kingdom that regularly hangs people for selling, or using, the wrong kinds of drugs," observed the alien-girl. "But there are many things in this 'America' that do not make much sense. At least *one* of those, however, I mean to deal with, today. Oh, look – it is Sylvia... time for more lies, I suppose."

The Russian nodded, as the lights again began to dim.

"And now," announced the white-haired man, "For the *second* half of our exciting presentation tonight, I'd ask you to welcome Ms. Sylvia Abruzzio. Sylvia?"

A wave of polite applause swept through the audience.

Misha clapped unenthusiastically, while his companion did so carefully, seemingly trying to avoid making too much noise.

"Hello, everyone," spoke the spare-framed, prettier-than-Cher Bono lookalike, as she adjusted the height of the podium back up from where it had been with Ramirez. "NASA has asked me to give you my impressions of the alien named 'Karéin-Mayréij', from a scientific perspective, and I'll do the best I can... but I must tell you, ladies and gentlemen, that it's difficult to come to valid conclusions, about a being who you have only been able to observe over a long-distance video-link."

But in a few short moments, Sylvia... thought the Storied Watcher.

"Furthermore," went on Abruzzio, "And this is something that Hector has already alluded to, thank you Hector – for much of this period, our attentions were understandably concentrated on dealing with the 'Lucifer' situation; so, unfortunately, some of the time that we might otherwise have spent on learning about 'Karéin', had to be spent on stopping the comet."

Abruzzio stopped to clear her throat, then said, while sounding as uncomfortable as Ramirez had, "In the end, that turned out to have been the right decision... since if the Air Force, working in partnership with NASA, had not stopped 'Lucifer', we all wouldn't be here to talk to one another... right?"

There were a few cheers from the audience, but the response was surprisingly muted, as if the local yokels had heard it all before.

"When we first made contact with this alien," explained the NASA scientist, "We attempted to communicate with, uhh, it, as best we could, keeping in mind that we had in no way prepared for such an eventuality. We would have wanted to have spent more time exploring the cave on Mars in which she had been found – but that had to be put on hold when Captain Jacobson, uhh, carried her back to the *Eagle* spacecraft."

The Storied Watcher rolled her eyes and got the Russian's attention, with a gentle elbow. "Another pointless and irrelevant falsehood!" she grumbled. "It was *Commander Sam* who was carried back to the landing-ship, along with dear Cherie Tanaka... and that was done by Devon and Brent. So many lies – how can I even *begin* to correct them?"

"A futile task – as many who have attempted the same, have discovered," cynically replied Misha.

"As you might expect," remarked Abruzzio, "Given the unprecedented nature of the discovery, a lot of things about 'Karéin' were new to us. For example, she learned English with *amazing* speed – it only took her a few weeks to do that – but despite much effort on both her part and ours, it has so far proved very difficult for us to learn anything of her own language... which seems to be based on sounds and concepts that have no counterparts anywhere on Earth."

The alien-girl leaned over toward the SVR-man.

"*N'ìm h'tä 'm tokhl'à u'wz'iêî, j'aaa,*" she whispered, with a wry smile.

"One day, you must teach me some of that," he muttered, philosophically.

"It means, roughly," she explained, "'Your language is difficult, too.'"

"Although externally her body appears to be, ahem, exactly like that of an ordinary young human woman," continued the scientist, "It was clear right from the time when we first encountered 'Karéin', that she's in fact *radically* different from *Homo Sapiens*. For example, when we tried to use some of our standard tools to examine her internal organs, all we got was, uhh, static. That's to say, there was something interfering with the signal emitted by our portable magnetic resonance-scanners; X-Rays didn't work, either. To tell you the truth, we can't even tell if she's really a conventional living creature – or if she's just some kind of very sophisticated robot, under that human-looking exterior..."

A bemused smile came to the young-looking woman's face.

She leaned over to Misha and opined, "I really *must* give these Americans due credit – they are experts in devising creative lies... but, did I feel much like a clockwork mechanical-person, to you, my love?"

"Feelings such as you bring about," he whispered back, "Cannot be made by any device; but if they could, I would want to build a thousand copies of you."

"However," elaborated the professor, "We *were* able to accomplish some basic research into Karéin's physical appearance. She is approximately 172 centimeters, or around 5 feet, 8 inches, tall, and, based on comparisons with our databases of standard human body types, resembles a blond-haired, green-eyed, Caucasian human female of between 17 to 19 years old – although, according to her own statements, she's *much* older than that, as much as 2 to 600,000 Earth-years, if that's to be believed. These estimates of her age are based on drawings that she made of the positions of objects in the Martian night-sky; we calculated the relative rate of positional drift of some of these stars and planets... assuming that she's not just making it up, of course."

"And you do not look, ah, a *day* over 18, or so," joked the Russian.

"Well... I *do* look after myself, after all," deadpanned the alien, with a low giggle.

"Another interesting thing is," noted Abruzzio, "Despite the fact that 'Karéin' has, ahem, a really nice, medium-slender build, teenager-like figure – hey, folks, I'm just relating what my male friends down at JPL were telling me! – we measured her weight at about 88 kilograms, which is about 195 pounds, for those of you not up on metric. This kind of weight would be next to *impossible* for a human female to carry on such a trim, spare frame as she has... so the theory here is that her body is considerably more dense than ours is, for the same internal volume."

"Is that true?" inquired Misha.

"How would I know?" parried the Storied Watcher. "I have never seen my body-insides, opened up for inspection. Though, many enemies have tried to do so... unlike me, they are no longer alive."

He leaned back in his seat and smiled.

"Like I said before, said the scientist, "I should mention that the DNA-sequencing that we have so far been able to do on the alien's tissue, has produced some truly *amazing* results. Although it has some similarities to the human equivalent – for example, it is carbon-based and is somewhat like that of a higher ape – Karéin's DNA is very different from *anything* that we've so far encountered, anywhere in this solar-system. That's probably a good thing, considering that it would make her almost invulnerable to ordinary human diseases, and would conversely make any little bugs that she's carrying, very unlikely to affect us; which is almost certainly why the crew of the Jacobson Mars mission didn't get sick by being in her physical presence."

"Many of the divergences are highly technical and I won't bore you with them here," continued the professor, "But two, in particular, stand out. First, some of her cells, as well as the DNA within them, seem to mutate at will; there's definitely a pattern and a purpose to this, but we're currently at a loss to figure out what that is. A lot her ordinary body-cells are kind of like human stem-cells – they're able to become anything that's needed, at a given point in time. The second interesting thing is her DNA-sequence, and some of the chromosomes that result from it, are *extremely* complex – for example, some of the samples that we examined, have over five times the number of strands that a normal human's would have. We have no idea at all, what function this extra complexity plays. But, as you can imagine... it's a fascinating new area of exploration for us."

"Finally," concluded Abruzzio, "What this all shows, is that we need to leave all of our expectations about alien life behind, when we start investigating it. 'Karéin' *looks* like us... but, in reality, she's *very* different from you or me, as different as you or I would be from a whale or a honeybee. Like Hector, I deeply regret that we had only a very short time in which to become acquainted with her. But in that time, we gained scientific knowledge that we otherwise might only have come upon, centuries in the future... if ever. Who *knows*, what other, fascinating things that we'll find, as we push ever further out into the universe?"

She stopped, pensively observing the crowd, for a second or two.

"And *that*, ladies and gentlemen," stated the scientist, "Concludes my presentation, for today."

In only a moment, everyone was on their feet, applauding wildly.

He let the enthusiasm go on unabated for twenty seconds or more; but eventually, the white-haired man again mounted the stage, and, advancing to the other side of the podium, he took hold of the microphone and announced, "Well, folks – that was certainly quite *something*... wasn't it? Think you got your money's worth? Let's give our guests another sign of our appreciation!"

After the obligatory roar of hand-clapping, he mentioned, "Now, it's time for questions from the audience – Hector, come on up again – yeah, right on the other side, here. If anyone wants to ask a question, raise your hand, and when we point to you, one of the hotel-staff will bring a microphone over to where you're sitting, then you can stand up and fire away. Just one thing... there are a few subjects that are still off-bounds for reasons of national-security; if we hit one of those, we'll tell you – then you can either ask a different question, or just pass the floor on to the next person. Those of you who don't want to hang on for the question-and-answer session... you're free to leave, if you want, and thank you very much for attending our seminar today. Does everybody understand?"

"What does 'pass the floor' mean?" whispered the Storied Watcher.

"An English expression which means, 'yield the opportunity to speak, to someone else'," explained Misha.

"Okay... so, let's have the first question," called out the white-haired man, surveying the audience.

Pointing to the other side of the floor, three rows or so behind the Russian and his exotic companion, he indicated, "Yeah, *you*, there – third chair from the left. Go ahead."

"Oh," she said, under her breath. "Listen, 'Michael'... I need to ask you something."

"And what would *that* be?" he replied, only half-wanting to hear the answer.

The droning voice of some down-home suburbanite from behind them, started asking a question about "Did this-here Martian-girl ever say anything about sports... like, say, football?"

They could hear Abruzzio attempting to answer, while evidently trying to avoid laughing.

"I must warn you that the American spies are, uhh, 'on to us', as dear Bob would say," advised Karéin-Mayréij, her beautiful eyes looking at him straight-on, though not with the bewitching-trick. "You have every right to flee, now; but... I would have you *stay* with me, whatever happens here."

"We have been *over* that, before," he protested. "I am an – I have, another job. More than that, in fact. You want to know something funny, 'Rosalie'? I am under orders from my government to make it easy for the Americans to find you, track you... if necessary, to *kill* you. Telling you that, would probably earn me the firing-squad, if others at home were to find out. But I *owe* it to you, that you should know the truth... which is, my own 'Empire', is really not that much different from this one. They fear you – and from fear, come terrible mistakes."

"Despite this... I will defend you from all perils," countered the newcomer. "Will you follow your orders and try to kill me, or help others do the same, 'Michael' of the other Empire?"

He lowered his head and wearily shook it.

"No," he quietly admitted. "And you did not need to ask me that."

She took hold of his hand – an embrace whose supernatural warmth, Misha had somehow forgotten – and offered, "I will not ask you to renounce any oath, for doing so would be without honor; but your destiny follows a *different* path, from today on, dear 'Michael'."

The Russian could not think of anything to say, so he just stared forward.

"Folks," joked the white-haired man at the podium, "I think we've established that this alien probably can't tell you who won last year's Super Bowl... right? Next question... okay, you, at the front."

The young-looking woman and her reluctant companion now fell silent, as they patiently listened to off-base inquiry after evasive answer, one following upon another, for many long minutes.

Finally, after the crowd had thinned to perhaps a third of its original number, the announcer again took over the main microphone and said, "Well, that's been quite a few questions, now, so I think it's time to wrap things up... oh, wait a minute... do we have one more, back there?"

To Misha's combined amazement and horror, the one called 'Karéin-Mayréij', was holding her left arm, up high.

Blood On The Carpet

"Yes, young lady?" requested the white-haired emcee, as a hotel-orderly promptly walked over to stand on her right side. "Here, stand up please – okay, there's the microphone. Go ahead."

Sweating, Misha searched desperately for an escape-route.

There will be at least four, probably ten, trained CIA assassins firing at her – and at me, he nervously realized.

A second later, another feeling – one of, he considered, half-insane power and confidence – infected his soul, as he perceived a haunting tune, in the back of his mind.

Regally, the Storied Watcher slowly came to her feet, and the SVR-man noticed that she had advanced forward, by perhaps a half-meter.

"A few modest questions, have I," she began, her eyes gazing straight at Abruzzio and Ramirez, "And behold them now. Why does your President refuse to speak honestly, with the one who you call an 'alien'? Why does he mislead this world, about what she has done at great risk, on behalf of all those who call the Earth their home? Why do his sycophants torment her poor friends in well-hidden dungeons? And – last but certainly not least – why has he tried to *murder* her, for no sensible reason, whatsoever?"

Misha noticed several dark-suited men and women muttering quietly into mobile-communicator units, while they discreetly moved from one position to another.

"We... uhh... well, Miss – what's *this* all about?" complained the emcee. "This meeting concerns the alien from Mars... not the President. Do you have a question that's on topic, please?"

"Oh, I am 'on topic'... I can *assure* you of that, sir," purred Karéin-Mayréij, as she stood, proud and straight.

With a saturnine smile, she doffed the baseball-cap.

Her hair – now as gold-yellow as the Sun – fell in long, flowing locks over her shoulders, matching in perfection, her complexion and eyes, which had also reverted to their true, not-far-from-godly norms.

"Hi, Hector... Sylvia," called out the Storied Watcher, with a half-curtsy that would have only been familiar to a select few. "I am *so* happy that we can finally meet, in-person. Do you remember how I promised that we would, ahh, 'do science', together?"

What's that music coming over the intercom? noted a big, tough-looking, long-haired man, several rows back.

Fuckin' great rock... but what band... and where?

Abruzzio's jaw dropped, and it was matched by Ramirez' look of shocked, but overjoyed, surprise.

Sylvia, Hector – open your minds to me, the alien-girl tried to send in their direction.

Though I cannot properly prepare you... I pray that you can learn and keep the truth.

Bewildered, the emcee turned quickly to whisper something in the direction of the two NASA scientists, while an agitated discourse went on at, and behind, the front platform.

The Storied Watcher turned her head, first to the left, then to the right, addressing the remaining crowd.

"Ordinary people of Tucson," she calmly but forcefully pronounced, "It may not henceforth be safe for you, in here. I would advise that you should leave, as soon as possible."

Torn between destiny, duty and common sense, Misha moved two or three chairs further to the left.

A few of the more perceptive attendees started to uneasily head for the exits; but a good fifteen or twenty more, evidently wanting to witness something 'exciting', hung around anyway.

"Did you not hear what I *said?*" she again broadcast to the crowd.

"What's the *problem?*" demanded the huge, square-headed, leather-faced, tattooed man with long hair and a goatee beard, who was nursing the last dregs of a cup of beer on the unoccupied chair next to him.

"So you mouthed off about the President," he grunted with a shrug, flexing his bulging biceps. "Big fuckin' deal! Man's got a *point*, though – if you ain't got nothin' real to ask, lady – why don't you *say* so, so we can all go up and get us a few more autographs?"

"You have no *idea* how funny that sounds, sir," answered Karéin-Mayréij, with a sharp, malevolent smile. "Very well – but I cannot be held responsible... you have been *warned.*"

"Warned about *what*? You mean, about you wasting yet more of everyone's day, young lady?" complained a waspish-looking woman, near the front of the audience.

She is not even trying *to hide them, anymore,* mentally noted the Russian.

Even the Americans *cannot be so stupid as to miss what* that *means!*

"Why not ask our two guest-speakers, Madam?" remarked the newcomer. "I think that they will attest, that this is not wasted time."

With a newly-pale complexion to match his hair, the emcee, his hands fumbling a note that had just been passed to him, stammered over the microphone, "Ladies and... gentlemen... I... uhh... have a special announcement... due to a terrorist threat that we've just received, we have to ask you to immediately leave this building – please line up in single file at the main exit, remain calm..."

A whiff of fear passed through the crowd, and most of the attendees started to stand and rapidly collect their belongings; but, at that precise moment, the Storied Watcher's eyes flashed, and every exit-door slammed loudly shut, as if kicked by some unseen force.

Still fixed in her original position, Karéin-Mayréij called out to all of them, as the air became thick, electric with some kind of atmospheric adrenaline.

The music – a subtly-rumbling, exciting rock-beat – was now echoing in minds both inside the locked room and out.

"By now, you have all made your choice," she taunted. "Sit down and enjoy the show. Oh, and... 'duck when necessary'."

Misha could not help himself from laughing, although he silently prayed that none of the American spies would notice.

Aghast, some of the seminar-goers went back to their seats, while others clustered around the exits, which seemed to be quite impossible for even two or three grown men to force open.

"And now I address the many spy-warriors of the U.S. Empire, who hide in ambush, all around here," called the alien-girl. "Leave me and those who I love alone, and let me just talk to my friends Sylvia and Hector. I promise that I will not strike the first blow – but, be of no doubt – I can and *will* defend myself. Try again to kill me, and *you will die!* Let us meet in peace, today, this I pray –"

Suddenly, there was a loud shout, from behind and to her right.

"*To Hell With The Devil!*" it screamed.

In quick succession, two shots rang out, followed by three or four more seemingly coming from different directions behind the Storied Watcher, as the panicked crowd dove under tables, chairs or anything.

There was the reverberating sound of a ricochet, and – with small sparks flying from the point of impact – the newcomer was instantly knocked forward over the chair directly ahead of her, as if punched hard in the small of the back. Oddly, though, no blood issued forth.

As she gasped and sputtered, dark-suited secret-agents, guns drawn, issued forth from either side of the front platform. They advanced rapidly down the periphery of the room on either side.

Grimacing and reaching her arm around to feel her back, Karéin-Mayréij righted herself and wheeled in place, rapidly half-singing, half-chanting,

"*Ahn-JAY-YE! Faya-GAR-yoo! EE-YA-beh!*"

Her body disappeared for a half-second, and the clothes that had formerly adorned her, vanished in a dull flash; but, in the next eye-blink, a new and radically *different* creature, terrible in weirding war-garb, appeared before the amazed, frightened, overawed onlookers.

Ooo – Oooo – Ooooo – wailed an entrancing, electric-Celtic-sounding melody, its susurrating, pulsing, subtle back-beat issuing simultaneously from somewhere and nowhere.

Did her eyes glow more brightly than what adorned her frame? Such questions would be worthy of debate, for the mighty Storied Watcher was now clad, head to toe, in the fortress of *Vîrya Ahn'jë*, her thousands of tiny, infernally-hot, scale-mail plates each shimmering with a subtly-different color : a translucent, shifting, black-and-silver-and-gold-and-everything-else pattern, looking akin to a picture taken slightly out of focus.

Arcane runes glowed dimly on the skull-cap that protected the head of this latter-day 'Destroying Angel'; and crimson-red, admixed with blue and dark green, shone the blade of the former *katana* – now transformed into something radically more potent – named *Fàiagàryuu*, who had secured himself to a belt-clasp on the right side of silver-black-gold-hued *Ahn'jë*.

The shield, who she had named *I'ëà'b'*, was grayish-blue over black upon her left arm, while the yellow-orange-over-ebon dagger named *Ksé'l'ch'* was subtly affixed to the outside of the lower part of her left leg, with his 'brother', purple-and-navy *Ss'éth'ch'*, taking an opposite position on her right shin-side.

Oddly, the cape-part of *Vîrya Ahn'jë* was mostly rolled-up around the shoulders of the Storied Watcher, although enough of its scale-encrusted black-and-silver still flowed out to cover the top half of her back. Her hair was now bound in pony-tail-fashion, by still another aspect of the Storied Watcher's youngest war-child; securely hidden behind *Ahn'jë*'s body-armor was secretive *Vîrya Quü'j*, eldest and wisest of them all.

Striking a deadly-determined, martial pose, but wheeling in place without moving a muscle, the alien-girl looked quickly behind her and toward the concession-table, tracking the rapid advance of the spy-men on either side of the room.

While doing this, she noticed a commotion of some kind going on around the front platform; a loud argument of some sort had erupted.

Meanwhile, three rows back from her own position, stood a big, tattooed guy, holding a still-smoking handgun, his feet firmly anchored in classic "ready-to-fire" mode. The man's weapon was pointed at the remains of a bullet-riddled chair on the other side of the center aisle.

Below the chair, were the bloody remains of a nondescript-looking, middle-aged Caucasian man. This unfortunate also had evidently wielded a handgun – a smaller, composite weapon – still gripped tightly in his dead hands.

Inertia – or gravity – caused the corpse to roll over, and out of its surrounding clothes fell a pear-sized, green-colored metal object. It bounced along the conference-room floor, and, a second later, more panic ensued as several of the onlookers realized what the thing was.

"Chill out!" ordered the big gunman. "Yeah, I see it too... but the pin's still in. It ain't gonna blow, 'less you're stupid enough to pull it out."

Now, both the Storied Watcher, and the tough-guy, were penned-in by six or seven dark-suited government agents, all with various kinds of hand-held weapons pointing inward, toward the mass of folding seats.

"Put down your weapon and get down on the floor – hands behind your back!" gruffly shouted one of the agents, from the left side of the room. "You are now in the custody of the United States! Surrender – you're *surrounded!*"

"Hey, boys, let's not get *personal* 'bout this!" parried the big man, not changing his stance. "I'm just a bounty-hunter – Wolf's the name – saw that sonofabitch over there start shooting at the chick in the Hallowe'en disco-ball suit, so I dusted him with good ol' plastic Betsy, here – well, we got a 'pre-emptive self-defense with firearms' law in this-here state, you know? I got every *right*... but I don't want no trouble... don't want to lose my license. I'll get down, okay?"

Slowly, he started to bend his knees. He shoved his gun across the floor toward the agents.

Terrified though he was, from his perspective to the young-looking woman's side, Misha could not resist the urge to laugh, however softly.

A 'bounty-hunter', he thought. *With a gun. In here, with...*

God, get me out of this insane country – it has *to be safer in front of a firing-squad in Moscow!*

But his reverie was interrupted by another invocation coming from Karéin-Mayréij.

"KSS-AY-elsh! sss-AYthh-CHH!" she hissed, through fanged lips.

Faster than any could perceive, a deep-blue-and-violet-colored dagger, accompanied by an unnerving, wailing sound, issued from one of the alien's leg-pieces, with its bright orange-yellow counterpart, singing its own chiming, staccato song, flying from the other.

The blue weapon flew into her left hand, with the other one depositing itself into her right. She now stood with her arms outstretched, pointing these weapons at the dark-suited men who pointed their guns at her, from either side of the room.

With a mixture of fascination and fear, Misha observed that a sheen of hoarfrost was starting to envelop the alien's left gauntlet, while the right-hand one glowed dull red.

How can she hold *those ungodly things?* he pondered.

I am several feet below and to the left of the blue one... and I can still feel the hellish cold of it going right through *me.*

It felt like every ounce of warmth in his rapidly-numbing head and arms was being sucked outward, upward, toward that accursed thing.

Do not worry, sounded a thought in his mind.

Væran Ss'éth'ch' is trying not to hurt you... but make sure to be far away, from where he strikes.

"No, spy-men of the American Empire, it is *you*, who do not understand!" growled the Storied Watcher. "Indeed, there *are* captives here – and they live at the whim of their captor, who now addresses them. Put away your weapons – *all* of them, including the little plastic guns and poison-darts, that you have hidden in various places on your bodies... sit down, and let me explain my purpose to you. Then, I *might* let you go in peace."

Misha noticed that the blade of the sword at her waist was giving off an alternatively orange-red and blue-green glow.

One of the secret-agents, his other hand still holding a gun pointed at the alien, unhooked a small portable-communicator from his belt, held it up to his lips, and started talking, under his breath.

"Target acquired," he whispered. "But armed with unknown weapons, and uncooperative. Request procedure update."

For perhaps ten seconds, the stand-off continued, with half of those in the room holding their breaths.

Eventually, the lead spy-man, having heard something through his ear-piece, turned to address the young-looking woman.

"You're instructed to immediately allow all non-combatants to egress this facility, lay down your weapons and surrender!" he demanded. "The National Command Authority assures that you won't be harmed, and that the President will communicate with you in due time. Do you understand?"

"Tell your President," spat the Storied Watcher, "To, ahh, 'fuck off'! He can negotiate with me right now, – over that fancy little speaking-box that you have with you. And tell him that he *severely* tries my patience. His time has run out, and if he does not free – *ohhhhh!!!*"

With a look of severe pain, she suddenly stumbled, as if gut-punched by a heavyweight.

"*Tommy!*" moaned an agonized Karéin-Mayréij.

"*Go!*" shouted one of the agents, as guns blazed, the spies lunged forward,and utter confusion reigned over an impromptu battlefield.

Panicked seminar-goers crawled toward the periphery of the room on hands and knees, as quickly as they could.

An electric-rock song – or something like a song – pounded its beat into Misha's head; and, until his conscious mind pulled him back, he was about to leap up and attack, all by himself.

In the shuffling madness, of the locomotive...

A hail of bullets tore through the air toward the alien-girl; but, a microsecond before they left the gun-barrels, the two daggers each screamed toward her tormentors.

A fraction of a second later, the little shield shot from her arm. With a hundred times the speed of the fastest tornado, it orbited her like some kind of mobile armor, deflecting each projectile as it invaded the newcomer's space, sending lethal ricochets in all directions.

A well-built, brush-cut Caucasian guy with a pock-marked face, dressed in a conservative business-suit subtly different from those evident on the other agents, sneered and shouted something like "*Kill her!*"

Stepping quickly forward, he threw a small switch on his pistol and it began shooting like a machine-gun.

Evidently, the man meant to overwhelm *Vìrya I'ëà'b'* by sheer weight of firepower; but his gambit was short-lived, as dark-blue *Ss'éth'ch'* impacted with the gun. In the next half-second, a choking, numbing wave of cold beset the entire room. Misha tried to take a breath, but the pain of the super-chilled air as it entered his lungs, made him involuntarily exhale. Coughing and sputtering, he doubled over.

As he tried to regain his balance, the Russian looked up in shock, at what the blue dagger had done. The assailant had been instantly frozen solid, and, along with the pillar of icy air-condensation that covered his remains, he shattered into something resembling a ghoulish parody of a Bloody Mary On The Rocks, as the dagger's inertia took it right through the center of what had, a half-second before, been a living human being.

Meanwhile, with *Vîrya I'ëà'b'* still encircling her slumping figure, two of the dark-suited men dived at the newcomer – and were instantly, horrifically mangled by the shield's sharp edge, which sliced off one agent's nose and forearms, and another's right arm, ear and leg, like some kind of mad, free-flying skill-saw-blade.

Blood splattered everywhere, with the two critically wounded spies thrashing their lives away on the floor.

On the opposite side of the room, the orange-yellow dagger flew right into the pistol-barrel of a hulking, black Federal agent, melting it instantly into flaming slag. The man screamed in pain as he tried to use charred, blistered hands to put out a fire that was rapidly spreading over his suit-sleeves, but some kind soul managed to throw the remnants of a cup of beer at the spy, and he collapsed to the floor, wailing in agony.

Oddly, both of the weirding daggers, as if uncertain what to do next, stopped attacking and returned to a position high over the battle-scene, hovering ominously.

"Immobilize and terminate!" came a shout from the confusion, and a steel-reinforced composite net, fired from some hidden location and dripping with some kind of green goo, bloomed like a mushroom over the alien-girl.

The shield impacted with this on its way down; and – though *Vîrya I'ëà'b'* tried mightily – her nascent skills could cut but a few strands, before the net had floated down to completely envelop her erstwhile "mother".

Though none of the humans – save Misha, whose mind perceived a weird, edge-of-consciousness wail – could hear, *Vîrya I'ëà'b'* cried out to the Storied Watcher in frustration.

"Grab her!" ordered the lead government agent, and two or three of the biggest remaining spies again rushed forward, jumping on top of the net like in a rugby-scrum-for-keeps. To their dismay, they felt their clothes and exposed parts of skin start to sear, upon coming into contact with her armor.

The shield retreated to its resting-place on the Storied Watcher's arm. Now – despite the weight of several hundred pounds of sweating human flesh on top of her – she rose up like a leviathan, cruel and powerful, underneath this restraining-device.

"Think you have *got* me, pathetic humans?" contemptuously snarled Karéin-Mayréij, through fanged lips, as they each pointed drawn guns at her head, not a meter from it.

In a split-second, a burst of energy, akin to a huge electric short-circuit, shot out from the alien, throwing each of her shocked, singed tormentors back by a good three man-lengths.

With blindingly-fast sword-strikes from *Væran Fàiagàryuu* – whose blade, Misha noted, was covered with little, dancing motes of blue-green flame – the Storied Watcher effortlessly cut the net to shreds; it simply disintegrated, as the sword hit each strand. Then, palms outstretched as if praying for a benediction, she caused the shards of the net to rise up all around her.

The creature's eyes flashed, and these shattered remnants flamed and melted into charred dust.

From one side, came another call.

"*Send the mechs!*" it ordered.

Those in the room heard faint 'clicking' sounds, and one or two even saw from whence this noise issued – strange, box-like things, each about the size of an old-style tower-PC, suspended on six articulated, metal legs.

At least four of these robotic machines rapidly closed the distance, illuminating the Storied Watcher with pencil-thin laser-beams, which were followed a fraction of a second later, by yet more bullets, fired by a Gatling-gun like contraption on top of each unit.

The alien-girl let out a whooping martial-arts shout and, in a heartbeat, propelled herself five meters or more into the air, with the projectiles fired by the mechanical killing-machines alternately melting and ricocheting from her protective bubble.

She wheeled in mid-air, facing downward for a second, and instantly, the shiny insect-like things were all gathered into a single, clicking, whirring, gun-firing mass, which was thrown hard against the high conference-room ceiling, when, in the next second, her rotation again faced upwards.

Boom! came the sound of a powerful explosion that shook the entire building and blew a five-meter hole in the roof of the room; the shrapnel would have shredded many of those below, were it not to have been blocked by the young-looking woman's force-field.

Gypsum dust and small pieces of metal and wood rained down from above.

Her shimmering, electrified figure framed by the flowing, now-unfurled cape of *Vîrya Ahn'jë*, Karéin-Mayréij landed on compressing legs, her feet impacting with the floor with the sound of thunder.

"You cruel *swine!*" she cursed. "Your war-boxes would have killed all in the hereabouts! Send your cowardly *masters* to fight me... if they dare!"

The few Federal agents who were left in anything like operational condition, had the presence of mind to retreat and hide. One of them pulled out his mobile-communicator-box.

He whispered, "Headquarters, we need to *sanitize*, ASAP! Advise estimate, time-on-target."

SNAFU Report From The Hotel Tucson

Notwithstanding the fact that he had been given plenty of advance notice about the seminar with the two scientists – and despite the balm of two of Air Force One's best stiff drinks ahead of time – the President still jumped nervously upward, when his mobile-communicator showed "ANDERSON" on the incoming ID-display.

"Yes, General?" he asked.

"Mr. President," advised Anderson, using a professionally-smooth tone, "I'm afraid we have a *situation*, down in Tucson."

"I'm afraid to ask," quickly responded the American leader, "But... what *kind* of situation?"

"We're still not exactly sure... reports from the scene are sporadic, and they don't make a lot of sense," explained the General. "But here's what we *do* know, so far : it looks like that the alien *did*, indeed, show up to the seminar – the second, afternoon one, which was due to have been over and done with, by about now. Evidently she showed herself in full view of the audience just as the question-and-answer period was about to come to an end, and then started demanding to speak with yourself, directly, but –"

"Well then – why haven't I had a call from her, yet?" demanded the President.

"As I was about to say, Mr. President, sir," continued Anderson, "Things get confused, at this point. Apparently shots were fired, and –"

"'*Shots were fired*'?" retorted the President, his voice furious. "What the hell do you *mean*, 'shots were fired', General! By *who!* I *specifically* gave orders that no action was to be taken against the alien –"

"I understand your concern, sir... but we just don't *know*," pleaded the General. "Except that there have apparently been some casualties – CIA is reporting that it has four agents down. They're saying that some kind of weird, uhh, 'music' started playing; then the alien deployed some kind of previously-unknown weaponry against them... their own weapons have, uhh, proved completely... ineffective."

"*Jesus Christ!*" angrily exclaimed the U.S. leader, a faint sheen of sweat breaking out upon his brow. "Isn't this *exactly* what McPherson warned would happen? I *knew* that some kind of bullshit like this was going to happen, I just *knew* it! Alright. Look – what's going on right now? Is the alien still in the hotel?"

"From what we can tell," remarked Anderson, "This has now degenerated into a hostage-situation, with this so-called 'Storied Watcher' holding at least twenty civilians, plus the close-in teams from CIA and FBI, plus McPherson's two associates from JPL, as 'human shields'. The Agency claims that she's threatening to kill all of them if her demands aren't met –"

"*What* demands?" interrupted the American leader. "And why, in God's name, has she become so goddamn *confrontational*, all of a sudden? I talked to the bloody alien *myself*, while she was in that Mars ship, uhh, the one that Jacobson was in charge of. She was all sweetness and light –"

"It's a mystery, for sure," interjected the General, "Although one of the early reports had her saying the same stuff as quoted from the incident at the TV station – you know, 'free my family' and so on. I should warn you, we're getting reports from the FBI-team that's also on the scene, that somewhat contradict what CIA's saying... they have her being more conciliatory... I wish I could reconcile these for you, sir, but as you recall, Defense wasn't allowed to have soldiers there, because it would have –"

"Okay... *okay*," muttered the President, "Let's cut to the chase, here. Where's Jerry Kaysten? Wasn't *he* supposed to be down there? And what about our military assets?"

"As far as I know, the Chief of Staff *is*, indeed, down there at the Hotel Tucson," confirmed Anderson. "That's the good news. The *bad* news is, we can't get in contact with him – all the local cell-connections are saturated. He might even be in the seminar-room, which would mean that *he's* now a hostage, too. As far as for military forces in the area, we can offer you almost anything that you want in terms of air-power – gunships, fighters, stealth-drones with precision-guided munitions, even one of the low-yield nukes that we spoke about in our last meeting; and General Blanshard informs me that he has at least a battalion of ground troops at Davis-Monthan. It would take them about 40 minutes to get fully deployed to the vicinity of the Hotel Tucson – but there, we have a bit of a complication..."

"And what would *that* be?" mumbled the President, looking dejectedly out over the aircraft's wing.

"Well, sir," noted the General, "The task of defending the building's perimeter has been, ahem, 'subcontracted' to GrayWar Corporation – they have several hundred, uhh, 'soldiers' there. In the past, when we've sent regular troops in to relieve them, there have been problems every time... up to and including shooting-incidents."

"Too bad. Get 'em out, as soon as you can," ordered the U.S. leader.

"By the way," warned Anderson, "We seem to already have had one such situation – details are sketchy but it looks like two of GrayWar's people and a civilian – a young woman similar in outward-appearance to the alien, were shot – dead by a sniper, as the evacuees exited the building. Several more are seriously wounded."

"I don't *understand*," remarked the President. "I thought that DoD didn't have any people covering the building?"

"Correct – we had no sharp-shooters there, although some are now on their way," commented the General. "Maybe this was some kind of screw-up on the part of the Tucson Police SWAT team? We're investigating, of course. And as this is an emergency, we can contact Mr. Duke at GrayWar and have him issue the 'get out of there' order personally. However... that'll take time – maybe an hour or so."

"Do so!" demanded the President.

Another circuit lit up on the communicator, and this time the ID, to the President's immense relief, showed "J-KAYSTEN".

Immediately, and pleased that he had mastered this technological feat, the U.S. leader pressed a button and cross-connected the two lines.

"Jerry? *Jerry?* You there?" asked the President.

"Yeah... Kaysten here," came back a ghostly voice.

"I can hardly hear you," complained the American leader. "Where are you?"

"I'm down here across the street from the hotel, in our temporary control-center," said the Chief of Staff. "All the cell-phones down here are acting up, so's a lot of the other wireless stuff. There's some kind of weird interference – spooks are trying to track it down and compensate for it... so far, no dice."

"We'll just have to live with that," directed the President. "Listen, Jerry... I have Anderson on the line, as well – what the *hell's* going on down there, for Christ's sake? This was supposed to be a *low-risk* operation – at least that's how it was sold to me."

"Your guess is as good as mine, sir," explained Kaysten. "I got no idea what's happening inside the seminar-room – I was in there with Abruzzio and Ramirez up to near the end of the question-and-answer section... looked like nothing was going to happen, so I stepped out the back door to answer the call of nature... got out of the bathroom, was on my way back, heard some kind of big commotion inside the room and I noticed a bunch of people charging out in a total panic."

"Jerry, you've *got* to get in there and talk to this 'Karéin' creature, or whatever she's calling herself these days – from what I hear from the General, this situation is spinning out of control, and I need somebody in there who I can *trust* –" demanded the President.

"Sorry – no can do, sir," argued the Chief of Staff. "I already *tried* to get back in... but shortly after that weirdo music started coming from inside the conference-room, the door that I went out, *all* of them leading back in there, in fact, are... well, it's like they're just *glued* shut – damnedest thing, we had four big guys on 'em, can't even budge 'em. Right after that, we heard shooting and the FBI-team that we had outside the room hustled us off to this place across the street. So here I am."

There was nothing but static on the line, and for a second or two, the President was afraid that he had lost Kaysten's signal.

But eventually, the Staff Chief's voice again sounded, faint as ever.

"If this makes any difference, now, Mr. President," he apologized, "I'm... *sorry*. We planned this one out as carefully as we possibly could... but it got away from us. I have no *idea* how that happened – no idea at all –"

"Apologies and ass-kickings later, Jerry," grumbled the President, "Right now, we don't have time for all that – we have to try to stop this fiasco from deteriorating any further. From what you can tell, is the alien still holed up inside the hotel – in that conference-room, I mean?"

"*Think* so," confirmed the Chief of Staff, "At least, that's what the local FBI guy is saying – he's been in contact with Bureau H.Q.. Both the Agency and the Bureau have people trapped in there, and I've been trying to shake information out of them – but here again, we're running into this weird communications-thing – the closer that you get to the hotel, the weaker the signals get... it may be impossible for the agents in the room, to get a report out."

"Listen," inquired the U.S. leader, slowly and deliberately, "General Anderson has informed me that the alien may have been responsible for as many as four deaths... maybe more. Oh, and she's threatening to kill more hostages, if her demands – whatever those are – aren't immediately met. Is that true?"

"Can neither confirm nor deny those claims, sir," came back Kaysten's static-laden voice. "And probably nobody will be able to, until we can get in there and do a head-count. But judging from all the shooting that I heard, I'd have to assume that there *were* casualties, Mr. President, sir. As to who shot first and who got hit... well, the only thing we pretty much know for sure is that the alien herself is still standing... otherwise we'd already have dealt with the situation."

There was a long silence, then the President stated, "Okay... I understand. One other thing – what's going on, PR-wise? Who knows about this, so far? If we had to use military force, how much control would we have over what gets out into the media?"

"Well, sir," explained Kaysten, "Tucson City Police are already on-scene within the hotel, and they've been instructed to use the terrorist angle as a cover-story; standard procedure, that is, we've got more latitude to invoke 'national-security' to shut down the media from reporting on it, than if we had, say, called it a gangster shoot-out. We've noticed a few amateur photographers and voggers standing around, and of course we've confiscated their equipment – but in the last ten minutes I heard a rumor that several of the local TV stations are sending reporters down here... I've dispatched some Secret Service people to all of the Tucson stations, ordering them not to run any reports on what's going down, but as you'll recall from the Miami incident, this stuff is *bound* to leak out, sooner or later... really a matter of 'when', not 'if'."

"Put a lid on it, Jerry!" demanded the American leader. "I don't care how you do it... just *do* it – you go that?"

"10-4, sir," confirmed the Chief of Staff, "From my POV, bottom line here is, if the situation remains just inside the conference-hall, we've got a fair chance of containing the media fallout... if it goes past that, there may be *nothing* we can do, short of arresting half of downtown Tucson."

"We may have to do *just* that," grimly stated the President. "We can *not* allow news of what's really going on, to hit the national networks. We might end up with a total breakdown of state authority, overnight."

"I'd tend to agree with that, Mr. President," agreed Anderson. "And in that light – as little as I'd like to admit it – if we use more than minimal military force against the alien while it's in the Hotel Tucson, there may be *significant* civilian collateral-damage. The building-staff are apparently trying to evacuate it as we speak, but.. well, I suppose I don't have to explain the risks, if we, say, drop a bomb anywhere near there..."

"No – you certainly don't," muttered the President.

"If it's of any interest," added the General, "I'd have to say that I'm gaining some respect for the alien's ability to think strategically. She – it – must have calculated that revealing itself under these circumstances, would constrain our military options, given the collateral-damage issue. These are *classic* terrorist tactics, Mr. President... and what's significant from a military point of view is, it may mean that she isn't strong enough to take us on out in the open. In my opinion, that's something you should take into account, when planning our own next move."

A smartly-dressed Air Force lieutenant now interrupted the meeting.

His face wore a look of urgency.

"Mr. President, sir," he said, "President of the Russian Federation on the Hot-Line."

Crossing A Fateful Line

With the blood-covered floor squishing underneath *Vîrya Ahn'jë's* war-boots, a tense and angry Karéin-Mayréij bent over the two limbless agents that had fallen afoul of *I'ëà'b*'s edge.

"Fools – you were *warned!*" she spat out through a fanged grimace, at the pitiful, gasping, nearly-dead creatures. "I should let you slowly die here; however, perhaps it is better that you live, as a warning. But your life-essence spills. I will stop that – though not so as to give away my blessing, which you deserve not."

She looked upward.

"*Ksé'l'ch'*," she invoked.

The mangled agents screamed, as the orange dagger cauterized what was left of severed arms, legs and arteries; then it, as well as the blue one, flew back to its resting-place on the alien's lower leggings.

"Try to keep them alive, *Vîrya Ahn'jë*... no more," ordered the Storied Watcher, as, carefully ensuring that her flesh did not make contact with their own, she laid an armored-glove hand on each of her victims.

"*Vîrya I'ëà'b*," added the newcomer, "Provide the same to the man over there, who has felt the burning kiss of thy brother, infernal *Ksé'l'ch'*. Then help those others who have been wounded, by the foolish gunfire of these warrior-spies. But if any more raise a hand against us – remove that, and any else that needs be, with thy edge of sharpness."

The shield flew from the alien-girl's arm and landed on the black man.

Within three seconds, his breathing became more normal, and his moans reduced to whimpers.

The buckler returned to her mistress.

Now, Karéin-Mayréij looked over at the still-frozen, shattered remains of the dead spy.

"My first, down here," she quietly observed, with a tone of genuine remorse. "How many *more*, before all is done? This accursed path, I have trod before."

Her voice rising to the accompaniment of an other-worldly dirge, in the direction of the hidden scientists, she wailed, "Am I then not *terrible* in my might? Have ye not reason enough, to fear me? For there are some wrongs, that can *never* be made right."

As her chin trembled and a feeling of utter despair radiated from the creature, a tear dropped from her eye; but after a second or two, the alien-girl had evidently regained her composure, and, after observing that the three crippled agents were no longer at death's door, she walked over to the bounty-hunter and crouched down to address him.

"Thanks for shooting that gun-assailant, on my behalf," she mentioned. "I am sincerely in your debt, though in fact his bullet did little more than pain me with a bruise. Oh, and..."

"And... uhh... what..." stammered the stunned gunman, used as he was to using his size and strength to be the man-in-charge.

"My war-child, *Vîrya Ahn'jë*," explained the Storied Watcher, "Asks, 'what is a Hallowe'en disco-ball suit'? She inquired of her, ah, grandmother, *Vîrya Quü'j*, about it... but even *her* wisdom fails in this matter. Is such a thing, famous armor? *Vîrya Ahn'jë* hopes and expects that it has seen many victorious battles, if she is to be named with its legacy."

The bounty-hunter lowered and shook his head.

Thinking as quickly as he could – but not knowing if he dared to laugh – he managed, "It's... uhh... yeah, it's, like, uhh... really good. It's, uhh... like that stuff they make them big Army tanks out of... you know?"

With inscrutable sincerity, Karéin-Mayréij smiled at the man.

"She is pleased with your answer," she remarked. "Which is fortunate, for you."

"Well, that's... uhh... great," he evaded. "Listen, lady – like... what the fuck *are* you, anyway?"

Again, a pleasant, saturnine half-grin appeared on the face of the newcomer, with an odd dip of her head to one side.

"You can think of me as someone," she answered, "Who can either *save* your little Empire of the United States, or set it on fire, from end to end... depending upon how wise your President turns out to be, in the next few minutes."

"*Riiight*," he uneasily replied.

The Storied Watcher now rose to her feet, accosting the still-armed agents, who had barricaded themselves behind whatever obstacles – overturned chairs, the edge of the front platform, *et cetera* – were most convenient.

"I hear you conspiring with your leaders, over those voice-boxes that you wear," she called out. "Now hear me well! Your fool-hardiness has already resulted in the needless death of one of your fellow-warriors – and several more may yet not survive to see the end of this day. It is near a *miracle* that none of the common-folk in here, have been fatally wounded; but the next time that you make an attempt on my life, my war-children will be even *less* restrained. *You and your miserable little American army do not stand a* chance *against me!* Give yourselves up – or, at least, throw me a voice-box, so I can speak with this 'President' of yours. If he has any honor, he will act as a true leader, and parley."

She paused for a second and, in a loud voice, added, "Sylvia, Hector... I know that you can hear me. I am *so* sorry! I will do all that I can to avoid hurting you, but... you should hide, as best you can..."

The alien-girl fell silent, then again shouted to the black-suits, "I give you sixty seconds; and at the fifty-count, you should make your peace with your God."

"*Karéin!*" implored the hushed voice of the Russian, from under his chair. "Stay your hand – I *beg* you! These agents probably have no authority – they do only what they are told, to disobey means death, for them. But I have an idea..."

Without moving a muscle, Karéin-Mayréij slid over to be in front of where Misha had hidden.

"And what would *that* be?" she inquired, *sotto voce*, her gaze never leaving any possible route from which an attack could issue.

"I have my own mobile-communicator," he hastily disclosed. "If you approve, I will call Moscow on it – then ask the leader of my own country to make an emergency call to his American counterpart. We can then connect the two calls together, so that you can talk directly to the American President."

"Just like I did with the phone-switch at Bob's work-place," acknowledged the newcomer. "But he refuses to speak with me, over his own soldier's talking-boxes. Why would he do differently, under your scheme?"

"Because, the United States and Russia have a long-standing rule, that when my own *President* calls theirs on a priority-channel, the latter *must* immediately reply," stated the Russian. "It was put in place to prevent an accidental war with atomic bombs."

"Hmm... it *might* work," she allowed. "I hold little hope for this plan – but though I *always* make good on my threats, I desire no more human-blood to stain my hands – the stink of wrongful death turns my stomach and pollutes my soul. Do it – and quickly!"

Nodding vigorously, he pulled out a small cell-phone-like-device and quickly dialed a number on it.

A second later, a crestfallen look appeared on Misha's face.

Looking up at the Storied Watcher, the crestfallen SVR-man explained, "It is being jammed – the signal, that is. I should have *known* – this is standard procedure for those in my profession."

"Dial it again... and hold it up to me," she requested.

Her gaze still on the tensed, crouching American agents, she called out, "A ten-minute reprieve has been granted. Make no hostile move – he who does, will be instantly cut down!"

The agents made no reply, although there was clearly much communication going on, judging from the sounds coming from behind the front platform.

While Misha's arm was still heading upward, he felt the communicator being yanked away, by some unseen force.

It was now in the Storied Watcher's left hand.

Her eyes darted between her opponents and the display on the phone's screen, as she directed, "Take my grasp, Misha – and do not let go. I will re-enter the commands that you just put into this little speaking-box, while you hold it in your other hand; and, as I have smelled the radio-waves that it sends out, I will make them stronger... the signal should break through the Americans' chaos-waves, now."

The device drifted down to where he could snatch it, and he watched the buttons of the key-pad self-depress as he embraced this fearful being's left hand.

So now you see my fine-tuned arts of death, came a thought.

My crimes disgust me... and I must eventually make account for them.

But sometimes, only cruel actions can bring justice... or, survival.

A faint voice – weaker than that to which he was accustomed – sounded at the other end of the link.

In Russian, it announced, "Alexi here – 'hearing aid' engaged. But your signal is poor... what is your report?"

"I am in a Class *Dvina* emergency situation, with the Storied Watcher right next to me," advised the Russian spy, in his own language. "Alexi – I need you to patch us in to the *Presidient*, immediately – and tell him that he needs to initiate a Red-Telephone-call to the American President, to connect with the one that we are on now. Do you copy?"

"Copy," sounded the voice. "But... *surely*, there are details? What, precisely, is this situation?"

"No time!" countered the SVR-man. "Except – tell him that *disastrous* violence will result, if he cannot mediate a solution between the U.S. President, and the alien. This situation is escalating *rapidly* out of control... do you copy?"

"Copy," affirmed Alexi. "No doubt you know the consequences, for a false alarm, here. Cross-connecting, now."

"That is rather funny, really," mentioned Misha, in English. "How could the consequences be much worse?"

Softly, Karéin-Mayréij counseled, "Easily... for example, the Americans could drop a large airplane-bomb on this building – as their warriors are now discussing with their leaders, at the other end of this room. Hence the ten minutes. I will need only a few seconds to make my escape, but you and the others would need more..."

"Hey," shouted the bounty-hunter, himself crouched down as low as comfortably possible. "What's goin' on?"

"Quiet!" retorted Misha. "Can you not see that she is *busy?*"

"Do I have a connection, yet?" demanded the young-looking woman.

"Not yet," muttered the Russian. "Still trying to get my own *Presidient*, then –"

Addressing the bounty-hunter, but neither moving nor changing her constant scanning for the slightest hint of movement on the part of her opponents, the Storied Watcher asked, "You said that your name is 'Wolf', and that you are a hunter of humans... is that correct?"

"Yeah," affirmed Wolf. "But I only go after the bad-guys. You know, druggies, bail-jumpers, illegals and such. I don't do gangs, though."

"Why is that?" she idly inquired.

"Too dangerous," he answered. "Them gang-bangers is *mean.*"

"'Too dangerous'!" muttered Misha, with a nervous, rueful laugh. "'Too *dangerous*', he says... now *that*, is funny. Tell me, Mister 'Wolf'... have you looked around here, lately – "

Then, suddenly, he changed to his native language, and began to speak something in rapid-fire cant.

"Come over here, 'Wolf'," requested Karéin-Mayréij. "But stay low. If they fire, I must as well. I would not want my war-children to, ah, make a *mistake*, in your case."

She slightly changed her stance, to address the platform, or, more precisely, those arrayed behind it.

"*Hector! Sylvia!*" called the alien-girl. "I cannot go over there to meet you, without again risking a 'misunderstanding'. But I beg you – *please*, come here to advise me on how to deal with your 'President'. I give you my word – you will not be harmed, on my account!"

Even the humans in Storied Watcher's vicinity, could hear a furious argument breaking out behind the platform; but, to her obvious dismay, no-one issued forth.

The big man, his head and shoulders still partly above the chair-top line of sight despite bent knees and a crouch, awkwardly shuffled over until his was about as far from the alien on the right, as Misha was on the left.

"Yeah... so, what you want?" he asked, uneasily looking up at her.

This man was not the type to openly acknowledge being outmatched, but Misha could see the combination of awe and fear in his eyes.

What is the matter? thought the Russian.

Have you never been side-to-side with an angel... a goddess?

A second later, he mumbled, "*Akh du, tovarisch Presidlent, ya –*" and held up a hand.

"You said that you do not try to apprehend gangsters – bandits, brigands, of the violent and lawless type that I see on tee-vee around here, all the time, because the risk is too great... is that right?", asked the newcomer.

"Yeah... more or less," confirmed Wolf. "It ain't that I'm *scared* of them – one on one, I can take 'em man-to-man, pretty much any day. It's just that they *all* got guns, they ain't afraid to use 'em, and they usually never go out alone. Top of that, you whack *one* of 'em, the rest of them have a habit of taking it *personal*. I got only one life to live... I'd kind of like it to end later rather than sooner, you know?"

"Thus I have reasoned myself, over ten times a thousand human lifetimes, or more," observed the alien-girl, with the hint of a smile. "I am still here, and I mean to survive my stay on this world, as well. So let me be straightforward, man-named-'Wolf'. Not just because I am in your debt, I would offer you the chance to –"

"Karéin!" interrupted the Russian. "We are connected! But I am concerned about the stability of the link. You had best speak quickly... I do not know how long it will remain working."

The special SVR mobile-communicator flew out of his hand and into her own.

"This is Karéin-Mayréij – the Storied Watcher of the Thousand Worlds, here," she calmly and deliberately announced, although Misha could somehow tell that something was worrying this creature, by the way she stared off introspectively into space. "Who do I address?"

"You are now speaking to the President of the United States," came back a ghostly, static-beset voice, followed by another, only slightly more audible.

"And I, am the *President* of the Russian Federation," the second voice explained. "I have used the special, reserved communication-line between the United States and my own country, to facilitate this conversation. I sincerely hope that you are able to resolve your differences. I will not again speak, unless I am asked to, since this situation is the problem of my American friend. Sir, I pass the floor over to yourself."

"Thank you," stated the President. "May I go ahead?"

He sounds nervous, she sent to Misha.

"What the –" exclaimed the bounty-hunter. "Thought I heard somethin'... but in my head –"

"Shhh!" admonished the Russian.

"Of course," replied Karéin-Mayréij, to the U.S. leader.

"First of all... let me say that I regret whatever misunderstandings have occurred, between yourself and the government of the United States," apologized the President. "The situation that we are now discussing is absolutely *not* what I had hoped would occur."

"Nor I," she parried.

"Well, if that's the case," he continued, "I have consented to this conversation – over the strong objections of many of my military- and intelligence-staff – so we can work out our differences, without any further hostility or violence, between yourself and my country. Are you willing to discuss matters, with that as a starting-point?"

There was an unusually long pause until the Storied Watcher replied, as if she was pondering something.

"Yes – but we may not have much time," she warned. "And as to the question of violence... out of honor and gratitude to dear Sam Jacobson and his adventuring-team – since he apparently answers the call of duty to this 'United States' of yours – up to now, I have, though sorely tempted otherwise, refrained from retaliating against your warriors. Despite this, so far, soldiers and spies in your pay have tried to *kill* me, at least twice, possibly three times, including today, not a half-hour before now. Not to mention, your hirelings have kidnapped five of my most dear human-friends... and they are being abused by your palace-torturers, as we speak. Were I to try the same against yourself, how do you think that *you* would react, sir?"

Something is wrong – both I and three of my war-children sense it, she sent to Misha.

Your little cell-radio-phone is giving off a strange signal, it is going upward, to the sky.

Tell the Wolf-man to be ready to move, on a moment's notice.

"I can assure you, Karéin, that I have given *no* such order!" protested the President. "Can't we work together, to get to the bottom of this? If you promise to lay down your arms, accept our protective-custody and not show yourself to the public, I give you my personal word of honor that I'll put the intelligence services of the United States at your disposal, to try to track down these friends of yours –"

"Let us now speak plainly, 'President' of the United States Empire!" brusquely interrupted Karéin-Mayréij. "I did not land on this world – neither upon your conceited little kingdom – seeking a fight; the opposite, in fact. When I was in the starlit darkness, I spoke with you as a friend, and thought that the same honor would be done in return, to myself, when I crashed down to Earth, with the misfortune of landing in this 'America'. At first I was weak, and only narrowly did I escape the repeated attempts on my life; but, sir, I am *not* helpless any more! I tell you now, so that there can be no mistake, you *cannot defeat me* – the greatest demons and devils, far worse than anything on this world, have tried : all have failed. You *cannot* kill me – not even with the air-bomb which I now perceive to be coming in this direction. Here... I will show you what I mean."

She turned to the platform.

"This is not an attack," shouted the newcomer. "Hold your fire."

She looked skyward, and said something in her alien tongue. Neither the Russian spy nor the bounty-hunter could understand a word of it, although Misha did hear something that sounded like, '*Ksé'l'ch*''.

Along with the back-beat of the Celtic-rock music that was again reaching a crescendo, his mind perceived another strange thought.

Take no risks, my fire-child, it cautioned.

Thou are still young, disable it, do not let it use its death-bang –

The yellow-orange dagger shot out of the alien's hand, and, shining with a painfully-bright glow, it flew straight upward, through the hole in the roof.

From his vantage-point, after wiping both a shower of gypsum-dust and the sweat of inchoate, 'one-step-from-the-Great-Beyond' fear from his brow, Misha could just see what must have been the hot-dagger rocketing skyward. It must have been at least five hundred meters distant, probably more, when there was a huge shower of sparks, rather like what the Americans were wont to do on their 'Fourth of July' holiday.

Perhaps three or four seconds later, the dagger, followed by a trail of smoke, came back down through the hole. Its glow was gone and its color was marred by black charring.

The dirtied yellow-knife deposited itself into the Storied Watcher's free hand. With a thoroughly weird, maternal look, she held it close to her breast, kissed it – even though, the damn thing was still boiling-hot, Misha could tell this even from as far away as he was – and mumbled something.

The whole episode had taken no more than a few seconds.

Thou pass the test, great Ksé'l'ch', she congratulated.

And thy power thus waxes, she sent, in the Russian's direction.

I never doubted thee, valiant child.

"*Tell* me, Mr. President," spat Karéin-Mayréij into the communicator, "Do your courtiers now tell you what has lately happened, hereabouts? I doubt not that they urge yet another such act of treachery. Maybe more bombs – say, five or six – all at once? How about one of the atom-smashing ones – those that immolate an entire city? By all means, send them my way! Any that my war-child *Ksé'l'ch'* cannot immediately burn to cinders, they will miss... at least, they will miss *me*. Regrettably, I cannot protect all the innocent peasants who are unfortunate enough to be here, now. If you care so little for *my* life, then my only plea can be for theirs. How many of your subjects will you slaughter, in the vain hope of a lucky shot against one of my kind?"

"Your... war-*what*?" stammered the bewildered American leader. "Please... uhh... please stand by," came back his faint, desperate-sounding voice.

"You have one minute," she evenly stated. "Less, if even *one* more false move is made against me."

The Storied Watcher addressed the SVR-man.

"There is no more Eng-lish speaking on the line," she commented. "Only Russian-talk. Here, I will give it to you – please tell me what your leaders are saying."

The communicator again flew to his hand.

The newcomer bent her upper-body, to call out toward the platform.

"*Hector! Sylvia!*" she pleaded. "Please – *please* – come here, right now! I only want to *talk* – I will neither hurt you, nor anyone who accompanies you! Please, *come!*"

Turning to the bounty-hunter, she added, "The time is short... so I will come directly to the point. Man-called-'Wolf', I offer you the chance to join the disciples who follow me, who learn from me... who *belong* to me. I will teach you arts – not just of war but also of many other ingenious and guileful things –

that you could not comprehend, in a *thousand* human lifetimes. I would make you my bodyguard, as well as the greatest 'boun-tee hunter' in the history of your world. What *say* you?"

There was more argument, rising to impassioned, back-and-forth shouting, from behind the platform.

Though he was trying to concentrate on the faint phone-conversation, Misha thought he heard something like the English phrase, "That's an *order!*" from the front of the room.

"I... uhh... like, from what I see, lady – don't take this the wrong way, ya know, – but... uhh... it don't look like you need too much help to keep the bad-guys off your back." uncertainly replied the bounty-hunter. "I got a girlfriend, no kids, nothin' serious, but – tell you the truth, I'm not sure that the 'belongin' part of it is what I'm lookin' for... you know?"

"*Shto*?" they both heard Misha exclaim. "*Da, tovarisch Presidient, ya ponemayu, a nyet, ya ne –*"

"What is he saying?" demanded the Storied Watcher; but in the same moment, the Russian handed the communicator back to her.

"The American President is back on," advised the SVR-man, an ashen look on his face.

"I am here," spoke the newcomer, into the receiver.

"Okay, Ms. Mayréij," sounded the faint voice of the President. "What if I told you that we can give you a video-link to this, uhh, 'family' that you mentioned, earlier? What if we could show you that they're in good health, that they're not being harmed? Would that help you make a positive decision to deal with us in good faith?"

"Considering what you have *already* done to them, a great debt remains to be paid," guardedly countered the alien-girl. "But stopping an evil, is the first step to expunging it. What do you propose?"

"Just a moment... yeah?" stated the U.S. leader, to someone else at his end of the link. "What's that? Well, she – fine, *fine*, I'll ask... listen, something that we're curious about... just how *is* it that you suspect that this 'Billings' man and the others, are being mistreated? I mean, you haven't seen them since –"

Abruptly, he stopped dissembling.

"He is lying," whispered Misha.

"The Government, tellin' a *lie*? You don't *say*," grunted the bounty-hunter.

If he once told the truth, came back a mental message, *I should die of surprise.*

"You will just have to believe me when I say, 'I know'," countered Karéin-Mayréij, in straight-forward manner. "I have many ways that you comprehend not. Including the one that tells me of the several bomber-airplanes that you have circling overhead, as we speak, Mr. President. I advise you to call off the latter, forthwith, for it would grieve me to have to destroy them. It is the act of a coward who hides inside a castle and sends foot-soldiers, to die against a foe that they cannot possibly defeat. But as for the show of my family – I will certainly oblige you. Where should I look, to see dear Bob, Whitney, Tommy, Curtis and Melissa?"

"You know, young lady," admonished the President, "If I used insulting language like *that*, against yourself, you wouldn't be too happy with *me... would you?*"

"I suppose that you have a point, sir," admitted the alien-girl. "If I challenged you to meet with me in one-to-one combat, so we could resolve this with risk only to ourselves and not to those who we command – that would not be too courageous of me, either, would it? Even if I truthfully promised not to employ my weirding-powers and fought only with the war-skills of my hands and feet, you would not stand a *chance* – you would be dead before you could make a move. Therefore I withdraw my accusation against your personal bravery. As to your *integrity*... that remains to be seen, does it not?"

"I could argue that too... but I'd like to move on, if you please," complained the U.S. leader. "I have ordered that no action should be taken against you, as long as you don't act in a hostile manner, yourself. Right now, my intelligence personnel are connecting a mobile communication-unit, to the large display-screen which I have been told is in the conference-room. This will be hooked up to a video-feed from where your, uhh, 'family' is being kept. You will be able to see them, all together, there. Hopefully *that*, will provide you with the assurance that you're looking for."

Is it possible that he is honestly trying to make amends? wondered the Russian.

"Did you not earlier say that you would 'help me look for' Bob, Tommy and the others?" curtly retorted the Storied Watcher. "My, *my*... how *efficient* your search-parties have become, all of a sudden, sir. So... you thus acknowledge that Bob, Tommy and the others *have* been in your custody, all the while? Oh, and please excuse the comment about 'you could not make a move'. That must sound... *threatening*, from your perspective. I do not mean to be any more provocative than is necessary."

She has had thousands of years in which to learn the arts of negotiation, mused Misha.

I wonder if the American President understands this.

"That's, uhh, good," replied the President. "And as to the matter of the captives – yes, we *do* have them, but, I can, uhh, explain all about that," he bluffed. "But I'd prefer to do so later, if you don't mind. We've, uhh, had our share of communications-issues back at this end."

"Umm-hmm," commented the newcomer, with one of her trademark half-smiles.

"Please stand by," requested the U.S. leader. "My people tell me that you should be seeing something on the conference-room screen, in the next few seconds."

Speaking away from the phone, Karéin-Mayréij called to those behind the platform, "Listen, all of you – I withdraw my deadline, for now; there is no need to remain in hiding... at least not on *my* account. The American President and I are communicating with each other, and he promises to show my family on the big tee-vee screen, just behind the speaking-stand in front. Perhaps we can resolve this dispute – but, none the less, I advise all you spy-men not to try any more tricks. You have already seen, where *that* will lead."

Slowly, she started to move toward the center aisle. Motioning to the big man and the Russian, she asked, "Will you come with me?"

"Yes," confirmed Misha. "For, if this is of any interest... I now no longer have anywhere to go."

The alien-girl sent a compassionate look at the SVR-man.

"I *know it*, dear friend," she acknowledged. "And you have made the right decision; for blindly following cruel orders, is not the way of honor and power, but that of stupidity and weakness."

Now, her stare caught the bounty-hunter. "And what decision will *you* make, 'Wolf'?" she pressed. "Will you retreat into your comfortable, obscure life of tracking down petty criminals... or will your feet walk the path of enlightenment... of *greatness?*"

The view-screen in the front started to flicker, although there was as yet no discernible image upon it.

Wolf looked genuinely torn, but after a few seconds of pondering his fate, he spoke up.

"Lady – you sure have a *way* of saying that," he muttered.

Throwing up his hands in mock-surrender, he added, "I have a feeling I'll regret this, but... what the hell – if I go for it, maybe I'll get one of them book-deals... or somethin', you know?"

He rose to his feet and walked toward her, and all could see how he towered over the alien-girl. She looked like a child in an elaborate October 31 costume, compared to the bounty-hunter's massive, muscular bulk.

"Or... *something*," she remarked, with a knowing smile. "And, by the way, you can call me 'Karéin-Mayréij', which is my name; although, the custom down here appears to be just 'Karéin'... that will do, as well."

"Pleased to meet'cha, 'Karéin'," he said, offering a handshake.

Vîrya Ahn'jë, I pray thee, quench thy fire, sent the newcomer, to the scale-mail.

These humans are not yet ready for it.

But help make them so.

Bemusedly, the Storied Watcher extended her own hand, but just before the two made contact, she warned, "I think that I should advise you, 'Wolf', that my touch will seal our pact, in ways that you do not yet understand. There is *no* turning back, when we embrace. Will you then accept my gift?"

Uneasily, the big man just nodded, as he grasped her hand.

Instantly, Wolf's jaw dropped. There was a look of unnerved astonishment on his face.

"Holy... *Shit!*" he gasped, upon breaking the connection, sweating and trying to prop up his upper body with palms supported by on thighs.

"Welcome to my world, 'Wolf'," amicably remarked Karéin-Mayréij, turning her attention to the video-monitor, where an image was taking shape. "Excuse my conceit. Welcome to, *our* world."

"Yeah... right," the big man managed, shaking his head as if trying to recover from a punch. "Damn... that glove was *hot*... but I guess I got away without no burns..."

"That is just the first taste," advised Misha, allowing himself a smirk. "Wait until she shows you the, ah, 'main course'."

The bounty-hunter just stared forward.

"Hello... Karéin-Mayréij... can you hear me?" sounded the voice of the President, from the speakers on the large video-monitor.

"Yes," she replied, into the communicator.

"Good... I will put them on, now," announced the U.S. leader.

There was some static on the screen, and the picture shimmered and broke up several times, before it finally became stable enough to make sense of.

Sure enough, there were five figures, standing straight up, looking at the camera – a middle-aged Caucasian man with rather too much around the waist and thinning hair; a spare, Afro-headed African-American woman, approximately in her mid-thirties; a black girl in her early teens; a black schoolboy, and, finally, a young, tan-skinned boy, about the same age as the African-American one.

As if spontaneously, they all waved at the camera.

As near as any human could have discerned, they looked exactly like Bob K. Billings, Jr., Whitney Claremont, her children, Melissa and Curtis, and, of course, the boy, Tommy George.

"Thanks be to the Holy Light!" breathed the Storied Watcher, tears coming to her eyes. "At least – they are alive. Despite everything... they are still *alive.*"

"You see?" came the voice of the President. "This whole issue has just been a big misunderstanding – and, for the record, it's one that I sincerely regret. I hope we can now trust each other and start over with a clean slate. Does that sound good?"

"There is still much that must be accounted for, sir," answered the alien-girl, as she wiped her eyes. "But for now... all I want to do, is talk to them. Then, if you so require, I will accompany your warriors to a place of your choosing, on two conditions : One, that eventually, I will be re-united with Bob, dear Tommy and the others; and two, that both you and your army understand, that I will be your guest of my own free will – that is, I will not be a prisoner. Do not worry about my leaving suddenly, without discussing the matter with yourself – I seek not to rule humans, nor to dispute your authority... so I will try to be discreet about the fact that I am here. What say you?"

"That's, uhh, *great,*" answered the American leader.

After a strangely long pause, in which those in the room could just hear some kind of discussion taking place at the other end of the line, his voice returned.

"I'm afraid that we can't arrange for you to speak with these folks, right now, due to technical reasons," he stated. "The thing is... we only have a video-feed to the location where these friends of yours are currently residing. But later, we can –"

"Could you not relay a message to my family, on my behalf, sir?" inquired the Storied Watcher. "Specifically, about how ashamed I am, that I was not able to find and rescue them, before now –"

"I'll, uhh, yes, I think we could do that – Harry, can you set up –" he slowly replied.

"And just *one* more thing," pleasantly requested Karéin-Mayréij. "Can you ask Whitney – what the name was of that nice song that she taught me, on the way back from the army-camp, up north? I seem to have forgotten it... which grieves me, because I would like to sing it again, with her and the rest of my family."

With a knowing half-smile, the Russian turned his head, to look at the bounty-hunter.

"Did I mention," he whispered, "That trying to mislead this creature, is *not* a good idea?"

"'Specially for a dumb fuck like that jackass President," mumbled a still-befuddled Wolf.

"Karéin," cautioned the President, "We both have to be *reasonable*, here. I've gone way out on a limb, against the advice of my military and intelligence staff, to show you that we have what you want – uhh, *who* you want – and that they're doing just, uhh, fine. There's nothing that I would like more, than to get you in touch with Billings and the rest of these people – and that *will* happen in due course – but for the time being, you'll just have to take my word that everything is above-board –"

"Sir... you *must* have some warriors or courtiers, at the site where my friends are being held," pressed the Storied Watcher. "Why can you not pass on my apology to Bob, Tommy and the others, simply by asking your servants to relay it to them? And as for the song – you can have any one of my friends write the name of it on a piece of paper, then hold that in front of the camera-eye that now beholds them. Or just have one of them say the name of the song – I am skilled at comparing sounds, to the movements of lips and tongue that form the corresponding words. Surely, *that* can be easily done –"

He hides the truth from me, she sent to Misha.

Children, be again at thy guard.

A second later, an astonished bounty-hunter stammered, *sotto voce,* "Whoa! What the – I heard – no, *didn't* hear, but –"

The Russian held a finger to his lips and made the "Shush" gesture.

"She said, 'welcome to our world', Mr. Wolf," he whispered. "How do you like it so far?"

"Fuckin' voodoo *magic*," was all that Wolf could think of, to say.

"Look, these people – your friends, I mean – they've been through a *lot*, lately," evaded the U.S. leader. "My advisers are telling me that reminding them of anything that might have taken place over the past month or so, might be, uhh, *stressful* for them, traumatic, even... so if you can just take me at my word and wait until –"

"*Ohhhh!*" suddenly groaned Karéin-Mayréij, as she immediately doubled up, wincing, drooling and holding her waist in obvious pain.

A second later, she was on her knees, sweating and coughing.

"*Tommy... Bob... oh Gods Above... hang on, I beg you...*"

The poor thing looked as if the wind had been knocked out of her by a sucker-punch.

Her hand loosened and the cell-phone fell to the floor; luckily, it did not appear to be broken, since the President's voice could still be heard faintly issuing from it, with perhaps a quarter-second delay compared to the version of his speech that was coming from the front-platform monitor.

"Karéin!" exclaimed Misha.

He rushed over to her, accompanied in this by the bounty-hunter.

"Whoa, lady, – you don't look too good there," he commented.

"Karéin? Karéin? I'm not hearing you – please come in!" issued the voice of the President, from both the phone and the view-screen. "What's going *on* down there?"

Slowly, the Storied Watcher, her countenance showing a terrible fury, rose to her feet.

Ethereal music again sounded, as she hissed a riposte, through clenched, fanged teeth.

"Those people who you have on your big tee-vee screen, Mister... President," spat the alien-girl into the communicator, which now hovered directly in front of her. "They look like they are nice and healthy – they still smile at me, wave to me... do they not?"

"Yes... of course," said the voice from the monitor and phone. "They're fine, just like they've always been. What's the problem?"

"*Ohhhh – Ye Heavens!!*" moaned the newcomer, again suffering some kind of terrible, invisible blow. "*Tommy* – send you my power – use your mind – stronger than your body – *uhhhh....*"

Gasping for air, she staggered back and forth, but then again regained her composure, perhaps a second or so faster than she had, previously.

The eyes of Karéin-Mayréij now were glowing brilliantly, as was her armor – her entire *being*, in fact, shone like a hibernal sun; but there was an ominous red tinge to it, this time.

Music – akin more to an electric-guitar howl, than a symphony – rose in gain and tempo, all around.

"You should tell the schemer who crafted this despicable pack of lies," she angrily shouted, "That he or she should have refrained from torturing my *real* friends – wherever they are – while you paraded these false puppets in front of me!"

"But – *but* –" desperately prevaricated the U.S. leader, his voice barely audible over her invective.

"Now mark me well, you cruel, lying, so-called 'President'!" admonished the enraged Storied Watcher, "You have used up your *last* chance, just now! I am coming first for my family, then for you; and if I find Bob, Tommy or the others dead, or harmed beyond repair, *I will first kill you – then, I will kill everyone around you – then, I will kill every single one of those responsible for this!* I give you forty-eight hours in which to bring my friends, in unharmed condition, to the top of the mountain, where I first landed on this planet. If they choose to grant your life, I will do so. If they do not – or if any of them are not delivered in good health – then I would suggest that you make your peace with your God. *Do you hear me? Do you* hear *me! Answer!*"

But there was naught, save static, over either audio-connection.

"We must away from here, immediately," she warned. "An attack – a big one – is on its way. I can defeat it... but you might not survive the battle."

Karéin-Mayréij now turned to address those who hid behind the front platform.

"Hector... Sylvia!" she called, with sadness and frustration echoing everywhere, "My heart breaks, that it has come to *this*... but they are too close to you, and they have weapons – they might shoot, before I could – when all is over, I will beg your forgiveness, with my tears."

For a second, the alien-girl paused, as if concentrating in the direction of where she had last seen the two scientists, and, from behind an obstruction, a few heard a low moan, followed by more pandemonium, with the sound of a body slumping to the floor and shouts of "get her!".

"Now *leave* this place, as quickly as you can!" exclaimed the Storied Watcher, addressing those who were hiding. "The doors will no longer bar your way. Tell everyone in the ho-tel to flee, as well. *Go!*"

All of the humans in the room, save the two next to her, ran in panic for the exits.

From the door in the far front, Misha thought that he heard something like, "fuckin' *puto idiots, let me* – *!*" followed by, "shut him *up!*".

"Come beside me," demanded Karéin-Mayréij, as the music pounded out, everywhere. "Grab my waist and hold tightly on – do *not* release your grasp, unless you have a parachute and a hiding-bunker, at the ready. And fear not the dark that will envelop you, so all will appear as in blackest night; but this same thing, is what will protect us. Hurry, time is short!"

"You're nuckin *futs*, lady!" protested Wolf. "Look at that armor – we'd be *roasted!*"

"*Vîrya Ahn'jë* will tamp down her fire as much as she can, and already are you greater than ordinary men," explained the alien-girl. "Fear her not. You will be proof against her essence... though, perhaps not *comfortably* so."

Each knowing that the only likely alternative was probably a quick, shrapnel-riddled demise, the bounty-hunter and the Russian rushed over to either side of the young-looking woman and took hold of her as best they could, though her head came up only to Wolf's shoulder, so he had to crouch to get a decent grasp.

In the next second, the two men felt an iron-like grip securing their bodies to her own, as their minds swam with incomprehensible thoughts. Neither could understand how they could be in contact with a fire-brazier, yet not be harmed in so doing.

"Oops," they heard her sheepishly admit. "Eventually, I shall have to give my war-children a rest – and it might be, uhh, *distracting*, for me then to have no peasant-clothes."

She shot a glance at the discarded track-pants, shirt and baseball cap, and these instantly were compressed into a mass no larger than a soccer-ball, which floated up to nest under her cape.

A shroud of utter darkness fell as an ebon curtain, perhaps – as far as either could tell – three to five feet from the cluster of bodies, alien and slightly-more-than-human, in its center.

"*Vîrya Ahn'jë*, use all thy arts!" requested the Storied Watcher. "*Vîrya I'ëà'b'*, make thee the Hurricane!"

Instantly, the buckler flew off her arm, and it started to make the rapid, encircling-pattern that they had seen earlier, in the conference-room; evidently, the shield did not go outside the dark-cloak, because both men could just see it, hurtling back and forth.

"*Jaysus H.*," exclaimed the bounty-hunter, as he realized that his feet were no longer in contact with the floor.

He felt himself, no doubt the other two also, going up, faster and faster, like on the upward side of a circus Ferris-wheel.

In no more than a second, the smell of the air changed from the antiseptic, artificially-cooled stuff inside the hotel, to the hot, Southwest breeze telling of the outdoors.

"I must call upon my greater powers," warned the alien-girl, the volume of her voice obviously kept low on purpose. "Else, we are in danger that one of my enemy's weapons will score a, uhh, 'lucky hit'. Scant minutes ago, to have been so close to me, when I do this, would have meant a quick and painful death, for both of you. As it is now, it will be merely, ahh, *unpleasant*... but take heart. The *Fire* that you will feel, later will make you great and powerful, far beyond the ken of mortal man. Do *not* resist it – *love* it, *accept* it, let it come into you, let it flow through your nerves and mind. And do not forget to keep holding on!"

"*Knew* this was gonna be a *bad* day," ruefully grunted Wolf, while the Russian rolled his eyes.

A second later, both men echoed the Storied Watcher's earlier cries, as charges of some other-worldly energy shot up and down her body, occasionally jumping over to the two hangers-on, illuminating their psyches with combination of burning pain and luxurious ecstasy, that not even the most expertly-brewed synth-drugs, could ever *hope* to equal.

Far below, they heard the thunder of a huge explosion, followed by two or three more.

There were the sounds of debris impacting her protective bubble, followed a split-second later by the shudder of a shock-wave.

"Drink it in – take of my *life*," counseled Karéin-Mayréij, the Destroying Angel, her voice mighty and purposeful.

"For, go we now to... *war!*"

Karéin's War

Let's Put On Our Group-Thinking Caps

The face of the President was stone-grim, as, from his RF-sealed chamber on Air Force One, he called the emergency video-conference to attention.

"Mr. Secretary – I need an *immediate* status report," he demanded. "Where's the alien now?"

"I'm sorry, Mr. President, sir," replied DeWitt, his image still slightly fuzzy on the view-screen, "But we just don't know... it might have been in the hotel when our emergency surgical-strike arrived – but, given the previous history of this creature... I wouldn't count on it. We have a forensics-team going over the ruins right now... if they find anything, we'll let you know immediately."

The gaze of the U.S. leader, icy in its demeanor, now focused on the image of the CIA director. "Can CIA confirm that? What about FBI?"

Impassively as always, the CIA director looked straight at the camera and said, "Sir, we can't add a lot to what the Secretary of Defense has stated, except for one thing : although our agents were, obviously, preoccupied with making an expedited egress from the building just before the second strike arrived, we have a couple of reports of the alien having blown a large hole open in the roof of the Hotel Tucson's conference-room. It's possible that it escaped in that direction, because our local energy-tracking teams noticed a surge over the roof of the conference-center, shortly before the bombs took out that part of the hotel. Unfortunately, the shock-wave from the attack destroyed much of our equipment – this is 'one-of-a-kind' stuff, I'd remind you – and a lot of what's left, will take some time to repair."

"Okay... I *get* it," muttered the President, raising his hand to demand silence. "Director Ochoa? Does FBI have anything to add to this?"

The Hispanic man on the view-screen shook his head. "No, sir," he stated. "When the shooting-started, our agents' top priority was to protect Abruzzio and Ramirez, since they're important assets in this case. Our field-team was mostly hidden behind the speaking-platform during the altercation, although Agents Chu and Boatman *did* get a good look at the alien from time to time... if that helps."

"It doesn't," growled the President. "Alright... is Anderson there? General, do we have any idea of where the alien's going, or where it's hiding? And how the hell is it managing to *evade* us like this? I don't think I need to tell you – I'm getting *very* tired of having this damn creature making fools of all of us, by showing up whenever and wherever it wants, with no advance notice. There has to be some way for us to track down and corner it. There *has* to be!"

"Don't we wish, Mr. President, sir," answered Anderson, clearly trying not to respond to his superior's provocation. "But it's not a simple task. For example, at one point, we were *sure* that we had a lock-on, and we were about to slave the missiles' guidance systems to the target co-ordinates that we so obtained; but then, the signal cut out completely. About ten seconds later, the signal showed up again, and once more, we got a lock – only to find the signal starting to come from all *over* the place, as if the alien's energy was being bounced off interior walls, nearby buildings, in some kind of random pattern –"

Fred McPherson's face looked genuinely amused, as he cut in.

"Guess *what*, General?" he sardonically commented. "She's *jamming* you, that's about the only reasonable explanation. Welcome to fighting an opponent with *thousands* of human lifetimes under her belt, in which to perfect the arts of war and deception. She's not playing by our rule-book – and she's quite a fast learner, when it comes to our military technology... wouldn't you say?"

"As little as I like admitting it, Mr. Science Adviser," replied the General, "Professionally, I'd have to admit that your theory, while as yet unproven, is certainly plausible. I'm hoping you're wrong – because if you're *right*, I'm not sure where that leaves us, vis-à-vis what to do with the alien."

"Fine... whatever," complained the President. "Let's take a step back. How the hell did it get into the building, in the first place? How did it get into the conference-room? I thought the whole idea was to try to deliver our carefully-crafted message to the alien, in a discreet manner. Now... *this*. Does anybody have any answers?"

"FBI has been going over *that* one, again and again, Mr. President, sir," offered Ochoa. "But as you might imagine, our task has been complicated by the fact that there was an uncontrolled mass-exit from the hotel, both just before the bombs hit, and in the panic afterward... it has proved very difficult to track down eye-witnesses who could give a clear account of what was going on. We're still investigating, but evidently, this 'Storied Watcher' creature has some kind of advanced hiding-capability – maybe it can easily disguise itself. Or something."

"Well, last picture that I saw," unhelpfully commented the Vice-President, "She looked pretty much like any girl you'd see in a centerfold."

There was a pause, and then again, the American leader spoke up.

"I've already told all of you," he gravely warned, "That I am going to require a secret commission to investigate that sequence of events – one that occurred in stark contrast to my *expressly*-stated directives – and that there will be *serious* consequences – up to and including trials for insubordination – once I find out who disobeyed my orders. In the meantime, pending the outcome of that investigation, I need as complete an analysis as possible, as to the military capabilities that the alien demonstrated during the altercation... along with any possible counter-measures that we can deploy to negate these abilities. Do we have an accurate casualty-count, yet?"

"The Bureau didn't lose anybody, thank God," mentioned Ochoa. "Although we had a number of light injuries caused by flying debris, after the second air-strike."

"None from the military, either," added DeWitt. "GreyWar wasn't so lucky – they had five killed by the surgical-strike. They're suing us over that, by the way."

"They know where they can stick *that* summons," joked the Vice-President.

"How about CIA?" asked the President.

"Not so good," replied the CIA director, with only a hint of compassion in his voice. "We have three agents unaccounted-for and presumed dead; these were seriously wounded as a result of the alien's attacks, and were rendered immobile. We have to assume that they were killed in the second strike, since they wouldn't have been able to egress in time... we may never know for sure, as there isn't a lot of forensic evidence left at the scene. Oh – and I should mention – there was also an individual, dressed in professional-attire, who was killed directly by the alien's advanced weaponry. Our people first believed him to be one of our own, but this doesn't correspond with our duty register for the day – perhaps he belonged to FBI?"

"Negative," disputed Ochoa. "As I said... luckily, we didn't lose anyone down there. Our field-team led by Agent Chu also noted *that* attack, due to its unusual nature... we'd have to assume that he was plain-clothes from the Tucson police... or maybe Secret Service."

"Civilian casualties?" asked the American leader.

"At least thirty, maybe as many as fifty, with a hundred or so wounded," glumly advised Kaysten, with his remote image superimposed on part of the screen. "Mostly hotel-staff and customers who got caught in the air-strike, or its after-effects – but at least four civilians, also some of the GrayWar mercs, seem to have been shot by a long-range sniper as they exited the building... the Tucson cops are still trying to figure out the meaning of that. They're combing the downtown... needless to say, it's hard to believe that the alien had hired a hit-man."

"Well... I suppose it *could* have been worse," mused the President. "But need I say it out loud, it's *not* good – not good at all – that we're dealing with an enemy who's now clearly demonstrated, that it's willing to *kill*, to get its way. Throws the whole thing into a new light, in my opinion."

"I know I'll be outnumbered in saying this," opined McPherson, "But I find it very hard to believe that the Karéin-Mayréij with whom I'm familiar, would have launched an unprovoked and fatal attack, of the type we're apparently discussing. Before we label her as a 'murderer', I'd strongly suggest that we know *all* the facts."

"You're *right*, Mr. McPherson," icily retorted the Vice-President. "You *are* outnumbered! How many times does this damn thing have to threaten to kill your Commander-In-Chief, not to mention everybody in his immediate vicinity, before you start to take it seriously?"

"I won't respond to that," countered the Science Adviser. "Except to say, 'aren't you the guy who told us, that she'd only be armed with a pea-shooter'?

Seems that more than *one* of us have made claims about Karéin that we've lived to regret, later."

"Enough!" interrupted the President. "We've got no time for recriminations."

McPherson turned to address the President.

"Sir," remarked the Science Adviser, "I hope that by now, you've noticed a pattern developing here. First, we get the government's most skilled secret-agents deployed at the hotel, but the alien comes bedecked with God-knows-what type of her own gear, and – guess what – we have no way at all to cope with any of it. She even shoots down a smart-bomb, but we have no idea how she detected it, in the first place. Then, despite our having the facility under relentless watch by our most sophisticated detection-gear, she simply *vanishes* –"

"What if the bitch is dead... lying in bits and pieces, down in the rubble of the hotel?" half-rhetorically suggested the Vice-President. "Have we ruled that out, yet?"

"With all due respect, sir," interjected DeWitt, "Based on the events so far, we think that outcome – however desirable – is *highly* unlikely."

"I had to *ask*, you know," grunted the Vice-President.

"Appreciated," said the U.S. leader. "Fred? Make your *point*, please."

"Okay," answered McPherson. "And to get right down to it... you *saw* what she did with the weapons that she arrayed against us – but put on your thinking-caps, ladies and gentlemen... what about the ones that she *hasn't* shown us, yet? This is a creature in possession of many *thousands* of years of strategic and tactical knowledge, possibly gained in environments that we can't even imagine – it's not even *remotely* rational to imagine that we can outwit her."

"For example," continued the Science Adviser, "Consider her 'deadline' for producing this 'Billings' guy and his entourage. Pretty smart of her to give us so little time in which to examine and analyze how to counter all these new weapons that she showed up with, earlier today... wouldn't you say? Here, I'm reminded of reports coming off the Mars mission, in which the cosmonaut mentioned that after only a few games, 'Karéin' started winning all the chess-matches, even though her opponent had played it all his life –"

"Mr. McPherson," politely noted Halford, "I believe that you're advocating capitulation to the alien... or do I have you wrong?"

"No – I'm not proposing anything of the sort," retorted McPherson, "I'm suggesting that we stop a strategy that's obviously failing, before we make things even *worse*. All we're doing, is angering and provoking 'Karéin' even more, each time that we try to confront or defeat her. Why don't we just give her what she's asking for, now that we've found this 'family' that she's apparently willing to fight us over?"

"I think things have gone a bit beyond the 'trying to make nice' stage, Fred," countered the President. "You've *heard* the recording. 'Karéin' said in no uncertain words, that she – it – is planning to *kill* me – and, if it's of any interest – probably everybody in my Cabinet, as well... including, presumably, yourself. Given what we've already seen, namely, thirty or more people dead down in Tucson, we simply don't have the luxury of trying to 'reason' with this being, any longer, I'm afraid."

"Hear, *hear!*" grunted the Vice-President.

"Okay," argued McPherson, "Let's say, Mr. President, for the sake of the argument – and I'm not saying I agree with this – but suppose we really *do* have no choice but to try to kill 'Karéin'. Nobody sitting at this table has yet proposed a plausible attack-plan. If we don't want to – and I use the word reluctantly – 'appease' her... then what's the plan to eliminate her? And – more importantly – what's the fall-back plan, if she outwits us yet *again?* We've got forty-eight hours, or less, before she comes looking for –"

"I'm not going to worry about an arbitrary deadline imposed by an adversary who has already promised to kill me," stated the President.

"But," he added in the direction of Anderson and DeWitt, "To Fred's point... I haven't heard a military plan that's likely to succeed."

"For the time being," said DeWitt, "We have to concentrate on your own safety, sir, until we can devise adequate countermeasures – I'd suggest that you transfer as soon as possible, from Air Force One, to one of the unmarked National Air Command Post aircraft that we had prepared to mitigate a terrorist situation. We have no reason to believe that the alien can track you even as far as the regular Air Force One ship – but just to be prudent, it would be unwise to assume that it can't. After we're reasonably sure that you're secure, then we can try to plan a counter-attack. The Joint Chiefs and I have already initiated emergency planning to define strategies that might be effective against this creature."

"All well and good," interrupted the Vice-President, "But what the hell are we going to tell the *public?* Damn Democrats are mouthing off again about 'where's the President, in this hour of economic crisis'... and once the Tucson incident leaks out, as surely it will, the rumors are going to spread like wildfire unless you can show up on the boob tube and tell the voters 'don't worry, be happy'."

"He's absolutely right, sir," echoed Kaysten. "There are rumors all over NeoNet to the effect that 'the Muslims have already gotten to the President, he's hiding from them'... the Tucson situation will only make it worse. We have a lot of leverage over the old-school news-channels via the No More Subversive News Act – after all, we can simply pull their licenses to report on the news, throw 'em in jail if they keep writing stories – but with all the voggers on Neo with their live, 'always-on' video-feeds, our options are limited... there are just too many of them."

"Shut down NeoNet, if you have to," ordered the American leader. "Although I'd consider that as a last resort. We'd be better off just cutting off all feeds from outside our borders, with the domestic stuff being regulated by FBI or Secret Service people who we can station with the television-networks. After all... they're the only ones that ordinary citizens are allowed to connect with, to get on the NeoNet at all... right?"

"Pretty much so," confirmed the Chief of Staff. "Except for a few who are getting illegal feeds from places like Canada, Québec and Mexico. Problem is that then they cross-connect with the main NeoNet trunks and the unauthorized stuff gets distributed all over the place."

"Well – track those down and throw 'em in the slammer," ordered the President, while addressing Ochoa. "Use any excuse you want – movie-piracy, spreading birth-control propaganda, using European computer-software or those – what do you call them – data-scrambling programs... *whatever*."

"We'll get right *on* it, sir!" confirmed the FBI director, with relish.

"So Jerry," inquired the President, "Just off the top of your head... what's your solution on the PR front?"

Kaysten leaned back and shook his head rapidly, as if trying to clear his mind for some quick thinking.

"I was *afraid* you'd ask me something like that, sir," he quipped. "Okay – here's what I've got, not much – but *maybe* we can make it work.

"What if," proposed the Chief of Staff, "You make a very quick, secret trip to the White House, stay there only long enough to make a few recorded speeches that were clearly by yourself and that were *unmistakably* done in the real Oval Office... these would be generic, like, 'My fellow Americans, I can assure you that the Muslim threat in Tucson is well under control, and despite the recent events that you may have heard about, our Armed Forces have captured or killed all the terrorists' – we'd have to record a few of these, so they could be activated as necessary. We could add in a staged press-conference or two, with hand-picked fake 'reporters', maybe a couple from the major networks for credibility – who we'd threaten with 'disappearing', if they spilled the beans."

"So far... so good," stated the U.S. leader. "*Then* what?"

"Then, when all the media-circus-stuff is done with," advised Kaysten, "You get out of Dodge as quickly and secretly as you came in, we put in the stunt-doubles for you and the First Family to make it look like you've never left... that buys us 'normalcy', 'President's staying at his post, he's in charge'... all that crap. *Huge* confidence-builder, there! Secondly – needless to say – it keeps you out of harm's way. We could have you on the unmarked air command-post, twenty-four hours per day, indefinitely, and the dumb voters'd be none the wiser."

"Fine," interrupted Bezomorton, who had been biding his time. "But if the alien's serious about 'coming to get you', and if it sees the 'real you' showing up in the Oval Office – that's *exactly* where it'll be heading next. What I'm trying to say, Mr. President, is... it could be very dangerous for you even to set *foot* in the White House, right now."

"Yeah... you got a point there, John," uneasily commented the President.

"On the other hand," argued DeWitt, "It would be a perfect chance – maybe our *only* remaining chance – to get a good shot at the creature. The tactical advantage would be all ours. Except for the issue of collateral-damage, of course."

"Quite correct," added the impassive voice of the CIA director. "We now have better intelligence on the alien's capabilities... its habits, its weapons. We could set a trap for it –"

"Can't make an omelet without breakin' a few eggs," cackled the Vice-President. "Besides... as long as we avoid any bombs falling on K Street and so on, we'd only hit the slums and the Capitol... whack a few Democrats as well as a pouting little Martian-girl – hey, that's just icing on the cake... right?"

"We should be so lucky," cynically remarked the President, "Jerry – I'll go for this 'canned speeches' idea of yours, but I'm not going to spend one *second* longer than I have to, in D.C. – after that, I guess I'm on the plane until further notice. Arthur – make sure that the Joint Chiefs and DoD get their tactical-plan to me, ASAP – the *next* time that this 'Storied Watcher' being shows up, I want to know that I can take her, uhh, it, out. John, Arthur – both of you work with CIA and the other agencies and do the best job that you can of strengthening our defenses at the White House... maybe we'll get a lucky shot at the alien, if and when it shows up there. Incidentally... any news on the Muslim bomb situation? Since we're blaming the whole 'Karéin' mess on those Islamic maniacs, I suppose we should find out what *they're* up to, these days."

"Not much new after we last spoke about this," commented Bezomorton. "The remaining nukes seem to have just disappeared off the face of the Earth... I wish I could say that's what really happened to them... but I can't."

"No new leads from CIA," that Agency's director stated.

"Nothing from FBI," added Ochoa, "But we're using every available asset on that one... except, of course, those dedicated to the 'alien' thing."

"Navy has been trying to intercept and inspect every ship we know to be on the high seas," noted Halford. "We're pretty sure that nothing's getting through in the North Atlantic and, sort of, in the North Pacific; but the Southern Hemisphere and around the equator – that's another story. Seems like every second ship we get near down there, has an escort, either by the Chinese, the Indians or the Brazilians. They've been refusing our demands for boarding-parties, too."

"Why don't we just sink 'em – you know, 'shoot first and ask questions later'," growled the Vice-President. "I thought those new subs that we're paying a half-trillion bucks each to build, could run rings around *anything* these stupid Third-Worlders have."

"We have to watch our step," Halford pointed out, suppressing a frustrated sigh, "Because if we did, Mr. Vice-President sir, there's a good chance that we'd end up on the losing end of a high seas shooting-war. Yes, the new *Gingrich*-class boats are state of the art... but we're outnumbered between three and four to one in the southern oceans, depending on who you're talking about as the opponent. And anyway, submarines aren't a very good ship-inspection tool."

"Heard and understood, Kyle," appreciatively offered the U.S. leader. "Well, all we can do is continue to monitor the situation, and the minute that we get any new information... make sure that I get notified, ASAP... understood?"

"Understood, sir," came back two or three voices.

"We're done, then?" asked the President.

After a few nods and some silence, he added, "Very well, then. Dismissed."

Dirty Deeds Done Dutifully

The President could see, over the Air Force One view-screen, that all but Halford, Bezomorton and the CIA director had trickled out of the remote room, with Kaysten's signal dropping almost instantly.

"Sir," interrupted the CIA director, "There's something else that I need to discuss with you... in *private*, if you don't mind."

The other two men stopped.

"Is this something that Admiral Halford and I should be aware of?" inquired the National Security Adviser.

"No," passively answered the CIA director, staring straight forward, not looking at the General.

"Mr. President?" suspiciously grumbled Bezomorton, with an arched eyebrow.

"It's okay, John," counseled the U.S. leader. "If it's relevant, I'll update you myself."

"Very well then, sir," politely replied the Adviser. "I'll start working on the 'reception party' in D.C., just in case our friend 'Karéin', shows up there."

"Very good," offered the President, as Halford and Bezomorton got up and walked out, with the Admiral slowly closing the door behind him.

After a second or two, the President offered, "I kind of get the feeling that this is something *important.*"

"You could certainly say that, sir," replied the CIA director.

"Go ahead," requested the American leader.

"I'm bringing this information to you with some reluctance, sir," began the director, "But given the situation that recently developed at the Hotel Tucson, I have determined that withholding it further, might not be... *appropriate.*"

"Well – now you've got me interested," mentioned the President. "What's the news?"

"You'll recall," explained the CIA director, leaning a bit back in his chair so as to be looking more directly at the view-screen at his end, "That the alien's demeanor became rapidly less positive, shortly after – on your instructions – the Agency showed her the image of the individuals who she referred to, as her 'family'... correct?"

"You have a talent for understatement, there," ruefully confirmed the President. "And frankly, I *still* can't understand what the H set her off, at that point. I mean – didn't we all figure that she'd be *happy*, elated, even – at seeing this 'Billings' guy, the black woman and the three kids in there with them? I've already told the Cabinet, DoD, your Agency – anybody who'll listen, and many more who won't – that I was *sure* this thing would get worked out, when CIA finally located this so-called 'family', where was it, you said –"

"We found them being held captive in a locked-down ranch outside Tucson, gangster-stuff," prevaricated the CIA director. "*Maras*, probably... they had already left when we showed up. But, Mr. President... that's not what's important, now. What I need to explain to you – and this is for your own ears only – is well, the group of people who we showed to the alien over the video-link to the Hotel Tucson conference-room, was *not*, in fact, the real thing."

"What? What the...?" stuttered the U.S. leader. "*Now*, you've got me thoroughly confused! I thought you *did* have Billings, Claremont and the three kids – ?"

"We did, sir," replied the director, "And we *still* do – Billings and his group are being kept in a secure location. However... the ones that we showed to the alien were 'stunt-doubles', surgically- and chemically-modified to as closely as possible resemble the original individuals, very much the same concept as we use with yourself to provide a number of false targets for the terrorists. This was the main reason why we had to request that you not give the alien direct contact with them, as the idea was to –"

The President rolled his eyes.

"For Christ's *sake!*" he complained, "You did all of this without asking *me*, first? Who thought up *that* bright idea?"

"*I* did, sir," claimed the CIA director, staring at the screen and standing his ground. "But 'thought up', is giving me undue credit. I'd remind you that tactics such as this are standard Agency procedure – we do *not* need specific National Command Authority authorization to implement same. It's been so for many years, both for reasons of operational efficiency and for plausible-deniability... all that good stuff."

"Well, henceforth – you *do* need my permission to try any of this crap, where the alien is concerned... you *got* that?" demanded the President, irritation obvious in his voice. "Whatever you had intended, it didn't work out too well, did it? This 'Karéin' creature obviously saw through your little trick, and now we've got her on the warpath against us. Damn it anyway – if you had just *told* me –"

"*Sir*," interrupted the director, "While the Agency will take your orders into account as best we can, I'd have to correct an assumption that you just made, and this is the reason why I chose to disclose the fact that we had used the 'stunt-doubles'. While it's certainly regrettable that the alien reacted in the way it did, that fact is actually *crucially* important. It may be the key to how we can defeat 'Karéin', once and for all."

"*Do* go on," sarcastically retorted the American leader.

"Alright. Here's what we've got," explained the CIA director. "Now, as background – and here again, this is for your own *exclusive* knowledge, sir – for some time, the Agency has been using our standard, ahem, 'enhanced' interrogation techniques against Billings, Claremont and certain of the Claremont children, also, more recently, the Amerindian boy named 'Tommy', in hopes of inducing them to reveal intelligence data on the alien's abilities, its characteristics, its goals and motivations, and so on –"

"*Jesus Christ!*" gasped the President. "You mean you've been *torturing* these people? I thought we were only doing that to the gangsters and the Muslims! Don't tell me, let me guess – 'all standard procedure, not requiring my approval'... right?"

"You got it, sir," confirmed the CIA director, with the hint of a satisfied leer on his face. "As I believe you were briefed upon taking the Oath of Office, ever since the G.W. Bush Administration – interrupted, of course, only by that little 'blip' in the 2010 time period – the Agency has traditionally had considerable autonomous discretion, on matters such as this."

"Your discretion has just been revoked!" growled the President. "I don't want so much as a *scratch* on them, from this point forward. That's an *order*."

"Can we return to that later, sir?" unctuously requested the CIA director. "Because I have to explain to you something much more important, that was indirectly revealed, as a result of these interrogations."

"Please don't excuse my French," shot back the American leader, "But this had better be fucking *good!* I don't know what could *possibly* make up for – "

"It *is*," evaded the director, a vacuous smile on his face. "Although we didn't get anything really useful from the interrogations themselves – both Billings and the rest of them, seem to have some kind of unusual ability to withstand, ahh, 'discomfort', at a level far outside what we would otherwise consider normal for a bunch of ordinary civilians – as is standard procedure in these operations, we kept meticulous records of what coercive methods were used, and at what times."

"So *what?*" challenged the President. "So you're keeping notes of when you put on the electrodes... bully for *you*. For the record, I've never *liked* this crap – I agreed to it reluctantly, and only then, because the goddamn Muslims are doing worse, to our boys over there in Pakistan. Bloody dirty business, if you ask me."

"Anyway," continued the CIA director, not taking the bait, "During the Tucson Hotel incident, some of the Agency's field-teams noted that the alien had suffered a, uhh, 'seizure' – similar in some ways to an epileptic fit, or maybe a bad drug flashback, in other words, a sudden, incapacitating physical spasm – just prior to the outbreak of shooting inside the conference-room."

The U.S. leader was listening intently, now.

"Another such episode," noted the director, "Was evident, during the abortive discussion between 'Karéin' and yourself, shortly before it started cursing and threatening you, after which of course we had to cut the link for your own safety. In each case, the alien seemed to be in genuine pain, and also seemed to be at least partially unable to defend itself... but unfortunately it seems to be able to recover rapidly from whatever caused these seizures. Hence the outcome of the shoot-out in Tucson."

"So?" asked the President.

"Our people in the Agency are good... *very* good," self-congratulated the CIA director. "One of them had the bright idea to go back and try to correlate these 'seizures', with other events that might be time-synchronous. You'll never *guess* what the match-up, turned out to be."

"People dumping stock on the Dow and buying gold?" quipped the President. "Nah. That's been going on for a year or more, now."

"Sir," stated the CIA director, plainly and directly, "Each of the alien's incapacitating spasms, was correlated almost perfectly – to the *microsecond*, in fact – with the onset of our use of enhanced coercive physical stimuli, on members of the Billings group."

The President fell silent for a few seconds, as if pondering the impossible.

"You mean to tell me," he half-gasped, "That each time you put the thumb-screws to Billings, or Claremont, or those kids of theirs... the *alien* got hurt, too?"

"Yes, *indeed*," confirmed the director. "And the greater the physical pain inflicted – although, as I mentioned earlier, the symptoms exhibited by the detainees were strangely muted – it appears, the greater the corresponding effect on 'Karéin'."

He, too, fell silent for a second or two, then added, "Of course, you must know what this implies : the process may be our one *really* effective weapon against the alien. Internally, the Agency has been running a number of computer-models to simulate this effect... and the results have been *most* interesting."

"I'll *bet*," quietly observed the President.

"As near as we can tell," neutrally stated the CIA director, "It appears that while inflicting moderate physical pain on a single detainee can only incapacitate 'Karéin' for a short time – no more than six to ten seconds, at most – if we were to find some way to either cause overwhelming unpleasantness to one member of her 'family' – or to do the same to two or more of them – we'd have a good chance of crippling it long enough for our conventional weapons to finish the job... the alien's defenses would be temporarily disabled."

"Meaning that the Air Force could get a shot at her... right?" stated the U.S. leader.

"Precisely!" eagerly confirmed the director. "Furthermore... we're speculating that if we were to either cause *agonizing* pain to the entire 'Billings' group, or to terminate all of them at one precise moment in time, this might *permanently* cripple the alien... or, even kill it outright. I should caution you that we can't be certain about any of this, because there's obviously no way to test the theory, prior to trying it operationally. But within the Agency, we have a unanimous consensus that the basic concept is a sound one, because it's a simple extrapolation from one quantum of effect to the next. We believe that it's worth a try. And there's *another* thing."

"What," breathed the President, his face ashen.

"It's reasonable," explained the CIA director, "To assume that the cause of – for lack of a better term – the psychic link between the 'Billings' group and the alien, is prolonged, close physical contact with it. If that's the case... then there's *another* group that would also presumably have the same ability to inflict damage on 'Karéin'."

The American leader's visage showed depths of horror.

"I'm referring, of course," droned on the director, "To the Mars mission astronauts, wherever they're now being kept. The point here – and, Mr. President, you have to appreciate that I find the next part just as distasteful to say, as you do to hear it – is, if these tactics do in fact work, their effectiveness would be *far* greater if the same were to be used on the Jacobson team, simultaneously. Within the Agency we're calling this the 'One-Two Knockout Punch'. We have a high level of confidence that if doing away with Billings and the four others in his group won't do the job... adding the Mars group to the equation should kill the alien for *sure*."

A sad look appeared in the eyes of the American leader.

"Do you *understand* what you're asking me to authorize?" he angrily demanded. "Not just the *cold-blooded murder* of five otherwise innocent American citizens – but now, also three Air Force officers and a civilian professor... not to mention a unique being who... well, you know..."

"Mr. President," argued the CIA director, "I'd remind you what's at stake, here – *nothing less than the survival of this Republic*. If this creature isn't stopped – and soon – it'll be coming not only to kill *you*, but also anyone associated with the Executive Branch... maybe, everyone in the whole *country* – after all, hasn't 'Karéin' threatened something like *that*, as well? I'm sorry, sir, but the logic here is *inescapable*."

"Are you sure... there's no other way?" pleaded the U.S. leader.

"*Very* sure," persisted the director. "You've seen how ineffective the military has been against this monster – any honest observer can see that's not a viable alternative. Sir – think of similar, difficult decisions that your predecessors have had to take! For example... Truman and the atom bomb, or J.E. Bush and the Selective Domestic Enemies of the State Elimination Program. Both of these were morally-challenging – but in a dangerous world, sometimes there's no place for sentimentality. I'm afraid this *is*, one of those situations. Oh... and if it would help on the plausible-deniability front, the Agency's willing to disclaim your knowledge of the operation... that is, we can take full responsibility upon ourselves, if you so direct."

The President slumped back in his chair and pondered the options, for about ten long seconds.

"No... no, this is something that I'll have to do myself," he remarked.

With a nervous laugh, he added, "That's why they pay me the big bucks... right?"

The U.S. leader stopped for a second or two more, then said, "Listen... it goes without saying that we have to keep this operation *absolutely* secret. And I have to tell you... I'm thinking seriously of giving the alien one more chance to surrender, if we could just –"

"Doing that would be *most* inadvisable!" protested the director. "Mr. President – you've already had a vivid demonstration of how quickly this creature can adapt to, and negate, our tactics. What if it figures out what we're planning and improvises some kind of way to block out the, uhh, 'negative feedback', from whatever we do to the Billings and Jacobson groups? Any competent military strategist will tell you, the most potent weapon of all, is, simply... *surprise*. If you give the alien another chance – particularly if it guesses what we're doing – you'll very likely be throwing away our last, best hope of stopping 'Karéin'. It would be *unconscionable*, sir."

"You mean more 'unconscionable' than torture and premeditated *murder?*" spat the President. "You said it yourself – there's no way to know if this little page out of Al Capone's play-book, is even going to *work*, in the first place. I'm sorry, Mr. Director, but let me be clear about one thing – *I'm* giving the orders here... and *I'll* make the final decision as to how, or if, we're going to proceed. Do you copy on that?"

"I copy, sir," affirmed the CIA director, with his usual infuriating passivity. "My observations and concerns on this matter have been noted. Please do not take too long to inform the Agency of your go-forward plans, as there are some rather severe logistical issues associated with the necessary preparations, particularly if we are – as I strongly suggest – going to add the Mars mission astronauts into the program. That said... do we have anything more that we need to discuss here, sir?"

"No," weakly concluded the President. "I'll try to decide before noon tomorrow, and I'll inform you immediately when I do. Dismissed."

"Very good, sir," offered the CIA director.

The U.S. leader pushed a panel-button, and the screen went almost as dark as his beleaguered moral compass.

Now alone in the Earthborne video-room, the CIA director flipped a communicator switch and spoke quietly in his trademark monotone.

"This is Top Dog, ID value is Anthill 456, Geranium 89, Torus 3A," he said. "Operational instructions follow. Confirm identity."

"ID value here for HQ Gopher is Inkwell 7C92, Hen-house 11, Unity 2E18," crackled a remote voice. "Confirmed at this end – I'm seeing your token as well, sir. Go ahead."

"One-Two Punch now a 'go'," stated the director. "But C-In-C is giving us trouble on some of the details. I'm preparing an Agency 'go-it-alone' finding. Consider it pre-authorized with value Romeo 14A, Orion 072. Copy?"

"Copy, sir," replied the remote voice. "We'll get the five stretchers set up in no more than an hour. Do you want separate containment-rooms, as we've been doing up to now?"

"No, common area is mandatory, in this case," requested the CIA director. "But there's one variance to your set-up, anyway."

"Yes, sir?" asked the voice. "What is the variance?"

"Plan for four more stretchers," came the order.

Nightmare Channel CB

Again, Cherie Tanaka let out a cry as she woke up from an afternoon nap, a cold sweat oppressively enveloping her like a too-soon burial-shroud.

Her wail – with an odd echo to it, as if coming from somewhere else – was even louder than the other one had been, scant hours ago. It left the woman gasping for air, like the wind had been knocked out of her by a rough tackle.

By now – even though Tanaka's eyes were tightly closed, as she tried to make sense of the mental images that had so badly troubled her – she could tell that both Jacobson and White were just outside what passed for a privacy-door in this plastic-and-metal gilded-cage.

"Another one?" asked the worried former Mars mission commander, as he barged into the room, followed a footstep or two behind by the black astronaut.

"Worse... and different," sighed the woman, as she slowly opened her eyes to behold the two men. "I don't know whether it was a just a really bad regular nightmare... or another... *vision*."

"Do you remember any of it?" inquired Jacobson.

"Yeah," muttered Tanaka. "I was tied up, confined... couldn't move... and I wasn't... *me*," she rambled. "I think I was a *black* woman, for however much sense *that* makes – I got a look at my arms, and they were the same color as yours, Devon –"

"Well, congratulations on your promotion, Professor," quipped White. "Although I've always thought of y'all as a soul sister... and I mean that both ways, don't you know."

"Cherie?" now asked a concerned Boyd, as he followed the other two into the quarters of the former Science Officer.

"Another bad dream, Brent," she answered.

Boyd's face looked on, in in stunned surprise.

"Yeah, but there's *got* to be a deeper meaning here," replied Tanaka. "In *this* nightmare, I looked up... there was a man in a smock, like, you know, a dentist or something... he had a sadistic, cruel look on his face, then he took out some kind of huge needle – like a regular one for drawing blood but *much* larger, with something green in it – the last thing I remember was seeing this accursed thing in his hand, he was about to hit my stomach with it... I screamed in pain... no, that's wrong – I *know* this is going to sound impossible, but *we* – Karéin *and* I, we *both* screamed... I could *feel* the impact of it on her consciousness as well as mine... then I came to... I guess my mind couldn't handle the feedback, if that's what it was."

Boyd, his shoulders slumped in an odd combination of relief and fatigue, plunked himself down on the cot, next to Tanaka.

"So *that's* what was going on," he introspectively commented. "Maybe I'm *not* going insane, after all."

"What y'all mean, man?" uneasily inquired White.

"What the Professor just described," explained the astronaut, "Is pretty much *exactly* what I just went through – with the exception that in *my* dream, I was a little boy... other than that, it's the same scene. I guess I'm not as good a vocalist as she is, but man – that was a *really* unpleasant experience."

"So what *does* it mean?" asked Jacobson.

"I don't know," stated Tanaka, her Asian-American countenance wrinkled in contemplation.

"The only explanation that makes sense, to yours truly, anyway," offered White, "Is that maybe it *was* somebody else who y'all was on the same mental CB-channel with, Professor. Somebody who themselves got in a bit too deep with the Savior of this dumb old planet, I'd bet."

"Makes sense," added Boyd. "But *who*? And why'd they be tortured like *that*? And if they *were* being abused, why wouldn't the Storied Watcher come to save them? She's not the kind to abandon people like... us... right?"

"Well... she hasn't showed up on our doorstop, yet," reminded Jacobson.

"Which implies," noted Tanaka, "That she doesn't know where we are."

"Considering that we're being kept prisoner in what's probably a very out-of-the-way, heavily-guarded and shielded place," observed Boyd, "That shouldn't be much of a surprise."

"Or she doesn't care," unhelpfully commented Jacobson.

"But then how's she sendin' us all these bad dreams, Brent?" demanded White. "When we all were up on *Infinity* and *Eagle* – Lord rest their tin souls – Karéin didn't have much of a problem homin' in on radio-beacons that were millions of kilometers away. Somehow it just don't make a lot of sense to think that she can't find us, when we're no more than half a planet away, at most."

"There sure *are* a lot of unanswered questions," said Boyd, "But from my perspective, the biggest one is, 'when the hell are we going to get out of here'. Apart from the boredom of having to tell the same thing to these so-called 'scientists' that they keep sending in here, every day... I'm worried about the escalating magnitude of these bad dreams. Maybe I'm a bit better able to handle it than Cherie, simply because I got a *lifetime's* worth of bad alien-goddess karma in that first incident back on the *Infinity*, but if these dreams start coming back at us, every night..."

"Yeah – no *kidding*," agreed Tanaka. "I haven't had a nightmare like the one I just woke up from, since I was a little kid. I don't fancy putting up with stuff like this, *ad infinitum*."

"But what can we do about it?" complained White. "They got us cooped up in here better than in one of them 'ultra-max' jails they started buildin' in the '20s. You'd need a tank to get past those walls without a key."

"I've been *thinking* about that," remarked the Science Officer, looking pensively away from the three men. "Because there was *another* message that kept coming at me – I had another burst of it about an hour before I decided to conk out this afternoon. It came back even *stronger*, when I had the bad dream... kind of like background music... it was like I was hearing it while I was tied helplessly up to this stretcher..."

Her voice trailed off.

"Don' tell me, let me guess," interjected White. "Somethin' 'bout, 'y'all can do it, the power rests strong within y'all, now'?"

Tanaka looked up, searchingly.

"Yeah, Devon," she confirmed. "Pretty much *exactly* what I was thinking."

"That message might not even have been *meant* for us, you know," cautioned Jacobson. "And in any event, I shouldn't have to remind you of the consequences associated with a violent attempt to escape this facility. Apart from the fact that it would be *mutiny*... they probably have this place surrounded by a company or more of heavily-armed soldiers. Unless you've figured out how to use our new little bag of tricks to stop a few hundred bullets flying your way, I'd suggest we belay the 'jailbreak' talk."

"Well, what are we supposed to do, Sam – just sit around in here until Doomsday, hoping for them to get bored with us and send us packing on our merry way?" argued Tanaka.

"Doomsday already been and gone, I'd remind y'all," joked the black ex-astronaut. "And we all got through *that*... with a little help from our friend."

"Hah!" chuckled Boyd. "You got a point there," he said. "But so does the Professor. We're not accomplishing *anything* in here, and judging from what's been going on in my head – assuming, all the while, that these 'visions' are a halfway-accurate representation of reality – it looks like something very big, and very unpleasant, is happening on the outside. So why don't we at least *ask* the damn Air Force about what's going on, and demand to get some straight answers. The worst they can say is 'no', although we'll have to think up a cover-story if they in turn try to find out –"

His voice was cut off by a loudspeaker-announcement.

"*Attention!*" it exclaimed. "Paging Commander Jacobson and his team. We have orders directing that you will shortly be moving out. Please begin immediate packing of personal effects for departure – ETA, fifteen minutes."

"Hey," continued Boyd, with an joyful smile, "Now *there's* the power of positive thinking... wouldn't you say?"

"Won't take *me* long to pack," happily echoed Jacobson. "Considering how little we all got back to Earth with. Holy Cow... I just can't *believe* it's over!"

White matched the other man's grin and did it two or three better. "'Bout damn *time*," he said. "I can hardly *wait* to see the missus, not to mention Martin 'n Francelle. Looks like we outlasted 'em!"

But the elation of the faces of the two Air Force Majors was quickly negated by a look of dark gloom, on Tanaka's own.

"What's up, Professor?" uneasily requested White. "Y'all gettin' used to the hospital food in here?"

"I want out, just as much as anyone," answered the woman. "But something tells me we've got no such luck. In the back of my mind, I keep having a feeling like it's 'out of the frying pan, into the fire'."

"If that's so," countered White, with a suddenly strange, determined look, "Like I said before... we been through a bigger fire, before. We'll deal with it."

"It wasn't *us* that put out that fire, you know," observed Jacobson.

"She and us were a team," countered Boyd. "*Are* a team."

"Captain," added the black ex-astronaut, his visage still grim but serene, "We'll deal with it. Y'all just got to have *faith*."

"Yeah," agreed Jacobson, his voice quiet and resigned.

For a few seconds, the former Mars mission crew sat in silence, their thoughts not recorded in these pages.

"Well then... we had better get packing," ordered the Commander.

Delivery At Progreso

As little as the short Mexican with the long beard had wanted to admit it, man-handling this damned thing from the freighter, across the dock at Puerto Barrios in Guatemala, had actually been the *easy* part of this leg of the project.

There had been an unending series of problems after that, ranging from a broken truck-axle, to having to pay *la mordida* to six or seven different groups of gangsters, just for the 'privilege' of crossing their territories, to almost dropping the precious, unnaturally-heavy box down a steep-sided gorge, at a hairpin turn in the still-potholed back-roads of the Yucatán.

Despite all this, driven by their faith in Almighty Allah, the short man and his small and very discreet group of true-believers – disgusted with the corruption and depravity of the Catholic Church, repelled by the *Yanqui*-loving theology of the Protestants – had persevered, and now, just over the north horizon of the Gulf of Mexico, beckoned the ultimate goal... the ultimate target.

Bueno, he reflected, as, sweating despite the cool ocean-breeze, he dismounted from the truck-cab and leaned back on the front motor-casing, looking out over the placid sea on the other side of the city-square statue.

That accursed woman-devil from Mars prevented Allah's righteous revenge against the Great Satan.

But His martyrs will strike again, none the less.

His reverie was interrupted by the sound of a motorcycle. A few seconds later, it roared up to the other side of the *carro*.

A kick-stand went down, and, slowly, the motorcycle-rider, also a Mexican man and also bearded, but taller, with intense black eyes, walked around the front of the truck, until he was a few feet away from the truck-driver.

"*Soy apenas una gaviota,*" he said. "*Estoy buscando un mosquito.*"

"*Sí,*" replied the truck-driver. "*Soy mosquito aquí. Continúe,*" he requested.

"*Estoy listo para recibir los artefactos,*" explained the other man.

The short Mexican nodded a silent "*Si*", as he stroked his beard and again got back in the truck's driver-seat.

"*Sigame,*" called out the man on the motorcycle.

The truck revved up its engine and followed dutifully behind, heading toward the boat.

Only The Best Stuff, For Mr. Wolf

"Any more ups and downs and I'm gonna *puke,*" complained the bounty-hunter.

"Consider how much *worse* it would be, if you could see how far we are from the ground," replied the Storied Watcher, matter-of-factually. "But anyway... it is late in the day and I become fatigued – defying the gravity of this planet *is* challenging work, you know. We have gone a good long way from the city – so just a bit further and we will, ahh, how would Bob say, yes – 'put down'. Misha, how are you doing?"

"Better than he is," philosophically answered the SVR-man. "But then, back in the old country, when I was *Spetsnaz*, we were accustomed to jumping out of airplanes and helicopters, sometimes two or three times a week."

"'*Spetsnaz*'?" inquired Wolf. "That somethin' wrong with yer nose?"

"I was in the Russian army," patiently explained Misha. "Like your Navy SEALS, or your 'Green Berets'."

"No shit?" grunted the big man. "Well – them SEAL boys *is* tough... but I didn't see you doin' too much back there."

"That, my gun-loving American friend," indifferently replied the Russian, "Is the difference between 'bravery' and 'stupidity'."

"Enough of this!" protested the alien-girl. "It is time to land – I see a waterfall ahead. We can wash and drink there. Brace yourselves; going down..."

Feeling as if they were in a rapidly-descending elevator with all the interior-lights off, the two men had no choice but to hold on for dear life.

After perhaps twenty to thirty seconds, they felt the cool wash of water-spray.

"Hmm," they heard her remark, "I detect a little cave, to one side of the cascading water. We can stay there for a while and rest."

The motion now changed to a sideways flight-path.

"How do you see anythin' at all, lady?" demanded the bounty-hunter. "It's darker than midnight in a coal-mine in here. I can't see worth *shit!*"

"The kinds of light-waves that you people can see – at least, until your abilities, ahh, 'mature'," she answered, "Are a small fraction of what is revealed to my eyes. And unlike you, I can choose which types of energy-waves that I will perceive and process. I have to do that quite frequently... it is difficult to make sense of everything, when one has so many images in one's mind. Brace yourselves – we are landing."

Mercifully, they felt solid ground confront the bottoms of their feet, although Wolf stumbled a bit, as the floor of where they had come to rest was uneven and covered by small rocks and stones.

Down came the ebon shroud, and the two humans blinked furiously while their eyes tried to adjust to the beams of sunlight streaming in to this place, from an oval entrance about three meters from their landing-place.

"Man, it feels *good* to be back on solid ground," offered the bounty-hunter. "That whole thing was like floatin' around the whole Southwest, without a parachute. Where *are* we? If you don't mind my askin', of course."

"Hmm," commented Karéin-Mayréij, "To tell you the truth, I do not exactly know, 'Wolf'. Though I studied furiously to learn as much as I could about this planet called 'Earth' – as well as this 'United States' Empire, in which I now unfortunately find myself – there was a lot to commit to memory... and, no doubt, I missed much knowledge, in the process. I believe that we are in the Big Canyon, and that we are facing north. We are also to the west of the Tucson-city. If either of you knows more about this place, I would be in your debt if you would tell me."

"It is called the '*Grand* Canyon'," noted Misha. "The biggest one on Earth."

"One of the 'Seven Wonders', you know," chimed in the bounty-hunter. "Keeps them tourists comin' – or at least it *did*, until they pretty much closed the borders up tight."

"Oh," acknowledged the alien-girl. "Well... it certainly *is* big – but there is a much larger one on *Mailànkh;* were you to stand on its rim and look down, you could scarcely see the bottom. In the old days, it was filled with water, and I would dive into its depths, from time to time..."

"'Fraid I can't help you a lot on this, but – oh... *wait* a minute," said Wolf, as he approached the cave-entrance and peered outside.

"Hey – that's a damn big waterfall," he exclaimed. "Heard of this place, once... think we're in Injun territory. You *can* hike here, if you pay off the natives, but I never got this far in... usually I'd just drop by them stores they got on the highway – 'bout the only place in the Southwest you can get old-fashioned cigarettes, anymore. They'll sell you even better stuff, for enough money... but I never went for *that* shit, you know."

"'Injun'... you mean the same tribe that Tommy belongs to?" hopefully inquired the newcomer.

"How would *I* know?" mentioned the bounty-hunter, leaning his arm on the side of the cave-entrance. "He from 'round here? Like, Hopi, Navajo... that kinda thing?"

"Unfortunately, I do not think so," answered the Storied Watcher, a sad, far-away look on her otherwise serenely-beautiful, heavenly-princess face. "He is from the northern fief of 'Ne-bra-ska', I believe."

"That's a thousand miles or more from these parts, as the crow flies," remarked Wolf. "Ain't no way that we're gonna... oh... *right*," he sheepishly added.

"He is not there – on this 'reservation', that is – any more," explained Karéin-Mayréij.

She sat down on a nearby rock and looked up at the two men.

"Your damn-ed President and his lackeys have Tommy, Bob, Whitney and her two children, hidden away in some filthy dungeon, where they are being cruelly-tortured!" she angrily remarked, "No doubt to make them give away imaginary secrets about myself."

"Why don't you just go there and knock a few heads together?" asked the bounty-hunter, now taking a rough seat, himself. "From what I saw back there, they couldn't fight you if they were sittin' in a Westmore tank takin' pot- shots out that big gun it's got on it"

"You may be correct about that," interjected Misha, "But she does not know *where* her friends are being held. Nor – for that matter – does my own government. In case you had not noticed... the American state has many secret prisons, where people go when the President wants them to 'disappear'."

Wolf suspiciously regarded the Russian and pointed out, "Yeah... I *had* noticed. In my line of work, you don't, and you got a short ol' career, pardner."

The Storied Watcher cast her gaze first to Misha, then to the bounty-hunter.

"I hold and trust that you will not reveal what you now will see, to *anyone*, save that I so permit," she commanded, slowly standing up as she spoke.

"*Ch'éyl Vîrya Ahn'jë, oomènyé oye'hà'à,*" she half-sang, half-spoke, and in no more than the blink-of-an-eye – had the humans been fast enough to have noticed the details – the cape flew off her back, making a place for the rest of her war-gear, as each piece of the latter – first, the body-armor called *Ahn'jë*, then the two daggers, their union hissing and popping as the cold of violet-and-navy *Ss'éth'ch'* came into contact with the orange-yellow of hot *Ksé'l'ch'*, then the sword, *Fàiagàryuu.*

This was finally covered by the shield *I'ëà'b'*, and all came to rest on the cape, which formed a shroud tightly compressing and enveloping all of these items, into something no larger than a child's school-backpack.

The alien-girl was now clad only in a bikini-like undergarment composed of the same weird stuff as was the armor-suit named *Ahn'jë*, except that it was perhaps not as dark-hued as the outer-armor; and this left very little to the racing imaginations of the two humans, who stood, googly-eyed, in front of her.

"Oh, *mann*," gasped Wolf. "Where's the saltpeter? My girlfriend's nice... but *you*, girl – I mean – if we was *alone*..."

"Actually," she primly explained, "These undergarments are part of *Vîrya Ahn'jë*, my girl-child fortress... I decided to keep wearing them, since, although I claim no foolish modesty – you are both well-acquainted with the pleasures and soft body-curves of woman, are you not? – I felt that going completely nude here, might be too, ahh... *provocative*."

"Good judgment on your part," ruefully agreed the Russian.

"You might find it interesting," noted Karéin-Mayréij, "That you are making *Vîrya Ahn'jë* herself, rather aroused, as well; she perceives your manly-emotions, and they bestir her own female-instincts, but she knows not how to interpret them – or what to do with them. *Vîrya I'ëà'b'* – my girl-shield – would also feel thusly; however, she sleeps beside her war-brothers, right now."

"You... uhh... mean that yer bikini, and that chain-mail stuff that you were wearin' a few second ago... it's gettin', *hot*, for us?" asked the bounty-hunter.

The alien-girl leaned back on her seating-rock and nodded with an amused grin.

"Pretty much so, Mister 'Wolf'," she confirmed. "If I correctly understand what 'hot' means, in this context. *Vîrya Ahn'jë* finds both of you most attractive, although in different ways."

"Well, if... you know... this armor of yours really got goin' – like, how would it – her – whatever – how would it *do* it... if you know what I'm sayin'?" pressed the incredulous big man.

"*Vîrya Ahn'jë* is yet but a *child*," counseled the Storied Watcher, "Thus, there is much that she has yet to learn. That said, I am sure that she would find a way, if the matter were urgent... though her body-fire might cause you some problems. For the time being, I have instructed her to be patient and wait until she understands more about the joys of lovemaking."

"What is the matter?" muttered Misha. "Have you not been in any of those shops that you Americans have on the seedier-side of Tucson? There are all *sorts* of artificial devices with which you can, uhh, 'do it' – this one that she speaks of, is *far* more sophisticated. But, Karéin... I must confess, seeing you like that... it brings back fond memories..."

Yet more astonishment showed on the face of the bounty-hunter.

"You mean," he demanded, pointing first at the other man, then at the newcomer, "That you did it with... *her*?"

The Russian just smiled, smugly.

Amazing! thought Misha.

I can feel the envy in his mind.

Like waves of heat coming from a campfire...

"Do not worry, 'Wolf'," cooed the alien-girl. "If the Gods so will it – you will have your chance. In the meantime... I suppose I that should use those clothes that were given to me by... well, there is no need to go into *that*, right now."

Her head flicked a quick nod; and, instantly, her frame was bedecked by the garments with which she had been gifted, back at the Losada household.

After picking up his dropped jaw, Wolf was barely able to respond, "Lady, that's the best thing I've heard all day – just don't tell the girlfriend... okay? Oh, and... didn't you say you had a bf, already? You know... this 'Billings' guy?"

"Oh-kay," she pleasantly answered. "And, yes, I do – I love Bob very much... and he has given me his solemn pledge of love, as well."

"That gonna be a *problem*?" inquired the big man.

"No," she stated.

"Really?" he pressed. "Like... if *I* was your old man – just speaking hypothetically, you understand – well, I'd probably be a bit more, uhh, *possessive*... kinda like if you're lucky enough to shack up with a movie-star – you don't want to have 'em wanderin' on you... right?"

"You humans have much to learn about love, sex, pleasure and the differences between all three of these," countered Karéin-Mayréij. "Where *I* come from, we have seven different words for 'love' – one, for example, means 'deep, abiding love of woman for man', of the type that Bob and I have, while another means, 'two people giving freely of themselves, for the pleasure of the moment', while still another, is the love that I have for my adopted son Tommy, or that *Vîrya Ahn'jë* and her brothers and sister have for myself, as their mother. There are other words, with other meanings, as well. It is pointless to try to rank one of these above another; they all have a place of rightful honor in how kind, happy people relate to one another. Thus, is how I live my own life. Bob knows this."

"The natives of northern Russia, have twenty words for 'snow', you know," observed Misha.

"Take your word for it," grunted Wolf, as he found a place to stretch out on the cave floor, "So, now that we got *that* over with... what's the plan?"

"Storied Watcher... I had been meaning to ask you the same thing," echoed Misha. "Did you not say something about a demand that the President should produce your family, near a mountain, to the north? And you set a fairly short deadline. If this place is far away, we should not stay here too long – America is a *big* place."

She bent forward, resting her palms on her knees.

"Two reasons," spoke the alien-girl. "First – as I said some time ago – I am tired from the journey, thus far. It is difficult *enough* to bend the gravity-waves so that I can stay airborne; and to ensure that my skills continue to return, I have had to – uhh, how would you say in Eng-lish – 'push it'... that is, whether or not you noticed, as we went further away from Tucson I tried to go as high and fast as I could –"

"Which is?" interrupted the Russian.

"As you measure these things," she explained, "About a thousand meters above the ground, and a few hundred kilometers per hour. But I am improving rapidly. I must balance the rate at which my skills return, against when next I dare risk a confrontation with the battle-machines of this 'President'. I already have more than enough power to defeat these, should I have to do so... but I prefer not to try, without the ability to out-fly and out-maneuver his war-planes and robot-rockets."

"We must consider," continued Karéin-Mayréij, "That the President may have been reluctant to drop an atom-smashing bomb on top of us, when we all were in the hotel, because in so doing, he might have killed more of his subjects than even *he* would be comfortable with slaughtering. He may not be so restrained about a battle in the countryside. Depending on how big it is, I probably *can* withstand a nuclear explosion, provided that it does not go off too close – but it is obviously not something with which I want to experiment. And that leads to the *second* reason why I stopped here..."

Her trailed off, and she stared intently at the two men.

"I kinda get the feelin' you're about to say something that we might not like hearin'," uneasily mentioned bounty-hunter.

"Yeah," she confirmed. "You got *that* right, 'Wolf'. I will not lie to you... nor will I mislead by omission."

"We have been through a lot already, some of us more than others," commented the Russian, with a sidelong glance at the big man. "What do you mean, Karéin?"

"It is like this," counseled the alien-girl, "If I favor someone, when they dwell with me, abide with me... *lie* with me... this makes them stronger – indeed, it changes them into something neither human, nor full-blooded greater *Makailkh*, as I am, but instead into something in between – far more powerful than a normal being, hard to kill yet still quite able to be killed, long-lived and healthy yet still, ultimately – mortal."

The SVR-man's face wore a look halfway between elation and panic.

"You mean this process has already... *affected* me, Karéin?" he asked.

The Storied Watcher nodded affirmatively and said, "Even so. The longer and closer that people are to me, the faster and more forcefully the change becomes. Different people end up at different stages of this wondrous transformation; I can neither fully control it, nor, frankly, do I completely understand how it works – I only understand that it *does* work, and that once it starts, it *cannot* be stopped, or reversed. It has already started with you, Misha; but as for *you*, Wolf, since the time is likely so short, there is another bridge you must cross – and you must do so voluntarily. Would you hear of it?"

"Thought I had enough weird stuff to last a *lifetime*, when I first took hold of your hand, girl," muttered the big man. "But go ahead... I s'pose I ain't goin' anywhere fast anyway, considerin' it's a hundred feet or more down from the mouth of this-here cave."

The alien-girl came over, sat down next to him, and, to Misha's scarcely-disguised displeasure, side-saddled next to the bounty-hunter, squeezing his hand.

"'Wolf'," she softly instructed, "You can come with Misha and I without agreeing to what I will shortly request, if that is your choice; but unprepared as you are, now, you will be vulnerable to the many attacks that the American government might direct against us. There is a good chance that one of these – for example, gas that would wreck your nervous-system and kill you in a few seconds, or certain kinds of radiation – might quickly cause your demise."

"Not to mention all them bullets 'n bombs that we had flyin' all about, back there," added the man. "They was more than enough for me, right there."

The Storied Watcher giggled a bit, but then her visage returned to serious guise.

"Another thing is," she noted, "When my powers of flight fully return – and that hour is not far off – I will be accelerating, decelerating and maneuvering at velocities that would crush every bone in your body, if you were holding on to me during that time."

"Remind me just to take a bus," quipped Wolf.

"But there is a way around it," she went on. "If you consent to the 'change', while I will still have to be careful – this applies equally to you, Misha, incidentally – I will have much more latitude in how I behave, while you are near to me. I can make you stronger, much more powerful, much more able to resist harm of almost any type... *but...*"

"It's always the 'but' parts that I hate," grumbled the bounty-hunter. "You usually find 'em just before the fine print in a car-warranty."

The Storied Watcher again allowed herself a subdued laugh.

"This is no sneaky contract," she stated. "But it *will* be a leap into the unknown, if you want to undertake what I now propose."

"Get *on* with it," demanded Wolf. "What I got to do? Is it like one of them 'hazing'-ceremonies?"

"Not... *exactly*," explained the newcomer. "As I mentioned, if you had been with me as long as has Misha, you would already be on the path to power... but matters being as they are now, I must hasten the process. Other than making love – something that we can do as soon as we have some privacy, out of respect to our friend – by *far* the most potent way for me to, uhh, 'jump-start' your transformation is to share one of my most special body-fluids, with you."

"If yer on the rag, I ain't goin' down on you – no offense, you understand, but I ain't no Angel," he retorted.

"No... *I* am the 'angel'," she argued. "Or... so I have been told. I know what 'on the rag' means, because Bob translated the phrase – however, that female problem *never* happens with me. But what is 'going down'?"

The Russian burst out in gales of cynical laughter.

"Karéin," he barely managed between guffaws, "First of all, I think that our big friend means, the 'Hell's Angels' motorcycle-gang – they are notorious for having unpleasant initiation-rituals. Second, as for 'going down', well... a man uses his tongue in a certain way, on a woman... remember back in the motel?"

The alien-girl put her hand to her mouth and giggled, girlishly.

"Oh... I *see*, now," she remarked. "Where *I* come from, we call doing *that*, 'kissing the *mèlepang*' – it is a fruit whose sweetness becomes stronger and stronger – and its flesh becomes firmer – the more that one puts one's tongue to it. An apt comparison... would you not say?"

She winked at him.

"Indeed," agreed Misha. "I would like to visit that waterfall – I think that I need a cold shower."

"I'll join you, if and when she lets us outta here," snorted Wolf.

"So," continued the Storied Watcher, "This body-fluid issues from somewhere else... *from* these, specifically."

Immediately, four cruel-looking fangs extended; and – as the alien looked up at him, trying to appear like an innocent, big-eyed teenager – the bounty-hunter jumped back in shock and surprise.

"*Shit!*" he shouted. "I got myself stuck in a cave with a fuckin' *vampire!* You stay away from me – *hear?*"

"What is your *problem?*" indifferently asked the Russian. "Did you not see the Storied Watcher's, ah, pointed teeth, back in the hotel?"

"Didn't get too good a look at 'em – but I thought it was all just an *act*, you know, falsies, same as that disco dancin'-suit she was wearin' – but they're real... ain't they?" protested Wolf, with more than a trace of a shudder.

"Just as much a part of me as your incisors are a part of you," offered the alien, trying to sound friendly and matter-of-fact. "And I will not force you to do anything. If you allow me to inject my empowering-fluid, I would do that in the arm or the thigh – not in the neck as your 'vampire'-legends tell... you would get a potent and quick-acting dose, and you would be more or less able to function after no more than an hour or so. Alternativel..., I can make a few drops of it issue forth from my teeth and then I can use my finger to apply these to your tongue. The effect will eventually be the same – but it will not act as quickly, and there may be some, ahh, *unpleasant* side-effects."

"Like what?" grunted the big man. "Like I maybe turn into a bat?"

"*Oooh!*" peevishly retorted Karéin-Mayréij. "*Enough* of this stupid superstition! All that would happen, is that you would fall asleep, for a short time."

"Yeah... *right*," warily replied the bounty-hunter.

"Is there anything else that you want to know about it, 'Wolf'?" she asked.

"Not really," he said. "No, on second thought... how far you say it was down to the ground?"

"Oh, come *on*, for Heaven's sake!" complained the Storied Watcher. "You are being an *idiot*, man! I offer you the chance of a *lifetime!* Do you *know* what an honor it is to be given this gift?"

"If this means anything, my friend," interrupted Misha, "I refused Karéin's offer to follow her, at first; more than that, I refused an order to engineer her death. I am therefore now a traitor against Mother Russia – if they catch me, the firing-squad will be the *least* unpleasant of my possible fates. I could not care less if you accompany us... but I thought you should know that."

"All it says to me," argued Wolf, "Is that she's got you snake-fascinated, pardner. Who's to say that this Martian spit doesn't fuck up your mind, so you can't *think* worth shit, forever and a day?"

"It is a type of, uhh, *venom* – not saliva," countered Karéin-Mayréij. "And, again so as not to mislead you – yes, sir, it definitely *does* affect your mind... but not as you now speculate. You will think faster – see the world in more colors, be far more in control of your own body – and a thousand other things beside. All of them are greatly beneficial. Ahh, how can I *explain* it – I am not the one who is changed by being in my favor, anyway! Misha... can you find words to describe this?"

"I have not partaken of any of this, uhh, 'fluid', either," commented the Russian. "However... I *can* honestly attest that since I first met you, Karéin, I have continuously felt better, more alert, even, *younger*... each and every day... until the time when you left. Since then, I have not become any stronger, but neither have I weakened. All I can say to Mister 'Wolf' is – have you never experimented with a recreational drug? How can you say that it is a 'bad thing', if you have no understanding of what effects that it brings?"

"Wouldn't know," parried the bounty-hunter. "I don't do drugs. At least... not any more."

"Well?" impatiently pressed the alien-girl.

"So you want me to just take your word for it... all this, '*El Permanante* Steroid Treatment', courtesy them nasty little teeth of yours... 'zat right?" requested Wolf.

"Yeah," she plainly affirmed.

"Do I have a choice?" he asked.

"Of *course* you do!" she answered, with a sigh. "But only if you are, oh, how did Brent Boyd say it... yes, only if you are a, uhh, 'dork'."

"Then... no," he said. "Hey... you don't think I'm, like, a 'dork'... do you?"

Karéin-Mayréij rolled her eyes.

A second later, Wolf backtracked, "Okay – maybe just a *little* taste, you understand? It's like them drugs, you don't want to get *totally* shit-faced... uhh, whoops..."

"I thought you do not 'do', drugs," sneered the SVR-man.

"I don't," shot back the bounty-hunter. "Not for years – but when you're a teenager, hey, you *try* things, you know?"

"Um-hmm," knowingly nodded the alien-girl. "Well... if it is of any interest, it would be nice to 'try' one or more of these substances and have it affect me, the way they evidently do for you mortals. Unfortunately – or more likely, to ensure my continued survival – my body usually dissolves this kind of foreign substance before it has any effect, for either good or ill. I do not believe that I have been 'drunk', or 'stoned', in several thousand of your Earth-years."

"Should sign you up for the Christian Temperance League of Southwest Arizona," grunted the big man. "You'd be their poster-girl."

"I do not think I would like to see you 'out of control', Karéin," observed Misha. "Not for one single second."

"Yeah," she ruefully agreed. "Unfortunately... you have good reason to be of that opinion. I have a few very faint memories of being 'out of control', though not to alcohol or drugs... *bad* things happened..."

"I can just *imagine*," shuddered the Russian.

"So how exactly does this all work?" demanded the bounty-hunter.

"What happens," described Karéin-Mayréij, as she re-positioned herself on a nearby rock, "Is that I concentrate – and hope that the right stuff issues from my teeth. Shall we, ahh, 'give it a try'?"

At this, she closed her eyes, as if meditating.

"What... uhh... happens, if the 'wrong' stuff comes out of these teeth of yours?" inquired Wolf.

"Depending on what it is," explained the newcomer, matter-of-factually, "It can be a fluid that heals even the worst wounds, when death is near; or something that bestows a blessing and makes you, uhh, 'compatible' with the Fire, or, a liquid that dissolves flesh, indeed, stone, like fiendish acid, or a nerve poison that would kill you in a few seconds... or, other things that whose functions that I seem to have forgotten – or whose purposes, if any – that perhaps I never really *did* come to comprehend. You must understand that I do not go around biting people, very frequently. I will need to rely on instinct, here."

"You're nuckin' *futs*, lady, if you think I'm dippin' my tongue in *that* shit, if you don't even know what it *is*," protested the bounty-hunter.

"If you want... I will be your 'taste-tester', Karéin," stepped in Misha.

She looked up at him.

"Thanks," she said, "But why are you willing to take that risk?"

"I have... *faith*, in you," he replied, plainly.

"You are dear to me," quietly remarked the alien-girl, looking at the SVR-man with a loving glance. "Especially as you remind me of another, whose faith is also thus. But it will not be necessary... I know how most of these substances from my teeth taste. Once I have the right one, it will be completely safe."

"Suurre," countered the big man. "I believe you... millions wouldn't."

The Storied Watcher opened her eyes, followed rapidly by her mouth. She touched her index-finger to the tip of one of her top fangs, from which had issued a drop of something that resembled water.

Rapidly, she deposited the liquid on her tongue and closed her eyes; but a second or so later, her visage was clouded with an unpleasant demeanor.

"Ugh," commented Karéin-Mayréij. "Nerve venom, and... oh – I forgot to mention – I have boosted it with rattle-serpent poison... you know, the kind that would liquefy your flesh, destroy your muscle tissue... I took it into my body, taught my fangs to manufacture it... I *do* that kind of thing, you know. How do you say – yes, Tommy taught me the phrase... 'my bad'!"

The Russian snickered. "You, uhh, *do* that kind of thing, you say? Well – of course! I teach myself all sorts of new things too, all the time, Storied Watcher."

Wolf incredulously shook his head.

"This is gettin' like one of them TV movies that you turn off at 2 a.m., when you had one too many and forgot to hit the remote," he muttered.

"Time for the next scene, then," continued the alien-girl, not missing a beat.

Again, she closed her eyes, seeming to be deep in thought; then she repeated the fang-harvesting technique, this time with a drop of faintly green-tinted something-or-other.

And again, a pained look appeared on the newcomer's face, when she tasted the stuff.

"The burning-fluid," she grumbled. "You would not want to have *that* on your tongue – unless you desire to speak no more."

"There's probably a lot of folk who'd think that'd be a big improvement... but I'd still like to be able to order a pizza," quipped the bounty-hunter. "Look – you *sure* we ain't just wastin' each other's time?" he complained.

"Patience," counseled Karéin-Mayréij. "I *will*, ahh, 'get it right'... sooner or later."

"Right," he sarcastically replied. "'Sooner' would be a lot better, if it's all the same to you, lady."

For a third time, the Storied Watcher sat and concentrated, her face serenely composed in close-eyed meditation.

Then, as she had done twice before, she touched the tip of her index-finger to the tip of her fang, this time, the opposite one from the right-hand tooth that had previously been tested.

A liquid with a subtle topaz-yellow sheen to it, appeared on the extremity of her finger.

A smile came to her face.

"Try *this*," confidently requested the alien-girl. "It is the, uhh, 'real shit'."

"I *know* I'm gonna regret this," self-warned the bounty-hunter. "Listen... do I gotta lay down, or somethin'? I mean... there's some of this shit that if you're standin' when you take it, you end up flat on your face... or maybe with your face lookin' down into some puke..."

"Perhaps you had better do so," amicably suggested the newcomer. "Just with your fore-body propped up against something. And as far as I know, it does not make one nauseous... but, uhh, 'better safe than regretful', as Bob used to say."

"It is... oh, forget it," interjected Misha. "We do not have so many idiom phrases in my language, thankfully."

"Let us not tarry," commanded the Storied Watcher. "It will evaporate, after a short time. Here, 'Wolf'... open your mouth."

"Always preferred to smoke it, rather than –" he started to say, but as the alien's finger deftly flicked her fangs' output on to the man's tongue, he abruptly stopped speaking.

Leaning back against the cave wall, Wolf looked up, with dilated pupils, and an odd expression, halfway between contentment and fear.

"Ohhh..." he moaned. "Got snake-bit, one time... like that.. gotta sleep..."

With a soft thud, the bounty-hunter, with the muscles of his huge body suddenly relaxing, keeled over.

Pickin' Up The Pace

By now – despite a regime of torment that would undoubtedly have driven him, or any normal human being mad, had it been imposed so much as a fortnight ago – Billings was feeling almost confident.

His beleaguered body had been injected with foul chemicals, subjected to increasingly-potent electric shocks and a fair share of good old-fashioned physical abuse – starting with face-slapping and progressing rapidly to simply having the shit beaten out of him, by two burly parodies of a male nurse – but *nothing* had, as yet, made him beg, cry or spill the beans on *her*.

Even having needles slowly inserted into delicate parts of his anatomy, or having deep scalpel-gashes made into the same, hadn't done the trick. The salesman – to his unending amazement – had watched it happen with morbid curiosity, like watching a dentist pull out one's teeth, after a good shot of local anesthetic.

Okay – the sleep deprivation and the 'waterboarding' *had* come close to breaking him; but whatever witchcraft that she had laid upon him – the thing that reduced what should have been screaming agony, down to a dull ache – evidently couldn't completely offset the exhaustion of a burned-out brain or the primal need to breathe. But for Billings, apart from it now being a matter of pride – she had done *her* part, he was bound and determined to do his own – there was an unanticipated fringe-benefit.

Namely... the look of wild frustration on the faces of his torturers, as each of their techniques came a-cropper.

Secretly, each time he heard them curse his obduracy, Billings felt a surge of perverse satisfaction.

He'd have done a victory dance, were it not for the arm-, leg-and head-restraints.

They keep telling me, 'this is going to hurt us more than it's going to hurt you', he found himself thinking.

Never thought I'd hear myself saying this – but I think the bastards are right...

Still groggy from yesterday's beatings and endless, uncalled-for sleep-interruptions, the salesman's brief reverie was shattered by the familiar feeling of rough hands on his collarbone.

"Well, *well*, Mr. Billings," came the unctuous voice of one of the nerdy, bespectacled *faux* 'doctors' behind the two thugs who were now man-handling him to his wobbly feet, "Have we learned our lessons, yet? You've been one of our slowest students, over the past few days... and we're now *way* behind schedule. I'm afraid we're just going to have to pick up the pace – nothing *personal*, you understand – but, well, we're answerable to the higher-ups, and you're going to get *us* a bad report card, too! Why don't you just make it *easy* on everybody and start talking? This can all be over in an hour or so... it's up to you!"

His tongue mercifully telling him that all of his teeth were still intact, despite several hard punches in the mouth, through swollen lips, Billings was able to mumble, "fuck you", to the sadist-doctor.

"Okay," continued the man, with mock empathy. "We'll do it *your* way, then, Mr. Billings. It's all the same to us – 'same old same old', as the saying goes – and, as we've tried to reason with you before, we have an *unbroken* track record, for these kinds of things. Mr. Smith, Mr. Jones... if you will, please."

The iron grasp of the two big, crew-cut, white-garbed Caucasian orderlies yanked the salesman off his cot.

Though he knew he could – after a fashion – still stand, Billings had no intention of co-operating, so he feigned 'rubber legs'. This availed him not, as the orderlies dragged him down the corridor outside his cell, by arms and shoulders propped up by the armpits.

How long the journey to the black-site torture-chamber lasted, he neither cared about, nor paid any attention to; for Billings had already begun the secret mental preparations that, so far, had proved an impregnable bulwark against the worst that they – whoever they were – could throw at him.

He first thought of *her*, then, of everything that they had done together, in those few, halcyon days; then, finally, he concentrated upon the few, precious words that she had given him, when explaining how to defend against her 'mind-fuck' ability.

Your mind is an iron tower, a high fortress, an iron tower, a high fortress, an iron tower... rinse and repeat as necessary...

In furtherance of the 'all-but-beaten' routine, Billings had been keeping his eyelids half-shut, and had been practicing his best glassy-eyed, well-past-sanity, stare.

Actually, the ruse was not far off the truth, but he tried not to think in that direction; too depressing, especially considering that, given her absence for – what was it, days, *weeks*, now? – he was confronting, well, *forever* in this parody-of-Hell, delivered courtesy of Uncle Sam's fine, 'government of the people'.

In keeping with the act, the salesman allowed himself only the slightest hint of a smile, as they dragged him into the chamber. But a second later, along with the usual coterie of two white-smocked torturers and three black-suited guards, he saw something that came near to shattering his defenses, all at once.

Tommy.

The boy – a gagged, terrified-looking, tear-streaked, wild-eyed remnant of the child that Billings had previously known – was strapped securely on a gurney that had been hinged head-upward, so that nothing that was about to transpire, would be left to the imagination. One of his nipples had apparently been forcibly removed, and there were small, cigarette-sized burn marks at random intervals all over his body.

The only mercy – if one could call it that – which had been afforded this pitiful creature, was a urine- and feces-stained pair of underwear, arranged loosely around the boy's upper thigh.

"Okay, Mr. Billings," sounded the mock-sympathetic voice of one of the 'doctors', as the salesman was himself affixed to a gurney, set up to directly face the one containing Tommy, "Since – as we said – you haven't been making very much progress lately... we thought it might be useful to bring in one of your classmates... somebody who can help you get up to speed, you know."

The 'doctor' walked over to the boy, and laid a creepy-friendly hand on his shoulder.

"Now, Tommy, here," he commented, with a thin smile, "*He's* needed some encouragement, too, but I'll tell you, Bob – say, you don't mind if I call you 'Bob', do you? Great! Thought we might as well be doin' the first-name thing... you know, it's a bit more *intimate*, that way, isn't it – ah, but silly *me!* Here I go, getting off-topic, again. You'll have to forgive me.. just something I have to work on... you know? We've *all* got things that we can do a lot better... isn't that right, Bob?"

No, sent Billings in the man's direction, *I'm* not *going to let* her *tear you limb from limb.*

I'm going to do that, myself.

He glowered at the 'doctor', and right then, an idea came to his mind.

Trying to keep it as inaudible as possible, he started to mumble, 'Sari... Sari... Sari', before a whack to the side of his face stopped this gambit, cold.

"Ah, Bob," quipped the torturer, "We're glad that you're trying to say you're sorry – but, well, 'there's no excuse for *you*'... right, guy? Just between you and me, though, keep it up – I *like it* when my 'patients' apologize for all the trouble that they've caused me. Kind of makes my job feel worthwhile."

"So... back on track, as it were," he elaborated. "As I was saying... little Tommy here – he's getting *way* ahead of you, that's the only way to put it, see? You have no *idea* of the stuff that he's been telling us! Like, for example, about this Martian chick that you all fell in with, how she can re-program computer-chips in a blink of an eye, and how she can breathe underwater, and about that lil' ol' removable left eye of hers... you know, the one that can fly out and see around corners?"

You smart *little bugger!* mused Billings, trying desperately not to show any sign of smugness.

Something true, and a lot that's not. She taught both of us well.

Hold on, kid... hold on...

"I don't know what you're talking about," whispered the salesman, through clenched teeth. "And I wouldn't tell you if I did."

"Oh – but I think you *do* know, Bob," countered the 'doctor'. "And Tommy here, with a little help from yours truly – he's going to give you that little old 'push' that you need, to loosen your tongue... help us sort out fact from fiction, as it were. See... the thing is... we've heard a *lot* from that nigger bitch Claremont – unfortunately, she's not talking much anymore, little problem with a slip of the wrist while we were working on her vocal-cords – hell of a thing, but if it's of any interest, the doctor in charge really got his wrists slapped for *that* one – oh, pardon, there I go again... getting off-subject! *Stop* me when I do that... okay?"

Waves of hatred, mixed with gut-sinking guilt, washed through Billings' beleaguered psyche.

Oh God, Whitney – please forgive *me, for ever introducing you to her...*

The man now moved close, so that his foul, stale breath washed over the salesman's prone face.

"So where *was* I... oh, yeah... the story from the rest of your sad, in-over-their-heads little troupe," he elaborated. "Now as for the nigress' two kids, the teenager's been quite talkative – after we gave her a few hard-drivin' shots of the ol' white man's pork-sword, *that's* always fun duty for our boys to pull rank to get, after the blood-tests come back negative, of course – and the nigger boy, well, *he's* told us almost as much as your friend Tommy over there, but... not all of these stories match up. So I'm thinkin'... if we can just get you and your little kid Friday over there, to fill in the blanks together, we'll all be right back on schedule! Sound like a *deal*, Bob?"

Billings said nothing, staring straight ahead.

She said that she could kill with a thought, he mused.

I wonder...

"Ah – you're a man of few words, Bob Billings, pathetic little fuckin' two-bit floor tile nobody salesman from Tucson, Arizona," cursed the 'doctor', with his professionally-maddening tone. "But – deep down – I *know* you're gonna wake up and see the light... and it's my job to guide you there. So what say we get *going*, Bob old boy? Not a *moment* to waste, you know!"

He nodded to his counterpart, who had moved over to Tommy's gurney.

Stay with me, son, sent the salesman, hoping that the child would pick up, and hoping that the bastards couldn't see the tear welling in his eye.

Cry out to her – *but send the pain to* me.

Uncle Bob will bear it all, for you.

The other *faux*-'doctor' held some kind of sparkling, ozone-smelling instrument up to the poor little boy's one remaining nipple.

Through the gag, Tommy screamed.

Blessed Leader, You *Warned* Us Sinners

"So what *happened*, Brother?" demanded the voice on the special secured phone, deep inside a hidden Tucson bunker.

The tone was unusually subdued, even, disappointed; which, the man listening at the other end knew, was unusual.

The Boss, he was *never* disappointed. Not, that is, in front of anyone who had *lived*, to see him that way.

"Still hard to say, revered Brother Harold," responded the man known as 'Brother Martin'. "Have you seen any of the reports coming over the computer-network, yet?"

"A couple," came back the remote voice. "They're hangin' it all on the Muslims. Not that those devil-worshipers don't deserve the bad publicity... but it's just a cover-story, of course."

"Well, sir," answered Brother Martin, "As yet, we have only a partial story, but I'll tell you what we know down here in Tucson, and this is mostly based on the radio-code transmitter that we had planted on the first martyr –"

"So he made it into the conference-room? With the gun?" interrupted the man calling from elsewhere. "And the back-up martyr? What 'bout *him?*"

"It appears so, for both of them," confirmed the younger man. "As for the first one, we were pretty sure of *that* part of it working, sir – I had our best people put together a special composite-and-plastic weapon, we were pretty sure it would get through the checkpoints, anyway. What we *didn't* count on, unfortunately, is that just after the first of our two Lambs sacrificed for the Lord, we lost the signal... so our recording from inside the hotel conference-room ends, at that point. I guess the government must have started jamming everything... but I'm getting ahead of myself, here."

"Go on," ordered the remote voice.

"Bottom line is, revered Brother... near as we can tell – I should mention that this was just an audio-feed, we couldn't get one of those little button video-cameras working in time, and we had concerns that a video-feed might be more detectable – it appears that although the Devil-Girl *was* hit, she... *survived*. We base that supposition on the fact that we can still hear her voice on the recording, even after the next event; there are more shots – maybe from government agents who were in the room, maybe from somebody else, could be a civilian –"

"Wait just a *minute*," interrupted Brother Harold. "What do you mean, 'a *civilian*'? And who was this person shootin' at?"

"Not sure," answered Martin. "He calls himself a 'bounty-hunter', but I'll agree with you, sir... it doesn't make a lot of sense. It sounds like he's talking with the Devil-Girl for a few seconds after the shots are heard on the tape, then the signal goes dead... jammed, possibly, or maybe the bug that we planted on the martyr got damaged... your guess is as good as mine. We have no good picture of what happened after that, or what, if anything, our second martyr was able to accomplish. I don't know what to *say*, sir."

"There are a few things here," commented the remote voice. "First, we have to consider the possibility that – in addition to us, and maybe the government – there's somebody *else* who wants the accursed creature dead... the Muslims, possibly? Or another Christian group – one that disputes our God-given primacy over the flock? The voice of the Lord that guides all my decisions... tells me that somethin's goin' *on* here. What happened afterwards? From what I see on the computer-networks, the whole hotel got leveled –"

"Yes, it did, sir," explained the man with the phone in the bunker. "It's unfortunate that we don't know what went on in the conference-room, from the time when both of the recording bugs gave out, to the time when these big explosions happened. And just before the hotel got blown up, they evacuated the building; our sharp-shooter thought he saw several females matching the Devil-Girl's description, issuing from the front entrance... so he opened up. He's doing penance right now, in the cell next to the one I'm in."

"But you did *not* see a definite kill of the Devil-Harlot itself – is that correct?" demanded Brother Harold.

"Well, sir," answered the other man. "Looks like there *was* an Air Force missile-strike, or something similar, against her... but no, sir, I honestly can't make any such attestation."

"Then," growled the remote voice, "We've got to assume that the monster was still alive, at that point – unless they had already got her and were just tryin' to get rid of the evidence. Brother... do they think these missiles, bombs n' such, did the job?"

"May the Lord forgive me for having to say this, sir," replied Brother Martin, heavily, "But... *no*. The chatter we're picking up from our internal sources – mostly, within DoD – is all about 'it got away, what do we do next'... that kind of thing. It's obviously hard to get the flavor of these discussions without having direct access to the sources, but the impression I'm receiving is that the government is now really scared about the Devil-Girl... in one of the reports, I heard the phrase, 'we're at war, now'. Maybe that's a *good* thing, sir... maybe we're all on the same side?"

"Well, if they're scared of her, they're a day late and a dollar short!" snorted Brother Harold, his voice rising in disgust and rage, with each passing word. "The fool atheists, agnostics and unbelievers – if they had just *read* their Bibles, Revelation, especially, they would have *seen*, plain and simple as the Lord can write it, that this spawn of Satan had to be *dealt* with – and *quickly*, before it could get its goat-hooves strongly planted on God's good Earth! Now, it's on the loose, and – just like we had feared – its infernal powers are on the rise. Didn't I *tell* you this was gonna happen, Brother? Didn't I *warn* everyone!"

Now echoing the other's anger and frustration, the man in the Tucson bunker replied, "Yes, blessed leader, yes – you did. You saw it all... and they *waited,* they *hesitated,* they tried to *reason* with it, just like the Apostles tried the same with Judas – and look where *that* got them. But the worst of it, sir – from my limited point of view, down here – is that I don't know where we go from here... other than to pray. How can poor sinners like me, or us all, defeat a monster like this?"

"'A Mighty Fortress Is Our God'... remember that song?" quickly remarked the Christian leader, his voice now one of a tutor, a mentor. "Especially, the part about facin' Satan, on the field of battle? It's no *accident* that the Lord put *that* one in the hymn-book, you know. He set it in there, exactly for times like these, so that His Holy Warriors would have the guts to stand brave, in front of the Devil himself... or herself. You understand?"

"Yes... I see what you mean, blessed sir," sighed Brother Martin. "Now, only Lord Sabaoth can guide us – but with His help, God's warriors may yet triumph. Whew! For a moment there, despair was almost about to overcome my faith. Thank you, Brother... thank you from the bottom of my heart."

They both fell silent, but eventually, the man in the bunker again spoke up.

"So what is to be done?" he inquired.

"I'm prayin' for divine guidance on that, as we speak," noted Brother Harold. "And it may take some time for the Lord to make His plan clear to me; but in the meantime, what we got to do is pull out all the stops, to find out what the government intends to do now. Usin' my former military training as a guide, I'd expect that their Number One priority would be to find some way of tracking the monster down – so what we need to do is get our inside-folk concentratin' on any news – however limited it might be – 'bout that. Secondly – they'll have to draft a plan for killing Satan's spawn, once and for all... see where I'm goin' with this?"

"I think so, master Brother," answered the man in Tucson. "But please make it clear for me."

"Alright," confidently hypothesized Brother Harold. "I'm guessin' what happened down there at the hotel was, the government had the firepower, but not the *will* to *use* it – probably because they were afraid of gettin' their limp-wristed lil' ol' hands dirty and droppin' a Big One in the middle of the city... but I ask you, Brother, of what importance would be a million or so civilians – most of 'em heathen unbelievers and Catholics, anyway – compared to the gravity of having Satan's own child, walkin' on the face of this Earth?"

"Can't argue with you there, sir!" agreed Brother Martin. "God's Holy Fire, coming down on the perverts in those two cities... it's all in the Bible."

"*Exactly!*" confirmed the Christian leader. "Now... we're in the exact opposite position – *we've* got the confidence of the Lord to guide us, and we're *not* afraid to mete out His stern judgment – but what we're lackin' is a good arsenal. And, upon reflection on this whole situation... I think what Jesus is tellin' us, is that our whole approach has just been too... *timid,* that's the best way to put it. So we need to figure a way for us to get our hands on one or two of the Big Ones... I mean, the *really* Big Ones, you understand what I'm sayin'?"

A gasp came from the other man. "I... do... blessed Brother... but... well..."

"But – *what*, Brother?" quickly came back the interrogation.

"I was going to say, sir," stuttered Brother Martin, "That those are some of the most well-guarded military assets in the United States... it's a capital offense to be caught with unauthorized access to them, and all that... even so, sir, there are many practical problems. From what I'm hearing, the government itself has only a few left after the comet episode, although they're on a crash program to produce more. In any event – these weapons are *heavily* guarded, and they can't be fired unless you have access to the... what was it called, now..."

"I'll save you the trouble, Brother," answered Harold. "Remember... I used to be in the military. It's called a 'PAL', or 'permissive-action lock'. And you're right – tryin' to figure a way around such a thing might take us longer than we have left, before the Devil-Girl gets really too powerful for even something like *that* to affect her... but it's not what I had in mind. What we gotta do, is get one or two of our people in the right positions – not necessarily bein' the actual authorized guy with the key, you understand, all we have to do is git someone close enough to pull a pistol-trigger or two and then get their hands on the firin'- and targetin'-mechanisms – and the rest will take care of itself naturally."

"An ingenious plan, sir, if we can make it work... but it would be a *huge* challenge, at the best of times," remarked the man in the bunker. "And on top of *that*, blessed sir, this entire project is based on the assumption that the government *will*, eventually, figure out a way to accurately target the Devil-Girl. What if they can't?"

"I'm already thinkin' of another way of accomplishing the same thing," answered Brother Harold. "But, regardless of that... do you have *faith*, son?"

"Yes, sir, I *do!*" came back the affirmation, from the bunker, as if by rote. "I have complete faith in Lord Jesus... and in you. Didn't John the Baptist say that God could make Sons of Abraham, out of the stones in the field? If He can do *that*... surely, He can guide us to victory."

"You're gonna make a fine leader of our flock, someday, son," congratulated the Christian leader. "But in the meantime... it's time we both got workin' on this-here project."

"I'll check the database, then I'll make a few calls," promised Brother Martin, his voice earnest and authentic.

Have *I* Got A Deal For *You*

"You *sure* you're good to talk?" inquired Minnie Chu, in the direction of the lanky, black-haired woman, whose torso was now bent over the table in front of her chair, as if ready to puke. "You *fainted* in there. We can do this later, if you want –"

"No... it's okay," countered Abruzzio.

She looked up with an ashen countenance and added, "Just a *doozy* of a headache – that's all. I'll have that coffee, if you don't mind. Black, please."

"Comin' right up," said Boatman.

The big black man popped out the door, in the direction of a vending-machine.

"How about you, Mr. Ramirez?" asked the FBI-team-leader. "You don't look much better than she does. If it's any consolation, it's nothin' to be ashamed of. For a civilian, traumatic experiences are –"

"With all due respect, Ms. Chu," objected the short, Tex-Mex guy on the opposite side of the table from Abruzzio, his own color almost as drained as her own, "I would remind you, that both of us had to deal with what happened at Mission Control, shortly after the comet got popped. *That* was traumatic enough... but nothing like *this*."

"Well, I wouldn't want to argue," retreated the Asian-American FBI-agent, "But, however bad *that* was – we all just about lost our lives back there in the hotel... in addition to that other very bad outcome..."

"Yeah," commented Hendricks. "Son of a *bitch*, no doubt about it. *So* close. I mean, everything was supposed to be going according to plan. We had it negotiated down to the last detail – rules of engagement, inter-Agency stuff – the works. Excuse my French, but... what the fuck *happened*, back there?"

"We may never know," remarked Chu. "There are a lot of unanswered questions, that's for sure – starting with 'who the hell fired the first shot, when doing so was explicitly forbidden, by Presidential order', going all the way to, 'why did she suddenly turn so hostile to us'. But what the Director wants, now, is for us to pick up the trail... ha, ha."

Boatman had caught the tail-end of this, as he walked back through the door, steaming beverage in his massive, bear-paw-like hand.

"Didn't they say, they figure she's invisible... and that she just *flew* out of there?" mentioned the black agent. "I don' want to be the one to tell the Director the bad news, Minnie, but, well... I 'spect that they didn't teach you how to track a fugitive like *that*, back in the Academy... I know that they sure as hell didn't teach *me*."

"No *shit*," morosely echoed the third agent.

"We've just got to be *professionals* about this, and do the best we can," directed Chu. "So, if Mr. Ramirez and Ms. Abruzzio feel up to it, maybe we can start the de-brief. If nothing else, it'll help pass the time, until we get other news."

"More than that," mumbled Abruzzio, staring absently, but forcefully, straight ahead.

"What do you mean?" asked the FBI-team-leader.

"I'm... not... sure," answered the scientist. "Before I go any further with this and make a total fool out of myself, I'd like to try a little experiment, if that's alright with you."

"Don't see why not," offered Boatman. "Minnie, you got any objection?"

"Nope – but what *did* you have in mind, Ms. Abruzzio?" inquired Chu. "This isn't a lab... there's not a lot for you to work with."

"Not a problem," answered Abruzzio. "All I'm going to do, is say the first part of something that, uhh, came to my head, while we were in the conference-room, and I want Hector to try to fill in the rest of the sentence. I'll give you two seconds to reply, and if you can't think of anything to say, then we'll just go on to the next part... okay, Hector?"

"Sure," agreed Ramirez. "But," he added, with an odd look in Chu's direction, "I already *know* what she's going to be saying, so I bet I won't need the two seconds."

"I don't know what this is supposed to prove," grumbled the Asian-American FBI-agent, "But I don't have a lot better to do... so go ahead."

"Here goes," started the scientist.

She stared at Ramirez, and stated, "Dear Hector and Sylvia, forgive my intrusion..."

"But you are my last chance, to set this right...", immediately answered her counterpart.

"Your President-king is either a tyrant..." continued Abruzzio.

"Or his courtiers betray him..." intoned Ramirez, not missing a beat.

"I ask you to plead my case..." chanted Abruzzio.

"Tell all who will listen – 'the Storied Watcher wants no war'...", the Hispanic scientist went on.

"For if need be and danger threatens..." said Abruzzio, her voice now hesitating, as if worried about repeating what came next.

"Close your eyes and chant my name out loud, for as long as you can..." said Ramirez.

"And the Destroying Angel, shall come to your side, swift as the Four Winds," concluded Abruzzio.

The FBI-agents, all three of them, fell silent for a few seconds.

Then, Boatman managed, "*Wow!*"

"Sylvia," asked Ramirez, "Not that I have to confirm this, but... how did I do?

"Perfectly – down to the last word," noted Abruzzio.

"So did you," commented Ramirez. "I knew *exactly* what you were gonna say."

"Soo..." inquired Hendricks. "Is this supposed to be some kind of, uhh, mind-trip that she laid on you two? You know, while we were all in the conference-hall?"

"Must've been," uneasily affirmed Abruzzio. "Judging from the headache. It hit me all at once, just after she unlocked the doors. Which may have been lucky, because like I tried to shout to those black-suited goons who hustled us out of there – against my will, let me state for the record – I was about to go up and try to *reason* with Karéin-Mayréij. If they had just *let* me, dammit –"

"We already been *over* that, Ma'am," interjected Boatman. "No doubt you'se speakin' out of conviction – but the fact is, there was a *shootin' war* breakin' out in there. Worth our badges to get a 'protected Government asset' hurt, in that kind of situation, you know."

"Well, what's worth more, your 'badges'... or the fate of the whole *country?*" peevishly argued the scientist.

"We're not going to solve *that* issue, here, or now," parried Chu. "But, anyway... Mr. Ramirez – did this, uhh, 'effect', happen to you, as well?"

"Sure *did,*" confirmed the Hispanic man. "Didn't hit me as hard as Sylvia – guess I just got a thicker skull, or something like that – but, like, it was this big idea showed up in my mind, all of a sudden; I could hardly think about anything else, for a minute or two... you guys notice how stunned I looked?"

"*Tell* me," complained Boatman. "I had to practically carry you all out of there."

"Wait a minute... *wait* a minute," interjected the FBI-team-leader. "We're doing a *lot* of speculation here. Mr. Ramirez, Ms. Abruzzio, I know you both *think* that's what happened, but... well... I also know how disappointed you must be in what transpired at the hotel – with the alien I mean – so isn't it possible that this dialog was just the result of, uhh, wishful-thinking, or something like that?"

"Sorry... no *way,* Ms. Chu," countered Abruzzio, pointing a finger at her own forehead. "It was unlike anything that's ever been in *this* noggin, before... you'll just have to take my word for it."

"You ever get the same kinda thing in your head... *believe* me, lady," added Ramirez, "You'll know right away, what we're talkin' about."

"Yes, but I'd have to remind you," noted Chu, "That neither of you had ever previously met the alien in-person... and even assuming that she's capable of telepathy – something that we have absolutely *no* evidence for, from the existing records – why would she single out just the two of you, for this 'message'? And if she did, how would she send it only to you, without it also showing up in the minds of the twenty or so other people that were around you, including myself, Will and Otis, here? Why wouldn't she just say her message, out loud? This is an *awful* lot to believe."

"Minnie's got a point, you know," offered Boatman. "I mean, no offense here, but you all are... uhh... kind of *minor* players, in this whole thing – not that we're any better, mind you, but if she had sent this little ol' Martian mind-telegram into one of us, or better still, into one of them CIA-boys, there'd have been a greater chance of it gettin' to one of the higher-ups. This 'Karéin' girl ain't stupid – do you really think she'd make a mistake like *that?*"

"You *know* that Hector and I came right here, and that we didn't have any chance to collude or communicate, between the fiasco that went down in the hotel, and now... right?" Abruzzio pointed out.

"Sure," interjected Boatman, "But what's to say that you two didn't work out somethin' between yourselves, beforehand?"

"We were trying to memorize that tedious little piece of baffle-gab that the government wanted us to repeat to Karéin-Mayréij – you know, the one on the card?" protested Abruzzio, with irritation in her voice. "*That*, was bad enough. You think we had time to cook *this* up, as well?"

"Well," noted the third agent, "Recalling what went on in the hotel-room, at first, this 'Storied Watcher' chick *did* try to talk to Ms. Abruzzio and Mr. Ramirez... that didn't get her too far, and *if* she's trying to tell the President that he's been had, by his own people, no less – something that, for the record, we don't have much evidence in support of, but just for the sake of argument – she's not going to come out and say it right in *front* of all those Agency and military folk... is she? *If*, all of this is on the up and up, that is."

"Maybe she didn't mean for us to tell *you* about it," muttered Abruzzio.

"Little late *now*," amicably observed Chu, with an arched eyebrow.

"Well, I don't know how Sylvia feels about it, Ms. FBI Agent... but as for me, I thought a bit as we were on our way over here, and the thing is, if we were to withhold this information from all of you," mentioned Ramirez, "I don't know how we would get it to the President, anyway. So I guess FBI will have to be our spokesmen – spokespeople, excuse me – for all of this. I'm hoping that's a good decision."

"It is," confirmed the FBI-team-leader. "But it leads to a different question... listen, Ms. Abruzzio, Mr. Ramirez, would you mind excusing us, for a minute or two, please? Otis, Will, let's step outside and chat, if you don't mind."

The two male agents nodded and headed out the door.

"We'll only be a few minutes," advised Chu. "Could you wait here, please?"

"On one condition," requested Ramirez. "I want a coffee, too. Double sugar. I don't suppose you got any *Kahlua* to put in it?"

"'Fraid not," said the FBI-agent leader, professionally. "Doing that while on the job – not a career-enhancin' move, in my line of work. But the double-sugar, I can do. Refill for you, Ms. Abruzzio?"

"No, thanks," replied the scientist, mental fatigue etched on her face.

"Okay – back in five... or ten," said Chu.

The FBI-team-leader walked out and shut the door to the debrief-room, and turned to face her two compatriots, who had taken up back-to-the wall positions in the outside hall.

"So, guys... what do you make of all *that*?" asked Chu.

"Well," offered Boatman, "Intuition from a few hundred suspect-interviews tells me, they certainly *think* they're tellin' us the truth. Which is, needless to say, quite a different thing, from it really *bein'* the truth... it's not beyond imaginin' that they might make up a story or two, to keep us and the military from blowin' our friend 'Karéin' to Kingdom Come. Hell, Minnie – don't mind sayin', I kind of felt the same way too, back in there... I mean, you got to admit, this creature is *unique...* fascinatin'... all that good stuff. Even if she *is* a mortal threat to the country that's payin' our salaries."

He paused for a second or two, then added, "Of course... that ain't gonna change how I go about doin' my job, you know?"

The team-leader nodded, knowingly, her eyes lost in thought.

"Second that opinion," added Hendricks. "I'd say, if what we saw was a staged-performance – it was a damn slick one. You notice how the Latino-guy answered after Abruzzio, almost before she was finished saying her part? What I mean is... if they *are* trying to protect the alien, this seems like a pretty lame way to do it. *Way* too easy for us to test and disprove."

"Okay," continued Chu, "Now *if* – just for the sake of the argument, you understand, because I'm by no means convinced – if we assume that 'Karéin' *did*, in fact, plant this little message in the brains of the two scientists sitting in that room, it leads to a wide range of other questions..."

"Like... what?" inquired the black agent.

"Like... 'who – if anyone – do we tell about it'... and 'how do we tell them'," replied the woman. "If I'm reading it right, she – the 'Storied Watcher', I mean – clearly *did* mean this message – at least, the first part of it – *exclusively* for the President. If we just pump the results of what we just heard through the standard Project Red Rover channels, that would seem to go against the alien's entire intent."

"As well as makin' fools out of all of us, in front of the Director, if this all turns out to be nothin' more than just some wishful-thinkin'," observed Boatman. "I don't feel like losin' my badge over somebody's daydream."

"You got *that* right," agreed the third agent. "And something *else* doesn't add up – I mean, near the end of the crap that went down in the conference-room, this 'Karéin' chick was shouting out loud that she was going to take the President apart piece by piece and not put him back together again. That's pretty *definitive...* wouldn't you say? So why'd she plant a message in Ramirez and Abruzzio that's basically the exact opposite – you know, 'can't we all just get along'? She's supposed to be so damn *intelligent*, but all this doesn't look smart to me... just, *confused*, as if she can't decide whether to shit or wind her watch."

Chu smiled.

"Will, you have a *way* of putting that," she said. "And both you and Otis have accurately pointed out the contradictory things about the testimony that we just heard. But there's *another* problem..."

"We got *lots* of problems, Agent Chu," noted Boatman, with a shrug. "This one any more interestin' than the rest of 'em?"

"Yeah," confirmed the FBI-team-leader. "It *is*. See... according to Agency protocol, we have a standing obligation to report what Abruzzio and Ramirez told us, right up the chain of command. Want to lose your badge? Easy – just withhold evidence, from a high-priority investigation... and *this* one's about as 'high-priority' as you could *get*."

"Not followin' you here, Minnie," inquired the black agent. "Why would we withhold anythin'?"

"Here's the issue," explained Chu. "Our friend 'Karéin' has pretty much worn out her welcome within the National Command Authority, and that probably includes the Director... so he's not going to like hearing three junior FBI-agents telling them, 'wait, just forget all those death-threats that she made out loud, in front of the media – we have two people here who had a *dream* that she still wants to talk'. *Especially*, when we have no independently-verified proof whatsoever, that anything they're saying, is even half-true. See what I'm getting at?"

"What do you mean, '*three* FBI-agents'?" joked Hendricks. "I haven't been at this job as long as Otis... I don't feel like getting drummed out, before my pension vests."

"What do you mean, '*two* FBI-agents', paleface?" added the Boatman, for effect.

"Okay – *okay* – so we're all on the same page, here," remarked the woman. "We need *proof*. About whether the alien is on the level. *Sooo*..."

"Oh – wait a just *minute*, Minnie," immediately protested Boatman. "I don't like where *this* is goin' – not by a St. Louis ghetto *mile*! You *can't* be serious! What if it *works*?"

"What you talkin' about?" demanded Hendricks.

"Y'all got to learn about readin' what somebody's *about* to say... as well as what she just *did* say, Will my man," explained the black agent. "If I'm doin' so correctly, I'd ask you to recall the last thing that our two pointy-headed scientists mentioned in their little séance back there... you know, the one about, 'just say my name, and...'"

"*Whoa!*" gasped the third agent, as the realization came to him.

He shot an alarmed glance at Chu.

"Otis is right – you *can't* be serious, Minnie!" he echoed. "If not reporting their story up the line is a bad idea... this is the great *grand-daddy* of bad ideas. I mean, if they're telling the truth – and it really *does* work – we should have them do it, say, somewhere like in the middle of a big bulls-eye out in the desert, just to make it so those Air Force hot-shots, can't miss. You *saw* what she did to the CIA dudes back in the hotel-room! What if she shows and takes a dislike to us, too?"

"No shit," piled on Boatman. "We probably look just like them CIA-guys, to the alien, you know."

"Well, maybe not so much," quipped Hendricks. "They got better suits than us, man... better suits."

"*Look*," argued the Chu, "I'm not going to deny that there's a risk associated with trying this 'call my name and I'll be there' idea; but – as we just discussed – there's a risk with either not telling the higher-ups about what we heard from Abruzzio and Ramirez, as well as *with* telling them. I don't –"

"One risk is, 'we get busted down a rank or two'," interrupted the black agent. "The other is, 'we get reduced to a heap of frozen stewin'-beef-cubes'. Not exactly the same thing, wouldn't you say?"

"I'm *acutely* aware of that possibility," retorted Chu. "Although – for the record – what I was *going* to say when you cut me off, was, your original explanation is more or less on the money... I don't believe that *any* of this is true. Especially not the part about, 'just call my name'... I mean, if it was that easy, why hasn't she had these 'captives' that she's so obsessed about, call her up and ask her to spring them from wherever they're being imprisoned? And what happens if she gets a few thousand people doing it, all at the same time?"

"Yeah," commented the third agent. "Talk about an over-booked chat-channel."

"Minnie," pressed Boatman, sympathetically but forcefully, "Remember, we're talkin' about a creature that shattered a *comet*, and that a few hours ago, took apart a whole *roomfull* of CIA's best hit-men, without hardly stoppin' to catch her breath. If you're serious about this idea – and I hope you're not – you gotta think ahead to what we're gonna do if it really *does* work. Do we put her back in touch with the President, or the Director? What if she wants to go flyin' off to parts unknown, with them two scientists in tow... do we just let her? How would we stop her, or take her in? Point is... if we screw up on even *one* of these things, it won't be just a matter of losin' some rank; apart from quite likely gettin' killed, *if* we're still alive after it all goes down, they're gonna throw us in the deepest hole they got and throw away the key. I don't know, Agent Chu... I don't know. Seems like an awful lot of risk, for not a lot of reward."

"Look at the bright side," joked Hendricks. "We could get her autograph. Be worth a lot on the computer shopping channels."

"For your estate an' whoever inherits it, yeah," countered the black agent.

"Guys, I'll be honest with you... I haven't worked all of this out, yet," offered Chu. "But if it doesn't work – which, I'll repeat, I think is by far the most likely outcome – we'll have disproved the scientists' story, we can file it as a footnote to the rest of our report... case closed. If it *does* work... well, there, I agree with you, there are a lot of 'unknowns', but – as long as we can survive the initial encounter, maybe by groveling on our knees, dancing a jig for her, telling her whatever she wants to hear to whatever she asks, who knows – we'll have found a one hundred per-cent accurate way of summoning the alien to a particular place at a particular time. You think *that* might be something that the military might find useful, guys?"

"Great idea... as long as I ain't anywhere within about twenty miles, the next time you give her a call to 'come on over'," grunted Boatman.

"Make that fifty, for me," added Hendricks. "On second thought, two hundred."

The door to the other room opened, revealing Ramirez' round face, a bit more of the color now having returned to it.

"Hey, you guys," he complained, "You said only ten minutes! We're out of coffee, and Sylvia has to use the ladies'-room. You anywhere near done, yet?"

"Just finished, now," answered the FBI-team-leader.

"Yeah... we're 'finished', all right," sourly muttered Hendricks.

"And listen, tell Ms. Abruzzio... we've got a *proposal* for you," said Agent Minnie Chu.

One Hot Step From Armageddon

On the next day, the bounty-hunter had thought that he had been the first to awake, given the look of peaceful repose on the alien's face, matched or perhaps even exceeded by that on the visage of the Russian.

'Sposed to be fuckin' cold, sleepin' out in the desert, all night, he thought.

Yep, I feel it... no I don't. No chill.

Damn strange...

Yet, before the big man was able to take so much as a step in the direction of the other two, the Storied Watcher had rolled over and announced, "Good morning, Wolf; the sun rises for the first time, over your new greatness."

"Thanks... I think," he slowly replied, while trying to make sense of how the surroundings looked as if they had somehow been rendered in a richer palette, like a TV that had its 'saturation' control turned way up.

Them deep purples and reds, he silently reflected.

How'd I miss 'em, before?

Nah. Gotta be just all that risin'-sun stuff.

They must've been there, all the time... right?

Then he shot a rueful stare at the alien-girl and the other man, the remnants of the latter's clothes, draped over both of them.

"Seems you've had *your* fun, while yours truly had one too many and passed out. Well, wouldn't be the *first* time," muttered Wolf.

"Who is *that!*" exclaimed a startled Misha, as, his *Spetsnaz* training coming to the fore, he half-jumped up, only at the last moment thinking to take his pants around his waist and preserve some semblance of modesty.

"Oh," he sheepishly offered. "Sorry, there... I suppose that I must have dozed off..."

"Yeah – so did I," commented the bounty-hunter. "But looks like you had more fun gettin' there. Well... whatever she gave me, at least it don't give too much of a hangover... I can say *that* for it."

Fumbling for his underwear, as well as fumbling for the right words in English, Misha awkwardly replied, "Listen, 'Wolf'... you must understand... she and I have a, uhh... *shto govoriet po-Angliskii...* a 'previous relationship'... to tell you the truth I am rather ashamed of losing my self-control, in this way..."

"Stow it, pardner," indifferently answered the big man. "I didn't go to the damn hotel, lookin' to get laid, anyway. You want *that*, you gotta go for them cheap motels on the south side of town."

"All will be evened up, in the long-run," interjected Karéin-Mayréij, herself now propped up by palms, while shooting an affectionate glance at Wolf. She did up a couple buttons, covering up her breasts and the neck-pendant that lay between them, much to the secret disappointment of the two men.

"Misha," she requested, "Would you mind if I used this shirt of yours, as a temporary garment? My own clothes, uhh, ended up underneath *Vîrya Ahn'jë;* she sleeps still, and I would let her slumber on; she learned much from us, but found the whole thing rather... *overwhelming.* You tired her out."

"Oh – no problem," allowed the SVR-man. "Although, as I think I told you, just before – I found, uhh, 'doing it', in front of this 'living armor' of yours, to be an unsettling experience. I tried to ignore it, but all throughout, I felt a second 'voice' in my mind... thoroughly bizarre..."

"What the – oh, *I* get it," muttered the bounty-hunter, suppressing an incredulous laugh. "Ain't you ever 'done it' in front of a pet dog, or somethin' like that? Back home, me and the gf had a canary that, this is God's own truth, would start singin' out this rappin'-song, each time that she ca –"

"Just be glad that it was *Vîrya Ahn'jë,* and not any of my male war-children, who I had in there with us," bemusedly interrupted the alien-girl. "Her instincts are female and accommodating; and she is, for the most part, very obedient. *Their* personalities, conversely, are somewhat more... *forceful,* and difficult to control. I do not believe that they would have done you any permanent harm – but, had they become overly, ah, *excited,* they certainly might have spoiled the mood."

With a little nod, her own garments came back to her body.

"Thanks," she said to Misha, handing him back the shirt.

The big man now could not help but laugh out loud.

"You know, lady," he guffawed, "You and I ever do it, I want them fuckin' things put away in a suitcase, first, and I want somethin' nice and heavy on top of the lid."

"But you will *disappoint* them," pouted the Storied Watcher, with mock-indignation. "They are but *children.* They have *so* much to learn."

"That's fine," retorted the bounty-hunter. "Get 'em a book... or plug 'em in to NeoNet. You *did* build a computer-port into them, didn't you?"

"Sort of," she evenly noted. "As yet, they only know a little of techno-wizardry. But they are like me; they learn rapidly, and rarely make a mistake twice."

"Wonderful... I think," grunted the big man. "Anyway, there any way that we can get goin', anytime soon? To wherever it is, that we *are* goin'... that is."

"Why is that?" asked Misha.

"I gotta take a shit," explained Wolf.

"Oh," said the SVR-man.

"Bad drugs *do* that to me, you know," grunted the bounty-hunter.

"Hmm, well – I would not want you to be uncomfortable, on my account," remarked Karéin-Mayréij. "But it would be, ahh, *inconvenient*, to have us doing our toilet in here... I will tell you what. Why not let me carry you down to the bottom of the canyon, next to the little lake below the waterfall; you can do your, uhh, 'business' down there, somewhere... there are tree-leaves you can use to wipe yourself, and there is water for cleaning up with. Just call up in the direction of the cave when you're done and I will come down and retrieve you... oh-kay?"

"You might as well take me, too," uncomfortably stated Misha.

"For a while, it sounded like the two of you did not have much in common," joked the Storied Watcher. "I guess that I was wrong about that."

The bounty-hunter rolled his eyes.

"Anytime this week, then," he complained.

"If you are ready," advised the newcomer, standing up and moving to the cave-entrance, with the bottom hem of Misha's shirt riding tantalizingly just south of the top of her thighs. "There does not appear to be anyone outside... so put your arms over my shoulders, just as you did when we arrived here."

Both men shuffled over to her and quickly obliged, with Wolf on the right and Misha on the left.

The alien-girl shot a glance, backward into the cave.

"Thy mother leaves only for a few seconds," she called out, apparently to no-one. "Sleep restfully, children."

Slowly, the three rose into the air, drifting gracefully out into the open.

"Oh, it feels *lovely*, does it not – having the breeze on one's skin, especially the parts that are so often covered up," remarked the Storied Watcher, as she slowly guided them forward and down. "Such a *moderate* climate that you have on this pretty little blue-and-green world! You know, when one does this same thing in places where it is so hot as to melt metal, or so cold as to freeze the breathing-gas atoms, the feeling is also interesting, stimulating... but, quite different. I feel sorry for you humans, that you cannot share that experience."

"I'll take your word for it," muttered Wolf. "Wavin' my privates over a volcano, or the South Pole, ain't exactly what I had in mind for 'fun'."

She turned her face, shot him a goofy-looking grin, and gave the big man an affectionate kiss on the cheek.

"We both have limits, and we both respect them," observed Karéin-Mayréij, as they came in to touch down. "Mine are just a bit more, ah, 'flexible' than yours. But perhaps, over time, we can add some latitude to your own."

With the feet of the three now back on *terra firma* at the shore of the small lake, Misha also turned to address the young-looking woman.

"Karéin," he asked, with a worried tone, "You did not use that 'cloak' of yours, this time. Was that wise? What if we were to be detected?"

"I think that is unlikely," explained the newcomer. "Remember – we are in the canyon, below the line of sight from the surface of the land outside of here. I cast my long-gaze skyward, and did not detect any spy-planes or spy-moons; though, you should understand, this ability, too has a distance-limit. Also... the dark-cloak is not the *only* way I have to confuse those who might look on us, from above. Just a little bend in the light-waves above us... that would look like the shimmering heat of the desert... would it not?"

She smiled, in her trademark saturnine manner.

"You never cease to amaze me," started the Russian.

"Listen – *you* go ahead with the 'oohs' and 'aahs' there buddy... I gotta run," interrupted the bounty-hunter.

With a pained look on his face, he trotted off behind a group of bushes.

"Oh... no problem," pleasantly called the alien-girl, to Wolf's back.

She turned to address Misha.

"I shall leave you two down here, for a few minutes... I perceive *Vìrya I'ëà'b'* to be awakening," she remarked. "And I should return to the cave – elsewise she and her siblings will be worried and may come looking for me, and yes, that *would* be something that perhaps the Americans' devices, if they are keen, might be able to detect. Five minutes, then?"

"That should be enough," answered the SVR-man.

Like an erotic parody of a latter-day Tinker-Bell clad only in a man's cheap golf-shirt, the Storied Watcher effortlessly levitated into the Grand Canyon air and wheeled in mid-flight, her figure rapidly receding into the distance, toward the cave-entrance.

Well, I suppose I had better do what I came down here to do, mused Misha, trying all the while to suppress the unnatural pangs of regret at seeing her – *feeling* her – leave his side.

She is like a drug, he ruefully admitted to himself.

Every bit as addictive.

Off he went, taking care to find a pack of bushes as far as possible from those that the bounty-hunter had chosen.

What does she see in that semi-literate, muscle-bound buffoon? reflected the Russian, as he set about to relieve himself.

Then again... this 'Billings' fellow – he was nothing but a small-time American salesman.

But it is crazy *for me to have these feelings of jealousy... she is probably reading them right now, at long distance...*

Eventually, he was done, and – his butt protesting at every turn, as the leaves found around here were slightly abrasive, or maybe had some kind of stinging sap – Misha went back to the waterfall-pool, finding the bounty-hunter there ahead of him, busy washing hands in the water.

"No soap," grumbled Wolf. "That's 'roughin' it' for ya, I guess."

"Well," commented the SVR-man, trying to sound polite, "When they put one through *Spetsnaz*-training back where *I* come from, one becomes used to such privations; they drop you in the Siberian *taiga* in mid-October, with nothing more than the summer uniform on your back, and a single hunting-knife. The objective is to return to the nearest outpost of civilization – which is at least 300 kilometers away – before the winter snows come. If one is alive at the end of the trip, he 'graduates'; if not... then Mother Russia has one less weakling-soldier to worry about –"

Suddenly, a terrible cacophony – halfway between a wail and a shriek – issued from the direction of the cave. Its chilling, mournful tone echoed dolefully across the canyon-walls.

"*Jaysus H. – !*" shouted Wolf.

In the next second, a shower of sparks, accompanied by wisps of flame at least ten feet long, shot from the cave-entrance. The ground reverberated, as if afflicted by a minor earthquake, and the wailing sound gradually gave way to ethereal music, ominous in its martial-air.

"What the *fuck*?" loudly protested the bounty-hunter. "They *get* to her? But *how?* Didn't see no bomb or rocket –"

"No, not that – I was *afraid* of something like this," counseled an immediately-worried Misha. "They must again be torturing her 'family'! Listen, 'Wolf' – if you value your life, I would advise you not to stand in her way... Karéin becomes very... *angry*, when she feels them doing this –"

"Whaddya *mean*... oh, wait a minute – *I* get it," commented the bounty-hunter. "You mean, like what went down in the hotel... when she doubled over, all of a sudden?"

"Yeah – that is it," confirmed the Russian.

"Uh-oh – here she comes," he warned.

A terrifying sight now beset them; as Karéin-Mayréij – bedecked in her full, flaming war-garb, its glow so bright as to pain the eyes – floated down toward the two frightened men. Her eyes shone brilliant yellow-red, and bolts of other-worldly energy shot up and down and occasionally outward, from her body. Each charge thundered a warning-cry, to all around.

The drumming beat of her psycho-music, its import telling of action and power, raced through their minds like thrice-refined adrenalin.

"'Best behavior' time, I guess," mumbled Wolf. "Thank God I had to take a dump – wouldn't have wanted to be up *there*, when –"

Reflexively, both men moved back from the edge of the pond, making enough room for the Storied Watcher to alight in front of them.

This was a prudent move, because as she approached, they saw the very rock beneath her feet hiss and char; they felt the heat and hate – or, was it the both of these, intermingled? – emanating from her figure, bathing them in its infernal radiance.

It hurt, terribly. But it also felt... *luxurious.*

Through a fanged, sinister snarl, the newly-fearsome being spat out,

"That is *it! This* time, the fools really *have* pushed me too far, and, moreover – they have unlocked my greater powers! Now – your damnable so-called 'President' will discover what happens when he tortures my *son!*"

"Great Saint Seraphim of Sarov – have *mercy!*" gasped Misha.

He fell on his knees, trying to avert his gaze.

"Karéin," stammered the Russian, "I will not beg for their reprieve, or their forgiveness; for they deserve what comes to them. All I *will* ask is – 'remember that not *all* Americans have done this to you'. Do not crush those who this President, oppresses, along with Tommy and the others!"

He noticed that the fire in the ground was inching toward where he and the bounty-hunter, were standing.

"You have made this plea of me, before," she growled. "Too late, Misha... *way* too late! Not even the entreaties of *Vîrya Quü'j* – my most faithful companion – can turn me now from this purpose. They will *pay!*"

"What you whimperin' about there, Russkie?" demanded Wolf. "99 per-cent of us Americans couldn't give two shits what happens to the President, anyway. No skin off *my* ass, either."

"You do not *understand*," shot back a panicked Misha. "She warned the President, that if he continued to torture her family – especially her adopted son – she would destroy *the entire United States!*"

The fire in the rock edged ever-closer.

"*Whoa...*" exclaimed the nonplussed bounty-hunter.

With a jaundiced eye, he regarded the Storied Watcher, asking, "That *true?*"

A second later, he added, "Oh, yeah... when you was talkin' at the big screen... but you didn't really *mean* that... right? I mean, people always say all sorts of shit, just for *effect*... don't they?"

"I shall blast this cruel empire, down to the last rock and *stone!*" hissed the alien-girl, her fangs showing evil upon her lips. "And had you failed to notice – I am *not* a 'human-people'... nor do I make idle threats. When I am finished, the face of this 'America' of yours, will be akin to the Moon up yonder, in the sky!"

A second later, she stated, "Take off your socks and shoes... and roll up the bottoms of your pants."

"*What?*" requested a confused Wolf.

"It makes no difference to me," said Karéin-Mayréij, with an indifferent shrug. "Unless you would like to have them burned and melted on to whatever would remain of your feet."

"This is all happenin' too fuckin' *fast*, Karéin!" quickly protested the bounty-hunter, as he tried to remove the footwear, tossing each piece some distance behind.

The move had been anticipated by the Russian, who was already down to his socks.

"Do you trust me?" she demanded, staring at them with glowing eyes.

"Do I have a choice?" argued Wolf.

"No," stated the newcomer.

"Then... I guess I do," he muttered, nervously watching the heated part of the stone as it approached the tips of his toes. "Trust you, that is."

"On *no* account look down; instead, pay attention only to me, and I will guide you," commanded the Storied Watcher, her voice surreal, hypnotic. "And do not fear the *Fire*; if you feel a little of its sting, *welcome* it, take it into you... drink it in, *love* it... *feel* its noble, burning caress."

With a queasy feeling in his gut, along with the Russian, the bounty-hunter noticed that the creature who he was addressing was – no other way to put it – *afire*.

Little tongues of flame danced all over her strange, multi-colored armor, and this was no cheap illusion : standing in front of the creature, was like being too close to a blast-furnace. The only respite from the inferno was a small spot near the outside of her right shin.

Trying to keep his mind off what was likely to be his feet being burned into cinders, Wolf started, "Listen, lady... Karéin... whatever you're callin' yourself, these days..."

"Yes?" she replied, with haughty indifference.

"Just before I get my toes burnt off," he remarked, "About this business with the good old U.S. of A.... I'm not gonna get down on my knees or any shit like that – not my *style*, you know – and besides, I don't want to get my legs roasted, neither, but... you're goin' *way* overboard, Karéin, if that's what you're really fixin' to do."

"Heard all of this before," countered the Storied Watcher. "And I *tire* of these facile excuses, while my blameless, trusting child, suffers in agony! Keep your eyes on me. Do *not* look below my face. You too, Misha."

"Ohh, what a weird feeling," interjected the SVR-man. "But a good one. Like the warmth of vodka, all the way down to the feet..."

"Nah... Bourbon..." commented Wolf.

"For *God's* sake, lady," he continued, "How can I put it... okay. Look – you 'n me, we ain't too far different on this thing. For near my whole damn life, I've been goin' after the low-lifes, the druggies, the sex perverts, gangstas, the lot of 'em; and more than once, I've seen the folks they hurt, sometimes, that they kill... it's been all I could do, to avoid just *wastin'* 'em, first chance I got. But I never *did* – even when I knew, it might mean they'd just be back on the streets, two weeks from, whenever. It's what makes me, *me*, and what makes them, *them*. Otherwise, they're just some fuckin' thug with a gun – and so am I. Oh, *shit*... that's one *strange* feelin', you got that right, Russkie..."

Somehow, the bounty-hunter resisted the urge to look at his feet, and instead, concluded, "I don't know about you – I'm not much up on all this 'goddess' or 'angel" business, you know – but I'd have a hard time lookin' at the mirror in the mornin', with *that* kind of shit on my conscience. For whatever it's worth."

"A grand speech," offered Karéin-Mayréij. "Would that I had heard such, from your mighty 'President', and not from a Tucson, Arizona, boun-tee hunter. So you want me just to let him get *away* with it? How would dear Bob – if lives still, Holy Light so favor – how would *he* put it? Ah, yes. 'Fuck You', would be what he would say."

"No," proffered the big man, as humbly as he could do. "He *deserves* what he's got comin'... I won't dispute that. I seen enough of what them assholes in D.C. do to us here down in the poor seats – people just 'disappearin' all the time, good men comin' back from fuckin' wars all over Hell's Half Acre, missin' arms 'n legs 'n balls 'n whatnot – so I couldn't give a rat's *ass* what you do to him, or *all* of 'em, up there, for that matter. All I'm askin', is... 'don't boil the baby with the bathwater, Karéin'. Hold off with that terrible swift sword you got hangin' by your side. Give 'em a taste of what you're capable of doin', without hurtin' any of us innocent bystanders."

"And just how should I do *that?*" she half-teasingly demanded. "Maybe I should send your President another nasty ee-mail, or perhaps I should again take over another tee-vee station, and say some swear-words, about him? Sorr-ee – but we are *way* past that point."

"I have an idea," suggested Misha.

"Umm-hmm," chimed the alien-girl, staring intently at him. "Oh... and you may now look downward. And put on your footwear, if you so desire."

Half-dreading what they would see, both men turned their gaze to their feet, which were covered with a fine, charcoal-dust.

Looking side-to-side and slightly backward, Misha and Wolf saw – to their mutual amazement – that they had been standing at least a meter inside the area that had been superheated by the Storied Watcher's fire-aura.

"If you are interested... the stuff upon which you are standing, had been warmed to – I am not exactly sure, but this is close – about four hundred degrees, perhaps five or six hundred, on your Celsius scale," noted Karéin-Mayréij. "Remember how I told you, 'I wish that you could feel how pleasant these other environments, can be'? Well – now you know of one such. Furthermore – do you not feel a little tickle on your skin, now and again?"

"Yeah," confirmed Wolf. "Figured it was sweat evaporatin'. You know – that whole, 'stress', thing?"

"Not that," contradicted the newcomer. "You sense the energy-glow given off by me and my war-children. From where you now stand, you are exposed to a hundred times what would quickly kill a normal human. *Feel* the power, my two new-found brothers! Drink of it, revel in it... learn to tame it! Thereby, you will be great. Oh, and by the way, do not worry about having to wash your hands after, uhh, 'doing your business'. Any microbes that may have ended up on them, have now been irradiated to oblivion."

"*Incredible,*" managed the Russian, not knowing whether to laugh or to cry. "And, I suppose that we should say, 'thank you', for the empowerment. But of what use will this be, if we can only use it in a devastated country?"

"Yeah," agreed the Storied Watcher, with an air of indifference. "I confess that I had not thought *that* one through. Oh, well... is there anything more, before I set this foolish 'United States' afire, from end to end?"

"At least hear me *out*, Karéin!" cried a fearful Misha.

"Umm-hmm?" she responded.

"Our friend 'Wolf' has a valid idea," spoke the SVR-man, thinking as fast as he dared. "You do not *need* to kill anyone – either directly or indirectly – to impress upon the President, that he is over-matched. Why not start by destroying visible landmarks that have only a symbolic or historical function? Strike at the symbols of American state power, rather than its substance, at least, at first. You can always escalate to more... *serious* targets, later, if necessary."

"Such as?" warily inquired Karéin-Mayréij.

"I am not very well-versed in American landmarks," stuttered Misha. "Wolf, do you know of any? That would not have many civilians around them."

"Shit – don't ask *me*, I don't do a lot of travelin'... 'cept I took the gf to Disneyland, one time," evaded the bounty-hunter. "No 'collateral-damage'? That kind of rules out the White House, most of D.C. as well... lots of tour-guides and tourists... you know? No, wait, *I* got one... how about that place in – where is, it, yeah, it's in South Dakota I think – the one with all them big faces of the Presidents? There's tourists around *there*, too... but not right up on the side of the mountain. Yeah, *that'd* do it... you could write 'Fuck You Mr. President' all *over* it, and nothin'd get hurt 'cept his feelin's. Or... why not take out a few of them satellites? The TV ones, I mean... only thing that would get killed, would be a few old Clean Christian Sex Channel re-runs, no great loss there –"

"Too high," countered the alien-girl. "I am not yet capable of consistently maintaining even a low orbit, or of obtaining escape-velocity. *But...*"

"But?" nervously asked the Russian, hoping against hope.

"Your idea does have merit," she slowly stated, with an inscrutable stare. "Misha, my love – I am *furious* at what I have felt happening to my poor child, Tommy – how can I make you *see*...yes, I could touch you, and share the cruel experience – but I will not. I would not inflict *that*, upon anyone who I do not want to hate me."

A tear fell from one of her shining eyes and was quickly evaporated by the raging fire upon her breast.

The creature gave off successive waves of palpable rage and terrible sorrow, and she sat down on a nearby rock, the very touch of her bottom causing the thing to hiss and crackle.

"*Why* can I not just find Bob and Tommy, and the others besides!" moaned Karéin-Mayréij. "*Why* do they not *call* to me and lead me to them, in their hour of tribulation? What witchcraft does your government use, to hide them from me? Through all the Many Worlds, I have *never* had to deal with subterfuge, akin to this! I near my wits' end."

"I wish that I could offer some wise advice, Karéin," counseled Misha. "But if you are at a loss, it would be foolish of me to suggest what to do. All that I can think of right now, is the remote possibility that someone *other* than the American government, is in fact the group that holds your family hostage, and that so abuses them."

"Well, that's all fine and dandy," argued Wolf, "Except that they were all right up there on that big TV thing, in the conference-hall, even if she thinks that them guys were stunt-doubles. And our great fearless leader himself, said that he had 'em all bein' kept nice and safe and secure. Why the hell'd he say somethin' like *that* – take the blame on himself, I mean – if he didn't really *have* this 'Billings' fella, and the rest of 'em? I mean... talk about takin' the fall for somebody else – if that's what you're suggestin' is going on here – this is the great *grand-daddy* of all times that somebody took one on the chin for the team, wouldn't you say?"

"The President may be so desperate that he pretends to be in charge of these people, just to stay your hand, until he can think of a better strategy," proposed Misha. "And a great deal about this does not add up... such as, 'why is my own government collaborating with yours, to kill the creature who saved our entire *planet*'? Answer *that*, if you please."

"I hardly know what to say when they pull me over for doin' 150 in a 130 zone, pardner," grunted the bounty-hunter. "Don't ask *me*."

"The American President *is* the one who commands life or death, safety or pain, over my friends and family," firmly stated the Storied Watcher. "Of *that*, I am certain – I do not know exactly *how* I am sure, and my vision is cloudy... but I *am* sure. It is not just intuition, but another of my abilities, that speaks to me, in this manner... so justice *must* now be done, and must be done severely. And I have every *right* to fully carry through with my warnings to this filth-of-a-coward-king that you call, 'President'."

She stopped for a second or two, lost in thought, then continued, "But... bless the both of you... there was a time – whose memory curses me still – when I would easily have slaughtered a thousand – a *million*, even – to provide relief to the few who call me friend... who call me, 'master'. I will *not* go back to the dark soul who I was, in those haunted days; but *neither* will I stand for the cruelty that has now been wantonly inflicted on my... son. I *will* avenge him, in a way that your 'President' will not soon forget!"

The alien-girl rose up; and again, the two cringed at the fearful majesty of her waxing aura, its infernal heat and invisible shroud of killing radiation, bathing them in a mixture ten times ten lethal to ordinary men.

"I will start with this 'face-mountain' that you speak of, Wolf," she vowed, as the psycho-music rose to a penultimate crescendo. "And then, I will go on to other things – until your 'President' comes to me on his *knees!*"

"*Wait!*" shouted Misha. "What is to become of us, Karéin?"

"Yeah – it's a bit far to walk back to town, you know," mentioned the bounty-hunter. "And, didn't we have a contract, or somethin'?"

"As for you two," explained Karéin-Mayréij, with regal satisfaction accompanied with a weird-looking smile in Wolf's direction, "By the bond of my gift and my blood, I grant you the right and duty to communicate and intercede, on my behalf. Go and retrieve your shoes."

Quickly, the men grabbed their foot-gear, only holding the shoes and socks, not bothering to put them on.

When all had been taken in hand, Wolf and Misha felt themselves rising in the air. They were drawn continuously closer to this terrible creature, as the party went upward and started nearing the top of the canyon; but, to the dismay of the two men, thin wisps of smoke began to issue from Wolf's jacket and Misha's trousers.

"Put us down!" yelled the SVR-man. "We are catching *fire!*"

"Oops," came back the reply. "*You*, are made proof against me. I forgot that your clothes are not. *Væran Ss'éth'ch'*, if you please..."

Faster than an eye-blink, the blue-violet dagger shot from the lower part of the Storied Watcher's right leg. It stationed itself between her and the two she had in tow, and instantly, both felt a blast of brutal, ultra-Arctic frigidity.

Now, Misha stared at the coating of frost that was quickly forming on his upper-body. A sideways glance showed that the bounty-hunter's long hair and beard were also encrusted, as if the big man had just been dug out of a glacier.

Ye Gods, marveled the Russian.

The cold is far worse than the deepest Siberian blizzard – I should be screaming in pain, at frost-bitten fingers, nose, earlobes, frozen eyeballs – but it is almost the same sensation as with the fire-walking trick.

Cool, this time, and... pleasant.

So this is how a super-being does it.

"Indeed," confirmed Karéin-Mayréij, as they cleared the top of the canyon and came down about ten meters away from its rim. "A 'super-being'... like *you*."

To the nerve-wracked ears of a turncoat spy, against whom his government's best assassins, were no doubt now being arrayed, this sounded like – well, it sounded like a *chance.*

Fine, take your best shots, if you must, Oleg, Katya, and others beside, mused Misha.

Maybe, you will receive more than you bargained for.

The Storied Watcher turned to address the bounty-hunter, while the dark-blue dagger darted back and fell into her grasp. The alien – hoar-frost forming for a second or two, on her lips – caressed it, whispered something, then bade it go to its hiding-place on her leg.

"My war-child *Ss'éth'ch'*, says that he is *most* impressed with the two of you," she commented, in as straightforward a manner as if describing a school report card. "His frigid breath came down scarcely less than against the spy-man in the hotel-room, and you did not flinch. He requests that when again we meet, you and he should touch, so that he can inquire about what it is like to be a 'boun-tee hunter' or 'spionage agent'. Like his brother, whose kiss is fire, poor *Ss'éth'ch'* does not have many with whom he can safely communicate, in this manner."

Wolf had half bent-over, shaking the ice from his beard, with his upper-body propped up by palms on knees.

"Let me get this right," he coughed, batting his eyes to get the frost from his eyelashes. "Your... knife, the blue one I mean... wants to have a, uhh, little old man-to-man chat, with us?"

"Umm-hmm," noted Karéin-Mayréij. "He states that both of you have interesting, ah, 'jobs'... and furthermore, he *likes* you especially, Wolf... while his brother seems more partial to Misha. Have neither of you had a young boy as a son or nephew, who aspires to grow up and have an exciting occupation... like, a warrior, a healer, a police-man or a temple-priest?"

"Yeah – but most of the ones *I* know, have two arms, two legs and a head," quipped the bounty-hunter, still wheezing to get the last wisps of super-cooled air from his lungs. "Little hard for us to, uhh, *relate*... know what I mean?"

"Shhh!" remonstrated the alien-girl. "You will *upset* him! As yet, he does not know much about how unique he is; neither does *Væran Ksé'l'ch'*. I would have my children learn these things... *gradually*."

"Well," allowed the big man, shaking his head and trying not to laugh too loudly, "Tell him we'll have to take a rain-check on that."

"More like an 'ice-check', to abuse an American saying... would you not say?" smartly proposed the SVR-man.

"Oh-kay," replied the Storied Watcher, with a wan smile. "In the meantime, you may want to practice by finding some liquid nitrogen and seeing how long you can dip your fingers in it."

After all the provocation... she still has a sense of humor, reflected Misha. *Thank God.*

"I probably should not ask this," he inquired, "But, uhh, what about the yellow one? *Please* do not tell me, that *it* wants to 'chat' with us, too."

"I do not yet know," serenely replied Karéin-Mayréij. "His cold-brother is communicating with *Væran Ksé'l'ch'* right now. You may want to try grasping a few bar-bee-cue briquettes, when their fire glows bright red, as well. But start with only one or two – or maybe, if you are not ambitious, try snuffing out a cigarette in the palm of your hand. If you burn, that will help your body adjust for the next time, and then it will be easier. Nothing valuable is achieved without sacrifice... right?"

"How will we know when we, uhh, exceed our new abilities?" requested the Russian.

"Easy – it will hurt," she replied, matter-of-factually. "More so than would be called for, that is."

"If you do not mind... how much *should* it hurt?" he pressed.

"I do not precisely *know*," evaded the newcomer. "But *you* will. Your body will tell you – just like when you dip your toe into a bath-tub filled with water that is too hot for an ordinary human to tolerate. It is the same idea with the gift that you have been given... except for a few hundred degrees, that is."

She arched an eyebrow and sent them an "ask a stupid question" smirk.

"This has *gotta* be worth a book-deal," muttered the bounty-hunter.

"Most Americans do not know how to read, anymore," sniffed the SVR-man.

"Wolf," continued the Storied Watcher, "Would you mind lending your jacket to Misha? He is closer to your size, and though I checked my fury, I did so somewhat too late... I seem to have, ah, *vaporized* the shirt that he earlier gave to me. My own peasant-clothes are oh-kay, if, a bit, uhh, singed – they were underneath *Vîrya Ahn'jë* when the knowledge of my loved-ones' torment fell upon me – and lamentably, I have not yet taught my war-fortress-child the gentle arts of fabric-weaving. Her grandmother shall have to do that, as she and my newborn go a-journeying. Later, I will repay both of you for this favor. I hope it is not too much to ask..."

She has just been talked out of vaporizing an entire nation, thought the astonished Russian,

And here she is, worrying about a cheap shirt from the Tucson, Arizona, Goodwill Thrift Store.

How is one to please a being like this?

"By learning about me, bit by bit, as I learn about you," she affectionately riposted. "And by being my conscience... when mine own is absent."

"Thank you for the compliment," offered Misha, "Though, as I look back on the things that I have done for Mother Russia, it is hard for me to imagine myself, as anyone's 'conscience'."

Wolf removed his jacket and handed it to Misha, scanning all around.

"I want it back, but you might want to wash it, when you get a chance, pardner," he remarked. "I don't spend much time at laundromats."

The bounty-hunter looked hither and yon, over the landscape.

"There's a lot of 'nowhere' around these parts, you know," he added. "So, uhh... where do we go from here, Karéin?"

"You still have some money... right?" she asked.

"Yeah, I guess..." he confirmed.

"Walk south and east and you will encounter a road, then a town, about six leagues from here," she instructed. "Once there, purchase something to eat and drink – then make your way back to Tucson. Go to the K-GUN tee-vee station and tell them to warn your people, that one new 'monument' will be destroyed each day, until the President meets my terms; and – should he refuse – in a week from now, it will not be only statues and monuments, that will be rendered unto ashes. If he does all of that, I *might* let him live. Understood?"

"He ain't gonna *like* hearin' that," warned the big man. "I thought we was goin' on this thing all together... I mean, what's to say that the Feds don't just do to Mr. Russkie and me, what they've already done to this 'family' that you're so bent on helpin'?"

"Wolf," she requested, staring deliberately at him, "I am about to close my eyes, and when I do, I want you to repeat my name, out loud. Keep doing it, until I tell you to stop. You as well, Misha. *Begin.*"

"Never *did* like the Hare Krishna stuff," complained the bounty-hunter, "But, okay, here goes... 'Karéin... Karéin... Karéin...'"

"You are doing it incorrectly," impatiently retorted the alien-girl, her eyelids apparently shut. "Use my full, *real* name."

"What you mean? Isn't that your whole... oh, yeah, you said somethin' back in the hotel, I think..." he said.

"It is, '*Karéin-Mayréij*'," advised the Russian.

He started chanting these words, and a few seconds later, the big man chimed in.

Another saturnine smile came to the face of the Storied Watcher, as she opened her eyes, revealing a painfully-intense glow.

"Much better," she congratulated. "Now listen carefully. As with all my disciples, you, Misha, and you, Wolf, both of you are linked with my mind – I have a limited ability to feel your thoughts. This is an old and great skill and, though its use has been of inestimable value from ages past, I unfortunately do not have a great deal of control over it – at least not at anything but very close range, that is, within eyesight. Sometimes it works over great distances, most of the time it does not, I do not really know why... but one thing that almost always *does* work is, if you call my name out loud, and you keep doing that for a minute, an hour, longer, if possible, I will know where you are, and I *will* come swiftly to your aid. Use this gift only when you are in immediate danger, for life and limb. Do you comprehend?"

"Yeah, sort of," confirmed the bounty-hunter. "The psychic GPS-2 location beacon. Fuckin' *ay*."

Misha rolled his eyes and shook his head.

"That is *one* way to put it, I suppose," he muttered.

"You may tell whomever captures you, if it comes to that," explained the newcomer, "That if they harm you, they will be reduced to atoms; but do not tell them that if you but chant my name, I will find you. What they *should* do, is simply let you go. I will convey my messages to the American government through one or the other of you, and – at a time and place of my choosing – I will reunite you with the rest of my company of followers."

"With you so far," acknowledged Wolf.

"In the meantime," she continued, "Try to stay low and try not to be taken in, if you can avoid it. If it is possible... may I request that you somehow make contact with Hector Ramirez and Sylvia Abruzzio? They, too, are friends, and I would entrust them to communicate on my behalf, as well. You will find that your bodies and senses will be rapidly improving, so it should not be so difficult to stay out of trouble... the American spy-warriors probably think that you're both dead, blown up in the hotel, anyway."

"What if they grab us, we call *you*, and then they drop an H-bomb on top of our whole little garden party?" challenged the bounty-hunter.

"It will not work," replied the Storied Watcher, fire all over her being. "And woe betide he who tries it. Your stupid President has not yet guessed that I *cannot* be surprised – at least, not in guile of war – and that my powers usually adapt and increase as needful. It may take many hard lessons, for him to, ahh, 'get the message'... but so be it, in that case."

"Hey – *I* believe you," offered Wolf, throwing up his hands in mock-surrender. "I just wish you could send him a nasty NeoNet e-card to let him know ahead of time, so we all don't have to get our hands dirty."

"Tried that... sort of," she parried. "Maybe he does not read his, uhh, 'ee-mail'. Unfortunate, would you not say?"

"Now you should *go*," commanded Karéin-Mayréij, again terrible in her might, with the psycho-music echoing across the desert and into the great canyon. "I have not cloaked myself, and that is deliberate. Make haste to be away from this spot – put at least three leagues between here and where you end up, an hour from now, and use your wits from there on in."

Momentarily, her stern, godly guise lapsed, and they saw a sad look on the alien-girl's face – the familiar, pretty-peasant visage that they had come to so appreciate.

"I would embrace you both to say 'goodbye, for now', dear friends," she softly called, "But though you are now far more than mortal men, still would you be consumed. To later, then... when we may again touch, with the powers of *Fire*... and of, love."

Humans have a saying, 'great minds think alike, and fools never differ', came a warm thought.

We all pass the test of conscience, dear friends... and thank you, for walking there, by my side.

I owe you a great debt, which I will *repay... though I know not how.*

The two now-more-than-men involuntarily squinted, as they felt the overwhelming surge of a rainbow of energy extending from one end of the spectrum, well past the other, as the very *being* of Karéin-Mayréij began to shine, lighting up the Arizona desert with an incandescence even brighter, than that of the overhead sun.

The sand beneath the war-boots of *Vìrya Ahn'jë* began to blacken and burn, and both Misha and Wolf involuntarily stumbled backward, smelling smoke issuing from their clothes; though, only minutes ago, these had been nearly frozen stiff.

"*Revenge!*" they heard, as she rocketed skyward, a meteor in reverse.

As the brilliant point of light receded, Misha breathed,

"For the sake of God... s*pare them*, Destroying Angel."

Hold The Cameras

The President put up his hands, trying to fold his elbows so that the video recorders – if they were still on, and he hoped that they weren't – couldn't see the perspiration staining his underarms.

"Look – I've done *five* of these damn things, already," he protested. "Can't we take a break?"

"Okay, sir," came the voice of the Chief of Staff, from behind the glare of the studio-lights. "But if we're going to stay on track, we've got to keep it to ten minutes or less – otherwise we only get seven done instead of eight. *If*, that is, we don't take a chance with the schedule."

"What's *one* fake speech, more or less?" muttered the President, as he got up from the leather-bound chair behind the Oval Office desk, and wiped the sweat off his forehead.

Immediately, two makeup artists came over to fix the damage, but he waved them off, requesting, "When I get *back*, please. Mention that to the blow-dry guys, if you don't mind."

"Yes, Mr. President," answered the obliging voices of the two underlings.

They trotted away.

"I need a *drink*," sighed the American leader, as he took a few long strides and opened up the liquor-cabinet. "My throat's getting dry, or maybe it's all this made-up stuff... I'm used to these speeches being, ahem, 'less than the full truth', of course – but *this* little scam's kind of going the next mile. Do I look as unconvincing as I think I look?"

"Never better," reassured a grinning Jerry Kaysten. "You're a *pro*, sir."

"Thanks... I *think*," replied the President. "Where's the ice?"

An orderly quickly brought over a bucket with some ice-cubes.

"Mr. President," sounded a loud voice from the back of the room, behind the large crew of sound and video technicians. "Call for you on Secure Line 3."

"Can it wait?" he retorted. "We've only got three more to do, then I'm out of here – I need a few minutes."

"It's General Anderson, sir," remarked the voice. "He says it's highest priority."

"Fine... *fine*," muttered the President. "I'll take it back there."

Bourbon on the Rocks in hand, he pushed his way through the crowd, and accepted a handset from a clean-cut young Air Force officer, who entered a code into the device's keypad, then tapped a push-pin on a small, silver-colored thing about the size of a fat quarter, on the reverse-side of the phone.

The American leader positioned himself so that he was half on the arm of a nearby futon, and spoke into the handset.

"Yeah, Harry?" he stated. "We're just finishing, here. What's up?"

A second later, the color drained from the President's face, and a shocked, worried expression took over.

"*Jesus!*" he gasped. "You *sure*? Wait a minute, I missed that... can you say it again? What the – twenty-five *hundred* miles per hour? Hold on a minute, will you?"

He motioned to Kaysten.

"Get these people out of here, *immediately!*" commanded the President.

"But sir, we've still got three –" argued the Chief of Staff.

"Right now – that's an *order!*" repeated the U.S. leader. "The taping-session is now over with."

Kaysten – having built a career on reading the man's meanings – acted quickly.

"Everybody *out!*" he demanded, in turn. "Get your gear later. *Now!*"

Rapidly, the video teams were escorted out the of the Oval Office.

"Okay, Harry," continued the President, "Please don't tell me that it's on its way toward – oh, thank *God* – but why the *hell* would it be heading in *that* direction? What I mean is... there's nothing there except cows, and... sure, you've got a point – but don't we have a lot more missiles on the submarines? And the ones out there don't have any nukes on 'em, anyway... right? Well then... what's it *doing*?"

He stopped talking and listened for a few seconds to Anderson's remote voice.

"Yeah – I *hear* you," spoke the President into the handset, his tone still worried, but less so. "Obviously. Okay... I'll catch up with you once I'm up there. In the meantime, we need a one hundred per-cent accurate track, shadow it with the secret black planes, and... no, no *way* – you hear! Only two exceptions : one, it goes for *me;* two, it heads out of our airspace, we might not get another shot... what's that?"

There were a few seconds in which the American leader remained silent, evidently listening to more counsel from his top military brass.

"Yeah, I suppose," he said, "But it has to be *large-scale* damage – not just a few dead civilians... I'm leaving you in charge of that, until I get up in the plane and can get info in real-time... what? Look, Harry – I *hear* what you're saying, but you'll just have to *trust* me, I have an alternate strategy... no, I can't, not here, I'll brief you as soon as I can... we're all making this up as we go, you know... Yeah. On my way now. Over and out."

The President looked up, but Kaysten didn't have to ask.

"The alien... right?" he offered.

"Air Force just picked up what they think is its track," replied the U.S. leader. "It's *gotta* be the alien... it's giving off a heat-signature like no tomorrow – sure doesn't appear to be hiding – and it's flying at well over two thousand miles per hour, northeast from a point in the eastern Grand Canyon, toward... we're not exactly sure, where. It's heading out of Arizona, toward Utah, maybe Colorado, right now."

"They gonna shoot it down?" inquired the Chief of Staff. "Wouldn't that flight-path take it over SAC headquarters?"

"Not unless it heads right for yours truly, or it tries to fly off somewhere, or it starts killing large numbers of people," explained the President, as he collected the papers on the desk and made ready to leave. "The track doesn't seem to indicate an attack on Colorado Springs... Anderson and his boys haven't figured out what it's up to, but at least it doesn't appear to be heading toward us... *yet.*

They're scrambling fighters as we speak, and Air Force has at least three AWACS, plus an *Aurora-II*, on the way."

"But if it's out there over the northern Prairies, there wouldn't be a lot of collateral-damage, we could even use a nuke –" proposed Kaysten, holding the Oval Office exit-door open. "Why don't we just fire a Big One right on *top* of it, after it's over Canada? Even with fallout, there'd be no *way* those blue-state wannabes up there, can do something like complain to their Congressmen – zero risk on us domestically –"

"I *know*," interrupted the American leader. "But we've got a better plan."

He went through the door and started down the hallway.

"Like *what?*" pressed the Chief of Staff, as he helped the President put on his bomber jacket. "One of the secret anti-missile lasers, maybe? Or some new missile? From what I had gathered, the damn thing's just about invulnerable to anything we can throw at it..."

"Nope," answered the President, with Kaysten, the latter man burdened with carrying the bulk of the American Leader's gear, huffing and puffing to keep up with his boss as they exited the White House and strode across the Rose Garden towards a waiting stealth-helicopter.

"*Everything*, Jerry," he commented, with perhaps the hint of a smile, "Has a weak-point. The trick is finding somewhere to hit it, where it *hurts*."

He paused for a second, then added, "And *this* one... this one, is going to hurt, like no tomorrow."

To the *thump-thump-thump* of the helicopter-blades, the two men got on board, leaving the White House to their not-so-lucky stunt-doubles.

The Worst Kind Of Lesson

With the friction of the dense, cold air making the front of her 'bubble' glow with fierce incandescence, the Storied Watcher cruised at what was, for her, medium speed, heading toward the place with the big statues.

Some twenty minutes, as they reckon time, yet to go, she mused.

Shall I just remove their heads, or, perhaps, write a rude message, or... both?

From her vantage-point of some five thousand meters above the ground – the bare minimum needed to keep a safe distance over the peaks of Eastern Rockies – the Storied Watcher's own, addressed the six little minds.

Be ever-vigilant, my children, she communicated, *and learn how my senses scan up and down, side to side, ahead and behind, for signs of trouble; especially ahead, since the shield of my mind burns as it protects and enriches us.*

But the war-machines of the enemy can smell this fire and track upon it, unless we put on the dark-cloak...

Now turn thy perceptions upward : observe the sky-machine three leagues above us, the one that follows our every move?

I choose that we let this one see us, for sometimes in war, it is useful that we reveal a small part of our capabilities, that our enemies falsely think this to be the totality of what we can achieve.

Know, however, that ye shall have only scant seconds to respond, if our opponent chooses to attack, though my battle-music that now sounds in thy minds, will change in a trice before.

Strangely, there is no assault, yet... but let not down thy guard...

Suddenly, the alien-girl felt a hateful, overwhelming, stabbing pain afflicting her chest, and a numbing wave of fear, dread and shock descended upon her psyche.

Tommy – oh Tommy! reverberated her mind, as, in a fetal position of misery, she tumbled from the sky, trying desperately to stop a black mantle of unconsciousness from ending her days.

Son – call your prison to me! was the last thing that she could cry, as Karéin-Mayréij spiraled toward the scenic mountains, far below.

Encounter In A Colorado Roundabout

Except for the chapel-steeple some distance off, the most interesting thing that one would normally see at Aspen's 'Lefty Leftist Traffic Circle', at the junction of Castle Creek Drive and the other streets, would be the occasional car-crash, maybe with a little blood-and-guts to spice things up for the 6 o'clock local news.

And, to tell the truth, there *was* almost such an accident, today; but the cause was anything *except* the usual story of 'too little attention, with too much speed and booze'.

Johnny D. Masterson, landscaping shift manager of Denver, Colorado, saw it first, from behind the wheel of his newfangled, fuel-cell-and-electric SUV; the damn thing fell headfirst out of the sky, like a parachutist who forgot to pull the ripcord, only slowing down slightly before it hit the pavement with a shower of sparks, some fifty feet in front of his vehicle.

"Jesus fucking Christ!" yelled the man, as he swerved to avoid the strangely-glowing package that had just been deposited in front of him and ten or so other motorists, going each way.

He almost ended up rolling the car as he went off on the shoulder, but since these 'eco-friendly' jobs couldn't go that fast in the first place, Johnny managed to keep everything upright.

Mrs. Danielle R. DuBois, proud entrepreneurial proprietor of the Aspen Down-Home-All-You-Can-Eat-And-Keep-Standing Restaurant, and Emilio Moreno, lucky-to-be-working-at-all delivery truck-driver for the Aspen And Vail Overnight Laundry Service, also saw it, alternatively gasped and swore, and themselves pulled over and stopped, as the rubberneckers momentarily slowed down, then sped off, bored at the apparent lack of blood, shattered glass and ambulance-lights.

Masterson was, naturally, the first to get out of his cab and rush out to the middle of the road, in the direction of the... *thing*, but he was followed close on by DuBois and Moreno; and, thankfully, the Hispanic had the presence of mind to bring along a couple of flares to warn the oncoming traffic.

At first, the previously-flying-thing was glowing so brightly that he and the others could barely look at it. But after ten seconds or so, it had dimmed enough to look like... well, they weren't sure *what* it resembled.

"What the *hell*...?" exclaimed Masterson. "You see that thing come down?"

"*Sì señor*," answered the Mexican-American. "It look like a meteor... but no crater. It slow down, just before it hit the road..."

"Saw it too," echoed the woman. "Hey, looks like it's cooled down, now – whoa! What you make of *that*? I can see a pair of feet, or boots sticking out from under that... uhh... parachute... or whatever's over top of it. You think that person's still alive? Somebody had better call 911 – you got a communicator? Mine's back in the car –"

"Mine too," remarked Masterson. "Look... before we call the ambulance, let's go over and see if there's any point, poor bugger hit the ground pretty hard –"

He stepped forward, but in the next second, there was a flash like the discharge of an improperly-grounded power-cable, and the man was knocked back on his heels.

"*Shit!*" he cursed, running his hands over his face to feel the singed tips of his eyebrows and hair. "What the fuck was *that*? Felt like I got hit by one of those personal stun-gun things!"

"Look!" warned the Hispanic man. "He's getting up! Oh... sorry... *she's* gettin' up –"

They heard a retching, coughing sound, as the figure – much of it still obscured by a flowing cape – propped itself up on knees and palms, gradually tried to right itself.

"Hey, *you!*" called out Masterson. "You *okay* over there?"

Mutely, the figure, its face still obscured as it look straight down, shook its head.

A few seconds later, the three onlookers heard a low, pained moan, followed by something being forced out in a thoroughly foreign-sounding language.

"I'd come over to help," continued the landscaping manager, "But, something zapped me good, when I tried –"

Finally, they heard something intelligible.

"Sorr-ee," came a light, melodic-sounding voice, with gasps between words. "It will not happen again. My, uhh... my children, thought that you wanted to hurt me, when you approached so fast. Just give me a few minutes... I will be, oh-kay."

"So we *can* come and help you, now?" asked DuBois.

"Yes... but I do not require any help," replied the figure. "Except, maybe..."

"Maybe what, *señorita*?" inquired Moreno, as the figure now managed to sit up, revealing a beautiful, teenager-like face framed by flowing blond hair, encased in something that resembled nothing so much as a tight-fitting suit of ebon-scaled mail armor, complete with sword and a small shield on one arm.

"Do you have anything to eat?" requested the crashing-to-Earth creature, as the three hurried over to her side. "Like... a chocolate-bar?"

They noticed that the pavement underneath where she had landed, was pock-marked with small, blackened indentations, some of them still hissing with wisps of smoke issuing forth.

"I think I have one back in my car," stated the restaurant-owner. "But it's in the glove compartment, my kids put it there last week – might be a little gooey, it gets hot in there, when I have the windows closed –"

"Well, now I've seen *everything*," remarked Masterson, as he bent down over the armored-girl. "Where the hell did *you* come from?"

The wail of an oncoming car honking in frustration came and went, as it, and several more sped by.

"Tucson, by way of the planet *Mailànkh.... pick* one," muttered the female, taking deep breaths as she spoke.

"Mai-*whaaa*?" asked the delivery-truck-driver. "*¿No es Inglès?*"

"Forget it," she morosely answered. "And no – it is definitely *not*, 'English'."

"We better get off the road, here," suggested Masterson. "Flares are burning down, and cars around here ain't gonna be expecting us. You want we should call 911?"

"Uhh, no... that will not be necessary," said the strange being, as she tried to stand upright, on wobbly legs. "Listen... could you please bring those burning-sticks over here?"

"*Sì, pero porque –*" said Moreno.

The armored-girl waved her hand, and, to the astonishment of the three humans surrounding her, the flares started coming toward her of their own accord, as if they were iron filings drawn to a magnet. Moreno and DuBois stepped gingerly out of their path, and then they saw the being take hold of the flares. A second later, their flames were extinguished.

The pained look on the face of this weird creature lessened, slightly.

"You are correct," she offered. "Here – I can walk over to the side of the road."

Slowly, followed by the three now-fascinated humans, the fallen-girl stumbled forth, eventually leaning against DuBois' sedan and staring dizzily out into space.

"Here... I'll... I'll get you your chocolate-bar," stammered the restaurant-owner. She hit a button on her key-chain and unlocked the doors, heading around to the passenger-side to rummage for the candy in the glove compartment.

"Listen, lady," mentioned Masterson, "We... uhh... we didn't see a parachute, and... well... what's *that,* you're wearing? If you don't mind my asking."

"You want the truth?" asked the strange girl, still staring into the sky.

"Sure," he confirmed.

"What I am 'wearing' – that is the closest word in your language, but it is not really a very good translation... I suppose, 'traveling with', might be a better way to put it," she explained, "Are my beloved war-children, *Vîrya Quü'j, Vîrya Ahn'jë, Væran Fàiagàryuu, Vîrya I'ëà'b', Væran Ksé'l'ch'* and *Væran Ss'éth'ch'.* It is they, two of them, specifically, who broke my fall and otherwise saved their mother. I owe them my *life*... as they owe me. Thus we are bound. And..."

"And?" pressed Masterson.

"I guess that I owe all three of you, too," continued the creature. "As you saw, it took me a few minutes to shake off the effects of... the... *thing* that beset me... that drove me from the sky. Had a car or truck impacted with me as I lay here, *I* would have survived – my... uhh... 'bubble' would have stopped it – but whoever drove that vehicle... it would have been like driving into a stone wall. I should not wish that to be on my conscience."

"Here it is," interrupted DuBois. "Like I said, not much to look at... it got melted."

"No matter – I am now more in your debt, kind woman," answered the armored-girl.

Again, the three humans looked on in amazement, as the chocolate-bar flew all by itself to the creature's hand, shedding its wrapper in the process.

"Mmmm," purred Karéin-Mayréij. "That tastes *so* good, you have no idea..."

The suit of armor now started to give off a dim glow, which, they noticed, with the fear starting to claw at the fringes of their consciousnesses, was being matched by a glow from this being's eyes.

"Señorita," demanded the awed Mexican-American, "Who *are* you?"

Warmly, she smiled at them, as she noted, "You can think of me as a friend... a very *powerful* friend, who is trying to set right, some things that have gone terribly wrong. Listen – I do not have much more time here, and I need you to do one more thing for me, if you will."

"Uhh... sure, I guess," said Masterson. "What?"

"Can you each close your eyes and think of your names and places of residence, please?" asked the armored-girl. "You do not have to say them out loud. Just think of them, as if you are about to fill out a, umm, let's say, a 'crediting-card' application form."

"Huh?" uneasily stated the delivery-truck-driver.

"Just *do* it," she implored.

"Well... okay," agreed DuBois.

All three closed their eyes, concentrated for a second, then opened them to look at this weird creature, who, to their alarm, was now glowing like a set of halogen headlights.

She pointed at each of them, in turn.

"Johnny Masterson, of Denver," she indicated, in the direction of the SUV driver.

"Danielle DuBois, of Aspen," she said to the woman.

"Emilio Moreno, of Glenwood Springs," she called, to the Mexican-American.

"Holy *shit*," gasped Masterson. "How the hell you *know* all that? None of us told you our names!"

"I told you – I am a very *powerful* friend," explained the armored-girl, with a kindly smile. "But it pains me that right now, I do not have enough strength to safely give you the gift that I would otherwise happily bestow. So I would ask that you would accept – ah, how would dear Bob put it – yes, accept a 'raining-check' on it; I will visit each of you when my current quest is finished. We will settle things then, and speak and rejoice as new friends. Will you accept my promise?"

"Uhh... wow, *sure*," evaded DuBois. "I got a restaurant... you want a free meal? Be great publicity – whoever you are."

"Would it be oh-kay if I brought along a few extra friends?" inquired the strange creature.

"No problem," confirmed the restaurant-owner. "Oh, except... food's on the house – you gotta pay for your own drinks, though. Civic ordinance – not much I can do about it."

"Dear friend," commented the armored-girl, with a wan smile, "I have had far more than my fill of the rules of this 'United States', but in this matter, I will obey, out of respect to yourself. Now... I must be on my way, so you should all back away from me – at least ten meters – to be safe. Any closer, and you would be... uhh... *harmed*."

As she completed this, the fallen-girl's countenance became godly – frighteningly so – and her body began to show flecks of fire, up and down.

Weird, exciting, improbable music began to reverberate in their minds.

"Don't know about *you*," shouted Masterson, "But I don't think she's kiddin' – I'm *outta* here!"

Rapidly, he and the other two ran off, up and down the shoulder of the road.

A second later, they had to shield their eyes, as something too bright to behold, again shot skyward.

No Quarter For You, Ms. Karéin

The President had just buckled the seat-belt.

As he heard the engines of this unmarked, nondescript substitute for Air Force One – neither the sleeping-quarters, nor the wet-bar, were nearly as nice as the amenities within the real thing – firing up, out of the corner of his eye, he saw an Air Force lieutenant approaching from behind.

"Excuse me, sir," announced the clean-cut young man, "But it's the Secretary of Defense – he's demanding to speak with you, right now."

"Well, we're just taking off, aren't we –?" remarked the U.S. leader.

"I have a headset for you, here," stated the lieutenant. "I'll switch the secure link in to the port on the arm of your seat, you can just plug in the jack on the headset and speak into the microphone."

"Oh... okay," said the President, accepting the headphone-like contraption. "Just a second... where *is* the damn thing... oh, wait a minute, *there* it is... yeah, put him through, I'm good to go, I think."

The lieutenant hit a button on a remote controller, wrote something down on a portable tablet-communicator, saluted and then walked away.

"Hello... Arthur... you there?" asked the American leader, seemingly speaking to no-one in particular. "Yeah, it's me – we just took off from Andrews... okay... what's the update? *Really?* Just like *that?* She – it – *what?*"

He fell silent for a few seconds, then continued, "Listen, Air Force didn't take any pot-shots at it, did they? You *certain?* Well, then – what the hell *happened?* You're right... damn peculiar, but what *I'm* really concerned about is, losing track of the accursed alien... yeah, I'll stay on the line, no rush here... sure."

The President's face looked out a porthole, into the approaching twilight.

For as much as ten minutes or so, he remained thus; until again, a distant voice sounded in the headphones and the conversation resumed.

"Yeah, I'm back... okay," remarked the Commander-In-Chief. "What did you say? Is that verified? Of *course* I'm glad that we're tracking it, again, but... no, not exactly... not that I know of... but I'll ask."

Another short delay ensued, then, again, the President addressed his understudy.

"Listen, Arthur," he went on, "You just have to *trust* me on this one – we may have gotten a bit ahead of ourselves here, but in the long-run, I'm taking this as good news... as long as we can keep our eye on it from here on in. What? Well, as I understand it, we're out over the Atlantic... okay, just keep me informed, and like I said – no unauthorized attacks, you *hear?* We've got something much *better*, cooked up – just got to get the last few pieces of the puzzle in place. What? Can you say that again, please?"

After a second or two, the President spoke up.

"Oh, for Christ's sake!" he grumbled, "Have Jacob tell the damn Russians and Chinese to go screw themselves – this is *our* ball-game, in *our* ball-park –

what don't they understand about *that?* Listen – they should be thanking *us* for dealing with the situation, not... yeah, loud and clear. Alright. Any change, you buzz me right away, no matter *when* you get the news. You got it. Thanks, Arthur. C-in-C out."

The self-proclaimed 'Leader of the Free World', put the back of his seat into 'full-recline' mode, and tried to relax.

When Uncle Sam fights dirty, he mused, a slight smile evident on his face, *He fights... to* win.

Just *Watch* Me, Human!

After the last, all-too-close episode, the Storied Watcher had steeled herself to recognize and cope with the plague of shared pain... although she was by no means sure that her mental defenses would hold up against the next such onslaught.

At least now, ye know the signs of it, she communicated to the strange 'children', whose bodies enveloped and protected her.

If thy mother should fail... take over from her, as ye did so well before, I pray.

Rocketing at some two thousand kilometers per hour – as the humans would reckon it – Karéin-Mayréij dodged and weaved just over and beside the peaks of the Black Hills; and when she first perceived the distant presence of her objective, she slowed until she was moving somewhat above the speed of sound.

They need to see, after all, she mused. *And to hear this, the first of my war-songs.*

Now a sound – low, haunting, Celtic-cadenced, beautiful in another context – issued from all around, though not from her lips or lungs.

Ooo, ooo, ooo, it rang up and down the valley, echoing off the mountain-sides, as she cleared the last set of peaks and gazed directly at the monument ahead.

There – just off the road with the cars – that *is where the empire's peasant-people enter,* she reflected.

Very well, Mr. 'President'... that shall also be, where they first shall know.

Like a miniature comet with a purpose, the alien-girl circled the front-entrance of this temple of American ancestor-worship, dipping low and slow enough to induce a sonic boom over the parked cars and advancing tourists, so that none could fail to notice.

"Holy *shit...* what the hell's *that?*" she heard coming from several different places on the ground, and – though none save her war-children could so perceive – the newcomer allowed herself a wry smile.

"That a *missile?*" shouted a worried voice from the car-park. "Maybe it's a Muslim attack! Somebody call the *cops!*"

Oh no... not these 'Muslims' who you hate and fear, thought Karéin-Mayréij.

You behold something much *worse, in the long-run.*

Ooo, ooo, OOO, came down a crescendo of stirring, yet ominous, psycho-music, as the Storied Watcher's brilliant, godly figure righted itself and slowly descended to a crash of thunder and fire, in the middle of the plaza, just road-side of the big gray enclosure entitled,

'M O U N T R U S H M O R E N A T I O N A L M E M O R I A L".

She held *Væran Fàiagàryuu* in one hand, his blackish-red-and-green blade flickering with flame subtly-different to that which similarly bedecked the most part of dark-scaled *Vîrya Ahn'jë.*

Her visage was grim, determined, savage, and the concrete underneath her feet began to smoke and hiss, for well-nigh three meters in every direction.

Hold back thy powered glow, as will thy mother also, advised the alien-girl to her children.

For these humans, not like our friends Wolf and Misha – their flesh is weak... it would die from the touch of thy energy, and they feel it not, until too late.

A large crowd of astonished onlookers quickly formed around the now-mighty Karéin-Mayréij, who just stood serenely in place, saying nothing.

Some of the braver ones tried to approach, but the sting of her infernal aura stopped them in their tracks, long before they could get very close.

Someone yelled out, "Who are you?"

For a few seconds, the newcomer kept the crowd 'shivering with anticipation', as she answered not; but at length, she replied, "I am called the 'Storied Watcher'; and I am the Fire-Bringer, who your fool President has wronged, and who he wrongs still, even at this very moment. I come now to show the fate that will befall you all, should your leader not relent and make peace and penance, according to my modest demands. But – before I do this – I must ask you two questions."

"What questions?" asked another voice.

"This is *great*, man!" came still another.

"One," requested the Storied Watcher, "Do any of you have a vid-ee-oh camera, or other such device, so that a record may be made of what will transpire here?"

Several of the crowd enthusiastically answered to the effect of, "You *got* it lady, I'm taping *all* of this."

"Good!" firmly and forcefully stated the alien-girl. "Make sure that you send it *immediately* to your Neo-Net, for your government will soon try to tell lies about this event. The truth is – I have warned your President about what I would do, if he persists in mocking and deceiving me; the more so, for cruelly afflicting my family. Shortly, he will see a small morsel of the doom that comes quickly upon him... and, if he relent not, upon all of you."

The Storied Watcher stopped for a few seconds to let the impact of her words sink in, then pointed at the huge carvings on Mount Rushmore and continued, "And two, concerning the rock-face upon yonder mountain, which contains the statues of past Presidents – do any humans venture there, right now? For I would not yet hurt any who have not grieved me, except by blind followership. That fate comes last, and I pray it come not at all... but it is not up to me."

There was immediate confusion in the crowd, but eventually, a tall, mustachioed man in a 'Smokey-The-Bear' hat stepped forward and announced, in a loud voice, "Look – whoever you are, the answer's 'no' – it's a National Monument, you have to have special permission to rock-climb there – and we don't have any permits issued for another month and a half. Listen... you're, uhh, causing a *disturbance*, as well as damaging State property – the concrete, I mean. I'm afraid we're going to have to take you in for questioning. Please turn off the furnace-act and come with me... don't make me have to call the police."

Savagely, a star-eyed Karéin-Mayréij laughed out loud, her fangs part-extended, as a fearful wave of heat washed over the crowd, driving them yet further back.

"Man, nice music," somebody from the crowd interrupted. "Jamie – what channel?"

"I think *not*, man-with-the-wide-brown-hat!" derisively answered the newcomer. "But I *will* allow you this much : you are indeed correct about the 'damaging-State-property' issue... only you do not yet comprehend the fullness of it. And one more counsel I would give, here, today, for all those in your empire, who see me approaching in *Fire* and glory. I would not harm ordinary Americans, if the choice to avoid this is practical; but it would be wise for you to leave as fast as you can, when I make it plain what will be the vehicle for my next 'message', to your President."

"What's all *that* fancy-dancy B.S., supposed to mean?" shouted the park ranger.

"Just *watch* me, human... if you dare!" snarled the Stored Watcher, as she half-crouched, with the cape of *Vîrya Ahn'jë* flowing from her back like a dark spinnaker.

The fire all over her body, now became inter-mixed with charges of some lightening-like thing, that shot back and forth, up and down.

The heat was suddenly unbearable, and the crowd retreated in a confused, panic-stricken mob.

Ooo, ooo, OOO, echoed her war-cry, as Karéin-Mayréij became a streak of light stabbing the clear blue sky, bending its path a few hundred meters overhead, toward Mount Rushmore.

A Friendly Chat With Mr. Bennington

"I ain't got *nothin'* to tell you, lady," muttered the big, tattooed man, as he steered his gaze away from the attractive, Asian-American countenance of the FBI-team-leader, toward the beam of light entering this dingy interrogation-room, from the half-open top-part of the window facing outside. "Except... if you're smart, you'll let me go and have it done at that."

"And what's *that* supposed to mean, Mr., uhh... 'Wolf', it is, I believe?" contested Minnie Chu. "Some kind of *threat?*"

"Yeah... you could call it somethin' like that," replied the bounty-hunter. "See, I got money – and I got a lawyer on retainer... in my line of business, you need one on call, pretty much all the while. You ain't got *nothin'* on me. I mean, Crissakes – if I had somethin' to hide, you think I'd be ridin' a *bus?* Just let me get to a phone, give me my one call... and I'll be out of here."

"Oh, you *think* so, do you?" taunted the woman.

"He's never failed me before, and I've been up on all sorts of stuff – B&E, 'excessive force', 'concealed gun' – that one was before they loosened the rules, of course – and various other shit," countered Wolf.

Chu leaned back in her plain, wooden chair, looked across the barren hardwood table, and, uncharacteristically, let out a hearty laugh.

"Mr., Mr. – what *is* it, now, yeah, Mr. Bennington – Darryl D. Bennington, right? Which name should I use, your real one, or your stage-name?" she inquired, with a bemused smile.

"'*Wolf's* the name," growled the big man. "I ain't been called 'Darryl' in twenty years."

"Very well, then," sighed the FBI-agent, "'Wolf', it'll be. Now, let me give it to you straight – first of all, I don't know how much reading up you've been doing on the Emergency Laws –"

"I don't do that much readin'," interrupted the bounty-hunter.

"No... I guess *not*," allowed Chu, with a sardonic grin. "Well, let me clue you in, my friend – under the enlightened, secret laws that have been in effect since the bad-stuff that went down in Miami a few years ago, us Federal folk don't have to *let* you make a phone-call, and we can keep you well and truly locked up for as long as we like, no questions asked... that's pretty much 'it'."

"*Really*," he challenged.

"Really," echoed the FBI-agent. "Now... I can understand how you might not be quite up to speed on this, since we rarely get down to this neck of the woods, and we usually don't have to intervene in local law-enforcement – where, it's true, you're probably still working under the old rules, on a day-to-day basis. But clear your mind of all that. You're playing in the *big* leagues now, mister!"

"Bully for *me!*" answered the bounty-hunter. "I ain't scared of you. Never was before... and much less so, now. And as for this bein' the 'big leagues'... well, lady," he added, with a malicious chuckle, "You sure got *that* right. If you knew *how* big, you wouldn't want to keep me in here one *second* longer."

"Before you go way out on a limb, saying things like that," advised Chu, "Would you like me to tell you why you're in here?"

"Seems like I got nothin' else to do for the time bein'," he quipped.

"Okay... so here's where we're at," resumed the FBI-team-leader. "We have two reasons for wanting to become, uhh, better-acquainted with you : one, you were observed in the hotel-room with the alien – by some accounts, you even spoke with her – just before the little altercation that happened shortly thereafter; and two, would it interest you to know, that the other man who we picked up from the bus at the roadblock, was a *Russian?*"

"So *what?*" evaded the bounty-hunter. "Could have been worse... he could have been a Mexican... right?"

"Not only that," explained Chu, now standing and resting her hands on the top of the chair, "But we have good preliminary information, that he may be a deep-cover operative of the Russian SVR. Oh – if you're not up to date on this kind of thing, that's their equivalent of the CIA. In other words... we believe that he's a spy. What you think of *that?*"

"Good for *him*," shrugged the big man, trying to sound indifferent. "But if I was you... I'd let him go, too."

"What's *that* supposed to mean, Mr. Bennington?" shot back the FBI-team-leader.

"Just a *feelin'*," replied Wolf, with a feigned smile.

"Okay," replied the woman. "Listen... you don't mind if I have a couple of my friends join us for this conversation, do you?"

"All the same to me," he stated.

Chu spoke out loud, to nowhere in particular.

"Otis, Will... can you come in now?" she called.

More dust showered down from above the dingy, rust-hinged door that opened, allowing a huge but only mildly-overweight, bald-headed black man, and a much trimmer and considerably-younger Caucasian agent, both dressed in cheapish-regulation FBI business-suits, to join their boss, at the table.

"These are Agents Boatman and Hendricks – my partners on my special team," remarked the senior agent. "Will, Otis... this is Mr. Darryl D. Bennington, otherwise known as 'Wolf'... he's a bounty-hunter, by trade."

"Pleased to meetcha," offered the black man, with as convincing a smile as he could muster.

"Likewise," added Hendricks.

"Gentlemen," said Wolf, leaning back a bit.

"Hope Ms. Chu here hasn't been too tough on y'all," mentioned Boatman.

"Oh, everything's been fine... just *fine*," small-talked Wolf. "Except for that little matter of me bein' able to call my lawyer."

"Look," demanded Chu, leaning forward with the hint of impatience in her eyes, "I don't think you *understand* how, uhh, relatively lucky you are, to have been taken in by the Bureau, as opposed to the several other... agencies, that might have grabbed you. All we're asking for, is some straight information about what transpired between you and the alien in the Hotel Tucson conference-room, as well as a truthful and verifiable explanation of how you got out of there, without being killed. *And*, how you managed to be on a bus from an Indian reservation back to Tucson, with a Russian spy, less than a day later. If it's of any interest... your girlfriend is beside herself with worry about what's happened to you, she thinks that you didn't make it out of the hotel –"

"I guess I'll just have to take your word about that, since you won't let me near a phone, to speak with her, myself," sarcastically argued the big man. "And it's nice to see that all of you FBI-folk are so concerned with my well-bein', but... well, let's just say, I'm pretty confident of my chances of stayin' alive, on the outside. Oh, and one *other* thing... I'm stayin' in here, more out of courtesy, than of necessity... know what I mean?"

"Mister, you're in a *jail* – or hadn't you noticed?" countered the third agent. "If Agent Chu decides that you ain't goin' – you ain't *goin'*. I'd have thought that if you're so familiar with the law, that wouldn't be too much of a surprise."

Again, the self-satisfied smile showed on Wolf's visage.

"I'm well aware of the surroundin's," he offered. "I'm just sayin' that you all ain't the *only* ones holdin' an ace or two up the sleeve."

"It's probably not to your advantage to be playin' games with us," warned Boatman.

"It ain't a *game*," retorted the bounty-hunter. "Of that, I can *assure* you."

"Why don't you just answer our *questions*, sir?" shot back Chu, frustration rising in her voice. "You just tell us the truth... it's some mundane story, it checks out – you walk. If you've got nothing to hide, what've you got to lose?"

The big man now came forward and rested his palms on the table, staring intently at the Asian-American agent.

"Like I told you right out front, lady," he stated, his tone low and cautionary, "Not only do I got rights, but... I got no assurance whatsoever, that if I level with you, you ain't gonna just throw me in some deep dark hole and then throw away the key, like them *Federales* do to people down here, every so often – I need *guarantees*, before I'm gonna tell you jack *shit*, that's *my* bottom line. *Capiche?*"

"So if we promise to let you go... you'll talk?" bargained the FBI-team-leader. "And how do I know that you've got anything worthwhile to tell us, anyway?"

"I guess you'll just have to *trust* me," he answered. "For what it's worth, I think you'll find it *mighty* interestin'."

"Before I take a break and discuss this with my associates," requested Chu, "Is that everything?"

"Yeah," confirmed Wolf.

As the three agents got up, he again spoke up.

"Hey, *lady*," he called. "On second thought... there *is* somethin' else."

"What?" inquired Chu.

"You know that Russian dude?" said the bounty-hunter.

"Yeah," replied the woman. "What *about* him?"

"You better bring him in here," recommended Wolf. "So he can back me up."

"I thought you said you didn't *know* him...?" challenged the team-leader.

"I don't... not *exactly*," indicated Wolf. "It's... *complicated*... that's all I can say."

"This is *highly* irregular," protested Chu. "He's a foreign national, suspected of illegal espionage inside the United States. It's a summary death-penalty offense... were you aware of that? He's in this office – that's true – but the SSG boys are going over him right now, and after that, he goes off to the Agency... I wouldn't count on seeing much of *him* again, afterwards. I'd be going out on a limb to try to get him in here, even for a short time. Why's he so important to you, anyway?"

"He ain't," offered the big man. "Let me ask *you* something, lady – you said that your little threesome here is chasin' the alien... right?"

"You *got* it," interjected Boatman.

"Then... he's *important* to you... right?" suggested Wolf.

"Why?" asked Hendricks.

"Guess you'll have to wait and see," insouciantly replied the bounty-hunter. "But I'd be obliged if you'd get his sorry ass in here, none the less."

"Right," sighed Chu. "Please excuse my team and I, would you?"

Wolf nodded in mock politeness, as the three FBI-agents marched out of the room. And thus he sat for perhaps an hour, idly wondering if the events of the past day and a half were real, or if he was just on some kind of particularly potent synth-drug trip.

But eventually, he heard voices – more of them than before – outside the translucently-glassed door. It opened, and in trouped Chu, Boatman and Hendricks.

They were followed by Misha. Unlike Wolf, the SVR-man was in handcuffs and leg-restraints.

"Thanks for the bus-fare, my friend," muttered the spy, as he awkwardly took a seat at the long end of the table, corner-on where the bounty-hunter had been situated. "I *knew* that it was insane to take your advice and take public transportation back to the city; but then, it is not the *only* insane thing that I have been doing lately."

"Nice to see *you*, too, pardner," evenly mentioned Wolf. "Hey – they got you trussed up better than a roast pig at the State Fair."

He turned to address Chu.

"Ain't no point in puttin' all that gear on him, you know," argued the big man. "He ain't goin' nowhere... if he don't *want* to, that is."

"You must really get off on speakin' in riddles there, Mister Bounty Hunter, sir," offered Boatman.

"Oh... they ain't *riddles*," countered Wolf.

"Okay," interrupted Chu. "We've brought in your friend – something that I had to cash in a *lot* of chips to accomplish, I'll have you know – so it's time for you to keep up your side of the bargain. Let's *hear* it, please."

"Fair enough," agreed the big man.

He turned to Misha.

"So what'd you tell 'em so far?" he asked.

Reluctantly, his eyes avoiding contact with anyone, the Russian replied, "Nothing."

"Well... now's your chance," proposed the bounty-hunter.

Misha sat stone-faced, looking straight ahead.

"I guess cat's got his tongue," opined Wolf, "So I'd reckon that's *my* cue – but if I get anything wrong – I never *was* much for rememberin' stuff, that's why I used to always carry around my notepad, when I was bustin' them druggies and bail-hoppers, y'know – you set the record straight... okay, pardner?"

"Fine," mordantly grumbled Misha. "No doubt I will soon be shot, either by the American government, or by my own. Perhaps they can recruit a squad made up half from each nation... then we can see whose bullets are more effective, for this purpose."

"Quite a lead-up," commented Boatman. "So... out with it."

"Okay," started the bounty-hunter, "It's like *this*, you see. You all remember that heavy shit that went down in the hotel? In that fancy-ass conference-room, I mean."

"How could we ever *forget*," answered Chu. "We almost got *killed* in there! A lot of others weren't so lucky."

"Yeah, well, shit *happens*, you know," sniffed Wolf. "So, anyway... yours truly – either the smartest or stupidest decision I've ever made in my life, and I'm not yet sure which it is – well, I'm off work for the day, just did the late-shift the night before, and I'm sick of the video-game-thing and the TV-thing and the NeoNet hidden-channels porno-thing... so I decide to try somethin' different, and I see this ad for these scientists givin' some big speech about this space-alien that they say them astronauts let loose on Mars, before the comet, that is... so I say, 'what the hell, I'll go down there, grab me a beer, zone out, catch some sleep, maybe even *learn* something', you know?"

He looked up at Hendricks, who was furiously taking notes, and asked, "Am I goin' too fast for you, there?"

"No... *no problemo*, man," answered the third agent. "We're getting this on tape, anyway."

"Right," said the big man. "So where was I?"

"In the Hotel Tucson conference-room, listening to the Abruzzio-Ramirez lecture about the alien, I'd assume," reminded Chu.

"Oh... yeah," grunted Wolf. "Well, this lecture goes on and on and on, three beers and I'm almost comfortably-numb – I never *did* go for all this science shit, you know? – but then, just as things are about to wrap up, just ahead of me and to the left, up stands this real *cute* teenager or twentysomethin', nice blond hair 'n such, and she starts mouthin' off some long-winded stuff about 'you know who I am' or somethin' like that –"

"Excuse me," interrupted the Asian-American FBI leader, "But did you say you knew this woman, from before?"

"Nope," replied the bounty-hunter. "Never met her before that day. *Wished* I had, though – damn prettiest girl I *ever* saw. Hey – don't tell the gf about that... okay?"

"Not as long as you keep talkin'," promised Boatman. "Go on."

"So," continued Wolf, "Here's where things get... *strange*. Bit after this cute chick starts up with the speech, all of a sudden, this mousy little guy in big glasses, a short-sleeve shirt and business slacks a few chairs down from me, he pulls out a piece and squeezes off a shot – might've been more than one, don't know, exactly – at the girl, hits her in the back, just below the neck, impact throws her forward a bit... but I gotta tell you, at that point, I was just fuckin' *amazed* at how she had a neck left at all... I mean, this guy's shot hit *flesh*, but the slug bounced off as if it was one of them fancy bullet-proof chest-covers, you know? I ain't surprised any more, mind you – but I'm gettin' ahead of myself..."

"What happened next?" inquired a fascinated Hendricks.

"Well, I guess reflexes kind of got the better of me," explained the big man, "Or somethin'... don't really know *why*, bein' as I had just *met* this chick, but I was really mad about the whole thing – Crissakes, it was pre-meditated *murder*, or attempted murder, y'know... so I just grabbed ol' Betsy – my custom-throated and ramped ten-milimeter concealed-carry, and yes, I *do* got a State permit, I told 'em so when I was down there – and I, uhh, let loose on this little prick who shot the girl, that's the bottom line. When I was finished, he wasn't movin' – *that's* for sure."

Chu turned to the Russian.

"Does this account of the early events in the conference-room, correspond with your own, sir?" she asked.

"Yes," he stolidly replied.

"Continue," ordered the FBI-team-leader, in the direction of the bounty-hunter.

"The rest of it shouldn't be much that you don't already know," Wolf offered. "So I'll only give you the part that's, uhh, *unique*, to yours truly. All of a sudden – too fast for me to figure out how the fuck she managed it – this chick has outfitted herself in that funky suit of armor that you're no doubt already familiar with –"

"Don't make that assumption," interrupted Chu. "We'll ask you more about that later, but keep going."

"So she comes over to me and says 'thanks for trying to save my life' – makes sense I suppose – and she, uhh, offers me her hand. Then, well..."

"Umm-hmm?" queried the woman.

"This is kind of hard to put into words, lady," elaborated Wolf, "But, when I touched her – well, *that* was quite a trip. How'd I describe it... okay, let's try it this way. It was like you instantly knew her – trusted her – as if you'd known her all your life, even though consciously, you were perfectly aware that you'd only met her five minutes ago... shit, I don't *know* how to explain it, exactly. Except to say, I was also very well aware that she was somethin'... *different*, you know? Not just from the psychedelic handshake, but also from how she took them Men in Black apart and didn't bother to put 'em back together again, without so much as breakin' a sweat. Damn *impressive*, I'd say."

"You ain't just fuckin' whistling Dixie about *that*, mister," half-joked Hendricks. "Listen, 'Wolf'... do you have the slightest idea of who you were *dealing* with, in there? I think that we'd better set you straight, so you know how out of your depth –"

The big man looked up at the third agent, and slowly and deliberately commented, "Sure *do*, pardner. Her name is 'Karéin-Mayréij', and she goes by the title of 'Storied Watcher', whatever the hell *that* means. And if you're interested, Mister FBI Agent – it's *you* all, the whole damn *government*, that's out of their depth, here. You know what she did to them fancy-ass Federal dudes in the hotel? Oh, by the way, sorry, if any of 'em was from your agency, but like I said, 'shit happens'... but what I was gonna say is, you only saw a *fraction* of what this space-chick is capable of. You have no *idea*."

"Oh... I think we've got a pretty good idea," argued Boatman.

"No, you do *not*," quietly contradicted the SVR-man.

"Would you care to elaborate on that, sir?" asked Chu.

"I will let my friend do the talking, for now," evaded the Russian.

"Fair enough... but we *will*, of course need to hear your full story, later," demanded the FBI-team-leader.

Misha nodded, his eyes staring blankly forward.

"May I continue?" requested Wolf.

"Please," directed Chu.

"So... now mind you, this rest of it went on over some time, while the President was makin' a horse's ass out of himself, tryin' to bullshit our little Martian goddess about this 'family' of hers – bad, *bad* mistake there, by the way," continued the bounty-hunter, "But, bottom line, this 'Karéin' girl, well, she offers to make my Russkie *amigo* and yours truly, kind of her, uhh, 'followers', 'disciples', whatever you want to call it, and she notices that our friendly Air Force is about to bomb the ratshit out of us and everythin' within three city-blocks... so she sort of airlifts us up and out of there, lands us up in the Canyon, where she explains what she's all about and what she's fixin' to do to get even. With the government, that is."

"Which would be...?" grimly inquired the team-leader.

Wolf looked at Misha, out of the corner of an eye.

"Tell me if I got this right, will you, pardner?" he asked, to a nod on the part of the Russian.

"Okay... so here it is," said Wolf. "First, she wants Mr. Russkie 'n me to walk clean out of here, since we're kind of actin' as her mouthpieces, go-betweens, that kind of thing. Oh, and she also mentioned that if you all so much as part our hair the wrong way, she'll –"

"'Reduce you to atoms' – I believe that those were her exact words," helpfully interjected the SVR-man.

"I... *see*," remarked Boatman. "Certainly has a way of makin' herself clear, wouldn't you say?"

"You don't know the *half* of it," confirmed Wolf. "Next, she wanted him 'n me to hunt down them two scientists – maybe arrange a meetin' with 'em – because apparently she spoke with them while she was in outer space, and she more or less trusts 'em. What she wants to talk to them *about*, I got no idea. I'm not sure if that request is still, uhh, 'operative', though... since it was assumin' that we didn't get captured."

"*Interesting*," offered Chu, with a sideways glance to her fellow agents. "Hey – maybe there's *one* request that might be do-able."

Boatman winced, while Hendricks rolled his eyes.

"Okay," went on the big man, taking note of the agents' demeanor. "Finally, we get to the nub of the biscuit... I'm afraid that our fuckin' genius President has really rubbed the Storied Watcher the wrong way, on this little problem about her 'family', the salesman and his various hangers-on, *especially* the boy – what did she say the kid's name is, again –"

"Tommy," noted Misha. "She considers him, as her adopted son."

"Yeah... 'Tommy'," continued Wolf. "Now you all had better listen up good, here, Missus FBI Lady – through some weirdo shit that neither Mr. Misha nor yours truly has any chance of understanding, it seems that when the government hurts this salesman guy – uhh, 'Billings' is his name as I recall – even worse, the 'Tommy' kid – well, it sorta gets channeled through to Karéin... and the results ain't pretty. In fact, it's drivin' her fuckin' *crazy*, both physically and emotionally, and she's gettin' less and less rational, each time it happens –"

"Excuse me," interrupted the FBI-team-leader, "But you say, 'hurting' Billings and his party? What do you mean by that?"

"Just what he *said!*" shot back Misha, his eyes sullen with anger. "The American intelligence-agencies have been *torturing* those who they took away from Karéin-Mayréij – and have been doing so ever since they captured the Billings group. If this of any interest, my own government has known about it almost from the start... but we have been helpless to prevent it."

"Why the hell would they do *that?*" incredulously demanded the third agent. "What'd they have to *gain?*"

"*You* tell *me*, pardner!" retorted the bounty-hunter. "But I can *assure* you... if they keep it up, it'll go down as the most fuckin' stupid thing ever done in the whole sorry story of human history... that is if there *is* any more history, a month from now. The President and his jackass advisers have no *clue* of what they're provoking... no clue at all."

"She *did* threaten the life of the President, you know," argued Chu. "That a good enough reason?"

"No," contradicted Misha, shaking his head.

Boatman got up and paced around a bit.

"I dunno," he noted, "I seen them boys from the 'Secret Branches' do some pretty tough stuff, from time to time, but 'splain me this – why would the President authorize them bein' continually tortured, when he's got a lot to *lose*, by doin' that, and a lot to *gain*, by *stoppin'* it? That is *if* any of this was really *happenin'*, in the first place. What facts do you have to back up the belief that the alien's grievance is legitimate? What if she's makin' it all up, as an excuse to take us over and set herself up as some kind of damn queen, or somethin' like that?"

"She ain't," countered Wolf.

"And you expect us to just *believe* you, on all that?" asked the black FBI-agent.

"Guess you'd have to get to know her a bit better, to know that she ain't bullshittin' us on all of this," stated the bounty-hunter.

"Go on," quietly asked Chu. "Did the alien give you any clear idea about what specifically she was going to do next?"

"To give you some idea of the bullet that you all just dodged, at least for the time bein'," warned Wolf, "As of the last little episode – this was when we was all in the Canyon, mind you – well, that was the one that pushed her over the line, I guess that's how you'd say it. She was all set and prepared to... uhh... waste the whole fuckin' *country*, take it apart brick by brick, melt us all to slag... whatever. We, managed to get her to back off a bit – credit where credit's due, that was mostly my Russian *amigo*'s doin' –"

"Is that true?" queried a nervous Boatman, looking straight at Misha.

"We both *begged* the Storied Watcher not to make good on her most serious threat," answered the SVR-man. "And – as my good friend said – we *were* able to convince her to, uhh, *moderate* the amount of destruction that she will inflict on the United States... but she only agreed to this on a temporary basis. Hopefully there will be little or no loss of life... but if your foolish government keeps abusing the captives, especially 'Tommy' – I would not want to *see* what will happen then."

"*Shee-it*," muttered Hendricks.

"Just a second, Will," ordered Chu, "We don't –"

"Please listen to me now, FBI-agents," interrupted an agitated Misha, "*Whatever* happens to me – I am well aware of the fate of an unmasked spy – you *must* convince your government to, how do you say in English, 'lay off the captives', and sue for peace with the Storied Watcher! She is *far* past your ability to fight or defeat – the very *existence* of your nation – possibly my own as well – is at stake here!"

"That's pretty... *definitive*," offered the black agent.

"No *kidding*," added Chu. "But assuming – big 'ass, you and me', here – that this story is one hundred per-cent true, with nothing left out... what exactly, did the alien say that the President has to do *now*, to make her, uhh, back off? I'd remind you that she *did* have a chance to speak directly with him, back at the hotel, I mean... and that little dialog didn't turn out terribly well."

"You think that might have been because them spy-dudes in the dark glasses and the Men in Black suits, tried their best to *kill* her?" sarcastically retorted the bounty-hunter. "I don't know about *you*, lady – but I usually get a bit *impatient* with people who's firin' guns at me, or at civilians and bystanders. As that freak who got the whole ball rollin' by shootin' at Karéin, found out the hard way."

"The Storied Watcher has already made her terms quite clear, I believe," added Misha. "You would do well to act on them... and *quickly*."

After a few seconds of aghast silence, Chu remarked, "You know... the President would *never* agree to anything like what we've so far heard; apart from the fact that he'd have to sacrifice most of the Cabinet and the senior leadership of both the intelligence-agencies – possibly including the Director of our own FBI – and of the Armed Forces, he'd be completely *humiliated*, having to beg for his country, and maybe his own life, in front of this creature. *No* political leader could possibly survive such abasement – it's out of the question!"

"So I guess that counts as you *admittin'* that they're all *in* it – that is, all this shit about tryin' to pop the Storied Watcher, like them Feds do from time to time to the gangstas and the Muslims, as well as the bull that they're doin' to the salesman and his folk... right? Gotcha!" needled Wolf.

"I'm not 'admitting' *anything*, Wolf," shot back the woman. "I'm simply trying to outline reality for you. This historical record is clear – governments like ours *don't* back down, in situations like this. Think of the Cuban Missile Crisis, 9-11, or our response to the Pakistan thing –"

"We'll *see* about that," answered the big man. "Because there ain't never *been* no crisis like *this* – and our dumb-ass President ain't never dealt with anyone like Little Miss Flyin' Unguided H-Bomb, up there. From my point of view, the only interestin' thing is, 'how much of this here United States of America does she have to do the shake-'n-bake treatment on, before he gets it through his thick head that –"

The door flung open, revealing a look of combined fear and amazement on the face of the junior FBI station-staffer who confronted those in the room.

"Excuse me, Ms. Chu," he exclaimed, "But we got a TV-feed from up north – there's something that you'd better see... right *now*."

Bye-Bye, Mr. Lincoln

"This *live*?" queried a passer-by, as the downtown Boston crowd congregated around the department-store flat-screen, 3-D holo-TV display.

"*Think* so," suggested a rotund, matronly woman, reluctantly depositing her shopping-bags on the uncomfortably-warm pavement.

"What the fuck's *that*?" asked a street-vendor.

"Don't know – can't hear the audio... it's behind the window," complained the woman with the shopping-bags.

"Here – I got Disney News on my wrist-communicator," offered a smartly-dressed businessman, shooting his arm forward, revealing a watch-like contraption with a flexible fold-out screen, that immediately revealed a 3-D television signal with a voice-over.

Immediately, a crowd pressed in on the lucky ones who were close enough to see what was going on, on the screen.

Faintly – the speaker *was* the size of a shirt-button, after all – came the voice from the wrist-TV.

"Ladies and gentlemen," it announced, with an immediately-obvious sense of gravity, "We're bringing you the crisis that's now unfolding at Mount Rushmore National Monument, live – the situation's still somewhat confused... what's that, Ewell? Right – yeah, okay... yes, we've got the telephoto on screen, now –"

After a second or two, there was a cry of alarm.

"Oh my *God* – look at *that!*" intoned the anchorman. "Holy S*h* – the Washington statue? Oh, sorry – I stand corrected, that one was Jefferson – look out, here it comes again – wow, oh... *wow!* Ladies and gentlemen, just to bring you up to date, about five minutes ago, something – we're still not sure what – started to attack the National Monument; and so far, it has used some kind of, uhh, I don't *know* what, to destroy the statues of the Presidents, one by one – this weapon, if that's what it is, it's too bright to look at directly... it seems to be flying right at the Monument, then we see a deep gash being smashed through the face of a statue, then it just, uhh, falls *apart,* I guess that's how you'd put it... there's some kind of strange music playing in the background, on all local channels, by the way... yeah, okay – you got an update? Well... does the government have any comment at all?"

"Jesus!" breathed the street-vendor. "Bye-bye to *you*, Mr. Lincoln!"

"Shh!" admonished the shopper-woman.

The businessman whistled in awe.

"Okay... Phillips here again," babbled the announcer. "Yes, ladies and gentlemen... I'm afraid that what you're seeing is the end of a fine national treasure that has inspired and uplifted Americans for many years, now – I have to ask myself, 'who would engage in such a senseless act of vandalism' – what's that, Ewell?"

There was another short pause, and then the voice-over continued, "Well, thank God for *that*... uhh, folks, our man at the scene is reporting that to the best knowledge of the Park Service, there haven't been any casualties among the many tourists there... hold on... now *this* is incredible! Can you see this, ladies and gentlemen? It's uhh, *writing* something into the side of the mountain, where the statues of the Presidents were, until about a minute ago... listen, Ewell, can you make that out? Yeah, zoom in a bit more, if you don't mind?"

The on-site camera's field of vision narrowed, until the scene showed what was left of Mount Rushmore, with a brightly-glowing *something*, streaking back and forth, across the rock-face.

"Will you look at *that!*" gasped the announcer, "It's firing a yellowish beam of light – the rock's just *melting* underneath, as it goes up and down – yeah, okay, I think I can read it, now... I don't know, folks, this makes no sense at all, but so you can make up your own minds, I know it may be a bit hard to see from where you're watching – it says, 'FREE MY FAMILY, NOW'... no, wait, there's more, something else is being written underneath... okay, I can see this, too... it says, 'OR YOUR COUNTRY WILL BURN'. What the *hell?*"

"You figure out what's goin' down, man?" requested a Hispanic voice.

"Damn – must be the Muslims, I figure," argued someone. "We *fucked*, *hombre!*"

"Quiet! He's saying something else," noted the shopper.

"Okay, folks – we're going to show you the last part of this incident," said the announcer, "Roll tape... there it *is* – you can see this, uhh, thing, just shooting off the top of the screen, like a missile or something. Ewell – can you get any closer? Oh, I see... yes, just to explain to our audience, the Park Service and another government agency are now closing off access to the Monument... sure, get yourself out of there, no problem, good work there, Ewell."

The anchorman turned directly into the camera.

"Well, ladies and gentlemen," he concluded, "You've just seen a very unusual event, live and in 3-D color on the Disney News Channel, and to provide some background and analysis, we've gathered together our distinguished panel of science and terrorism experts –"

All of a sudden, the screen flickered and went blank.

The businessman shook his arm in a futile attempt to wake up the somnolent gadget, but to no avail.

"Yo!" shouted out someone from the periphery of the crowd, "All them TVs in the department, they done gone dead, too. Oh, wait a minute –"

When the businessman again regarded his wrist-display, for a second or two, there was just the familiar, mouse-hat test pattern of the Disney News Channel, along with its trademark slogan, "All The News That's Fit To Entertain"; but shortly, something else started abruptly playing : a scene from a light-hearted comedy, featuring the cheerful face of Blaine Maine, the entertainment mega-conglomerate's latest pre-teen starlet.

"We now resume with our normal program-schedule," stated a voice-over.

"Here, let me try another channel," muttered the businessman, as he fumbled with the too-small controls on the device.

"Will you look at *that*," complained the shopper-woman. "They've *all* got that stupid movie, playing, now."

No Deal, *Puto*

"*Caràjo*," cursed the stocky, sweating, bandanna-garbed Latino, as he spat and wiped his hands together to try to get the pressure-wounds out of them.

He looked at his companion in the twilight, in the endless sand-and-scrub about twenty meters behind a nondescript Texas roadside gas-station, its half-lit neon sign announcing, "Yes, we DO have gas and water, max 1 gallon each per vehicle".

The proprietor of this fine establishment – having discreetly gotten a quick look at the two tough-looking men camping out in the hinterlands behind the station – wisely put up a placard in the front window saying, "Closing In 15 Minutes, Back Tomorrow Morning".

"*¡La mierda, hombre!*" protested the short *bandito*. "That big box thing in the van – it weighs a *ton*. Pushed down the suspension so much I just about busted an axle when we went over that set of potholes, three miles back, at the junction. At least it got handles... without them, no way, *señor*. What the fuck's *in* that thing?"

"Don' know," indicated the other one, a taller man, as he rubbed his heavily-muscled, tattoo-bedecked biceps. "Came off the boat with the other shit – you know, that *yayo* that *el jéfé* gonna send up Chicago-way. It ain't the *usual* stuff, *that's* for sure – I hear somebody say that it's 'heavy weapons'... you know, even out things with the Man... but how they gonna get it to L.A. and the other places – don' ask me, *hombre*. All the big man tell me is, 'be at the gas *cantina* by 7:30 p.m.... so here I is."

"You mean it might be them new guns, rockets... *ese tipo de mierda?*" inquired the first thug. "We got all we need here... you seen what kind they are? Like maybe the ones that go right through that fuckin' armor they got on the cop-wagons these days?"

"*Yo no sabe, hombre*," remarked the second gangster, with an indifferent shrug. "It's sealed tight... welded, I think. I asked Roberto – you know he's the *compañero* who do the boat-runs – and he said there'd be some New York bangers who was gonna be by to pick it up, no later than tonight. But we ain't s'posed to let 'em even *see* it, until Emilio and his 817 posse get here to back us up, if there's any... *trouble*."

"Yeah... no shit," echoed the short gangster.

"*Bueno* – I'm ready, *con mi cuete*," he added, patting the artfully-hidden sub-machine-gun under his vest.

"*Calmese, hombre*... this is supposed to just be a business-deal... nothin' more," cautioned the taller man.

He bent over and pulled out a rolled-up bubble-gum wrapper and a short straw, but, at this, the other man complained, "Hey, *hermano* – you got some nose-drops? Don' be a pussy – come on, share it with your homies."

"*No hay problema*," replied the bigger gangster, in as friendly a tone as one would ever get from the likes of him.

"Plenty of *yayo* to go around, *compadre*," he amicably stated. "You know the drill, *hombre* – the 'snow', *el jéfé* got all he can use and then some, he don' mind if some of it go missin' – but the synth and the guns, *that* we gotta account for. Here, you can use my tube."

As he took a deep snort, his eyes closed in happy appreciation, the short gangster echoed the sentiment.

"*Yo soy* just a soldier, but I *love* the fringe-benefits you get for bein' a *Mara*, *es mi vida loca*, I been to the curb too much before," he commented. "Makes my fuckin' day go a little bit easier, *that's* for sure. *Pero oyeme, hombre*, I'm just curious – I mean, the guns, when we get 'em, and that's not too much, you know, 'cuz we can buy 'em right 'round the corner here, anyway – they usually don' wrap 'em up as tight as *that* box. Didn't nobody tell *el jéfé* what's in it? Reason I ask is – you know him, he don' like *nothin'* goin' through his turf, if he don' know *exactly* what it is. If he don' know, he don' get his cut... and I don' want to be the one who tell him, *usted lo sabe*?"

"I *hear* you, *hermano*," agreed the second gangster. "All I really know is – and I have this second-hand from that *cholo* who do the boat-runs – is, they got intercepted by one of them 'volunteer' Coast Guard yachts, just south of the coast, and it took some pretty big *mordida* – lot more than we usually pay for a regular delivery of the product – to make 'em look the other way. Ah... it don' mean shit to me, *hombre*... all I want to do is get this deal over with, get the fuck out of here and back to them three little *chicas* that I got waitin' back in the barrio... *comprende*?"

"*Claro que sì*," echoed the short man. "I only got two – but one of 'em's thirteen, and she's *muy caliente*... she *tight*, you know?"

"Ah, you got me beat there, *hombre* – fifteen was the best I could do," grinned the big gangster.

The two *Maras* shared a good old-fashioned belly-laugh, and then set about to waiting.

After a good half-hour more of idle talk, with the darkness falling over the East Texas desert rapidly, they saw three cars'-worth of headlights, and, following standard procedure, the larger man crept out of sight, while the shorter *Mara* gangster stood in the glare to confront whomever was in this convoy of vehicles.

"*Hòla*," he called out, squinting to make out shapes and faces. "*Mi nombre es Joaquìn. ¿Còmo se llaman*?"

"*Es mìo, Emilio, con el posse*," answered a voice from the lead car.

"*¡Amigo!*" replied the short thug. "*Yo ve al bandera*. Good to see you, *veterano*."

"*Sì*," agreed the voice. "*Hombre*, I hope we ain't late – them bitches from the East Coast shown up yet? *El jéfé* say, in no uncertain terms, that we was 'sposed to get here early."

"Nope... you ain't late," noted the short gangster. "We ain't seen *shit* since we got here. Park yourselves, *amigos*."

Rapidly, a group of eight more tough-looking Latino gangsters, most of them looking deceptively overweight, though – if the truth be known, most of it was muscle, not fat – exited from the convoy, then the leader issued an order to the three drivers who were left in the vehicles.

"*¡Que vamos, muchachos!*" he announced.

Each car did a quick turn and ended up as one part of a semicircle, with headlights, now turned off, lined up precisely so as to illuminate the van with the mysterious cargo.

"Okay, so we set up now," said Emilio. "Listen... did *el jéfé* tell you anythin' 'bout this deal?"

"No *hombre*," came the voice of the larger of the two original gangsters, as he briefly emerged from the shadows.

"*Hòla, Carlito,*" called the leader of the second *Maras* group. "Well... just before we goin', I get a message from him sayin' that them pussies from New York, they gotta pay in *gold* – that's the arrangement, none of this "guaranteed clean thousand-dollar-bills" shit – *el jéfé* get ripped off two weeks ago by them nigger Bloods down Houston-way, Secret Service used some fuckin' smart-chip shit to track the first cash-in down to our mules, it was a *mess, hombre*... whole payout went down the toilet. These East Coast *Norte 14 perritos*, they don't got the gold – an' I got some science-stuff on me, you just push the button and it tell you if it's the real shit or just bricks they painted up – an' they goin' *down*... *comprende*?"

"*Sì hombre*," growled the short gangster. "*¡Que à ellos vamos que dales duro!*"

"*Bueno*," directed Emilio. "But hopefully – this bein' a clean transaction – it not comin' to that. Yo... *usted tiene* some *yayo* there? Let yo' old *hermano* have a toot... okay?"

"*Por supuesto*," complied the short gangster, handing the nose-candy and its associated paraphernalia to the leader of the second group of *Maras*, who did two lines quickly, shaking his head with violent ecstasy as the cocaine-rush fortified his confidence.

"*¡No hay nada còmo este!*" he grunted in satisfaction. "It's *clean*, man – an' so you got to do a little curb service for it now and then, no big thing... that synth-shit – I don' trust it, you know? Fuck with yo' mind *permanente*... *comprende*?"

"*Còmo no*," confirmed the short guy. "Anythin' they make with them fuckin' computers, *hombre* – I figure the Man *gotta* be takin' his cut off us *cholos*, before it even hit the street. I hear from one of them LK'ers that the government makin' it themselves, they handin' it out to them nigger Crips n' Bloods when they wan' to stir things up on the street, fuck up the distributin' arrangements. Well... at least we got ol' *Señor Nieve* to fall back on. The Man got his ass thrown out all over *Suramèrica* – he ain't gonna get back into the supply-chain down there."

Emilio did not reply, this time, as he was in the clouds, already.

They settled down to more waiting, with a few of the less disciplined of this Texan branch of the *Mara Salvatrucha* playing Mexican *narco-trafficante mariachi*-music on their car-radios.

Finally, after perhaps an hour more – with the sun now completely below the horizon – one of the lookouts, who had been encamped on a car rooftop, shouted,

"*Veo una línea de tres coches, todos junto. ¡Pienso que es ellos, jefe!*"

Shaking himself not completely out of a cocaine-induced stupor, Emilio now commanded, "*Bueno muchachos – que tenemos nuestra fiesta. Ustedes saben la señal. Si digo que es sólida... después los dejamos alejarse. ¡Si digo que es amarilla – es tiempo para bailar!*"

"*Bueno*," confirmed a number of voices from hiding-places in the dark.

"You the shot-caller, *veterano*," he heard Carlito add to the chorus. "*Mi nueve* is ready to go."

Unsurprisingly, the next three minutes seemed longer than the previous hours all put together, but eventually, the three cars that the sentry had seen coming down the highway did, indeed, turn off the road and proceed to the meeting-place behind the building.

As they pulled into the open area, even in the darkness, the vehicles' tinted windows and garish bling, clearly marked them as something other than ordinary domestic automobiles; and several of the hidden *Maras* idly wondered how the newcomers had evaded what must have been repeated inter-state roadblocks and police-traps, in the trip from 'wherever', to the here and now.

Slowly, the three cars came to a full stop, with the largest one – a big, black SUV of some sort – in the front, and the two others in flanking-positions to each side, slightly behind.

Nobody got out. Instead, a voice, probably from a concealed exterior speaker, blared, "*¿Tienen ustedes el paquete especial que está para nosotros?*"

Joaquìn realized why Emilio was the leader – at least around here – as well as why he needed a little 'something' to fortify his courage; for it was *one* thing to welcome a fellow group of *Maras*, but something else entirely, to be the point-man against heavily-armed thugs from a different gang.

Especially, a gang from a long way away – one that they knew little about.

With the headlights of two of the *Mara Salvatrucha* cars painting his back, Emilio now boldly strode up into the lead vehicle's glare, and, staring straight forward at a counterpart who was still securely hidden behind the tinted glass, he replied, "*Posiblemente... si ustedes tienen el envío del oro que fue prometido al jefe.*"

"*Bueno*," came back a metallic voice from the car, and its doors started to slowly open, revealing the hulking shapes of another apparently-Latino gangster and his three bodyguards.

As these no-nonsense types slowly entered the illuminated area between the two facing-off car *laagers*, all of Emilio, Carlito and his shorter side-kick could instantly tell that these guys were not *Maras*, not *ALK*, not *Nuestra Familia*, not *Ñeta*, not even *G27* – not *anything* with which their branch of MS-13 were familiar; the demeanor, and the colors were all wrong.

There was not a single tattoo visible, anywhere on them.

It was unnerving.

I don' get what he's flashin'... and 'unknowns' my bad for a gangsta, mused Emilio.

Bueno... get the gold, give them this fuckin' heavy piece of shit, get outta here pronto... go back an' do a little well-deserved machinin' with my cute little toss-up back in the barrio.

The *Mara* walked up to a point almost close enough to look the other leader in the eye. The man was maybe slightly more than his height, with a crooked nose and an oddly long beard, and he had a weird, quizzical stare to go along with it.

Three muscle-bound, shaved-head bodyguards, each also bearded, stood behind this man. It was no secret that they were heavily – if discreetly – armed.

"I'll be doin' most of this transaction mostly in English, yo'," offered Emilio. "Less chance of any... misunderstandin's... *comprende*?"

"Acceptable," answered the other man, with an accent that the gangster couldn't quite place. "Where is it?"

"Over here, in the van," indicated the *Mara* right-hand soldier. "An' listen, *cholo* – I know you'se packin'... es *bueno*, but we got everythin' covered... *comprende*?"

The other lead-gangster just nodded, first giving some kind of 'stay put' signal to the other two cars, then giving a different wave to his bodyguards, who joined him in following Emilio to the van containing the unknown object.

The *Mara* opened the rear-door of the van, revealing the strange, heavy container within it.

"There she is, *muchachos*," he said, with an indifferent shrug. "You wan' examine it?"

The long-bearded man just motioned to one of the bodyguards, who pulled an odd-looking instrument – akin perhaps to one of those new-fangled digital tire-pressure gauges – out of his jacket-pocket.

This guy entered the van, searched around the side of the box and then inserted the instrument into what must have been a small opening in the side of the container. He examined the LED-display on this tool, turned his head and nodded to the leader of this strange other gang.

Carajo, considered the semi-concealed Joaquìn, from the shadows.

Could have sworn *there ain't no holes in that thing.*

Where the fuck *they hide one?*

I could have put my eye up to it, seen inside...

"We are satisfied that you have brought the correct goods," remarked the East Coast gang-leader. "Back up this vehicle into the middle-area that is in the lights... we will back our own behind it, so the package can be transferred from the one to the other."

"Whoa – *espera por un minuto, amigo*," countered Emilio. "We got a little matter of *el dinero*... you know? You bring it up here into the lights, we count it, we got a few little *pruebas* of our own that we got to do... *si todo sea aceptable*, we shake hands, all get back to the *barrio – comprende*?"

The other gang-leader just stared at the *Mara* gangster for an uncomfortable few seconds, then slowly stated, "That can be arranged."

Again, he gave an unfamiliar hand-signal, and, a few seconds later, a rear-door on one of the two other vehicles of his convoy opened, revealing a fourth bodyguard, big, bearded and surly like his three counterparts. This man was carrying a brushed-aluminum suitcase, as he walked briskly toward and into the headlights.

"Here it is, as requested by Don Morales – ten million," mentioned the Eastern gang-leader.

"Open it," demanded Emilio.

"You don't *trust* us?" replied the other man, in a subdued, but surly, tone.

The *Mara* lieutenant just smiled.

"Open it," ordered the other gang-leader, to the man carrying the suitcase.

The bodyguard strode forth, un-clicked a few catches on the handle side of the suitcase, and held it up to the light, causing a flash, as the sheen of gold bricks reflected into the Texas desert night.

"Just like we promised," commented the Eastern leader.

"*Bueno*," answered Emilio. "*Para comenzar*. I just got *una poca prueba* to do here, *muchacho*."

He retrieved his own strange-looking, pseudo tire-gauge instrument and held it up in front of the other gang-leader.

"*You* don' mind... do you?" he queried.

The other man nodded affirmatively, but in so doing, he shot a quick glance toward one of his bodyguards, to no apparent effect.

Fumbling more awkwardly than he'd have wanted to – for all the while, Emilio knew that he had to keep one eye on the other group, reading their body-language, which was already making him more than a little uneasy – he clicked a switch, and a pencil-thin beam of light issued from one end of this small contraption, striking a gold brick inside the suitcase but not reflecting much off it.

The *Mara* lieutenant looked at the read-out.

"AU-79 CONFIRMED", it indicated.

"Hmm... *es bueno*," said the gangster.

But check two or three of them, he remembered the instructions, from the *Mara Salvatrucha South-West jéfé*.

You don' *fuck with the Don, Emilio* said to himself.

Not if you want your balls and your tongue, still attached, by the end of the day.

"Jus' bein' *thorough, usted lo sabe,*" he temporized, while sweeping the light-beam across the gold bricks, striking two or three more in turn.

"AU-79 CONFIRMED" came back once, twice; then, just as the gangster was about to do the third brick, as he maneuvered the beam from the second ingot to the one next to it, going over a very thin gap in the process, the instrument's display showed something different.

"5-LAYER EU CURRENCY, GENUINE", it read.

"Yo!" grimaced the *Mara,* quickly returning the testing-gauge to his pocket and mentally recalling his quick-draw technique, as he spoke. "Hey *perritos,* you wan' to pull out them top three bars there? Yeah, those ones – I gotta see down to the bottom of the case."

"There a *problem?*" demanded the Eastern gang-leader. "This has *already* taken too much time."

"I'm not seein' gold all the way down," complained Emilio.

"Five million in gold, one half-million in Euro-verified bank-notes, equivalent to five million U.S.," retorted the other gang-leader. "That was the agreement."

"*Y que*? I don' think so, *perrito!*" shot back the *Mara* gangster, backing off by four or five paces. "*El jéfé* give me *clear* orders – it *all* gonna be in gold, or no deal. He already been racked up over that Dead Presidents shit... an' he ain't doin' no more of it. Tell you what – same place, same time, next week, you come with *el oro,* everybody kickin' it, we do business. *Comprende?*"

Emilio turned and started to walk away, saying a silent prayer that the other group couldn't see the cold sweat on his brow.

Chill, cholo, *keep it together,* he reflected, as he considered where he would dive to.

Fuck them – gonna be gettin' off the gate, any second...

"We can't let that happen," the *Mara* heard the other gang-leader say, as he had almost made it to the rear left side of the van, the two halves of its back door still open.

"The package is... *essential,*" the Eastern gangster demanded, his voice rising. "We can send one of our cars back to get the payment converted, but this may take time. We can wait here. So can *you.*"

"You *loc, vato?*" protested Emilio, half-turning so as to see the Eastern gangsters. "You can't be chillin' out here in daytime – neither can me 'n my *hermanos* – we stick out like a fuckin' big bright sign with '*cholos aqui*' all over it... might as well just walk down to the station an' make things easy for the Man. No way, *hombre!* We doin' the ghost, *pronto.*"

Breathing heavily, the *Mara* lieutenant stepped forward, his over-shoulder gaze still on the other man, who was slowly backing up toward his own vehicle-*laager,* with a weird, glassy stare issuing from his eyes.

Emilio was now within jumping distance of the van. He took a last glance, just in time to see two of the other gang's bodyguards starting to move their arms to reach inside their vests.

"Hey *puto*," shouted the *veterano*. "*¿Usted es amarillo?*"

He dove for cover, reflexes practiced the hard way, time after time, now his best defense.

Wild gunfire erupted from both directions, as if on cue.

"*¡Mátelos todos, muchachos!*", came a yell from the *Mara* side of the battle.

Shots pinged from the car-body and the thing inside the van, and for a few brief seconds, Emilio thought that he had literally dodged the bullet – but then he let out a combined curse and moan, as an agonizing rush of pain issued from his left leg.

It felt like his foot had been bitten off by a shark.

Sweating and swearing – with blood pouring out of his boot – he managed to crawl underneath the van and pivot, so he could see the carnage going on above and behind. He retrieved his gun and unlocked the safety, pointing it toward the lighted area, although by now only a few headlights remained functional.

The scene was every bit as ugly as this gangster had ever seen, with bodies – most of them riddled by multiple bullets – spilling blood all over the otherwise-cool Texas desert sand.

As near as Emilio could tell, to his relief, it appeared as if his *compadres* were slowly winning the battle, with the faint traces of two or three *Maras* using time-tested street fighting techniques to flank the enemy gang, on both sides; the others appeared to be pinned down in and around their vehicles, although they were still shooting hard and fast.

The mysterious Eastern gang-leader – having taken at least three shots to the chest – lay on the ground, his head propped up only by the body of the guard who had previously held the money-suitcase, its precious contents now alternatively glittering on the ground and wafting off in the soft breeze.

Somehow, the long-bearded man still had enough life left in him to raise a feeble finger and then shout an invocation, its words hard to make out but definitely neither in English nor Spanish.

A second later, the lead vehicle of the enemy gang gunned its engine, heading straight toward the back of the van containing the strange box.

Carajo! cursed the *veterano*, as he tried desperately to shuffle out from under the van that he had, a few seconds ago, hoped would protect him. But he could hardly move his shot-up leg, and he was moving much too slowly to get very far.

"*¡Emilio está por debajo la furgoneta!*" he heard someone shout.

It sounded like Carlito.

The rest of the East Texas *Maras* opened up on the SUV with everything they had – a fusillade that would have shot any lesser automobile instantly to pieces; but *this* one must have been well-armored, because it simply shrugged off the cop-killer slugs and barreled forward like a juggernaut, its big tires crushing the life out of the Eastern gang-leader and his fallen bodyguard, as it bore down on the back of the van.

A second before it hit, Emilio had the presence of mind to cross himself.

Orgulloso morir como un gángster – con mi arma en mi mano, he reflected, a strange sense of peace and pride resting upon him.

And the last thing that he *heard*, before a huge explosion – a conflagration that, he would never realize, could have been much, *much* more destructive – lit up the East Texas sky, was a phrase now all-too-familiar, to even the least-informed of Earth's human inhabitants.

Allahu Akbarr! it screamed, a half-second before Emilio went to the next life.

All The President's Yes-Men

"So... what are our options? On the PR front, I mean," muttered the President, again addressing the crowd in the bunker via secured video-link, from his vantage-point above the clouds, in the unmarked jumbo-jet that now served as an *ersatz* Air Force One.

"I don't know if you've yet seen the press-speculation, sir," stated Bezomorton, "But there is already a widespread rumor that the Muslims have somehow seized control of the 'Sword of Freedom' weapon that we had – err – been claiming to have in our own arsenal. It's already gone viral on *MyTubeSpace* – and although the Anti-Subversion Office is of course deleting the videos involved as they show up, some of them are bound to escape our attention – after all, we only have about 15,000 full-time staff on internal censorship duty. And it gets worse..."

"How could *that* be?" complained the President, his voice weary.

"I'll show you, sir," replied the National Security Adviser.

Bezomorton hit a button on a recessed panel, directly in front of him on the bunker conference-room table. Immediately, an apparently cam-corded, hand-held still frame, showing a scene with a black-suited... *someone*, standing in front of a crowd, with a long, low concrete structure, adorned with faintly discernible writing in the background.

"*This*," he noted, "Is probably our more immediately serious public propaganda issue, sir. May I run it?"

"Do I have a choice?" weakly joked the U.S. leader.

"That's why they pay us the big bucks, having to rub elbows with the Great Unwashed at election-time... as well as to have to watch crap like *this*," replied the Vice-President, from down in the bunker.

"My bucks aren't worth anything, anymore, anyway," moped the President. "But I suppose I got to. Okay, John... roll it."

The President in the airplane, and the rest of his at-pleasure courtiers, as well as a few others, below, now both silently beheld the video that had been taken in front of the entrance to Mount Rushmore National Monument, starting with a few jerky shots of the brilliant figure of Karéin-Mayréij streaking over the parking-lot of the place, then progressing to the alien's speech in front of the crowd. The ground-level home video had apparently been appended by other eye-witness recordings, showing the Storied Watcher's destruction of this American icon, at relatively close range.

"Jesus H. Christ," *breathed* the President, as the presentation ended. "How long has this been out on NeoNet?"

"At least 24 hours, sir," explained Bezomorton, professionally. "Here again, we've pulled the plug on it as best we can... but – short of completely shutting down NeoNet – a move that I think we now have to *seriously* consider, despite the substantial effect that action might have on commerce –"

"Like, 'shutting down whatever little domestic commercial activity we still have *left*, after closing the borders to foreign-trade'," interrupted the Treasury Secretary.

"NSC's well aware of that, and we aren't suggesting something like this, lightly," retorted Bezomorton, "But as we all know, an *unprecedented* situation is now upon us. I'm not going to debate the pluses or minuses of it here – I just wanted the President to know that it's an option."

"I hate to sound like a broken record," interrupted Kaysten, "But about the Muslim angle –"

"It'll never fly," countered McPherson. "Pun intended."

"Well... okay," amicably replied the Chief of Staff. "I guess I'm just in the habit of blaming the Muslims for *everything* – down to and including having my steaks ending up being overdone on the BBQ."

A few laughed at this *bon mot*, and the President added, "You aren't the *only* one who's been thinking that way," to more chuckles from the table down in the Earth-side bunker.

"Jerry – you try to figure out some kind of plausible cover-story," he requested, "But in the meantime, we've got to consider the real problem... namely, what the hell do we *do* with this damn ' Karéin' creature? Arthur... what's the state of DoD's intelligence-gathering against the alien?"

"We *have* been making some progress, sir," replied DeWitt, as he opened a previously-sealed set of documents. "First of all... there's now no serious doubt that the creature *is* deliberately trying to suppress its energy-signature – I just wish *we* had a stealth capability like *that*, frankly. That said, we now have some confidence that we *can* track 'Karéin' – at least while it's flying at hypersonic-speed – meaning that, in theory at least, we *can* use this capability to use guided munitions against the alien. This is, in my opinion, a significant improvement in our tactical situation."

"How?" asked an evidently startled McPherson. "Are you tracking her, I mean."

"Well, at first, it was giving off an IR-signature that we could hardly *miss*," explained the Defense Secretary, "But later, it just dropped off the scope – showing pretty convincingly that the alien *is* masking its track... and very effectively. However, it seems that it can't completely escape the basic laws of physics. When it accelerates to speed – around Mach 3.7 or so – it starts to give off a faint thermal-signature... even if it's invisible to radar. The heat-trail is far less prominent than it *should* be – somehow, it's like about 98 per cent of that heat-energy is just going into a 'black hole' of some kind – but the other two per-cent *is* leaking out, and we think that we can home some missiles in on *that* little oversight on the alien's part. With any luck, when it next tries the vandalism-trick, we should be able to shoot it out of the sky."

The Science Adviser just sat there, ashen-faced, but the President inquired, with less than what one would have expected in the way of excitement, "You don't *say*... well, *that's* good news. Tell me... what types of weapons could you use for that?"

"We're swapping out the ordinary AR heads on our AIM-145 air-to-air missiles, the type that we use on our stealth-fighters, in favor of some field-modified, multi-band IR-seekers, as we speak, Mr. President," interjected Air Force General Harry Anderson, with typical gruff, military confidence. "Even a near-miss by one of these weapons within – say – fifty feet of the target, we believe, ought to cause fatal damage to the alien. And note that we wouldn't just be using *one* missile... the idea would be to saturate the creature with as many as we can get within range."

"What about nukes?" interrupted the Vice-President. "We got any nukes that we can fry her with?"

"You have *such* a way of putting that, sir," offered Bezomorton.

"Well... *somebody's* got to say it," argued the Vice-President.

"The long and short of *that*, sir," remarked Anderson, speaking in cool, measured tones, "Is that while we now *do* have three nuclear weapons in our arsenal, and while we're on a crash program to enrich sufficient fissile-materials so as to rebuild the rest of our pre-'Lucifer' inventory... even the smallest, lowest-yield thermonuclear weapon, isn't compact enough to fit into the very restricted form-factor of an air-to-air missile. This would have been the case even *before* 'Lucifer', and the only bombs that we have been able to put together since then, can't be carried by anything smaller than a strategic cruise missile."

"Furthermore," he went on, "The alien is a small, *highly* agile target, with – as far as we can tell – reasonably good situational threat-awareness capabilities; it would probably see a large, slow missile like a nuclear-armed cruise, coming from far away, and would then just zip off somewhere else. But we do have another 'secret weapon – namely the 'hard-kill' lasers deployed aboard our airborne ABM-systems... the energy-beam on this weapon is capable of cutting an incoming ICBM warhead in half – so if we can bring it to bear against our opponent, it's a 'look-shoot-kill' situation, in our opinion."

"*Impressive,*" commented the President, "Especially if we could combine it with... but, anyway... for the time being, I want to be clear on something – under *no* circumstances do I authorize the use of nuclear weapons against the alien, if the engagement is to take place on or over American soil. Apart from the chance of accidentally vaporizing one of our own cities, the public might take it as a Muslim bomb, even if it went off over an unpopulated area... there'd be panic, for sure. Harry – do we have any idea of where the alien is, now, after the Rushmore fiasco?"

"Sort of, sir," replied the General. "After it attacked the National Monument, it did a quick 'pop-up' maneuver, as if it were assessing the tactical situation, checking for signs of an imminent attack on our part – of course, due to the surprise nature of the situation, we were in no way prepared to deploy any significant assets in the area – then, it again descended to very low altitude and streaked off in a north-easterly direction. We lost the trail just as it entered Michigan airspace."

Now, McPherson seized the floor.

"Excuse me, Mr. President," he remarked, "But – even though I'm sure I won't win any popularity-contests around here for raising this issue – I need to point out that there *is* another option that we haven't considered here."

"And *that* would be...?" queried the American leader.

"Well... why don't we just airlift this 'Billings' guy and the rest of these people who she's so interested in, up to the mountain that she specified?" proposed the Science Adviser. "Why the hell don't we simply do what she *asks*? How hard can it be? I mean, by Karéin's own words, 'they're just a bunch of ordinary people' – it makes no sense *whatsoever* to risk the safety of the whole *country*, over a salesman, an African-American woman and three kids! I've yet to hear a sensible reason why we don't do this, and then deal with the other issues later... when she's had a chance to cool off and come to her senses."

"We *don't* give in against terrorism, or appease people who threaten to destroy us – remember?" sneered the Vice-President, in McPherson's direction.

"The matter is academic, anyway," commented the indifferent-sounding voice of the CIA director. "We don't even *have* 'Billings' and the rest of the alien's supposed 'family'. Don't you think that would have been our first course of action, if we *did* have these civilians?"

The President tried to hide his wince, upon hearing this lie.

"*Wait* a minute," argued an obviously suspicious Science Adviser. "We showed a live video-feed of the 'Billings' group to the alien, at the hotel, just before everything went south, at that event. What seems to have set Karéin off, in that situation, was that she accused you of trying to 'fake' having the 'Billings' group at your disposal – the point is, either we *do* have them or we *don't*... or are these 'fakes' all we've really got? Mr. President – if you want us to give you worthwhile advice on what to do with the alien, we've got to know exactly what the *truth* is, here!"

Unexpectedly, Ochoa now jumped back into the discussion, stating, "While I don't necessarily want to support Mr. McPherson's plans to go 'how high' when the alien says 'jump', sir, I think it would be very helpful to the Bureau, also, if we knew the facts. From a field investigations point of view, that is."

With an eyebrow unsubtly arched at the CIA director, the U.S. leader replied, "I'm afraid, Fred, Cesar, that for reasons of national-security, there are some rather... *strict* limits on what I can say to the Cabinet, on this matter. I *can* confirm that the individuals portrayed to the alien over the video-link to the Tucson hotel, were *not*, in fact, the original, authentic 'Billings' group. Beyond that... I'm afraid there's not a lot more that I can add."

"Is that because I'm under *suspicion*, here, sir?" shot back McPherson.

"No – of *course* not, Fred," quickly answered the President. "This has nothing to do with you personally. It's simply that we're trying to keep a few of our plans regarding the alien, limited to certain people, on a 'need-to-know' basis... come *on*, none of this is new – it's 'standard operating procedure'... that's all."

"Well... if that's how it's going to be, then I guess that's how it's going to be," muttered an exasperated McPherson, throwing up his hands in mock defeat. But a second later, he pressed on, saying, "Well then – what about Jacobson and *his* crew? The Mars mission team, I mean... why not enlist *them* to talk to the alien, on our behalf?"

"Fred... you already *know* why we can't do that," protested the President.

"What do you *mean*, sir?" interrupted Ochoa. "Are we facing a contamination-issue, here?"

"No... not *exactly*," evaded the President. "I'm afraid I can't go into any more depth on this situation, either."

The FBI director was not the only one to show a suspicious, puzzled look, upon hearing this.

"Yes... I *do* know," indicated McPherson. "And I'm aware of the risks. It just seems that in view of the situation that's unfolding right now, the risks of *not* using all our available assets, are considerably higher."

"I'll take it under consideration," mentioned the President. "But don't get your hopes up."

The silence in the air was now so thick that even the Storied Watcher's vaunted side-sword would be challenged to cut it; but, eventually, the American leader again spoke up.

"Listen, everyone – we've more or less talked this subject to death, by now," he opined. "Just so we're all on the same page – John, Arthur, if the alien surfaces again, you have my authorization to try to shoot it down, subject to the following conditions : one, *no* use of nuclear weapons; two, if it tries to hide in a heavily-populated area, such that significant collateral-damage might result even from a conventional strike, there is to be *no* such attack, without me first being advised of the tactical situation, and then me giving my okay; and three, if the alien leaves our airspace, conditions one and two don't apply. You got that?"

"Copied and understood, Mr. President sir," confirmed DeWitt, with a nod, for his part, from Bezomorton.

"What if it flies over Toronto, or Monterrey, sir?" quibbled Hyndman. "What are we going to do, drop an atom bomb on a Canadian or Mexican city?"

"To paraphrase a famous Secretary of Defense," snickered the Vice-President, "'Stuff happens'".

"We'll cross *that* bridge when we come to it, Jacob," answered the President. "All I'll say for the moment is, 'my duty is to preserve and protect *American* lives... not those of foreigners'. I'd expect the Canadian and Mexican governments to understand that."

"Easy for us to say, when it's *us* nuking *their* cities, and not the other way around," unhelpfully muttered McPherson.

"Two other things on the agenda," continued the President, obviously trying to change the subject. "First – we need to discuss the status of the Pakistan bomb situation; second, can whoever's in charge of it, please make sure that the link stays up after everyone else vacates the bunker down there – I have something that I have to discuss with CIA... and the rest of you will appreciate that this is a national-security issue... so I'll have to ask you all, except the Director, to find your own way out... okay?"

"Okay," unenthusiastically answered a number of them.

"Shouldn't NSC be involved?" complained Bezomorton.

"In theory, and in the fullness of time, yes," replied the President. "In practice, and in the near term, no... I'll brief you later, John."

The National Security Adviser stewed, with mistrust all over his face.

"Very well, then," said the American leader. "So what about the 'loose nuke' problem – any updates on *that* front, gentlemen?"

"Only anecdotal things," offered the CIA director. "We were working on a possible connection through the Québec New Republic last week, we passed the information on to the Navy – Admiral, I believe that one came back as a negative... am I right?"

The normally-quiet Halford now spoke up.

"That's correct, Mr. Director," he reported. "The missile-destroyer *U.S.S. R.H. Limbaugh III* intercepted a vessel, name of *Le* Petit *Québec Libre*, that outwardly resembled an oceanic dragnet fishing-boat, just inside the three-way disputed waters in the Gulf of St. Lawrence. It attempted to outrun us on a track back to Natashquan; but after a few warning-shots, it came to, we boarded it, and although it *was* loaded with light weaponry – automatic-rifles, machine-guns, land mines, even some gas and a few ATGMs and MP-SAMs... there weren't any nukes on board."

"So what'd we do with all the guns and so on?" idly asked the President.

"Oh... we let the ship go, of course," replied the Admiral. "No business of ours – Canadians complained no end... but that's really between them and the New Republic, after all."

"Well what the hell do they need with all that battle-gear?" said the President. "The Frenchies, I mean."

The CIA director answered, this time. "Our sources tell us that the weapons are probably meant to reinforce the New Republic's volunteer army – don't know if you remember, but they're fighting a low-end counterinsurgency campaign against the Indians and Eskimos in the northern part of Québec. They can't afford heavy weapons – their economy has kind of been in the toilet, ever since they declared independence from Canada."

"There *is* someone who's doing worse than we are?" came an anonymous voice, from the bunker-table.

"Never could figure out football on three downs... but anyway, no other news – am I right?" inquired the President, looking at Ochoa.

"No sir," said the FBI director. "Not on the 'loose nukes' file, that is – we have a lot of leads and some background-chatter – none of it of very high quality, in our opinion."

Now, Ochoa's visage measurably darkened, as he added, "I should mention, however, that developments aren't very good on the Southern California front – we've been able to take back some of the suburbs... but even with reinforcements from the Army and the Guard, we're *far* too thin on the ground to push much further toward central L.A. Frankly... some of our analysts are recommending that we simply sit tight and let the *Maras*, the Crips and the Bloods wear each other out... there are reports of scores of casualties being taken by each of the gangs, every day. Of course there's no medical care to speak of, as all the hospitals are basically barricaded-up."

"Sounds good to *me*," quipped the Vice-President. "Can we at least take back Beverly Hills and Bel Air?"

"Those two areas are currently under the control of GreyWar Corporation, apparently with the active co-operation of the 'White Aryan Resistance' and elements of the Klan – that's also true of much of Hollywood," explained Ochoa. "They're doing a passable job of defending property – but beyond *that*, well... we have reports of minorities – mostly Hispanics and African-Americans – being thrown into swimming-pools containing pet sharks and alligators, being used as bait in dog-fighting contests, being, uhh, 'impaled' on the tops of flagpoles, and, if you can believe this, they're making kids as young as *seven* –"

"We get the picture, Cesar," interrupted the U.S. leader. "Keep me advised... okay?"

"Yes, sir," answered the FBI director.

"Okay, folks," said the President, "We're already running over time here, so the economic-stuff will have to be pushed to our next meeting. Unless anyone has other issues to raise, I'll call an adjournment for today... for all of you except CIA, that is. Anything else?"

All he saw was a room full of shaking heads and polite silence. "Very well, then... thanks, everyone. Let's get going on the PR-stuff as soon as we can, we're working against the clock on that front. Dismissed."

We Report To Ourselves, Sir

One by one, the people in the bunker shuffled out, leaving the President apparently alone with the CIA director.

"Listen," started the American leader, "I wanted to tell you... I'm having second thoughts about this 'One-Two-Punch' idea that we discussed. At least for the time being."

The CIA director sat in stony silence for a few seconds, then replied, "And why would *that* be, sir?"

"Two reasons," explained the President. "First, we owe it to DoD to let them have their shot at the alien – Arthur seems reasonably confident that the Air Force might be able to drop 'Karéin', using just the weapons currently at their disposal... you heard him, yourself. If we could do *that*, we could preserve the lives of Commander Jacobson and the Mars mission crew, and doing that is *very* important, from a national-security point of view –"

"I'm afraid I don't understand," countered the CIA director. "While no doubt the Government has invested significant resources in their recruitment and training – and while explaining their permanent disappearance would cause some public relations issues – they're just a bunch of Armed Forces personnel, after all... we lose *lots* of soldiers, every day. What makes Jacobson and so on, so special?"

"Let's just say," stated the American leader, as he tried to hide how much he relished knowing facts that his country's most feared secret police agency was apparently ignorant of, "That these former astronauts are considered by the Pentagon, as a *key* military asset. There are reasons behind this, that I can't go into, right now."

"With all due respect, sir," argued the CIA director, "I think that you really *should* – that is, explain what's doing on, to myself, right here, right now. The essence of Operation One-Two Punch is correct *timing*, between when we initiate the, uhh, 'procedure' on the Billings group, and when we – if necessary – do the same on the Mars mission astronauts. If anything interrupts that timing, or – worse still, that would imply we're to get less than complete co-operation from other branches of the Government – the entire *plan* could fall apart. If you'll just *tell* me the facts here, then CIA would be pleased to –"

"I've *already* informed you of the situation!" retorted an irritated President. "Certain facts concerning Jacobson and the rest of his group, are considered to be a National Command Authority only, military secret – that's the bottom line. You'll have to work with the others only, for now. Do you *understand*?"

"Well – that may be a *challenge*, sir," replied the CIA director, his monotone even more frustrating than usual. "Under the authority that you delegated to me as of our last conversation, a sequestration order has been issued to have the Mars mission group taken to a secure holding-facility – the same one, as a matter of fact, where the Billings group is being kept. My understanding is that Jacobson and the rest of the astronauts should either be there already, or should be arriving shortly –"

"Then *countermand that order!*" demanded the U.S. leader. "Get Jacobson and his people out of there, *immediately* – you can return them to the Air Force facility where they were previously being held, and make sure that General Anderson is made aware of their return – you *got* that?"

"I don't think that would be... *advisable,* sir," contradicted the CIA director. "There are logistical issues associated with aborting the mission; and if Jacobson, Boyd, White and Tanaka have already been delivered to the facility, they're probably aware of some of our... *special* interrogation-procedures, by now. That knowledge could prove to be *highly* problematic, if they were later to be released and were to tell the media. You have to *appreciate* – this is a facility built like a 'roach-motel', that is, 'you check *in*, you don't check –'"

"*Look,*" half-shouted the President, "You don't seem to be getting the *message* here – I'm not interested in excuses, I simply want the Mars mission astronauts put back under *military* control, and I want that done ASAP – is there something unclear about my orders, here?"

"Mr. President... *Mr. President,*" unctuously cooed the CIA director, "I had hoped that we'd never have had to come to this point in our relationship... because when you and I work *together,* we're much more effective than when we work at cross-purposes."

He paused, with the slightest of a lick-of-the lips, and continued, "But with that said... we both need to understand and acknowledge certain basic facts. One – although I *do,* indeed, answer to yourself from a dotted-line perspective... need I remind you that institutionally, CIA has had almost *complete* autonomy in its operational procedures, for decades now. I'm afraid that the Agency can't allow an individual political leader to backtrack on that commitment, especially under the current, difficult circumstances –"

"Are you refusing a *direct* order by the *President of the United States?*" growled the American leader. "If so, you're asking to be fired, mister!"

"Oh... I wouldn't put it *that* way, sir," smiled the CIA director. "A more accurate description would be, I'm simply asserting the authority of the Agency to conduct affairs that are *clearly* under its exclusive jurisdiction, without our operational procedures being micro-managed by transitory political authorities, who aren't aware of the consequences of their demands. So let me explain the 'bottom line' from my perspective, sir : to put it crudely, 'you look after your back-yard, and I'll look after mine'. Is that clear?"

"*Here's* what's clear – as of right now, you're *fired!*" cursed the President. "I want you out of your office by the end of the day tonight."

"*Sir,*" chuckled the CIA director, "Aren't you forgetting about National Security Directive 23-179?"

"I have no interest in discussing this with you further," the President shot back. "You serve at my pleasure – like any other Cabinet-member – and as of ten seconds ago, that status has just been revoked! Hand over the keys to your office, to the Deputy Director, and tell him to give me a call, when that happens."

"Well, sir," explained the other man, with contempt clear in his voice, "You see, under NSD 23-179 – which, I don't know if you've been reading your secret National Security Council internal history-books, but feel free to check up on it, if you want – the President is *prohibited* from the non-voluntary removal of anyone in my position, or the Head of the Joint Chiefs of Staff, or the Secretary of Defense, for that matter, in a 'time of national crisis'... if memory serves me correctly, the rule was put in place to avoid a rogue President acting, ahh, 'intemperately', in a confrontation with a nuclear-armed foreign power."

The President fell momentarily silent, while the director elaborated, "I'd certainly say that having a lethally powerful alien flying around, combined with possible atomic terrorism, would count as such a 'crisis'... wouldn't you? This has been established precedent, for thirty or more years, now... and I believe the rest of the Agency and the NSC will back me up on it. In view of that, would you like to discuss how we can get back to working with each other, sir?"

"That's *bullshit!*" angrily shouted the President. "Even if there *was* such a directive – which I highly doubt – it was agreed to by a previous President, and it can be over-ruled by *this* President. I don't know what's so hard for you to understand about 'you're fired' – do I have to send the military and the Secret Service down to Langley to escort you out? Or do I have to explain the *consequences* of treasonable insubordination against your Commander-in-Chief?"

"I think you'll find," amicably countered the director, "That you'll have a hard time having that kind of an order *enforced*, sir. I'll tell you what... why don't we just 'agree to disagree', for the moment... and when you've cooled down, Mr. President, then we can get back in touch with each other and come to an understanding about the rules of engagement – that is, between the Agency and the Oval Office."

"Like I *said*," muttered the U.S. leader. "So we can keep this nonsense out of the media, I'll give you until sundown to clear out your desk quietly – and just to show you how forthcoming I am, I'll even instruct the Deputy Director to tell the public that you're still in charge. You want to 'discuss' things? If I find you sitting at that desk by tomorrow morning, our next discussion will be with you in a military brig. You *got* that?"

"This conversation is at an end, sir," concluded the CIA director. "But I'll leave you with one *other* thing, to consider, before you try to make good on all these demands. Namely, the track record, longevity-wise, I mean, of Presidents who have acted in a manner contrary to the Agency's interests... well, that hasn't been very *good* – you know? Just think back to that messy business that went down after 2016, and you'll see what I mean. Do you think what happened there, was an *accident?*"

"You *dare* to *threaten* – " inveighed the President.

But then, all of a sudden, the video-link went dead.

Unhappy Landings

"We *there* yet, Dad?" quipped ex-Mars-astronaut Devon White, repressing a yawn as he spoke, in a reprise of a joke he had made at another time, in a place very far away.

It was almost hard to hear him, over the poorly-muffled roar of huge jet-engines outside the cabin; but somehow, the newly-sensitive ears of the three others – or some other sense – could easily understand what he was saying.

"Beats me," offered Boyd, as he twitched and churned to try to shift the position of the over-tight seat-belts and cables that confined him in place. "It's been five hours, or more... I'd have thought that we'd be there, by now... wherever 'there' is, that is."

He fidgeted some more. "Man... these body-restraints drive me *nuts*," he complained. "I guess I had forgotten how they made the ones in *Eagle* and *Infinity*, ergonomically fitted to yours truly's *corpus delictus*."

"Well, it's a military transport – not first-class on U.S. American Air," reminded Jacobson. "But you're right... I can't figure exactly where we might be, but we've *got* to be landing soon – from almost any point in the continental United States, we could have been to almost any other point, by now. *Peculiar*, I'd say."

"*Damn* peculiar," echoed an obviously-worried Tanaka. "Unless we're going in circles, of course."

"Of course," said White. "Makes sense to me."

"No... it's not that," commented the former Mars mission commander. "We're out over sea... over the ocean, maybe."

"Pitch dark outside, and above the clouds, Commander," remarked Boyd. "How you know that?"

With a pensive look, Jacobson replied, "I just know, Brent... I just... *know*."

Boyd nodded, in mute acknowledgement.

"Hawaii, then?" proposed White. "Damn – and I forgot my surfboard."

"No," stated Jacobson. "North of that. Feels *cold* outside."

"Yeah," confirmed Tanaka, a distant look in her eyes. "Listen, Brent..." she started.

"Umm-hmm?" responded Boyd.

"Just wondering," inquired the woman, "Were you, Devon or Sam able to figure out exactly what Army, or Air Force, or... whatever, unit, those guys who loaded us on to this aircraft, belonged to?"

"Didn't get a good look at 'em, but something tells me that they aren't the real thing," replied the man. "Uniforms are all wrong... and aren't Marines supposed to have a shave each morning? Commander – how about you?"

"Your guess's as good as mine," parried Jacobson. "Maybe Special Forces? I looked for recognizable insignia, too... but didn't see any..."

A second later, they felt a bank in the aircraft's path; then, it started to descend.

"Goin' down," commented White. "Any guesses as to where?"

"Beats *me*," said Boyd. "But the Captain's right. I can feel the outside environment too – and, we've *got* to be way north."

"Sam – what the *hell's* going on?" demanded the woman, her attractive, Eurasian face, querying the man, relentlessly. "I'm getting a very *bad* feeling about this."

"I have no idea," answered Jacobson. "And I don't mind the rest of you knowing... I've been *very* disappointed with the Air Force, regarding the amount of information that we've been receiving since – well – since we got back. This little field-trip could be considered the icing on the cake, I suppose."

"Yeah... you got *that* right, Commander," agreed the black ex-astronaut, his voice unusually subdued, now.

"Brace yourselves!" announced a voice over the transport's intercom. "Coming in for landing-pattern."

The former Mars astronauts were quiet for a minute or two, as the aircraft came down, its glide-path unusually steep, or so it seemed.

Boyd looked out the window.

"Socked in *tight*, the must be landing on instruments," he noted. "*Thought* I caught a glimpse of open ocean out there, though."

The transport bumped and rocked.

"Same here," confirmed White. "And for what it's worth... I sure wouldn't want to be tryin' to land this thing with *that* rainy pea-soup out there – bet y'all it'd be easier to land good ol' *Eagle* on *Mailànkh*."

"Funny how you put that," observed Tanaka, with a forced half-smile.

"In honor of, Professor... in honor of, don't you know," quietly added the black man.

Tanaka nodded, her eyes again, far away.

With an abrupt 'thump', the aircraft touched down, and their minds felt the surge of engine-power outside.

"Whoa," exclaimed Boyd. "Reversers on full bore. Must be a pretty short runway, for them to have to do *that*, right on landing-gear contact – especially considering how lightly-loaded this crate is... just us and that bunch of MPs, or whoever they are, in the back."

"Really bad feeling, now," whispered Tanaka, with a tinge of sweat on her face. "Really, really, *really* bad!"

"Yeah," answered White, the jocular stuff gone entirely from his demeanor. "Cherie –" he started, but his voice was cut off by a second announcement.

"Escort team – stations!" it barked. "Jacobson crew, prepare to disembark. No discourse allowed from this point on. You are to speak *only* when directed to do so. Eyes forward, no questions. Ten seconds allowed to retrieve your gear. That's all."

"I *love* the Air Force," muttered Boyd, but he saw Jacobson's 'shush' gesture, and stopped.

Mutely, all four of the former Mars mission crew grabbed duffel-bags and backpacks, as the aircraft finally shuddered to a full stop.

Scarcely before they could look up, they were half-surrounded by a team of ten or more big, heavily-armed guards in desert-issue camouflage-uniforms, blocking any route backwards into the cargo-hold.

"Front exit," one of them, probably a sergeant, ordered.

Jacobson stood, saluted the man, gestured "come on" to his team, and proceeded to the front egress-hatch.

Gingerly, he stepped down the stairway, and – obeying the letter but not the spirit of the commands that he had just overheard – he surveyed the scene as he descended.

The air was cool, bordering on cold – and sodden, and it was made worse by a half-gale-force wind; but although Jacobson was clad only in a thin prison-issue uniform, this bothered him not in the least.

The terrain past the runway – no, "landing-strip" would have been a better description, the thing was clearly far too small to have been anything like what you'd find at a major airport – was almost uniformly tundra-like, with only a few rolling hills visible in between patches of near pervasive surface-level fog.

Once the three men and one woman had reached the tarmac, they were quickly flanked by the guards. Their leader – a sergeant, as near as could be told – shouted out, "This way!"

There was a military transport-truck waiting. To its front and rear were two similar vehicles, apparently intended as an armed escort.

"In the back," ordered a guard.

"Where are we *going* –" demanded Tanaka; but she stopped talking as several of the MPs, or whatever they were, began to aggressively brandish weapons.

Reluctantly, the four ex-astronauts clambered aboard.

The back of the olive-khaki-colored, but otherwise unmarked, vehicle *did* have rudimentary, un-cushioned sitting-benches on either side; but, other than for a canvas top, it was well-nigh open to the elements. As it began to head off down a rough-hewn gravel road, all of them could immediately feel the clammy chill of the maritime air of this place – although, strangely, the cold did not really produce any serious discomfort.

Anxiously, Tanaka opened her arms and shook her head, in a "what the hell" gesture, toward the others. White just shrugged and Boyd did more or less the same.

For the next fifteen to twenty minutes, they silently remained like this, as the truck careened back and forth on the winding road, scarcely at ease while searching for any sign of civilization, in the barren, lichen-and-wildflower landscape that they could see behind them.

Eventually, the vehicle came to a stop, and the leading guard barked another order.

"Disembark!" he shouted. "Rules will be *strictly-enforced*! Any attempt to escape will be met with lethal force!"

The rear gate dropped and, one by one, Jacobson and his compatriots jumped to the ground.

The guard pointed to a low, nondescript building, looking more like a maintenance tool-shed than anything else.

Sam, came a familiar voice into his head, as he walked.

Can you feel the warmth, coming from all around us?

It feels like... energy... don't you think?

Weird, responded another, clearly that of White.

Not too much of it – and it's damn cold – but the little glow feels...warm.

Go figure.

I thought I saw 'GrayWar Legion' on one of those guys' uniforms, sent Boyd.

Figures. Next trip to Mars, they'll 'outsource' that to the effing mercs, too.

Acknowledged... but let's keep the mental chit-chat for when we really need it, Jacobson tried to broadcast.

Ten minutes from now, I figure, came back the mind of Boyd.

After a trip of perhaps a hundred meters or so, they were at the front of the building, a structure no more than fifty feet long by half that wide. There was a locked door, but the place looked empty, deserted; no light, or other sign of life, issued forth from inside.

"Put down your possession-bags," ordered the sergeant. "We'll handle them from this point on. Arms behind your backs!"

"Now look here, this has gone just about far enough –" protested Tanaka.

Instantly, a hand was roughly slapped over her mouth, and her arms were pinned behind her back. In no more than a second, they had handcuffed her.

Stunned, White and Boyd would have made a move; but – simultaneously – they were themselves set upon by two guards apiece.

"Hey, y'all – go *easy!*" attempted the black astronaut, as he was wrestled to the ground so he could be handcuffed.

"What's your *problem!*" shouted Boyd. "We weren't trying to resist!"

"Shut up, prisoner!" retorted the sergeant.

"A formal protest *will* be registered against this *outrageous* and inappropriate treatment!" growled Jacobson, as he tugged at the restraints : they had used inappropriately-small handcuffs, and the accursed things were digging into the flesh on his wrists.

"Mister," he angrily continued, "I hope you've got a damn good military defender, for your court-martial! That is – if whoever you work for, has any legal jurisdiction here, at all – which I doubt. You *do* know that false imprisonment of a commissioned officer of the Armed Forces, is a *capital* offense?"

The man laughed, derisively.

"I'll make a note of that, Commander," he mentioned. "But our directions come from as high up as you can *get*."

He stepped back and nodded to one of his subordinates.

"Bag 'em!" he commanded.

Headin' West, With *Un Gran' Regalo*

For purposes of this transaction, a more or less new vehicle – a plain "like-from-the-factory" white van, with appropriately-doctored license-plates – had been stolen to order, off the streets of Houston. It bounced and rumbled across the Arizona back-roads, each and every bump making the dark Hispanic eyes of the driver involuntarily wince.

"This would be a lot easier if *el jéfé* let us take the Interstate, you know, *hombre*," complained the *Mara*. "I can' do more than fifty, without losin' a wheel or an axle. That thing's fuckin' *heavy*, man!"

"*Usted* still good to drive?" asked the scar-faced Latino gangster in the passenger-seat. "Been three hours since the *Nuevo Mexico* border, *cholo*."

"*Necessito el yayo en unos minutos...* but I'm still fresh – *lo juro*," attested the driver.

"*Còmo no, muchacho*," replied the other gangster, as his gaze swept over the trackless, sun-scorched wastes of the south Arizona desert.

"Anyway," he commented, "Ever since the Wall come down after all that 'comet' shit, this here's *our* turf – *usted sabe*, the Man, he don' dare poke his *cabeza* this far south. *Jéfé* say we good, 'long as we stay this side of – what the name of that fuckin' place – oh yeah, Gila Bend, *that's* it. North of that, INS got roadblocks everywhere, 'specially up 'round Tucson. Let me see that map, *de acuerdo*? I *think* we still in the pipe... but I don' know..."

"*Carajo, hombre... you* s'posed to be the one who's navigatin', here," argued the driver, with a nose-sniff and a rueful shake of his head. "If that's all you know, we just as likely to drive right into some Crip town, they have our balls for dinner... *comprende*?"

"*No se preoccupe, cholo!*" countered the *Mara* in the front passenger-seat. "I ain't never been this far west – 'least not in the desert, I mean... I done some curb-duty down Phoenix way years ago, but we be okay... *¿No es verdad, muchachos?*"

The alternately bearded, gold-toothed and battle-scarred faces of four more *Mara Salvatrucha* gangsters, each heavily-armed but only dimly-visible on the inside walls of the darkened rear-compartment of the van – all called back in the affirmative.

"*Seguro*," said the driver. "*Pero, mira...* didn't you say we goin' cross Injun-country? I don' like the sound of *that...*"

"*Jéfé* cover the bases there, too – all we gotta do is hand off them AK's we got under the floor-boards – old shit anyway, riflin' mostly gone on the barrels – an' the reserve-boys gonna gas us up, point us past California border," explained the navigator. "Injuns ain't stupid – their turf, but since the Wall come down, lot more of *us* than *them*, in these parts, they need *somebody* to do the policin' of the whole thing. Man ain't had his troops in there for twenty years, besides. Where you *think* all them synth-labs hangin' out, anyway?"

The driver let out a hearty laugh.

"Hadn't thought of it that way, *cholo*," he allowed. "Good fuckin' business-arrangement!"

"*Claro que sì*," confirmed the navigator. "*Used sabe...* sure sounds like *el jéfé* pull out all the stops, for *this* one... I ain't seen hardly no sign of the Man since we set out – not even none of them State Patrol fuckers, an' they usually all *over* the place... *el jéfé* must have paid 'em off good, *sin duda*. I bet you it some high-test shit in *esa caja* in the back. He tell you what's in there, *hombre*?"

The *Mara* in the driver's-seat wiped the sweat from his brow, and, never taking his eyes from this dilapidated back road, replied, "*El no me dice nada, hombre.* He just say some shit like, '*este es mi gran' regalo* to them fuckin' Bloods, delivered to their doorstep *por mis compadres de Los Angeles*'. Funny, though... Pablo back there say it's feelin' warm to the touch. Hey... maybe it's one of them new portable synth-lab things, you know? I hear they use lots of juice, you gotta tap in to a main power-line... *cholo* down near Houston got fried doin' that, last month, you know..."

There was silence for a moment or two, then the navigator remarked, "*Bueno*, if *jéfé* sendin' us *this* far... I figure somethin' *muy grande* comin' down."

"*Sì hombre*," echoed the driver. "*Algo de grande... muy grande.*"

The van lumbered out into the desert, on a westward heading.

You Could Say, "I Just Dropped In"

By slowing until we are no faster than a gliding-bird, and by using the most-part of the cloak of darkness, dear children, sent Karéin-Mayréij to the five little voices who needed this tutoring, *we can likely evade the air-army of the 'President-king', who rules over this Empire.*

That, and staying close to the ground, weaving in and out of the trees... I read about this, on the 'Neo-Net' picture-boxes.

The lesson is thus : know thy enemy – seek out his weaknesses, before you go to battle. Victory, o ye new to life, goes not to the strongest... but to the most stealthy, wise and guileful – for the most potent weapon of all, is, 'surprise'. Followed only by that renowned second man-at-arms... 'preparation'.

I should rest, mused the newcomer.

It has been near-on a full day of testing the searching-skills of the President's sky-army, and so far, none of his air-chariots – not even those who we approached – have discerned our proximity.

The great abilities return quickly – but I dare not be caught at less than my full well of power... hmm, a long road, low-cut grass fields with little flags all about, and a barn-like structure, with the name of a man, 'Earl Bottoms', on it... people are going in and out, some are carrying packages of food, I can smell it from here... ah yes, that must be 'take-out', as Bob explained, back in his vehicle.

Very well, then – nourishment to enrich the inner fire.

But no song to announce my coming... let us tamp that down, though doing so aches my head...

Moving no faster than a couple kilometers per hour, now, the alien-girl landed behind a tree, righting herself as her feet made contact with the earth.

Time to hide thyselves, children, she counseled.

For here, I need adorn myself in peasant-garb.

With a quick nod of her head, Vìrya Ahn'jë and the rest of the Storied Watcher's war-children compressed themselves into a tight mass, enveloped and bound by the armor's cape, as her disguise-clothes came upon her body with equal alacrity.

With the light-bending trick making the war-bundle all but invisible, the alien woman took it to float behind and inspected her appearance.

Hmm... the rest of the vestments that I was given by Freddie of the Losada clan, considered the newcomer.

Surely do I look the ragamuffin, but it will have to suffice for the time being.

A pity that the people of this place only wash their clothes in machines, not in the fresh air... it were much easier to, ah, 'borrow' what I need, if they just did that...

Oops, she realized.

They will want money here.

Vìrya Ahn'jë , *if thou should be so kind...*

From seemingly nowhere, shot a tightly-rolled packet of genuine U.S. of A. common currency, still warm to the touch, as *Ahn'jë's* ability to protect what she cached within her hiding-places, was not yet perfect.

A second later, out popped a pair of wrap-around, mirror-sunglasses – their lenses still soft to the touch, their folding ear-arms discolored from the young living-armor's incomplete ability to protect them from the heat of the journey.

Ahh – drat! considered Karéin-Mayréij.

That nice, shiny-stuff is part melted-away... but they are still the color of a bright silver-blue coin, and these attractive little spectacles have now absorbed some of the spirit, being so close to Vìrya Ahn'jë *and myself, nestled as they were in the recesses of my war-daughter...*

So – if I use my arts to fortify such, spread the mirror-coating, make it and the glass to grow in affinity with my eyes, with my gaze of destruction...

Though none were around to hear, an invocation in an utterly alien tongue, sounded at the limit of human audibility, as the Storied Watcher displayed a wan smile and donned the sunglasses.

Welcome to the team, she sent to the spectacles, despite knowing that they could only dimly comprehend.

When thee feel the burning light come from mine eyes, learn to move thy particles of being, quickly out of the way, and strive to mold thy form as needs for disguise.

For now, though... I should be content for thou to learn how not to interfere with what I am able to see, with these eyes. Later, take my seeing to heart and learn to do it thyself.

Girl-child, Venerable One – please tutor and lend a mote of thy intellect.

And remind me to bind the babe with my hair-locks, should cause arise.

Now, the alien-girl peeked out from behind the tree and saw no-one, so off she set for the door, rapidly traversing a waste-rock-and-limestone gravel parking-lot. In another few seconds she was inside.

To all regards, she was just another traveler wishing a seat at this cavernous, 'down-home cooking highway rest-stop' place, to join the several hundred already deposited at various booths and tables within.

Reminds me, she reflected.

That kind family, who first took pity on me – Catherine, Mark, and their children – should check up on them... I hope that the President has not persecuted them, on account of me... where did they say that they came from?

Ah yes... 'Mee-shee-gan'...

Fortunately, though people were coming in and out all the time, there was next to no line-up, and in less than a minute, the round, friendly face of an African-American host appeared in front of her.

"Table for one, Miss?" he offered.

"Ah... yes," she answered. "And I ask you to excuse my appearance. I have been on a long and rather – ahh – 'busy', trip, without a good chance to clean myself up."

"Don't worry 'bout that," suggested the man, as he pulled out a menu card and ushered the young-looking woman around a central structure that had a sit-down bar, extending around it on three sides.

"You're not *half* as bad as some of them truckers we get in here, after they just done fixin' the brakes on they rigs, you know," he explained. "Sometimes we gotta get the cleanin'-lady in here right after they get up an' leave, just to get the axle-grease off the seats. 'Sides... I like them glasses you got on – if you don't mind me sayin'."

"Oh, not at all," demurely replied the Storied Watcher. "They are, ahh, kind of my special pair – my, 'custom proscription'."

"Pro – oh, I get it," he answered, with a grin. "This way."

The host showed the newcomer to a small, two-place table, on one side of a low partition that she was easily able to look over top of, even when sitting down.

The table was near the middle of the large room, closer to the bar than the outside wall. From this vantage-point, she could see most of what was going on in the restaurant – especially, her attention was quickly drawn to the bright colors of the OLED-technology television above the bar, which was displaying some kind of game-show.

The people on that tee-vee show seem very excited – they are jumping up and down, as if overjoyed – oh, I see... they have won a prize, she thought.

One would think that they would have to prove their skill at something like a chess game, or maybe solving number-puzzles – but all they had to do was spin that big wheel, the one with the little ball that bounces back and forth...

What is this about 'sorry, you'll have to take the cash, since the pleasure-cruise option isn't available right now'... oh – wait a trice – did I not hear something about that, back in Tucson, about the President sealing the borders of this kingdom against foreigners?

It is regrettable that ye cannot also see the moving-painting-pictures up there above the sitting-counter, sent Karéin-Mayréij to the complaining, invisible bundle that was fidgeting on the seat of the chair, on the opposite side of the two-person table.

But if anything important transpires, I shall leave ye see through mine own eyes.

Now... shush! Else shall ye draw undesired attention, children – mark my words and be calm.

The faint vibration on the other chair came to a halt, though not without some mental whining being reflected at the Storied Watcher.

"Miss? *Miss!*" implored the host, trying to get the alien woman's attention.

"Oh... sorr-ee," she apologized. "I was just watching the tee-vee, up there, and I was telling my – oh, uhh, *nobody*, that is. I suppose that I must seem a bit absent-minded... I have, ahem, a *lot* on my mind these days. What did you want to say, sir?"

"Just that Minnie over there, she'll be your server... okay?" indicated the man. "She'll be right over there."

"Good," replied the newcomer. "Oh – one more thing – do you accept, uhh, Ew-Ess twenty-dollar bills, as exchange, here?"

"Sure *do*," answered the host, with another grin. "Lot of places only take the cards these days... but what with the truckers and the kinda girls that hang around 'em –"

Taking another look at her clothes, he quickly shut up.

"Hey, no offense, you know – " he stammered.

"Oh – none taken," reassured the alien-girl. "I do not ride with those who drive the big trucks... at least, not any more."

"Sure," he retreated. "But listen, Miss... one other thing, I forgot to mention... boss is tellin' us to remind everybody 'bout this – you didn't park your car over on the far right side of the lot, did you? Because that whole side's reserved for the golf-course – they catch you *there* without a sticker, you can get towed... so you might want to move your vehicle over closer to the restaurant."

"That is oh-kay," replied the Storied Watcher. "Actually... I do not have a car, so that is not a problem for me."

"Yeah, super," offered the host. "Then you can take your time eatin' dinner – next bus ain't along for another two hours."

"I did not ride a bus to arrive here," she remarked. "That is a good means of transportation if one cannot afford a vehicle of one's own... but when *I* travel, I must be free to journey where I want to go – not where the bus-driver says that he is going."

Shush, she pleaded with the invisible, giggling bundle on the other chair.

"Wow, Miss," exclaimed the man. "It's sure a long way to walk, to get here from Coldwater."

He paused for a second.

"That's funny," he added. "Thought I heard somebody laughin', or... no, *didn't* hear it, but still..."

He looked perplexed.

"I did not walk, either," she commented, with a bemused smile. "And, to answer your next question... I sort of, ah, 'dropped in', you might say."

Vîrya Quü'j, speak some sense to them, I pray, ordered the Storied Watcher, as a gale of just-below-audibility laughter issued from the cape-bound package.

"Yeah, *whatever*... right," muttered the host, with a half-interested shrug. "Well, Minnie will be over here in a minute... I gotta get back to the front, or boss'll have my hide... okay?"

He left the menu on the table.

The alien-girl shot an insouciant thumbs-up sign to the host, and he rapidly disappeared back in the direction from which he had come.

Drumming her fingers on the table in front, as she waited to be served and began to idly pay attention to the television – *a bad habit*, she ruefully noted, that she had somehow picked up from poor, abused Bob Billings – the Storied Watcher descended into people-watching, with one eye periodically checking the televised goings-on above the bar.

The clientèle here was mostly white and, by all appearances, lower-middle-class, nuclear families, with a smattering of other types, ranging from the occasional minority and some farmers and truckers to a smattering of teenagers who were noisily chatting and playing with some kind of portable, 3-D video-device.

The alien-girl's more-than-human senses overheard a variety of conversations, mostly of pedantic subjects like sports-score and local goings-on, although a few *were* talking about "all that stuff that went down on TV yesterday, until the authorities shut it up real fast", and – to her satisfaction – one group of restaurant-goers actually mentioned "that space-chick... I wonder what she's got to do with it".

Her reverie was interrupted by a bored-sounding exclamation, from one side of the table.

"Take yer order, Miss?" announced a middle-aged, average-looking *hausfrau*, dressed in some kind of *faux* milk-maid type of uniform.

The woman looked over the newcomer with thinly-disguised envy; even in disheveled, rec-room clothes, and despite the alien's conscious attempts to avoid it beaming through, her inner, near-godly beauty could not help but leak through to offend the waitress' perspective.

"What?" replied Karéin-Mayréij, silently remonstrating herself for the bad example of being startled by an ordinary mortal.

"Oh, uhh, yes – for *sure*," she answered, rapidly opening the menu and regarding what was contained within it.

"Excuse me," queried the Storied-Watcher-in-mufti, "But why are all these items on the food-choosing list, crossed off? Can one no longer order them?"

"You sure *are* from out of town," cackled the waitress. "Ain't you heard about the 'embargo'... or whatever they're callin' it? Since that announcement from the President that was on TV a while back, things have been harder and harder to get, up here in these parts – lot of the stuff that they used to import, we ain't seen none of, for *weeks*. Hey, but we still got steak, milk and coffee... one dollar surcharge per cup... but at least you can *order* it here. Couple a places in town ran out two days ago – same damn thing – can't get any more from down south, wherever. You ready to order, lady?"

"Hmm... I should like the... uhh, yes – here it is – the 'toast and jam', if you please," requested the alien-girl. "It is not crossed off... is it still available?"

"Sure *is*... but is that all?" asked the waitress.

"Yes... but *lots* of jam, if you do not mind," said the Storied Watcher.

"We got a ten-dollar minimum," warned the woman. "Stops the rubbies from comin' in and just loiterin' all day."

"A... uhh... 'ten-dollar min – ee – oh... I see," noted the newcomer. "The least money that one can pay, and still be allowed to spend one's afternoon here... is that right?"

"That's about the story," confirmed the waitress.

"I suppose that the 'toast and jam' would not cost ten dollars?" asked Karéin-Mayréij.

"Only seven-fifty," lazily answered the woman. "We got a special this week. Which is a great deal, the way food prices have been goin' up these days."

"Oh-kay, then," said the Storied Watcher. "Do you have something that, ah, does not have any animal-meat in it? It is rather difficult to tell from this menu-thing, I mean, I would not order a steak, but a lot of these items do not describe if –"

"Oh... so you one of them 'veggie' people?" sniffed the waitress. "Well, you might want to try the vegetarian pizza... customers tell me it ain't too bad, I wouldn't know myself, of course, I can't *imagine* it without the pepperoni and anchovies, you know? Just like Mom used to make it."

"Ansho-what?" started the alien-girl. "Never, ahh, mind. I would imagine that one would be most at ease eating the food that one was raised with... but as for me, I, uhh, I 'get around' a lot, I have to try new things quite frequently – very well then, the 'veggie' pizza, if you please. How much does it cost?"

"Small one's fifteen... big one's thirty, war-tax and gratuity out," spoke the waitress. "Best prices you'll get on the road in these parts. Most places got 'em for twenty and forty."

'Gratuity', silently thought Karéin-Mayréij. *Ah, yes – a special gift for those who serve.*

At least one knows how much of a hidden fee to pay, in this *kingdom, saves one the awkwardness of offering too little or too much of a bribe...*

"Fortune favors me, then... I shall have just the little one," she indicated. "That and the toast, should be, ah, within my budget, as my boyfriend says."

"You got it," agreed the woman. "Anythin' to drink? Coffee, tea, Killer Stimulant Cola or beer, maybe?"

"Juice of the orange, please," requested the newcomer.

The waitress shrugged.

"Yeah... yer lucky there," she commented. "Still got some of that up from Florida... ain't had none of it from California for a while, though... they're tellin' us that the trucks aren't gettin' through, or something."

She wrote something down on her computer-tablet and turned as if to go, but was interrupted by her customer.

"Excuse me," asked the alien-girl, "But would you mind explaining something, just before you ask the cooks to exercise their craft?"

"What?" responded the waitress, with a tone of mild annoyance.

"Please excuse me – but while we were talking, I noticed what was going on with the, uh, 'gaming-show', up there on the tee-vee screen," explained the Storied Watcher. "The em-see is saying that one of the people has won a 'brand new car', and they all seem *very* excited about that. How is a 'brand new' car different from one that is just 'new'?"

"It's, like, 'new – right out of the showroom – or somethin' like that," stated the waitress. "'Newer than new', or... hell, *I* don't know," she groused. "It's just one of those things that they say to make you think it's somethin' real special."

The woman paused for a second, searchingly looking the newcomer up and down, then added, "Listen, girl... you aren't from around these parts... are you? You got kind of a strange accent, if you don't mind me sayin'."

"No... I am not," replied Karéin-Mayréij, with a saturnine smile and subtly-arched eyebrow. "From around here, that is. I am from, ahh... Tucson. As for my accent – well, I suppose that it must be due to the influence of all those, ahh, 'illegals', that we have down in the principality of Arizona... there are, ahh, *way* too many of them, down in the southern regions... you know?"

Tucson, by way of the Many Worlds, she mischievously sent into the waitress' mind.

As the psychic giggles reverberated, the Storied Watcher counseled her war-children.

Humor, dear ones, is a quality that adds immediately not to the arts of war; but neither is it of no worth.

Such things mark us as different from, better than, dull living things who perceive naught but the mundane needs of day by day.

Confused, the waitress stumbled off in the direction of the kitchen, muttering something about "Damn flashbacks, just tried the synth stuff *once...*", too low for human ears to comprehend.

What did dear Bob say? reflected the young-looking woman.

'There goes your five – or was it fifteen – minutes of fame'.

But thank you for serving me, none the less.

There is honor, children, in doing a humble profession, if it is one that helps others to survive and be happy.

For the next twenty minutes, the newcomer sat and waited, watching the *kitsch* of the game-show with a mixture of amazement at, and incomprehension of, this shallow, gaudy spectacle of American consumerism.

All these 'commercials', six or seven of them for each five minutes of the gaming-show, she spoke to the invisible package.

See, ye – use mine eyes, if you will – how the riddle is really, 'how would one tell the gaming-show from the commercials, mixed into a chaotic jumble as they all are?'

Ha, I see that ye are perplexed...

Well, the answer is easy, in fact : the gaming-show is where the people are presented with baubles and trinkets, for which there is no need, but they are given money, with which to buy all these indulgences; whereas, in the 'commercials', it is the same, except one is instructed to waste one's own money on 'a brand new car' or the such-like.

It is all about using shiny electro-boxes and driving-chariots for a trice, then throwing them away in favor of another that is more or less the same, while the many have no money to buy a first one... that is how people like dear Bob claim to have 'made it'.

But I would gladly watch these boring entreaties to shallow wastefulness for a thousand Earth-marked years, she miserably reflected, *If I could but have Bob, Tommy and the others, to hold close to me, in front of the tee-vee for that time.*

Tears us lay thy on, Mother, quickly responded five small, neither-human-nor-*Makailkh* voices.

Family first ours kin of are too ours... well grieve we as.

Wiping her eye, Karéin-Mayréij gently stroked the little amulet that still adorned her neck, as she laid an affectionate hand on the invisible bundle on the other chair-seat.

Should misfortune make me leave this world entirely and live out my ages on some cold rock in the void, she silently called to them, *I would still have all of ye.*

And we would sing to one another – now until forever – blessed, beloved little ones.

Mercifully, the game-show ended, and after a flurry of fast-talking commercials, a 'Report on Sports' program came on.

"Here's yer dinner," interrupted the waitress' voice, as she placed a mid-size pizza, several slices of toast, four or five small jam-packages and a large glass of orange juice, in front of the Storied Watcher.

"Thank you very much," appreciatively answered the alien-girl. "It looks – how did Bob say it, again, oh, right – just 'scramptious'."

"I think you mean, 'scrumptious', Miss," indifferently mentioned the waitress. "And that'll be... let's see... twenty-six fifty, plus ten per-cent war-tax, plus eight per-cent gratuity – no point in askin' any more, boss just skims it anyways – yeah, thirty-one twenty-seven. If you don't mind paying up front, that is... I'm off shift in half an hour."

"Oh, no problem," replied the newcomer. She rummaged around in her track pants, coming up with two twenties.

"Will that be enough?" she asked.

"I got change," said the waitress.

She pulled a five-dollar bill and some coins out and handed them to the apparently ordinary woman seated at the eating-table.

"Just the paper mon-ee... you can keep the coins," offered Karéin-Mayréij, pushing a few quarters and other small change back toward the woman.

"Don't like carryin' a bunch of coins around?" inquired the waitress, quickly pocketing the change.

The face of the Storied Watcher wore an inscrutable expression, as she replied, "That is right, 'Minnie'... they make too much – ahh – noise; and they do not, ahh, *compress*, very well, when one needs to travel with a light load. You know what I mean?"

Nonplussed, the waitress said, "Not really, Miss, but... well, you enjoy your food... if you need me, I'll be at the take-out counter... okay?"

The alien-girl just smiled warmly and nodded as the waitress turned and walked away.

Quickly spreading some jam on a slice of toast, she wolfed most of it down in only a few seconds, hoping that none could see her sharper-than-everyone's incisors.

Take what ye need in sustenance, as I replenish my body, she murmured to the invisible bundle on the next chair.

Ye need such, for thy might to come to full flower.

But in the mid-time, I pray that ye maintain the watch in my stead; now, I would drop my guard and take some little leave as repose.

For the next few-score minutes, the Storied Watcher happily munched away at a mediocre vegetarian pizza, aware that it was half the size of what had been depicted on the menu, as well as of the fact that the cheese on it was mostly beeswax or some other equally unpalatable substitute. She did not care very much, about this chicanery.

The alien-girl would have noticed herself, a fraction of a second later, but her eye had strayed elsewhere, when her meal was interrupted by the patient, wise thoughts of *Vîrya Quü'j.*

Sword-mistress – observe – moving-painting-box – above – table – long – tankards – upon, advised the ancient relic.

"We interrupt this program," spoke a voice-over on the television, "For a special public announcement. We take you live, now, to the Press-Room of the White House, where the Press Secretary is about to speak."

"Damn it!" someone cursed, "They were just about to show the highlights from the Bengals' game yesterday!"

"Somebody change the channel!" demanded another.

The barkeep shrugged his shoulders. "I *would*, mister," he apologized, "But waitress dropped the remote in a jug o' beer last week, it ain't worked since then. I'd have to climb up there – just live with it – these things usually ain't that long, anyways."

A scene, heretofore unfamiliar to the eyes of Karéin-Mayréij, was now displayed on the overhead monitor. There was a pudgy, conservatively-dressed Caucasian man at a podium at the front of a rather crowded room, with rows of fold-up chairs, each occupied by an equally formal businessman; almost all of these where also from the dominant racial-group, and only a few of them were female.

A crowd of five to ten people now started to congregate below the television, some cracking a joke or two, some just standing there, silently observing with folded arms.

"The President has issued the following statement," announced the man at the podium, "Regarding the events that occurred at the Mount Rushmore National Monument, yesterday."

Most of those within eyeshot or earshot, in the restaurant, now had stopped eating and had started to pay attention.

"This incident," claimed the spokesman, "Was the result of the unauthorized theft and misuse of certain classified high-technology-assets of the Department of Defense, evidently by a disgruntled female member of the military. This misguided young woman has, obviously, since been taken into custody; the President wishes to assure the public that the matter has been dealt with swiftly and effectively, and that no further incidents of this nature are anticipated. He also wants to make it clear that contrary to the rumors that have been going around the media lately, this was *not* the work of subversive groups, nor is it in any way related to the violent shoot-out between U.S. and Muslim terrorist forces that unfortunately caused severe damage to the Hotel Arizona in Tucson."

"*Laws*," exclaimed a farmer. "Damn Muslims is *everywhere!* Oughtta nuke 'em all, that's what *I* say."

"Now... as I'm sure that all responsible representatives of the mainstream media in this room will understand and appreciate," continued the man at the podium, "Since we're dealing with some *highly*-classified weaponry here, I'm afraid I won't be able to respond to questions as to its nature and capabilities, and there may be a number of other areas in which I won't be able to comment. With that in mind, I'll take the first question... yes, Mr. Wilson, go ahead."

"It's all bullshit, man!" countered a seedy-looking country-time teenager with a dirty T-shirt and a baseball cap. "I saw the video on Neo, just before they cut it off and put that Disney Channel shit on it. That *weren't* no Army-girl in that-there suit. Not 'less they figured some way to set her on *fire*, that is."

"Aww, come *on*," argued one of the black waiters. "They prolly did all that fire-stuff with a computer, after they did all the shootin' on a set, somewhere. That NeoNet stuff's *all* faked... y'all see that clip they had week before last, with the dog flyin' over a house so's he could catch a squirrel? Or how 'bout that one that was on 'till they pulled it too, they said it was, 'The Guiness Record For The World's Biggest —"

"It's the *President* saying so, young man," interrupted a middle-aged woman in horn-rim glasses, whose prim tunic was adorned with a "St. Ann Coulter Memorial Club" button. "It's the *patriotic* thing to do, to believe what your government tells you."

"Hey, keep it *down* for a sec," admonished a middle-aged family-man. "I wanna *hear* this."

"...That's true, Mr. Wilson," droned on the spokesman, "But it's also about as far as I can go with that line of questioning... okay, Jackson Sawyer from Disney News... go ahead."

A dapper-dressed young white man, stood up and the camera focused on him. "Mr. Secretary, can you confirm that the equipment used by this renegade member of the Armed Forces — and here, I'm referring to the suit of armor, plus the shield, and the, uhh, cape and all that — is part of the 'Sword of Freedom' weapon that the President has spoken about, earlier?"

"I'm afraid I can't comment on that, Jack," replied the man at the televised podium, "Except to say that it's reasonable to assume that our military has a range of advanced technology-assets that the President can deploy quickly, depending on the circumstances of a conflict. Yes — okay — Billie-Jo Parton, back row. Go ahead."

A large-busted blond woman with an unruly mass of platinum-white hair, sitting near the back of the room, stood up and addressed the Press Secretary.

"Well, Mr. Secretary," she bubbled, "I'd like to say, what an honor it is, to be able to address y'all, and how nice it is that the President is tellin' the country what's goin' on, and so soon —"

Back in the restaurant, one of the onlookers muttered, "How the hell does somebody like *that*, get on TV? In the White House, I mean."

"Easy, depends on who you pay," said a trucker.

"Or who you *blow*," smirked the country-boy, to a look of disgust on the part of the woman in the glasses.

Quiet, ye children, remonstrated the Storied Watcher, as she felt the other chair vibrate with poorly-repressed mirth.

"I'm sure the President appreciates hearing that," commented the man at the podium, with a faked smile. "Now, as to your *question*, Ms. Parton –"

"Oh, yes – of course," stammered the platinum-blond in the Press-Room. "Well, I just wanted to ask the President... like, what can he tell us about this woman who stole the special weapon... you *did* say that it was a female, didn't you? I mean, why would a *lady* do anythin' like *that*? And what was she doin' in the Army, in the first place?"

"Well... as you know," explained the Press Secretary, "Following on Congressional approval of the Returning Traditional Gender-Roles for the Armed Forces Act some time ago, this Administration has been actively discouraging participation of women within the Department of Defense; however – as you can probably appreciate – given the fact that about forty per-cent of the military was female at the time that this law was passed, it has been a slow process. As of our last count, we still have about thirty per-cent of DoD being comprised of women."

The spokesman cleared his throat and went on,

"Clearly, there's still some way to go, before we can fully comply with the legislation. Frankly, these moves – necessary though they are – have caused some tension, and, while we still don't have complete information on what precisely motivated this young lady to carry out what is, technically, an act of *treason* against her country and her President... we think it's reasonable to assume that resentment about the phase-out of female combat-roles, may have been a motivating-factor here. I hope that answers your question."

"Excuse me," persisted the blond, "But what is the government going to *do* to this woman? Assumin' that she's guilty, that is."

She giggled a bit, batted her eyes and sat down.

"As you also know, Ms. Parton," answered the man at the podium, matter-of-factually, "The penalty for treason is normally death by hanging, which can be commuted to life imprisonment by special order of the President. I should note, however, that because of the special national-security considerations of this situation, it's likely that the Department of Defense would opt for a closed-session trial under military law, with penalties assessed by the Uniform Military Code."

"Probably means they fire her out of one of them battleship-guns, ass-first," joked the farm-boy.

"Yeah," confirmed the African-American waiter. "Or they use her for target-practice on a firin'-range. Rumor is they already doin' that with some of them illegals."

Ah, children... how swiftly the peasant-folk believe the lies, sent the Storied Watcher, to her war-family.

But observe, how, both in the arts of Vrùn-Ch'é *and those of politics, sometimes, the most effective technique is to turn an enemy's attack, his lunge and strike, back on himself.*

Shortly, I shall show ye how.

While this counsel was being tutored, the televised session had gone on to another question. "No, Mr. Beckson, we don't," heard the group in front of the screen. "We're counting on you guys and gals to do your patriotic duty and *not* broadcast or repeat this kind of thing – especially when we need to concentrate the full attention of our police, our armed forces and our intelligence-agencies, against the very real and very serious threat of Muslim terrorism and aggression. The President and your country expect that you'll do no less. And that, ladies and gentlemen, will be all for today – thank you and good afternoon."

A cacophony erupted inside the remote briefing-room, as dozens of reporters shouted questions at the Press Secretary; all this was, of course, to no avail, as the man quickly exited the scene, surrounded and protected by several big, glowering Secret Service bodyguards.

Mother, understand not we, echoed a bewildered query, inside the Storied Watcher's psyche. *Refute easy untruth to. Why?*

"We now return to our regular program-schedule," said a voice from the video-monitor, "Please stand by for the last half of 'Couch Potato Sports Line', after a few words from our sponsors."

At this, the picture on the television reverted to its normal fare, namely, a commercial about a coffee and beer additive promising to "Make Every Man Over 40, Perform Like He Was 20 Again (Call Your Doctor For A Free Prescription *Today!*)".

Because these people are conditioned not to ask questions, she patiently sent back.

So... we must help them to inquire... by giving them much to ponder upon, and far too much to ignore.

"So whaddya make of *that?*" queried a middle-aged man, to the rest of the small crowd that had remained up at the bar, after the better part of them had dispersed when the press-conference ended.

"Like I *said*, Mister," proposed the farm-boy, "It's all *bullshit*. 'Member how they told us that we was gonna take over that Paki place, they'd all say 'thanks' to good ol' Uncle Sam for comin' and throwin' out the terrorists? My brother signed up the next day. He never came back, and they're *still* tellin' us that we won. Well if *that's* true – then how come they can't even get his *body* back?"

"That's another subject, young man," imperiously retorted the woman with the horn-rim spectacles. "Besides... how would *you* know? You don't look like you spent a lot of time in school. You should have a little *respect* for our President – you *heard* that 'Press' guy! We have a serious *problem* with all that 'terrorist' stuff – what with the Muslims, the gangsters, the subversives and all that. The police can't be spending all their time chasing around over-educated college kids trying to get rich by faking 'flying rocket-suits' and the like, on NeoNet. The very *thought* of it!"

She snorted in contempt.

At this, the Storied Watcher wiped the last traces of the food from her lips and slowly got up, taking care not to appear as if she had overheard or taken interest in the conversation.

Children – repose is over, silently advised the alien-girl, toward the invisible bundle that now floated close behind her.

She rounded the table and came to rest her elbow on the raised demi-wall that had separated her seat from the open area in front of the bar and the television.

"Well... I'm on *MyTubeSpace*, like, three times every day, lady," countered a petite, perky-looking mid-teens girl wearing a "I DRANK – NIAGARA FALLS" T-shirt, "And *everybody* that I vid-chat with, says that weird thing that went down at Mount Rushmore, like... it was *real*. My boyfriend's into all the 3D-video-stuff – he's, like, trying to get into movies, you know – and he had, like, one of the guys who was right there, upload a, uhh – what'd he call it again – yeah, a 'first-gen copy', up to his computer... and he looked at all the special video-codes and whatnot, and he, like, says that they all check out. Like, *nothing* was messed around with – y'know – like how they do to make it look like crazy things happen, when nothing really did –"

"Oh, *please*, Miss!" sniffed the 'St. Ann Coulter Club'-woman. "*Surely* you can't be so naive as to imagine that they didn't doctor those images. You *heard* the Press Secretary – all of these things on the computer-networks are just childish pranks. And besides... let's just suppose, for the sake of argument, that these unauthorized, unpatriotic, so-called 'citizen journalism' videos, *weren't* altered or staged... yes, I saw a bit of it too, so I know what I'm talking about, didn't watch all of it, of course, but my son had it on *his* computer... anyway, if the event wasn't staged, then who *was* it, there, in front of the Monument? Can you answer me *that*?"

The teenager looked down, and, blushing a bit, forced out, "Somebody said it was, like... the... uhh... the space-alien... or, like, she – the girl in the suit, I mean – that she was, uhh... an angel... or the Devil..."

Her voice trailed off.

"You *see* how ridiculous it sounds... don't you?" crowed the spectacled woman. "You can't even tell me who it *was!* Which only makes sense, because it never *happened*, in the first place."

"Well... a *lot* of weird stuff been goin' on lately," offered one of the barkeeps, from behind the counter. "People seem to be forgettin' that a month ago, we was all ready to say our goodbyes to each other."

"Sure got *that* right," echoed the family-man. "Hard to believe it really happened. Sometimes I wake up thinkin' it was all just a dream."

"*That*, was a perfectly explainable set of events," argued the 'St. Ann Coulter Club'-woman. "Yes, I'll allow that none of us will ever forget that time... but in the end, the brave Christian men of the U.S. Air Force saved the entire *world*, by shooting down that terrible comet. Not, of course, that our country ever gets any credit for doing it... all I'm hearing about is those filthy, Christ-hating Muslims trying to blow *us* up, because –"

From her leaning-on-the-little-wall vantage-point, slightly ahead of and to the left of the most-part of the group, the alien-girl now spoke up, her voice melodious and clear, but also restrained and polite.

"How can you be so *sure* of that, Madam?" she challenged, and in the next few seconds, all eyes were upon the Storied Watcher.

That Familiar Old Poppin' Sound

Several of those at the Earl Bottoms Restaurant, including the 'St. Ann Coulter-Club'-woman, turned to regard the newcomer, who had barged, unrequited, into the conversation.

Whoa... why didn't I notice this *chick before,* silently cursed the farm-boy, in a thought-pattern involuntarily repeated by all the male humans in the vicinity.

She's a '10', for sure... man, can't take my eyes off her... wonder if she's one of them truck-stop girls... nah, ain't none of them who's that pretty...

"Why... err... what do you *mean* by that, young lady?" asked the older woman.

The alien-girl stood up straight and took a step toward the rest of them.

"You all see my counsel delivered, not by the well-trained liars who answer to this 'President', but instead by other of your fellow ordinary Americans, in recorded testimony," she remarked, "But you are so used to timidly believing whatever your king demands, that you put the truth far from your minds... I tell you now, what you just heard in this 'press-conference' – that is simply nonsense, put out by your President, to mislead the gullible and witless... nothing more."

"Well, I suppose that you're entitled to your opinions, Miss," complained the woman in the horn-rim glasses. "Although I must say that if I wasn't a forgiving person, I'd consider that last statement just *this* far from being subversive. Do I have to remind you that spreading unpatriotic rumors, is a *crime?*"

"It is?" interjected a black waiter, with mock surprise.

"An *awful* lot of things around here seem to be crimes," offered Karéin-Mayréij. "One can hardly wash one's hair or go to the market, without breaking one or another of these rules."

"Is that kinda crime, like, worse than bein' stoned all day?" quipped the farm-boy.

The alien-girl allowed herself a bemused laugh, with perhaps too much of a sharp tooth showing, for a half-second.

"Thank you for the kind advice, Madam," she offered. "But being accused of 'subverting' your government... ah, that would be the *least* of my list of supposed transgressions. If, that is, I cared to respect the self-serving laws imposed by your President, after what he has done, and continues to do, to my poor, innocent friends and family. Lest it need be said... I do not."

"You aren't making any *sense*, young lady," protested the spectacled woman woman with the "St. Ann Coulter Club" button. "We were talking about how the Air Force caught that renegade female who stole the secret weapons.... remember?"

"Nothing was stolen, in fact," countered the Storied Watcher, not taking care to hide how she was relishing the discourse. "From your government, that is. As for those who had to, ahh, 'donate to the cause'... they will be handsomely repaid, in time... and when they see what noble new life has in turn been born, I have no doubt that they will consider themselves greatly-honored."

"I'm getting *tired* of playing games with you, Miss," complained the apparently-older woman. "Especially, all this 'your President' business. What do you mean, '*your* President'? He's *everyone's* President – Democrat, Republican and Independent, alike – which is why we all have to pull together and do what he asks of us. Each and every U.S. citizen is supposed to know that. What's the matter – you not from around here?"

"Oh... you could *say* that," deadpanned Karéin-Mayréij.

"Bill," shouted out a voice from down the bar, "Can you get up there and give that damn TV a whack? There's some kind of music-interference on it, crowdin' out the audio. I don't even *like* that – whaddya call it – 'Celtic' crap."

"Hey," interrupted the "NIAGARA" teenager, the nervousness in her voice rising with each syllable, "You, girl, you look just like – on the video – I mean, without that armor –"

The Storied Watcher shot the youngster a grin halfway between goofy and cruel, pointing back in unstated confirmation with two index-fingers held out in mock pistol-style.

Inexplicably, the atmosphere in the place started to thicken, as adrenaline began to pour into human bloodstreams.

"What you *talkin'* about, kid?" requested one of the family men. "She's got a funny accent, I'll give you *that*, but... well, what *are* you talkin' about?"

"*Shit!*" exclaimed the teenager. She turned to look at a table near the middle of the room.

"*Keith!*" she shouted, and as a teenage boy roughly the same age slowly got up from his seat, the girlfriend motioned furiously to him, and he paused, then retrieved a finger-camera from a carrying-bag on the floor.

"Can you, like, please wait – *please!*" pleaded the 'NIAGARA'-girl.

"Oh... *certainly*," serenely replied the Storied Watcher. "I would not *dream* of going anywhere else, right now. *Unless*, of course, someone's 'Air Force' people, were to try to drop a bomb on my head."

"Turn that goddamn music *off!*" shouted a man at the bar.

"*What* music?" demanded somebody else. "Oh, yeah, I can just hear –"

"What's with *her*? The girl in the 'Falls shirt, I mean," inquired one of the family-men, uneasily, in the direction of the country-boy.

But there was no immediate answer, as the latter was just staring, smitten with the overpowering attraction that was, despite the newcomer's best attempts to conceal it, leaking out from her disguise.

The man elbowed the farm-boy.

"What's the matter... you get *stoned* all of a sudden?" he asked. "If so, take it outside – this is a *family* place."

"Oh, no, man," mumbled the country-boy, *sotto voce*. "I was just, uhh, *lookin'* at that chick, that's all... kinda hard to take yer eyes off of, if you know what I mean."

"Yeah," agreed the older man, nodding his head.

Arms folded in front, the alien-girl accosted the group.

"*She* knows who I am," she purred. "The rest of you do not, ahh, 'get it'... do you?"

"Get *what*, Miss?" growled the horn-rim-glasses-woman. "Nobody here cares about your subversive, anti-American, lib-ral ranting! Why don't you just get a move on, now, and while you're at it, find some *appropriate* clothing –"

Karéin-Mayréij closed her eyelids, then opened them; and the subtle, blue-green glow flowing from within stopped all who could see, squarely in their tracks.

"Are you *getting* this, Keith?" whispered the delighted, though frightened, teenage girl, as her boyfriend pointed the mini-cam over her shoulder.

A second later, the alien woman turned her head to stare at the two head-on, freezing them with a fine mixture of fear and excitement.

"I hope that you are so doing," she remarked, speaking directly into the camera. "For thus, you will carry my second warning, to the fool who calls himself, your 'President'."

Meanwhile, the woman in the horn-rim glasses had moved to the back of the scrum, and she turned to the barkeep. In hushed tones, she commanded, "Call 911 *immediately!* And call the Army! We have a subversive event going on here. Have you got a gun behind that counter?"

"Yeah, lady," he whispered back, "But it's only s'posed to be used in cases of a robbery – and how the hell should *I* know what the number is for the Army –"

"Then just get the gun and call 911!" cursed the 'St. Ann Coulter-Club'-woman. "I've got one in my purse. We'll *corner* her!"

"Lady – that-there 911 thing ain't been workin' since they changed over to –" he tried to explain, but the woman had turned and double-timed it back to her table, where she began furiously rummaging around in an oversize handbag.

"So, like, okay," requested the teenager standing in front of her boyfriend, "Since you're, like, on camera right now, would you mind telling us who you are?"

"Oh... not at all," replied the newcomer, with a characteristic, recovered dignity in her voice. "My name is 'Karéin-Mayréij', and I am the Storied Watcher of the Many Worlds, who was freed from a long sleep, by kind Sam Jacobson and his space-faring team, on the planet that you call 'Mars' and that I call "*Mailànkh*", a brief time ago. I now live among the people of Earth – and wish to continue doing so – acting as the guardian and tutor for you and your fellow human-creatures, for ages yet to come. As soon, that is, as I teach this 'President' of yours, a hard lesson about crossing me."

"Like... you're a *space-alien*?" gasped the video-girl. "Like, a *real* one?"

"Umm-hmm," confirmed Karéin-Mayréij. "A very real and very powerful one, more ancient and wise than you can know or understand. I may *look* human, but do not let that mislead you – I am the same as you saw on your tee-vee screens, the signal sent first from the surface of *Mailànkh,* then on the space-vessels commanded by Sam Jacobson and his crew, and then, as the comet bore down upon this beautiful green world..."

Her voice became quiet, as if she was lost in thought.

A second later, she turned her gaze to confront the horn-rim woman, who was standing to one side, with a small handgun trained unsteadily at the Storied Watcher.

"Alright, you – *you* – whoever you are – put your hands up where I can *see* them!" bellowed the 'St. Ann Coulter-Club'-woman. "And *don't* think I don't know how to use this! I'm a charter-member of the NRA in my community – I've taken all the courses!"

With a shrug, her eyes glowing like a LED lawn-light as she rolled them in contempt, Karéin-Mayréij elevated her palms in a mock-surrender gesture.

"My, *my*," she taunted, half-suppressing a bored yawn, "I see that I am taken captive by, ahh, 'overwhelming military force'... is that not how your American warriors describe it? Perhaps – oh mighty lady-soldier – you would be so kind as to inform me what you propose to *do* with me, before my arms become too tired?"

The ranks of the crowd were now multiplying quickly, and it was obvious that several others in the vicinity were also armed – the guns seemed to come out of concealed holsters like cockroaches from an untended trash-can.

"Lady – what you think you're *doing!*" protested the video-teenager. "She isn't threatening *anybody!*"

"Turn that camera off, right *now!*" ordered the spectacled woman with the gun. "We'll let the police and the Army decide what to do with her... somebody call 911!"

"Fuck *you!*" cursed the boyfriend with the video-camera. "Nobody elected *you* cop around here!"

"You want to get *shot*, keep *that* up, sonny!" yelled the glasses-woman.

"I got a gun on both of you," came a shout from a man in the crowd, to the side of both the Storied Watcher and the armed woman.

"I got one too," called the barkeep. "First person to squeeze off a shot, gets one from me. This is a *family* establishment – come *on*, everybody, just cool it, let the weird chick get on with her life! No need for anybody to be threatenin' anybody else."

Shaking her head with her arms still in the air, the newcomer sighed, "Shall the future rank this scene as enlightenment, tragedy... or farce? I mark it more the latter, peasant-citizens of the American kingdom."

The Storied Watcher turned to address the barkeep.

"Thank you for the support – everyone," she offered. "But worry not... this person cannot harm me. Therefore, I counsel you just to put down these weapons. I cannot protect *all* of you, if more than a few persons are so foolish as to start shooting."

"I'm giving you to the count of *five*," growled the woman with the horn-rim glasses, "To lay down on the floor and put your arms behind your back. *You* there," – she motioned to one of the African-American waiters, by waving her handgun – "Go and get me a pair of handcuffs!"

The waiter replied, "Handcuffs? What you *talkin'* 'bout, lady? We ain't got *nothin'* like that here!"

"I'm not joking!" she hissed. "Get something that we can tie up the fugitive with."

"May I put my arms down, now?" quipped Karéin-Mayréij. "I do my best to suppress the odors of my armpits, but even so..."

"*Shut up!*" angrily shouted the pistol-toting woman.

To the waiter, she demanded, "Get *anything* – *surely* you've got some rope. *Go!*"

"Lady, you're just makin' a *scene!*" argued the barkeep. "Why don't we just talk it out with her – besides, she ain't *done* anything."

"Except spreading subversive disloyalty to the government, as well as being high on those prohibited new narcotics – don't you see her *eyes?*" inveighed the 'St. Ann Coulter-Club'-woman.

To the alien, she shouted, "*You* there – count of five, on the floor, or you *get* it. Remember the laws that say, 'illegals, terrorists, drug-dealers and gangsters wanted, dead or alive'? *Five!*"

"Listen, everyone," called the Storied Watcher, her gaze sweeping back and forth so as to address the entire crowd.

"*Four!*" spat the woman with the gun.

"Please move back so she cannot hit one of you," requested the alien.

"*Three!*" warned the other woman.

"When she is out of bullets," counseled the newcomer.

"*Two!*" exclaimed the woman with the gun, anger rising in her voice.

"Try not to be too rough with her," asked the Storied Watcher.

"*One!*" howled the woman, her voice shaking with rage and indignation.

The alien-girl lowered one hand and patted a yawn, as the Celtic-rock music sounded dimly in the minds of nearby mortals.

A half-second later, the woman with the horn-rimmed glasses started firing, squeezing off five or six shots in quick sequence as the barkeep ducked and everyone – save the videographer, who merely crouched – dove for cover.

Pop-pop-poppity-pop-pop! reverberated a sound as familiar as that of milk on breakfast-cereal, to all Americans.

Her opponent's aim was better than average, as all but one bullet – which went careening off a chandelier somewhere – were right on target, directed to hit Karéin-Mayréij full-square in the torso and abdomen.

But instead of the usual splattering mess left by the impact of a ten-millimeter hollow-point, all that registered on the senses of the nearby humans was a series of brief, painfully intense flashes of heat, as – one by one – the otherwise lethal projectiles were vaporized or stopped by a near-invisible, shimmering aura surrounding this enigmatic, glowing-eyed creature.

"Jesus H. *Christ!*" whispered someone in the crouching, dispersed crowd.

"Are you *quite* finished, Madam?" inquired the Storied Watcher, with a bored, pitying tone. "I counted five... and I would not burden you with the task of more proof... I understand that each of these bullets is quite expensive. Why not use your mon-ee for better purposes – say, a pleasant-tasting mixed 'booze' drink... or a nice new hat?"

The boyfriend with the camera, slowly coming out of his crouch, could not resist the urge to laugh out loud, upon hearing this.

Several others, though still beset by the tension of having witnessed the confrontation, also dared to poke out their heads from various hiding-places.

"*Let me out of here!*" cried the gun-woman, as she dashed for the door.

She was stopped after two or three strides by some other, invisible force. With a pained look, the assailant rotated in mid-place, being somehow forced to stand, otherwise completely paralyzed, to face the being that she had just tried to kill.

Addressing the crowd, Karéin-Mayréij announced, "Now... the situation of this woman who, out of blind obedience to false authority, latterly tried to murder me... I present this to all of you, as an example in miniature, of what has been going on, between your rulers, and myself, on a grand scale."

"*Wow!*" was all the family-man, next to the farm-boy, could manage.

"Although," continued the alien-girl, "As has also been done with your so-called 'President' – she was clearly warned otherwise, with the swagger and arrogance of one who has never had to confront a superior opponent – she *thought* that the power of life or death, was held by her, over me; but in fact, the opposite is the case."

A cruel, severe, sharp-fanged smile was on the face of the Storied Watcher, as the gun-woman, held in the vice-grip of an unseen telekinetic power, began to gasp for breath.

"I can kill her with just a *thought*," ominously threatened Karéin-Mayréij, "As I can do the same to your entire *country... should* I?

A pall of fear washed over the crowd.

"No – *don't*, lady!" pleaded the teenager, who had moved back beside the boyfriend with the video-camera.

The ethereal music was subsiding.

"*Why* not?" rhetorically-postulated the newcomer. "She – like your whole arrogant, pathetic government – just tried to *kill* me, for bad, stupid reasons that do not stand up to so much as a *second* of honest scrutiny. On the other hand, I have *good* reason – namely, that this person has *already* tried to treacherously *murder* me... and she may again do so, the moment when she next thinks that she can. Should I tighten my grip, and slowly crush the life out of her, hearing all the while her bones shatter and her flesh compresses to liquid? Or should I be merciful – relatively so – and just disintegrate her into vapors and dust? It would then be all over too quickly for her to feel much pain... what *say* you, loyal, 'patriotic' citizens of America?"

"*Nooo!*" wailed the 'NIAGARA' teenager. "Like – stop *hurting* her! She can't hurt you... you just proved that! Why – like – *kill* her, just out of spite!"

Somehow – though she was still held in an invisible, tight-fitting prison – the gun-woman was now again able to breathe, albeit painfully.

"Ahh... you are *wise*, child," murmured the Storied Watcher. "You have guessed the meaning of today's lesson. Why not tell everyone, so to make it clear for your fellow-peasants and your posturing little President-king?"

"Don't, like – uhh – *fuck* with you?" nervously stuttered the female teenager.

"I probably would have tried to make it a bit more – ahh – 'elegant-sounding'," opined Karéin-Mayréij, "But that will do nicely."

The alien turned and slowly walked over to where the gun-woman was being uncomfortably-imprisoned.

"Now... as for *you*," stated the Storied Watcher, "I will let you out, in a second. But mark you not stride for an exit – for if you do, the *next* time when my mind lays its trap... you will regret even more, having allowed yourself to be – how did dear Bob say it – yes, 'two dress sizes too big'. Try any more tricks, and I will show you how quickly that I can make you fit into a nice bee-kee-nee outfit. Oh-kay?"

The gun-woman slumped to the floor, drooling and gasping for breath, as the newcomer released her grip.

In a loud voice, Karéin-Mayréij addressed all within earshot.

"You can all arise and come out now," she advised. "The shooting is over with... I hope. And as for this woman – she is not permanently harmed, except perhaps for pride. That, too, is a lesson for the situation of your entire empire – at least, for now."

"What do you *mean*, lady?" asked a balding, rotund, forty-something family-man in a white shirt, as he got up on wobbly legs.

Much to the man's chagrin, the alien-girl walked over to address him, standing rather too close for comfort.

"You can call me, 'Karéin-Mayréij', if you like; or, just 'Karéin' will do, since you people seem to like first names with only one word," remarked the Storied Watcher, her demeanor changing quickly to one of familiarity and ease.

"Hi, Charlie Green," she continued, in a friendly, non-confrontational tone. "You asked me what I mean? Well... here it is. Are you listening?"

She sent a "come hither" gesture to the teenage boy with the video-camera.

"Let us sit and talk," requested Karéin-Mayréij, as two chairs, propelled by her telekinesis, self-levitated from nearby tables and deposited themselves beside the alien and the family-man.

She gestured for him to take his place on the other seat.

"You may all grab a chair and gather round, if you like," she proposed. "And bring my assailant, too. She, and others of her like, *especially* need to hear and understand this."

The gun-woman, her face ashen with panic, was prompted forward by two rather large, no-nonsense-looking black bus-boys.

Several onlookers, including the videographer and his girlfriend in the 'NIAGARA' T-shirt, hastily retrieved seats from tables in the vicinity, not a difficult task as the ordinary activities of the restaurant had now more or less come to a complete halt, with a crowd eight to ten persons deep having clustered around the Storied Watcher and the ones who had been with her, just prior.

"It is like this, Mr. Green," explained Karéin-Mayréij. "And I have already attempted to communicate what I am about to share with all of you, directly to your President, in private; but he has obviously chosen to ignore my warnings and instead broadcast lies to all his subjects. So I take it now to the ordinary citizens of this empire that you call 'America', that you may – if you are wise, and you value your own futures – force the hand of your foolish leaders, make them deal honorably with me."

"What do you, uhh, *mean*, Karéin?" asked the family-man, his composure slowly returning.

Nervously, he looked up at the crowd and tried to joke, "Hey... I feel just like one of those talk-show hosts... you know?"

The newcomer smiled at him.

"Maybe the most important 'talk-show' that your neighbors and colleagues will ever see," she agreed. "Let us start where I last was, when I was, uhh, 'interrupted', by this woman with her fine enn-arr-ay gun-training. You now sit beside the one who, very nearly at the cost of her own life, destroyed the 'Lucifer' comet and thus who saved your planet –"

A gasp issued from all around.

The 'NIAGARA' teenager exclaimed, "You mean... that was *you*? Like, the shiny-thing that was, like, on the replays that we all saw last month? Because the President said that it was, like, some new space-ship from the Air Force –"

The Storied Watcher nodded affirmatively.

"Yes – it *was* I!" she declared, with majesty resonant in her voice. "This talk from your government about the wonderful new weapon, are simple, old-fashioned lies. As to the comet... I had to unleash my greatest powers to shatter it... I can scarce comprehend or control the forces involved, and I almost died in the attempt... *almost*."

While the amazed and fascinated humans hung on her every word, the alien-girl continued, "Then, I fell to the surface of your planet, unconscious and terribly-wounded, and – by some quirk of fate that history may record as bad luck – landed somewhat north of here, within this 'America' empire. I befriended a number of people who have become like a family to me, including one boy who I have adopted as my own son; but during the time when I was still weak and without access to most of my powers, my friends and son were captured and taken hostage by the servants of your President. Since then, your government has been cruelly abusing my family –"

"*Wait* a minute," argued someone in the crowd. "How you *know* that? And if you're so powerful – why don't you just go and spring all these folks? Looks like they ain't gonna stop you with no guns..."

Karéin-Mayréij caught her questioner in her gaze, and he froze in the belated recognition of who he was interrogating.

"A fair set of questions, sir," she offered. "As to the first, you will just have to believe me, when I say that I have... *ways*, to be aware of when my friends are being hurt. My problem is that wherever your President is imprisoning my family and son, it is *very* well-hidden; as yet, I cannot precisely locate it."

"But," she warned, "I *will* find this dungeon, eventually; and when I *do*, if my family and son are still being tortured there, *I will track down your President and his courtiers... and I will smite every last one of them, even unto dust! If* the President releases my friends forthwith, and comes to me on bended knee to sue for peace, *then* I might be lenient. Between now and then, *I will slowly destroy your country*, piece by piece, so that both you all and your President cannot doubt that I mean *business*. Thus it shall *be!*"

"That's, uhh, pretty *heavy*," nervously observed the family-man. "You really expect him to do that? Just give up, that is."

"I do not *care* if he is not disposed to beg for forgiveness," shot back the Storied Watcher. "If he is stupid enough not to come to terms with what he is up against, *then he will die* – as will all those who fight for him. Perhaps also all who are unfortunate enough to be within a few-score leagues of wherever I catch him. That choice is not up to me."

At the edge of her hearing, came a small voice. "Mommy – push my chair – I want to see," it pleaded. This was followed by remonstrations by an older, female voice.

"And besides – like, why would he *want* to hurt your family, Ms. Karéin?" demanded the 'NIAGARA' teenager. "Why wouldn't he, like, want to be nice to you?"

"Ask *him*... not me!" curtly retorted the newcomer. "I can only guess at his motives, although this is a pattern that I have seen all too many times, in ages uncounted past – a tyrant becomes set in his way of abusing people who can not, or will not, effectively fight back. Then he comes upon someone who *can* do so, but understands not the peril of offending that person. Well, peasant-citizens of America... that day has now come to *your* empire. It shall be up to *you*, to make your rulers come to terms with it."

"If you almost, like, *died* to save the world," pressed the 'NIAGARA' teenager, "Why would you be, like, so mean to America... to us? What'd *we* do to you? It doesn't, like, make any sense! You can't be nice *one* day, and then be cruel the next!"

"I do not *think* like you do," parried the Storied Watcher. "I am an... 'alien'... remember? We see the same things, but in different ways – my perspective is, *different* – and whether you like it or do not... you cannot ignore it. Risking one's life to secure the future of an entire planet, an entire race; *that*, I considered to be a noble pursuit. Now, I will risk the material comforts – maybe even the lives – of many thousands who I do not know and hold dear, to save the lives of the few who I *do*. I consider *that* also to be a noble cause."

"You aren't, like, making any *sense*," protested the teenager.

"I certainly *am*, from my point of view," contradicted the alien. "And I do not *care* what you – or anyone here – thinks of the merits of my case. You need to understand that the way in which you perceive such issues, is not necessarily how others do; thus, *whatever* transpires in the next few days and weeks, the people living elsewhere on your planet will go on long into the future, with myself as their guardian and protector. Your 'America' empire can either be so protected... or it can end up as a ruined wasteland."

"I *still* don't understand!" whimpered the 'NIAGARA' teenager.

"You do not have to," stated Karéin-Mayréij. "The only one who *does*, is your President. This dispute is between me, and him. You all just happen to be in the way. That is a pity, and I am truly sorry that it has come to this – but I will *not* back down! All hope is lost for you, if your President does not heed my warning."

See, children, how it is done, she silently sent to the invisible package floating just behind the chair.

A cruel king has loyalty like a fruit-skin – bright and visible, but so thin as to peel away with but the least effort.

These humans support their ruler mostly out of fear – but if there is one who they have good cause to beware yet more...

"I can't see – there are too many people –" sounded the child-like voice from the far edge of the surrounding crowd.

The Storied Watcher arched an eyebrow.

"President's got better weapons than just a pistol," remarked one of the waiters. "You sure that you can beat the whole *U.S. Army, Navy and Air Force*? What if he drops one of them big bombs on you?"

"I shattered a *comet!*" she haughtily retorted. "Ask anyone who is familiar with the natural laws of science, as to who wins a battle between 'atom bombs', and the former measure of power. And – since as this is being recorded and will therefore come to be known within your kingdom by many millions – would you like to see some of my weapons of war? Perhaps *that* will help convince you?"

"Yeah – *sure!*" enthusiastically exclaimed the videographer.

"Very well," serenely replied Karéin-Mayréij.

She stood up, took a half-step forward, and held out her arms and legs in "X"-fashion.

There was a flash that set all about to blinking away an after-image, and when the human eyes re-adjusted, they beheld the Storied Watcher now clad in a suit of shimmering, dark-scaled, slightly glowing armor, complete with a petite skull-cap, gauntlets, war-slippers and flowing cape, with her hair bound with a dark tie into a pony-tail.

She had an enigmatic half-smile on her face.

And she looked like a demigod; or maybe, a demon.

"*Damn*," gasped the video-taking boyfriend. "She's the chick that did all that shit that went down at Rushmore!" he commented, rather too loudly.

"Excuse me, sir... can you let me through, please?" requested the little voice.

There was some muttering and grumbling from the back of the crowd, at this point.

"I am indeed – and I am just starting, in that campaign," answered the alien-girl. "You see me now garbed in my war-child, *Vîrya Ahn'jë*. She is the Burning Adamant-Mountain, who can never be pierced or defeated –"

"*Wait* a minute," interrupted the family-man, looking up from his seat. "You said, 'she'? And you gave this, uhh, suit of armor, a name? What's this all supposed to mean?"

He wiped his face with his hand. "Man, it's gotten *hot* here, all of a sudden –"

The Storied Watcher looked down and replied, "In my language, the word 'Vîrya' means 'Princess' or 'High-Born Lady'; it is her title. Ahn'jë is her given name. 'Væran' means the equivalent, for a male. Sorry about the heat – the Flame is one of Ahn'jë's attributes, as well as my own. I will ask her to refrain even more than she has already... difficult though that is for her. But she is not alone with me; no, not by any means! Observe."

There was another flash – not quite as bright – and now, the newcomer held a sword, its reddish-green blade crackling ominously with little blue motes of some kind of energy discharge.

"This is *Væran Fàiagàryuu,*" *she* explained, to the delight of many in the crowd. "His is the realm of reaving and shattering; none can withstand so much as his most moderate strike, should he mean it in anger. I believe that the President's spies and assassins have already discovered this, to their misfortune."

Væran Fàiagàryuu was released from her grasp and rapidly moved to adorn the Storied Watcher's side-belt; then, several flashes occurred in quick succession, and when all was over with, the alien-girl was bedecked in the fullness of her war-garb, with silver-gray *Vîrya I'ëà'b'* on her left arm, Stygian-cold, dark-blue *Væran Ss'éth'ch'* on her right leg and infernal, yellow-orange *Væran Ksé'l'ch'* on her left.

"Oww!" shouted the man on the chair, as he suddenly jumped up to get out of the way. "Lady, just bein' *around* you hurts like *hell!*"

Her eyes were glowing brightly and there was more than a hint of a sharp tooth showing within her mouth.

"I suppose so," amicably replied Karéin-Mayréij. "Would it help to know that what so beset you, was but a tiny *fraction* of what my war-children can emit, when it suits them? Should I release just a little of it, everything within many hundred strides of here, would be instantly reduced to a charred ruin."

"You... uhh... don't *say*," warily observed the family-man. "So... where does that leave us, uhh, 'Karéin'?"

The Storied Watcher motioned for him to sit down.

"Please," she requested. "Come as close as you can tolerate. I restrain my war-children as much as I and they, can do."

A second later, she again took a seat, and there was the smell of melting plastic and rubber.

"Where it leaves us," commented the alien-girl, "Is that I will shortly leave to give my next little, ahh, 'demonstration'. When you see – however briefly, as I have observed how your government is of the habit of suppressing information – what I will do, you should demand of the President that he sue for peace and return my family unharmed. If he refuses, I will continue with my next target, and the next one, and the next... sooner or later, I will run out of places and things that I can destroy without endangering human lives. I will try as hard as I can to get my message across without killing anyone – but I can not and *will not* guarantee that nobody will ever be harmed."

She fell silent for a second or two, then quietly added in a compassionate voice, "I want all of you – and all American peasants – to know that I would much prefer to be your friend and guardian... not to be someone who brings terror and destruction. I seek no personal gain, and I have not the *slightest* interest in ruling over you... I do not, ahem, make a very good Empress. But I will *not* compromise on this matter, and I *will* rescue my family and son. All those who hear these words, should not doubt my resolve!"

"Woww," came a young voice from behind a forest of legs.

Karéin-Mayréij bent forward and to one side, as if trying to determine the source of the exclamation. The glow in her eyes changed subtly.

"Child – come unto me," she commanded, beckoning with her hand and fingers.

Purgin' And Scourgin'

"So how are we *doin'*, Brother Martin?" asked the severe-looking man in the huge room, its gloomy lighting and very size accentuating its funereal atmosphere.

His tone indicated that he did not expect a positive answer, and that was what he got.

"Well, sir," stated the younger man at the other end of the secured, dedicated-circuit computer phone-conversation, "We're doing about as well as we had anticipated... our operatives are slowly working their way toward the command-and-control apparatus... that's the good news. Unfortunately – and this is the bad news – it looks like the military is now working under some very tight constraints about firing off one of the bombs –"

"Not good – *not* good," muttered Brother Harold. "But we got to keep workin' at it – that's all there is to it. If I wasn't so good a Christian, I'd probably be sayin' somethin' that'd get me into a lot of trouble with the Lord, right now... alright. Listen, Brother – what about the previous option; that is, 'get one for our own use'? Anythin' you think we can do on that front?"

"We *have* been following up on that angle," commented Brother Martin, "Several of the faithful have come pretty close – for example, we have two in deep-cover at Kirtland in New Mexico, and they were making good progress, which was encouraging because until recently this was the main depot – but I'm afraid that they kind of hit a brick wall in terms of security, neither of them have the necessary clearances... they're reporting that if they push their luck, they'll *certainly* be caught."

""Scuse *me*," interrupted the shadowy-man, reflexively running a hand through his black, Brylcreemed hair, "But didn't we say that they need to take some *chances*, on this initiative? Problem we got is, these guys don't *believe*... they don't have any *guts*, and we're runnin' out of *time*. Didn't you see the pictures from up Rushmore way, what with the desecration of a national monument? The Devil-Thing looks like it may *already* be past the ability of conventional weapons to bring down, if we don't act soon –"

Taking an uncharacteristic chance, the man on the other end of the line interjected, "I *did* see that awful episode up north, Brother Harold, sir – and you're probably right about what kind of firepower needs to be used – no, let me take that back – you surely *are* right, but the situation isn't quite as bad as you may think... I accept the blame for not having kept you as up to date on it, as perhaps I should have."

"Go on," requested the Christian leader.

"See... the thing is," explained Brother Martin, "Although it has proved impossible to get our hands on one of the devices – *yet* – our intelligence about what the military is, itself, doing with them, is much better. Their problem is that after the 'comet'-thing, they're short of bombs; and because they don't know where the Devil-Girl may strike next, their only practical strategy is to disperse the few devices that they do have, so that there's at least one reasonably close by, in the event that she – sorry, it – happens to show up in the vicinity. That may open up some *opportunities* for us, sir. For example, one of them is about to be shipped to Barksdale... the Air Force base, I mean. That's in Louisiana, which is a friendly place for us – we've got a lot of local volunteer-observers around there, so that when the goods get delivered, we'll know about it –"

"Wait a minute," interrupted the severe man. "You think we could make an interception, at that point? I mean – before it gets delivered to the base and gets all bunkered-up?"

There was a short pause; then the younger man answered, "I don't know, sir – just thinking out loud, I don't think we'd have a problem getting info on the precise time and route... but in the past, these things are always sent in a convoy, with plenty of hand-picked MP's and other guards around... on the other hand, we've got *hundreds* of the faithful in that state, and of course there wouldn't be any shortage of firearms, it's bedrock NRA-country... but it'd still be pretty risky..."

"'Who dares, wins' – that's how the sayin' goes," countered Brother Harold. "Listen – where are the other ones headed? I'm just thinkin' that we might be able to go after another one, just in case we miss the first target."

"Other than for two that we know are in Kirtland," elaborated Brother Martin, "And for the bomb that we found out is being moved to Barksdale, we're not that sure about the fourth one, sir. Various reports have it either at Grand Forks – North Dakota, that is – or somewhere in the Pacific Northwest, Bangor in Washington, possibly... that's where they put the missiles on the submarines. I know that time is of the essence, but the other thing worth keeping in mind is, our sources are saying that the military might have as many as twenty bombs, by this time next month –"

"If we don't do *somethin'* soon, Brother," growled Brother Harold, "There might not *be* a next month – at least, not for us Christians, that is. We wait any longer, and the Anti-Christ – ably assisted and abetted by them accursed Muslims – is gonna set up its dominion right here in God's chosen country, and when Lord Jesus shows up to do the final battle, He's gonna have some mighty tough questions for us all to answer – such as, 'what did *you* risk in the fight against Satan, when my first set of Apostles all went and got themselves thrown to the lions in Rome, for My sake'?"

"As the Lord is my witness, sir," earnestly remarked the younger man, over the secure-phone, "I wouldn't know *what* to say to my Savior, if that were to happen – I'd be lost –"

"Right... and I don't know about *you*, Brother," the severe man inveighed, "But I don't want to have to be makin' excuses about *that*, to Lord Jaysus... remember, there's no doubt that He's gonna win and then cast the Deceiver, and his harlot female offspring, into the Lake of Fire; but there *is* a question, as to who's going to be thrown down in there, as well. You and me, we aren't like the average lay follower in the flock – at least *they'll* be able to plead ignorance of the situation, in front of the Lord, and beg for His mercy; but as for *us*, the burden is one hundred per-cent, on *our* shoulders – and we had better *not* shirk the duty that God has laid upon us. See what I mean?"

"I sure do, sir," acknowledged Brother Martin "The risk of trying and failing, that may be death; but the risk of *not* trying..."

"*Damnation* – for all eternity," confirmed the Christian leader, as softly as he ever would. "*That's* what's at stake, for the both of us."

"You know, sir," offered the man at the remote end of the line, "When I accepted my first promotion, I never thought I'd be carrying a responsibility like *this*... with such awful consequences, I mean. I don't mean any *disrespect*, sir – but if I had it to do all over again, I'd have been smarter just to have stayed as a humble believer down in Spartanburg. I'm just a *sinner*... not a godly leader of men, like you are, sir; I don't know if I'm up to it... I just don't *know*."

He fell silent.

"I'd remind you," counseled Brother Harold, in a fatherly way, "That Saint Peter was just a fisherman, until the Lord selected him, for great things. Every one of us that have heard the call, why, we've all had the same doubts – I'll let you in on a secret here, Brother – even *me*."

"Even... *you*?" asked the other man, incredulously.

"Even *me*," admitted Brother Harold. "It happened to me just before we purged 'n scourged all those fence-sittin' half-believers, and confiscated all their property, 'bout twenty year ago. But I prayed and prayed and *prayed*, and the Lord spoke to me and gave me the confidence to rise up and lead the flock, to show them the way. It will be the same with you... just you wait. Afterwards, you're gonna *know* what your purpose in life is, and you're gonna *know* that *nothin's* gonna keep you from fulfillin' it. Just do the best that you can to follow my orders and implement our plans, and you'll succeed – I have *faith* in you, Brother; that's why I picked you as my second-in command. And if you do your duty well, when the Lord calls me home, I mean for *you* to be my successor. Did you know that?"

"Me... *me*?" stuttered the younger man. "But, blessed *Brother* –"

"As surely as Moses passed the mantle on to Joshua, so many years ago," reflectively added Brother Harold. "You know, son... I've been doin' a lot of prayin' lately, and the Lord keeps sayin', 'it could be any day now, when you must lay down your life in this world, so to begin your *real* life, with Me'. It's not a message that I particularly *like*... but that decision's not up to me. It's my duty to listen, accept and do what my Savior tells me to. And for the record – wherever He leads me, whatever He bids me do... I'm ready."

"Praise the Lord," intoned Brother Martin. "With God's help... so am I."

"Okay," said the severe man, now back on track. "Now, speakin' of plans... here's what I want to do, from here on in. You need to get this-here Barksdale thing goin' the minute we get off the line, but I got some special instructions – you got somethin' to write with?"

"Ready and able," enthusiastically answered the acolyte.

I See A Light

In the damp, humid heat they waited, some anxiously, while the ones of greater faith had no qualms at all.

The blackness of this rural Louisiana night was only dimly offset by the illumination of a quarter-moon, and this leaked but feebly, through an overcast Southern sky.

Something rather "un-Christian" was heard, the sound coming from behind the heavily-armed, SWAT-geared man, who was crouching, along with the rest of the first echelon, behind a dense stand of bushes next to the state secondary-highway.

"Keep that *down*, Brother!" admonished the armed man. "Air Force sometimes sends advance teams – remember?"

"Sorry, Brother," apologized a voice from the third rank, ten feet or so behind the combat-geared man near the road. "It's just these, uhh, blessed mosquitoes... they're eating me *alive!*"

"Me too!" complained another voice, this one closer to the SWAT-garbed man. "We've been camped out here for four *hours* now... and there's *still* no sign of them. Are you *sure* this is the right place? What if they changed the route?"

"*Patience!*" counseled the dark-clad warrior. "They'll be here. Martin said so – and he has a direct-line to the Leader. I spoke to Brother Martin yesterday, and he said that the only way we can miss, is if they cancel the entire transfer. He's one hundred per-cent certain about it."

"How's that possible?" demanded the voice from the third rank. "*Nothing's* one hundred per-cent for sure... unless the Lord's behind it."

"The Lord's with us, and we have a tip from the GrayWar folk... remember?" stated the SWAT-man. "How do you think we're going to know which truck the goods are being kept in? We got more than a *couple* of the faithful on the inside of that outfit – and they have the exclusive on driving the vehicles. Just one quick toss of a Day-Glo paint-balloon and we know where to go. Don't you remember the briefings we had back in the Temple?"

"Well... the convoy's already more than an two hours late... so what if they *did* call it off, and how would we *know* –" argued the man in the second rank, before he was interrupted.

"*Silence!*" commanded the lead-warrior. "Something's coming in!"

He hit a hidden toggle-switch on one of the small electronics-boxes that were attached to his Kevlar-II flak-jacket, pushed an earphone back into position and started talking into a chin-mike.

"What's that? Oh... good," he whispered, the excitement in his voice rising with every word. "Yeah, I'm synchronized already – check on the 11:37. I *know* – but those GrayWar boys are drunk or stoned, half the time... okay, *okay* – I believe you... I just wanted independent confirmation. We're ready... absolutely. Just have the shielded transport ready the second that I give the signal... you know the drill. With the Lord's help, we *will* prevail! Out."

He uttered a command : "Lay low – and prepare to die for the Father God!"

Now all eyes turned to look at the far end of this second-class Dixie road, its macadam and asphalt receding into the oppressive haze in the distance.

But shortly someone called out,

"I see a light."

Now I Am Become...

Reluctantly, a few people in the front ranks of the crowd made way, revealing a young boy, tan-skinned and dark-haired, with East Indian or Hispanic blood in him, perhaps ten or eleven years of age – confined to a wheelchair, with thin-looking legs covered by a blanket.

Upon beholding the Storied Watcher, his jaw dropped, and he just sat there, regarding her with an awed, astonished stare.

"I bade you come hither," she demanded, with the insouciant arch of an eyebrow.

The boy in the wheelchair made no response, for a second or two; but then, he let out a sound like "whoa", as the chair was drawn toward the alien-girl by some unseen force.

Now he was right in front of her, all eyes of the crowd upon them both.

"I am Karéin-Mayréij," she self-introduced, in a friendly voice. "This man to the side of me, here, is Charlie Green. What is *your* name, young man?"

Just to be polite, she communicated to her war-children.

Of course, I know this already... but he is just a young one, like all of ye...

"B-Bobby," he answered. "Bobby Sharma, that is. Sorry about pushing my way through, with my chair, I mean... I can't walk."

He paused and then stammered, "Are you the – the – the, *angel*-lady?"

"Yes, I am," she evenly replied.

"Uhh, Karéin," interjected Green, "What... what exactly do you *mean* by that?"

"Just what I said," she replied, matter-of-factly. "*I am the 'angel-lady'.*"

There were a few gasps and murmurs, from within the crowd.

"Bobby," inquired Karéin-Mayréij, "Why did you come here? To see me, I mean."

"I... I don't know," he said. "Just to *see* you, I guess... I didn't think you were *real*. Oww... being so close to you – like being too close to a fireplace. Can you let me move back a bit... please?"

"Well, I am *very* real – and no, you did *not* come here just to, 'see' me... did you, Bobby?" she countered, her gaze holding him in a withering, overwhelming presence. "But you cannot go back, son – you have come too far, already. Instead... you need to come even closer. Come and sit on my lap, child. Take my hand."

"*What?*" fearfully exclaimed the boy, "I can't do *that!* I can't walk, and you have fire all *over* you – there's smoke coming off your hand, from that black metal glove –"

"Umm-hmm," patiently acknowledged the Storied Watcher.

"Somebody make her *stop!*" shouted the wheelchair-boy. "I'll burn up!"

From the back of the crowd, a desperate, female voice sounded. "Let me through – oh, Bobby, why did you – let *go* of me!"

"STFU," cursed another voice. "You want to get us all *killed*?"

"Kid pushed forward," muttered still another. "Serves him right! This is gonna be *ugly* to watch."

"Karéin –" pleaded Green, holding one arm up to ward off the shimmering waves of heat coming from her direction. "For the love of *God*... have pity on the boy – that armor of yours looks like it just came out of a blast-furnace –"

"Quite right," agreed the alien-girl. "Those who touch *Vìrya Ahn'jë* without her favor, will be burned – even to charcoal-dust. As will they who touch my person, without the same blessing. That is actually a *mercy*, you know. Worse, slower, more painful things can result, to those who mean ill to my war-children and I."

"But the kid –" stammered the man. "Please, *please* – don't hurt him!"

Spirit guide me , silently prayed the alien.

Send the Immortal Light.

Mother, why ? queried a host of enigmatic, private voices.

Search thy hearts... and ye shall know, she sent back.

"Bobby," counseled the Storied Watcher, staring intently at the child, "I will ask you two questions – and you must answer them with your truest heart. Oh-kay?"

"S-sure," whimpered the wheelchair-boy. "Can I go, then? It's really starting to feel *hot*."

"Bobby," she continued, "I am different from everyone else on this beautiful little blue-and-green world. Neither you, nor your parents, nor your grandmother or grandfather, have *ever* met someone like me. I can do *wondrous* things. Do you believe that?"

For a second, he looked entranced, but eventually he tearfully replied, "Y-yes".

From somewhere off in the distance, an ethereal tune started to play, its notes haunting, beautiful and dignified.

"Bobby," she pressed, her inspired eyes enveloping him, touching his soul, "I will *not* hurt you – and neither will my war-children. The pain will be there – I will not deny that – but I will make you safe against it. No-one else on Earth can do such a thing, that is, 'pain-and-no-pain, all rolled into one'. Do you understand?"

A strange look of peace fell over the child's visage.

"Yes," he mumbled.

"Take my hand," commanded Karéin-Mayréij, extending her right arm. "And close your eyes."

The wheelchair was drawn yet closer, and as the boy leaned forward, he was slowly levitated out of his seat. In a second or two, his fingers made contact with her own, and he let out a deep sigh.

"You will smell some smoke, but do not worry," she softly counseled, with the hint of a wry smile. "Although after this day is over, you may need a new set of clothes. Perhaps this shall be your 'burnt offering'? They tell me that the priests around here – at least some of them – still call for such."

He was surrounded by her infernal heat, little tongues of fire licking greedily at his hair, body and clothes, with wisps of smoke and a scorched smell issuing forth; but neither was he consumed, nor was he harmed.

Instead, Bobby lazily opened his eyes and looked up at the Storied Watcher.

A shimmering blue glow surrounded them both, now, while a gentle, haunting, healing song, played subtly in the background.

"My *God!*" breathed a voice from the crowd, as they saw the boy, his withered, useless legs dangling to one side, come safely to rest on the alien's lap.

"Why isn't he being burned *up?*" someone whispered. "Damn clothes look like they're gonna flash any *second!*"

Neither was that bush up on the mountain, the waiter dared to think.

"Ohhh," he moaned. "I feel the fire – so *hot* – but it doesn't hurt," he offered, as if in a trance. "That's neat..."

"It is... is it not?" she replied, maternally. "Now let my power rest upon you, son. Let it flow into you, take it in, *drink* of it – when the pain of my *Fire* comes to you – do not jump away from it, do not hide; instead, welcome it... like how your hand becomes used to the warmth of a hot bath. Are you ready?"

Take him as one of thine own, children, sent Karéin-Mayréij, to her strange creations.

Dreamily, the boy just nodded.

A second later, he let out a pitiful yelp, but this lasted only a half-second, as he then slumped into unconsciousness.

"What – what the hell are you *doin'* there?" demanded one of the family-men.

"He is resting, now," introspectively commented the Storied Watcher, as she gently stroked the somnolent boy's hair. "And his body waxes strong."

She paused for a few seconds; then, staring far out to space, with a tear welling in one dimly-glowing eye, she added, "You know, he reminds me *so* much of my own son... my Tommy. Oh, where *are* you, little one... where... *are*... you. My heart calls out to you..."

An overwhelming wave of sadness and loneliness, tempered with mystic things, washed over the crowd. Several almost fainted, and it was all the teenager with the camera could do, not to drop it.

"Like, get *ouut!*" gasped the "NIAGARA" girl.

Near-absolute silence now fell upon the scene. All that was heard, other than for human breathing and the faint after-echo of the Storied Watcher's healing-song, was the low crackle of *Ahn'jë's* body-fire.

After perhaps a minute or two, the boy's eyelids again flittered open, and he whispered, "Hey."

"Hey," she echoed. "How are you feeling, dear child?"

"Warm. Good," he replied.

"*Vîrya Ahn'jë* tells me that she has become quite fond of you, Bobby," observed the alien-girl, with a patient smile. "She says that your ailment was much easier to remedy, than that of the last young one, who she and her sister were called upon to help."

"What do you *mean?*" he inquired.

The boy looked down and noticed that his hand was resting on the ebon-glowing scales of the body-armor, and he almost took a start when he saw the little flickers of flame washing over his fingers.

Yet the Storied Watcher's own hand moved quickly to rest over the boy's, and she remarked, "See – did I not *promise* that the *Fire*, and the pain, would be made to be friendly? But I would caution you not to try stirring a camp-fire with your fingers... at least, not yet. The flame of my war-child is different – more subtle and intelligent – than the talisman of the fearsome Incandescent Lord, and it will take you and your people some time, to grasp it as you do the essence of young, mighty *Vîrya Ahn'jë.*"

She looked down at the boy from the wheelchair.

"You can go now, Bobby," she directed. "Though, we *will* meet again, when the times are more forgiving... and after I have, ahem, paid a visit to the rather long list of people to whom I have run up a debt."

"But I don't *want* to," protested the boy. "It's so nice and *warm* here in your arms."

"You're on *fire*, kid!" someone had the nerve to shout. "Would that be a *problem?*"

Bobby shrugged, indifferently and snuggled deeper into the newcomer's grasp.

"Here," she mentioned, taking him by the shoulders, her grasp causing more smoke to issue from the child's already ruined, black-stained clothes as she held him almost off her lap. "Son – nothing would please me and *Vîrya Ahn'jë* more than to hold you for a day, a week, a year... but if you stay in my grasp much longer, your clothes would burn up. That would not hurt... but you do not want to walk out of here in the *nude*, do you? Besides, your mother waits in frantic state behind the crowd, and it would be cruel of both of us to deny her love. Go to her, now."

"I don't *want* to, but... okay... I guess... but... I need my chair..." he requested.

"No... you do not," countered Karéin-Mayréij. "I will put you down. Your legs will feel strange... they will tingle, like your arms do when they have been left too long in one position. But put one foot ahead of the other, and make sure to keep your balance. Instinct will take over from there. Go."

The boy's feet hit the floor and instantly his knees crumpled, resulting in him sitting in woebegone fashion, looking up in desperation at the Storied Watcher.

"Pick me up – *please!*" he wailed.

She got up and bowed down over him.

"Arise," she commanded.

"I *can't*," he whimpered.

"Yes, you *can*," contradicted the alien-girl.

"I had an accident – when I was little," he tried to explain. "Since then –"

The music, akin to a far-off *Ave Maria*, started to play, again.

Ooo-ooo-oooo...

Now, the Storied Watcher went down on one knee, regarding the child straight-on.

"Bobby," she compassionately instructed, "A few minutes ago, I asked you to sit down in a brazier of fire – the cauldron of my own being, and that of *Vîrya Ahn'jë* – yet not to be hurt. You overcame both fear and doubt and did something *extraordinary*. Now, I ask you to do something much easier – if you will only *believe*. Do you trust me, son?"

Her eyes were glowing gold, as was the aura coming from all about her.

This ain't no damn *TV space-alien*, realized the barkeep, as awed gasps issued from the crowd.

The filial look again appeared on the boy's face.

"Yes... yes... I... *do*," he said.

"Then get up," demanded Karéin-Mayréij, beckoning with her hand, just out of reach.

While the audience held its breath, the boy painfully came to his feet, his atrophied legs looking impossibly thin to be supporting his more muscular upper-body.

Squinting with discomfort, he regarded the alien-girl and forced out, "Ohh, this is *so* much harder than touching the fire."

"No less a miracle," whispered someone in the back of the crowd.

"My war-children and I believe you," encouraged the Storied Watcher, to no-one in particular. "And we believe *in* you. A short time ago, a very long way from here, some dear friends did the same for *me*, and I did what I thought *I* never could. Now – so will you."

The music reached a hallowed crescendo but then gradually tapered off, as the newcomer pointed to the place in the crowd from which the wheelchair had emerged.

"Your Mom is back there, Bobby," she remarked. "Go to her, now – and give her my love. Your legs grow stronger with each second... but take your time."

Step by special-effort step, the boy stumbled forward. Halfway to the crowd, he turned and looked at the wheelchair, then at the Storied Watcher.

His face beaming with gratitude, Bobby disappeared into the forest of humanity.

Now, Karéin-Mayréij looked up at the crowd and proclaimed, her voice resonant with revelation, "See how the Burning-Angel leads you onward in the long journey; your ancestors surpassed their animal beginnings, by daring to use the Flame as a tool and weapon... but you could not touch it, you could not *be* one with it..."

The entranced crowd hung on her every word, as she explained, "Now, with time, willpower and learning and – yes, I will say it, a little, uhh 'magic' – your people can take the next step... the one that will empower you to visit the very stars in the firmament. For without this gift, I warn, ever will you be bound to this beautiful, but, ultimately, *finite*, little planet... oh-kay, possibly, also, her sister-worlds, who likewise encircle yonder Sun. And all this shall I do for you, and so much more; if only you will trust and respect me... if only, you will make your 'President', safely return those who I love."

"You're, like, *wicked* neat, lady," piped up the girl with the "NIAGARA" shirt. "So what you gonna do now?"

The Storied Watcher arose from her chair – the charred, scalded thing looked like someone had built a bonfire on it – and slowly walked over to the teenager, with fear more and more visible on her visage as the alien came face-to-face with her.

Pointing at the 'NIAGARA'-girl, the newcomer disclosed, "Ash-lee... Ash-lee Kras-now-skee... right?"

Dumbfounded, the teenager fell tongue-tied for a second or two, but eventually managed to respond, "Y-yeah... holy *crap* – how'd you, like... *know* that?"

"I know a *lot* of things," answered Karéin-Mayréij. "By means that you will have to, ahh, guess at."

The "NIAGARA"-girl inquired, "So... like... where you goin' now? You don't suppose I could convince you to come to the studio with Keith 'n me for a real interview – okay, it's not really a *studio*, it's, like, just his basement – but he's got a direct link up to Neo down there, bar-fridge that you can have anything you want out of, and –"

A friendly look now adorned the Storied Watcher's face, as she countered, "I do not think that would be a good idea, Ash-lee – your government has tried to kill me every time that they know where I am, or think they know; and though

I could probably protect you and Keith, I likely could not do so for the entire city-block where you live, and be of no illusion, the President would not hesitate to kill everyone in the vicinity, to have a chance to strike at me. You would be, how do they say, 'coll-at-ral damage' – the loss of which they give not the slightest care about."

Uh-oh, mused the barkeep. *If they do* here, *what they did at that hotel down Tucson way –*

"Even now," noted the alien-girl, "I have probably overstayed my welcome at this eating-hall, since the President's spies are listening to all the mobile conversations coming from here – his death-rockets and armored war-chariots may already be on their way. So must I also prepare my travel-wings, and I would advise all around here to do so, as well. There is no need to panic... I will tell you if I detect an imminent attack."

Despite her counsel, more than a few started heading rapidly for the exits.

The Storied Watcher shook her head in rueful acknowledgement and half-turned to address those who remained.

"So much good food and drink left unconsumed," she commented. "Well, better a meal not to be eaten, than it be one's last, I suppose."

To the barkeep, she apologized, "Sorry for the chair, sir... you can add the cost of replacing it to my account here, for the next time when I return."

"Oh... that's okay," he answered, obviously somewhat at a loss. "We'll, uhh, write it off, like for when they get broke by somebody too fat, sittin' on it... happens all the *time*, you know."

He reached for a microphone and threw a switch.

"Ladies and gentlemen," he announced, "We regret to inform you that due to – uhh – unforeseen circumstances, the restaurant will be closing for the day, in five minutes. Could you all please leave your payments in cash on your tables... or failing that, leave a phone number where we can reach you tomorrow. Thank you for choosing Earl Bottoms for your eating experience today, and you all have a safe drive home... you hear?"

"Thanks," acknowledged the Storied Watcher. And again she turned to address the ten to twenty people who had tarried.

"Praise be to all of you, for lending your ears to my counsel and story," she called out. "I have said it to many across this land, but I will say it again : sooner or later, all disputes come to an end, and when *this* one does as well, I hope that you will understand my ways – and that you will forgive what I now must do. In the meantime, tell your 'President' that he plays with a *Fire* that he cannot control; his time is up; he *must* sue for peace. He simply... *must!*"

Her eyes turned downward, and she started speaking an intonation in a thoroughly foreign tongue, as if to no-one; but in fact, had the humans understood, they would have heard,

"*Prepare thyselves, children; for the past tests were just practice-tilting... do ye feel the warning?*

Ye are ready now – and the metal-and-glue death-birds approach, as yet far away – but they close rapidly upon us.

Shall we teach them why to fear the offspring of the Makailkh?

Gird thyselves for war!

"She's talkin' to that smokin' *armor* of hers," whispered a country-boy.

"Yeah... give anythin' to know what she's sayin'," quietly offered one of the bus-boys.

"Betcha so would the President," muttered Green.

The alien-girl turned and marched purposefully toward the door, each footstep leaving an dark boot-print of melted floor-covering, steaming as she went.

Many of the humans tagged along, keeping a respectful distance behind.

"What she call herself... 'Burnin' Angel?" inquired a bus-boy, *sotto voce.*

"Either that... or she's the 'Burnin' *Devil*'," confided a country-bumpkin.

"No devil," protested the former wheelchair-boy, who had stumbled with awkward determination, his mother in tow, behind the alien-followers.

"I got to know her... she kinda got inside my head – she's not a bad lady," he added.

"*I* believe you, son," said a family-man, "Millions wouldn't."

A second later, he stopped dead in his tracks for a second or two, as a totally unfamiliar, unrequited thought impressed itself into his psyche.

Never a devil, nor divinity, nor demon, it advised. *A riddle, why? Thus the answer – I have seen and fought all three; and far beyond thy ken*, human of mortal birth, *are they. As am I, who speaks as a friend, to thy mind.*

Now, she had reached the outside, and as she advanced into the open area of the parking-lot, a few, including the videographer, were incautious enough to follow her even to here.

From every direction, other-worldly music, martial yet uplifting and beautiful, began to beset the senses of the humans.

A high wind started to move the trees, where there had previously been none.

Karéin-Mayréij wheeled, her eyes shining like an arc-torch.

The ground around her for several meters began to fume and darken, and one or two of the onlookers realized that their cars, parked nearby, would shortly need a new paint-job.

The wind around her, akin to a nascent tornado, began to kick up a haze of dust, which flickered and sparked as the inflammable particles within it were overcome by her surging heat.

"Wish you a painful death? Stand *back*, far back!" commanded the Storied Watcher, her voice now resounding with the timbre of godly – or, perhaps – demonic, majesty. "Else you be consumed by my *Fire* – to say nothing of those energies that you cannot see. The latter are slower to kill... but no less effective."

"*Jesus, Mary and Joseph!*" breathed one of the family-men, as he swapped one hand rapidly for the other, trying to protect his eyes while avoiding having the top sides of his fingers from being blistered. "It's like openin' a gas-barbecue too slow, after it's been on 'high' for an hour –"

The music now echoed furiously from all around; it even seemed to be coming from the overhead speakers, back in the restaurant.

The Storied Watcher, her feet and body planted in fighting-pose, her arms held outward with *Væran Fàiagàryuu* and *Vìrya I'ëà'b'* adorning the right and left respectively, looked up to the heavens and exclaimed,

"*Mark me*, President-king, tormentor of my loved-ones! You send your war-birds on my trail? They seek to find me... to do *battle?* No need, anymore – here, I will come and find *them*... and *you;* for now, I am become – who I *am!*"

The heat became too great for even the most hardy of the onlookers – too savage was it even for the child who, not a half-hour before, had laid comfortably in the Storied Watcher's burning embrace. He, along with all the other human onlookers, crashed back through the door, falling clumsily one on top of another, in a pain-driven panic to avoid permanent damage.

But a few had had the foresight to regard the scene from behind a window. Though even from *this* vantage-point, they were still beset by the cruel energy that streamed from every point on the fearsome being's frame, they were still able to see a shimmering, faintly blue-green shroud, looking for all accounts as delicate as a huge soap-bubble, envelop the mighty and enigmatic one called, 'Karéin-Mayréij'.

A second later, their eyes were involuntarily-shut, as a brilliance too great to behold, lit up everything for miles around.

It streaked into the sky, leaving nothing but memories of the impossible, and little wisps of fire, here and there.

Comes The Fire; Comes The Thunder

An ordinary man – or woman – would probably have been terrified by having a black, eyeless 'special-rendition'-hood jammed over his or her head, and, no doubt about it, the minds of all four of the former Mars mission astronauts raced with shock and disorientation, as their mundane senses were totally cut off from the outside world.

But 'ordinary', was the wrong word to use, today.

I was way too optimistic, issued the angry thoughts of Brent Boyd.

I said ten minutes... it was more like five.

Sorry.

"Drag 'em on," barked the sergeant.

Jacobson, Tanaka, White and Boyd each felt the grasp of a guard on their uniforms, as they were pulled forward, towards... who *knew*, where.

What the fuck *we s'posed to do now, Commander?* thought White.

Just go and get our necks stretched?

Trying to think, fast, broadcasted Jacobson.

Can't see, but I... perceive the scene, heading toward... hard to make out from the little shining pulses... looks like one of those elevators, the cage things that they use in building constructions.

Can the rest of you feel the scene, too?

I want to tear them limb from limb, wailed Tanaka's mind.

How much is too much?

And yes... damn, God bless you, Karéin, this must be infra-red, or something like that... goes right through these stinking 'rendition'-hoods.

Sam... let me do it!

There was a rattle, then a muffled curse.

Through the hood, Jacobson's enlightened eyes could see that they had thrown White against the cage-wall of the elevator, which now started to descend.

No – don't be stupid, Cherie, mentally cautioned the former Mars mission commander.

They're armed... we aren't.

We have to play this smart and find out what the hell's going on.

Just wait, he sent to her.

I just resigned from the Air Force, silently growled Boyd.

Goin' down, and fast, communicated White.

Brent, if I don't quit... do I get your pension?

It was all the rest could do to avoid laughing, but at least, the gallows-humor smiles were hidden by the black hoods.

The elevator was descending rapidly, now.

Jesus... this thing is deep, sent Boyd.

And I'm feeling those little flecks of energy more strongly now.

Commander – when do we pull the plug?

I don't think they mean us to come back, from wherever we're going.

Their ears heard something being mumbled into a microphone. It sounded like "Jacobson detainees ingress, one minute."

I won't issue any orders from here on, Jacobson broadcasted, his thoughts laden with sadness and the anger of betrayal.

But if you want to know what I plan to do... if it looks like they're about to murder us – God knows why – I will fight for my life.

Just don't ask me how...

I'm closing my eyes now, Sam, lest they see the glow, reverberated Tanaka's mind, across those of the other three.

Sensei, guide my steps... this I pray.

Let thy power flow to my brothers.

Make them strong... make them ready.

"What was *that?*" demanded one of the guards. "Whoever you are – belay that noise *immediately* – you're on a dedicated channel!"

Fuckin' ay, Professor, sent White.

I pray along with y'all, sister – first-blessed by the Hammer of God.

Send us the Fire!

To the minds of all four, the music sounded like something that they had heard before, far out toward Mars.

A faint voice came back over what must have been a small speaker within the elevator-cage.

"Copied but not understood," it declared. "We're playing *nothing* from down here, Sergeant!"

It feels like when I first touched minds with her – came mental gasps from Boyd's struggling psyche.

Barely able to keep standing, he half-slumped against the side of the cage, but luckily, none of the guards either noticed or cared.

"I say again, *belay that music!*" gruffly ordered the leading guard. "I hear any *more* of it and I'll give you the 50 lashes, *personally!*"

My God, Cherie! reflected Jacobson.

How long have you been this way?

"Checked carrier and sub-carrier," replied the remote voice. "We've got nothing but static. Must be a crossed wire, or something. We'll have a look at it when you get them off the lift... copy?"

As of about ten minutes ago, she sent back.

She said it would happen this way.

When you really need it, then, it comes... and you'll know that the time is right.

I just know, *Sam.*

Oh, can you feel *it? Can* you?

"Copy. You better be *right*, mister," grunted the sergeant. "ETA ten seconds... get 'em ready, Binks.".

I thought I knew Amaiish, mused Jacobson. *I was* wrong.

No wonder *she* warned *us about the* Fire.

It burns *in my mind, it cries to be let loose* –

How do we use it, Professor? silently asked Boyd, his mind slowly coming out of a thick haze.

With a loud 'clang', the elevator-cage hit what must have been the bottom of the shaft.

She said, 'imagine what you want to happen', I think, communicated Tanaka.

Just a guess – but I'd bet you were at least a hundred feet below the surface, Jacobson mentally commented to his team.

"Okay, get 'em out," ordered the mercenary leader. "Single file, right into the operations room. Hand-off to base personnel at that point."

Again, they were roughly grabbed and swung into place, then dragged forward.

I try not to imagine things like that, muttered White, mentally.

But maybe today – I'll make an exception, y'all know?

"Rodge," said another voice, evidently from a gendarme at the back of the group of guards.

Awkwardly, the four hooded captives, who had, not an hour before, each been proud, loyal professionals, each in his or her personal way – shuffled down what, to them, seemed to be a featureless, office-style corridor, with white tile everywhere and florescent lights on the ceiling, roughly at ten-meter intervals.

They traveled for a considerable distance – Boyd tried to count the footsteps, but gave up after several hundred – around three or four turns and bends.

Finally, they arrived at a door inset into the wall, its outlines barely visible to the dim special-sight that Jacobson and his crew had been relying on, ever since they had been hooded.

"We're here," announced the sergeant, speaking to his own men.

There was a knock, and, through the black sacks enveloping their heads, the Mars astronauts perceived the figure of a man, smaller by at least a head compared to the goons from GrayWar, dressed in a garment looking somewhat like a supermarket meat-department smock.

"Who's – oh, hello, there!" remarked this man. "I see you've brought our new 'guests'... *excellent!* Right this way."

"Duty-detail ends at this point," indicated the gruff voice of the sergeant. "I have a release for you to sign, acknowledging receipt of Samuel Jacobson, Brent Boyd, Devon White and Cherie Tanaka, previously of the Air Force Special Holding Facility. After this is completed, our hand-off process will be complete. Understood?"

"Oh... *certainly*," answered the smock-man, and there was a slick, ghoulish smoothness in his voice that put the hackles immediately up on the back of Jacobson's neck. "Just lead 'em in here... we have our own people to, ahh, keep things under *control*. Where do I sign?"

"Here," mentioned the sergeant.

He motioned to two of the guards and ordered, "Willets, McTavish – escort them into the room, execute hand-over to local prisoner-control staff. Ten second turn-around."

"Any problems so far?" inquired the man in the smock. "Have they been good little boys and girls?"

"Just a little back-talk at first," noted the sergeant. "But after we set 'em right about who's in charge... no, they've been pretty quiet, I'd say."

Along with the others, Jacobson felt a rough push in the small of his back, effected, probably, by the butt of an automatic-rifle.

Unwillingly, followed by Boyd, Tanaka and White, he slowly proceeded into a large, circular room.

The walls were covered with various storage-cabinets and electronic items, and there were four stretchers, or gurneys, or something like that; more than anything else, it looked like a hospital operating-room.

Along with the man that had signed off on the manifest, there was another like him and also four gendarmes, each armed in a similar manner to the ones that had hustled his crew down the elevator, but different, somehow – although the details were hard to make out, the uniforms and weapons were not the same as those of their former captors.

Commander... what's that smell? came White's thoughts. *Like blood, or sh –*

"That's *it!*" angrily protested the Mars mission leader. "I *demand* to know whose custody we're being assigned to! If you don't tell us what's going on –"

He didn't see the rifle stock hit the back of his head.

Dazed, and feeling blood leaking from the top of his neck, he crashed to the floor.

"*Shut up!*" cursed a voice. "You were *ordered* not to speak!"

Though every bone in his body wanted to lash out, something told Jacobson to hold off.

Slowly, he staggered back to his feet.

It's okay, team, broadcasted the former leader, to his team.

Quite a whack he gave me there, but I... uhh... seem to be healing pretty quickly, these days.

Let's find out what the hell is going on here, first.

"Well, I said that they *had* been co-operating," grunted the voice of the GrayWar sergeant, from outside. "I'd suggest that you let 'em know who's *boss*... but that's up to you. We'll be topside, if you need us."

That was their last *chance, Sam,* Tanaka sent back.

"I don't think *that'll* be a problem, Sergeant," replied the smirking, unctuous voice of the smock-man. "Here at the Agency, we've got an *excellent* track record in that department. Of course... we *do* have a few 'oopses' here and there, when our boys end up knocking heads *off*, when we tell 'em just to knock 'em *together*... ah well – accidents *will* happen, you know?"

"None of our business, sir," replied the sergeant. "Channel 231 on the box, if you need us. Okay, Legionnaires – we are *leaving!*"

They heard the door shut and the sound of marching feet receding in the distance.

We need to think about tactics, and fast, Professor, sent Boyd.

I count four armed guards – we can't afford to let one of them get a clear shot without being tied up... I'll go for the guy near the door.

Devon – can you take the one on the left?

White would have replied, no doubt in the affirmative; but at that moment, after a perfunctory gesture from the man with the smock, the four gendarmes advanced behind the captives and yanked the hoods from their heads, at least as roughly as these crude instruments of humiliation and psychological torment had been put on, in the first place.

Their mundane senses automatically taking over, the Jacobson team re-surveyed the scene.

It was as they had first observed, but they could now see that a number of medical-looking instruments were arrayed by each gurney, and there were restraints everywhere – a person probably couldn't move more than an inch in any direction, once tied down by this sinister gear.

And they could see the face of the smock-man.

Like the other one, he was a middle-aged, balding Caucasian guy; he looked like nothing more than a family-doctor – no, on second thought, he looked more like a dentist.

"So... here we all are," he offered, with a leer. "Your new 'home away from home', as it were. First order of business is for each of you to pick your own stretcher. You're the leader – right? You can go first, then."

"Alright," growled Jacobson. "It's time for some *answers*, and they'd better be *good* ones, mister, because our patience has just about run out! What the hell is going *on*, here?"

"Want me to teach him a little *respect*?" shouted the gendarme behind the former Mars mission commander.

Got the fucker on the left, telegraphed White.

Gonna shove that piece up his pussy ass.

Excuse my French, Professor.

"No – not just *yet*," replied the smock-man. "Remember... he's handcuffed, like the rest of 'em. 'Sticks and stones hurt my bones', *that's* how it goes... right?"

None taken, came back Tanaka's seething mind.

I'll help you, as soon as I deal with the one behind me.

Want another gun to go in with that, sideways?

"Answers!" demanded Jacobson.

That leaves the one behind you, White sent to his former commander.

He wants 'respect' – why don't y'all dis' him, sir?

That'll be my reason for...

"Of *course!*" smirked the man, as he leaned his back against one of the gurneys, "There's not a lot I *can* tell you – rules, *protocols* – all that silly old stuff. Drives *me* crazy, too, you know? But... let's just say, the guys who I report to, don't want you dead – not *necessarily*, that is. See, thing is – and here, I'm afraid that I'm going to have to leave a lot of it out, but... well, the way that I'd put it is... 'no pain – no gain', you know?"

"Why were we brought here?" exclaimed Tanaka. "Commander Jacobson isn't kidding! You need to let us out of these handcuffs, this place, and the lies, not necessarily in that order, but *immediately!*"

"Yeah, *look*," interjected Boyd, "Apart from this being the most outrageous abuse of authority that I've ever seen in the military – and I did two tours in the Middle East – what do you guys, whatever 'Agency' you claim to be – possibly have to *gain*, by treating us like this? Why the hell didn't you just *ask* for our co-operation? The Captain, Major White and I are all loyal Air Force officers – or we *were*, prior to today. This is *stupid*, in addition to being absolutely, completely, illegal!"

"Brent's right," echoed White. "He and I, Commander and Professor too, we flew all the way to Mars and back, for our country – and *this* is the way you say 'thanks'? I don't know what y'all fixin' to do here, but you're pushin' your luck, my man. Not too late to make it right, but pretty damn close... closer than you know."

"Questions, *questions*... so many *questions*," complained the smock-man, throwing his hands up in mock-exasperation. "The best way how I could answer that would be to say, 'I guess the higher-ups – including your good ol' Commander-In-Chief, I might add – thought that you all would be, ahh, somewhat unlikely to give us the kind of 'co-operation', that we need here."

With a thoroughly sinister-looking grin, he continued, "Let me give you my own perspective, speaking as a fellow... *professional*. You smart-talking little Air Force boys, plus our esteemed guest Professor Cherie – you don't mind if I call you 'Cherie', right? – you all aren't the *first* people that we've had on this project. And that's sort of why we had to tell you, '*come on down*'!"

The black woman and the man, Tanaka thought, to her colleagues.

It's starting to make sense.

A scream, just audible to their ears, though probably not to those of the guards and smock-men, accosted the minds of the Mars mission crew. It seemed to be coming from another room, far down the outside hall.

"But... *why?*" plaintively expostulated the woman. "We've committed no crime! What could we possibly have *done*, to justify the government... *torturing* us? How can you stand to do something like this, to your fellow human beings?"

The man got up and started pacing back and forth, raising his index-finger as if giving a university-lecture.

"You want to know?" he remarked. "Well... our problem has been, that our *last* bunch of 'guests', well, we threw just about *everything* we could at 'em... but the strange thing is – how could I put this – well, they weren't *responding* as we had hoped, and – that being the case – it hasn't been having the full *effect*, that our illustrious United States government had counted on it having. What good old Uncle Sam is planning, by bringing the four of you to *my* humble doorstep, is kind of getting you, and our previous guests, all together, then, well... 'it takes a village'... *that's* the idea."

"Bottom line is," he continued, sucking his lower lip for effect "If the hurtin's enough to bring the, ah, *target* down, once and for all, then it's 'kiss kiss bye bye', we all go our separate ways... no hard feelings, you know? If it *doesn't* – well, at *that* point, we may have to go to the next, uhh, level. Nothing *personal*, you understand; it's just what I *do*, what your friendly government *does* – come on, dont'cha try to pretend that you didn't *know*, you'd have to be pretty dense not to see how the game has been played, for the past few years. Just *business* – you've got yours... I've got mine."

"You son of a *b –*" started Boyd, but the ex-astronaut was cut off by the smock-man's concluding statement.

"But let me... *amend* that last statement, just a teensy tiny little bit," he unctuously opined. "Yeah – it *is* just my job, that's true – but you know what? It can be *fun*, too! I got to admit, I sort of get a kick from it – 'a thrill's a thrill, even in Paradise'... isn't that how the song goes? Well, folks, this *ain't* Paradise, I'm afraid... as you're about to see. Oh – and just by the by – this here is just your *first* stop in your all-expenses-paid vacation-excursion. The idea is, you're kinda best off getting as much as you can get done, up here, on Level One; if we're not satisfied with the results in *this* office, well, we gotta pack you all off to Level Two, and then Three, and, down she goes... by the time you get to Level Four, I'm afraid there won't be much left of you to do any thinkin' or talkin' *with*... so if I were you, I'd want to get off the ship at the first port of call. Whaddya *say*? That a deal – or *what*?"

Tanaka shut her eyes and started humming something low and haunting, but it wasn't the *only* new sound to issue from everywhere and nowhere.

Comes the Fire, she silently inveighed. *Comes the thunder!*

The other three tried to hold it together, as the power raced through their enervated, energized bodies.

"Did somebody turn on a player?" inquired a bewildered smock-man, in the direction of his colleague. "Hey, *I* like Celtic-power-rock too, but we're really not into Muzak, down here –"

Jacobson's face, matched in ashen tone by that of Boyd and White, now bore a look of terrible sadness, as if he had come to a bitter decision that had been avoided once too many times.

The waxing sound of the strange music was changing to something ominous... something, *foreboding*.

A tear welled in the eye of the former Mars mission commander.

"You can't be *serious!*" he softly pleaded. "*This* isn't the Air Force – the *country* – that I pledged my *life* to defend."

When I send the word, he communicated, as waves of an adrenaline-like feeling washed over all four comrades.

We're on our own now, team... hit 'em with everything you've got.

The smock-man smiled at the four former astronauts, but addressed Jacobson personally.

"'Fraid it *is*, there, big guy. Sorry – but that's the way of the world, these days – has been since the turn of the century, in fact... *you* know, that little business in Florida, where they set the pattern for what's to come? Too bad it took you until now to figure it out."

He nodded to one of the guards.

"Let's get 'em up," he requested, with a cruel, thin, smile.

A *tsunami* of fury roiled the signature-placid mind of Sam Jacobson, broadcasting a message of war, to the rest.

Go!

Angels Fight Best In The Clouds

Empowered by her war-song, with the lethal – yet luxurious – weirding-flame enveloping the very fiber of her being, Karéin-Mayréij hurtled at bone-crushing speed into the sky. This same *Fire* lit up the heavens, a torch of thousands of degrees burning from the surface of her protective bubble.

Clearing the cloud-tops – and very much aware that her incandescence must be easily visible to the humans' war-machines – she came to an abrupt stop.

Slowly rotating in place – not just in the horizontal, but indeed in the vertical and diagonal as well, as if weightless in the depths of space – the Storied Watcher shared the fullness of her senses with the half-magical beings who encased and defended her.

They need a lesson, she sent to the armor, shield, sword and daggers.
Hence shall we show our full glory.
A challenge to the air-warriors!

U.S. Air Force Major Anthony "Big Stick Tony" Antonio, Wing Commander of the Wright-Patterson Provisional Midwest Air Defense Group, spoke into the built-in microphone of his oxygen-mask in his F-32E stealth-fighter, as it super-cruised through the Midwest U.S. sky.

"Rover Down Leader to Rover Down wing," he broadcasted over the encrypted, plane-to-plane link. "Target acquired, 13,140 feet, grid-setting Golf Tango 398," he indicated. "Uh-oh, it just *disappeared* – oh, wait a minute, still on IR and MR – what the hell, looks like it stopped – PD-track gave out, no lateral-motion... switching to CW-mode... okay, target re-acquired, good clean lock, up-linking to ACP. This is really *strange*... it's not even *attempting* to maneuver, as far as I can see... Rodney, Dan, Mario – can you confirm that? A Leader over."

"B Leader confirm," spoke a ghostly voice. "Appears to be stationary. I don't think it *sees* us, sir. Over."

"Check EW status, showing status clear here," commanded Antonio. "Over."

"D Leader negative," confirmed a faint voice. "But we're about at range, sir – squadron, military power for ten seconds, then re-check."

"B Leader negative," stated another voice. "ECCM shows no gate-spoofing, no noise, nothing on the side-lobes, either... IR-signature is off the *chart*, should be an easy shot for the heat-seekers. Over."

"C Leader negative," echoed the fourth. "But I'm getting some kind of background-noise on this channel... isolating... damn... sounds like *music*," he continued. "Squelched it. Over."

"Rover Down Leader requesting confirm of lock-on... wing, do you copy?" requested the wing-commander.

Several of the voices called out over the intercom.

"Copy," came back the unanimous response.

"Copy that," remarked the lead fighter jockey, his voice involuntarily rising with the tension of the moment. "B wing, C wing – engage at will. Fox 6 at 80, Fox 7 at 40 – assess, follow up with strafing-run against corpse on my say-so. I say again, *permission to engage*. Copy?"

"Engage – copy," responded several voices.

A second later, he heard a chorus of excited-sounding exclamations.

"*Fox 6! Fox 6!*" came simultaneously over the link, from scores of fighter aircraft.

From all points of the compass, the U.S. Air Force's stealth-fighters opened their weapon-bay doors for the briefest of times, loosing dozens of battle-proven air-to-air missiles, against a faint, but well-tracked, beyond-visual-range, human-sized target. Some could home in on reflected radar-emissions, while others traced out a deadly flight-path with an imaging infra-red mechanical eye. Still others looked for a magnetic resonance-signal, while a few were "track-via-missile" guided toward their target by the much larger, more sophisticated sensors of the aircraft that had released them.

A good enemy might figure a way to fool *one* guidance system – a really competent opponent perhaps two or three; but *this* kind of volley had never previously failed to win control of the skies for the elite of the U.S. Air Force.

At twenty million dollars per rocket, Antonio had just fired off something close to the entire yearly budgets of several Third World nations.

But for *this* hunt, Uncle Sam would spare no expense.

Let's see you get your way out of this, *bitch!* grimly vowed Big Stick Tony.

War-birds in all directions, except dead above and directly below, counseled Karéin-Mayréij.

Now mark this; the electro-books tell of them firing seeking-arrows, each tipped with a point of blast and fire – these are akin to thee all, children, except far less able to think and move, and not alive, as ye are.

So wreck them as are ye best able; but as for the war-birds themselves, they each contain one living human – and I would prefer that ye not spill their blood, if at all possible; rather, cut the wings from their flying-cars...

Ah, there – feel the tickle of their many electro-eyes... see ye them, now?

Out come the arrows – and they close as fast as these man-weapons can, upon us.

Recalling the lessons from the research that the humans had so foolishly let her undertake, she counted off the seconds.

Can ye understand how I calculate, children?

The electro-feeling grows in a minor way, each second... 60, 59, 58... by comparing it with how far they were when launched from these modern flying-bows, we tell that they travel about two and a half-piece of a 'kilometer', as the humans reckon such things.

Be ready for when I invoke the slow-skill, if needs be... 40, 39, 38...

What is that, my blessed son?

A second later – though none were here to see it – a wry smile showed on the Storied Watcher's face.

Comprehend, sent the young-looking woman to the orange-hot fighting-knife that adorned her left leg, *that 'thirty-eight' is a number of the threes and tens, higher than thou has had to this time, needed to count.*

When thy mother regains all her power, much larger concepts shall ye have to master, to number the leagues over which she shall fly.

Now gird ye... 12, 11, 10...

As the sensors of the fighter-planes, still scores of miles distant, all lit up with a riot of overstimulated data – as well as a strange, Celtic electric-rock-like beat – the Storied Watcher, *Amaiish*-lightening shooting all over her body, began to rotate in place.

Faster and faster now she spun, her features becoming a blur, the force of her mind and the incandescent heat of her bubble, drawing the air-atoms toward her, as a mini-hurricane formed high over the Michigan skies.

9...8...7... Seek ye weak prey, death-arrows?

Then soar after her!

Suddenly – with acceleration never imagined by Earth's tacticians – the alien-girl rocketed upward, scant seconds before the vanguard of the air-to-air missiles converged, perhaps twenty meters from the point in space that she had previously occupied.

Many of the missiles came to a sudden end right there, as the roaring winds tore off their wings, causing, a split-second later, thunderous explosions as multiple proximity fuses detonated. But dozens more weapons were still on their way, having been launched slightly after the first volley, and these adjusted their course, streaking after the Storied Watcher as she fled upward toward the stratosphere and beyond.

We can, of course, incinerate all of these smart-arrows, with but a thought, she counseled.

But I would see how high they can go.

Upward toward and past the tropopause she climbed, taking care not to go so fast as to out-distance the missiles.

Five and a half-measure kilometers... six... seven... eight... nine... ten... behold, children, the last of them fall, their propelling-blood spent.

Conversely, we feel comfortable at home here... do we not?

Shall we continue higher still, even into the cold, dark void?

Ahh – leave that to later, silently communicated the young-looking woman, her hands playing lovingly over *Vîrya Ahn'jë*, the weirding-electric pulses echoing also in the minds of the rest of her war-children.

There is much left to do – the war-birds sent us their worst.

Now – let us pay them back!

From a vantage-point some forty-five thousand feet in the air, the Storied Watcher's regal, godly perceptive gaze washed over four groups of fighter planes, one approaching from each point on the compass, and climbing rapidly as well.

Like a meteor with a deadly purpose, she dove toward the unlucky ones coming from the north-west, her speed increasing to unimaginable levels in the blink of an eye. But after only a few seconds on this intercept-course, more missiles – this time, heat-seeking ones that homed in on the roaring friction of air-molecules, as the latter self-incinerated on the Storied Watcher's protective bubble – issued from the fighter-planes, and these projectiles tracked unnervingly well.

Her mind invoking the slow-time-skill, Karéin-Mayréij issued a hasty command, while reducing her cruise to a scant few hundred kilometers per hour.

Væran Ksé'l'ch', give them something more pleasing to an Umnàhr'é-*eye, then suppress thyself –* Væran Ss'éth'ch', *cool our aura,* she sent.

About a tenth of a second later, the orange-dagger rocketed upward to a distance of several-score meters, its other-worldly fire expanding into a huge, ballooning orb of incandescent heat-energy. Meanwhile, the blue-dagger flew an encircling-pattern around the Storied Watcher, instantly dropping the temperature of the surrounding atmosphere far below what was ambient for this altitude.

Perhaps two dozen missiles flew after the newly-appearing fireball, while the the infra-red signature of the hot-dagger dropped rapidly, as it exited the superheated air that it had just created.

Then, the alien-girl's psyche felt the panic that had gripped the half-mind of *Væran Ksé'l'ch',* for he was unable to fly far or fast – nor, indeed, to use most of his other abilities – without invoking at least some of his deadly elemental power; but, mercifully, the little orange war-knife was still well within reach of his mother's unseen, telekinetic grasp.

I would never abandon thee, she gently-reassured, as *Væran Ksé'l'ch',* was quickly drawn back to his resting-place on the newcomer's lower left leg.

With both of the daggers now retrieved and the light-bending skill at its maximum power, the Storied Watcher hurtled downward at a shallow angle, seeing – through one or two bandwidths randomly chosen, second by second – the fighter-wing pass unaware above her.

A split-second later, she abruptly reversed course, again rising and accelerating.

Now Karéin-Mayréij unleashed the fullness of her war-music, with its exciting, driving beat echoing in human, and near-human, minds, for many miles around.

She dropped the opacity of her bubble to visible light – though not to other types of radiation – and flew at over two thousand kilometers per hour, to catch up with the gaggle of fighter-planes, directly ahead of her.

You wish to hunt me, *weak, pathetic humans?* she challenged with angry determination, as pulses of *Amaiish*-power illuminated up and down her body like some kind of weird short-circuit.

Behold your prey – how she becomes the... huntress!

The TacAir Engagement Control Chief, sitting in front of his 3-D integrated holographic display in the AWACS-II Airborne Command Post, as this 747-derivative circled high over the Midwest skies, was the first to suspect that all was not going exactly according to plan.

"Rover Down Leader, Rover Down Leader, this is Sky Castle," he called out. "I have Tac update and link to Evil Eye. Do you copy? Over."

"Copy – Rover Down Leader here," replied a faint voice. "Fox 6 away, we have presumed kill but no positive, so closing for Fox 7 as mop-up. Interference on all voice-channels – I know how this sounds, but it's like... *music,* and it's becoming progressively louder. Over."

"Rover Down Leader, copy that – we're getting the same stuff here, attempting to isolate... we can confirm no kill – I say again, *confirm no kill,* target is –" warned the controller.

"Sky Castle – this is Rover Down Leader, 'scuse me sir – but what do you mean?" interrupted the distant Major Antonio. "We had 20 plus confirmed hits observed at this end, *nothing* could have... over –"

A second later, his intercom was overwhelmed by a bizarre combination of pounding, Celtic-rock music, intermixed with panicked shouting coming from other fighter-pilots.

"Rover Leader, Rover Leader – *emergency!*" shrieked the voice of the C squadron leader, the syllables of the man's speech barely-discernible over the cacophony of unrequited music that had invaded every command-channel. "Maneuvering-combat now – we're under *attack! Fox 7! Fox 7!* Jack – *look out,* it's on your *six!*"

"Can't see *anything* – it's like mag-flares e*verywhere!*" responded a befuddled pilot.

Trying to maintain a semblance of control, the Control Chief responded, "Confirmed, Lieutenant Bannon, we'll direct Evil Eye –"

"Wingman – break right – break *right!*" sounded over the link. "It's *behind* you, *pull up! Shit!*"

"Can't hear – fucking music –" complained a pilot.

"I see a chute," came a previously unknown voice. "Was tracking, but it went off to port –"

Another voice, fainter still over the thundering music, shouted, "I got a track! Under minimum for Fox 7 – gun now! Firing! *God damn*, did you see that *turn –*"

Then, this report went dead, as the exclamation was cut short by yet another one.

"I'm on fire, repeat, on *fire – holy shit*, what's *that –*" bellowed the C squadron leader, just before his own channel went off the air, with the sound of wind roaring in the background.

Again, Karéin-Mayréij allowed the infernal heat of her bubble to wax brilliant and incandescent. She attacked by weaving a wide cosine-wave-pattern right through the middle of the squadron, alternately diving from the "Hun In The Sun" position above, then attacking the fighters' blind-spots below and to the rear, like a gyrfalcon tearing apart a lumbering flock of game-birds.

Though the F-32E fighters were well-shielded against nuclear radiation – a feature that saved many lives, on this day – neither the aircraft, nor the flash-blinded pilots within them, could cope with close proximity to the alien-girl's scorching, dazzling, war-singing being.

Nor, alas, could they contend with the lethal edge of *Væran Fàiagàryuu*, whose strikes methodically sliced off ailerons and elevators, rudders and tail-planes, vectoring jet-nozzles and engine-parts, while the cold-blast of *Væran Ss'éth'ch'* – unwittingly aided by not a few misdirected thirty-millimeter Gatling cannon-rounds – un-flamed those turbofans that his elder-brother had missed.

One by one, the relaxed-stability computers that allowed the stealth-fighters to fly at all, could no longer provide even a modicum of handling-authority, and these elite aircraft began to tumble helplessly from the sky.

Now the C squadron leader made a near-fatal mistake : namely, flying straight and level for a few seconds, as he watched all but one or two of his fellow F-32Es being literally torn apart.

Luckily for him, the fearsome being whose boots crashed heavily down on the top fuselage of the fighter-plane, slightly behind its gold-tinged, semi-transparent canopy, had the mercy to tamp down the most-part of her deadly aura, just before her mailed, burning fist smashed through its rear-part.

A second later, the fighter-jockey yelled, "*Holy shit*, what's *that –*", while turning his head to behold the flaming, ebon-armored, fang-toothed figure of the fearsome Storied Watcher, as she came down on one knee and ripped away the remnants of the aft half of the canopy.

Over the roar of hurricane-force winds, from which he was inadequately protected, he half-heard, half-thought,

Next time, it will not be the wind-shield that I rip from its moorings, human.

Tell that *to your brave generals, wherever they safely hide, while you and your comrades, risk your lives.*
Now go – I attack not children, imbeciles, peasants, or... para-choots!
Wisely, the C squadron leader pulled his ejection-seat lever.

I believe *that they all jumped overboard... though I did not count the survivors,* sent Karéin-Mayréij to her war-children, as she rocketed up through the stratosphere, again aiming to survey the situation from a high vantage-point.
Chivalrous of us all to but cripple the mount – not kill the lance-knight, would ye not say?
There was a proud, contented murmur in return; but a second later, her bubble was struck by a brilliant, coherent light, and the surprised Storied Watcher yelped as she felt the heat of thousands of degrees Celsius impacting on her protective shield. Though the bubble indeed did stop almost all this unexpected energy, a fraction of it nonetheless leaked through, illuminating all within with an brutal brilliance.
Mother – burning thrill! shouted two or three little minds, starting an immediate squabble.
Oh... hold thy tongue, Væran Ksé'l'ch', interjected the alien-girl.
Not all thy siblings enjoy this – even thy sister, the Adamant Mountain, does complain.
A death-gaze – and quite a strong one, she explained, trying not to reveal the amusement that she felt upon hearing the dispute.
But fire is part thy essence, too, even for thee, Cold-Dark one... remember?
Fear not, it is only seeing-waves with much force... it can be drunk like fine mead, and can be bent just like ordinary light –
With a thought, the megawatt laser-beam of the Pentagon's most powerful airborne weapon flowed harmlessly around the Storied Watcher's bubble like creek-water around a pebble.
Let us see how it tracks, she mused.
The newcomer moved a few hundred meters to the north, and a little *Amaiish*-power was allowed to leak through the bubble, then a little more, then a lot more, but still, no laser-light shone in this direction.
It came from the west, two hands and a finger south of where the sun goes down, reflected Karéin-Mayréij.
Can ye see me, O sky-dragon?
Let us find out how.
And yes, children – I, too, see the fighter-planes, as they approach.
They will be dealt with, in due time.
Now the Storied Watcher began to weave a cork-screw path around the approximate center of the laser-beam, allowing her bubble become transparent first to blue light, then to yellow, then to green. She continued across the entire

spectrum, until a line was crossed between deep-red and the color that came next.

For a second time, the bubble was bathed in a death-ray that could have cut a missile in half; but this time, to her satisfaction, her mind perceived naught but a slight grumble from *Væran Ss'éth'ch'*.

Hah! Ye see in brighter Umnàhr'é, she remarked.

Well... ye shall shortly have all ye can ponder... and then some.

Sword of Flame – again to my hand!

The alien-girl, her eyes shining almost as bright as her force-field, started to dive and accelerate toward the south-west; but as the shock-wave of an instant sonic boom resounded off the clouds, it did not in any way overcome the chords of her war-song.

"Rover Down Leader – we have new TacEval here," countered the remote controller. "Target is undamaged – I say again, *undamaged* – it took at least two shots from the laser, then –"

The controller's voice was interrupted by an even more alarmed-sounding one, barely audible over a background of deafening, martial-rock music.

"Sky Castle – this is Evil Eye," it shrieked.

"*Declaring emergency!*"

The President Can't Talk Right Now

The path of her flight was now bent to the center-point of its arc, another maneuver whose bone-crushing G-forces would have killed any lesser being; then, the Storied Watcher hurtled to the west, streaking faster, by far, than any human aircraft – or, indeed, any human missile – could have done.

The battle-song of this intimidating creature, now echoing for leagues in all directions, mightily reinforced her contempt at the weakness of the humans; and this momentarily loosened her psychic preparedness, allowing a heat-signature to leak from the bubble. Her absent-mindedness was rewarded by two more rapid shots from the Air Force's most powerful ABM laser – equally to no avail as its otherwise-deadly beam, was directed away from the newcomer's protective force-shield.

In under a minute, she could perceive the hulking form of a 747-sized aircraft, dead ahead, and adjusted her course so as to streak right underneath the belly of this huge, four-engined air-fortress.

Ksé'l'ch', directed Karéin-Mayréij.

No more instruction was necessary; the left-leg dagger, its orange-yellow glow waxing to incandescent, white-shining fury, howled its own song of war, rocketing from the Storied Watcher as she passed under the AL-2C "Long Whip" Airborne Anti-Ballistic Laser Mission Platform.

In a fraction of a second, *Væran Ksé'l'ch'* effortlessly pierced right through the bulbous laser-focusing unit on the front of the aircraft, burning and melting it to a steaming, charred ruin in a shower of sparks and flame; but he continued his flight to an ellipse, above and then behind the AL-2C, meeting up with his 'mother' like some kind of weirding boomerang.

Even the Storied Watcher herself, flinched a little, when this infernally-hot weapon met her gauntlet.

Terrible are thee, Fire-Fang of the Many Worlds, she communicated.

Thou shalt soon burn and fuse the very particles of being!

Homage pay we all... but patience, O Hell-Deeps-Frigid-One... a chance to show thy own arts shall surely come, as well.

Now she abruptly reversed course again, accelerating to come dead astern of the lumbering 747-derivative, paying scant attention to the magnesium-flares and small grenades that it fired as a desperate, last-ditch defensive-measure.

A portal, ahead of and just below the tail-wing, noted Karéin-Mayréij.

Hear me, children...

I, too, am sorely tempted just to send this air-fortress crashing down, those within then to face their destiny as belief guides them.

But many on board are there only by compulsion – and it is chivalrous to parley and warn.

Ha... they open not the door, for us?

Let us then enter – invited or not!

Keeping exact formation at several hundred kilometers per hour, the alien-girl flew parallel to the door on the side of the aircraft, close enough for the brutal heat coming from her own being, and that of *Vìrya Ahn'jë*, to blister and discolor the AL-2C's outer skin.

At first, she bent her telekinetic will to unlock the door's pressure-resistant mechanisms, but the latter were complex and sealed with many artful safeguards. A second later, the mechanism's electronic circuitry was bathed in wave after wave of high-energy radiation; but still, it held.

Shielded against the unseen death-shine, I see, she mused.

Stupid me, children – this war-plane is meant to stay aloft even in a war fought with the atom-splitting bombs... I should have figured on that...

I could outwit its codes... a fond memory comes to mind, a first step into the dark void and Commander Sam's friendly space-vessel.

But I am in a hurry.

Despite the fact that it was almost perfectly-recessed into the aircraft's fuselage, the door's extent was marked by a thin outline, which now became a template for an attack never anticipated by human beings.

Ah, my children, if the great power ye shall now see, had only come back to thy mother, earlier in this sad adventure, she counseled.

Much grief would thus have been avoided.

A thought – in a thoroughly alien tongue, yet all too easily comprehensible to the Air Force soldiers on board the AL-2C, none the less – reverberated in the minds of humans and living-weapons, alike.

The Gaze of the Khùl-Algrenàthi'i *looks cruelly upon ye!*

From white-glowing, lightening-silhouetted eyes underneath a balefully-furrowed brow, flashed out two pencil-thin, parallel beams of scintillating, incandescent, *Amaiish*-powered... *something.* These impacted upon the outline of the door, following it up, then down, melting a furrow for the door's full vertical extent; then, the Storied Watcher fired another burst at its locking-mechanism.

Oooh – pray Mother we that us teach, pleaded a cacophony of little voices, inside the newcomer's preoccupied mind.

Ye shall have to learn to project thine own essences first, she tutored.

As the stare of fearsome Væran Ksé'l'ch' *and his sister, the Ebon-Mailed Mountain shall be fire; and that of his cold-brother be, ice.*

It takes much practice... ye are not yet ready... but soon...

As warning-klaxons shrieked within the aircraft, the alien-girl first extended her bubble over the area that her gaze had just impacted, then pulled on the portal mechanism. It flew wide open, and with the roar of her war-music – though without the explosive-decompression that would otherwise have ensued – she returned *Væran Fàiagàryuu* to his place at her side and floated through the entrance-way, into the aircraft.

Tamping down the fire that she shared with her war-child *Ahn'jë,* Karéin-Mayréij forced the door to shut, with the hot-dagger re-welding enough of it to ensure continued – if precarious – air-tightness.

She called a warning to the humans that she sensed just around the corner, down the carpeted inner passageway directly ahead.

"Shoot holes in your air-ship – go ahead, do!" echoed the voice of the Storied Watcher. "Thus your deaths will be not by *my* hand!"

"Evil Eye, this is Sky Castle," shot back the Engagement Control Chief. "We copy your emergency status. We need contingency classification – do you copy?"

"Sky Castle! *Sky Castle!* Do you *hear* us?" sounded a panicked, remote voice.

"Copy that, Evil Eye... but we're getting the same sound-interference on your audio – sounds like electric-rock, becoming louder all the time, can you switch to an alternate channel –" requested the Control Chief.

"No time!" came back the voice. "Sky Castle, we have damage – main array is out – I say again, main array is *non-functional* – RWR's showing strong EMP aft... hold on... reporting intruders on the lower deck –"

"*What?*" exclaimed the startled Air Force officer in the AWACS-II. "Evil Eye – we thought we heard 'intruders'... but you're thousands of feet in the air, for God's sake... is this a stowaway situation? You got *terrorists* on board? We need confirmation of your status – turn that damn music off *please –*"

"Sky Castle, this is Rover Down Leader," interrupted the pilot of the lead interceptor. "We saw Evil Eye strike... target has vanished – can you confirm kill?"

"Rover Down Leader, that's a negative – I say again – *negative...* keep channel clear, we have an emergency on –" started the controller.

"*Jesus,*" came a gasp from the AL-2C, now increasingly difficult to make out over the pounding, Celtic-rock-beat that seemed to be issuing from every speaker and headphone. "What the fuck's *that*? Yeah – well get them down there, *shoot it*, for Christ's sake! What didn't you understand about that – *shoot it!*"

There was a pause of two or three seconds, then the voice, even fainter than before, continued, "Sky Castle, I'm looking at one of the internal-security cameras, lower deck – I can't *believe* this, it's *her –*"

"Evil Eye, did not fully copy your last transmission," queried the Control Chief. "We track you descending rapidly – do you require crash-team? What's your abort-destination? Over!"

The next incoming message from the airborne-laser aircraft was so garbled as to be almost unintelligible, as it was all but impossible to make out the words – evidently shouted by several people in the AL-2C over an open microphone, all at once – over the pervasive, stirring back-beat of the Storied Watcher's war-song.

There were curses, combined with a noise that sounded like firecrackers, and the Control Chief thought he heard someone yelling, "We'll crash this ship, before –"

Then, following a pattern, the signal went dead.

Though she had suppressed her *Fire*, and that of her girl-child, as much as possible, the fine all-seasons carpeting of the AL-2C's inner corridor still bore the smoking trademark of her passing, as Karéin-Mayréij turned the corner to face the Air Force warriors – three numb-faced, shocked technical functionaries, one female, and two more martial types, both male, with pistols drawn – who stood in her way.

"Military police – *freeze!*" they yelled, palms in front of faces against the heat. "Hands up, or we'll *shoot!*"

With a bemused, fang-bedecked half-smile, the alien-girl paused, crossed her arms and addressed the group.

"Dear air-warriors of the American Empire," she counseled, "If your little pop-guns were of any use, I would already be dead, many times over. Did you not hear my warning? Your bullets cannot hurt me... but they *might* damage this aircraft – perhaps badly enough to cause its destruction. Tell me... did you bring some para-choots with you, today?"

"D-don't *push* me, lady," bluffed one of the gun-men. "Get on your knees!"

Indifferently, the Storied Watcher sniffed, "Shall we get this over with, then? I am on a, ahh, rather tight time-shed-yool."

She took a step forward, only to run into a hail of bullets, each of which was no more effective than every other one that had previously been fired at her.

Upon seeing this, the Air Force staffers who had confronted the newcomer, turned and fled behind a bulkhead, going, apparently in the direction of the bow of the aircraft.

But one of the females, a young red-head with a star and three little wing-stripes on her shoulder, had tarried by one or two inadvertent seconds, and she was thus trapped between the passageway in the middle of the bulkhead and the figure of the Storied Watcher.

With terror all over her face, the staffer was methodically forced into the corner at the junction of the bulkhead and the aircraft's inside fuselage, as the alien-girl slowly advanced.

Now, Karéin-Mayréij drew so close that her infernal radiation immersed the Air Force crew-girl in an agonizing wash, pain that was even more amplified when the newcomer's sinister gauntlet shot upward – the crew-girl was a few inches taller – and grabbed the other's jaw, with smoldering glove-tips instantly burning a red-blistered pattern on her cheeks.

The young Air Force staffer screamed and, mercifully, the Storied Watcher released her grasp.

"Shot your stupid little *guns* at *me*, eh?" commented Karéin-Mayréij, with a cruel, fanged smile. "Now... what should I do with *you*? How about a nice new, ahh, how would Bob put it, face-lifting, by burning off the top ten layers of your skin? Oops, I forgot... that much melted from your eyeballs, would... oh, well. *Unfortunate.*"

"Oh God – let me *go!*" shrieked the crew-girl. "It hurts – it *hurts!*"

"Well," teased the newcomer, "I did some research, you know... you are but a foot-warrior; that I can see from the mark of your rank. Tell me... would it be glorious to die, right here and now, for the sake of your 'President'? The slower I kill you, the more your honor... that is how it goes... is it not?"

"Please, *please* – don't *kill* me," pleaded the crew-girl. "I'm on my last tour – they're throwing me out of the Air Force because of that new law about 'no women' – I'm just a radio-operator!"

"If you were a big, powerful Air Force general, crewman 'Northcott' – and by the way, your first name is 'Patricia', right – would it then be oh-kay to reduce you to ashes - 'toes go in first'?" maliciously threatened the Storied Watcher.

"*Nooo!*" cried the staff-girl. "I mean, I don't – I don't know – please, *please*, I have two kids – I only joined the Air Force to get a college-degree –"

A saturnine smile appeared on the face of Karéin-Mayréij.

"Put your mind at rest, foot-soldier Patricia Northcott of the Ew-Nighted States Air Army," she counseled, her voice, all at once friendly and reassuring. "I do not slaughter peasants, or the ordinary sword-fodder soldiers, who cowards like your 'President' hide themselves behind... that is, if I have a *choice*. Luckily for you – I *do* have such here... but do not count on it always. Now... I have some friendly advice. Are you listening?"

"Y-Yes," stammered the crew-girl, through a haze of pain and tears.

"One," instructed the alien-girl, "Tell your superiors, and your 'President', not to, ahh, 'fuck with me'... none of you understand who you are dealing with. Better stop *now*, while you still have a country left! You *got* that, Patricia?"

"Yes... I think... oh, my cheeks *hurt*..." whimpered the young Air Force staffer.

"That is the second thing," explained the Storied Watcher. "My touch can be pain and death... but equally – life, health and power. Use your gift wisely; for I will be back to check up and make sure that you do. Your third child, who you now carry within – she will be great, for my mark lies inside you, as much as on your face. The latter will heal, eventually; but the former... that will be forever."

"I... I don't *understand*..." whined the crew-girl. "Boyfriend used *protection* – we can't get the Pill anymore, of course, but –"

"You *will* understand, shortly," countered the newcomer, with a kind of weird compassion in her voice. "And perhaps, some day, you may call me, 'friend'. Now, if I were you... I would find a para-choot, as fast as possible. Leave here, Patricia – go to the back of the airplane and jump out as soon as we get low enough for you to breathe... I can feel that the airplane is already starting to descend. You do not want to be in front of me, when I go forward."

Seeing the way open, the crew-girl, her face ashen with fear and pain, dashed by her erstwhile tormentor, heading for the tail-compartment of the AL-2C.

Now, with her war-song again rising, Karéin-Mayréij passed through the partition and headed for the front of the aircraft. The passageway was narrow, being crowded with electronic-gear on both sides; but these ingenious devices all met an abrupt end, as the alien-girl's fearsome aura of heat and radiation disintegrated circuitry, melting internal components into smoking, useless slag.

But halfway down the corridor, the Storied Watcher suddenly doubled up in pain, as if having taken a sucker-punch to the waist.

Tears – boiling-hot not just from her fire-imbued essence, but even more so from empathy, guilt and frustrated, bottled-up distress – spilled over the floor, slowly vaporizing as the waves of heat made steam.

Mother – we it pain too feel – nowhere from but – Mother Blessed, us cruelty punish let who sends this, us heal let thee – instantly sounded a bevy of worried, concerned, half-alien mental-voices.

Not so bad, Storied Watcher – not so bad, she tried to convince herself, as she gasped for breath, coughing and wheezing in between freely-flowing weeping.

You must shut it out, put up the barrier, harden your heart, your mind –
Oh, but Gods – my son, my son – can not shut out my son!

Oh-kay – it is passing, I am learning, I am adapting... no, I do not want to, do not want to defend against this, must suffer with them, for them...

O my children, bless ye in return... thy minds protect me, keep the worst of it at bay –

Just a few seconds more, I will be back on my feet, back in charge of my senses...

Gods of the Light, I want to kill all these people, want to blow this fucking airplane into smoking shards! she inwardly cursed.

They are behind this... these nobody human sword-fodder yeomen richly deserve it – after what their scum dungeon-masters are doing to my lover, my son!

It would be so easy!

Why should I forebear!

Things in all directions started to steam and smoke, as her fury expressed itself in waves of burning heat.

Them – spare – greater – because – thou – them – are, demanded the voice of *Vîrya Quü'j.*

My patience melts away with each cruel stroke they inflict upon helpless little Tommy, Venerable One, sent back an angry Storied Watcher.

I will defer to thy ageless wisdom... but this wicked, soul-less world burns out my morality like the desert sun on a spring-flood creek.

Soon it will be gone altogether, old friend; and then – mark my thoughts – the humans will come to know why they should fear me.

Us all fear they should, added some little minds.

Yes... fear us all! savagely agreed Karéin-Mayréij.

But not today... not right now.

I concede thee that much, good companion of the Many Worlds...

At least... until the next outrage.

Raising herself up while shaking off the dizziness, the alien-girl came up to a second bulkhead, its hatchway locked tight, and – with a furrowed-brow look of contempt, this barrier shattered into a thousand pieces, its plastic-and-metal construction rent apart by the Storied Watcher's mental forces.

A second later, her bubble was struck by dozens of automatic-rifle-rounds, fired by a Marine guard-unit that had taken up a defensive-position just ahead of the stairway going upward to the top level of the AL-2C.

"You want to *die*?" shouted the alien. "Then keep *that* up!"

Her warning was answered by another fusillade, and this time, several shots struck the walls, making deep indentations; but no breaches in the aircraft's pressure-hull were immediately visible.

"I give the count of three down to one," hissed the newcomer. "Then I open fire, and Gods rest your souls. Three... two..."

Hear ye the fear in their minds? she communicated to her war-children.

They have good reason.

Five or six more shots impacted upon her bubble.

Try ye to strike only to cripple, not kill, she instructed *Væran Ksé'l'ch'* and *Væran Ss'éth'ch'*.

But... do not try too hard.

"One..." warned the Storied Watcher, and when the last syllable of this word left her sharp-fanged mouth, two small daggers – each giving off a lethally-potent aura of its own kind of elemental-energy – rocketed from the alien's leg-braces.

In less than half a second, Stygian-cold *Væran Ss'éth'ch'* and infernally-hot *Væran Ksé'l'ch'* criss-crossed flight-paths, each striking the trigger-finger of a different Air Force crewman.

Screams issued from the scene in front of Karéin-Mayréij, as two men, one with charred stumps that had previously been his fore-arms, a second man with frost-shattered remnants of the same, collapsed on to the carpeted floor of this compromised airborne-laser fortress.

"We'll crash this ship before you can take over!" yelled someone at the back of the firing-group.

"Go right ahead!" retorted the alien-girl. "And send my greetings to the Lord of the Dead!"

More automatic-rifle rounds flew at the Storied Watcher, as she steadily advanced at walking-speed, with fabric and plastic fuming and discoloring as she passed.

With little wisps of lightening accentuating her glowing eyes, she fired a lethal gaze at two more Air Force crew-members, the first having her weapon sliced neatly in half, with its hapless user having most of one hand removed in the process; the second, who was in the process of removing a sidearm from its holster, had the weapon and its carrying-piece instantly blasted to smithereens, with the unfortunate side-effect of having at least an inch of the man's left hip reduced to a smoking mass of burned, bleeding flesh. The two or three who were left turned tail, slamming the door shut behind them.

The newcomer tarried momentarily as she surveyed the toll of human wreckage that her attacks, and those of the fire-dagger and cold-dagger – the both of these still hovering ominously over the wounded, bleeding, gasping humans – had wrought.

She got down on her knees, addressing them all at once.

"You are a bunch of fucking *idiots!*" castigated Karéin-Mayréij, her countenance a bizarre combination of vampire-like fangs, other-worldly beauty, compassion and contempt. "It is not as if I had not *warned* you – how much proof do you humans *need*, before you learn not to oppose me? It is no glory, crippling and slaughtering peasant-soldiers who do not stand a chance – this type of battle demeans me! Here... *Vîrya Ahn'jë – Vîrya I'ëà'b'* – do what ye can for them... I give ye thirty seconds. Make them live at least to a few more hours. This craft descends... perhaps they will be near a healer, when that time is up."

The Storied Watcher looked around, trying to see which of the grievously-wounded humans was least so. Eventually she settled upon the man whose side had been blasted open by her deadly eye-gaze.

"*You*, there," she commanded. "Is there a speaking-box around here, which I can use to address those in charge of this air-fortress?"

"W-what?" mumbled the afflicted man, as he lay on the other side, his hand over the wound in a futile effort to staunch the ooze of blood that already had him falling into shock.

"A speaking-box – an 'inter-come' – that kind of thing," pressed the alien-girl. "Be quick about it... or I rescind my generous offer to have my war-children lend you their succor."

"Lend me... lend me... oh, right... over there, on the counter... switch's under those papers that fell down when..." gasped the man, his face as white as a sheet.

"*Vîrya I'ëà'b*' – come thee to this one, forthwith," ordered Karéin-Mayréij. "His life drains away."

The buckler flew from another savagely damaged, prone figure, and deposited itself over the man's wound.

His head fell to the ground, drool pouring from his mouth as consciousness finally left him.

Now the alien-girl arose and floated over to a console to her right, with a stack of papers vaporizing at her first touch. She picked up a microphone, hit a switch and began speaking.

"Calling the captain of this vessel," she announced, mentally tamping down the electro-Celtic war-music reverberating through the U.S. Air Force's command-channels, to a dull roar. "You now hear the voice of Karéin-Mayréij. Respond, immediately!"

There was a pause of a second or two, then a voice, still faint over the cacophony of the alien's background-song, sounded over the link.

"This is Major-General Schweicker... commander of the AL-2C National Ballistic Missile Defense Weapon System, Omaha Wing," stated a remote voice. "Who's this? What do you want?"

"I *told* you who I am!" shot back the newcomer. "And what do I want? Simple – I will shortly arrive on the – ahh, how would one say it, yes, the 'bridge' – where you command this vessel. I seek only to use the communication-systems of the aircraft, specifically to speak to your 'President', but I want no more of the nonsense that I have so far seen down here on the lower deck –"

"You're ordered to lay down any weapons and submit to arrest," barked back the voice of the general. "Any attempt to make your way up to the command center will be met with deadly force."

"Oh, *please*, Mister 'Major-General'," spat Karéin-Mayréij, "*Spare* me the pathetic bluffing, will you? There are four peasant-soldiers cruelly wounded and close to death, by my hand, arrayed in front of me, down here. It is only by my mercy that they live at all. Do *not* make me give you another demonstration of my war-skills – because if you send any more sword-fodder to their doom, I will *personally* throw you out of this air-plane minus your clothes, your ears and your manhood. Do I make myself *clear?*"

"Seal upper-deck entrance," was all there was to hear; then the link went dead.

"Fine," muttered the alien-girl.

She stood in front of the locked hatch.

A second later, with the music again rising, the door disintegrated, the victim of two impossibly-fast blows from *Væran Fàiagàryuu.*

The Storied Watcher called out into the darkness ahead, not outwardly remarking that she could easily see six more, pistol-armed crew-members crouching behind upturned chairs and equipment-boxes, at the far end of the next corridor.

"Do not shoot," she implored. "I will simply walk by you... and I give my word that no harm will come, if you leave me alone."

"We... we can't *do* that," answered a frightened-sounding voice. "We have *orders!*"

"Then you have a choice to make, foot-soldiers of the American Air Army," warned the newcomer. "Your fellow-warriors have, no doubt, told you what will happen, if you try to resist me. Be of no illusion – I can and *will* kill, if I have to... but I do not *want* to. This is between your 'President' and I, only. There is no honor in letting oneself be slaughtered in futile cause – so just let me pass. Here I come."

Slowly, the Storied Watcher went forward, each footstep leaving a hissing, burned memento in the airplane's interior-carpets. About halfway down the corridor, the frantic whispers of the last vestige of the AL-2C's security-detail caught her ears.

"*Jesus!*" intoned one man. "What the fuck we do *now*, man?"

"We *gotta* open up on her!" answered a terrified another. "CO gave orders – we don't do it, Air Force gonna string us up anyways."

"Fuck *that*, man!" argued a female voice. "You see what she did to Billie and Frankie back there? I'm *outta* here!"

"Sit tight," ordered the second voice. "Look, maybe if we –"

"Where'd she *go*, Jack?" demanded a panicked female voice.

"Shit, it's *hot*, all of a sudden –" nervously observed the first man.

To which Karéin-Mayréij insouciantly replied, as she dropped her hiding-cloak and appeared right behind the troupe,

"I can make it much *hotter*, you know."

"Don't – don't *shoot* – *please!*" whimpered one of the men, holding his arms up high. "We – I mean I – I give up!"

"We *all* give up!" echoed two others, also showing the sign of surrender.

The alien-girl bid *Væran Fàiagàryuu* to her grasp and held out the weirding-sword, pointing it at each of the erstwhile security-guards in turn.

"See... here is the thing," she explained, with a thin smile. "It is *suicide* for you to follow the orders of your commanders and war against me... it is pitiful and unworthy for me to slaughter the helpless. Do yourselves a *favor* and find someone more, 'equal', to risk your lives against – and make sure to tell this to everyone who you meet. Do you understand?"

"Y – yes," stammered one of the Air Force staffers.

"And one *other* thing," added the Storied Watcher.

"What?" uneasily inquired the female crew-member.

"Tell your friends back there – those whose bodies have been rent by my fury – that I am truly *sorry*," apologized the newcomer. "These days – when I become angry – when I am foolishly-defied... at such times, it is not at all advisable to show one's face, or to stand in my way. I wish that your fellow-warriors should recover... I really *do*."

"Yeah... sure," was all the Air Force staffer could think to say.

Heading for the spiral stairway leading to the upper-deck of the aircraft, the Storied Watcher turned away from the group of shaken would-be air-soldiers, the back-wash from the flick of her cape touching lightly upon them.

"Now go and get some para-choots, or the like," she ordered. "For I know not if your superiors are sufficiently insane to carry through with the threat that I heard, a few moments ago. In that case, your deaths would not be on *my* account... but still, would I regret them."

The Air Force crewmen ran rapidly toward the rear of the airplane, only one of them daring to look over her shoulder.

Now Karéin-Mayréij, serene confidence marking her countenance, walked calmly and deliberately up the staircase. Reaching its top-most part, she reached a hatch closed tight, looked up with her palms outspread as if giving a benediction, and observed the barrier shattered by the rending powers of her mind.

"Do not shoot!" she exclaimed through the opened hatch-way. "I am here to *talk*, not fight – but if you choose the latter, that will be your last choice on this world!"

A second later, she levitated through the passageway, coming to rest on the floor of a darkened command-center just aft of the AL-2C's cockpit.

Armed Air Force officers – most of them senior to those who had been unfortunate enough to encounter the alien on the lower-decks – crouched in the shadows in every direction; but – no doubt mindful of what had just happened – they did not immediately open fire.

Now, with her ethereal bubble all but invisible in the half-light and her war-music subsiding somewhat, the Storied Watcher confronted the Air Force lieutenants, captains, majors and others who commanded this high-tech airborne war-machine.

"Who here among you calls himself 'Major-General Schweicker'?" she boomed. "Let him come forward!"

After a brief delay, a fit-looking 50ish, Caucasian man with silver-black hair, stepped out from behind two other officers.

"I'm Schweicker... and I'm in command," he stated, sounding as brave as would have been possible, considering the circumstances. "Your presence is unwelcome here, and you have committed crimes against the United States of America – for which you must be held accountable. What do you want?"

"Sir," curtly replied Karéin-Mayréij, "Your definition of the word 'crime' does not, ahh, appeal to me, I am afraid; and as to my being 'unwelcome'... well, *that* fact has been apparent since I was unlucky enough to end up in your pompous little empire. Anyway... I am not disposed to chat about such things, right now. You ask what I want? Here – I will tell you. I believe that you have the ability to open an, uhh, 'direct-line' to your President... is that not correct?"

"*Theoretically*," answered the general. "But arranging that kind of communication-channel would take time and would require a *very* important message. I'm not sure that I can –"

"Begin work on it!" countered the Storied Watcher. "If you want a good reason, tell whomever that answers, that you have ten to fifteen minutes, before I tear this aircraft into little pieces... then proceed to flatten whichever American city happens to be closest by, down on the ground. Did you, ahh, 'get' that... or do I need to repeat it slowly, so you can better understand?"

See, children, how, when one has carried through on a small threat of violence, one is then credible for more severe, false threats, she silently instructed.

If what but, Mother – came back a fire-crackling little voice, from the direction of the newcomer's lower left leg.

Let us hope that he does not call our bluff, she mentally answered.

Ye know that I seek them to fear me... not to hate me as a murderess.

The AL-2C commander hesitated for a second or two and for that time, the alien-girl worried that he would dig in his heels, but eventually, Schweicker grunted, "Very well then – I take back nothing that I've so far said... but to avoid further loss of life, I'll try to set up your communication-channel. You should be aware that it will be voice-only, and that I can't guarantee *anything*. Is that clear? Oh, and, uhh... how do you want to be introduced? I could simply call you 'the alien', but –"

"I am Karéin-Mayréij, who is the Storied Watcher," she replied. "I would prefer that to be my title – but as dear Bob Billings used to say, 'you can call me a cab, for all I care'... I think that the President will want to hear what I have to tell him."

The general nodded to one of his subordinates, who sat down at a console, entered some commands on a keypad and began mumbling something into a microphone.

"Attempting to establish secure link via MILSTAR-35B," announced a heavy-set, African-American communications-technician. "Sir... this is gonna be difficult – we're gettin' a lot of interference... channel's unstable, I can't get a lock on the carrier. I'm tryin' to compensate for it, but the pattern's showin' up all over the spectrum –"

"Oh... sorry," interrupted the newcomer, in a *faux*-pleasant voice. "I will – how does one say – 'turn down the volume'. See if it is any easier, now."

The communications-technician again turned to his console and adjusted the settings on a dial-control.

"Better now – not one hundred per-cent, though," he remarked.

Turning his head with a look of astonishment, he added, "You mean that was... *you*?"

The Storied Watcher, her fangs peeking cruelly out from under a self-satisfied half-smile, did a little half-bow in the man's direction.

"She's – she was – *jammin'* us," muttered a staff-lieutenant, from his post at a computer display on the other side of the command center.

"No fuckin' *way!*" whispered a more junior, Hispanic attendant to the senior officers. "How does she do something like *that*, with just a sword and shield –"

"Did you think that I would just sit around and let your smart-rockets and electro-wave seeing-devices home in on me, like a tracking-hound sniffs out a rabbit?" sneered Karéin-Mayréij, as the wicked smile returned to her face.

"I was planning to tell your President this... but now that we are on the subject, perhaps you can relate it on my behalf," she added, driving home the point. "If I am forced to fight his army, including all of those who now hear this, I will *not* wage the kind of warfare that *you* seek to fight... that is, with the advantage all on your side. I will, instead, fight *my* kind of battle – and I will fight to *win!* Sadly... some of your comrades have already found out what happens, when I must do this. I pray that no more must fall... for it demeans me to hurt an ill-equipped enemy."

"*Sure* you will," warily offered Schweicker.

"Sir, I got a proxied connection back to Air Force Ghost – uhh, I mean, to the President," interjected the communications-technician. "It's faint... but he should be able to hear you, if you speak clearly. Should I enable?"

"The word 'proxy' means, incidentally," advised the general, addressing the alien, "That we are bouncing the signal between a number of different relay-points. Thus it will be futile to try to trace back the direction of the radio-waves, to –"

Waving her mail-clad finger in the air, as if a teacher giving a lesson to a schoolboy, the alien-girl interrupted Schweicker. "To find out where your President hides, ahh – how would Bob say it – 'his sorry ass'. *Clever* of you – that I must admit. I concede one, ahh, 'pawn-piece' to your side."

The general wisely did not reply to this provocation, and merely directed to the console-operator, "Enable."

"By the way," added Karéin-Mayréij, with a *faux*-polite smile, "I am sure that you can use the same method, to – ahh – 'home in', on me. Be equally aware that if your friends use that to guide weapons in my direction... it will not be *me* who dies as a result. Had you noticed that I am rather difficult to surprise?"

"You don't *say*," deadpanned the general.

A few more status-lights flickered. "Channel's open, sir," stated the communications-technician. "But there's no answer... just a second... hello, hello, this is Evil Eye, priority call to C-in-C," he spoke into the microphone.

Holding one headphone to his ear, he continued, "Yes, this is Evil Eye... well it was *confirmed*... right? He's... *what?* He's *busy?* Look, sir... this is above my rank – can I put you through to the General? Okay... hold on."

The technician looked up at Schweicker.

"Somethin' *weird* goin' on over there, sir," explained the technician. "Link's active – and we're live – but they're sayin' that the President is, uhh, 'busy with a critical issue'... whatever *that* means. You want to talk with them, sir?"

"*Here*," growled the aircraft-commander, through clenched teeth, while the alien-girl observed the impasse with thinly-concealed, malicious amusement.

Schweicker quickly seized the microphone and headset.

"This is General Schweicker of the AL-2C Long Whip, call code 'Evil Eye'," he began, calmly but with force. "I'm requesting a direct conversation with the President, top priority... what's *that?* You want a *reason?* How about, 'I have the alien standing about two feet away from me on board this aircraft, she has just crippled or killed half my crew', and she's –"

"I have killed *nobody*... at least not that I know of," interrupted the Storied Watcher. "But you had better get one of your, ahh, 'medicine-men' down to the lower-decks; else my claim may eventually prove to be false."

Schweicker nodded to two of his subordinates and they headed down the hatch and stairway.

"Did you *hear* that?" demanded the general, still speaking into the microphone. "What do you *mean* – 'you don't believe me'? Mister – if you don't get the President right now, I'll make sure that you spend the rest of your commission cleaning *latrines* – look, don't take *my* word for it. Here... speak to her yourself."

He held the microphone out in the newcomer's direction.

"I know how this is going to sound," complained Schweicker, "But the President's aide-de-camp doesn't believe that you're here with us – apparently there's some kind of *other* crisis going on right now, and the Commander-in-Chief is, uhh, 'one hundred per-cent busy'. Would you like to speak to his assistant? Remember, we have your digital voice-print on file... they should be able to compare what you say now, to that, and verify your identity in that way."

"I suppose," answered Karéin-Mayréij. "And thank you for the free spying-advice. I will have to remember to sound different, for our next meeting."

The frustrated general rolled his eyes, though he tried not to show it.

As the alien-girl took the microphone, in so doing facing the communications-console and bending too closely over the technician seated in front of it – the man got up with a yelp and stumbled to one side, as her burning presence singed the top of his head – she added, "*Væran Ksé'l'ch', Væran Ss'éth'ch'*, watch ye my back, if ye please; and for the two of you Air Force soldiers who were starting to draw your guns, I would advise you to remain prudent and living warriors... rather than dead fools."

Instantly, the two little daggers flew to a spot just behind the alien woman, hovering there malevolently, at the ready.

"No hostile action except on my say-so!" quickly commanded Schweicker. "That's an *order!*"

"You now speak to Karéin-Mayréij, the Storied Watcher of the Endless Worlds," gravely spoke the newcomer, into the microphone. "Which courtier of the American President do I address?"

She listened to some faint words for a few seconds, then continued, "Hmm... I see, I *see*... well, that may *be*, young man – but you speak now with someone who is disposed to wreck your entire *country* from end to end – would *that* be a good enough reason to ask your President to parley for a moment or two? *What*? Of *course* I know that he already knows that! Listen here... what could be *more* important than – oh, just a *minute*. Would you please stay on the line? Oh-kay."

"Looks like the President's got a full day today," whispered one AL-2C staffer to another, with a scarcely-concealed, wry smile.

The glowing-eyed alien-girl turned to address Schweicker.

"It seems, General," she grumbled, "That your President has given orders that he is not to be interrupted from his present meeting, for *any* reason. And here I was to think that I had a monopoly on his worries – how *foolish* of me! Perhaps I should do something more – ahh, 'spectacular' – to gain his attention? How about turning a city or two, upside down? Or maybe cause one to sink into the ocean? Let us be *creative*, here... what types of ideas appeal to you, sir?"

"You're obviously speaking rhetorically... I *hope*," stiffly evaded the general.

"Rhet – what?" inquired the Storied Watcher. "Oh – you mean, like a joke... right? Well, I hate to disappoint you... but it is not."

"Let me have the mike again, please," requested the general.

The newcomer obliged and he again started to speak.

"This is General Schweicker, again – *look*, Mister!" he inveighed, "I *demand* that you put us us through to the President – we have a *crisis*-situation here on board Evil Eye – or if you can't, at least get me General Anderson, *he'll* know what to do – what's that? For *God's* sake... just a minute."

The Air Force mission commander looked up. "Now, I'm being told that General Anderson is *also* tied up, he's my –"

"Your 'boss'... the, ah, 'head-honcho' of your military organization," interjected the Storied Watcher. "I believe that I have spoken directly with that person, in happier times."

"Right," noted Schweicker. "Apparently he's in with the President... in the same meeting, that is. But I'm told that he – and presumably the President – will be out, 'real soon now'. Do you mind waiting?"

"Do I mind..." incredulously echoed Karéin-Mayréij, with a bemused head-shake. "Oh... of *course* not! I mean... I am *only* someone who has crushed demons and demigods with her bare hands, who can kill all of you with just a *thought*, who is one more torment away from reducing your nation to smoking wreckage – and who saved your whole *planet* from being shattered by a comet. Why would *I* mind waiting my turn... be that a minute, an hour or a day from now? I hope that you have a toilet-room located conveniently near, just in case. Say – have you, ahh, 'read any good books lately', sir?"

The communications-technician could not restrain his nervous laughter, upon hearing this; but the mirth was quieted by Schweicker in a like manner to the Storied Watcher, as she imposed self-control on her war-children, when her mind perceived them becoming distracted by the discourse.

"You hear somebody laughin'?" one Air Force lieutenant asked another, *sotto voce*.

"Yeah – sounded kinda like the Chipmunks... what the f, man..." the second staffer whispered back.

Desperately, the general half-shouted into the microphone, "We're running out of *time*, here! The alien is threatening to *kill* us, unless she gets to speak with the President, *immediately* –"

"I threaten not *you*," amicably corrected the alien-girl. "I promise to kill your *President* – and anyone else who has stolen and tortured my new-found human kin. I suppose that *might* include you *after* all, if you are stupid enough to stand in my way. Oops! Sorry for any, ah, 'miss-under-stand-ings'."

She showed a cruel, sharp-toothed smile, upon saying this.

"Did you *hear* that?" exclaimed Schweicker. "This situation is *critical* – oh, really? For *sure*? Thank God. Okay – yeah, I think she'll wait that long. I'll hand the line back to her... the next voice you hear will be the alien's."

He was about to hand the mike back to Karéin-Mayréij, only to find it pulled mysteriously from his hand, afterward floating through thin air to meet the alien's own.

"Meeting has just broken up," he remarked. "President will be on, in no more than a minute or two. I hope that's acceptable –"

"It will have to be," she replied. "As long as you understand... all the while I have been estimating how long it will probably take your government, to plan and execute their next attack upon myself. We are gradually nearing the end of that period, as we speak. When it comes – it would not be wise for you to be anywhere *near* me. As I believe that I said before... when I fully activate my war-skills, *I* am in no danger... but as for all of you... well..."

Again, they saw an indifferent, haughty smile, coming from the ethereally-beautiful, but intimidating, visage of Karéin-Mayréij.

Schweicker turned to one of his subordinates.

"Set a clock running on the computer, starting now," he commanded.

Say 'Hello', To...

As the first guard approached Jacobson from the rear, Former Mars Mission Science Officer Cherie Teruko Tanaka wheeled to face the gendarme positioned just behind her.

She quickly opened her eyes.

Which now were shining as bright as Venus in a clear summer night-sky.

"*You were **warned**!*" shrieked the more-than-woman.

A blinding flash of some kind of other-worldly energy thundered out from the half-clasped hands at her midriff, catching the guard as he was about to open fire. He went flying off to one side, the bones in his body giving off a sickening 'crack', as if he had been body-slammed by a rhinoceros.

Blood and smoke poured from the hapless man's SWAT suit. He convulsed on the floor, underneath a red smear slightly above, on the wall.

With the psycho-music pounding out an exhilarating beat, White's mind tore through the handcuff-chain on his arms in less than half a second, then turned to face the guard on his left, who already had an automatic-rifle half-raised.

But – yanked by some unseen force – the weapon flew from his hands, its magazine and various small parts falling from it in the process.

The gendarme jumped at the black man, thinking White to still be restrained; but the Air Force astronaut's hands were now free – and, despite years of other work – he had forgotten neither his ghetto street-fighting skills, nor the more formal martial-arts that he had learned within the military.

While the guard fumbled for a concealed combat-knife, White's boot caught him hard in the crotch, and then, a second later, the man collapsed in agony, as White grasped him on the shoulders.

Something terribly *cold* issued forth from the former Mars astronaut's hands, instantly freezing the gendarme's upper arms – as well as half his neck – into a perfect simile of an unprotected trip to the South Pole.

"*Fuck you!*" cursed White at his frozen, near-dead victim, as he turned to help his team-mates.

Boyd's task had been to deal with the one guard who had the sense to head for an exit, perhaps to warn the rest of those defending – well – wherever they happened to be. The man's hand had been reaching for the door-handle, but some unseen force seemed to prevent him from getting a solid grasp.

Worse still, the gendarme felt himself being involuntarily turned in place. As he raised his gun at Boyd, he saw the latter's face, which had an odd, grim smile on it.

"*Going* somewhere, motherfucker?" spat the Air Force major, catching the guard in an evil, dull-glowing stare.

The next second, the struggling, astonished man was being simultaneously levitated and spread-eagled, with his combat-helmet, gun and knife being methodically removed from his body.

"I'm getting a headache from this!" hissed Boyd, in the gendarme's direction. "Here – let's share it!"

The gendarme screamed and then fainted – blood pouring out his ears and nostrils – as the force of Boyd's mental powers pressed on his skull.

For his part, Jacobson, too, had quickly wheeled to face the guard who had been assigned to force him on to the gurney, and, as the man stepped forward, the Mars mission commander felt the mind of his former science officer and erstwhile lover, rend the connecting-cord of his handcuffs, in two.

The guard raised his gun and got two shots off, one of which struck Jacobson in the upper thigh; and though the fact of this registered on his mind, strangely, it just felt numb – as if some other force was shutting off the pain and shock.

None of the funny light and fire business from me, raced Jacobson's determined, furious mind.

I'm just going to beat the shit *out of you!*

With the force of a pile-driver and – for the briefest of seconds – a faint blue-green flash, Jacobson's fist smashed almost dead-center on the gendarme's chest.

The Mars mission commander was quite a big, heavy-set man to begin with, and he had won his fair share of boxing-matches, in earlier days; but what he hit the guard with was something far more than an ordinary sucker-punch.

With the sound of ribs cracking underneath a shattered Kevlar breastplate, the hapless man was propelled backward like a rag-doll shot from a cannon, halfway across the room. He impacted against a storage-cabinet with a muffled crashing-sound.

Bottles, test-tubes and other bric-a-brac fell out, covering the guard's apparently lifeless body underneath.

"Commander – you're *hit!*" shouted White, as he hurried to Jacobson's side.

In mid-stride, he noticed that while the second smock-man – who hadn't previously said anything – had hidden somewhere. His counterpart was dashing for a control-panel of some kind.

"*Professor!*" called the black ex-astronaut, pointing at his prey.

"Calling for *Daddy*, you worthless piece of *shit?*" screeched Tanaka.

Instantly, the second smock-man was stopped in more or less the same way as had been Boyd's assigned guard. The more-than-woman's mind dragged him backward, levitating him a foot off the floor and forcing his arms behind his back while so doing.

In three or four seconds, he was right in front of Tanaka, and her hands had been freed in the same way as for White and Jacobson.

The man's face was frozen in terror, as the former science officer forced him to face her.

She dropped him to eye-height, placed her hands over his ears and snarled, "I could kill you with a *thought* – but you don't *deserve* to die quickly... do you?"

better hope that your continued existence as a witness for the upcoming atrocities-trial, would be worth more to us than the satisfaction of seeing you die, slowly and painfully."

He paused, allowing silence to come down for a second or two.

"Any *questions?*" he growled.

Wide-eyed, the smock-man just shook his head.

"Well said, Commander," offered Boyd.

"Okay, then," said Jacobson. "So let's start with – when's the next regular check scheduled for what was supposed to have been done to us, in here? That is – how long do we have, before someone comes knocking on the door, out there?"

"Oh... not for another four hours," replied the smock-man. "Our techniques take *time*, you know. Although sometimes we get done early."

"I'll *bet* you do," muttered Boyd.

The former Mars mission commander shook his head in disgust. "Where *are* we?" he requested.

"Look – they'll *kill* me, if I tell you any more of this!" argued the captive, sweat breaking on his brow.

Jacobson used his index-finger to send a 'go ahead' motion to Boyd.

Instantly, the smock-man doubled over in agony, as the alien-power of the Air Force astronaut's mind simultaneously compressed his skull and built up pressure in his nasal-passages.

It lasted only a second, but that was long enough to leave him doubled-up, coughing and drooling in pain on the floor.

"How's it *feel*, asshole?" cursed White, squatting next to the poor creature. "I'm sure that my old friend Brent can keep it up for hours – *days*, in fact – if y'all want to go that route. Frankly... if I was in your shoes, I'd want to take my chances with the Man out there, rather than the four of us in *here*, seven days a week."

"Special... Agency... Interrogation... Facility..." gasped the captive.

"Where?" demanded Jacobson, his voice rising. "On the map."

"Aleutians... Amchitka..." said the man, as he tried to sit up.

"There's *another* thing that just started making sense, Commander," observed Boyd. "Remember how it felt... *warm*, out there?"

"Yeah," answered the Mars mission leader. "Residual radiation from the tests... that's *gotta* be it."

"You mean we're at a nuclear test-site?" asked Tanaka.

"You *got* it, Professor," confirmed White. "Underground blasts... they set off some pretty big bombs here, back in the 20th century, if memory serves yours truly, right."

"I wouldn't be surprised if this whole *facility* is built down one of the test shafts," observed Jacobson. "Kind of makes *sense*, don't you think? Would have been quite cost-effective to build – excavation's already largely done, ha ha – and who *cares*, if the background-dose is a little on the high side? Whoever's running the place, wasn't counting on anyone coming back up... either detainees or torturers."

"Yeah, be awkward for 'em either way... and it's conveniently far from the hustle-and-bustle of society," commented White. "Ain't no nosy reporters going to be wanderin' around topside... *that's* for sure."

Jacobson turned to address the false 'doctor'.

"Which leads me to the *next* question, my friend," he remarked. "Who's in charge, here? Who do you report to?"

"I guess... I guess I'm a dead man... already," started the smock-man.

"Y'all a fuckin' *genius* there, bro'!" spat White, in his direction.

"So... to answer your question, Commander Jacobson sir, it's... it's the Agency. The *Company*. Special Interrogations Branch. We're *all* Special Branch down here... except the boys from GrayWar, that is. They just deliver the new ones to us, then they leave... they don't know anything about Special Branch – 'need-to-know' and all that."

"CIA... right?" posited Boyd.

The man nodded.

"How long has this been going on?" muttered Tanaka.

The smock-man shot her a "what planet did you just get off", look.

"Why... since '02, of course," he stated, as if reciting facts out of an encyclopedia. "Although I don't know if this place was up and running then... it took a while to get everything planned and built – not the kind of thing that you can just go out and hire a contractor for, you know? Things *did* tail off a bit for a time around '010, or so I was told – apparently the President at that time didn't know about the facility or its other counterparts around the world, standard Company procedure when we don't have someone *reliable* as C-in-C. Anyway, all that was way before *my* time... I signed on about ten years ago, and we had been going full steam for *years* before that. Last few years, we've been *so* busy, we've had to turn some of them away –"

Maybe he couldn't read minds like the four astronauts did; but wisely, the smock-man saw the disgust on their faces and promptly shut up.

"How many people are you holding in here?" demanded the Asian-American woman. "Who are they? And *where* are they?"

"Oh... I wouldn't *know*," answered the man, indifferently shaking his head. "My... colleague and I, we're only tasked with the... uhh... Billings party – the salesman, that – and the four that were with him; and we're of course in charge of... uhh... yourselves. As for the others in here... God, there could be *hundreds* – I remember hearing the number '250', once, a few years ago... we got *everything*, from foreign terrorists, illegal immigrants, ghetto-gangstas, music- and movie-pirates, patent-infringers, *et cetera*, to abortionists, queers, dykes, race-mixers, birth-control-peddlers, porno-peddlers, subversives, traitors – you know, all the pond-scum that Uncle Sam just wants to be rid of –"

"I'm gonna fuckin' *kill* you!" shouted White, as he ran toward the immediately-cowering smock-man.

It took all the skills of Boyd and Tanaka to restrain him.

"We're only enforcing the law, you know!!!" quailed the smock-man.

The only reason I'm holding you back, Devon, sent Tanaka to White's furious mind,

Is that I don't want you being the only *one who gets the satisfaction of offing this son-of-a-bitch!*

We're into revenge, not murder... *remember?* cautioned the silent counsel of Jacobson.

"You're skating on *very* thin ice, mister," advised the Mars commander. "If I were you, I'd try sounding a little less... *positive*, about the contribution that you and your friends are making to American society. Now... we need you to answer Professor Tanaka's other questions. Where are the other captives being held – especially this 'Billings' guy – and those who you brought in with him? I need *precise* descriptions of all who belong to this other party of detainees. Then, I need a five-minute summary of the layout of this facility... in particular, all possible means of ingress and egress. Start *talking!*"

"I'm not sure that I can – *ohhhh*," moaned the man in the off-white lab-coat, as Boyd shot a wave of pain into his head.

"Okay – okay – I *get* it!" he gasped. "Billings – Bob K., salesman from Tucson, Arizona – he's Caucasian, actually looks a bit like you, Commander Jacobson, well, he's almost your height, anyway – middle-aged, dark hair, brown eyes. When we brought him in, he had a nig – I mean, a black woman – from Detroit, with him, goes by the name of 'Whitney Claremont', 30ish, thin build, Afro-haircut... she had two kids, boy of about ten, name of 'Curtis', teenager named 'Melissa'."

"You get all that?" requested Jacobson to Tanaka, over his shoulder.

"Definitely," confirmed the woman, holding a pen and writing-pad that had been scrounged from the surroundings.

"About the facility..." continued the captive, "It's all on a 3-D smart wallet-card in the desk-drawer over there... this is a *big* place – we carry these around with us so we don't get lost, *bad* idea to get lost in the wrong area, you know... you just press the little button on the card and it shows you the next level... it cycles between 'em. Oh, and it also can get you into some of the rooms – not the ones where the *real* fun goes on, of course, but –"

Boyd was about to do something unpleasant, but the smock-man quickly shut up.

With a wave of Jacobson's finger, White and Boyd set to rummaging through the storage-drawers.

"Found three of the things," indicated White. "And they work. Damn – he ain't *kiddin'*... this place goes on and on... hah, check out the title on th' card... 'R.B. Cheney Memorial Federal Interrogation Facility' – *that's* where we're at. *Figures!*"

Tanaka mumbled a curse and shook her head.

"Where's the Billings party?" demanded the Mars mission commander. "And is that all of them?"

"Yeah," answered the captive, "Far as I know, they're being confined in separate cells, one level below this one, except when we're... uhh... doing the *business* on them... that goes on generally one level further down. Oh... and there's one more in that group – an Indian kid, 'bout same age as the Claremont boy, called himself 'Tommy Tanak' at first, but after we did him a few times, he said his original name was 'Tommy George' –"

"Just a *minute*," interrupted Tanaka, her tone instantly alarmed and alerted. "This last child – what did you say his name was?"

"George," replied the smock-man. "Uhh, 'Singing-Bird' George, or some Injun-nonsense like that... sorry, there... said he was from Nebraska, a reservation... I think."

"No, *before* that – what did he say first, when you asked him his name?" pressed the former Mars science officer.

"*Jesus*," breathed Boyd. "The *visions* –"

Tanaka, with watering eyes, nodded in Boyd's direction.

"Uhh, 'Tanak', or something like... oh, *shit!*" stammered the smock-man. "Listen, missus, if we had known that he was *your* kid... honest, we'd have told Headquarters, asked for a 'bye' –"

"What *else* did this 'Tommy' tell you?" retorted the Asian-American astronaut. "I need *everything* – and *fast!* Or, so help me *God*, I'll pull it out of your brain, the hard way –"

The captive mewled in fear, and quickly added, "Not a lot that made sense, really – none of them gave us worthwhile information – remember, that's why the boys up in the executive-office sent you all down here? He... uhh... he cried a lot, wet his pants, par for the course... also gave us some stupid made-up story about 'the angel-lady is my mommy now, and when she gets here, she'll kill you all' –"

Gasping, Tanaka slumped to her knees, tears pouring down.

"Karéin... oh God, Karéin... your *son*! Sam... Devon... Brent... don't you *see?*" she sobbed. "It all comes *together*, now! She must have used *my* name, when she arrived down here – and *he's* the little boy in our dreams –"

White crouched down to comfort his colleague.

"Cherie," he quietly counseled, "I *know* what y'all is gettin' to... and I promise you, we'll find this 'Tommy', and the rest of 'em too. As the Lord's my witness... I *swear* it!"

"And when we *do*," glowered Boyd, barely able to contain his contempt while stooping over to stare at the man in the smock, "We're going to let the boy, and the rest of them, decide what happens to you. I'll be *more* than happy to carry out the sentence. Put *that* in your pipe and smoke it, dickhead."

The captive just trembled.

"But... if we're getting the visions," continued Boyd, worry all over his voice, "Then it's reasonable to believe that Karéin is, too, and *that* means –"

Jacobson, his eyes staring pensively out across the room, allowed himself a nervous half-laugh.

"Cherie," he slowly commented, "If you're right about this – and something tells me you *are* – based on our own knowledge of her... can you *imagine* what the Storied Watcher would do to someone – or a government – that she believed responsible for offenses like we almost suffered, ourselves? If they were done against a child who she considered to be a *son*?"

The smock-man saw a pall of dread descend on the faces of the four more-than-humans that surrounded him.

"*Jaysus H. Christ,*" breathed White. "And sorry old boy upstairs... but sayin' that, fits, here. Knowin' her as I do... she'd flatten everythin' between her and this 'Tommy' kid. Probably throw in everythin' for twenty miles on either side, just so the perps can't miss gettin' the message. She'd do the same if she thought *we* were in trouble – I'd bet y'all good money on that."

"Yes, but..." countered Tanaka, her own gaze as far-off as that of Jacobson. "She warned us over and over again about the allure of *Amaiish* – how it would tempt us to use it to destroy, how it would make us drunk with power – and how she had learned to discipline herself, how she would *never* hurt anyone if she could possibly avoid doing so. You're asking me to assume that she's suddenly changed into some kind of a *monster!* Every *fiber* within me refutes that. I don't believe it... not for a minute."

"Am-*what?*" asked the captive, looking up.

"STFU, asshole!" ordered White. "You all's *way* out of your depth here, my man. *Seriously* out of your comfort-zone."

"If only you *knew* how far out of your depth," muttered Boyd.

"None the less," observed Jacobson, "While I'd *like* to believe that what you're saying is right, Cherie... I think we have to seriously consider the possibility that Devon is closer to the truth. None of that, of course, justifies or excuses what the Government has been doing down here... but if Major White and I are even *half*-right, we have to think our next moves through, very carefully. We may be the only ones who can defuse the situation, before she... *well*. This is all just *speculation*, after all."

"Yeah... just *speculation*," repeated White. "Y'all sure got *me* convinced, Captain."

"Well," suggested Boyd, "Whether or not Devon and the Captain are right about this – we'd better act as if they *are*. I mean... one way or another, it's reasonable to assume that this 'Billings' guy and the rest of his group – the 'Tommy' kid especially – are probably being held in this same facility."

He crouched down beside the smock-man.

"Is that true?" he queried.

The man nodded.

"Alright," continued the ex-astronaut, "Just out of human decency, we have a moral obligation to get the Billings party, and as many others as we can safely accommodate, out of here – don't we? And I it would be better for us to have this

'Tommy' in our custody, as opposed to that of our little home-grown Gestapo crew here, when the Storied Watcher comes calling... wouldn't you say?"

"Probably," agreed White. "Unless, of course, God's little Destroyin' Angel leaps to *conclusions* when she sees it – like, she thinks that *we're* the ones who was pullin' her kid's fingernails out. I sure hope she gives us some time to explain what's been goin' down."

"Just a minute," argued Jacobson, as, grimacing, he tried to slowly come to his feet. "I hate to sound like the advocate for the U.S. government here... but, are we sure that it's a good idea to go around simply popping open all the cage-doors? Billings and *his* crew are completely innocent – these creeps undoubtedly wanted *them* for more or less the same reasons as they wanted *us* – but there may be a lot of genuinely bad actors – *real* terrorists, gangsters, and so on – being held down here. If we go around freeing them, willy-nilly, we could rapidly cause a totally out-of-control situation."

"You can say *that* again, sir," chirped the captive.

"Didn't I tell you to shut the *fuck* up?" spat White. "But hey – maybe I was too hasty there, peeps. Why don' we just chuck your sorry lil' lily-white butt in with all them gangstas and see how sympathetic they are –"

The smock-man looked down in terror.

"As little as I like to say it," remarked Tanaka, "I think that Sam's right, here. My moral instincts tell me just to free *everyone*, but we have to be practical – there may be hundreds of prisoners in here, most of them probably innocent, but freeing all of them at once without some way of preserving order, might quickly degenerate into a riot. Let's just find Karéin's friends, get them out, then tell the media about what's going on up here. When all this hits the news, they'll *have* to free the rest of them... at least those who haven't done anything. Can we all agree on that?"

"Yeah... 'cept for one little thing," retorted White.

"What would *that* be, Devon?" asked the Asian-American woman.

"Once we get us, and whoever else that we're takin' with us, and once we get to the surface – assumin' of course that we *live* that long – how the hell do we get *off* this damn island? That big old transport's probably long gone back to the mainland," noted the black ex-astronaut.

"Hadn't really *thought* of that," wryly admitted Tanaka.

"*Figured* y'all hadn't," observed White, with a gentle smile.

Now Tanaka turned her attention to Jacobson.

"Sam," she queried, "Are you *sure* you don't want to take it easy for a while, yet? You just got *shot*, for God's sake! Not a good idea to be putting pressure on it –"

"I'm *fine*, Cherie," countered the former Mars mission commander, though he was still wincing as he leaned back against one of the gurneys. "Well, okay, maybe 'fine' *is* a bit of a stretch, but... this is kind of hard to explain... it's like the more that I try to ignore the pain and make it work, the faster I feel it doing so.

I'm pretty sure that I can walk, now... don't be surprised if I can't quite keep up with you at more than a fast trot."

The three others could *feel* the power issuing from him.

"Anyway," continued Jacobson, with his apparent health waxing with every word, "So far, nobody seems to have noticed the little altercation that we just had here, but I don't think it would be wise to push our luck – we had better get going and looking for this 'Billings' guy, sooner rather than later. Brent, Devon – can you check what's left of those prison-guards. – you know, the ones in the black suits... if it looks like they're about to come to, we'll have to tie them up. Also, see if we can salvage their weapons and anything else of use that they might have on them – especially keys and things like that."

"Workin' on it, Captain," mentioned White, as he went over and examined the man that he had attacked.

This unfortunate creature was lying in a pool of cold water – undoubtedly the remnants of the former Air Force Major's assault – mixed with the faint pink tinge of blood.

White dragged the man out until he was lying face-up.

Quietly, he stated, "I think he's daid... or, at least, he ain't long for this world. No pulse."

The black ex-astronaut went silent for a few seconds, with the trace of a tear apparent in his eye.

"You know, Captain," he commented in a heavy voice, "I ain't wasted nobody, up to now – cracked a few heads down in th' hood and even *shot* a man – just self-defense y'all understand, but that one lived... 'thou shalt not kill'... 'member that? Didn't *mean* to, not really... don't know how I'm gonna answer for this..."

His shoulders slumped in remorse.

Tanaka hurried to his side and put her arms over him.

"Devon," she compassionately spoke, "He certainly would have killed *you*, if he had had the slightest chance... and he probably willingly participated in the murder and torture of countless innocent people – *all* of these sons of bitches did. You did exactly what you *had* to do... no more, no less."

She looked over at the other gendarme who her own burst of *Amaiish* had left lifeless.

"Having said that," she pensively added, "Where did I hear, 'it's a hell of a thing, to kill a man'. It looks like you're not the *only* one who will one day have to answer for her actions."

Share the guilt with me, Tanaka sent to the black man.

I feel like I'm about to puke, he mentally replied.

"I *know* what you two are thinking, and feeling," observed Boyd. "I was flying a jet, first for the Navy, then the Air Force... but I have no doubt that I'm responsible for some deaths, maybe people who didn't deserve it *nearly* as much as these guys did. All I can say is – 'it will pass'. But you never really *do* get rid of it, entirely. You *remember* it... that's just the way it is."

"You know," offered Jacobson, his voice equally quiet and reflective, "I can second Brent's point – I flew combat-missions for the Air Force, too – and... don't we all sound exactly like *her*, today? Remember what *she* said, about 'carrying the guilt of all my terrible crimes, wherever I may go'? Maybe, my friends, we've now got something *else* in common with our angelic mentor."

"Not somethin' I *like* to have in common," muttered White, the color slowly returning to his face. "When she laid all the special-power-stuff on us, I kinda didn't count on it endin' up like *this*."

"Yeah – and I'd bet you good money that the tab ain't finished being run up, yet," warned Boyd, as he surveyed the sprawled body of his own opponent. "Don't know how hard I hit this guy, but he's breathing... I guess he'll live, so we might want to tie him up, before we get out of here. Gun and other stuff looks like they're all still functional... I'll strip him of all of it – just give me a minute or two."

He set about to work.

"Guy that I hit, there's stuff missin' from his gun... we might be able to fix it, but that'd take time," noted White. "Maybe not worth the effort... I dunno."

Still somewhat favoring the shot leg, Jacobson slowly shuffled over to the pile of detritus, under which his assailant lay dormant.

He kicked a few boxes and bottles off the man, knelt down and extended a hand.

"Got a pulse... but it's faint," remarked the former Mars commander. "And barely breathing, there's blood all over his chest... must have broken some ribs. Maybe internal damage..."

His tone was reminiscent of what had been heard from White a few minutes before, and Jacobson quietly mentioned, "It's *different* when you do it from ten thousand feet, I guess... you don't get to see their faces – the blood's only *theoretical*, not real... ah, I don't know what I'm blubbering about here, I'm – or, until recently, I *was* – a member of an organization that's all *about* killing people..."

His voice trailed off.

Tanaka went to Jacobson's side, as she had with White.

"You're saying that because you've got a *conscience*... because you're a human being, Sam," she counseled.

"*Am* I, Professor?" retorted the Mars commander, his eyes looking searchingly up at the more-than-woman.

"Are you... *what*, Sam?" she rhetorically inquired.

"A human being," he said.

"No... on second thought – I guess *none* of us are, anymore... *are* we?" admitted Tanaka, while the smock-man stared in worried amazement.

"I'd like to *think*," observed Jacobson, taking a deep breath, "That whatever I've become – or, whatever I'm *becoming* – there will always be enough humanity left, to feel awful after doing something like we've – *I've* – done here. Even if it *was* necessary."

"'Amen' to *that*," chimed in White. "Killin' folk's what *they* do... ain't what *we* do... right?"

"Anyway... gun and gear off this poor soul seems mostly to be salvageable," noted Jacobson. "I think I'll leave his helmet and visor on, if you don't mind."

"Yeah," said Tanaka. "Don't blame you for that. Here, I'll check mine... and, damn!"

She fell silent, then added, "And that *definitely* makes two of us with blood on our hands, Devon... I don't want to be ghoulish, but it looks like this guard was dead before he hit the wall..."

The three men stared at her, without saying a sound.

"Look – I *know* what you're thinking," exclaimed the woman. "I just... *lashed out*. I didn't *mean* to kill him – not exactly – but this damn thing is hard to *control*... you know? If I hadn't used all that I had, it might have been *me*, lying over here... guys, you understand... don't you?"

"Of *course* we do, Cherie," sympathetically replied Jacobson. "We're all like a bunch of children armed with phaser-guns, and we don't know how much of a charge will just make them hurt, as opposed to making them die. It's just that when you did it, you looked like, uhh, her... the *bad*, 'her'."

"Yeah," pensively agreed Tanaka. "And you know what the hell of it is?"

"*Do* tell," grunted Boyd, as he set about collecting all the scavenged battle-gear in a pile in the center of the room.

"For a few seconds there, I kind of *felt* like the bad 'her', I think," commented the former Mars science officer. "One, two, three, senses working overtime, into overdrive – everything was slowing down, as if I had minutes – *days* – to make up my mind about what to do next... I looked around this room when my mind heard the 'go' from Sam, and all I saw were... uhh... were..."

"Were... *what*?" inquired Boyd.

"You all looked like... *insects* – that's about the long and short of it," she quietly remarked. "Like something I could step on and not give a *damn* about, because your lives were just so... *unimportant*. Maybe that's why I let loose against the guy who was about to attack me. Something just said, 'who cares – let him *have* it'."

Again, she got the measured, worried stare from the three men.

"*Look*, guys," protested Tanaka, "I'm telling you all of this because as a scientist, I have an obligation to report the truth – and because you have the right to know, both as friends and colleagues... whether or not the facts reflect well on me. I guess all I can do, is ask you to try to understand and bear with the changes that are going on inside me – if for no other reason than they might soon be affecting *you*, too. Oh... kay?"

White allowed himself a nervous laugh.

"That an *intentional* slip-up, Professor?" he asked.

A pained smile came to Tanaka's face.

"Sort of... I hope," she answered.

"So do we all," observed Jacobson, casting a sympathetic glance in the direction of his sometime lover. "I guess that may well be a bridge that we all have to cross, eventually – but in the short run, 'we got a job to do'... so I'd suggest we get around to doing it. Brent, what's the equipment-situation?"

Boyd laid out the gear in three neatly-arranged groups.

"Well," he began, "We got two assault rifles – ten-millimeter AR-180 plastic and composite bull-pup jobs, by the way – that seem to be fully-functional, and they got pretty much full clips, thanks to our stopping the guards before they could get too many shots off. The third one *looks* okay... but the diagnostic-display's showing an error – it might have been that it got partly hammered by the Professor's little light-show there... it *may* still be able to fire, though, so I'd say 'take it with us'... if only for deterrent effect."

"What about ammo and other gear?" requested Jacobson.

"Only one spare clip for each gun," continued the ex-Mars mission pilot, "I'd assume they didn't anticipate any prolonged fire-fights down here – with two more scrounged off the weapon that Devon did the Humpty-Dumpty trick on. Plus three gas-grenades, four combat-knives, two Kevlar-II breastplates and two working communicators... although I don't think answering incoming calls would be a good idea. Oh... and I got three computer pass-keys – undoubtedly for the doors – but they're those ones that you have to enter a PIN-code to use, so I'm not sure how much good they'll be to us. That's about it."

"If none of you have an objection," proposed the former Mars mission commander, "I'll take the marginally-functional rifle... Devon, Brent – you guys are probably quicker off the trigger than I am – so why don't you sling the ones that we know will fire. Cherie... you didn't want to carry a gun, did you?"

"Negative," stated Tanaka. "I think I'll be able to defend myself."

"You *think?*" quipped White, with a tone of friendly sarcasm. "Back on the *Infinity*, I told Miss Angel-Lady that I'd pick a gun over this weird shit she laid on us, ten times out of ten... just *another* thing yours truly might do some re-thinkin' on, y'all know..."

"You got *that* right," agreed Jacobson. "Let's divide up the extra clips between the three of us with the guns. The rest of the stuff goes evenly between all of us – except you and Brent get the flak-jackets, I doubt they'd fit the Professor... Cherie, I assume you know how to throw a gas-grenade?"

"I'll figure it out," she serenely replied. "And if it comes to that... maybe I'll see if I can learn to *breathe* that crap, too."

"That stuff 'sposed to make you puke your guts out, the second y'all get a *whiff* of it, you know," remarked White. "They made us try it out in Basic. I couldn't stand up for two hours, afterwards."

"Devon," commented Tanaka, with an eerie look in her eyes, "I just... *know*, that I can handle it. Maybe nerve-gas, too – though *that* one I'll maybe give a pass on. God, it's a weird feeling, knowing that my body's... *changing*, like this, watching it going on, waking up each successive morning, being able to do things that I could only fantasize about, as a child... I feel so powerful, so...

superior. Don't be afraid of hearing that, any of you – because you'll be here along with me, real soon now... you know?"

"*Right,*" apprehensively muttered White. "Anythin' y'all *say*, Professor."

"We've done a lot of improbable things as a team," noted Jacobson. "I suppose this one's just another that we'll have to add to the list."

"Well, when you figure out how to breathe water, make sure to take notes," mentioned Boyd in Tanaka's direction, as he presented the gear to his team-mates. "Because we may *need* to, if we want to get off this god-forsaken place."

He turned his glance to the smock-men.

"What do we do with *them?*" he asked.

"I could use my mind to try to knock 'em out cold," offered Tanaka, "But... like I said before... there's always the risk of me getting a bit carried away, and something *unfortunate* happening... like, 'their brains get par-broiled from the inside out'..."

"No great loss," said Boyd, with an indifferent shrug. "Probably a much nicer way to die than what they've inflicted on their victims."

The smock-man whimpered for mercy.

"I'd tend to agree with y'all, Brent my man," added White, "'Cept I'm sure the Professor could probably compress a *world* of hurt into a few seconds, don't you know. And it'd kinda be fun to see if I could maybe try my own hand – oh, 'scuse me, my own *mind* – in doin' the same thing to whichever one she doesn't want. But somethin' tells me that just out of fairness an' all that, we oughtta leave them to Karéin, when and if she shows up here. I mean... we can pick up them two muthas on the way out, can't we?"

"Yeah – just tie 'em up and gag 'em," directed Jacobson. "Devon may be right – I have a *feeling* that our friend the Destroying Angel will want to – *ahem* – have a little 'talk' with these guys... and they'd be too much of a burden to take with us, for now. Let's be quick about it – I want to be out of here in five, if possible."

As Boyd roughly grabbed the two smock-men, using some electrical-cords and network-cables to tie the unconscious one back-to-back with the one who was – after a fashion – still lucid, he coldly suggested, "I hope you took all that in, my friend. Because when *she* shows up –"

The man, his voice quivering, managed, "The... 'Destroying'... *what?* You mean... the *alien?*"

The former Air Force major pulled the restraints so tight that they almost cut off circulation, and replied, "Just think of us, as 'Bambi'... I guess that's the way that *I'd* put it."

"B-'Bambi'?" stammered the captive.

"See... with all you saw us do here, *we're* just lil' old Bambi, asshole," growled Boyd, his eyes staring intensely with hate and contempt against his would-be torturer.

"And when *she* gets here, say 'hello' to... *Godzilla.*"

A Fumble For The C-In-C

"So... let's have it," ordered the President.

Even through the distortion of the video-link – nearly at maximum-range, as it was, today – the U.S. leader's face had that "at wits-end" look.

"I'm afraid, Mr. President," grimly stated Bezomorton, from the ground-side bunker, "That none of the news is good."

"Well, *that's* hardly a surprise, these days," muttered the President. "The alien... right?"

"Not *this* time," answered the Security Adviser. "Might be worse, in fact. Have you heard from DeWitt, yet?"

"No," mentioned the American leader. "John – you're starting to *worry* me, if that's possible. What's going on?"

"Basically," said the adviser, his voice flat and analytical, "It appears we have a Lost Arrow situation."

"Lost... what the hell's *that?*" shot back the President.

"Basically, it's the code for a missing nuke – in this case, one of the Air Force's, down in Louisiana," explained Bezomorton. "What's worse is... the weapon may have been hijacked –"

"What the f – God *damn it!*" bellowed the President. "Where's DeWitt? Where's Anderson? Get them on the line, ASAP –"

"I've already arranged for that," quickly remarked the National Security Adviser. "Just a second – okay, engaging... they should be on your screen now."

Suddenly, on the other side of the still unstable video-display, there appeared the be-medaled, grandfatherly face of Air Force General Harry Anderson, along with DeWitt's leathery, ex-Marine visage.

Both men looked about a decade older than they had, not a fortnight ago; and, most uncharacteristically, Anderson's bushy white hair did not look like it had recently been touched by a comb.

"Mr. President –" started DeWitt; but he was cut off by his Commander-in-Chief.

"Arthur – what the *hell* is going on," angrily cursed the U.S. leader.

"God knows... I wish I *knew*," sighed a crestfallen DeWitt. "As I understand it, Air Force was transporting one of our very few available nukes... this one was a boosted W-88 Mod 5 – high kiloton-range, if that's of any interest – by joint Army / Air Force land-convoy, to Barksdale Air Force Base in Louisiana; standard procedure so that we have at least one usable nuke in each major geographic region... if you'll recall, that was to have it as a potential device against the alien. Information's still coming in, but as near as we can tell, looks like the convoy was attacked while transiting one of the back-country roads that we normally use for this purpose... now, we can't account for the bomb. I'm *very* sorry, Mr. President. I know there's no excuse for this sort of thing."

"You don't *say!*" retorted the President. "But attacked by... *who*? And do we have the damn thing back, yet?"

"There's a lot of contradictory evidence, sir – but what we have so far points to the Muslims," interjected Anderson. "We're getting reports of a suicide-raid and Islamic religious-paraphernalia being found on the few physical remains that could be identified, after the attack and fire-fight. As to the weapon physics-package itself, we still don't have a good trace on it, although we're pulling out all the stops. FBI and Louisiana State Police have sealed the entire state – all the border-crossings are roadblocked – and we're calling out what's left of the Guard, down there. We're doing everything we can."

"*Jesus*, Harry – how could something like this *happen*? You have to know that I have no choice but to hold Arthur and you *personally* accountable for the situation. The Air Force is *your* responsibility... right?"

"Mr. President... I accept full responsibility for this complete breakdown in Air Force security and discipline... and I have already prepared my letter of resignation," apologized Anderson, fatigue and frustration echoing with every syllable.

"Sir... I know that there's no excuse for what appears to have happened down near Barksdale – but in all fairness, I think that you need-to-know the following facts : One, this was a professional, very well-planned and well-executed attack... the assailants knew *exactly* where to launch their ambush, and their timing was *very* good."

"What do you mean?" pressed the President.

"Well, for example," continued the general, "They left a decoy-version of the physics-package, accurate down almost to the last nut and bolt, except for the fissile-material of course, down at the attack scene... *that* trick threw our recovery-team off by a good three hours, until they remembered to hook up our mobile PAL-gear and check to see if the unit was responding as it should have. Two – and this'll be the only request that I'll make, regarding the whole fiasco – *please* don't blame the Air Force boys that we had riding shotgun on the convoy. They fought bravely to the death – each and every *one* of 'em – but they had the rug pulled out by those useless party-animals from GrayWar, who turned tail at the first shot –"

"*Wait* a minute," interjected Bezomorton. "Did I hear the word, 'GrayWar'? Excuse my French, General – but what the hell was *that* outfit doing on a *nuclear weapons transport convoy?*"

"What were they doing?" shot back DeWitt, with wounded pride. "*I'll* tell you, Mr. Adviser – they were assigned the *exclusive* contract to drive all the vehicles – as well as to set up all the logistics for this, and every other such trip – that's been going on since the 'Private Enterprise Reforms The Military Act' ten or more years ago... remember?"

Bezomorton rolled his eyes and shook his head, as the Defense Secretary complained, "The Joint Chiefs opposed this ill-advised legislation at every step of the way – they warned the President's predecessor that we'd be opening up *huge* security-holes in letting these amateurs take over all the non-combat-roles – but we lost *that* battle to Mr. Horn and his political-games in the Senate."

"Horn told me that we'd lose Dixie if we repealed it, and that GrayWar was going to be limited to things like mess-duty," grumbled the President. "If he was here, I'd wring his neck... but we're getting off-topic... look, Harry, there's going to be hell to pay for this, but put the 'I quit' letter away, please – I might want to wring *your* neck, too, but I need you on the job – it's your responsibility, even if it's not your fault."

"And it's a responsibility that I fully accept, sir," quietly stated Anderson.

"Obviously," warned the President, "We now have to assume that the Muslims have their hands on a bomb, and are planning to use it as soon as they can – that's a situation that we have to avoid at *all* costs. What do you need to get the damn thing back? I don't care what it is, or what we've got to spend... but you need to tell me."

"The only thing that we really need now, sir," indicated DeWitt, "Apart from time – which is a luxury that we don't have much of – is to get the resources of NSA and CIA fully on the case. FBI's already working on it... but as you know, there are statutory restrictions on the use of the intelligence-agencies, domestically –"

"I don't give a tinker's damn about the rules, in circumstances like *this!*" demanded a frustrated President. "You go ahead and tell NSA that they're to tap every phone in the *country*, if needs be –"

"They're *already* doing that, sir," reminded Bezomorton. "Have been since the 9/11 incident, many years ago. The issue isn't having access to this kind of communications data; the problem is making sense of it... separating the wheat from the chaff, as it were."

"Tell them to drop *everything* until they trace down who's behind this!" snapped the American leader. "And when they find the effing Muslims, I don't care if there aren't any prisoners."

"What about the alien-project?" inquired the Security Adviser. "It's taking up almost all of our time, these days."

"No... not *that* one... I meant everything *else*, other than that," half-retreated the President. "But... put the bloody alien on the back-burner. She – or it – seems to only be defacing national-monuments... wouldn't you say we can take a few of those, compared to, say, losing all of New Orleans – or Atlanta – in a mushroom-cloud?"

"There's not much *left* of the Big Easy after the third flood, anyway," noted Bezomorton. "But I understand you loud and clear, sir – I'll have NSC convene an emergency-meeting right after we get done here... we'll co-ordinate operations. Oh, but, uhh... what about CIA?"

"What do you *mean*, 'what about CIA'?" guardedly asked the American leader.

"Are *they* in on this, sir?" asked Bezomorton. "Their resources could come in mighty handy."

"That's, uhh, a bit of a *sensitive* subject, currently," evaded the President. "You can call on them if absolutely necessary, but make it a last resort... for the record, I have to say that I'm as unimpressed with *their* performance, as I am with that of the Air Force. CIA was *supposed* to keep the goddamn Muslim terrorists out of the country and to warn us when they had something afoot – well, I'd say they've utterly failed in that department... wouldn't you? Oh... and have you been in touch with Cesar?"

"We're trying to contact the Director," spoke DeWitt. "He was tied up on a conference-call about the Southern California situation – we couldn't get through, but that meeting should be ending any moment now. The Bureau's Southeast branch is already devoting all their resources to this issue."

"Well – tell him to devote *all* his resources – everywhere – to tracking down the bomb," commanded the President. "Except – as I said before – for a skeleton-crew to keep track of the alien. You got that?"

"Yes, sir," confirmed the Defense Secretary. "Neither I nor Air Force will rest until we get to the bottom of this and retrieve the device."

Anderson added, "I know this is small consolation, Mr. President... but we may still have some time before the hijackers are in a position to actually detonate it. We think it's *highly* unlikely that they could compromise our PALs like they evidently did for the Pakistani weapons; our locking- and authorization-technology is *far* more sophisticated. It may take them weeks or months to figure out how to bypass it –"

"All true, General," interrupted Bezomorton, "But the Salvation League has surprised us before – and besides, even if they *can't* set the weapon off in the good old-fashioned way, that wouldn't stop them from using the fissile-material for another Miami Dirty Bomb type incident... would it?"

"Either outcome's *completely* unacceptable," forcefully responded the President. "We need to get the bomb back – period! Then we need to make those who took it, find out the *hard* way, about what happens to terrorists that play for keeps against Uncle Sam. And we need to do all of this, without the *slightest* hint of it becoming public. Listen... on the latter front, what's our cover-story?"

"Kaysten called me about that, a few minutes ago," explained Bezomorton. "We're depicting the roadblocks and the other lock-down activities, as 'being made necessary by the largest drug-bust in the history of the Southeast, but some of the filthy gang-members responsible are still at large', that kind of thing. Here – unlike the fiasco down in Tucson – we have the huge advantage that all the action seems to have happened far away from the TV-cameras. We've got the news-suppression teams staying on top of this, and so far, we seem to be in control of the situation. Score one for *our* side, Mr. President."

"Yeah, great, we're down by 21 and we kicked a field-goal," muttered the President. "Bully for *us*."

Wearily, he leaned back in his inadequately-contoured aircraft chair, paused for a few seconds, and said, "I guess I had better let you gentlemen get on with it. Is there any more?"

"No... I don't think so, sir," answered the Defense Secretary.

But a second later, the general looked downwards and pulled out a mobile-communicator.

"Just a second, sir – my 'Code Red' beacon is lit up... yes, it's Anderson here," he spoke into the device. "I'm in a meeting with the President, this had better be *important – what*? For God's sake, that's *all* we need right now... are you *sure* that... I mean, you have confirmed, haven't you – you *have*? She's commandeered the whole *aircraft*? But – no, never mind. Of *course* I will – this is a multi-hop link anyway. Just a second."

"You've *got* to be kidding!" exclaimed Bezomorton.

"What's *this*, Harry?" requested the President.

Over the video-link, Anderson's bloodshot, sleep-deprived eyes looked up at his Commander-in-Chief.

"Based on what I'm hearing... I'm afraid we no longer have the luxury of pulling resources off the alien-project, for the time being," he advised.

"What?" shot back the President. "I gave you an *order –*"

"I *know*, Mr. President, sir," parried the general. "And I intend to obey it, as soon as you work things out with the, uhh, *being*, on the other end of this line. She seems to have taken over one of the airborne-laser weapons ships."

Even through the static, both Bezomorton and the general could see the 'deer-in-headlights' look on the face of the American leader.

"I'll put her through now," proposed Anderson.

Bluffing With A Hand Of Deuces

The voice coming over the multi-hop, encrypted link was faint, but unmistakable.

"Do I address the President, now?" requested the melodious voice of Karéin-Mayréij.

"Yes," confirmed the U.S. leader. "I have you on speaker, and I have General Anderson of the Air Force, my Secretary of Defense, and my National Security Adviser, also listening in. What's the purpose of this call? As of our last conversation, it did not seem as if we had much more to discuss."

"The purpose is simple," stated the alien-girl, in a matter-of-fact tone. "Do you surrender?"

"Do I... *what*?" stammered the nonplussed President. "I, uhh... I rather think *not*, young lady... why would I, uhh, 'surrender', to you?"

"Have I not proven superiority of arms, sir?" countered the Storied Watcher.

"I don't know what you *mean* by that," stalled the President.

"Well... I stand now within the pressure-hull of one of your airborne battle-airplanes, which I have commandeered and which I can easily destroy," explained the newcomer. "As I have done to the many fighter-planes that you have sent against me. I have tried to be merciful in how I knocked the latter

lonely and call me 'mother' – is in no position to lecture *me* about 'right' and 'wrong'!" inveighed the Storied Watcher. "I *should* simply end this conversation right now and start toppling sky-scraper buildings... but I do not want to devastate your kingdom to prove a point, so here is an offer : Why not just return my loved-ones and let me take out my justice – call it 'vengeance', if you will – on those who are directly responsible for the abuse of Bob, Tommy, Curtis, Whitney and Melissa? I did not *want* to go a-warring against you – but you leave me no honorable way out! *Surely,* the loss of a few of your dungeon-keepers would not, ahh, 'keep you awake at night'? Why do you protect these sadists who plague my child... my friends? It makes no *sense*, sir!"

"That's, uhh... that's *complicated*," prevaricated the U.S. leader, to the consternation of all his under-studies. "We're doing all we can to locate and return the Billings party and the astronauts. "Besides... your own behavior looks plenty irrational from *my* vantage-point – you're threatening to destroy an entire *country*, for the sake of a few civilians. *Surely* a being as, uhh, 'sophisticated' as yourself can see the lack of proportionality in such conduct."

"What do you *mean*, 'complicated'?" pressed Karéin-Mayréij. "You are the 'President'... are you not? Give me access to Commander Sam and the space-farers so they can help in the quest – then issue an order that my kin be immediately released, upon pain of death to anyone who disobeys you –"

"It doesn't *work* that way," evaded the President. "I'm not at liberty to go into the details. Believe me – I wish I could be more forthcoming on this matter, but all I can do for the time being is ask for your patience –"

"While my *son* is being *tortured*, by lackeys who answer to yourself?" she hissed. "Then here is my 'final answer', sir : *go* fuck *yourself!* You had *better* find my family and free them, ay-sap – while you still *have* an army to command, and a country to rule. Now I must go... your Air Force is preparing another attack. And, ahh... 'have a nice day' – since you do not have many days, of *any* kind, left, Mr. President!"

Abruptly, she cut the connection, leaving a sombre, at-wits'-end President now in conversation only with his Air Force Chief of Command, his Defense Secretary and his National Security Adviser.

"Well... didn't *that* go just swell," muttered a disheartened President.

All Aboard, Going Down

"Time-check," requested Jacobson, in the low voice that he and the rest of his troupe had adopted, upon venturing out into the hallways of this sinister, underground fortress-cum-dungeon.

He held up his hand to signal a temporary halt.

"'Eighteen to twenty minutes since we left them assholes trussed up, back there," answered White, in the same subdued tone. "We gone quite aways – and if I got this right, just up there an' round the bend, there's another elevator goin' down to the lower levels... but I dunno..."

"What you mean, 'you don't know'?" queried Tanaka.

"Well, this pass-card 'n map-type-thing we got back in the fight-room, it's kinda actin' up," explained the African-American astronaut. "Not sure exactly what's wrong with it... it's like every so often when I get my fingers in the wrong place, the picture – of the map, that is – it goes all wonky... it breaks up."

"Didn't Sergei say something about when he was playing chess with *her* – ?" noted Boyd.

"Yeah," agreed the woman. "Her, uhh, 'aura', was how she described it – remember? Maybe that's *another* little attribute that we seem to be developing... lucky *us*, ha ha..."

"As I recall... she said that hers could, like, stop bullets 'n such, Professor," commented White. "Sure hope I don't have to test that theory any more."

"I'd settle for her cute little light-bending trick," remarked Boyd. "You know – the one where she just waltzed right by us and arranged a stowage-berth for herself in the *Eagle*. Damn corridors are lit up like a hospital-ward – sorry, bad choice of words there, I guess – and if they've got cameras hidden somewhere up and down 'em – we're sunk. 'Least we haven't run into anybody else... which I think is weird... where *is* everyone?"

"Haven't seen even *one*," offered Tanaka. "Nor have I, uhh, *felt* any, if that makes sense. Which is not to say that there isn't somebody sitting in front of a console somewhere around here, directing a few hundred guards to trap us in the middle of a hallway."

"You know, Professor... I kinda think that they ain't bothered too much with the whole internal-security thing," suggested White. "I mean – anybody who ends up spendin' so much as a day or two undergoin' the stuff that these guys been doin' to their, uhh, 'guests' – they wouldn't be in much shape to be goin' anywhere... and where'd they go *to*? Sooner or later, they'd get to a door that they can't open... and then it'd just be a matter of time. Let's face it – if y'all gonna make the mother of all jails... this'd be it."

"Which raises the question of, 'what do *we* do when we reach one of those same doors – that the card can't unlock, I mean?" inquired Boyd.

"Leave that to *me*, Brent," replied the former Mars mission science officer, with an ominously confident tone to her voice. "I can *feel* it, feel it within me... getting stronger with each passing minute... can't *you* feel it, too?"

"Yeah, Professor... I can," uneasily confirmed White. "Effin' *scary*, you know?"

"I... *know*," quietly mentioned Tanaka, her voice and eyes far-off.

"Well – we haven't run into any guards so far, although I wouldn't count on that *always* being the case," noted Jacobson. "Especially at major ingress- or egress-routes – of which an elevator would *definitely* qualify, so... you all got the drill memorized, folks?"

"Cherie and I give 'em the big headache, if they don't raise the white flag when you tell 'em to freeze – if you care to give 'em a warning at all, that is; fail either test, Devon fires first, asks questions later," stated Boyd. "Copy?"

"Copy," echoed the woman, while the former Mars mission commander just nodded.

He sent an interrogatory stare to White.

"No problems here, Commander," added the black astronaut, quietly but forcefully. "I seen my share of drive-bys – had one aimed at me, but they missed – *I* don't intend to. For the record – I don' *like* all this shit... but I 'spose there's been a lot of stuff like that so far, and we prolly ain't half done yet."

"You can say *that* again," muttered Jacobson, "On *both* counts. Alright... let's get going."

His index-finger motioned forward, and at this, White and Boyd, automatic-rifles held at the ready, began to half-crouch toward the turn in the corridor, which was perhaps seventy feet or so from where they were now.

After a minute or so of tippy-toe travel, Boyd peeked around the corner, then quickly moved back.

"Two guards in front of the elevator-doors," he whispered. "Both armed, but guns slung over their backs. They don't look too 'with it'... might even be half-asleep."

Shouldn't we just be thinking to each other, Brent? came the powerfully-unmistakable signature of Tanaka's psyche.

They might hear us...

Let's keep that as much of a secret as we can, silently cautioned Jacobson. *Less we use it, the easier to do that.*

They're too far away to hear, anyway, mentally replied Boyd.

"Anybody else close by?" asked the Mars commander, *sotto voce.* "They see you?"

"Don't think so, to both questions," Boyd whispered back. "Like Devon said – they're probably not expecting uninvited foot-traffic... I can see quite aways down the corridor past the elevators... nobody down there, as far as I can tell."

"God, I *hate* doing this – any time you go up against an armed opponent – well, I don't have to explain that..." complained Jacobson. "Devon... isn't there another way down?"

"Stairs – but they're all the way on th'other side of this level... it'd be quite a walk," whispered White, with a negative head-shake. "And it looks like they go through at least two locked gates, plus some shit that I'm not sure of... it shows up as a symbol on the card but there's nothin' 'bout it on the map-key. Unless y'all want to spend a *long* time gettin' to the stairs – I'm afraid this is it, Commander."

"I don't suppose we could use the gas-grenades?" proposed Jacobson.

"Even if we *could* heave 'em that far," warned Boyd, "Those two guys would have plenty of time on their feet in which to fire. And what if they simply run off and get reinforcements?"

"Not the answer that I wanted to hear, but it wouldn't be the *first* time," ruefully acknowledged Jacobson. "Okay, then – Cherie, Brent – on my mark, I count to three, you jump out on two and do your thing, Devon and I step out on three and do what we have to. We had better hope that there's nobody within earshot, if we've got to start firing – but in that case, let's get it over with, get into the elevators and worry about how the hell we get back up, later. You ready?"

"You're right... I *hate* this, Commander," quietly muttered Boyd. "But, 'ready'."

"Ready, oooh, *ready*," cooed Tanaka.

Her voice was weirdly serene, unnerving in its self-confidence, and somehow, its cadence matched that of the music that played ethereally in the backs of their minds.

Glad you're on our side, sent White to the Asian-American woman.

Her acknowledgement was a saturnine smile that White knew he had seen, somewhere else, before.

"One..." counted Jacobson, holding up his index-finger.

"Two," he commanded, and at this, Boyd, armed like a paratrooper, along with the slight, apparently inoffensive figure of Cherie Tanaka, wheeled into the line of sight of the two gendarmes at the elevator.

And let fly with an invisible mental assault – which had absolutely no apparent effect.

"Intruders!" exclaimed a guard. "What the *f* –"

Shit, flashed Boyd's mind, broadcasting the words faster than human lips could have made the requisite sounds.

Out of range – they're un-slinging their guns – Cherie, get down!

I'm oh-kay, came back the reply.

There's that music again, realized the former Mars mission pilot.

Inspiring – electrifying – but concentrate, for God's sake, Brent –

As his military training kicked in and Boyd knelt down in classic, stabilized weapon-firing position, to his dismay, he saw Tanaka, her eyes shining blue and white, walking calmly in the direction of the two guards, her hands held out in front, palms-forward.

"What's the *fuck's* she *doin'!*" gasped a horrified White, while Boyd raised his automatic-rifle and drew a bead on the guard ahead of him and to the left.

The former astronaut squeezed the trigger and was rewarded by two or three direct mid-body hits on the unfortunate fellow, who was instantly knocked prone by this lethal barrage.

Unfortunately, before either White or Jacobson could fire at the second gendarme, this man – evidently quicker off the trigger than had been his counterpart – managed to shoot several rounds in Tanaka's direction.

Some of these would certainly have cut her down; but instead, what first registered to the senses of the rest of the Mars mission astronauts, was a series of heat-flashes, as the guard's bullets hit something invisible to the eye – but none the less very *real* – at a point between four and five feet in front of Tanaka's figure.

There were the sounds of a ricochet or two, as well as the faint 'click' of the remnants of bullet-slugs, impacting with the antiseptic-white floor tiles of this benighted place.

"*Freeze!*" bellowed Jacobson.

But the gendarme – though nonplussed by the complete ineffectiveness of his first fusillade – stupidly elected to empty the rest of his clip in Tanaka's direction.

As six or seven more shots bounced ineffectually off whatever was protecting the woman, White dodged to the right, crouched and shot, using the time-honored ghetto-trick of aiming first for the crotch, then spraying bullets upward.

Did this luckless man die first from the fragmenting shell that splattered the contents of his face and skull all over the white tiles behind; or, was it, perhaps, the rainbow-hued lightening-charge that howled from Tanaka's hands, a microsecond earlier?

A thought to be pondered later, Boyd sent to the rest of the group, as he tried to mask the creeping fear that infected his mind, when he looked at the former Mars mission science officer.

No wonder *she's starting to think of us as 'insects'*, he mused, using all the tricks to keep the thought to himself.

By now, the former astronauts had advanced rapidly to a spot in front of the elevators. Hearts pounding while disgust stuck in their craws, they surveyed the scene.

"The one that Devon and Cherie opened up on, he's... well, what a *mess*," uneasily observed Jacobson. "The other one, here, let me have a look... ugh, not much better – not dead *yet*, but I don't think there's anything we can do for him at this point... I guess they must have upgraded their guns, or their ammunition, and forgotten to upgrade their body-armor in like measure. *Jesus*, Cherie – what the hell was *that*, that you hit the second one, with?"

"Well, 'scuse me for askin', Professor, but, like, why the hell ain't y'all *dead*? That guy shot right *at* you," added White.

"It's, uhh, hard to explain... as I think I've said before," responded Tanaka, her eyes still glowing dim-blue, as she addressed the men. "It's like something *told* me that his bullets couldn't hurt me... that they were, uhh, *inferior* – all I had to do was reach out, in front that is, fill my mind's touch with the *power* – and I'd be in control... I guess this must be how Karéin energizes her 'bubble', except that I could tell, mine was only protecting me from the front... and I when the bullets hit my, uhh, shield, it felt *good*, like the kinetic energy was feeding me – it was sort of like the feeling you get from a good massage..."

"Yeah, and you sure 'massaged' that poor bugger good enough," remarked Boyd, with a suspicious stare at the woman.

"*Look*, guys," argued Tanaka, "This shouldn't be a surprise – I mean, *you* use telekinesis too – all you have to do is reach out, the same way as you usually do when you're trying to manipulate a physical object... except *here*, you deliberately stop your reach and you then tell it to *repel* things – not grab on to them. Am I, uhh, making any sense, here?"

The music slowly waned.

"Not really," countered Boyd, "But I'm sure you'll get us dull schoolboys up to speed eventually... in the meantime, Commander, I think we'd better get the hell out of here, ASAP. There must have been quite an echo down the halls from all that shooting, and unless the Professor wants to try her hand at protecting us from a rocket or two fired up our arses –"

"Yeah... you got *that* right," agreed Jacobson. "Devon – you got that card-thing working, yet?"

"Think so – here goes," stated the black astronaut. "Damn, no response... oh, sorry, had it keyed in for the wrong level... shit, it's that BS with the aura... here goes again – yo, *bingo!*"

There were sounds of movement from below, and artfully-hidden, illuminated letters now appeared in the white tiles above the elevator-door.

"Interesting," observed Boyd. "Look at 'em *go* – 'SL-650' – 'SL-550' – 'SL-450' – not exactly like what you'd see in a hotel..."

"Ain't no ho-tel, or hadn't y'all *noticed* by now," cynically noted White.

"I'd bet you that those refer to 'feet below sea level', or maybe meters," suggested Tanaka. "Which would mean that the bottom-level, assuming that the '650' reading is it, is one *hell* of a long way down from here."

"An apt way to put it, Professor," opined Boyd.

"What do you mean?" she disingenuously replied.

"The 'hell' part," he commented.

"You might be right, Brent... you might be right," replied Tanaka, her eyes again staring in a far-off way. "But console yourself with the thought that if we're to descend into the Pit... at least you're doing it with the meanest son-of-a-bitch – excuse me, *daughter*-of-a-bitch – in the valley. I can *feel* the rage empowering me..."

There was a soft 'ding', and the elevator-doors opened.

"Wow – damn thing sure is *big*," remarked White.

"Yeah... more than large enough to take a gurney or two," coldly opined Tanaka.

But Boyd mustn't have been following the conversation, because immediately, he stepped inside, and, with clockwork efficiency, unleashed a fusillade against a small surveillance-camera located in the top right corner of the device, reducing the thing to smoking wreckage.

"Don't know if it was working, or being looked at," he observed, matter-of-factly. "But either way... it's taken care of."

Surveying the sparking, shattered remains of the spy-camera, Jacobson grumbled, "You can say *that* again! But let's watch the ammo-count, folks."

White added, "What they say back in 'Nam... 'we sure liberated the hell out of this place'?"

"I was Number Two in my class for weapons-training when I took Basic," commented Boyd, with a shrug. "It *comes* back to you, I guess. Kind of force of habit, you know."

"Like with th' Professor – glad y'all's on *our* side, Brent my man," joked White, as he walked in and hit the 'hold open' button. "Might as well start one level down and work our way lower, if we got to... didn't that asshole who we roped up back in th' front office, say that this 'Billings' guy and the rest of 'em, were one level below this one?"

"Yeah," confirmed Boyd. "That is, if they haven't been taken even further down for 'special treatment'... remember?"

Two of the others nodded, mutely, not wanting to explore this idea any further than absolutely necessary.

"You know, I've been thinking of Dante – the *Inferno*, that is – for at least the last hour," stated Jacobson, as he, followed by Boyd and Tanaka, entered the elevator. "I took it back in college years ago, loved every page... even wrote a term-paper on it. Can't help having it come to mind, in a place like *this*."

The doors closed.

"Can't agree with you on *that* one, Sam," introspectively countered Tanaka.

"Why not?" asked the team-commander.

"Because... if I remember correctly," she explained, "That story is, ultimately, about redemption... but the way it looks from *here*... I'm thinking more of Faust."

White hit the glowing button marked, 'SL-250', and all of them felt both downward motion, as well as steadily increasing levels of background-energy.

"All aboard for Hell," he announced.

Honorable Soldiers, Forgive Me

The Storied Watcher propped her fore-body up by mailed fists upon the instrument-panel, plainly not caring that the heat from contact with *Vìrya Ahn'jë*'s gauntlets, had already melted and discolored various of the knobs and buttons upon this device.

Ah, fortuitous, a good distraction – they see wisps of smoke but not the little electron-charges going back and forth, she silently sent to both the weirding-armor and the amulet.

Ye speak now to the dull-thinking-machines on this war-bird?

See what they have to say, force into their 'memory banks' if needs be... remember all – especially the 'crypt-oh' numbers, if ye please.

Hard – like us – not – tongue – ours – trying, dear Mother – came back the reply, though none of the humans heard.

The downward-hanging side-bangs of her hair partly hid the frustration and incomprehension on her face, as Karéin-Mayréij muttered a low curse in a language foreign to all but her special war-children.

"Sorry... I didn't catch that," mentioned Schweicker.

The newcomer turned her head, with weird-glowing eyes unnervingly evident, and addressed the general.

"It seems that I have been – ahh, how would Bob say it – 'stonewalled'... yes, I believe that is the term," she remarked. "I do not know how much of that conversation that you overheard, Mr. Air Force General; but your President wants not to bargain with me. I made him an *extremely* reasonable offer – but he rejected it out of hand, for nonsense reasons that he refused to explain or defend. I suppose that I should not be telling you this... but your leader has me *completely* bewildered."

"I'm sure that you can appreciate that from a military point of view, that might be considered as a *good* thing... not a bad one," evenly offered Schweicker.

Now Karéin-Mayréij turned to rest her arms behind, leaning back against the instrument-console, with little wisps of smoke or steam lazily issuing forth from where she made contact with it.

She looked up at the general, who, like many of the males on this aircraft, was considerably taller.

With a fang-bedecked half-smile, she explained, "What I *meant*, sir, is that I am used to being, ah, 'stonewalled' by opponents who are in a position to do so... that is, by enemies who actually *can* effectively fight back. Your 'President' is in the precise *opposite* situation – I can tear this country of yours *apart* with my bare hands, if I am inclined to do so – yet he bargains as if he holds an, ahh, 'hand of all big deuces' –"

The communications-technician, perhaps unwisely, spoke up, upon hearing this.

"What you all say there, lady?" he inquired. "About the cards, that is."

"Oh... I said that your President thinks he has all the better cards, because he has a hand of deuces," stated the alien-girl. "That is another word for 'devils', my boyfriend told me –"

"Yeah, but if he's just got deuces, that's just a bunch of twos – pretty much *anythin'* will beat that at poker," commented the technician.

"What do you mean?" querled the Storied Watcher.

"You see, to beat a hand of say three twos, all you gotta do is have three of a kind, or –" started the junior Air Force staffer.

"Well... I prefer chess, anyway," argued the newcomer. "And pawns should not be lecturing queens – a lesson both for your President, and yourself."

There were a few seconds of awkward silence, then Schweicker spoke.

"That will be *enough*, Specialist!" he ordered.

The abashed man slunk off into the shadows.

"Sanction him not, sir!" requested Karéin-Mayréij. "Every so often, a pawn who is brave enough to speak truth to power, is lucky enough to be promoted to a king, or a queen. Unfortunately... most of them die, before they reach the finish-line."

The technician looked like he was going to say something, but he wisely restrained himself.

"It is a pity that poor Bob had insufficient time to teach me the fine points of this 'poker' game, before your spies hauled him off to the dungeon," continued the alien-girl. "If he is still alive when I find him, I will surely ask for a few lessons in the fine points of playing-cards."

She stood up straight, with her infernal aura waxing so hot that both the communications-technician and all in her vicinity, scrambled for distance and cover.

"In any event," continued Karéin-Mayréij, "What I was trying to say was, your President is behaving *stupidly* – he bluffs, with no way to back up his threats – and both he and I know it. This is the mark of an inexperienced, foolhardy, or just insane, leader... not a wise one. I will have to give him another little demonstration of my war-skills... then see if he relents, at that point. Or at the next. Or at the next after that. We *could* end this easily – with minimal, ahh, 'collateral-damage', as I believe that you American warriors are in the habit of calling it – but your so-called 'leader' instead decides to dissemble, with your lives and those of your fellow-citizens, as his sacrifice in a futile cause. What a tragic, pointless waste!"

"You *know* that we will have to try to stop you," stiffly warned Schweicker.

"Go ahead and *try!*" sneered the newcomer, in open contempt; but then, a second later, she seemed to involuntarily move her mailed fingers over the breast-covering of *Vîrya Ahn'jë*; her shoulders slumped perceptibly, and her voice took on a different, regretful tone.

"No, on second thought... do *not!*" pleaded the Storied Watcher. "I beg you *not* to fight me – the more lethal the weapons that you employ, the more savagely I will reply – and be of no doubt, I *will* fight back! It is what I *do*; it is what uncounted ages of warring-experience against far more dangerous opponents than yourselves, have taught me *how* to do, all too well. At some point – under the pressure of quick decision-making – I will use powers so indiscriminate, that they cannot *fail* to slaughter large numbers of humans, warriors and civilians alike. I so much do *not* want to do that... but given the obstinacy of your President, I am running out of options. Do you *understand?*"

"What *you* need to understand," replied the general, trying to choose his words carefully, "Is that from our point of view, you're an enemy combatant who is threatening both the President of the United States, and our whole *country*, over a dispute that's outside our ability to resolve. *Our* job is to defend our Commander-In-Chief and our nation – and we *will* do that to the best of our abilities. We're all pledged to give our lives in the defense of our country, if necessary. That's what *we* do, Madam."

The alien-girl's eyes were watering, but then she regained some of her composure, turning to rapidly address one Air Force staffer after another.

"Honorable American warriors – do any of *you* know where my family is being held?" she cried in distress. "Do you *want* to die? Give me *any* clue, however minor, something that will lead me to my loved-ones! Or just let me speak with Sam Jacobson and the voyagers to *Mailànkh!* Give all of us, a way *out* of this!"

But all she perceived, was a stony silence.

After another few seconds, she added, "Then, indeed, I must go – your Air Force's next attack closes quickly in upon this place. I will survive it easily... you may not. Prepare yourselves!"

With the two elemental-daggers resuming their stations on her leg-braces, the Storied Watcher walked past Schweicker toward the hatchway through which she had come to enter the forward deck; the general had to quickly dodge out of the way, to avoid being burned as she passed.

Then she sadly advised him, "I will leave through one of the doors that you can seal from the inside... and I give my word that I will not cause any further damage to the aircraft, while I am inside it. After I am gone from your airplane, for the first hour, I will not war against you – unless I am attacked first from here; but if I am, I will use *all* the powers at my disposal. If I were you and I wanted to stay alive, I would not want to see that, happen. Do you understand?"

"Yes," grimly confirmed the general. "Nor can we give false assurances of your own safety, if you continue hostilities against the United States. For the record, I regret the situation – but I *will* do my duty... as will everyone on board this aircraft."

Now, the music started again, a susurrating, subtly exciting, ominous beat that seemed to echo from each molecule of the air in this place.

The alien-girl cast him a long glance.

"You are honorable soldiers," she called, "Since you make war in misplaced trust and loyalty... not for plunder or dogma. I pray two things : that fate may take you elsewhere, than against me; and that some day, you can... *forgive.*"

"That," offered Schweicker, with characteristic restraint, "Will depend on future events."

Karéin-Mayréij nodded in acknowledgment, but did not reply; instead, she disappeared down the hatch, in a wash of brutal heat, a roaring war-song and the blink of an eye.

As she did, a sextet of little mental-voices chirped,

Mother – more – their – war-talk – much – perceive – we – now.

And the Storied Watcher, after stealing quickly past the moaning, crippled results of her earlier attacks, tarried for a moment at the exit-hatch, replying in turn,

I promised the humans another lesson... a final *warning, before they reap the Pillar of Fire... and I mean to make good, on that pledge.*

This 'President' rules largely by terror, partly by the mislaid loyalty of his swordsmen – but more so, by the stolidity and gullibility of his peasantry...

They crave continuity... things being as they were before.

But if his 'White House' palace, his 'Oval Office' throne... if those were to be thrown to pieces by a superior power, with the Tee-Vee cameras arrayed all 'round...

Fly we to the East, little ones; for thy Mother, who is called 'Destroying Angel' –

*She has become... her **namesake!***

– End of Book Three –

Don't miss Book Four of *The Angel Brings Fire...*

Children of The Fire

www.ingramcontent.com/pod-product-compliance
Lightning Source LLC
Chambersburg PA
CBHW030931020726
47498CB00001B/200